FEAR THE SKY

MW01132042

Volume 1 of The Fear Saga

by Stephen Moss

"You did not bear the shame
you resisted
sacrificing your life
for freedom, justice and honor"
Inscription, Memorial to the German Resistance, Berlin, Germany

Contents

Prologue

On the outskirts of our solar system there is a ring of broken lumps of rock and ice. They form a roughly spherical border marking the outer reaches of the sun's influence, a loosely strung fence around our stellar home. Against this backdrop, a meteor the size of Central Park flies past.

Not that its size is particularly unusual.

Size, like speed and distance, can only be judged as usual or unusual when taken in context. So as we consider this particular meteor, even though it is the size of Central Park, or about three times the size of the largest aircraft carrier on earth, it is dwarfed by the multitude of extra-stellar debris relegated by chance to the cold, distant reaches of our sun's gravitational well, which, in turn, are made minuscule, negligible even, by the unfathomable expanse of the void beyond.

All that said, no human eye could compare them in order to judge the disparity. For even if someone happened to be in the vicinity as this particular meteor came by, its passing would be so fantastically fast as to be imperceptible, and would do little to break what would be a phenomenally boring existence for this lone stellar observer. For this is a place that any vessel we could build would take more than a lifetime to reach, and it would probably be even less interesting up close than it has been in the glimpses we have snatched by telescope. No, to travel from this point to the earth in the two months it will take this meteor to get there, you would have to be going at the blurringly astonishing rate of two thousand kilometers every second, at which speed you could circumnavigate the Earth twice in less than a minute.

Of course, this meteor's seemingly incredible speed is also not that exceptional, for an interstellar body, which, though rare, are not unheard of.

No, the only truly exceptional thing about this meteor is that spread out behind it by a complex, invisible web of magnetic forces is a vast, atom-thin surface, so thin that matter passes through it unhindered, leaving it unharmed by the cosmic dust that would otherwise tear anything so huge to shreds. Its delicate mesh reflects only a small wavelength of plasma. Catching and resisting this particular wavelength, however, in this ocean-sized parachute, means that the very sun the meteor is rushing toward is filling the thousand-mile-wide radiation chute with solar wind.

Indeed the only exceptional thing about this meteor is not its size, which is puny compared to its neighbors, or its spectacular speed, which, though rare, is far from unique. No, what would have astonished any spectator that could see this particular meteor is that this particular meteor is slowing down.

- - -

One month after passing the proxy border to the solar system, the meteor passes Jupiter. As it does so, the magnetic fields that form and control the vast sail behind it shimmer almost imperceptibly with the first hints of the active deep space detection systems coming from its destination. After a few hours of final adjustment, the magnetic ties holding the entire solar sail together collapse. In an instant, any possible hint of the parachute they had caused to form vanish like a puff of smoke in the wind.

Under the steadily increasing wash of radar signals, the meteor then begins to slowly and deliberately disintegrate.

Part 1

Chapter 1: Under the Radar

The walls of Neal's cube are the type that can be torn down and rebuilt, reconfigured to a hundred different formats, the quintessential faceless, formless walls that enclose millions of office workers across middle-class Eur-merica. You would not know from its creative shades of grey that this cube, and its dated Compaq PC, sit less than a quarter of a mile from the US Air Force Phased Array Antenna.

The magnificent and complex phased array was designed for deep space object tracking back in the 1960s by the finest minds in the world, when the finest minds in the world were all working on either looking into space, or getting into it. Four months before its completion, it was appropriated by the Air Force that had discretely facilitated its federal funding. They had covertly helped drive its completion in order to use it to track satellites, specifically Russian satellites.

In return for everyone's hard work a team of civilian scientists were allowed to monitor non-military targets with any unassigned bandwidth during off-peak hours. Sixty years later, with the finest minds now working at Apple, the once extensive civilian team had been whittled down to four doctorate students from a nearby technical college in Phoenix.

This is due, in part, to the fact that "unassigned bandwidth during off-peak hours" translated to being on site from 11pm to 6am every day for perhaps two or three hours of highly interruptible system access.

The only upside of the job was that Neal got to tell the young students at the university bar that he monitors space for the next planet-killing meteor. Unfortunately for Neal's love life, however, was the fact that while Armageddon may have made them all seem like superheroes, between each earth-shattering stellar event there are several million years of thoroughly unsexy peace and quiet, and it felt like he spent roughly that at the observatory each night looking up porn on the government's PCs, usually in a vain search for a photo of a doppelganger of one of his female PhD students doing unspeakable acts with a slightly balding 39 year-old like himself.

Interspersed amongst this carpel tunnel inducing work, he would somewhat diligently log the trajectories of random debris in the solar system, most of which would never come closer to Earth than our nearest planetary neighbors. Every few months he would track an incident, typically a cluster of rock and ice that would come close enough to be pulled in by our orb's mass, only to be consumed in the atmosphere like fireworks. So Neal was not particularly excited when his computer automatically shifted his view to the system monitoring control screen, interrupting his typing into Google search so that "…orority web-c…" appeared in the control field before he stopped his left-handed typing and looked at the data on the screen.

The screen was now filled with two windows. The largest one contained an inverted triangular graphic, which was an interpretation of the 3-D space in the hemisphere viewable by the array. To its left was a scrolling list of data apparently designed to be as unintelligible as possible, but which conveyed vast swathes of information to the educated eye.

The graphic showed the various objects being tracked by the system, at least those not denoted as 'classified' by the system's all-seeing military operators in another part of the building. At the extreme range of the device, a small cloud had resolved itself, highlighted in red as a new/unidentified/unclassified object.

The list of information on the cluster was lengthening as more data became available. Speed, estimated origin, estimated volume, estimated track; the last of which was bolded, and was the reason the system had automatically flagged the record and notified Neal's team. Collision potential: 16%. Neal was intrigued.

Clearing the command field, he typed "execute collision parameter analysis" and sat back. A new box overlaid the last with the automatically assigned number of the incident, the date, and the title of Neal's request at the top. The rest of the window remained blank while the system gathered more data. Normal turnaround time would be about forty-five minutes for something this far away, so Neal decided to get some shut-eye while the system worked.

After thirty-five minutes the phone rang. Neal started, it was now nearly four in the morning, and the only noise in the cramped space was the whirring of his antiquated hard drive and some Kings of Leon playing through his media player.

Neal put his circa 1975 brown office telephone to his ear: "Yup?"

"This is ANFPS85 control, please confirm identity."

"Errr, I don't mean to be a dick here, my friend, but didn't *you* call *me*."

"We have a system request from your terminal, please confirm identity."

"Neal," he said, then, "you need my number, wait, err…ID number: ANFPS85…err…65239." ANFPS85 Control waited a moment while Neal figured out that there was something else missing. "Oh, right, the cool part, right, yeah. My clearance ID password thingy is eleanorrigby66."

"Identity confirmed, please state the reason for your bandwidth request."

"The object …" he waited, expecting them to see what he was talking about, then continued, "it's kind of big and it's heading our way. Well, I think it is, at least the system thinks it *could* be, and I thought it best to get more data."

"I have the object record now, sir. At this range this would require more bandwidth from the array than is assigned to your program."

"Are you using it for something else?"

"You do not have clearance for that information, sir."

Neal sighed: the joys of working with the military. "Well, when will it be available?"

"Details of the availability of the array are classified, sir."

"Can I use the system when it becomes available ... please?"

"I can neither confirm nor deny that the system is currently unavailable, sir."

"Wait, let me get this ... you know ... clear: you cannot tell me whether the system is in use, so it sounds like you are telling me that whether it is or not, you wouldn't let me use it, in case me using it somehow informed me as to its being previously ... unused ... because you think that info would be useful to me in some way. My friend, I think this conversation is actually making me stupider."

The slight delay on the line was the strongest display of emotion from control that he would get.

"Your request is being reviewed by the site commander, sir. Would you like to stay on the line, or have us contact you when there is a confirm ... putting the commander online, sir, hold the line, please ..." a new voice came on the line, older, stronger, "Hey, Neal is it? This is Colonel Milton. I see from your file that you've been here for six years, huh?"

Neal frowned at this new turn in the conversation. "What, on this call?"

The colonel's skin was proverbially thin from years of having his ass unsubtly kissed by his subordinates, but also because of that his awareness of when he was being mocked was accordingly poor and the swipe passed over his head. "Yes, well, you've been given P5 clearance so I have the authority to decide whether you should see this."

"And ..." Neal said, expectantly.

"Yes, Mr. Danielson, we've run the full collision potential analysis you asked for, I'm sending you the data now."

With that, the Collision Analysis box populated with a string of data: number of objects in cluster, estimated trajectory, estimated entry time/point/angle of insertion. To get this much data this far out would take most of the array's huge number of individual antennae focusing on the object.

"So you don't have bandwidth to analyze the incident, huh?" said Neal.

"I wanted to see the results before releasing them to a civilian," replied the colonel.

"To get this much detail must have taken pretty much all the nine thousand antennae in the array, I guess you had some availability."

"Hey, like you said, it's 3:48 on a Tuesday morning, what else were we doing with the system?" The colonel laughed.

"Ah, facetiousness, wonderful. Why didn't your boy just tell me it was running?"

"Sergeant Cyr wasn't at liberty to tell you that, you are need-to-know on these things, and I decide what you need to know. Deal with it, son."

Son ... really, so we're doing *this* now.

"Well, *pops*, now that I can see the file, this looks pretty significant, what do you say you give me file edit rights and I can start an analysis and write-up."

The colonel paused a moment, then said, "The full data shows it isn't as large as it seemed at first, just a bunch of debris. We are downgrading to potential atmospheric incident. Assigning file to your team now, you can have it."

"So if it isn't going to kill people then you aren't interested, is that it?'

"Yes, son, that's pretty much it."

And the line died.

He was right, of course. It had potential: plenty of small pieces to burn up and create a bit of a show, but for the fact that they would probably be spread all over the place. Bits and pieces would slide in all over the globe, as its arrival was so oblique as to give all the random chunks of ice and rock long, arching trajectories. The few pieces that didn't bounce right off our ionosphere would burn up all over the stratosphere like a handful of pebbles hurled, en masse, across a lake.

Neal got on with typing up the entry:

NOTICE OF ANTICIPATED ATMOSPHERIC PENETRATION
Time logged: 0344 MST
Date logged: September 20
Location: AMFPS85 Radar Array
Noted by: Neal P. Danielson
Note Type: First Contact [He just loved typing that]
Est. Date of Atmospheric Penetration: October 4
Est. Volume: 2.5 km^3
Est. Mass: Not Enough Data to Calculate
Impact Probability: Limited, some debris
Est. Impact Location(s): Not Enough Data to Calculate
Incident ID: ColonelMiltonBlows

Chapter 2: Rude Awakening

The shades were drawn against the sun, and McDonald's breakfast wrappers were strewn across the coffee table. In the studio apartment the full bed doubled as a couch for Neal's limited friends. Also in the room were two unmatched armchairs, one an upright, stately number with a detailed, if worn, light blue and yellow floral pattern, and the other a puffy Naugahyde La-Z-Boy, its oversized pillows overhanging each other like the layers of fat that probably adorned its original owner. Both had been neighborhood front lawn acquisitions of a younger, even poorer Neal, and both were now covered in jeans, college tracksuits, and old T-shirts of once-cool bands: the apparent standard issue uniform of every research student Neal had ever met.

The VOIP phone rang on the old laptop Neal used as a phone/stereo/TV resting on top of the slew of outdated and unread aeronautics and engineering magazines that cluttered his coffee table. It was 11:15am, and Neal had been sleeping off his Sausage McMuffin dinner/breakfast for two hours.

After a struggle to realign himself in bed so he could reach the PC and answer the phone, a red-eyed, unshaven Neal pressed *enter*. "Who is this?"

Out of his PC's small speakers the stern voice of the Array's site commander came, "Danielson, Colonel Milton, not a fan of that incident ID. Rename it. Anyway, it's been a week and there is new data on our friend."

Animating now, Neal swung his legs off the crumpled sheets and his mind's eye tried to focus on the swathe of data and analysis he had prepared on the incident since its discovery. "Wait, so it is really coming? That is awesome. Is it as interesting as I have been telling you guys it would be?"

"We have several billion dollars of equipment up there that is about to come under assault by a hailstorm of interstellar rubble, I am glad this interests you."

Neal frowned again. "Colonel, the chances of coming into direct contact with an interstellar object are phenomenally low. This is the first time we have ever detected, let alone crossed paths with one, and you're worried about satellite TV. Scientists across the globe would kill to see what you are seeing right now."

"Yes, well, wish granted. There is a small briefing at 1300 hours. Come in the main entrance by noon, a liaison will meet you there and bring you to the con so you can look at the numbers beforehand."

"Wait … that's in …"

"Be sure to bring your driver's license and ANFPS ID, otherwise you will be denied entry, liaison or no."

After objecting for a moment more about the short notice, Neal realized that the colonel had closed the call. "Fuck me," he said as he stood up, and while sniffing for semi-clean clothes on the La-Z-Boy, he mumbled sullenly about the military, going into some detail about what Colonel Milton's mother would apparently do if strapped for cash in Tijuana.

- - -

Neal looked around the large main control room and thought to himself that it was as far advanced from his cube in the civilian section of the building as Einstein was from George W. A single huge screen about twenty feet across showed a huge graphical representation of 3-D space. In many ways it was the same view Neal could see on the small screen at his desk only with vastly more information displayed, and in far higher resolution.

As with his view, this vast screen's perspective could also be rotated to show the various views of the objects' approaches and orbits, their trajectories and speeds. Tracked simultaneously were at least three or four dozen satellites currently in this section of Earth's orbital plane, one basically functional space station, various USSR era million-dollar scrap heaps, and one impending meteor shower.

A female officer in her early thirties sat at the command console while her commanding officer, Colonel Barrett Milton, stood behind and to her left. He turned to size Neal up as he was escorted into the room, then the colonel turned back to the main screen as Neal walked up, staying focused on the screen as Neal was announced by the liaison. The colonel dismissed the thankless private without ceremony and waited a moment while Neal took in the information on the big screen.

The room was about the size of a squash court, oriented towards the inextricably cool main screen that no doubt cost more than Neal made in several years. Ten consoles faced the screen about fifteen feet back from it, in a room that clearly followed some military control center design standard: the walls were so as not to detract from the main screen, which in turn was faced by the array of computer stations in two banks.

At these stations sat grim-faced operators, waiting to respond to the commands of the two or three senior officers that could either sit at the central command console that none of them knew how to use, stand behind an unfortunate junior nominated to sit there for them, or bark orders from the balcony that ran across the back of the room about four feet above the main floor. Behind the balcony were two offices; both were glass walled so that the officers that typically sat in them could watch proceedings while pretending to do important things.

Neal neither noticed nor cared about the layout of the room, or the uppity way the colonel had greeted him, or rather, had not greeted him. He did not even see the somewhat elderly woman standing on the raised balcony, quietly watching the proceedings.

Despite his ignominious job and unimpressive resume, Neal was a surprisingly bright man. His downfall had been that he had always had trouble pretending to care what professors often stupider than he, always less intuitive, but nonetheless far more politically and socially aware had been speaking about. The fact that he had made it through his bachelor's and master's degrees in astrophysics almost in spite of himself demonstrated just how sharp he was. So when he was presented with a tool as impressive as this huge display and the computers supplying it, with such a plethora of information previously unavailable to him, he was, to say the least, engrossed.

After noticing several satellites he had notably not seen on his own views, he focused in on the object of his previous week's hard work. It had now resolved into a hazy cloud of what was, according to the system, 156 chunks of varying size, but few larger than a Volkswagen. Basic information was presented in a list to the right of each object in a small semi-transparent table. As the cluster of debris moved across the screen, the table moved with it.

"Like I said on the phone," the colonel began, still facing the screen, "we have a briefing at 1300 hours and I wanted you on hand to talk to the details of your report."

Neal was still trying to digest just how much he hadn't been privy to before, and which he had about thirty minutes to come to grips with before the briefing. Staring at the screen and speaking in a distracted tone, Neal said, "Yeah, I just wish you hadn't called me so early, did I really need to be here this soon?"

The colonel turned his head, looking at Neal like he was a pestering child, and tried think of a response, but he was neither practiced in, nor did he enjoy, banter.

At a request from the colonel the view reoriented to show the impending shower's approach on a cross section of the Earth and started scrolling to show each piece's trajectory. Of the cluster, about twenty pieces were singled out as large enough to survive entry into the earth's atmosphere, but very few of the estimated trajectories showed an entry, the rest all showed as bouncing off the atmosphere, due to their oblique angles of approach and limited mass.

Neal studied the figures and graphics. "Those trajectories are wrong, you haven't correctly estimated the mass of the objects; they won't all behave like that." He turned to the lady at the console, "Didn't you use the numbers in my report?"

Before she could speak, the colonel answered for her, "The computer estimated the weights based on data your civilian predecessors have compiled over the years. Were those numbers wrong?"

"No," Neal braced himself for a long, laborious explanation, then seemed to change his mind. "Look, there are other factors to consider that appear here but have not been seen previously. Maybe I could just …" Neal started towards the central console, but was intercepted by the colonel.

"Hold on there, Mr. Danielson. If you could explain these 'factors' to me before we go changing our estimates, I would appreciate it," the colonel prompted, standing in his way and turning, now, to face the scientist.

Neal sighed a moment, then elaborated, "The objects are behaving slightly anomalously. There is no larger, central mass, so some, if not all of them, must have been joined as a cohesive mass at some point. Some point not too long ago, in fact," Neal postulated.

"Why does there have to be a central mass?" the colonel said, shrugging slightly.

Neal mimicked the shrug and said, "Why would they be so close together if there wasn't? Listen, Colonel, these objects have come a phenomenally long way from whatever orbital mishap started them on their journey, if they were all separate objects then there would need to be something larger, *with enough gravitational pull*," he emphasized, "to keep them all together as they travelled. Otherwise they would have separated over time. Heck, over the kind of distances we are talking about, they would be light-years apart by now. Unless they had had some proverbial glue binding them."

"Well there clearly is no 'glue' now, so your theory must be incorrect."

Neal shook his head at the remark, but summoning up his patience, he went on, "There is that, but still, despite the apparent lack of a large mass, it is very clear that the objects are, even over the last week, pulling apart from each other. It is slow, but they are more spread out now than they were when we first spotted them. Given time I could probably extrapolate the time they separated." Neal was aware he was almost pleading, but this was the most interesting thing that had happened to him in a quite a while and he was so very desperate for anything in his life that might be termed interesting.

The colonel paused a moment, then said, "Mr. Danielson, this is all very well, but I still don't see how this would affect the mass calculations." In fact the colonel was wondering if he should be getting frustrated with Neal for wasting his time, or with himself for not getting it. He decided to remain passive until he found out, and by passive he meant obstinate.

The hitherto silent woman at the back of the room chose this moment to interject, stepping slowly down the steps from the balcony to the main floor and introducing herself as she went. "Neal Danielson, Laurie West, I'm an astrophysicist myself, on occasion."

Neal whirled to her, momentarily sullen in reaction to the apparent additional assault on his expertise. But his wariness wavered when her name came to him, and he tilted his head inquisitively.

"Dr. Laurie West ... of the Hubble Institute?" he said, his right hand starting to rise from his side to meet hers as she approached, but moving slowly, as if its cooperation were dependent on her response.

But she merely nodded and shrugged offhandedly, as though the title were a prank she had played in college which she hoped no one had heard about. They shook hands, Neal shaking hers with increasing enthusiasm as it sank in that he was talking to one of the premier physicists of this, or frankly any other time.

She returned the handshake in kind, not one to think that her title made her better than the clearly quite sharp man in front of her, and then said, "So your report posits that our estimate of the objects' masses should account for their having recently been a part of a cohesive mass. I agree that it is almost certain that they were, until recently, part of a larger whole. Too close together, as you say, and diverging even now." He nodded and she smiled, but then she frowned and carried on. "But why would this affect the mass estimates?" she asked, her hazel-grey eyes glittering with intelligence and curiosity as she released his hand but held his gaze.

Reticent at this rare opportunity to talk shop with someone that actually knew more than he did, Neal started in slowly, choosing his words carefully to try and avoid a misstep. "Well, it would seem to me that an object's mass would probably be affected by its environment over time, therefore if these were previously, recently, even, part of a larger whole, then they would have been compressed into denser mass, giving them a higher mass to volume ratio. Their volatiles would also not have been exposed to as much freeze-cracking and UV bombardment."

She didn't hesitate for a second, "But the exposure to vacuum that they are having now would have the same effect on their volatiles as it does on any other meteor, probably more drastic due to their previous lack of exposure, so wouldn't they have stabilized to something more like the mass norms originally estimated once separation occurred?"

Neal had had the benefit of thinking about this for a week versus her five minutes, but she was still only just behind him. "Well, that was my thought too," he said, "but then I reviewed the imagery that the array had compiled and noticed that, well, there is surprisingly little debris."

"And if there had been a sudden combustion of volatiles due to exposure, there would be a cloud, probably even a tail," she continued his thought.

"Exactly. No tail, very little debris." he said with satisfaction.

The colonel looked on, taking some small satisfaction in the knowledge that if she had needed to have it explained to her, then *his* ignorance was more than acceptable, and felt suddenly more comfortable interposing his own question: "Well, I guess I am still unclear why this would affect the estimates."

Neal looked to Laurie as if to say, would you like to field this? But she chose to deflect the courtesy.

"Please, go on." she prompted with a beneficent, almost parental smile.

He smiled in return and turned to the colonel, saying, "If they haven't exuded volatiles it means they don't, or rather didn't, have very much of them, which means that unlike typical interstellar masses they may not have the, well, the holes and gaps that escaping gases would leave behind as they either combusted or froze under the alternate exposure to the freezing vacuum and the sun's unfiltered barrage. Previous estimating tools assume that a significant proportion of an interstellar object's total volume is, in fact, empty, nothing there: fractures and gaps left by escaping gases."

He took a breath and continued, walking around the colonel to the console as the junior officer seated at it leant to one side to allow him to reach the keyboard. "Sooo, if these guys don't seem to have many of those gaps," he said as he typed into the machine, looking up at the screen as the mass estimates changed under his fingertips, and the computer began to recalculate the way the objects would react to the earth's atmosphere, "they may have a higher mass to volume ratio, they may be denser, in which case they … might … do … this." he said as he clicked enter on the last of the reconfigured estimates.

They all looked at the screen as the alternate entry statistics appeared.

The colonel's obstinacy was not born of ignorance or stupidity, as it turned out, but of long practice of authority, and he was just as quick as his neighbors to see the implications of the new numbers.

"Yes, this *would* make it more interesting," he said quietly.

Revised: NOTICE OF ANTICIPATED ATMOSPHERIC PENETRATION
Time logged: 0344 MST
Date logged: September 20
Time Last Modified: 1257 MST
Date Last Modified: September 27
Location: AMFPS85 Radar Array
Noted by: Neal P. Danielson
Note Type: First Contact [never gets old]
Est. Date/Time of Atmospheric Penetration: October 4, ~10am GMT
Est. Volume: ~1.35 km^3
Est. Mass: ~116k tons
Impact Probability: Scattered debris
Est. Impact Location(s): Multiple sites: all oceanic,
- North Atlantic, two impacts possible near Outer Hebrides, Scotland, and the Channel Islands
- Northern Pacific, two impacts possible across northern Pacific near Bering Strait
- East China Sea, impact possible northwest of the Okinawa archipelago
- Indian Ocean, two impacts possible: one in the Bay of Bengal near Sri Lanka, one southwest of the Kathiawar peninsula in the Arabian Sea
Incident ID: ColonelMiltonBlows

Chapter 3: Well-Lit Corridors

The colonel walked behind and to the right of the pair of scientists down a long, neon-lit beige corridor, herding them to turn left or right as required. Neal had tried to let the colonel go first as the man knew where they were going better than either Neal or Laurie did, but the military man's training would not allow him to have civilians walking behind him in the high-security facility, out of sight, as it were.

As they walked in relative silence, Neal noted that unlike himself, Dr. West had not tried to argue the point with Colonel Milton, and had simply started walking in the direction indicated by the colonel's outstretched hand. As she was clearly not one to blindly follow societal gender mores, it was obvious that she was simply more aware of which arguments could and could not be won with men like the colonel. The point was not lost on Neal, and he decided to try and follow her lead in the upcoming military briefing, noting with satisfaction that he was not as pigheaded as his ex-girlfriends typically said he was.

"We'll be taking this next left." the colonel interjected from behind them, continuing as they turned onto another uncomfortably well-lit beige corridor, "We'll be meeting in Teleconference Room B526 up here on the right."

As they approached Barrett Milton stepped to the door before them and, pausing as he clasped its handle, spoke in an aside to Neal, "Before we go in I just wanted to confirm that you changed the Incident ID on that report, I had meant to mention it in the control room but our conversation went a bit long and it slipped my mind."

"Yes," said Neal in a similarly low voice, remembering the report's less than diplomatic name, "about that." The colonel froze at Neal's hesitation and frowned very sharply at the scientist, apparently considering bringing his not inconsiderable martial training to bear on the man.

The colonel spoke quietly but sharply, "I like a joke as much as the next man, Mr. Danielson, but this is going in front of important…"

"No, Colonel, no. You misunderstand. I tried to change it, I really did," Neal held his hands up to placate Barrett, remembering his very real and quite frantic attempts to edit out his quip once the incident came into the spotlight as 'requiring further investigation.'

"But apparently once you submit a report," Neal continued, "you cannot edit its ID, something about 'tracking' and 'validity of data.'"

The truth was that Neal didn't dislike this Colonel Barrett Milton guy nearly as much in person as he had after their initial phone conversation. Plus the 'guy' in question was roughly six foot, his angular jaw and rugged features emphasized by a clearly enthusiastic athletic regime, and it was obvious to Neal that the man could happily beat the younger, but somewhat flabbier, scientist to a Tropicana pulp if the inclination grabbed him.

Like before, Laurie saw an opportune moment to interpose herself between the two men, this time physically as well as metaphorically, and as she pushed past them toward the door, she said, "We need not mention the title as we introduce the topic, Colonel, nor, I'm sure, does anyone read that part of the report."

As she said, this she remembered, with a well-hidden smile, the name of the incident, and hoped her analysis of the reading habits of the room they were about to enter was accurate. The colonel contemplated the number of far worse things he had baked into official reports as a lieutenant to spite his fellow junior officers and calmed himself. After a moment's pause, he released his grasp on the door handle so the doctor could enter the conference room, his sheen of professionalism and authority rising over his anger, like rising water snuffing a flame.

Neal followed Laurie into the room, apologizing silently to the once again unflappable colonel as he passed. The room contained a long table with about five chairs along each side, and one at the end nearest the door. An extremely large flat screen was at the other end with a camera mounted above it, and flat, omni-directional microphones were arranged intermittently along the table's length.

An air force technician sat about midway down the table at a small touch screen console, setting up the link with the meeting's other participants at the Pentagon. The screen itself simply said "WAITING FOR PARTICIPANTS" with the kind of infinite, machine patience that sentience simply won't allow.

Standing to one side was the colonel's aide, who had left the control room ahead of them to make sure the conference room was set up. As Laurie took a seat, the screen came to life and a gathering meeting showed on the other end. It was full of highly decorated senior officers and a couple of more expensively dressed, if less well-decorated civilians who were busy sitting their suited selves down, arranging their papers while they arranged their thoughts.

"The link is muted," prompted the technician as he went to leave, "the sound control is here," he said, pointing at a small button and volume control next to the microphone in front of the colonel.

The colonel looked at the button and nodded, but did not look up from his seat at the head of the table as the technician left. The colonel's aide went to the door and confirmed it was securely closed, per procedure, and then took one of several seats arranged around the outside of the room, leaving eight empty chairs at the large, immaculately polished conference table itself. Neal watched her sit on the outside, and was unsure whether he was happy to be at the grown-ups table, or annoyed at the triumph of hierarchy over practicality. Then he thanked the gods that he wasn't in the military himself, and took the seat opposite Laurie, with the colonel between them at the table's head.

"The meeting will be led by General Pickler of Air Force Intelligence," the colonel said, indicating the man at the head of the table on the big screen. "So you know, Mr. Danielson, they can see several other conference rooms from their screen. My report will be one of several that will be made at this meeting, and the objects of your report will be one of several I will be reporting on. You will speak only when asked to, and only on the topic of your report. This meeting will be classified level P5 based on the presence of you and some other low-level civilians. So you know, I checked and confirmed that your Armed Services Secrecy Act Agreement is up to date prior to approving your attendance here today.

Consider yourself informed that this meeting most definitely falls under the auspices of that contract."

Neal noticed the colonel was looking specifically at him as he said this. He nodded seriously, but inside him he felt two conflicting emotions coming to the forefront as the colonel spoke: firstly, how damn cool it was to be attending a classified meeting, but secondly, it was also dawning on him that he had clearly just signed up for what was probably going to be two hours of serious tedium. This would be a thorough test of his inherent allergy to monotony, delivered as only the military can deliver monotony. He only hoped he didn't actually fall asleep as he had so often in class. No, that would be bad, he thought. Shit, have to stay awake, he thought. Shit, what am I doing here, he thought.

The colonel then turned briefly to the doctor, seated calmly on his other side in her somehow smart white T-shirt. On top of the T-shirt she wore a knee-length, grey, thick-knit woolen cardigan, which framed an exquisitely well-polished silver necklace from a trip to the Mayan Riviera decades ago.

"Dr. West," he said, "as with all our meetings so far in your stay with us at the Array, this falls under the Agreement you are no doubt very familiar with. Level P5, as I said before."

Laurie nodded professionally and they all turned to the screen, where they too seemed to be coming to some kind of order. Barrett clicked on the sound button and 'Mute Off' appeared briefly in the center of the screen.

"… ime we got started, gentlemen, ladies." said the general at the head of the other table. The hubbub died down, the general nodded to his aide and scribe to his side, and began:

"Good afternoon, everyone, let's get started. Plenary Briefing of United States Air Force Intelligence, Surveillance Branch, September 27th, General Pickler chairing.

"We've completed our roll-call at this end," the general said, looking to his aide for a nod of confirmation. The aide leaned towards him, "Level P11, as usual, sir." he mouthed to the general, indicating the lowest level of security clearance at their end of the room.

"If we could start with you, Colonel Milton." the general prompted.

"Colonel Milton, Level 11, for ANFPS85 on the line, sir. Dr. Laurie West you know, Level 13, I also have a Mr. Neal Danielson for a spot analysis, Level 5 clearance, and Lieutenant Diorio, Level 11."

The various other unseen sites on the briefing call provided their information, acknowledged by the general as Colonel Milton had been, and soon the meeting began in earnest. Over the course of the next forty-five minutes the general ran through a checklist of agenda items that apparently all the participants at the other end were privy to. He stopped at various points to allow various parties, both seen and unseen, to contribute in a well-orchestrated interplay of highly educated experts, informing highly ranked and often equally highly qualified officers. Topics included reports, analyses and think tanks on a variety of space-related surveillance topics from satellite tracking and development to launch monitoring programs, both at home and abroad.

As discussion of each agenda item came to a close, it was either closed or tabled for review in closed door meetings as deemed appropriate by the general after a form of hierarchal democratic consent had been reached which only effective military organizations and the occasional medieval government have ever done well.

In the meantime, Neal considered his fellow classified meeting attendees. Laurie was, undoubtedly, extremely clever, what was less expected was her lack of conceit or patronizing tone. Of course, being very nice and inclusive is, in its way, a conceit of the extremely clever and accomplished, albeit a more pleasant one.

That said, he brimmed with a pride he'd not felt in some time when he recalled how effectively he had explained his theory to her, and not for the first time he longed for the higher echelons of scientific pursuit which a younger, more arrogant Neal had spurned. He envied the patience that he knew she must have displayed in the decades she had no doubt spent under people less gifted than her before reaching the level which she clearly now enjoyed. Patience he himself had always had trouble showing during his shorter and distinctly less exalted career.

As the meeting proceeded, he noticed that she would occasionally interpose a thought or suggestion, always to the attentive silence of the group at the Pentagon, but she never grandstanded. Colonel Milton proved equally surprising. He was not a dolt, as Neal had assumed, but a capable man who was actually in the right job here at the Array. He had demonstrated surprisingly little difficulty absorbing the new ideas Neal had proposed, and had shown virtually none of the inflexibility that Neal expected from a man of his rank and station. Within his arena the colonel's was clearly a strong mind, trained after years of rigmarole into a practical conformity that was no doubt appropriate to his rank.

While the stereotype had been wrong for the colonel, though, it was becoming clear it was very much applicable to General Pickler, Neal thought, as he looked at the general's corpulent face. Though he had a strong stature, his coloration showed that an abundance of a younger man's indulgences were still stubbornly allowed to pass his lips, and no doubt he would continue to insist he was fine till the day his seemingly healthy, five-mile-a-day body keeled over, his bacon and filet mignon soaked blood finally congealing in his veins.

Sadistically entertained though Neal was by this image after nearly an hour of painstakingly banal briefings, he was broken from his reverie by the sudden turn of the meeting's focus to the topic he was here to discuss.

"Colonel Milton," the general said, "you had some business from the Array's comet, asteroid and meteor review, I believe. Another Armageddon, is it, colonel?" the general chuckled as he made his little joke, bless.

Apparently the ridicule that Neal had encountered for what he did was not limited to undergrad guys at bars competing with him for the attention of their impressionable female counterparts.

The colonel breezed past the patronizing, if innocently intentioned joke by the general, "Yes, sir, I have called your office's attention to the report dated September 20th of this year from this facility."

"Yes, Colonel, we have the report in our packets." the general said, his aide handing him the copy.

"General, if I may," said the colonel, "we have made some additional calculations based on revised estimates that are not in the version of the report you have in front of you."

"New estimates? Based on new information?" the general questioned, looking through the screen at the colonel.

"Not new information, per se, sir, but different interpretations of the existing data by our experts."

Neal spoke up: "We didn't factor in a lack of gas cloud or debris, err, sir, so the original estimates were, well, wrong."

The general looked at the scientist as if unaware whether to acknowledge him and Neal looked a little disconcerted. Why had he suddenly felt the need to speak, exactly? He glanced back at the colonel only to be greeted by a foreboding expression not dissimilar to the one he had seen just outside the conference room not an hour beforehand.

"What my colleague from the Array's *civilian* team is trying to say, sir," interposed the colonel, returning his focus to the general, "is that we have a potential alternate set of estimates based on a theoretical new interpretation of the information."

"Do you and your team concur with this analysis, Colonel?" asked the general.

Neal, the general, and all of the briefing team at the Pentagon looked expectantly at the colonel, all except Dr. West, whose calm gaze remained passively on Neal.

"I have reviewed the data and the theory and believe it has foundation, sir." said the colonel diplomatically. "General Pickler, sir, I believe my aide forwarded a revised version to you before this meeting, if you would like to call it up on the screen."

"Well why wasn't it included in the original report put before this board?" inquired the general, and the colonel paused, making a mental note to black list one Neal Danielson, stopping him from ever being allowed in this meeting, or this facility for that matter, ever again.

"May I offer up a point, Michael?" Dr. West interjected to the general, the use of the senior officer's first name momentarily stunning everyone.

But Laurie smiled serenely, took the silence as tacit approval to carry on and said, "I have reviewed the numbers and the revised analysis that Mr. Danielson proposes. At this point I am in agreement with the colonel's insightful opinion that they require consideration. Unfortunately, my late arrival this morning from Washington meant we were unable to get these revised estimates into the copy of the report you are holding."

Neal and the colonel stared at her, as did the general, while everyone else joined the serene doctor in looking at the general for his reaction.

After a moment, the general duly said, "Well, then, we should certainly review the new data, Colonel." The room breathed an imperceptible sigh of relief, and the colonel made a note to upgrade his respect for the good doctor from high to downright inestimable, "Tell me, does this new analysis imply a danger of planetary impact?"

"Not on land, no sir, that appears unlikely, but if it holds true then it does imply that a potentially significant amount of debris could enter equatorial orbit in the same plane as our satellites, as well as entering the atmosphere."

The general looked grave, "OK, Colonel we have the report on-screen now," he said, his eyes looking to the left of the camera to something the colonel could not see. "Let's see, Incident ID: 'ColonelMiltonBl'…yes, well then," the colonel flinched, but the general moved discreetly past the title, "yes, I see the atmospheric entry location estimates. Colonel, why don't you tell us how you reached these conclusions?"

The colonel went to speak and then thought better of trying to explain it, saying instead with a cautioning glance, "Mr. Danielson, maybe you would like to go over the details of the new trajectories."

Neal took a breath, noted to himself that he really was every bit as pigheaded as his ex-girlfriends used to say, and then, after arranging his thoughts more cohesively, he began: "General Pickler, sir, what Dr. West, Colonel Milton and I decided after reviewing the data available was that there was a potential that this meteoroid cloud wouldn't follow the same mass estimating theories established in the past. You see, sir, there is a notable lack of both a central mass and a gas cloud. This is important here because we can see…"

Neal continued with his cogent explanation and found himself finally beginning to see how much easier it would be if he behaved a little more like the intelligent person he purported himself to be.

Chapter 4: Their Eyes Upon Us

300,000 miles out from Earth along our equatorial plane, the cluster's speed, though diminished, is still faster than any craft we have ever manufactured as it rushes to meet us, our gravity bending its path gently inward. It flies past the orbital radius of the moon without preamble and over the next few hours it enters its final approach to Earth. The vast majority of the chunks of matter are lifeless astral rock, the leftover building blocks of a trillion planets and suns. They are, as predicted by Neal Danielson, less riddled by the scars of gaseous escape and freeze-cracking than would typically be expected, but bar that, they are mostly unexceptional.

As the cluster's leading edge starts to brush the outer limits of the troposphere, the paths of eight specific pieces distinguish their trajectories in ways not dissimilar from the predictions of some of the more astute scientists at the various radar arrays and observatories monitoring the cluster's approach. Though far from smooth or regular, close inspection of these particular eight masses would show that in some of the cracks and dents that do dot their surfaces there appear to be patches of a smooth, matt material, as though inside these eight blocks something dark is hidden.

All eight rocks form part of the leading edge of the cluster as it dips farther into the atmosphere, and they begin to trace long, slow arcs across the night sky of Earth, rapidly approaching the dawning sun that is seemingly coming to meet them over the horizon.

As they begin to enter the atmosphere proper, the eight objects start to glow and smolder under the first signs of air resistance. Slowly, inextricably, their outer shells start to burn away, disintegrating under the barrage of a quadrillion air molecules after surviving a quadrillion miles of vacuum to reach this point. As their entourage vanishes into a glowing haze, the eight resolve into cylinders ten feet long, perfectly black; matt black as midnight in the densest forest, utterly and profoundly unreflective in a way no natural substance could be.

They continue to arc apart ever so slightly, but at their oblique angle of entry these slight differences in trajectory will give them vastly different impact sites.

As the ever-thickening atmosphere cloaks them in fiery balls, they begin their final approach, and as one by one their short-lived orbits disintegrate, they each drop to their watery graves.

High above, hidden amongst the remaining body of the cluster, out of the atmosphere's reach, four sinister pyramidal black objects begin to distance themselves. They are each forty feet across, and fifty feet in length and as they quietly and slowly separate themselves from the remains of the asteroid, they orient themselves toward Earth, with their peaks pointing down toward the spinning blue and green globe below them. As they slowly spread out around the equator their orientation presents no flat surface directly toward the planet, rendering them virtually invisible to any earthly radar. Each is the same pitch-black as their smaller counterparts fast approaching the ground, as black as the void that forms their backdrop, and slowly but surely over the next two weeks they will maneuver into geosynchronous retrograde orbits around the earth, equidistant from each other, encircling the waist of our world.

On the surfaces of each of the inverted pyramids several apertures smoothly irise open, and with phenomenally acute sight they begin to survey their prey for the first time. Despite the huge distances travelled by this cluster of rock and interstellar material, the globe below them appears massive and terribly beautiful as its surface flies by.

They look on, as across this canvas their eight smaller cousins blaze their meteoric fall to Earth.

Chapter 5: Blissfully Ignorant

The Waterloo Club in downtown Brussels is as well adorned as its frequent and honorable guests. Dressed in a tailor-made dark grey suit, crisp white shirt, and one of his trademark colorful bowties, François-Xavier Marchelier walked from his car to the back door, passing the familiar doorman of the club with a genial nod and smile. Two discreet armed guards stood to either side of the door, a series of cameras above it leading to a room where people identify which of the club's guests the guards should, or should most certainly *not* search.

"Bonsoir, Monsieur Marchelier." the footman said as he gently laid the club member's white cashmere scarf and calfskin gloves over his left forearm.

"Bonsoir, Arthur, tout va bien avec le dîner?" inquired François-Xavier.

"Naturellement, Monsieur, tout es prêt." says Arthur without a smile, his eyes momentarily closing as he nodded slowly to his esteemed guest.

"Excellent, Arthur, excellent." The minister smiled back, turning to make his way into the lounge.

Deep green, studded, leather chairs, older even than most of their inhabitants, dotted the highly polished, well-worn parquet floor in groups two or four, sometimes paired with matching burnished burgundy leather sofas. François-Xavier strolled amongst the auspicious men toward an unoccupied table with an old and faded 'reservé' sign.

"Ah, mon ami honorable, qu'est-ce qui se passe?" a man hailed as the minister walked passed. François-Xavier bowed gently to the man but did not stop, walking onward with an ingratiating smile. Arriving at the empty table, François-Xavier turned the reserved sign onto its face and sat, plucking a copy of *Inventaire* magazine from under his arm. As he started to read the magazine, a waiter appeared with a glass of chilled Versinthe, set it on the table in front the minister and then retired without a word, taking the reserved sign with him.

In a back room of the club, a group of drivers and assistants sat sipping free coffee from a set of glass pots on heating pads in a corner. Among them, First Lieutenant Jeanette Archalle of the French Army Intelligence Service, Special Assistant to the Minister of Defense, sat with her tablet terminal, running various encryption programs on e-mails coming in to the minister.

Attached to her wrist by a titanium handcuff and weapons grade two-foot stainless steel chain was a briefcase. The case literally never left the assistant's side for the eight hours she was on duty, at the end of which she would transfer it to one of her two colleagues using an additional chain, seeing to it that it was never separate from one or the other at any time.

Jeanette had commented to her cohorts at a briefing that it was surprising how quickly you forgot the briefcase was even there, as it literally and figuratively became part of your body for eight hours a day. They had agreed, but had mocked her for saying she thought she might miss it when she went on vacation the following day.

They had every right to mock her. Getting one of the jobs on the minister's team of three special assistants was extremely hard and very prestigious. The security process you had to pass was beyond rigorous, and because of that there were no substitutes. While Jeanette was away, the other two would have to make up for her absence by working twelve-hour shifts, and they had made sure Jeanette felt every inch of their gratitude.

But Jeanette hadn't been joking when she had said she didn't notice the briefcase anymore, and unless they were updating its closely guarded contents, or running a drill with the mock codes and protocols it also contained, she almost forgot it was there. Thus the briefcase was not the subject of the lieutenant's thoughts as she read the decrypted e-mail from the European Space Agency to the minister and decided that Mr. Marchelier would probably want an immediate update on its contents.

Standing up, she nodded at the two dangerous-looking members of the French Secret Service who made up her security detail while she carried the case, and walked through the main door, heading toward the club's concierge desk. They were behind her in an instant, maintaining a respectful distance and an ever-watchful eye on her as she asked to use the club's printer, transferring the now decrypted report she has just received to an SD card and plugging it into the printer's side.

- - -

The minister was engrossed in a lengthy article about Pascal Mercier's Night Train to Lisbon when Jeanette walked up and stood just out of earshot, awaiting permission to approach. Though he did not look up, he noticed her waiting. As was his way, he finished the paragraph he was reading, smiled a moment at a particularly erudite simile, and then looked up at his expectant assistant. At a wave of François-Xavier's hand, she stepped forward and whispered in his ear, handing him a report as she did so. He nodded, took a minute to flip through the multi-page report as she stood patiently at his shoulder, and then asked: "Has the navy confirmed this?"

"Yes, sir, their comments are at the bottom. It appears to be benign enough, but I thought I'd let you know there will be a bit of a show tonight when they enter the atmosphere."

"Oui, Jeanette, merci beaucoup pour votre diligence." he said, and she nodded to him with a polite smile and turned to walk away. The Frenchman read the report again. Apparently they were going to have quite the fireworks display tonight. He checked the probabilities of landfall and their relevance to France and her protectorates and nodded. Nothing to be afraid about, but still, something of interest.

"Bonsoir, Monsieur Le Minister." said a voice and François-Xavier looked up, smiling as he took in the visage of Sir Stephen Packsley, a colleague of his from across la Manche and without hesitation rose to his feet to greet his sometime acquaintance.

"How are you, Sir Stephen?" said François-Xavier, his English impeccable if heavily accented, "I didn't know you were staying in Paris or I would have suggested we had dinner together."

"I'm well, Minister, trés bien, merci. Et vous?" replied Sir Stephen, waving aside the Frenchman's apology but noting his colleague's ever-so-slight cringe at the English stiffness Stephen applied to his French. Why, thought Stephen, are we so forgiving of the wildly incorrect ways the French pronounce English when they so stringently criticize us for the slightest mispronunciation of an 'r' or 'ou?' Nonetheless, he smiled patiently as he shook François-Xavier's hand and accepted the man's invitation to sit.

They had spent the day in lengthy meetings along with many others, discussing a host of not-very-fascinating issues from immigration bylaws to farming subsidy reform, and neither of them had much of an appetite for discussing political matters. The meetings had been, as they often were, in English, the most uniformly spoken language amongst the group. Though François-Xavier was fluent in his sister language, it was still an added strain to have to speak at length in it, especially in a meeting that already strained his patience quite enough, thank you very much.

He sighed discreetly as he mastered his frustration over the subjugation of his mother tongue to its gruff Germanic neighbor. In more forgiving moments he had often been amazed at the vast array of words that English had at its disposal, and in fairness it was an extremely nuanced and versatile language. A word for the thousand variations of any given emotion. If he hadn't been essentially forced to speak it by its pan-global usage François-Xavier might have had some small respect for Shakespeare's mother tongue. But he *was* forced to speak it, and often.

As they sat in relaxed silence, François-Xavier glanced at the report he had just received, raised his eyebrow and smiled.

"I don't know if you have heard about it but apparently there is to be a meteor shower this evening." he said.

"Yes?" Stephen thought a moment and then memory of the report he had read a week beforehand came to him, "Yes, yes, I remember now. I received the same news. From what I have heard it is to be quite the show. They say some of the debris may even touch down … though not on land, I understand."

The Frenchman looked questioningly at his companion, "Oh, you have heard about it too? Good, I had assumed that you would not have had a chance to read anything since the meeting today." François-Xavier smiled and handed the report on the shower to the Englishman. It was in French but unlike most of his compatriots Sir Stephen's grasp of the French language was passably good.

But Stephen merely smiled and did not open the report, saying, "Oh no, I happened to read about this last week when the report came … out." Sir Stephen trailed off as he noticed the date on the Frenchman's report and realized that the information had only just reached them today. France had enjoyed a not-inconsiderable decrease in the cooperation of their US intelligence counterparts since their disagreement over the Iraq war, while the English were clearly still enjoying the benefits of America's more advanced space monitoring program.

But François-Xavier was first and foremost a politician and with feigned ignorance he skated over the issue and smiled benignly, "You know, the club has a roof terrace. Perhaps you would like to take a turn up there and watch the show?" he said.

- - -

The two suited gentlemen stood on the rooftop balcony, the evening skyline of Brussels spread out before them, dominated by the Gothic bell tower of the church in the central Grand Place. The orange-yellow streetlights illuminated the picturesque cobbled streets of the old town and restaurant district below. But the picturesque city that sprawled about their feet was forgotten for now as the two of them joined a growing audience, their eyes turned firmly to the night sky above them as two stark, golden flame trails traced the path of their burning sources as they shot towards the northern Atlantic.

They were blissfully unaware of their smiling faces being noted and logged by a synthetic eye as it passed, unseen, far overhead. Lit by the candles arranged tastefully around the terrace, their mouths moved in conversation, the movements of their lips interpreted, translated and reviewed from far above in an instant. As their conversation was logged, images of their faces were also analyzed.

Later that night they made their good-byes and walked across the club's private car park, their assistants escorting them to their cars. As Jeanette and her two armed guards helped the particularly merry Minister Marchelier to the door of his bulletproof Citroën, the eye watching them from above noted the briefcase chained to her side and sent a message to the interior of one of the fallen meteors.

It had analyzed the conversations of the two gentlemen and those around them, and the appearance of the case and the security detail it so clearly merited. It had sifted this from the sea of data it and its peers were already gathering as they watched the planet they now orbited. In databases already flooding with data, names, relationships, addresses, jokes, and idioms, in languages it was already decoding down to the colloquial level, the intelligences that watched from above surmised they had found a person of interest, and that one of the many primary, secondary, and tertiary mission parameters that it was so capably designed to fulfill was already clarifying itself.

It posited that it may have acquired one of its targets. It wanted the contents of that case.

Chapter 6: Over Arching Introduction

Over the heads of watching fishermen on board the small Indian fishing junker the *Nada Harashnu*, a smoking orange fireball plummets to the ocean halfway to the horizon. They hear its roar as it passes overhead, but they see it hit the water several moments before the terrific sound of its impact reaches them.

The plume of water it sends into the air casts a shadow a quarter of a mile across the dawn, and the fishermen stare wide-eyed at it, the boat wallowing on the gentle but irregular chop typical of these waters.

Thirty seconds later the bow of the shockwave rushes to meet them, a gust of air preceding the sudden swell of water. The boat rises, suddenly driven upwards by the wave coursing underneath it. The small waves that had gently rocked the boat a moment ago are shaken from the surface of the water as the low parabolic flies outward. The boat's sudden rise drives the fishermen to their knees as their very world moves violently at the whim of the shockwave surging through the water beneath it.

Though powerful, the shockwave begins to dissipate quickly as it expands outwards. The fantastic energy that had driven the meteor, like a javelin, through our atmospheric shield finally sighing its last breath as it is absorbed by the ocean's depths. It is reduced, in the end, to a gentle spreading swell as it rolls outward to wash unseen on distant beaches.

As the southern Indian fishermen look to each other for reassurance the water lowers again and settles around them, their ship gently swaying, as though the boat is as dazed by the experience as its crew. As far as the eye can see the ocean is now perfectly smooth, as though the hand of God has grasped the very corners of their world and shaken the wrinkles out, the shockwave like the waft of air flowing under a tablecloth as it settles down on the proverbial table beneath.

- - -

Though her mother did not know it, she had just made all of young Sowmya's dreams come true. Sowmya may not understand all the things they said at school, but she knew, for certain, that no day in her life would ever be as wonderful as today, two days before her sixth birthday. In her arms, too precious to wear, nearly too wonderful to touch, lay a sari. A new sari: purple with red stitching and gold sequins. It was obvious to Sowmya that it was by far the most beautiful sari ever made, and Sowmya marveled how her mother had accomplished such a thing when she had discovered it.

Surely the daughters of the Brahman would envy such a prize. She had discovered it in her parents' room while trying on her mother's pair of English high-heeled shoes which her uncle had brought home from Calcutta. Then she had seen the small card made out to her and realized this sari was to be her birthday present. She hadn't been able to leave it there, it was simply impossible; no feat of will power could have allowed her to put it back in its box right then. She would return it later, after she had kept it close for a while. So she had gently put it under her dress, close to her belly, and then she had run out of the house.

Arriving at the beach, she had taken it out, peering carefully around to make sure no one was there to see her treasure. There she had sat for half an hour imagining how it would feel to wear it, but worried that she may never be able to bring herself to put on such a marvel. And so she sat on the beach outside the small fishing town of Kodikkarai that was her world, elated, staring out across the water.

Her papa had told her that a large island called Sri Lanka was just over the horizon, where millions of people lived. She hadn't decided whether or not she believed him yet. After all, why wouldn't they just come and live here in India like everyone else, there was plenty of space. Her mother even had two spare rooms she rented out to laborers; some of the Sri Lankans could stay there. Of course, her uncle also said there were whole other countries, lands, seeming other worlds out there as well. None of it sounded very plausible to young Sowmya.

She was thinking about the imaginary Sri Lankans and how they could not possibly be as happy as she was right now, even if they existed, when, walking out of the gentle surf toward her, she saw one. The Sri Lankan looked very wet, but she didn't seem very tired for how far she must have swam. Sowmya could only swim about two meters from her big sisters before she was exhausted.

Behind her the Sri Lankan woman dragged what looked like a black plank nearly as long as herself and nearly as wide, but with a round cylinder seemingly strapped along about a quarter of its underside, scraping in the dark, wet sand. By the mark it was leaving it appeared to be very heavy, but it didn't seem to bother the woman as she gently picked it up and started folding it up. Actually it was like it was folding itself in her hands. After a moment the woman, who was about the same height as Sowmya's mother and older sisters, was left holding something that looked remarkably like the backpack her uncle carried when he went travelling, only black, as black as night, the girl thought, momentarily.

Turning, the Sri Lankan looked straight at Sowmya, who froze on the spot, utterly transfixed by the woman's black eyes. The woman started walking slowly toward Sowmya until she stood over her, smiling gently, like Sowmya's mother smiled at her.

"Hello," said the woman whose name would be Preeti Parikh, "would you like to show me where the train station is?"

Sowmya did not compute that the woman's hair was somehow already dry: in fact, so was the casual but exquisite sari Sowmya now saw the woman was wearing.

She merely said, "ok," meekly, and climbed to her little feet.

- - -

"Mother! Mother! I saw one, I saw one!" shouted Sowmya, running back into the house an hour later.

"One what, puppy?" her mother asked patiently, not looking up from her needle and thread as she replaced a button on her second son's school uniform.

Sowmya had walked in silence with the Sri Lankan all the way to the train station, where the lady had quietly requested and paid for a ticket all the way New Delhi.

"A Sri Lankan, Mumma! I saw a Sri Lankan. She swam over to India to go and live in New Delhi!"

Lifting her head with a patient smile as her daughter stood panting expectantly in front of her, Sowmya's mother looked at her, and then down at the object in the girl's hands.

Sowmya followed her mother's stare down to the sari still clasped at her tummy, creased now with being carried in her scrunched up little hands for over an hour.

"Oh," said Sowmya, crestfallen, "I found it."

- - -

Though Sowmya would be one of only a handful of folks to see them walk ashore, there were, in fact, seven other strange people who made landfall that day in different places around the world.

People would have been unlikely, for example, to see the Chinese looking gentleman stepping out of the surf north of Jiaojiang at 5am, or the apparently Pakistani gentleman climbing up a wet, craggy rock shore and then walking to the deserted coastal road toward Karachi.

Any onlookers would have been very curious and concerned to see the man washed up onto the beach in northern Scotland in October by the freezing North Sea tide. Likewise the woman who stepped lightly across a black pebble beach from the perilously cold waters near Seward, Alaska, or the dangerous-looking man who navigated the ice to stumble ashore in Petropavlovsk, in the Kamchatka region of eastern Russia.

That said, in the haze of swimmers enjoying the year-round warmth of the beach at Herzliya, north of Tel Aviv, quite a few people noticed the woman who swam ashore between the man-made rock islands preserving the beaches near the marina. However, the few that did were more focused on her striking figure and the revealing bikini she was wearing than the slightly strange black bag she was carrying.

Bill and Mandy Tubbington, on a late summer holiday in Guernsey with their two children were among the few who noted the slight but strong-looking man swim ashore there. Bill assured his wife and kids that because this man was carrying a bag he must be a scuba diver returning from a dive. Mandy recognized her husband's tone as the one he put on when he didn't know what the hell he was talking about, but did not make anything of it, as she was quietly enjoying the sight of the swimmer's bum as he walked up the beach toward the car park, his hair drying surprisingly quickly in the wind.

Leaving the beach later that day, neither of them would have the presence of mind to think of the man when they discovered that their rental car was missing. Especially as they would hear from the police within ten minutes of calling them that it had already been found, twenty miles away on the other side of the island, locked and unharmed, at the ferry terminal linking the island to nearby France. Without any evidence of a break-in anywhere on the car, the police would not waste much sleep on the investigation.

Chapter 7: Improbable vs. Immovable

In the same building as the conference room where Neal and Laurie West had reviewed their report not two weeks ago for General Pickler, Neal sits, alone now, reviewing his notes. He is back on the run-down, outdated civilian side again, seemingly so far from the state of the art equipment and brusque but efficient air force officers.

This part of the building is not maintained by the deep pockets of the US Air Force, but instead by the ever-shrinking coin purse of the university's physics department. Though the PCs are actually provided by their government-backed neighbors, it is clear that this part of the building represents the place that the colonel sends his outdated and unwanted PCs to die.

Over the past couple of weeks since the meeting with General Pickler, Neal had contrived to make himself unpopular again by incessantly demanding that the government look into retrieving one of the asteroids that had, without exception, landed near, but never actually on, land. Confounding what might have otherwise been a fairly reasonable proposition was the fact that they had all fucking well landed in deep water, thought Neal angrily.

But it *could* be done, he had said a hundred times. According to all reports from near the impact sites they had all survived the atmosphere to hit with apparently significant force, registering on seismographs around the globe, and causing minor but clearly defined shockwaves to wash up on nearby shores. This fact indicated that they were even denser than even Neal had speculated, making other theories that they must have disintegrated upon impact far from certain. Those theories were further refuted by the lack of any floating debris at the Alaskan site, which the coastguard had been dispatched to survey, or the Scottish site, which had been visited by the RAF and British Royal Navy.

But Neal's arguments had fallen on deaf ears. The colonel, who had caught some of Neal's enthusiasm in spite of himself, was controlled by higher powers that were more pragmatic and less curious than he, and both Neal and his theories had been brushed under the carpet.

So Neal had returned to his 1970s decorating nightmare of an office and worked his theories with his limited resources, sending his reports to any noted scientist he could find an e-mail address for. The only one who had responded was about to join him on the cheap side of the fence for a meeting.

Dr. Laurie West had found herself quietly impressed with Neal. But more than that, she felt the same shared pangs of frustration when she looked at him as she did when she remembered her own wasted shouts of protest before she had learned to play the surprisingly political game of modern scientific pursuit. Like it or not, the days of discovering life-changing breakthroughs in your basement laboratory were all but gone. The machinery necessary to explore the limits of our ever growing field of knowledge were simply too expensive to afford without navigating the bureaucracy of big business, or worse, big government. Nowhere was this truer than in astrophysics, Laurie thought as she climbed the stairs to Neal's floor, where people like her and Neal simply must have access to big toys to see what they wanted to see.

As she turned the corner, she saw Neal. He looked tired, but as he rose to greet her she saw the same eagerness in his eye she had seen the day they had met in the control room. Since then she had been back in Washington, in her usual office. Unbeknownst to Neal, she had been party to the calls between General Pickler and Colonel Milton, and she wondered if Neal knew how vigorously the colonel had pursued Neal's cause.

After receiving his latest reports, they had spoken briefly over the phone, but without the numbers and graphics in front of her it had sometimes been difficult to follow all of his arguments. Besides, it had been a while since she had found herself discussing a theory as interesting as this, and with someone as surprisingly capable as Neal was. Conversations like this were so much better in person. So she had arranged another trip to the Array a little sooner than she otherwise might have, and now found herself smiling warmly as she walked up to Neal, who watched her approach like a shipwrecked sailor sighting a sail on the horizon.

"Dr. West, I can't say how grateful I am to you for coming all this way." he said sincerely, taking her proffered hand.

"It's Laurie, please." she said with a friendly smile, "I have to say I was looking forward to it. You have some very interesting ideas, even if they are leading to some strange conclusions."

"Yes, well, it certainly seems that way, but the numbers speak for themselves, don't you agree?" he said, hopefully.

"Well apparently they aren't speaking a language Washington can understand." she said, laughing ruefully as she took a seat at the large table.

"Yes, well, maybe you can help me to translate it, or maybe just take out the big words." he said with a smirk.

She surveyed the table which Neal had sequestered for his research, and the slew of papers, piled statistical analyses, physics textbooks, and copious notes that covered every inch of it. She felt a surge of curiosity and excitement for the coming debate. Though she always wanted to believe even the most outlandish theory, she would never allow herself to follow one blindly, and her powers of perception were of such a high level that she could play devil's advocate to even the most well-founded and accepted theory.

While this one was currently accepted by only one man, she felt certain it still qualified as well founded, and looking up at the incisive eyes of that lone believer, she felt keen to start the battle of minds she sincerely hoped she was going to lose.

But before that, she would need some ingredients to stir the proverbial soup.

"OK," she said, "we're going to need coffee, cookies, water, a whiteboard, and more coffee."

He laughed out loud, feeling a surge of hope at the arrival of this prospective ally, "With pleasure, Laurie, with absolute pleasure!"

- - -

Three hours later, they had lost none of their enthusiasm and the room had become strewn with even more papers, while the three large whiteboards they had wheeled in were well covered with often conflicting equations, and diagrams depicting angles of entry and orbit. Laurie had brought so much rigor to his thinking that he was almost ashamed that he had presented his thoughts to anyone without putting them to this test first. But neither of them could doubt now that this rigor was only strengthening his conclusions.

Several things had kept Neal up after the meteors had made their scattered impacts on Earth, most of which were merely circumstantial: that they had landed near land, but never on it was curious, as was the fact that they had all landed in patches of deep water or underwater trenches that veered unusually near to land. But despite General Pickler's opinion of him, Neal was not one to wildly pursue conspiracy theories and these apparent coincidences had no more impact on him than they had had on a man of the general's unimaginative disposition.

The thing that had peaked his interest was that they had all made it to those oceanic impacts at all.

While an ultrasonic entry to an atmosphere as thick as ours is always destructive, you could never predict exactly how the vagaries of shape, mass, constitution, and density would combine with the prime factors of angle-of-entry and speed to affect an arriving meteor's ability to survive the onslaught.

You could, however, say that increased size also increased the probability that the mass would survive the introduction to our planet and make it to the surface. So at a given angle of entry, there was a size above which it was very likely that some part of it would make it all the way, and conversely there was a line below which it was inordinately unlikely that it would.

Between these two wannabe-absolutes was a range where factors like shape and density held more sway, though the degree to which they would affect the outcome was harder to predict than the blunter factor of being very big or very small.

"Our eight friends," Neal had explained to Colonel Milton, then to General Pickler, and had reiterated to Laurie's nods of understanding at the beginning of their conversation, "fall in the bottom of this range of mixed probability.

"Specifically," he had continued, "the odds were that they each had on average a roughly 1 in 46 chance of impacting the surface, based on our estimates of weight against the norms of meteor showers in the past.

"Now those are odds we have all faced many time in Vegas, sadly, but multiply that likelihood that one of them would impact to cover all eight making it and you have the same increase in probability that you will win eight times in a row at a roulette wheel.

"Specifically, the chance that all eight would impact is closer to 1 to twenty trillion, roughly." Or 1:20,047,612,231,936, as he had written on the whiteboard for effect.

Once again, Neal was not one for flights of fancy, but above one in a million, he started to get curious. At the very least this probability had to warrant some exploration. This had been the crux of his argument to Washington. General Pickler's counter, for he was not a complete fool, it turned out, or, at least, one of his advisors wasn't, had been that these estimates of likelihood were based on the relatively limited experience we had with interstellar masses, and maybe these were just of a type that we had not previously theorized.

While the general had agreed that this unusualness alone did make the asteroids of interest, he had then pointed out that the shallowest of the waters they had landed in was nearly two miles deep, roughly the depth the Titanic had sunk in. Given that it would cost a massive amount to raise any of them, but more than the difficulties of getting one of these rocks up, there was a much bigger problem. It was one thing to find one of the largest ships in history sitting on a rocky ocean bed, but the very thing that made these rocks of interest was their relatively small size. Finding them amongst their annoyingly also very rock-shaped surroundings presented a potentially insurmountable problem.

It was to these challenges that Neal had set his mind, and as he had discussed his ideas with Laurie, it had become enticingly clear to her that the problem had been a proverbial Pearl Harbor to his sleeping intellect, and had awakened a giant.

- - -

At 4am Laurie lay in her hotel bed, too mentally exhausted to relax. A late dinner of pizza had been eaten on a tablecloth of papers as they had gone through the final throws of their efforts to codify their conclusions. Eventually she had returned to the faceless Marriott Courtyard and collapsed.

She could remember the moment she realized his ideas were taking shape in her own mind. As she had started to defend them in ways he had not yet seen she had realized that she had joined him, and was now one of two people that believed that these objects could and should be found. It was an opinion that had lost him his short-lived respect at the Pentagon, but she had friends he did not. That and the fact that the two of them now had a plausible theory on how to find their quarry should make some measurable difference.

In Washington on Monday she would don a suit and bring to bear the powers of her title as Senior White House Scientific Advisor. On Monday, she would demand a meeting with the White House Chief of Staff, and then, hopefully with his blessing, she would go and see the president.

Chapter 8: Communicating with Hammers

Pei Leong-Lam stood up as the long, green and brown bus entered the processing center at the East Gate of Weifang Base, home to the 26th Infantry division of the Chinese Army and to their most prestigious officer training school. As the high, chain-link gate closed behind them and the six armed guards reassumed their positions in front of it, he reached up to pick up his large military duffle bag from amongst the identical piled bags on the rack above all their heads. He was careful to appear as strained by its weight as his cohorts were by their bags, even though his was essentially empty.

Up until two days beforehand the large duffle bag had contained only one item, itself another container of sorts, but now, though it appeared to be full, its contents were notably absent.

Pei Leong-Lam jumped down from the bus with his fellow officer candidates and formed up along a yellow painted line at the barked commands of the drill sergeant's team of squad sergeants. The drill sergeant walked silently among them, eyeing up the officer candidates, assessing them with long-experienced eyes.

His scarred face was of Tibetan origin, and he had grown up on the plateau, the son of a Sherpa, joining the Chinese People's Liberation Army years after it had first subjugated the Tibetan government. Eight years into his army career he had returned to his homeland with a rifle, and fought with cold calculation and efficiency alongside his fellow Chinese soldiers when they had reinvaded his home country to regain control.

As he surveyed the new meat, his calculating eye came to Officer Candidate Pei Leong-Lam. He noted the soldier's bolt upright stance, the controlled breathing that belied his obvious strength and physical conditioning, but most of all he noted the complete lack of emotion shown on his face as his black eyes remained unflinchingly forward while he was surveyed.

The drill sergeant decided offhandedly to make this one his first example. He would push this one till he broke, or till he met the highest possible standards, either way it did not matter to Drill Sergeant Shih. The others would see from this moment what was expected of them, and what happened when his standards were not met.

Assuming a stance not an inch from the face of the taller, younger Pei Leong-Lam he shouted, "Why do you not look at me? Am I not worth looking at? Am I not pretty?" he screamed with phenomenal volume right in the man's face, his spit flying.

"My eyes are front and center, Drill Sergeant." shouted Leong-Lam, without hesitation.

The drill sergeant tried unsuccessfully to place the accent on Leong-Lam's Mandarin even as he reeled at the quick and annoyingly correct response.

"Are you telling me my business, boy?" he said more quietly, with all the considerable venom he could muster.

"No, Drill Sergeant." shouted the soldier.

"Seems you think you already know the rules here, boy, maybe you think you don't need to go to Officer Training School?" he shouted, "Do you think you are going to be an officer, boy?"

"Yes, Drill Sergeant." was the shouted reply.

"Well, we'll see, won't we," said Shih quietly once more, then, back at his practiced and phenomenal top volume he screamed, "On the floor, give me fifty of your most patriotic, boy."

With the aplomb of the very strong and very supple, Leong-Lam dropped straight forwards, cushioning his fall with his hands, and proceeded to push through forty of his fifty push-ups with straight-backed ease. Drill Sergeant Shih looked on and started to get annoyed; this was not supposed to look this easy.

Sensing anger at his ability, Leong-Lam changed tactics and began to strain at forty, flagging at forty-five, and finally collapsing at fifty, wheezing, and struggling to his feet with feigned difficulty.

Though happy he had broken his new whipping boy, the sergeant also noted to himself that the candidate did not complain or seem even slightly dismayed at the clear injustice of his punishment. Good, he would certainly not go easy on him, but maybe this one had promise. Now the fat tub of lard next to him, on the other hand:

"Do you think you can do better?" he screamed as he brought his guns to bear on this softer target.

"Where did you get your clothes from, you disgusting lump?" he barked, "The zoo?"

- - -

Two days earlier, outside the town where he would eventually be picked up by the army bus and delivered into Drill Sergeant Shih's loving arms, Leong-Lam had stood at the bottom of a wooden telephone pole. In orbit above him an eye was watching him and his surrounding area, checking for coming traffic.

Lowering his now full bag from his back to the soft, wet soil along the side of the deserted road, he bent and looked at its featureless top. As he stared, a small opening formed on the bag's surface, revealing a pouch just larger than the inch-long device it contained.

Leong-Lam picked up the crocodile clip shaped device and clipped it to the collar of his white shirt. Sensing his readiness, the eye overhead confirmed that he was alone, and Leong-Lam turned and with the practiced ability of a chimp, or a beach boy climbing a coconut tree in some now defunct Caribbean ideal, he shimmied hand over hand up the telephone pole, eventually grasping one of the fat telephone lines with one iron-fisted hand. In this position he hung in apparent comfort as he unclipped the black object from his collar and attached it to the line.

The feeling of the wire's thick plastic coating was like a muffled opera to the tiny device, and it immediately reached out its microfiber probes to penetrate the wire's coating, seeking the meat inside. As they found their purchase within, the connection was complete, and the coursing information within sung through the small device like a burst dam.

The device did not understand its purpose, only its mission, and it hung on to the wire as tightly as Leong-Lam and wirelessly informed the black bag below of the successful connection. The black bag was a repository for a host of devices of varying sizes, but its cylindrical central core was of singular purpose. The subspace tweeter was the only communication device its makers still truly used, and though its inner workings were complex, its purpose was simple. Via the creation of a microscopic gap in what we perceive as space, it was possible to physically affect the very fabric of the cosmos.

The effect possible was, in reality, no more than a tiny vibration, like a radio wave, and it was all but imperceptible. Though theorists and science fiction writers liked to posit that it would one day be possible to open holes like this large enough to allow people or spaceships to step instantly from one place to another, such a thing was, even to our guests, still a dream.

But the vibrations they *could* send through the tiny gaps could be felt instantly, by anyone equipped to listen, anywhere in the universe. All that the device had to do once it had opened the hole was make a vibration significant enough to cover the radius it needed to encompass. The part of the tweeters designed to make these vibrations were referred to as 'hammers,' and the only thing simple about the multi-dimensional esotericism of this incredible device was that the bigger the hammer that was used to make the vibration, the wider the device's range.

The clip on the wire, seeking to relay the signal coursing through the cables in its grasp, needed only to affect a sphere large enough to encompass the bag below, and accordingly, its subspace tweeter was only a centimeter long. The black bag's hammer, however, was much larger, nearly three feet long and a foot wide. Large enough that three hundred miles above it, the proverbial thud of the bag's hammer as it relayed the smaller device's signal was felt by the exponentially larger subspace tweeter at the core of the black pyramid satellites orbiting stealthily above.

Because of the medium through which the signal travelled, the connection was not party to the limits and delays of normal three-dimensional communications, a benefit not even light waves enjoyed. The connection established was instantaneous, and in real-time. It was the same as if the entire fifty-ton supercomputer floating in space was somehow hanging off the small telephone wire itself.

Using this new connection, the artificial mind in orbit went to work executing a series of complex programs designed to hack the networks of several Chinese government agencies. It was able to monitor their progress in real-time, and make adjustments to the programs as they encountered firewalls and barriers. With its vast computational brute force the machine could easily have hacked our relatively primitive firewalls, but this would have set off an abundance of alarms in these heavily monitored networks. Though not nearly as advanced as the machine probing them, the firewalls and other defenses surrounding the databases were far from simplistic. So the virtual tendrils the supercomputer was sending out gently probed each barrier. They were seeking, with infinite patience, subtle and unobtrusive ways into the halls of power, for their whole purpose was centered, above all, on remaining unnoticed for as long as was necessary.

Finding the keys it sought, the computer deftly opened the locks to the People's Liberation Army's vast personnel database, and planted a record within. In an organization as leviathan as the million-strong Chinese army, no one could possibly notice the appearance of the somehow preapproved application of Pei Leong-Lam to enter Officer Training School. An administrator at the 26th Group Army Base at Weifang would briefly, but very quietly curse his superiors for adding a late entry to their cadre of new trainees. But the administrator in question would not be so foolish as to question a senior officer's wisdom out loud as he set up Pei's base record and assigned him a bunk and a standard-issue equipment docket.

The job at hand was complete. On some level, the supercomputer enjoyed this rich hard-wired access to information, but it would not be wise to leave its small black access point clipped to a wire out here for some telephone company worker to possibly find it. Its first directive was to get the operatives emplaced so they could begin to work towards the positions that their superiors needed them to be in. Soon the AI would have more permanent access points established by each of its Agents, but for now it notified Pei Leong-Lam that he could proceed with the next stage of his mission.

The device was duly unclipped, and then two things happened. The tiny microfibers projecting from its jaws retracted silently into their sheaths, and Leong-Lam released his grip on the thick wire it had hung from.

He promptly fell the thirty feet to the ground, landing with a thud. His firmly placed feet absorbed the shock easily, but were driven several inches into the soil by the force of the impact. Maintaining his balance with aplomb, he wrenched his feet from the soil one by one, with an audible squelch, and returned to his waiting black bag. Replacing the device in its cubbyhole, he lifted the black bag out of the military duffle it had been hidden in.

Though it was far from safe to leave the large subspace relay here, there was no way he could get such an ominous object past the base security he was about to face. So after extracting some of the more innocent looking tools and communications devices from the bag and placing them in his military duffle, he carried the heavy black object a few meters off the road into the muddy swamp of rice paddies that spread out over the surrounding countryside.

No amount of time in the water would harm or even mark the object, but it would not just sit in the shallow water to be potentially found by the feet of a field worker. As soon as it felt the muddy bottom the object started to bury itself, its sheath morphing in waves to move the mud around it outward and then back in over it, making it disappear slowly but steadily beneath the surface.

It eventually came to rest a meter down into the mud, far from curious eyes...or feet, as Pei climbed out of the paddy, gathered his now almost empty military duffle bag and starting to walk down the road.

While Pei's own internal subspace tweeter could receive signals directly from the overhead satellite, it had not been possible to put a 'hammer' inside a human analog large enough to send signals much farther than a few miles. It was for this reason Leong-Lam and his seven colleagues had been given the larger, more powerful tweeters to relay signals to the hub satellites orbiting above them.

It was an inconvenience to have such a large piece of equipment with them, but one that could not be avoided. Unfortunately the larger tweeters' size also meant that the Agents would often have to leave their relays behind when entering secure areas, but this was also unavoidable.

As Leong-Lam walked away, he left no marker, nor did he worry about the safety of the device. His subspace tweeter relay would be watched over night and day by a far more powerful guardian in orbit, ready to bring to bear a host of unpleasant defensive weapons if the buried relay were somehow discovered by an unfortunate field hand.

Chapter 9: Mr. Precedent

Except, perhaps, for the few people who work there every day, it really never gets old driving up to the White House. Pulling up the rear driveway to the parking lot after passing the security gate, Laurie found she could easily recall the giddy excitement she had felt the first time she came here.

It was just such a cool building, you would have to be half dead not to think so, and it wasn't a dose of patriotism that was driving her. She had seen several seats of government around the world, not least of which the ex-viceroy's palace in New Delhi, which now housed the entire Indian executive branch, such was its size and grandeur.

It was simply the surging power that emanated from places like this. That, and the fact that she was a part of that power.

Flashing her pass at the waiting Secret Service detail, she walked past them into the building proper and turned left along the row of offices leading to the West Wing. She had called Jim Hacker ahead of time and paraphrased what she intended to talk about. She was not foolish enough not to notify General Pickler that she was doing it either; he was not an enemy to be made if it could be avoided, and he was duly waiting when she arrived, his face passive.

She nodded at the somewhat familiar receptionist, then took a wild stab at her name, "Margaret, can you tell Mr…"

"He already knows you're here, Dr. West," the receptionist smiled at hearing her own name, "he will be with you shortly."

Laurie quietly congratulated herself on successfully buttering up the receptionist, who was, after all, the gatekeeper to one of the most influential men in the world, and took a seat on the waiting room couch beside the general.

Jim Hacker's office was linked to the bustling hub of activity that was the president's staff center by a heavy wooden door, but he also had a separate corridor to the reception area. It would not do to have every one of his wildly varied daily guests coming through the president's nerve center, both for their sake and his.

He finished refreshing himself on the doctor's and general's files, a habit that served him well, and then closed his laptop. He had studied the original request of one Neal Danielson that had apparently prompted this meeting after getting off the phone with Dr. West, the Senior White House Scientific Advisor and was, he thought, somewhat prepared for the meeting.

As they sat on the waiting room couch outside, the general, remaining facing forward, said to the doctor, "So I imagine there is some new information to consider on this?"

Laurie mirrored his lack of body language, but said in a quiet voice:

"New information of a sort, General. In much the same way as he did with our mass estimates not long ago, our friend at the Array has not found something new so much as brought a fresh perspective to existing data."

She turned now to him, and he met her gaze, "Michael, we have worked with each other for six years now, I hope I have always shown you just how much respect I have for the many factors I know you have to consider when making decisions on these things, and the dilemma which that poses for you."

The general was stunned by the sudden candor of his normally unflappable civilian colleague, but that surprise also opened a small gap in his professional armor for a moment, and it was through this gap that Laurie hoped to reach.

"I hope you have also gathered some measure of respect for me too, over the years," she continued, "and now I hope I can cash in some small part of that mutual respect for your trust when I say that we have something here. Something unusual, something potentially unique, and though I don't know what it is yet, when something like this lands just out of reach, I think it is our job, our duty, to reach farther. To keep reaching until we have it in our grasp."

She held his gaze, and he felt the full weight she was putting behind her words. Her powerful sincerity met him head on, and he realized that he did indeed have a great deal of respect for this woman. As his usual pragmatism struggled to reassert control over him, he was overcome with the knowledge that she had proven to him again and again that she had a formidable mind, and he had never seen her be unreasonable or behave like the stereotypical blinkered pursuer of truth at-all-costs. He had also never seen her lose her cool. This formidable woman was asking for his trust, and more than that she was asking for his help.

The moment was broken by the smiling invite from Margaret to go in, and the two of them stood, the general indicating for Laurie to go first. Jim Hacker was ready with handshakes and platitudes as they came in, prepared to talk the doctor down from what sounded like a potentially costly project.

He was not ready, however, for the usually pragmatic General Pickler to be on her side.

Chapter 10: Testing the Waters

Neal had never enjoyed living in Arizona, so the change of venue would have been welcome anyway. The fact that he was also working on something that was so cutting edge also helped make up for the fact that he was also, frankly, well outside his area of expertise.

Luckily the same skills that had gotten him through seven years of university with a pretty much constant hangover had served him well when he was invited to join Dr. West at the Marine Research Institute in Florida. Though this was officially a navy project, the Institute was actually a private facility. It owed a lot of its funding, however, to the US government. So when the navy had come calling they had put their best people on the project.

Laurie and Neal stood in overalls staring at the top of the huge tank emerging from the constantly soaking concrete platform surrounding it. Suspended from the steel gantry that ran over the tank, a bulky and irregular probe, covered in plastic and taping, was hanging by a thick cable into the water, pointing down into the dirty depths of the tank, scanning its hidden bottom far below.

The water had been filled with an unnatural amount of salt, sand, dust, and debris to simulate a greater depth of water than was actually present, for while the tank was one of the largest indoor tanks in the world, it was still a fraction of the depth they would be searching in.

Laurie looked at the specially field-hardened laptop in Neal's hands and nodded as he explained what was happening. The initial tests had proven their science sound, but their application amateur. Luckily the practicalities of ocean-bed analysis were the bread and butter of the experts here.

The Institute was, essentially, the final evolution in the hunt for oil, a hunt that was seeking with reckless resolve to extract every last drop of fossil fuel from the earth, no matter how deep, cold or, as was becoming more and more the case, war-torn its location was. Through long practice they had evolved sonar and seismology to a fine science, and were capable of viewing, analyzing, and categorizing almost any ocean bed on the surface on the planet.

The very nature of their business, however, meant that the larger the target they were looking for the better. Because of this, high resolution had rarely been a top priority for them as they had scanned the world's ocean beds for the telltale signs of hidden oil and gas reserves.

So when they had been presented with the parameters of the problem they were being asked to work on, they had actually been grateful for the introduction of an outside authority to help guide this new avenue of research.

Laurie had warned Neal, however, that these folks would not listen to him if they knew he held merely a master's degree, let alone one in an unrelated field. So she had introduced him as an anonymous advisor, his identity necessarily classified, and given him the pseudonym of Mr. Smith.

More than happy to play to this persona, Neal had joined the team and worked with their superior knowledge of sonar and seismology to seek the results he needed, guiding them like the hands of his mind's eye, imagining and then executing a barrage of ever larger tests and experimental machinery to aide him in his mission to find a way to locate the meteors.

Any concern she may have had over his ability to maintain credibility had been assuaged when she had heard him discussing part of the theory they had both developed with his new team.

"Because of interference, sea state and various other factors, it's clear that multibeam bathymetry data conceals too many outliers and simply won't get to the resolution we need. In order to process large amounts of data accurately and effectively, we're going to need a faster and automatable approach. To this end, Dr. Cavanagh and I may have defined the beginnings of an algorithm for detecting outliers based on density of points.

"Firstly, each swath of data should be projected along orthogonal and side direction axes. On each plane an initial point would need to be determined according to a corresponding maximum density. Then a whole region could be mapped and searched by the connected neighboring points on each plane. Then we adopt the erosion and dilation algorithms you have already developed to eliminate outliers within the larger region."

While Laurie had been somewhat confused by his logic she had seen that the group had been engaged as he spoke. The passionate debate that had been catalyzed by his theory had been one of many crucial steps the team had needed to make in order to realize Neal and Laurie's somewhat naïve plans. Once again she had found herself reflecting that Neal was smarter than even he gave himself credit for, though she had no intention of fueling his self-confidence and resulting dubious sense of diplomacy further by telling him so.

Two months later they had a prototype for the tool they would need to find the meteors, and she had come down to Florida a couple of days ahead of the generals, admirals, and other White House advisors who would be arriving tomorrow to view the demonstration.

They had spent the first day going over the theory and design of the scanner, or Gamma-supplemented Radar Sonar Seismographic and Planar Array. They had been incredibly creative in their thinking, and had come up with some fundamentally new ways to approach the problem, but essentially the system worked by combining multiple existing scanning techniques, and using them in unison. The readings of all of these were then cross-referenced using a series of complex algorithms developed by the team to single out features of the scanned area that met a series of criteria, each identified by a different part of the scanner.

That had been yesterday, but despite her interest in the scientific rigor, she was keen to see the machine in action. It had been necessary to bring her up to speed, however, as the team arriving would be looking to her for reassurance that there was meat behind what the civilian team was saying.

Though today they would see it in person, Neal had taken some pleasure in teasing her further by spending two hours explaining the tests they had developed for it. After all, before the navy would agree to dispatch the tool and the team to one of its vessels to go hunting, they would have to prove to the arriving dignitaries that it would work in waters that were really two miles deep.

With Laurie's patience running dangerously thin, Neal had eventually brought her from the meeting room where they had reviewed the countless equations, and out into the 'lab.'

As they stood there amongst the tanks and cranes, they were both starting to feel like they had chosen the wrong specialization, for no astrophysics experiment had used labs like this since the moon landing tests. Sure, they had their Hubble telescope, but you didn't wear overalls and a tool belt to work on things like that, you wore a full-body encounter suit and re-breather, and most astrophysicists were unlikely to be doing that anytime soon.

The probe dangling in the huge tank, which they stood watching, was scanning through the water. It sought a variety of identically shaped objects which had been strewn on the bottom of the tank, each of a different material and correspondingly different density. The test for the probe was to see if it could detect the position and density of each object in a series of controlled tests, with remote-controlled underwater cranes moving them between each running of the test.

The cranes would also rearrange a set of even smaller iron blocks into different patterns, testing the ability of the probe to achieve the necessary resolution for the greater vertical distances that would eventually be required.

All of this was done amidst a bed of sand and small rocks designed to mimic a natural ocean bed. This, and the debris in the water, should prove enough to demonstrate the machine's ability to see through everything, up to, and including, mud.

There was one other test that they would keep in reserve in case their audience was not convinced by this massive and impressive show. The second test was fairly expensive, a little strange, and very messy, so they would only show it if someone in the review board asked the same question that Laurie had asked immediately after Neal had finished explaining the first test.

While considerations of cost and clean-up affected the test's appeal for the Institute's administrators and financiers, Neal and most of his colleagues were hoping more than a little that they would have to go to plan B.

- - -

The next day, seated in three rows on white plastic fold-out chairs, the review board was arranged like a wedding, with the naval officers on one side, the air force's on the other, and the various civilian assistants and advisors to each dotted amongst them like their proverbial dates. The chairs had been arranged in the same spot Neal and Laurie had stood in only a day beforehand viewing the massive tank that housed their main experiment.

In the back row Laurie sat between General Pickler and an ex-naval captain who had joined the Institute full-time four years ago after being assigned there for two years as a navy liaison. The appropriateness of Captain Hawkson's assignment had been a little too good, it turned out, and his passion for the specific brand of naval ingenuity the Institute required had drawn him away from his career in the navy proper. Well, passion and a private sector paycheck. Laurie had met him when the project had been initiated eight weeks beforehand, and since then, he and Neal had clearly become friends. The night before the team had gone out for a drink after the dress rehearsal was complete and they had ended up polishing off beers into the wee hours. No doubt if they were successful today, they would repeat that this evening, but first they had seventeen pragmatic and dispassionate senior military men to show the light to. Considering the audience, they had felt it best not to set Neal loose on them, so they had picked one of the Institute's own to lead the demo.

And so, after introducing the project and the team, Laurie had handed over to the team's designated driver and taken her seat, winking at Neal on his spot on the other side of the tank from them. He was standing at the control panel that linked him with the remote cranes at the bottom of the deep well of murky water.

- - -

An hour or so later, the demo was going well, and they were approaching the end of the third and final repositioning. Dr. Madeline Cavanagh, the designated speaker and another member of the previous evening's celebration, continued her description of the way the tools worked, and how they had solved the multitude of problems they had been presented with.

Dr. Cavanagh was in her mid-thirties. She had started out as a marine biologist but her sharp intellect had driven her to branch out into different fields since then, and for the last three years she had been earning the respect of her peers at the Marine Institute. She had an excellent speaking voice and a clear, concise way of explaining even the most complex ideas. She also had striking blue eyes that contrasted her red hair, and which she was using to full effect to engage her audience as she talked. She had that rare kind of attractiveness that did not diminish her intellect, but instead served to heighten her outward credibility. She had been a force on the team over the past two months, second only to Captain Hawkson, who, unbeknownst to the rest of the team, she had been seeing for quite some time.

At Neal's confirmation in her ear, she wrapped up her explanation and guided the audience's eyes once more to the large screen where they were projecting the compound image from the probe. The image started out blank, then slowly but surely each element of the probe started to return data, the computer running simultaneous algorithms to sort the images into an ever more detailed picture of the tank's dark bottom.

Meanwhile, Neal was looking at the raw data behind the image as the computer zeroed in on the anomalous shapes it was seeing, determining their exact shape and density with ever-greater certainty. Even given infinite time the machine would never reach 100% certainty, but the margin would gradually decrease by ever-smaller amounts. For their purposes 85% or above had proven more than reasonable and soon the computer made its 'guesses.'

Neal relayed them to the main screen, and Madeline read them off to the waiting guests, who had each previously been handed the tests' layouts to compare against. As with the first two tests they were appropriately accurate. Neal and Madeline smiled. Laurie turned to James to shake his hand. As the group started to ask its final questions, they were clearly just going through the motions. The tests had been both impressive, and as close to conclusive as a system's test could reasonably come. While Neal did not want to invite undue criticism of his team or their work, a part of him still waited hopefully for that elusive question that would force them to go to Plan B. As the group's questioning continued along ever more banal avenues, it seemed less and less likely, and he was surprised when it eventually came up, not least of which because of who ended up asking it.

"I wonder if I might ask something of the team, Dr. Cavanagh?" asked General Pickler, standing and projecting his formidable voice to the podium.

"Of course, General." prompted Madeline.

"You've shown that the probe can see through all kinds of murk, and to a not inconsiderable depth. But two miles deep this tank is not. How do you know that the significantly increased signal distance won't simply refract your imagery beyond recognition?"

"Well, General," said Madeline, turning briefly to Neal to flash a smile at him, "that is an important question, and one we have battled with. We did come up with an experiment to test it, but it is a little … unconventional. If I may suggest we take a brief lunch break while we set it up, and then I hope we will be able to set your mind at ease."

- - -

As the group filed back in from their foray to the Institute's cafeteria, they were directed to a second part of the vast hangar that housed the various experiments the Institute was working on at that time. Though smaller in overall size than the main hangar, this room still ran the entire length of the back of the building. It contained only one structure. Originally designed for warping or "eccentricity" tests on the driveshafts of naval ships and cruise liners, the room held a single tube, five feet wide and 450 feet long. At any point along its length the hinged top cover could be opened to allow access, and the entire tube was mounted on rollers so that it could be rotated through 100° to allow for the removal of the test shafts onto railings that ran the length of the hangar.

The tube was empty now, its top covers closed, and in place of the stress engines normally placed at each end there were covers fitted to block the gaps. At one end a duplicate of the probe from the tank was secured into this cover, facing down the length of the tube. At the other end, they had arranged iron pieces on the inside of the cover, similar to the ones used at the bottom of the pool.

There were no seats here, so the review committee filed in and formed a line along the side wall. General Pickler was the first to speak: "Well, I guess I'm curious how this will help us anymore than the tank. How much longer is this, exactly?"

"Well, General," started Madeline, "the tube is actually only 150 feet longer than the tank is deep, but it is not filled with water."

"Well, what is it filled with?" he said to a mix of consternation and curiosity from the rest of the committee.

"Well, General, it isn't filled with anything, not yet, at least." She smiled at him without a hint of concern or patronizing tone, "To simulate two miles of depth we needed a substance much denser than water, but with some of the same properties.

"We can thank Captain Hawkson for his recommending something he had worked with in his navy days, which refracts at a degree twenty-three times greater than water."

As she said this, sirens could be heard approaching.

Two behemoth green and white airport fire engines pulled into the long chamber, one through the doors at the far end, and the other coming in through the big double doors right next to the group. They slowly pulled up to either end of the tube, as the committee stepped smartly out of the way.

"Ladies and gentlemen," shouted Madeline over the engines' low grumbles, "the dense foam these engines produce is just the substance we need, unfortunately it does not stay in its foam state for more than five or so minutes, so we were forced to wait till the last moment to have them come in and fill us up."

As she spoke, the engine operators climbed down from their cabs and began unwrapping the hoses, connecting them to specially installed valves on either end of the long tube.

With a radio confirmation from the distant second team the engine chief shouted commands to the hose team and both engines started pumping. Foam was squirting out of small gaps in the tube's side as it coursed from each end, and the stunned audience stepped back as it quickly filled the tube.

So that the tube would not explode when it was full, the team had removed the central top hatch and through this a thick jet of foam suddenly exploded as the two streams met in the middle.

The hose teams cut off the supply, and the probe was activated. As the compound image began to form on the screen, Madeline reiterated: "In the dossiers we gave your assistants, we included the consistency and refractive properties of jet-fuel fire retardant just in case, once again I reiterate that, for the purposes of our experiment, this amount of the foam behaves the same way as roughly two-mile-deep water does."

Slowly the image began to resolve on the screen and the military men confirmed it matched the predetermined layout shown in the previously unexplained depth test section of their dossiers. Happy and suitably impressed, they were keen to exit the noisy and messy room, and Laurie looked at Neal as they filed out the way they had come. He was laughing, along with his colleagues, as James Hawkson walked up to him and shook his hand, shaking his head and laughing as well. Neal and Laurie's eyes met across the room, he grinned boyishly and she chuckled, a small victory shared amongst new friends.

As Dr. West followed the committee members to their conference room to join the closed-door discussion about the project's future, James and Neal thanked the fire teams and they, in turn, exited the long room.

There was only one way to get the foam out of the tube and into drains in the concrete floor, so as the team enjoyed the success of the tests, and the fact they had gotten to use the giant airline fire engines, Neal walked quietly over to the tube's rotation controls.

"OK, enough celebrating, let's get back to business," he shouted, "time to clean this place up."

And with that he pressed the control that rolled the tube through 100°, its top hatches opening as it turned over.

Fifty-five thousand gallons of fire retardant foam flooded out, washing the team off its feet and covering them from head to foot. Twelve coughing, laughing snowmen got slowly up off their butts, wiping the harmless foam from their faces and surveying the foot-deep white pool that now stretched the length of the huge space.

Neal had held on to the wall mounted control panel and was only wet to the knees. He was now slowly moving toward the door, laughing, his relatively clean clothes the only color in a sea of white. James was the first to react, turning and sloshing after him. But Madeline was nearer the door and came to cut Neal's exit off as he laughed obscenities and tried to run.

"Come on, Mr. Smith," they all laughed as they pounced on him, "give us a hug!"

Chapter 11: Tested But Not Found Wanting

Drill Sergeant Shih considered the files in his hands. He had been working with the officer candidates for ten weeks now, and as usual, he had been summoned by the base commander to discuss their potential. While all were equal in the Chinese People's Liberation Army, he was discreetly tasked with identifying who among each class were more equal than others.

As the drill sergeant always did, on the first day of training Shih had looked for a strong candidate to abuse in order to set a standard of excellence for the group. Pei Leong-Lam had seemed to have all the required characteristics: strength, drive, and a measure of arrogance. But it had turned out his arrogance, if that was what it was, had been well placed.

Pei Leong-Lam was one of three candidates he had selected to present to the Base Commander, but Pei was as far removed from the other two as they were, in turn, from the rest of the class. He had consistently exceeded all targets for the school, coming close, but never quite breaking every record the base had. This final failure had not seemed to faze him, in fact his drive seemed to be utterly unflappable. The drill sergeant's shouts and abuse had also not served to allay his progress, nor make him angry. He had continued, utterly unaffected by Shih's deliberately unreasonable abuse.

As the buzzer rang on the base commander's secretary's desk, Shih rose sharply to his feet, his boots clicking to anticipatory attention, three crisp manila folders clasped in front of him. The secretary stood and, head bowed, opened the base commander's door. The door was made of thick but brittle wood, an opaque glass panel in the center framed the gold on black Chinese lettering showing the comrade's auspicious title. At a summons from within the office, the drill sergeant stepped through, the secretary closing the door behind him and resuming her seat.

- - -

On the other side of the planet, Lana Wilson sat on her bunk in her barracks at Annapolis and folded her uniform neatly. As usual, she was not participating in the revelry at the other end of the long room, as many of her other female navy officer-wannabes laughed and talked about the mischief they intended to get up to this weekend.

"All I know," said Marie Smulyen, leaning against her pillow on her bunk, "is that I am horny."

The other girls laughed and a couple nodded emphatically. "No shit, sister," said Latesha Harris from her perch on the end of Marie's bunk, "ten weeks in a room with you bitches is not my idea of fun."

Marie extended her leg and kicked her friend, "You love it, ya big dyke." she laughed.

"Hey," interjected KC Smith from the next bunk, "I'm with Latesha on this one."

"Sure you are!" laughed Marie.

KC did not look at Marie, but gave her the bird as she continued, "I have never seen so many naked women in my life. I intend to redress the balance this Saturday."

"You got a boyfriend?" asked another girl.

"Even if I did, I wouldn't want to have to explain to him the kind of freak I plan to get on this weekend. No, my friends, this will be strictly NSA."

Several of the girls shook their heads in disdain, their upbringing keeping them from sinking quite to the level of their male cohorts in the next building.

"Well," said Marie, "we have our first leave since joining the program this weekend, and I know some of you plan to have a nice dinner with some of the boys. Well, let me tell you, those *boys* are no good to me, so I'll be skipping that snore-fest and heading straight to the club. You fools can come on after and have what's left."

"I'm with you!" said Latesha.

"Hell yeah!" said KC, and the two of them reached over and high-fived.

Down the room, Lana did not look up from her bunk, but she was listening to every word of the group. In fact, she heard and logged everything they said, even the snide remarks and comments some of them made about her abilities. She had singled herself out from the class early on with her marksmanship and astonishing grasp of the navigational and engineering theory they had been forced to learn.

She was clearly going to be fast-tracked for promotion, and her colleagues were not foolish enough to doubt that she would one day be a powerful officer in the navy they planned to call home. But they were also not immune to some jealousy for her exceptional speed and intelligence. Physically, she appeared to be a match for most of the male officers; intellectually the school had no one who could challenge her.

So given her obvious focus and ambition, the other women in her barracks would have been surprised to learn that she was just as keen for the coming weekend leave as they were. But when the petty officer entered the room, she sprang to her feet just as quickly, and waited with equal anticipation for the official leave slips that the senior rating was handing out.

- - -

That Saturday morning, the roll call on the parade ground was more restless than usual. Marie and Latesha winked at each other as the master chief reeled off various information about where they could and could not go, and when they had to be back. Behind them, KC smiled a small but wicked smile to herself.

At the dismissal, Lana Wilson turned and walked directly toward the gate. In navy issue khakis she walked through the security checkpoint, flashing her pass, and down the street toward the bus station. As she was aware, the bus she planned to take was turning onto her street now and she broke into a sprint as she was informed in real-time what its speed and anticipated arrival time was. She slowed to a brisk jog as the bus pulled up to the stop just ahead of her, stepping in behind the last passenger as he climbed aboard. Though most of her colleagues did not plan to leave town that weekend, the few that had planned to take the bus to Fort Meade train station would be disappointed to find out that the next one was not for another twenty-five minutes.

- - -

Four hours later, Lana stepped off a regional train at the small, rural town of Parrsville. In a brief stop not dissimilar to the one Pei Leong-Lam had made on his approach to Weifang, Lana had also been forced to bury her conspicuous black bag as well. After a brief visit to a sporting supply store in the town center to buy a duffle bag, she began walking out of the town until she came to a spot along the road and stopped. She was exactly equidistant from the last house of the housing development on the outskirts of town and the first of the slightly dilapidated but still busy farmhouses that were the bread and butter of this area.

As she waited for the go-ahead from the ever-watchful eye above, she contacted her subspace relay waiting underground nearby, reinitiating the real-time connection with the orbiting platform. This allowed her to send instead of just receive information for the first time in ten weeks. While she uploaded her report on the Officer Training School where she had been sequestered for the last two and half months, the satellite confirmed that there were no cars in either direction for some distance and instructed the waiting black bag to extricate itself from its hiding place.

Lana watched as the object started to rise out of the loose soil at the side of the wheat field, its sides undulating, working it up out of the soil like a giant worm. Over the past two months it had been driven over twice by a tractor, and the farmer's dog had urinated on the soil over its head on several occasions as it sniffed at the alien presence below. But despite this, it had remained unharmed and, luckily for the farmer and his dog, it had also remained undiscovered. In a vineyard in France, a vintner had discovered a mysterious black bag there when he had begun to dig up an infected vine from one of his rows of Sauvignon Blanc. His end had been quick and gory, and the bag had simply shuffled itself to the side, reburying itself. It had remained there, unseen, while first the vintner's family, then the police had attempted in vain to discover the cause of the unfortunate man's death.

But Lana's relay had not been uncovered by fate, farmer, or mutt, and she now reached down and picked the large object up bodily with her amplified strength. She held it suspended as it vibrated momentarily at sonic speeds, shaking free the remaining dirt and muck from its sides, then pulled her newly purchased duffle bag over it, zipped it shut, and slung it over her shoulder, careful all the while not to place all the heavy black bag's weight on the wholly inadequate straps of the duffle that now held it.

- - -

Milt Mashford had never become used to the fact that the rugged appeal he'd enjoyed in his younger days had degenerated into a decidedly unappealing lecherousness in his sixties. So when he saw the attractive girl in khakis through the dirty windscreen of his ten-year-old F-150, he assumed he would be able to romance the girl into getting into his truck with him.

Due to Lana's time constraints, and the amount she still had to accomplish, it turned out he was right.

"Hello there, sailor-girl. Can I offer a ride to a member of our proud armed forces?" he said out of his window as he pulled up alongside her.

Lana did not hesitate; at the very least he could take her back to the train station in far less time than it would take her to get there on foot.

"Yes, that would be nice." she said, her face breaking into a radiant smile that stood in stark contrast to the blackness of her eyes.

- - -

An hour later, Milt had somehow found himself driving the attractive sailor all the way to what she said was her home some forty miles away on the outskirts of Annapolis. As they had pulled up she had leant over and given him a kiss on his cheek, thanking him for being such a patriot.

He had wanted to place his hand on her leg as they had driven, his lascivious instincts telling him he deserved a little grope for driving her so far. But something in her eyes had told him that it would be a mistake he would sorely regret. In the end he had watched her walk away without even looking back at him, and for want of a better option he had driven off, trying to work out if he had just been played, or even worse, had actually just done something nice for someone other than himself.

As the eye above notified Lana that he had turned the corner she also turned, walking down a side road. While she had been locked away on base for the first part of her training, the orbiting AI had used the peripheral links it could obtain by hacking the wireless airwaves and acquired her a house. It had also set up bank accounts for those of its operatives that were based in developed societies, and established several dummy corporations that it could siphon money to and from as needed. Finally, and perhaps most importantly, it had started the long and complex task of establishing a complete and verifiable background for each of the Agents. Lana was now going to be the first to establish a full and permanent land connection for the orbiting platforms, at which point their hacking and data manipulation would be able to start in earnest.

Arriving at the home she now owned but had never seen before, Lana walked up to the door and pressed her finger against the lock. The house was small and wooden, its aging white paint starting to flake along the edges of its slats from too many seasons spent untended. Inside it was little more than a living room and kitchen downstairs and a small single bedroom upstairs, but despite this it had all the things Lana and her colleagues sought.

There were, apparently, keys in the apartment, and in the future she would probably use them. For now, however, she would use the tool that had been built into her middle finger to allow her to open this, or any other lock with ease. Inside her finger ran four fibers that now started to snake through slits in the skin of the end of the finger pressed against the keyhole. They slid into the lock, seeking and finding the interior contours of the barrel and automatically forming themselves to the required shape.

With four independent fibers she could break even the most advanced multi-dimensional locks, but this was a simple deadbolt, and she opened it effortlessly. It would not be so easy for anyone else to get into the house once she left it.

Closing and bolting the door, she went straight to work, unsheathing the black bag and taking it upstairs to place it in an unimportant looking cupboard in the bedroom. The house had been left in a bad state, but she could clean it tomorrow. As the bag was placed on the floor of the cupboard, its own wires started snaking out of its casing. The layout and wiring of the house had already been downloaded from the easily hacked cable company's database.

Within minutes the wires found their way through gaps in the floorboards to the junction boxes it needed. The black cables latched onto the sockets like vampires on our information network's proverbial neck, and instantly began to suck. Easily bypassing the simple blocks erected by the cable company to stop illegal usage, the surge of data began to flow through the machine and via its subspace tweeter to eager machine minds above.

The connection complete, Lana began extracting some other devices from the black box's various compartments: a thick disc like an oversized hockey puck, a vial, a reel of cable, and a black block the size of a dishwashing sponge. When she was done, she placed the first device, a thick, flat, black disc, on the inside of the cupboard's single door and closed it. As the door latched closed the disc shot out six arms, each armed with a small but very sharp claw, which imbedded themselves in the frame around the door and then latched themselves to the door itself, locking it securely in place. The door could now only be opened by someone hacking it apart with an axe, but in the unlikely event that happened the disc would turn its six razor-edged hooks, effective in wood, devastating in flesh, to a far more brutal purpose in order to defend the bag within.

Walking to the bedroom's one window, Lana then placed a small dab of liquid from the vial on each of its panes of glass. Spreading from each drop, the glass began to turn opaque, blocking the view from prying eyes. More importantly, the reaction also began to harden the glass to something close to the strength of sapphire crystal.

Lana then extracted a length of the wire from the reel she had taken from her bag and laid it around the outside of the window, walking away after she had joined the ends of the wire together. As she walked down the stairs the wire started to sizzle, reacting with the caulking around window and turning first viscous, and then into an extremely hard glue around the frame, even as the spreading opaqueness of the glass blanketed to each pane's edge. She proceeded to do the same with each of the bottom floor's six windows, using the final part of the wire to seal the back door shut. She then returned to the upstairs cupboard, the disk protecting it forewarned of her approach, and rolled the still half-full vial under the sealed door to the waiting black box to be reabsorbed into its interior.

Coming back down the stairs, Lana opened the front door and used the malleable but impermeable tips of her fingers to unscrew the bolts holding the door lock in place there. Sliding out the old mechanism, she replaced it with the final device she had taken from the box upstairs. The small rectangular black box molded itself to the slot as she inserted it, taking the place of the vastly inadequate manual lock as the guardian of the house's only remaining access point. Unlike the passive tools she had used to seal the rest of the house's windows and doors, this device would actively monitor the only remaining access point to her 'home.' It would vet any key that entered the lock it now controlled, and would prove surprisingly stubborn should an unwanted guest attempt entry, becoming ever more violent in proportion to any intruder's vigor.

Along with its six-clawed friend attached to the inside of the closet door upstairs, it would be more than capable of defending the house's now hard-working contents against all but the most ardent attack.

- - -

Marie and KC stood at the bar and took a deep breath: this was going to hurt. Looking at each other once more for reassurance, they each dropped a shot glass of unpleasantness into their pint glasses, turning their innocent beers into boilermakers.

"Down the hatch." said KC.

"Fuck it." replied Marie, and they both started drinking.

"Wow", said Marie, grimacing, after slamming her now-empty glass on the bar.

"Ugh."

"That was disgusting." she shook her head, trying to clear it.

"I know," said KC, "fabulous isn't it!" They both laughed, wiping their eyes and mouths, and turned back to the dance floor. They looked at their friend Latesha who was getting very amorous with the man that had given them the money to buy the boilermakers, mostly so that he could get Latesha on her own.

Four of their male trainee counterparts were looking on from across the dance floor, commenting on the girls while trying to appear nonchalant. When the girls waved at them, they smiled, laughed, and turned away with feigned coolness.

"Amateurs." said KC.

"Well, we did say we wouldn't pee in our own bathwater," said Marie, "now what about those two civvies by the door."

KC was busy checking them out when her mouth dropped open in astonishment.

"Get the fuck out." she said in awe, still staring over Marie's shoulder.

"What?" said Marie and looked back at the two men. She was trying to figure out what had KC so shocked when she saw the ice queen herself walking across the dance floor. Lana Wilson, looking shockingly attractive, was strolling toward them.

"Evening, girls." Lana said as she came up to them.

"Lana." said KC in greeting.

"We thought you had done a runner after the way you walked off. Where did you go?" asked Marie.

"Had to run some errands … and to get some new clothes." said Lana.

"Yes, so we can see," they said, eyeing her striking figure, clad now in a one-piece black dress that did not run much past the tops of her thighs.

Lana turned and surveyed the room. She'd originally had no intentions of joining them tonight, much as Marie and KC had suspected. Not that she had actually been invited, of course. But when she had uploaded her report for analysis by the satellite-based supercomputer it had come back with some recommendations for her. It was virtually impossible to plot and codify the social workings of any complex society from without. However, with weeks to monitor and learn, an understanding of the behaviors and customs of the various nations the Agents were infiltrating was building that would be essential to the operatives' success. It was based on this ongoing analysis that Agent Lana Wilson had been informed that she should consider a more involved approach to not only her seniors, but also her peers.

It had been clear, based on the insults and comments made to and about Lana that she was not connecting with them, and this had to change. It had also been noted that she had a powerful tool at her disposal that she was not yet using: her looks. First things first, connecting with peers.

"I need a drink." Lana said as she turned to the bar, "What are you two having?"

"Hey, you're behind girl, we just had boilermakers." said KC, expecting Lana to balk at the idea.

"OK then. Hey! Sweetcheeks!" Lana shouted at the bartender, thrusting out her chest, "I'll need a round of boilermakers for me and my fellow soon-to-be-officers here."

"Whoa, we just had one!" started Marie, but Lana held up her hand.

"Fair enough." and turning back to the bartender again she corrected, "I'll be needing you to line up *two* of those bad boys for me, please."

The bartender stared, then shrugged, and continued pouring. KC and Marie glanced at each other, KC mouthing "Really?" at Marie. Dropping shots into two of the four glasses, she handed one each to Marie and KC, then dropped two more in the remaining beers and picked them both up herself.

Facing her cohorts, she smiled, then downed the first of her two pints in one swig. She held a straight face for a moment, then decided it was best to ham it up. "Yuck, that *never* gets easier!" she shouted, cringing.

"Atta girl!" shouted KC, "We didn't know you had it in you."

"Yeah, well, what about you two?" she said, putting down the empty glass and raising her second.

"Oh, it's on!" laughed Marie, and they all began drinking.

Ten seconds later the other two were doubled over, laughing and coughing at the bitter taste. Lana looked from one to the other with cold calculation, unfazed by the drink.

She broke into a smile as they straightened up. "Now," she said, "where is that Lieutenant Hamilton? He was supposed to be here, and he is cute."

The other two stared at her again. She was actually pretty cool, it turned out. But her black eyes were already busy scanning the room for Lieutenant Chris Hamilton, who happened to be the son of the powerful Admiral Hamilton. The purpose of all this fraternizing was to start building a network, and, she had decided, she should use all tools available to her to do so.

Laughing with his friends in another part of the club, Lieutenant Hamilton had no idea that his night was about to take an unexpected turn. Agent Lana Wilson was, of course, an amateur in the art of seduction and lovemaking. But she was also absolutely open-minded, very attractive, and inhumanly supple. It was not easy to make a man obsessed with you in one night, but Lana was, quite literally, like no woman Chris Hamilton had ever met, and he would find her quite intoxicating.

- - -

While Agent Lana Wilson was ingratiating herself with the natives, the orbiting platforms busied themselves with their newfound freedom. Nearly 90% of all the world's business, government, and military data is available over the internet, if you have the tools to get at it. The orbiting satellites had tools in abundance, and they set to work logging, tracking, and sorting through the reams of data that was finally coming available to them.

They were methodical, and they would work tirelessly, without pausing to virtually blink. But because of the way the world's communication systems worked it was inefficient and sometimes impossible to access all international data from one location. They also knew that if they attempted to access anything close to the volume they planned to review through one location it would set off alarm bells all over the world.

So while this installation was the first, it would certainly not be the last, as each Agent would eventually strive to set up their relays in such a way as to provide more access points across the globe through which to sift through our data. For now, though, they made do, sticking strictly to a predefined limit on the speed they downloaded data from the connection, and focusing the first steps of their behemoth task on that data most easily accessed from within the US.

Of course, while 90% of world's information was accessible through the internet, all the most critical information was, by design, part of that 10% that was not allowed to play on the world's information superhighway.

Where the orbiting AI's considerable abilities fell short, the Agents' part began.

Chapter 12: Mind if I Come In?

As the closed-door security committee meeting progressed, Laurie tried hard not to fall asleep. The halls of power were, unfortunately, often filled with morons, and for some reason the morons typically seemed to control the agenda. I suppose the business world is much the same, she thought, though it was not much consolation. Meetings were, almost by definition, the product of the indecisive mind, and so they were usually run, and often populated, by indecisive people.

As they finished up another agenda item, she was wondering what was next, when General Pickler nudged her subtly with his elbow. Oh, I guess it's us, she thought.

Admiral Hamilton had indeed just started presenting on the deep-sea probe project, and she knew she may be needed to interject at any point. She sat up and sorted her folders on her lap, she had several items with her which she could reference if there was a fight, and based on how things had gone over the last two days from a political perspective, a fight was entirely possible.

"After approving the second stage of the project in essence, Mr. Secretary," the admiral explained, "we began reviewing each crash site in order to select the one most likely to provide a successful result.

"We eliminated the crash sites in Russian and Chinese waters immediately as politically untenable, and the one off our own Alaskan shore unfortunately fell in the Aleutian trench, whose particularly treacherous currents and weather patterns would add several extra layers of complexity to an already complex task. While the experimental scanner may be able to find the object, it would prove very hard to retrieve it from this location."

"Yes, yes, I know about the problems there, Admiral, what about the others?" pressed the secretary of defense and chair of the meeting.

"Well, Mr. Secretary, that left the Eastern Mediterranean, Outer Hebrides, English Channel, and the two in the Indian Ocean. Of those the Eastern Mediterranean was the most practical, but we felt sending a naval vessel into the waters off Israel and Lebanon was less than wise, even a disguised one, so the next best options were the ones that impacted near the coasts of India and Sri Lanka, sir."

"Ah," said the secretary, sitting back, "so this is why I have been hearing about requests to enter India's sovereign waters with a minesweeper. Requests that, I understand, have been denied."

"Yes, sir, on the grounds that they intend to mount a retrieval project of their own, though we know from our own sources that they do not have the technology we possess to find the object, nor does it appear that they have dedicated the resources necessary to build such a device."

"So what do you propose, Admiral?"

Laurie was surprised that neither the admiral nor the secretary of defense had turned to her for further arguments as to why this needed to move forward; instead, the admiral opened another folder from the stack in front of him.

"Well, Mr. Secretary, as you know we had anticipated that we may have some trouble in this area, so we had formed an alternate plan, a plan that drove our selection of the Marine Research Institute as our vendor for developing the probe."

Laurie was intrigued; she had not been part of that conversation.

"As you know from the brief I sent you when the president originally approved the project, we have an asset at the Institute. I have since briefed said asset, and he is ready to execute the search covertly, using a civilian research vessel we have access to in the Indian Ocean."

Asset? Slowly it dawned on Laurie, and in retrospect it seemed painfully obvious.

"And you feel this is the best course of action, Admiral?"

"Yes, sir." confirmed Admiral Hamilton with a nod.

"And you, General Pickler," continued the secretary, "I assume you are in agreement with your navy counterpart?"

"Yes, sir." said the general gravely.

"Very well then, I will assume, Dr. West, that you have no objections either," she nodded, pretending she had known about the plan all along, "then let's move forwards." concluded the secretary, taking a breath and gathering his thoughts for a moment before going on.

"Gentlemen, though they will hopefully never know it, we are essentially talking about invading India, so I would like any civilian knowledge of this operation kept to a minimum. Your asset is to be the only civilian onboard, is that clear?"

"If I may, Mr. Secretary?" piped Laurie from her seat, "There is one civilian I would recommend sending on the mission, sir: the probe's designer, a Mr. Danielson."

The secretary frowned. "What is this man's clearance?" he asked the room in general.

Aides and assistants went to work, like automatons, looking up the information, but both Laurie and General Pickler already knew the answer, and the reaction it would get.

"Level 5, sir." said General Pickler, somewhat meekly.

"Out of the question." snapped the secretary, pausing a moment, then continuing, "If we must have an expert onboard, then surely Dr. West can assist this…" he looked at the memo in front of him "…Captain Hawkson."

She looked at him aghast for a moment then remembered herself. It would have to suffice. A level 5 would never be allowed on a mission like this, and Captain Hawkson, though he was apparently not quite what he had seemed, was still a very capable scientist, no matter what his ongoing ties to the navy actually were. She would just have to learn the system as well. And buy a lot of Dramamine.

- - -

It had been two weeks since Lana Wilson had set up her subspace tweeter relay in the closet of her proxy home. During that time it had acted as a conduit for over ten exabytes of data: ten billion gigabytes. The AIs were using a complex virtual routing system to throw off the local cable company's data monitoring systems and hide the amount of their bandwidth that was being taken up by a single location. It could not, unfortunately, reduce the effect this was having on the surrounding area's cable signals and the slight but rising number of complaints the company was inevitably going to receive, but it would make it nearly impossible for the company to trace the source of the problem, if the small, local provider was even proactive enough to seek it out at all.

As the information poured into the four supercomputers' memory banks it was sorted and dated in a complex relational database. Without politics or complaint, the four satellites dotted around the globe divided up the data and began wading through it.

For now, they had the time, capacity and patience to analyze all the data they could get, so they had yet to refine a set of criteria that would limit the search. At this stage they did not leave any stone unturned. Starting with e-mails, they began reading every message sent by every user of all of the major e-mail providers. Literally trillions of messages were sorted, read, and categorized, key pieces of information they contained tracked, logged and cross-referenced in a separate section of the database.

Addresses, bank statements, names, dates, meeting times; everything. When you have onboard memory equivalent to nearly half the combined capacity of every computer on earth, you can afford to start by storing everything you find, and worry about cleaning out the raw material once you have already gleaned any useful information from it.

Pictures were analyzed using complex facial recognition software, the computer determining with surprising accuracy the people in each photo by cross-referencing the e-mails of the sender and receiver over time, categorizing and noting relationships, lovers, family members, office flings, potential pregnancies, potential divorces. As the advanced artificial minds began to gain more understanding of their subjects and their cultures, they became capable of identifying compromising photos and situations, which were flagged for potential use later.

More private material and blackmail fodder was gathered in the two weeks after the connection was placed than by every secret service in human history combined. Admittedly, people worth blackmailing were far less likely to have bank details or naked pictures of their mistresses on their gmail account, but few people were completely infallible when it came to their electronic communications.

A subset of the limited data capacity available was dedicated to the much harder to access private files of the major military and government bodies that could be tapped into from this connection. Due to the aggressive encryption used by the armed forces, it took even these computational giants some time to crack each e-mail, so focusing too much of their still small available bandwidth on downloading them alone would have been an inefficient use of their time.

However, it was while sifting through some of the e-mails from one Admiral Hamilton that one of the supercomputers' subroutines came across a set of instructions to a former navy captain.

"Proceed immediately to Kodikkarai, India, airline and train vouchers en route under separate cover. Take command of Research Vessel *King's Transom*, load and test device, Dr. West to supervise device's dispatch and setup on *King's Transom*. DO NOT declare device's purpose, DO NOT declare mission's purpose, DO NOT declare US government involvement or awareness, mission will be denied under all circumstances, proceed to sea at earliest possible date with assigned team awaiting orders in Indian Ocean, locate target item or remains thereof, if successful notify this office of location, retire to international waters and await further orders."

The software had already discovered details of the earlier requests to India for access to their sovereign waters, but had not flagged them as access was not granted by the Indian government, and India had no machine capable of finding the objects in their deep sea graves. However, as this new information was analyzed and cross-referenced with the location of Kodikkarai, the subroutine automatically made the first entry in a hitherto unused section of the huge database: Potential Mission Threats.

The computer Mind overseeing all the processes and subroutines noticed the new entry with a part of its brain it had permanently dedicated to monitoring that section, no matter how empty it had been to date. Immediately the mind began to investigate. Soon the bandwidth limits for government data would be temporarily abandoned, and the combined abilities of four vast AI minds would start to seek out all relevant information and decide how to react.

The overriding goals of the supercomputers were the retrieval of the information they had been sent to gather and keeping themselves and the Agents they supported undetected until they were ready to use that data.

As an unfortunate vintner in France had unwittingly discovered, secrecy was a primary mission parameter.

Chapter 13: With Utmost Dispatch

"Now, I can't stress how important it is that you do not mention that you are from the Institute." James had reiterated to Neal and Madeline as the chartered turboprop had made its way to the small landing strip outside Kodikkarai.

"We get it, James, honestly, we get it." Madeline replied earnestly, "I am here as your bit of fun."

"Like a mistress...a concubine if you will." Neal put in with a sardonic smile. Madeline and James' relationship was not the secret they thought it had been.

James tried to reestablish control over the conversation, "OK, guys, I know I am being paranoid here, but..."

"How about we say," Madeline interrupted with feigned seriousness, "that I am one of the airline hostesses, and you just managed to bag me on the flight over?"

Neal and Madeline laughed, "You certainly dress like one...and that hair." said Neal, and she threw her empty plastic water bottle across the aisle at him.

Dr. West, sitting with Neal on the other side of the aisle from the two lovebirds, laughed. Then, in a more serious tone said, "Really you two, we've been over this before, but it is important that you understand how serious this is. You are not officially here. James and I are under strict orders not to bring any other civilians on board. The crew of the boat, though they will seem motley, will be all navy."

"So what are we *doing* here, then?" asked Neal, "Other than apparently joining the mile-high club with James, here?"

Ever the lady, Laurie moved smoothly past Neal's last comment and addressed his first question, "We still may need you to help configure the probe once we get it out of the back of this plane."

Through methods unbeknownst to the group, the large and cumbersome probe, and its larger wooden packing crate, had miraculously escaped inspection on the trip over. This was probably due to the pleasant, inconspicuous men who had somehow been waiting for them at each stop along the way, dispatched by the CIA to help 'expedite' their onward journey.

"Once we have the probe set up, with your subtle assistance, of course," continued Laurie, "you will have to stay on shore. We have to do the rest ourselves. It's one thing to get you on board while we're still in port as 'guests,' but the Admiralty will no doubt get a detailed manifest of who is onboard when we sail, and it would not do to have you on it."

"Now," said James, "what I have managed to bring along is a set of closed loop Military A-B radios. You two will have one with you on the shore, we will have the other on board the *King's Transom*. These things are precisely configured to each other; each has a matching quantum encryption algorithm that changes every tenth of a second in ways that only the twin machine can duplicate."

Madeline looked at him. He had emphasized to her that he could not explain why he was allowed to go on the mission and she was not. He had tried to say it was because he was ex-navy, but she knew him better than that. As he explained the clearly covert tool, her suspicions became ever more certain.

A government girl she was not, and she had never really understood how she had fallen for an ex-military guy, so finding out that he may still be part of that organization was more than a little disturbing. Of course, the fact that it appeared that he was now and had always been part of Naval Intelligence may explain why he seemed so different from other navy guys she had met.

Either way, as he asked her to trust him and forgive that he could not tell her everything, his pleading eyes had touched her. If he was some kind of spook, he was one for the right reasons, she thought, and that would have to do ... for now.

"Of course," interjected Neal seriously, "there is one important factor here that we have overlooked."

They all looked earnestly at Neal and he went on.

"If Madeline's 'cover' is that she is James' bit on the side," he said turning to Laurie, "what does that make me?"

They all laughed, Laurie shaking her head and wagging her finger as he pretended to lean in for a kiss. Though she was twenty years his senior, her timeless good looks and auspicious title made her still far, far out of his league.

"Hey," Neal said, as he continued trying halfheartedly to hug her, laughing as she spurned him, "I'll have you know I'm a secret agent. James Bond has nothing on me."

Madeline egged him on.

"Oh God!" Laurie groaned, laughing in spite of herself. Across the aisle, James closed his eyes and pinched the bridge of his nose with his thumb and forefinger, laughing in spite of himself. What had he gotten himself into, he thought.

- - -

That had been two days ago. They had since spent a two full days configuring the probe, Captain Hawkson dispatching the majority of his crew to get supplies while he snuck the two civilians onboard to help set things up.

But all that was behind them now. They had said their good-byes and now Madeline and Neal stood on the shore, hiding as inconspicuously as possible amongst the crowd of locals that had come to see the ship depart. They joined the crowd in waving at the large ship motoring out of the harbor, Madeline looking for and finding its captain standing rigidly on the bridge and smiling at the thought of the more amorous farewell she had given him in the wee hours of the morning.

As the helmsman steered the ship, the captain conning from over his shoulder, the whole bridge was surprised when the captain asked the first lieutenant to take the con and stepped out onto the port gantry. The *King's Transom* was nearly one hundred feet long, a converted deep-sea trawler that had been used as a marine research vessel for over ten years now. During that time, its owners had proved amenable to having it 'commissioned' by the navy for certain operations, proving discreet enough not to mention the changes of crew the missions usually required.

Its high bridge soared over an impressive bow, designed to brave even the toughest waters. As you moved astern, the sides got steadily lower, allowing ever easier access to the water for the host of cranes mounted on its open stern. The word 'transom' was the old navy name for the very back end of a ship, and such was the plethora of equipment, cranes, and even a functioning two-man submarine mounted on the *King's Transom*'s backside that the name had seemed appropriate.

Extending from each side of the high bridge were two gantries, designed to allow the captain or his lookouts to look over the side of the ship, or survey the horizon for signs of fish. Now, as Captain Hawkson stood on the port gantry, he surveyed the small crowd on the shore. Finding the two white faces hiding in it, he smiled. He then glanced down to the deck below to Dr. West who was looking up at him, smiling understandingly, and turned to head back onto the bridge.

Chapter 14: A Black Spot

It turned out Dr. West had not needed Dramamine for the relatively calm seas they would encounter. As they had left the harbor behind, she had met with Captain Hawkson, his first lieutenant, and the navigational officer, and they had gone over their search area.

Though satellite images had pinpointed the spot where the meteor had touched down, the vagaries of current made the range of its potential resting spots on the ocean bed significant. They had decided on a spiral search pattern. They would start at the center of their proposed search area, and then spiral slowly outward in an ever increasing circle. For the sake of testing the equipment, they had also run the probe while heading to the central start point.

The computer that they were using to plot the results was connected to the ship's GPS and it used that link to map the images it was receiving over a standard oceanographer's chart of the ocean bed. After three days, Laurie sat reviewing the results to-date. The image she saw was a chart of the southern Indian Ocean, specifically the area off India's southeast coast. In the bottom left-hand corner she could see the edge of northeastern Sri Lanka. Protruding from that was the bridge of relatively shallow water that joined it with mainland India, whose southeastern coast showed in the top left corner of the image on-screen.

Sprouting from a point on the Indian coast that she knew was the fishing town of Kodikkarai was the line of their path to the center of their search zone. Either side of the line was the detailed image of the ocean bed that the probe had gathered en route. Once they had reached their starting point, they had started their spiral outwards, making the whole image look like an ever-growing lollipop, its handle lodged in the port of Kodikkarai like it was clasped in the hand of a little girl.

She could zoom in on any part of the probe's imagery, utilizing its extremely high resolution to see the ocean bed in astonishing detail, all of it color coded by mass like a heat sensitive image or some psychedelic fractal. They had not found anything yet that came close to the density Neal and she had estimated the objects must have to all have survived their trip through the atmosphere, so Laurie stood up to join the captain on deck. They were only 15% of their way through the planned search field, after all.

- - -

That evening, as they both enjoyed dinner, the computer started beeping. It had found an anomaly. Looking at one another in surprise they put down their knives and forks and went over to the terminal. James let the doctor take a seat at the PC and watched as she zoomed in on the flagged part of the image.

Although the program had the ability to highlight that part of the image that it had flagged, that would not be necessary here. In the middle of the screen were two shapes, each completely black. The computer had not found the high-density they had expected. It had found nothing. These two spots on the ocean floor were sending back no image at all. Somehow the objects they were looking at were absorbing the probe's signals entirely.

- - -

"Let's not get ahead of ourselves, Laurie." said James calmly. They had returned to his cabin with a printout of the image so they could discuss it out of earshot.

"Not get ahead of ourselves? This is very strange, James. I'm afraid I can only draw a few possible conclusions from what we seem to be seeing here, and none of them are good."

"OK, *possible* conclusions, exactly. That's my point, we really only have theories so far, there is no need to be so … agitated."

"Captain, let me explain my concerns to you and I think you'll see why I am so 'agitated'…as you put it." Laurie frowned at him.

"OK, I'm sorry. I'm just, well, maybe I'm a little agitated myself."

"Look, there is only one thing that would return no signal to the probe that I am aware of. The probe has a very wide range of scanning ability, that is how you all designed it, after all; and, well, the only thing I can think of that would not show up, I guess, is some kind of superconductive material."

James frowned and she continued.

"When a superconductor is fully functional…and bear in mind we've only been able to do this in lab conditions with a separate power source cooling the material…it absorbs…or rather it *conducts*, pretty much all energy. So if you were looking at a perfect superconductor it would look pitch black, because it would be conducting all the light, not reflecting any of it.

"Now, here is where it becomes a little more disturbing: as I said, only a perfect superconductor would absorb *all* wavelengths and all energy, but we don't know how to make a perfect superconductor. They are purely theoretical. But what we are seeing here, well it looks like … a perfect superconductor."

"I don't like where you're going with this, Doctor." said James, looking at the pictures in his hands.

"Oh, I know, James, trust me, I know. I've made a career out of staying calm in the face of overly excited scientists. That is precisely why the president trusts me to give him balanced advice. But combine that thought process with the fact that this object we have found is more than likely the object we tracked from deep space to this spot and we can't help but go down a pretty disturbing road."

She paused. James glared at the images in his hands like they were pictures of his own funeral and Laurie bit her lower lip as she watched him absorbing it all. She had an impulse to desist, to leave him alone, but her own anxiety would not let her and she spoke once more, more softly this time, "But that is not all of it, is it, James?"

He shook his head, black or no, the image still gave them another key piece of information: the objects' shape.

"Now, James, tell me, what does that shape look like to you?"

"Two halves." he said.

"Two halves of what, James?" she prompted.

He sighed, not wanting to say. After a moment he met her intent stare and replied in a cold, quiet tone, his shoulders tensing as he spoke, "It looks like two halves of a missile, Laurie," he said, finally, "or…" and this took all his strength to say, "two halves of some kind of container."

They went silent, the implications too stark to warrant further discussion.

- - -

Above them, acute eyes tracked the *Transom*'s circular path, waiting. They were waiting to see whether the *Transom*'s probe discovered anything. They were waiting to see if the threat would pass, to see whether the team of humans would succeed in their task, or fail, saving them from having to take action.

They were listening to see what messages the ship transmitted home, ready to intercept them, ready to stop them from reaching their source if necessary, and ready to stop more from following if that was necessary. There had been some radio messages they had not been able to decode, but then there had also been several others that had been easily decipherable. As long as these messages continued to inform them of the probe's progress, they would let the ship be.

- - -

Each night since the *King's Transom* had left, Madeline and Neal had gathered in his small lodger's room at 11pm, the prearranged time when they would use their Secure Field Radio, or 'SurFeR' as they had been dubbed, to speak with James and Laurie.

It was now 11:30, and they had not heard anything. Madeline had always been very excited for these calls, and Neal had as well, to some degree. But some small part of him had always worried, slightly afraid of what they might discover out there. The silence of the radio this night had him spooked, and Madeline had subconsciously picked up on that concern and become unsettled herself, though she was keeping up an appearance of calm as they sipped a dubious local fruit juice and made small talk.

The sudden beep from the radio that lay between them on the single bed was startling. Madeline made an 'I-told-you-so' face as she reached for the green plastic radio that looked like a 1990s cell phone, complete with oversized rubber aerial.

"Where have you been?" she said into the handset.

"Yeah, sorry for the delay, we've been…" there was a pause on the other end, "…trying to figure something out." came James' voice over the two-way.

There was a slight delay as each of the radios went through the lengthy process of decoding each signal, and then thoroughly encrypting the return signal. The stilted conversation continued with Madeline asking, "What kind of something, James? Are you two OK?"

Over the next hour James and Laurie discussed the discovery with Neal and Madeline. Madeline was fairly incredulous at first, but that part of Neal that had been so keen to find one of the meteors had also been equally aware of what his original equations about their makeup had suggested. It was not long before the conversation moved away from whether the meteor was a natural occurrence and on to what to do about the strong possibility that it wasn't. Based on the object's description, Neal had posited three theories of what it could be.

First, it could have carried some kind of bomb, possibly thermonuclear, but it was unlikely that none of the eight would have detonated, so the group seemed to consider this possibility moot. Second was that it bore some kind of pathogen: a virus, or some other biological or chemical weapon. Laurie had responded immediately, "Yes, we thought about that, Neal, but surely if you wanted to disperse a pathogen effectively you would detonate the delivery device in the air."

"Maybe they did? Maybe this is just the remains of the capsule?" said Neal. Madeline wondered how they had so easily gotten to a discussion of 'they.' It had just never occurred to her as she had worked on the probe that it might find something…unnatural. But even as she struggled with this thought, Neal was moving on to his last, and most outlandish theory.

"My third thought is both the most ridiculous, and yet … perhaps … also the most plausible of the three." Madeline stared up at him, the radio silent as they all waited for his next words. "Well," he continued, "they may have been … landing capsules. For some kind of … machine."

James was instantly on the defensive against this seemingly preposterous thought, "Wouldn't they have *landed* on *land*, then, Neal?" he said.

"Well, no, James, they wouldn't, not if they didn't want us to know they had come." said Neal, Madeline still flinching each time anyone said 'they.'

Neal carried on, "If they wanted to arrive covertly, they would have planned to impact on water, but near to land. And they would have planned to leave what little evidence there was of their arrival in the most hard to reach place possible."

They could all see the same image in their minds: while they had been working on the probe back in Florida, Neal had posted a giant world map on the coffee room wall. On it he had marked with red pins the locations of each of the impact sites. It seemed so clear to them all now, so perfect how they had all landed in the deepest and most inhospitable waters in their given part of the globe. They had joked about it at the time: couldn't make it easy for us, could they.

Dr. West and Neal Danielson had noticed it way back in late October when they were analyzing the entry data. Neither of them had really discussed its implications, but it had been a natural extension of the conversation about how improbable it was for all of them to survive entry that they should comment on how improbable it was that they should all end up in deep waters.

But it was James who placed the final piece of the puzzle. His voice entered the silence after Neal's last comment, "It is clear we may have found something that is more important than any of us had expected. There is one more thing, though, that may be important here, and I am … sad to say it may also support your final theory, Neal. As I think about the meteors' locations, I think I can see an additional pattern on top of their landing in oceanic trenches."

Madeline was starting to freak out a bit and she was unsure if she could take much more of this. But Neal and Laurie were intrigued; where was the naval captain going that neither of them had already gone?

"Think about what land masses they actually landed near." James continued, and they all recalled the image in their minds again, "Scotland, France, the Eastern Mediterranean, China, Russia, Pakistan, the US, and, of course, here, near India."

They did not follow him, but his military training led him to an instant connection between the nations in question. "Let me put it this way," he rephrased as he waited for them to make the jump, "Scotland is part of the UK, and one of the most powerful countries in the Eastern Mediterranean is, I think you'll agree, Israel. So what do China, Russia, India, Pakistan, Israel, the UK, France, and America have in common?"

"Oh God." came Laurie's voice through the speaker, a moment before Neal figured it out. His eyes went slowly wide and his mouth began to drop open as realization came to him.

"WHAT IS IT!" shouted Madeline in frustration, half-crazy with fear and incredulity.

Her outburst shocked Neal out of his stunned state and he looked at her with eyes glazed with the implications of it all. In a quiet, measured tone, he told her what irrepressible fact James had led them to, "The nations James just named make the membership list of the most dangerous and exclusive club in the world." he said to her, "The capsules landed next to each of the eight countries with stockpiled nuclear weapons."

- - -

Though the four of them doubted they would sleep at all, they had eventually closed the connection and made the show of going to bed. They had concluded that the implications of what they had seen were too fundamental to be handled that night, or over the radio, no matter how secure the connection might be. They would bring the *King's Transom* back into harbor tomorrow and formulate a plan.

In light of the situation, James' navy instincts had told him to follow some old, battle ready habits. In the days of the Napoleonic wars, captains had been under strict orders to keep important documents in a weighted bag on their person, ready to throw overboard if they were captured.

While the need to throw documents overboard to protect them from falling into enemy hands had long since passed, a primal fear in James now made him do quite the opposite. For half an hour after the call ended, he had carefully loaded an orange dry bag with copies of their findings: including photos, a printed account of the mission, in cipher, and an encrypted DVD of all the files. He finished it with a personal note addressed to Madeline which he hoped would see the package to the right hands, then stood and left his cabin.

On board a deep-sea vessel such as this one, all life vests were equipped with an Emergency Position Indicating Radio Beacon, or EPIRB. The vests were designed to aid the recovery of anyone unfortunate to be washed overboard in the extreme seas the *King's Transom* was designed to face. Grabbing one of the vests from one of many racks around the boat, James attached the now sealed dry bag to it, knotting its straps securely through the bag's handle.

He then walked forward to the bow of the ship, where the ship's two anchors were stored safely in their deep lockers. At sea there was little reason to come to the wet, wind-swept bow of the ship, so James was alone when he laid the vest and its ward on the deck. He then laid a nearby, coiled rope on top of it, making sure the vest remained in no way actually attached to the deck, and returned to his cabin.

Chapter 15: An Indiscretion

Lieutenant Commander Richard Moore had not known any more of the details of this mission than the many previous covert missions he had been assigned to. Admittedly though, the location of this one had proven much nicer, and, frankly, so had the company.

After he had received his typically uninformative orders from Admiral Packenham he had read them with his usual haste. They never contained any important information anyway. He just hoped he picked up something more concrete on the base's grapevine. But the grapevine had been disturbingly quiet on this one, so he and his crew had gone to sea even blinder than usual.

They had taken command of the *King's Transom* from its usual crew after it had stopped in Diego Garcia Air and Naval Base for 'maintenance.' From there they had motored north in strictly civilian dress, as per their orders, to rendezvous with their soon-to-be captain and further orders in southern India.

Four days later they had made it to Kodikkarai where Captain Hawkson had joined them along with the civilian who had also been mentioned in the lieutenant's classified orders. Both the captain and his civilian cohort had been travelling with partners, and the captain had informed the lieutenant that these were part of their cover, and asked him not to note them in his report.

Ironically, it was precisely because he did not believe that they were part of the cover story that the lieutenant decided not to include them. These were clearly more than just cover stories (though what the attractive older lady saw in the shaggy, younger man she had brought with her was beyond him), but the lieutenant understood how hard it was for people in their line of work to maintain relationships and he had decided he would let this go unmentioned.

However, that indiscretion would be the only thing he would not note. Part of his instructions from the Admiralty had included specific orders to keep Admiral Hamilton abreast of the results of the probe's analysis. So each day Richard had supplied his daily report at 6pm, uneventful though it was.

A couple of hours after he had already sent today's report, he had noticed the captain and Dr. West talking animatedly before retiring to the captain's cabin.

Several hours later still, they finally went to their separate cabins, and Richard decided it would be a good idea to see if he could see what had gotten them so agitated. While the two of them were safely in their cabins he checked the probe's results from the past few hours. He was not sure what the significance was of what he was seeing, though it was clear his two auspicious guests were extremely interested in it, and it did look rather unusual.

As he studied the imagery, it looked to him like they had found the remains of some kind of missile. This certainly fell under the auspices of information the admiral would wish to be informed of.

Logging into the secure VPN account, Richard opened a new message from the in-box of the Admiralty e-mail account he had been assigned for the mission and began typing. He would attach the latest photos of the object, describe the way the captain had reacted, and send the addendum to Admiral Hamilton tonight.

Chapter 16: The Wrath of God

Ensign Weber was glancing at the autopilot on the bridge when he noticed a spark out of the corner of his eye. He was one of two ratings on the bridge as the rest of the ship slept. Lieutenant Moore, the officer of the watch, had gone below for a moment.

Looking forwards to where he had seen the captain walk past not an hour beforehand, the ensign was confused to see a bright orange circle appearing on the slowly rolling foredeck. Above the circle, a hazy, almost invisible line shot straight up, moving as the deck rolled, as though a small spotlight were shining on the deck from the stars above.

As he watched, his confusion turned to alarm as the circle started to glow bright orange, and its center started to melt, the half-inch thick steel of the deck apparently turning to liquid.

Instinctively, his hand reached for the red alarm button on the helm station and he flipped its cover open and punched it. As the siren wailed throughout the ship, he executed a textbook turn into the ocean's chop causing water to break briefly over the foredeck and hopefully quell the apparent small fire starting on the decking.

But the splashes of water seemed to vaporize as they hit the beam that was lancing down from above and the line seemed to track the boat's movements, keeping itself glued to the orange circle as it melted through to the deck below.

As the alarm rang through the ship Captain James Hawkson, like the rest of his crew, was leaping from his bunk and pulling on his clothes. In another part of the ship, a confused ensign stared upward from his bunk as a glowing hole appeared in the decking that formed the roof of his cabin. His three roommates were moving slowly away from it and from the ominous glow that was appearing on the deck below it.

As the frightened crewman edged around the small cabin's walls to join his friends at its door, a lurch of the boat sent him stumbling into the strange light that seemed to be shining through the hole. The others stared in horror as his entire body flared bright red and burst into searing flame.

"Terry!" mouthed one of his friends, stunned into silence as he watched the unfortunate man's body rapidly disintegrate, falling to join the smoldering orange circle that was now rapidly eating through the floor of their cabin.

"What the hell!?" shouted another of the stunned men, their internal alarms flaring in tune with the ship's wailing sirens. The heat in the cabin was becoming overwhelming and something inside them snapped and they started to run for fire extinguishers. But it was already far too late. As they ran from the cabin, the beam opened a second hole below the first down into the ship's hold under their cabin and the laser started to eat through to the very hull of the ship.

Lieutenant Moore ran from the main salon where he had been sat at the computer. He had only just finished sending his report a few seconds before the alarm had sounded. Running toward his post on the bridge he could hear screams and shouts from forward, and he went to investigate. As he walked forward along the deck he came to the incongruous hole in the thick steel deck of his ship, its edges now glowing white hot, and went to look at it. He approached carefully, leaning over to look down through the hole, imagining its source was below-decks.

The laser burnt cleanly through the back of his skull before his brain registered it was under attack. A moment beforehand, Captain James had arrived on the bridge and was about to ask for a status update when he saw the lieutenant through the window. He watched as his lieutenant's head evaporated, his body flopping forward and bursting into flame as it fell across the beam. The flesh provided only a moment's resistance before it was also obliterated, the relentless laser continuing its attack on the thick steel of the ship's hull two decks down as the lieutenant's lifeless, disembodied legs slumped to the deck.

Laurie West was not a dramatic person, she was not given to flights of fancy, but it was that very pragmatism that had led her to be so afraid of the potential implications of their discovery. Now, as she heard the screams of the ship's crew, something in her told her that their worst fears had been true.

She felt a calm come over her as she walked from her cabin, pulling her robe on over her pajamas as she went. Suddenly the boat lurched and seemed to settle. An almost subconscious sense in her told her that the floor she was standing on was starting lean forward, and she hastened her pace on deck. The boat was sinking.

James' instincts also told him the instant the hull gave way, and he was about to shout the order to abandon ship when a jet of steam erupted from the hole in his deck. Fresh screams from the few crewmembers not already on deck told him that the boat was filling with superheated steam from where the laser and superheated steel of the ship's hull had met the water as it rushed into the ship.

"Abandon ship!" he bellowed at the top of his lungs, hearing the call echoed by his crew as he grabbed a life jacket and ran for the gangway. As he ran onto the bridge's port gantry, he scanned the deck, assessing the number of crew he had left. The *Transom* was sinking fast, and they needed to get off now to avoid being dragged down with it.

Seeing the doctor in the small crowd on deck, his eyes locked with hers once again, just as they had when they had sailed from Kodikkarai harbor not long ago, and a sadness filled him. They nodded, knowing they had brought this hell down on the crew of the boat. He had no idea how the information of their discovery had leaked out, but it didn't matter now. He must try and save as many as possible.

- - -

A few minutes later, as they watched the ship finally go down, the drifting mass of floating people started to gather, organizing around the three inflatable life rafts they had managed to throw free before their ship sank.

As the crew helped each other aboard the rafts, a part of James told him that they were not out of the woods. His body continued going through the motions of helping his crew up and into the rafts, but in his heart he knew what must come next.

It started as suddenly as the first attack had, but the laser had no steel to contend with here, so instead it simply sliced straight across each of the life rafts in turn. Anyone already on board was cut cleanly in two, or worse, a couple of poor souls had their legs or arms partially severed, screams pouring from their mouths as the blood should have poured from their instantly cauterized limbs.

The panic and fear began afresh as everyone started swimming for their lives. But the harder they swam, the faster it found them, silencing them one by one. The beam was tracking down any movement, and the more frantic your flailing the sooner death came.

James and Laurie's eyes connected one more time across the water before she saw him cut down by the unseen, merciless blade, his head simply exploding in white flame like a match being lit, steam leaping from around his still moving shoulders.

"Run, Neal, hide," she sobbed into the night, as hell raged around her, "don't ever mention this to anyone. They've come for us." she said desperately, her eyes turning skyward as death found her.

Part 2

Chapter 17: The Other Shoe

The sun forced its way in through the woefully inadequate curtains like an unwelcome party guest, filling the room with an ever growing heat to match the stifling humidity. Neal alternately stood, fidgeted, glared at the silent radio on the bed, or paced back and forth in the small, dusty guest room, stopping at each turn to look out the window to the busy alley just below.

Madeline sat on the bed, not looking at the radio at all, like she was avoiding eye contact with a regretful one-night stand.

"I'm starving," said Neal, "we can't sit in here all day."

Madeline sighed, "I know, I know. I just thought we said we were going to talk further in the morning, why haven't they beeped us, or answered our pages?"

Neal paused before answering, "I'm sure they are just dealing with the crew and getting the ship back here as soon as they can. James said they would be back in port this afternoon. I'm sure we'll hear from them soon."

It was nearly eleven, and they had not left Madeline's room all morning, or strayed from the SurFeR that sat on her bed. Madeline had insisted on taking the radio to bed with her after they had all signed off, in the hope that James would take a moment to call her later on.

"How about this?" suggested Neal, "The radio is fully charged, I'll tuck it in my bag and we'll head to the market and get some food. If they buzz us while we're there we can be back here in a couple of minutes." he looked at her, but she did not look up from her seat on the bed.

He kneeled in front of her and took her hands in his, seeing in her face the concern and fear that he was refusing to acknowledge in himself. "Hey, come on." he said softly, "We'll both feel better if we get some food."

She nodded, giving in meekly, and they both stood. Unplugging the radio from its charging cable, he placed it in his small messenger bag and they headed for the door.

- - -

They sat in silence in the shade of a bleached old Coke umbrella, eating freshly cooked mushroom bhajis and sipping mango lassi. The heat of the summer in southern India was profoundly oppressive, and they felt it coat them, like a hot, damp blanket clinging to every inch of their skin.

Madeline eventually broke the silence, "Neal, you've been very diplomatic, but it's time we started to think about what could have happened to them."

His eyes connected with hers, his body remaining passive in the heat, and his mouth opened as if to utter another platitude. Then it closed again, a slight sag of his shoulders his only acknowledgment that he was having as much trouble deluding himself as her.

She continued, "There is simply no way James would have forgotten to contact us this morning, and even if he was busy on deck, which I find hard to believe with twenty-five trained navy sailors on board, then Laurie would have had plenty of opportunity to call us instead."

Neal decided to reiterate a possible option they had talked about when they had sat in her room earlier, "Let's not forget that they may have simply suffered some mishap with the radio, maybe it malfunctioned, or the batteries went."

"That is a possibility, but wouldn't James have used some other method to let us know they were OK?" She looked at him for some kind of reassurance, but he was running low on it too.

"Neal, last night we found pretty good reason to suspect that something has … arrived here from somewhere else." She still could not wrap her mind around it, but it was becoming steadily easier to say. "We all knew when we were talking about it that there was a pretty reasonable chance that whatever it is may not be friendly."

She paused, and he saw the next thought coming, watching her steel herself.

"If 'they' were watching last night," she continued, looking at her drink, "don't you think they would have noticed a ship patrolling the waters where one of their own had landed? They must have gone to vast lengths to hide whatever they are doing here, what wouldn't they do to keep it a secret?"

For the first time Neal felt what it was like to have someone jumping to conclusions faster than him, and felt some measure of the frustration that General Pickler and his colleagues must have felt when he ran off down theoretical roads in their meetings. He smiled ruefully, knowing he was about to deliberately be as pigheaded as they had always been to him.

"OK, let's hold on. We are going to need a lot more information before we can jump to conclusions like that."

She looked at him with the same frustration he must have shown a thousand professors. The difference was that all those teachers had all thought that he was being deliberately controversial, but Neal knew Madeline had no more desire to think these thoughts than he did.

As she went to speak again, they were interrupted by a commotion outside their boarding house down the street. Neal stood and peered down the crowded, dusty road to the small group gathering at its end. He saw the lady who had rented him and Madeline their rooms look down the street at him. He saw her say something to two officially dressed Indian military people standing next to her, and he saw her finger rise and point at Neal. The army men's eyes followed her outstretched arm, coming to rest on the only white man in the town, and the two soldiers both promptly began to run toward Neal.

He considered running too, he thought about grabbing Madeline's arm and dashing off down the street, but knew it would be pointless: two white people fleeing in rural India. He thought about saying something to her, warning her, but instead he stared mutely, her eyes posing a question at him and his obvious alarm.

The two men arrived, out of breath, a moment later, one of them replacing the hat on his head that he had held while running.

"Ms. Cavanagh?" he said to Madeline, his English pronunciation good, but stiffly lilted with local accent. She nodded, staring in fear and astonishment at him like he bore the plague, her worst fears trying to surface in spite of her.

"Ms. Cavanagh, please come with us. We have something most urgent to discuss with you."

She stood, starting to walk in the direction the soldier was indicating with the lack of will of a captured criminal, looking with pleading eyes at Neal. He followed her, suddenly feeling an overwhelming need to protect her.

"What is going on?" he demanded from the soldier. "Where are you taking her?"

"Please, sir, we have some urgent business with Ms. Cavanagh. She will not be harmed. You must let her come with us."

He tried to think of some reason for them to take him as well, and then blurted, "She's my sister. If you must take her, I demand to come with you as well."

The soldiers looked at Madeline, who was nodding emphatically, and then back to Neal. They were in no mood to argue. Their orders were to locate Madeline Cavanagh, who, according to their records had arrived into Kodikkarai with a James Hawkson a few days beforehand.

"Very well, sir, please come with us." one of them said, indicating a waiting green jeep.

- - -

The two of them sat in stony silence in a small air-conditioned room. The windowless space held one desk, four chairs, and nothing else. It was the first time they had been in air-conditioning since landing, and they felt like they had been pulled from an oven. Steam, Neal noted, was actually rising from their clothes.

But the pleasure of entering the cool office building had been but a moment's relief from their concerns as they had been led to, and then left in this hopeless room.

After five minutes the door opened and an officer in his mid-fifties entered carrying a folder and a fatherly smile walked briskly through it. He was followed by a younger man with more folders and a notepad, who closed the door while the officer introduced himself.

"Good afternoon, my name is Colonel Patel, of the Indian Coast Guard." he said as he seated himself across from them. "You must forgive my men for coming for you with no information, I am afraid that must have been quite alarming, but we had little choice, as, in truth, we do not have a great deal of information ourselves."

Neal and Madeline were confused, but they waited to see where this was going, unwilling to hurry the conversation to its potentially unpleasant conclusion.

The colonel got down to business, "You are Ms. Madeline Cavanagh of the United States?" he asked, acknowledging her nod with a note on a pad. "And you, sir, I am informed by my men that you are Ms. Cavanagh's brother?"

"Well, no, not really, but we are old friends, and I wanted to make sure I was allowed to come with her." Neal explained.

The colonel looked annoyed by this irregularity. "And you, Ms. Cavanagh. Are you as keen to have this man present as he clearly is to be here?"

"Yes, definitely, Colonel," she said emphatically, "Neal is a good friend of mine, and I very much want him here." Her candid desperation and vulnerability was obvious, and the colonel softened.

"Very well. You may stay at Ms. Cavanagh's request. May I have your full name for my records, please?"

"Danielson, Neal Danielson."

The colonel consulted his notes and, finding the name on the same passenger manifest that had linked Ms. Cavanagh with James Hawkson, relaxed his guard a little more.

He looked at them, summoning an air of professionalism, and proceeded, "I am afraid we may have some bad news for you."

Madeline cracked, a sob flowing from her in a fit, like a held back cough. Madeline was unable to reply for herself, so Neal turned to the colonel even as his arms went around her. The soldier was clearly discomfited by her reaction: it was as though she had been expecting him to say the worst, so Neal prompted him from his silence, "Maybe you could elaborate a little, Colonel?"

"Yes, well, we do not have many details. Last night, or rather early this morning at around 4am, we picked up a distress signal known as an EPIRB from about fifty miles offshore, actually many signals were registered, often a sign of a ship in significant distress."

"A coast guard helicopter stationed about three hours away was immediately dispatched," he continued, "though we were unable to get any response on any radio frequency. It is the coast guard's policy to investigate any EPIRB signal, even if no mayday is reported. Better to be safe than sorry."

He saw that Neal was clearly getting annoyed with his explanation, but he feared the man would not be happy when he heard what little more information the colonel actually had.

"When we arrived on the scene we found very little. Of the multiple signals detected at first, only one remained, and I am very sad to say it was not a survivor, but a single life jacket attached to a bag."

Neal looked at him, even Madeline stopped crying for a moment, her desperate mind grasping at the lack of concrete evidence that something had actually happened.

"Wait," said Neal, "where was the *King's Transom*?"

The colonel shrugged, "We found no sign of the actual ship, but her crew, well, they were …" he struggled to find words. He had seen the photos of what they had found, and it had shaken him to his very core.

He summoned his strength and soldiered on, "It appears there was a severe fire aboard the *King's Transom*, though caused by what, we cannot tell at this time. Though we could not find the ship itself, the crew were …. I am afraid there were no survivors."

He did not stop, he did not want to dwell on the image in his mind. He had one piece of information that was not completely terrible, and he wanted to move on to it.

"As I said before, the one remaining EPIRB signal that led us to the site was actually attached to a bag." he said, and then nodded to his assistant who stood and hurriedly left the room, returning a moment later with a large orange dry bag. Its attached life jacket, striped with soot like the rest of the floating debris and carnage, had been removed.

"You will understand that, for purposes of our investigation, we will have to ask you to stay in the area for the next few days while we complete our investigation. That said, in the absence of the actual vessel, said investigation will be … well … anyway."

He paused again. After a moment's silence, he nodded to his assistant who handed the bag to Madeline.

The colonel stood, slowly, saying, "Here it is," his sober tone displaying how little satisfaction he expected the bag to give them.

"Actually, it was the contents of the bag that led us to Ms. Cavanagh." he said, pausing for just a second more.

"Maybe I should leave this with you?" he said, finally, and turned to leave. Saying as he reached the door, "We will be just outside. Please let us know if you need anything at all."

The assistant wordlessly followed him, closing the door with a sympathetic nod.

- - -

The bag contained various items that they both recognized instantly as the shocking findings they had spent the previous night discussing. It was black comedy to Neal that the bag seemed so innocuous to the uneducated eye. The fact that they had been handed this by a government official without hesitation might have been funny to them both … on any other day.

Amongst the CD case, file folders, and rolled sheaf of printed photographs he found an envelope. On its outside, Neal read:

'To the reader of this message, I ask that you please place the contents of this bag in the hands of Madeline Cavanagh. She will be staying in the Ately Guest House in Kodikkarai. If you are not with the Indian Coast Guard, then I have no doubt Madeline will reward you well for the return of this bag's contents, which, though materially worthless, will be of great value to her.

Your servant,
-James Hawkson, aboard *King's Transom* at sea.'

Neal read the handwriting he had seen on so many notes back at the Institute. His heart sank for Madeline as he handed her the sealed envelope, knowing that its contents were, no doubt, meant for her.

She took it, looking back at him after reading its cover.

"Do you want me to leave you alone?" he asked.

"Don't you dare." she snapped, instantly regretting her tone. But he nodded understandingly and she duly ripped open the envelope. Inside was a note, and sure enough it began:

'Dear Madeline,

I hope I am the fool you have always thought I am. I hope you are reading this while I laugh in embarrassment next to you. No doubt Neal will give me a mountain of crap for being so paranoid. I really hope I am that much of a fool.

If I am paranoid then the proverbial alarm bells that have been screaming in my head since we saw what was lying down there will be just the result of spending too much time with lunatic scientists like you and Neal.

But deep down I fear they aren't baseless. If you are reading this without me it means that I have not made it home, and then I will not have put these files in this bag for no reason. If we have not made it home there is a chance, I suppose, that the boat sank for some innocent reason, but if you believe for one moment that this crew can't get this ship into port from here then you are a bigger fool than I.

I worked just as hard as you on that probe, and I know what its results mean. We have found something beyond important, and the pattern of where it and its friends landed is very, very worrying. I believe we have found something very dangerous. Something not-from-here has gone to great lengths to hide their arrival. They clearly possess a level of technology we don't if they can get here from wherever they are from, and I have to imagine they won't like us finding evidence that they have come.

We must tread very carefully with this information. If something has stopped me and Laurie from getting back to you then you must assume that that same something will be watching both of you too.

Tell no one, show no one, be careful. Hand all this to Admiral Hamilton directly and then go away and enjoy your life. Don't get involved.

Of course, I may be a fool. I hope I am a fool. But if I am not, if the worst has happened, don't be a fool as well.

I love you.

Yours forever,
-James'

Madeline handed Neal the letter, hung her head, and wept.

Chapter 18: Friends in High Places

Colonel Patel had been kind enough to leave Madeline to grieve, but had eventually had to pull Neal aside so that he could ask the many questions he was required to ask.

Neal's answers had been circumspect, but not unreasonably so. He was not a sailor, and had said this ignorance was the very reason he and Madeline had stayed ashore. It was several hours later that his assistant informed the colonel that a representative of the American embassy was calling from New Delhi, asking to speak to Neal.

When Neal was handed the phone he was surprised to hear a familiar voice.

"Neal, this is Tim Hamilton, at the embassy," Neal took a moment to recognize the name without its usual prefix, "no doubt this conversation is being overheard so I'll keep this brief. Firstly, are all of you all right?"

The voice of the senior admiral who had overseen the project, disguised as it was as being from a member of the American Embassy in India, had thrown Neal off for a moment. Then the admiral's suggestion of brevity sent a chill through Neal, reminding him of James' warning note. In thinking that they might be being eavesdropped on, the admiral may be righter than he knew.

He replied carefully, "Err … Tim, how are you? I didn't expect to hear your voice. Umm, we have had some sad news here, it looks like the boat James Hawkson and Laurie West were on has gone down, there do not appear to be any survivors." He paused a moment, the admiral silent at this confirmation of what had previously just been a rumor.

Neal, still fearful of the potential that someone other than the Indian government was also listening in, continued, "As of right now there doesn't seem to be any evidence of how or why this might have happened."

The admiral had hoped for some kind of explanation, but his training made him err on the side of action in the face of ambiguity, so he moved on. Sounding concerned but firm, he said, "Neal, we're going to overlook for a moment that you and Madeline were out there with them in the first place, and just be thankful that you didn't somehow make it onto the boat as well."

Neal sighed, almost relieved at the familiar stern tone of the admiral.

The officer continued, "I think it best that you and Madeline come home immediately. Take the next bus or plane back to New Delhi and I'll have one of the embassy staff meet you at the airport with your tickets home. Clear?"

"Absolutely, Tim, we'll see you in … Delhi," said Neal, and, hearing the line go dead, handed the headset back to Colonel Patel who replaced it in its cradle so they could return to the final questions the Indian officer had for his copious forms.

He did not discuss his imminent departure with the colonel, and it would not be till sometime later that the colonel would receive a call telling him to close the case and release the two Americans, appropriate pressure having been applied by appropriate people during appropriate meetings and phone calls. For the admiral was not idle after ending his call with Neal. After thanking the embassy in New Delhi for patching him through to the coast guard, he had woken up certain people within the Pentagon, initiating predefined protocols for extracting citizens from a friendly nation when they might hold pertinent or classified information.

The admiral had also placed a call to his longtime peer, colleague, and all round rival, General Pickler, to discuss this new turn of events, and his level of discomfort with them.

The extraction process, once started, took on a life of its own, long practiced procedures setting off a domino effect within the halls of power in Washington and beyond. While a representative of the secretary of state was calling his counterpart in Delhi, a government travel agency was locating the fastest possible route from Kodikkarai to Washington, DC. At the same time, the CIA was activating an asset on the ground in Delhi, dispatching him to the airport to meet the two citizens off the local commuter flight from Kodikkarai, ensuring they got to their flight home, and minimizing their contact with Indian officials, or anyone else, along the way.

And so Colonel Patel had been as surprised as Neal when a senior official had called him sometime later, ordering him to end his interview with the Americans and escort them back to their guesthouse.

"I am to help you collect your belongings," the colonel had said, somewhat bewildered, but nonetheless quick to comply, "then we are to drive you to the airport where a plane is, apparently, even now waiting for you."

Wow, thought Neal, the Pentagon doesn't fuck around. He had thanked the colonel, and then helped to escort the still distraught Madeline out of the coast guard building.

Arriving in Delhi hours later, they were accosted by a loud, middle-aged American tourist in a Hawaiian shirt and shorts. As they tried to politely get away from him, he leant in and shook Neal's hand, saying blithely that he was a friend of Tim Hamilton's. The shoe dropped, and Neal, squeezing Madeline's arm, said they should go and grab a drink with the man and talk about the States.

She was not far behind him, sensing his change of mood, and the tourist, who introduced himself as Bob, led them to a corner of one of the many airport bars.

They never discussed business, never mentioned anything about what had happened, Bob's stares telling them to keep the conversation simple.

As soon as Bob had seen the two getting off the plane in New Delhi, he had spotted the attractive Indian woman watching them. Sure enough, she had followed them into the bar and taken a seat at another table across the room. The fact that she did not have a bag with her had alerted Bob's instincts, but he was even more unsettled by her unnaturally black eyes. Whenever he glanced over they were on Neal and Madeline.

Bob assumed she was with the Indian government. He did not mention it to his wards, no need to worry them, but nor did he want them to start talking shop with a set of ears near them.

If a certain six-year-old girl in Kodikkarai had seen the woman, she would have told anyone that would listen that she was the woman who had swum ashore from Sri Lanka. But the six-year-old in question had still barely been allowed to leave her room since she had ruined her birthday sari.

- - -

Neal and Madeline were now five hours into their long flight home. Their VIP status and newfound friend Bob had gotten them into business class on the Air India flight to JFK, and they now sat in their large leather seats at 33,000 feet, semi-sober, the last few days seeming like an out-of-body experience.

They had scrupulously avoided discussing the incident since leaving Kodikkarai, their conversation coming in fits and starts as they tried to ignore the proverbial four-hundred-pound gorilla in the room.

Finishing his third Bloody Mary, Neal finally broke the silence, leaning close as he said quietly, "What are we going to do?"

"What do you mean?"

"I mean … what are we going to do with the pictures, the probe's findings? What are we going to do with what we know?"

Madeline in turn polished the last gulps of her own bloody mary, and said, staring into her empty glass, "I am going to do nothing, just like James said. I'm going to hand it over to people more powerful and more knowledgeable than me, and I'm going home."

Neal paused, he did not want to push her, but this would not wait for another time, "Madeline, I don't think it is going to be that easy."

She looked at him.

"We're involved, like it or not. This is … well … no longer something we can walk away from."

"Why not?" she said, pressing her call button to order another drink.

Neal looked at her. He was about to speak again when the flight attendant arrived. She had been very friendly since they had come on board, and had kept the alcohol flowing. Years of dealing with every imaginable walk of life had told the seasoned stewardess that the two of them were returning from something bad, and she had instinctively given them a little bit more space and a readier supply of beverages than their fellow business class passengers.

"What can I get for you?" she said with a warm smile.

"Another bloody, please, Shirley." said Madeline. Shirley glanced questioningly at Neal, and he smiled, raising two fingers in a peace sign to let Shirley know to make it two. Shirley nodded understandingly and headed off in the direction of the galley.

"Madeline," continued Neal as she departed, "whatever happened to James and Laurie out there, we have to assume that it happened because of what they found. We have to assume that either they were being watched or their communications were being monitored."

She grimaced at his words, and looked at him, asking with her eyes whether they had to talk about this.

"I'm sorry, Madeline, but please, hear me out. If you think I am off base I will never mention any of this again, I promise."

She thought a moment, then nodded dejectedly, reaching up like a child for her medicine as Shirley returned with their fresh bloodies.

Drink in hand, Madeline gulped at the cold drink a little too enthusiastically, and then cringed as the vodka and spice hit her.

Neal waited a moment, then went on, hesitantly, "Here is what I have been thinking: it seems obvious that something found out what James and Laurie were up to and reacted in a way that James was clearly fearing it would. Now, I've been thinking about how they could have found out, and it can only be either by watching them, from a satellite, or by eavesdropping on their communications."

A question leapt into Madeline's mind, and she asked, "Then why didn't whatever happened to them, happen to us too?" she asked.

"I was thinking about that as well, and I have to conclude that the SFR's encoding saved our particular conversation from being listened in on. After all, it uses two randomly assigned deteriorating algorithms for the encryption, each handset can only talk to its counterpart. It is supposed to be unhackable ... by anyone."

She seemed semi-placated by that explanation, nodding, albeit unenthusiastically.

He plodded on, "That theory is supported by the fact that we were able to talk for so long last night without ... interference. So given that I can't see how even the most detailed visual surveillance would have allowed them to see what was going on inside the boat's cabins, and they apparently couldn't hear our conversation, someone on board must have sent some kind of message about the ship's findings, and that triggered a ... response."

They both cringed, but Neal went on, "An update to Washington, maybe, maybe even sent by James himself, though I doubt he would have been so foolish." Instantly, he wished he hadn't used the word 'fool' for its unfortunate reference to James' letter.

She shuddered and Neal fell silent for a moment. But then Madeline suddenly took up his line of thought, her expression one of childlike fear, "They ... they were attacked from space." she said, reticently.

Neal had concluded the same thing, but he desperately needed to check his thinking, and so, despite how much it might hurt her to think of it, he prompted her to go on, saying, "Why do you say that?"

"Two things," Madeline continued, "firstly, the wreckage. A missile would have left some damage, pieces. But the ship must have been downed whole, taking everything that was bolted down with it."

An image filled her mind but she went on, driven now by a new emotion growing inside her: anger. "But there is more than that. Years ago, the Institute helped test a laser platform for the air force. It was going to be part of what Reagan stupidly used to call Star Wars. It was designed to be fired from space, but for testing purposes we fired it from an air force gunship. It ended up being scrapped because even minimal cloud cover cut the laser's effectiveness markedly.

"With more power we could have made it more capable, but we couldn't generate enough juice within the predefined weight limits. Anyway, I was part of the team that laid the targets for the laser, and picked them up afterward."

She turned to face him, clasping his forearm with her hand, "Neal, the burns on the bag, the soot, our targets from back then had the same pattern. It radiated from laser hits as the targets burned. The coast guard said it looked like there had been a fire," Neal could hear the venom growing in her voice, "they must have been burned alive as they tried to get away."

She looked into his eyes, her growing fury burning now as well, as fierce as he had ever seen, and he almost recoiled from her.

"We have to fight these fuckers, Neal." Madeline said in a low grumble, her lips and eyes set now in determination. "We have to fight them and we have to win. James was a good man, and I know you and Laurie were close. This was a terrible end for them."

She fixed his gaze and said, finally, "We need to avenge them."

He nodded, her resolve filling him, allowing his anger at Laurie's death to finally hit him. The emotion focused his mind into cold calculation, his uncommonly good instincts starting to guide his thinking once more. He thought about their next move.

"We will, Madeline, we will, but first we must survive this first storm. If they were cut down from above, that means we are always going to be vulnerable whenever we are in plain sight, possibly even when we are inside too, depending on who or what is watching. Either way, for now, at least, sunbathing is probably not a good idea."

She smiled, coldly, then added to his thought, "And e-mail is going to be out, as well. If they can hack comms from a navy boat in the middle of the ocean, they can certainly read our e-mails. In fact, to be safe, we are going to have to stop using any PC that is connected to the net, altogether."

They looked at each other. They had found salvation from their grief in seeking revenge. They would find a way to fight this.

"So I guess we're not going to hand this off to 'people more powerful than ourselves'?" Neal quoted her, a small, humorless smile edging at his lips.

"Those morons? Never."

They chuckled for the first time since it had all happened, and then Neal went on, "OK, so what *are* we going to tell the admiral and his friends? They are going to want an explanation."

Chapter 19: Conference of Equals

Since their arrival in orbit, the four satellite-based supercomputers had been constantly updating all eight operatives on the progress of the mission, while also monitoring their work down on the planet's surface.

After using devices like the crocodile clip to provide temporary connections to get the Agents in place, each operative had hidden their main subspace relays and proceeded to start integrating with their various target nations.

Leaving their relays behind had meant that they were unable to send significant amounts of information to the hub satellites in return until they were able to collect their relays and, like Lana Wilson, move them to more permanent locations.

In case of emergency, they were able to use small lasers aimed upward at the passing satellites to communicate covertly. But this method was cumbersome and limited, especially when compared to the instantaneously connected subspace tweeter that all their systems were designed around.

In the interim, most of them had buried the black boxes in fields near the military bases they needed to be billeted at for the first stage of their naturalization.

This was the case for Agents Lana Wilson in America, Preeti Parikh in India and Pei Leong-Lam in China, the same being true for the Agents in Russia, England, and Israel.

In France, Jean-Paul Merard had buried his relay in a vineyard, leading to the unfortunate if unavoidable death of the vintner, and forcing the Agent to wait several additional weeks for the police to clear the area before collecting it once more.

Shahim Al Khazar, on the other hand, was unique in that his orders were not to infiltrate a military or government organization at all. The political instability in Pakistan had led to the decision that it would be easier to nullify their military's threat by joining and helping the extremist forces in the mountains than from within the rigidly structured military itself.

Earning an Al Qaeda commander's trust had not been difficult; it had simply required that Shahim do something so atrocious that no one could doubt his resolve in the jihad they had all committed their lives to. After the explosion at the US Air Force base in Afghanistan had killed so many infidels, and claimed no fallen martyrs from the fighters' ranks, he had been able to carry his blanket-wrapped black box into the camp he was sent to unhindered, no one daring to stop him.

It turned out to be Pei Leong-Lam who was the last to be able to return to his relay, the closed doors of the Chinese Training Camp keeping him penned up for the entire officer training class.

After three months, however, Leong-Lam was also to be the first among them to be assigned to a base. Based on Drill Sergeant Shih's firm recommendation, he was to be sent to the prestigious Hong Kong Garrison. The day before deployment, he requested and was granted twelve hours leave by Shih out of respect for the way Leong-Lam had handled the drill sergeant's abuse, and as Pei came into range of his buried relay, the connection was reestablished, and the eight were united once more.

Since its inception, the plan to infiltrate the earth's superpowers had been founded on a very flexible set of parameters. No one could have predicted how earth's major societies would change over the years that would pass from when the attack was launched to when the advance party actually arrived, so into the various parts of the team had been built a series of checks and balances.

Like all civilized societies, the one that was descending upon us was as complex and multi-faceted as our own. Factions and political alliances were as much a part of its systems of government as any of ours. However, an unparalleled unity of purpose had come from the discovery of a weaker, conquerable planet within their grasp. This could be a fresh start for the planet's fiscal elite, a chance to expand out of the confines of their crowded, financially and politically saturated planet.

But as the plan to invade was formed, none of the prominent parties or dynastic families had been willing to give up control of the expedition to any of the others. So it had been decided that they would bake the same political diversity into the advanced team, and the invading army, which they 'enjoyed' in their own colorful governments.

The concession to politics had been further facilitated by the military decision to use a programming method known as personality-overlay to program the eight operatives, aiding their ability to appear less … robotic. Years of practice had led AI programmers, AIParents, or AIPs as they were called, to the conclusion that the fundamentally illogical nature of all animals was extremely difficult to fully duplicate in a fundamentally logical AI.

So this need to make the Agents more natural, combined with pressure from the halls of power to bake political influence into the invading force, had led them to decide to program the eight operatives of the advanced team with the personalities of actual members of their race, the minds to be nominated and voted upon by the very political entities that were vying for control of the whole enterprise.

The political battle that had followed had rivaled the greatest in any government's history, only just stopping short of open war. But, after six months of heated debate, short-lived alliances, betrayals, assassination, and unashamed commercialism, eight nominees had finally been agreed upon.

The satellite-based hub supercomputers would remain pure AI, their logic unquestionable, and would be placed in orbit around the prize, in charge of the day-to-day running of the operation, supervising the work of each Agent as they infiltrated the most powerful human militaries.

The supercomputers, however, would ultimately bow to the combined will of the Agents, whenever a virtual meeting of the Agents could be convened, the eight Agents' personalities, picked with great care and even greater expense, representing to varying degrees all of the main parties politic. They would vote on any decision that either they or the supercomputer chose to put in front of them, and this would allow the advanced team the strategic flexibility it would need to respond to any unforeseen developments once they arrived at Earth.

If a consensus could not be reached on how to react to whatever political or martial situations they found themselves facing, the AI would form the ninth, tie-breaking vote.

Now that Pei Leong-Lam had managed to return to his relay, the first full Council was convened since only a few days after their arrival. From now on, they would meet at least once a week, more often if the need arose.

The conference took place in a virtual meeting space, the personalities of the eight Agents represented by avatars created in their images, seemingly floating in a circle in empty space.

The AI that was creating the image and projecting it into the heads of the eight Agents was also the host of the meeting. It remained invisible, however, represented not by an avatar, but by virtual screens in front of each Agent, where it could place any image or dataset relevant to the conversation.

While this system might be primitive considering the machines' advanced abilities, the entire meeting would be conducted at phenomenal speed. The esoteric constructs inside each Agent that housed their personality copies were, after all, still computers, just with an animal consciousness overlaid on top of them; and they were still capable of operating at machine speeds.

None of them would ever struggle to recall an event or piece of information, or to calculate an equation; the answers would appear to them with the speed of any computer calculation.

So these meetings of the Council, while no doubt doomed to be steeped in argument, demagoguery and bile, would nonetheless only take a few seconds in real-time. While the meeting occurred, the Agent's on the ground, as long as they were within reach of their subspace relays, would only have to briefly excuse themselves from whatever they were doing, their eyes would briefly glaze over for a second or two while they participated, and then they would be back to the business of assimilating themselves in to their respective organizations.

So, as this first meeting of the Council was convened by the AI, around the world the eight Agents became momentarily distracted. Most had found ways to be alone, having been notified in advance by the AI that the last of their ranks was almost within range of his relay.

Agent Mikhail Kovalenko, in Russia, was unfortunately in one of many long meetings with his superior, both in terms of time and wind. The strict Captain Gorovchev would think the junior officer was about to sneeze, and would be thankful when, a moment later, Mikhail's eyes would focus again, allowing the captain to continue yet another of his frequent diatribes on the importance of discipline.

<Welcome.>

The word sounded from all around them, as their images resolved in the virtual meeting space. Because of the subspace tweeter, the signal travelled not through what we considered 'normal' space, but under its surface, so it was actually not burdened by the constraints of having to travel at all. It arrived instantaneously, and because of this a meeting would be conducted between eight people spread across the planet, without any of the delays such a meeting would suffer over our more primitive communications.

<I have created an agenda of items that seem pertinent. Agents are to keep additional topics for the end.>

The AI had orders on how to chair the meetings, and it was not flexible. A list blinked into existence in front of each of them, its contents immediately a part of their memory, sent as it was, and as all data was being, directly into their computer minds.

<The Indian Ocean Situation: Per updates provided, the research project was deemed a risk to Mission Security Parameters, monitoring revealed that Agent Preeti Parikh's landing capsule had been discovered. All operatives were not available to convene Council and decide action. Protocol was followed, research ship and all aboard were eliminated two days ago when message was intercepted indicating identification of the capsule by human scientists.>

Lana Wilson's avatar's virtual mouth opened to speak, the AI sensing this the moment she began. In the millisecond between her deciding to speak and the word forming in her avatar's mouth, the AI stopped talking and diverted her speech to the group. "Imagery of the action was conveyed to us," said Lana, "but not of the surrounding area. Was the destruction witnessed?"

<There were no witnesses, ship was not in visual range of other vessels. Radio distress signals were jammed. Automatic emergency location devices were not disturbed as no pertinent information could be transmitted through automated devices. All actions deemed minimum necessary to maintain mission secrecy.>

"I agree," said Lana, "and, yet, I feel we didn't go far enough. What about the other signals sent prior to destruction, the report you have already provided showed an encrypted radio signal from the ship that could not be deciphered. Who received this message?"

<Impossible to confirm. Available information shows a similar signal, also hyper-encrypted, coming from the shore at same time. Posit that this was reciprocal signal.>

Jean-Paul Merard, from France, interjected, "That must be the receiver, we should eliminate anyone who listened to that signal as well."

"My sentiments exactly," piped in Lana.

<Exact identity of listeners not confirmable. Posit that party that arrived with target vessel's captain were most likely receivers. Have monitored these individuals since. No further pertinent information to report.>

Preeti Parikh spoke, "I was closest to the incident, so I was able to go and intercept the other two humans in person when they were returning via Delhi, per my report. I monitored their conversation for several hours, they mentioned nothing of the ship, or its findings, during private conversations during this time, and, as I said, I watched them for quite some time."

She seemed to finish, then added, "Of course, I'm not saying that doesn't mean we shouldn't play it safe here." She was certainly not going to be the only one who cautioned inaction, even if it was, in fact, her sense that this was the right way to go.

"Why is this even being discussed?" said Lana, Jean-Paul nodding his agreement, "There is no reason to risk this. Kill them."

<Statement that there is no reason not to risk not entirely accurate.>

Lana visibly tensed at this. Effectively oblivious, the AI went on:

<Communications between senior military officials in the United States and their leadership body at the White House indicate a high level of concern over the disappearance of the research vessel in question. No parties have yet stated any suspicion of the reason for the sinking, or awareness of our existence, but further killing of members of the research team will significantly fuel further investigation and speculation, or worse.>

"Worse? How?" said Mikhail Kovalenko, "Surely they are more likely to suspect the Indian government of the deaths than us?"

<Reminder of Primary Mission Parameter: avoid, at all costs, potential military conflagration between nuclear capable countries.>

The penny dropped, for most, but others were less easy to deter, "Based on the political sensitivity of the effectively impotent 'NATO group,' they would never react so strongly to the loss of a few lowly scientists." said Lana, derisively.

John Hunt, speaking from his naval posting in Portsmouth in the UK, decided to speak, "Do not think that the people of Earth are so willing to … disregard the lives of their citizens just because they are not actually part of the leadership. The same political sensitivity that restrains the 'Western' countries from bold action on the international stage also drives them to protect, with vigor, even the most irrelevant of their people."

The English Agent went on, "I am not implying anything so outrageous as a simple incident like this sparking nuclear war. But whether that event is likely or not, we should not underestimate America's reaction if they believe members of their White House staff are being killed by a foreign power, not to mention an entire crew of navy seals and sailors."

Lana's avatar stared at him for a moment, their virtual constructs showing all the facial expressions of their copied personalities, a healthy dose of reciprocal disdain most prominent amongst them. But then she nodded, "Hunt is correct, they protect even the most negligible of their citizens because of their sad delusion of democracy." she almost spat the words, "I can only imagine how they would react if they suspected someone actually important had been assassinated.

"That said," she continued, "if either of the two remaining humans utters even the slightest suspicion of the truth behind the incident in India, it remains imperative that we eliminate them immediately. We will deal with any consequences, as appropriate, afterwards. Do I have quorum on that, at least?"

The group nodded, one after the other, her eyes meeting theirs until they came to rest on John Hunt's. "Of course." he nodded, acquiescing to the obvious majority with a virtual smile.

Sensing with machine accuracy the rooms' satisfaction with the topic, the AI moved on.

<Next Topic: The impending officer assignments of Agents Hunt, Kovalenko, and Merard: options for deployment.>

- - -

That initial part of the Council had taken just over 0.73 seconds in real-time. Lengthy debate followed afterward about the best assignments the British, Russian, and French Agents should seek in order to best position themselves for their respective missions.

After a further full second and a half the meeting was closed, a series of action items having been determined both for the AI, and for several of the Agents.

As Lieutenant Second Class Kovalenko returned from his apparently momentary lapse in concentration to his meeting with Captain Gorovchev, he looked to his superior, who was frowning at him with obvious impatience.

"You must forgive me, sir, I have not quite gotten used to all the trees here in the south, my allergies give me much dismay." he said, bowing to the captain's stern stare.

"Of course, Lieutenant Kovalenko. I imagine it would no doubt be funny to our soft Western European friends to hear an officer complain of coming *south* to Moscow, especially an officer as ... capable as you." The captain said it almost as an insult, such was his disdain for giving actual compliments. But the lieutenant's abilities could not be denied, especially within the area of intelligence.

"Anyway, enough of this chitchat. Where was I, Lieutenant?"

"I believe we were discussing potential assignments, Captain. You were extolling me on the very great importance of discipline, especially if I were to pursue a career in the Strategic Command Force."

"Yes, yes, Lieutenant, and very important it is. Normally I am very hesitant to use one of my few annual nominations to the SCF recruitment list. But in your case I believe you may be worthy of such an honor. I was a member of the StratCom myself; back when it really meant something."

The captain could not know that the lieutenant, via the AI's research, had accessed the captain's military record, including as much of the classified sections as were easily reached. So he could not know that the lieutenant was aware of the captain's five applications to the SCF, all unsuccessful, back in the Cold War when it had, indeed, been a much more elite force than it was today.

"Yes, Lieutenant, you may well be of SCF's standards, though I doubt you would have made it into the Old Strategic Command." said the captain proudly, the lieutenant nodding subserviently, making sure his face and deep black eyes betrayed none of his contempt for the pompous fool in front of him.

Chapter 20: Playing the Fool

"Come in, come in." said Admiral Hamilton. "Coffee?"

Neal and Madeline nodded emphatically. They had not slept in a bed since leaving the guest house in Kodikkarai, two days ago, and the admiral had been so keen to see them that they had been brought straight to the Pentagon from the airport.

Neal had asked that they be allowed to check into their hotels and freshen up, a sentiment that Madeline had echoed, but the driver had insisted that he was under strict orders to bring them directly to the admiral.

"Hey, I guess you two haven't slept, sorry. Lieutenant Martin should have let you check-in first so that you could freshen up." said the admiral. Neal felt certain that the lieutenant had been ordered to do no such thing; no doubt the admiral wanted them a little off guard so he could get the most information out of them.

Either way, they had both discussed at length how much they should tell the admiral, and their stories were well set as they gratefully accepted their coffees from the admiral's secretary.

"Now, maybe you could just answer a few questions and I'll let you head to the hotel, I'm sure you are both very tired."

They nodded at him. "Sure." said Madeline, and they both sipped their coffees.

The admiral looked at them. He did not like what he saw. They were clearly both tired, and more than a little unkempt. Neal in particular did not smell too fresh, and his thinning hair had gone a bit primal. But it was more that. They both seemed a little too … resolved.

"Neal, maybe you can start? I'm sure this is very difficult for you both, but why don't you start from how you both came to be in India in the first place. I assure you there will be no recriminations, at this point that would be … moot, but we want to know why you were both there, against the orders both Captain Hawkson and Dr. West received."

The two sleepy conspirators flinched at hearing the names, but Neal leaned forwards, glancing at Madeline quickly before saying: "Admiral, I am sure Laurie wouldn't mind me telling you, given how things turned out, that she divulged to me that she'd originally recommended I be allowed on board the *King's Transom* in her place."

The admiral remained steely faced at this violation of the military secrecy, and did not interrupt Neal, who, after a deep breath, went on, "I won't deny that there is a part of me that is happy the request was denied, but there was a reason for her recommendation. I, along with James and Madeline, here, were simply the best qualified to configure the machine.

"While we all knew that your orders prohibited our being on board when she sailed, Madeline and I helped with the set up beforehand, and then stayed ashore to answer questions via radio after she left."

"By radio?" the admiral exclaimed, "You exchanged classified information over the radio?"

"No, Admiral, not exactly. James ... Captain Hawkson ... was just as keenly aware of the need for discretion as anyone, so he brought along a matched set of Secure Field Radios for us to communicate with. You see, he and Laurie may have brought us along against your orders, but only because we had already worked on the probe, and knew full well what it was for. The 'SurFeRs' are, I believe, theoretically unhackable ..."

"Yes, thank you, Neal, I know the capabilities of the device in question." The admiral smiled slightly. He had to credit James with his thoroughness, even when he was disobeying orders he never forgot the intent behind them. "OK, Neal, so it seems you were in contact with the ship. Then maybe you can shed some more light as to what happened?"

Neal shook his head, staring at his cup in obvious discomfort, before replying quietly but earnestly, "Admiral, I only wish could. I am afraid when we last spoke with them everything was fine on board. I am sad to say we closed radio contact at around 2am, some two hours before ... *it* apparently happened."

Neal looked at Madeline, then reached out and squeezed her hand as he said the next part. "The next time we had any information about the *King's Transom* was when the Indian authorities found us."

"I see," said the admiral, quietly. Then, treading lightly, he probed further, "Then, perhaps you might have some information on what the results of the search were up until the ... incident?"

Neal paused a moment, and Madeline, not willing to let him bear this burden alone, spoke in his place. "We talked at length about the search the previous days, but not that night."

She sat up straight and seemed to gather herself, then continued, "Neal is being kind, Admiral, and more of a gentleman than, well, you'd expect." She shot a smile at Neal and he nodded, surprised, but, he couldn't deny, relieved that she had interrupted him.

"You see," she continued, "he wasn't on that final call, it was just James and I. It was late ... and the call was ... personal in nature."

She fixed the admiral with a powerful stare, her fatigue forgotten, her grief driving her forwards. Neal looked at her, astonished at her resolve. It had been Madeline who had come up with the cover story. He had fought her on it, but she had been as resolute then as she was being now, and he was mute with admiration for her.

The admiral and Madeline looked at each other for a moment, sizing each other up. Finally the admiral nodded, a look on his face as close to sympathy as you might hope to see on an officer dealing with blatant violations of orders and more than a few encroachments on the official secrets act. He made a note on his paper then looked back at Neal.

"I have to ask this, do you have any theories as to how this tragedy may have come about?"

Neal thought a moment. Madeline and he had debated at length whether to tell the admiral their true suspicions, but had decided that the chance that the staunch military man would pass them on was too great. That said, they had also decided that he was not a stupid or incapable man, in fact, Laurie had often referred to the admiral as an ally of hers in Washington, so they would try not to say anything that would burn their bridges with him, either.

Finally Neal went on, staring very deliberately into Admiral Hamilton's eyes. "Admiral, I cannot stress enough that we have no information that would allow us to make any conclusions about what caused the *King's Transom* to go down.

"However," Neal paused a moment to emphasize the next point, "nor am I able to eliminate any possibilities at this time."

The admiral stared at him. Through his own conversations with Neal, and through the candid and emphatic recommendations of both Dr. West, Colonel Milton back at the Array, and his normally unfazed colleague General Pickler, Admiral Hamilton had concluded that Neal's was an intellect not to be underestimated.

Long experience had also taught him that sometimes the question you didn't ask was what differentiated a thorough interviewer from a truly capable one.

He nodded, notably not writing anything on his pad of what he thought the scientist's comments meant. Then, suddenly, he got to his feet.

"Well, I think that is enough for today." They both stared at him in surprise as he rose and came around the desk. Then they stole a glance at each other as if to say: 'is it really that easy?' shrugged, and returned their confused stares to the surprisingly enigmatic admiral.

"I think it's best you both head back to the hotel." he said, "I will leave it up to you how long you remain in Washington."

Then to Madeline alone, "Madeline, I had not previously been aware of your relationship with the captain. Please allow me to offer my sincerest condolences. He was a very good officer, and, I believe, an equally good man."

She nodded at this, struggling not let her emotions get the better of her, not in front of this austere officer, not now they might be able to relax for a little while. So they all stood and shook hands, but as they turned to leave, the admiral suddenly said, "Err, Neal, the sad loss of my longtime colleague, and dare I say it, friend, Dr. West, has left a gap on the White House Science Team."

Neal turned to look at him as he continued, "I hope you do not mind that I have recommended your name to the president as a replacement?"

Neal's mouth opened, dumbfounded at the statement. He shook his head, unable to find words.

"I am assuming," the admiral said into the silence, "that you are planning to complete that thesis of yours ASAP? It would not do to have a lowly masters of science advising the president."

"No, Admiral, I imagine it wouldn't."

"Well, take a few days to think about it. The White House chief of staff will begin interviews in about two months, once candidate background checks have taken place. That should give you plenty of time to wrap up your thesis before you get the call. How long have you been working on it, now?"

"Oh, about … eight years … give or take." he laughed.

"Yes, well," the admiral frowned, "you should be about done then."

- - -

"What do you think, Admiral?" asked General Pickler as they spoke on the phone, not fifteen minutes after Neal and Madeline had left.

"I think that they're good people who've just been part of a clusterfuck, Michael … and I think they are afraid." said Admiral Hamilton.

"Of what?" General Pickler had watched the entire interview from a camera mounted behind a mirror in the corner of the slightly deceitful office they had met in. For unbeknownst to Neal and Madeline, they had not met in the admiral's office at all, but in one of many interview spaces in the building, this one designed to put people at ease by being set up as the office of the interviewer.

After Neal and Madeline had left, the admiral had picked up his brass desk nameplate and the two photos of his family and walked back to his own, notably less wired office. As he had done so, the 'secretary' stationed outside had disabled the cameras and microphones in the room and removed the admiral's name from the door.

"I don't know what has them scared, probably just seeing a boyfriend and a respected colleague die while in a very foreign country. Either way, we weren't going to get anything more out of them today, so I figured it best to send them home."

The general was silent for a while he pondered this, then he said, "And recommending this Danielson to the advisor's job? Are we sure that is wise?"

"Dr. West brought something unique to that team, a combination of extreme intelligence, rare creativity, and the balls to combine the two. She will be near impossible to replace, but if we can find it, we need someone who doesn't store his head up the scientific community's ass to make sure the president stays informed. Something tells me Neal is ready to be that guy."

"He's certainly got the smarts, I can't deny that." The general had been part of the review team for the probe and had seen the amount that Neal had brought to that effort, as well as being the only person who had correctly predicted the meteors' landing spots.

The general continued, "And I concur that he seems much more mature than when he was bumbling his way through my operations meetings. And anyway, I've got no one I'd rather have in there right now, so I'll guess support your nomination … for now."

"Thanks, Michael, I owe you one. You'll let me know if I can get you anything else on this." said the admiral, wrapping up the conversation.

"I know I'll let you know when you can repay me for supporting your boy." said the general smarmily, "Bar that, I think this whole project is better forgotten for a year or two. You don't think Neal and Madeline will push for another expedition to retrieve one of the meteors?"

"Something tells me neither of them plans on raising that topic again for a while. And I'll certainly dissuade them with some vigor if they try."

The admiral and general said their good-byes, closing the call, both satisfied with the conversation for now. The admiral had to meet his son for dinner. Apparently a new girl was in the boy's life, and the admiral always liked picking on his son about his unfortunate choices in women.

- - -

Having reviewed their entire discussion, and having hacked into and watched the meeting from the same remote view as the general, the AI transmitted to the eight that there was currently no need to further increase the mission's exposure by killing the remaining scientists. It would continue to monitor the actions of both Neal Danielson and Madeline Cavanagh, but for now the immediate threat appeared to have passed.

Chapter 21: It's Bad to be Home

Neal pushed opened the door to his apartment in Arizona and immediately reeled at the smell. It had been nearly three months since he had left for Florida.

Seeing a pizza box on the floor, he felt a wash of shame. That was bad, even for him. His mind went to whether he had emptied his fridge. He hadn't. But he had remembered to unplug his air conditioner to save electricity during the Arizona winter, such was the confoundable rationale of his sometime excuse for a brain.

Covering his mouth and nose with his grey T-shirt, he stepped over the mound of junk mail around his door and walked to the window, leaving the door open behind him. After wrangling the window open, cracking the flaky old paint that held it in place to do so, he grabbed his tall trash can from one side and pulled its bag out, itself another thing he had forgotten to empty. It was doing its bit for the aroma as well, no doubt.

The pizza box was damp through on the bottom and Neal feared it would collapse under its own weight, visions of a collapsing star coming to mind, and the relatively comparable destruction this box's unleashed contents would do to his floor. But he was spared that. It wasn't until he opened the door to the fridge that he was hit with a wall of pungency akin to, well, he didn't really know how to classify it: road kill, maybe? The puff of gas from a month-old corpse spontaneously combusting? No, that wasn't quite it. It was like an athlete's reused jock strap … dipped in excrement … and then baked.

He gagged, barely controlling himself, then set to making his home smell a little less like a French cheese shop.

He had seen Madeline onto her flight to Florida with a long and heartfelt hug before walking to his own gate for his flight back to Arizona. Neither of them had had the heart to talk more about what they were facing before they had settled their lives a bit, so they had agreed not to speak about it again until they were next together, which would be at James' funeral in two days.

No information had been provided to him about Laurie's funeral, though he assumed that, like James', it would sadly have to be closed casket, unable as they had been to identify any of the remains retrieved from the Indian Ocean.

He had not even started to think about the offer the admiral had made. He doubted that the White House would select him, even if he had the time to finish his thesis before the interviews started. Either way, he had bigger things to face than going job hunting.

He retrieved his old laptop from under a slew of junk on the coffee table and sat down on his unmade bed, the PC powering up as it settled on his lap, like a docile pet.

"OK, what do we have here?" he said to himself as Outlook came slowly to life on his screen.

"4,256 new e-mails, I'll get right on those, now how about calls. Two. Great, love to everyone too. Mom, three weeks ago. Shit, need to call her back. And ... Madeline ..."

He flinched involuntarily at the sight of her name, then clicked playback.

"Neal," came Madeline's voice through the PC speaker, "just to let you know I got back fine. Listen ... I wanted to say thanks ... I haven't said that yet. You know what for. You've been, just, you know, great." Neal bit his lower lip, uncomfortably.

Part of him had been unable to stop blaming himself for it all, like it was his curiosity that had gotten Laurie and James killed, but when he had tried to say that to Madeline as they parted she had, in a more forceful tone than he had ever heard from her, told him never to say it again. She had met his guilt with such stolid fervor that he had stepped back, but she had placed her hands on his shoulders and said, firmly still but with real affection as well, that he was not to blame for what had happened, and that both James and Laurie would be as furious as her to hear him say it.

Seemingly knowing where his mind was going, the voicemail continued, "I know you blame yourself for what happened, but, like I said before, we all went into this with eyes open. James was a big boy, and he wouldn't thank you for one second for implying that he needed you to protect him." Neal smiled at this, James would, indeed, have kicked his ass for presuming that this scientist should have saved the mighty naval secret agent.

"That said, you have been a rock these last few days, and ... well ... I just can't imagine what I would have done without you." Neal could hear her tears through the line, and now that she wasn't here to see them, his own trickled down his cheek as he felt her pain throb inside him.

He would not call her back, despite a pang in his heart to comfort her, she had already said more than she should. No, once he had booked his onward ticket to meet her in Florida, he would check in at the Array, maybe even head down there. He had to wrap-up things there, and maybe see if he could stop himself from being fired from the thesis program. He was sure that having access to the facilities like the Array would be more than a little useful as they tried to figure out exactly what had happened in the Indian Ocean, and what it all meant.

- - -

The colonel was surprised when his aide, Lieutenant Diorio, told him that Danielson had called the office. He had asked to be notified if Neal tried to contact the facility. Diorio had assumed it was because the scientist had apparently run off without notice, leaving his place on the roster empty.

But the colonel was not concerned with such things. He had rarely thought of the civilian team at the Array as much more than a nuisance. In fact, in his years running the complex facility he had only ever once had cause to fully admit the importance of its civilian arm at all, and that was when he had started working with Neal.

There was no doubt in Barrett's mind that someone like Neal would have been chewed up and spit out by any military force that would have had him in the first place. He was simply too lackadaisical to survive the kind of routine or discipline the colonel had come to find so reassuring.

But it was the very untamable nature of Neal's mind that had made him see the rarity of the atmospheric incident and to keep pushing for further analysis, an incident that had been viewed as nothing more than a liability to everyone else.

But now things had shifted again, and the call from General Pickler had thrown the colonel once more. He had not known this Captain Hawkson, or the crew of the *King's Transom*, but Dr. West had been a frequent visitor to the Array. The colonel was not one to dwell on losses, probably because he had suffered so many himself, but the deaths of too many friends over the years had left him with a profound respect for those left behind, and so he would go and visit Neal Danielson and see if there was anything he could do.

He would also follow the two specific orders of General Pickler: firstly he would see that there was no more talk of further expeditions for a while, and secondly he would … encourage the young scientist to pursue the job the admiral had put him up for. Certain people wanted another strong voice in that job, and they had decided that voice should be Neal's.

Standing, he went to the door, took his colonel's cap from the hook on its back, and walked out of his office.

- - -

Neal had given up on his junk-strewn hotmail inbox after getting through about 1% of the crap that filled it, and put his computer aside. He needed a black suit, white shirt, and a tie. He knew he owned at least one of each of these items, but now he had to find them amongst a sea of clothes which any self-respecting hobo would spurn in disgust.

Walking over to the taller of his two easy chairs, he started wading through the randomly piled clothes, of varying cleanliness and age. He was near the front door, and the pile of mail around it was proving even more annoying than its electronic equivalent in his inbox. He decided to find the three things he actually needed to attend to so that he could mail in his responses: rent, internet service and electricity bills.

As he kicked his feet across the pile looking for the telltale envelopes, two other pieces of mail jumped out at him. In amongst the credit card offers, coupon books and magazine subscription offers were two plain manila envelopes. The unusual thing about each was that the address on each was handwritten.

Like most of America, he hadn't received a personal letter since he was a child.

Picking them up, he returned to his spot on the edge of the bed and looked at the writing. It was phenomenally neat, but not familiar to Neal at all. There was no return address on them either, and they were on identical card stock. The only difference was that one had mailed two weeks before the other. He opened the most recent first.

'Neal,

You do not know me, but I know of you. I cannot explain who I am yet, or why I am sending you this note, but I can say with certainty that showing this note to anyone you do not trust absolutely would mean certain and instantaneous death for both you and them.'

Neal stared at the handwriting, as neat and regular as the envelope had been, and whispered, 'what the f..?' He read on.

'Do not e-mail anyone about this letter, do not talk about this letter to anyone on the phone, anyone at all. You are being watched. Talking about this will mean your death. Not at my hands, I assure you, but I will be unable to stop it.

Stay low, stay quiet, and tell your friend Madeline to do the same.

Soon I will be able to tell you more. Until then contact no one about this letter or about what happened in India.'

All thought that Neal had had that this might be a prank vanished when Madeline's name was mentioned. At the word India his heart simply froze.

'I have sent you another letter under identical cover but I know now that you did not receive it in time. Find it, and make sure no one else has seen it in the interim.

I give you these two final pieces of advice: do not talk about this to anyone when you are in the open, even Madeline. Never talk while looking upward. I think you may know why. And do not trust anyone with black eyes.

I will come find you soon. Until then, do nothing about this. Complete your thesis and do all you can to secure the job at the White House, it will be more useful than you can imagine in the coming months.

Yours sincerely,
A Friend'

Neal reread the sheet three times. Then opened the other letter, which was much the same as the first, only it contained a line imploring Neal not to go to India in the first place.

Dear God. Someone had known. Neal struggled to wrap his head around it. Someone was trying to warn him. Someone had known that the *King's Transom* would find something, and they had known what would happen when they did.

Suddenly there was a firm knock at the door and Neal literally almost soiled himself. The sensation was most unpleasant.

"Neal, are you there? I heard you were in town. Are you there?"

Who was that? Shit, Who The Fuck Was That?!

Neal scrambled to hide the letters, then recognition dawned on him, he had heard that voice on the phone too many times.

It was Colonel Milton. But what the hell was he doing here? Did he know? Was it him? Wait, he would not have sent the letters here, he would have told Neal directly. Let's not get paranoid, Neal, get it together.

"Colonel?" shouted Neal through the door.

"Yes, Neal, I thought I'd drop by and see how you are doing."

Neal opened the door the width of his body, standing in the gap to hide the mess behind him.

"Hi." said Neal.

"Neal. How are you? Listen, I heard about what happened in India. I'm sorry." said the colonel, his hat clasped under his arm as he noted the clearly distraught Danielson.

"Yeah, it got pretty crazy out there." said Neal, his mind still racing about the letters.

"Dr. West was a good person, I had known her for several years." said the colonel.

They both knew that Neal had only met Laurie a few months beforehand, but somehow they also both knew that Neal had grown closer to her in that time than the colonel ever had in much longer.

"Yes." said Neal, seemingly struggling to stay focused on the conversation.

"Well, Neal," said the colonel into the awkward silence, "I just wanted to come by and offer my condolences, and to pass on a message from General Pickler."

"Yes?"

"He says that you should try for that job in Washington, that he has put his name behind yours as well, and that I should help you with completing your PhD in any way I can."

Neal nodded, obviously brought to attention by this turn, but still mute. After a sigh Colonel Milton staunchly forged ahead once more into the resilient awkwardness, "Of course, as the air force liaison to your university, an institute which relies heavily on the Array's support, I imagine I will be able to be of very significant help, should you wish it."

"Wow, yes, err, that would be great." Neal said finally, realizing he was being offered help, help he sorely needed with getting his extremely rusty thesis past the university board.

Then he looked distracted for a moment, clearly thinking of something else, "Yeah," he said to the floor, "I've been hearing that I should take that job quite a lot recently."

"Well, that is because it is a very important job, and because the general, and Admiral Hamilton, I believe, have put their considerable weight behind you."

Neal looked at the colonel, he looked into his eyes. They were brown, dark brown to be sure, but not black by any measure.

"Yes, Colonel," he said, "it would seem to be a great opportunity. And it would certainly be very ... useful." He looked askance at the colonel to see if the word got a reaction, but was met with a blank, if slightly confused expression. One which soon changed to mild frustration.

"Yes, well, Neal. Like I said, the general wanted me to pass along that message. And I also wanted to give you this, as well." He handed Neal a slip of paper with an address, date, and time on it just under a week from today.

Neal looked a question at the rigid officer.

"It is the details of the memorial service for Dr. West. The president will be there, as well as the senior White House staff, General Pickler, Admiral Hamilton, and myself, amongst others. In light of your recent work together, I am sure she would have wanted you there, too."

"Thank you, Colonel. Thank you very much." Neal said looking at the paper, genuinely touched. Then looking back up, he continued, "I can't say whether she would have wanted me anywhere near there, but I'm certainly going to turn up anyway." he said with a rueful smile spreading across his lips.

"Yes," said the colonel, "something tells me it was just that attitude that made you so endearing to her." They both smiled sadly at each other, past conflicts momentarily forgotten, then the colonel nodded.

"Well, I am sure you are busy. Good-bye, Mr. Danielson. I'll see you in Washington, yes?"

Neal nodded, momentarily bewildered by it all. And with that, the colonel replaced his hat, gave a small salute, something he had never done to Neal before, and walked away.

Chapter 22: HMS *Dauntless*

The powerful, matte grey ship beat hard into the Channel swell as it invaded the deep harbor's entrance, brushing it aside as though a pest to be silenced. Standing in formation on her decks, any member of the crew of the HMS *Dauntless* not actively involved in crewing the ship 'lined the yards.' Back in the day, this would have meant three hundred men or more climbing her rigging and lining up along the sail yards and booms pitching high above the deck, an impressive sight designed as a show of skill and strength whenever a powerful sailing craft left or entered port.

The passing of the age of sail had left crews more deck bound, but improvements in their standards of both dress and discipline meant that the *Dauntless'* sailing from Portsmouth was no less stunning than in days of old.

Lieutenant 2nd Class Hunt was not part of the dress crew standing in formation along the decks but was, instead, more actively involved in the ship's current progress. Deep in the core of the ship, the vast diesel engines needed to power the frigate roared around him. His hair and face were thick with grease and dirt, its black coarseness ground into every wrinkle on his forehead and cheeks.

Standing on the bridge, the captain of the *Dauntless* was one of a few senior officers of Indian descent in the Royal Navy, and had worked hard against well-ensconced preconceptions of what a naval officer should look like. His relatively diminutive frame had forced its way bodily up the ranks, powered by a keen intellect and fearsome ambition. He had managed to do so against a tide of lighthearted racial slurs and offhand remarks, and against far more insidious prejudices, hidden, perhaps, but far from dead.

The prestige of the Royal Navy in an island nation still drove a certain kind of snob into its officer ranks. So when Captain Prashant Bhade met new officers like John Hunt, he instinctively balked at how clearly he fit the profile of what a naval officer 'should' look like that had so plagued a younger, more junior Prashant.

John Hunt had known about, and had been prepared for the captain's disdain for his carefully cultivated officer look. Courtesy of the AI listening from above, John had heard the details of the captain's call to his superior at Britannia Royal Navy Officer School, and the ensuing discussion of the then trainee's list of prolific skills.

Based on his reading of the captain's closed personnel file, John was far from surprised when he was initially assigned to one of the few parts of the ship that he had not demonstrated excellence at. Standing in front of the captain the day he had presented himself for duty, John had seen the glint in his eye when he said, "I see you are moderately proficient in a lot of the … easier parts of the duty roster. No doubt you will end up on the bridge in due course, but before that I think it would do you some good to take a more proactive role in the ship's operation."

Captain Bhade had smiled as he handed the fresh-faced new lieutenant over to his head of engineering, and watched him be led below to the engine room. That should wipe the smirk off his clean-cut face.

In truth, John Hunt never smirked. He never squinted or wept or wheezed or coughed or sweated even a drop unless it suited his purposes to do so. He had taken the assignment without complaint, and set to downloading the necessary data he would need for this job from the AI's data banks.

In truth, the role had been advantageous in many ways. The first of which being that it gave him ample opportunity to smuggle his relay on board the advanced destroyer before they left port. In the three days they had left to provision the ship for sea, John had been the first to volunteer for every task under the sun, including the arduous loading and fitting of several new and reconditioned parts for the engines.

Taking the usually unwanted role of supervising these jobs, John had been able to simply add his relay, coated in a wooden crate, to a pallet of equipment being lifted from the dock and then lowered down into the waiting mouth of one of the ship's holds.

Finding a place on board to hide it had been another matter, and if there were to be an emergency, the occupants of lifeboat eleven in starboard locker five would no doubt wonder what the black object in their life jacket locker was in the milliseconds before John, or one of the hub satellites above, was forced to deal with them. But, that highly unlikely event aside, it would hopefully remain hidden there for as long as it needed to be.

- - -

"So, how is he doing?" asked Captain Bhade of his chief engineering officer, as they motored steadily southwest, two days out from port.

The Welshman shook his head, "Well, sir, I cannot deny the lad has a head on his shoulders. You'd warned me of that, sir, and truer words were never said. But he is a worker as well, that one. First one in, last one out, that's him. I've had to remind him of the engine room time limits more than once."

Captain Bhade raised an eyebrow. The time limits in the engine room were due to the often dangerous combination of fumes and heat that had to be endured in there. All sailors had to take a turn on deck once an hour. In the first powered warships, it had been every twenty minutes, but then the fires of the old coal engines that they had used back then had made the engine room a giant oven. Longer than twenty minutes and the sailors started, quite literally, to cook.

Now the more efficient and cleaner diesel engines were safer, more efficient, more reliable, vastly more powerful, but the engine room remained a hellhole of fantastic noise, smell, heat and physical vibration. Your whole body shook for ten minutes after leaving it, your ears buzzing as the grease and carbon monoxide ebbed from your pores.

"A worker indeed? Well, we'll give him a few more months of working down there and see how he likes it then. Thank you, Shadley." The engineering officer, dismissed with a wave of the captain's hand, left the room.

The hardy Welsh career navy man had called various ships' engine rooms home for twenty-two years now, he thought, as he made his way back below the waterline, and was still pleasantly surprised by young Hunt. One thing about Lieutenant Hunt, he never copped the high and mighty with Engineering Officer Shadley, even though, as a warrant officer, he was technically junior to the young lieutenant.

No, John never patronized Bill Shadley, and that made him all right in Bill's book. Though the engineer would never dream of saying it, that smug prick of a captain could learn a thing or two from young Mr. Hunt.

- - -

A week later, John Hunt sat in his cabin amongst the four empty bunks of his fellow junior officers. He had just come off duty. His eyes were blank, and he was perfectly still, he had locked the door.

Inside his machine mind, the personality copy that was, to him, the closest thing he had to a soul, sat in its esoteric construct. It was, virtually at least, separate from the machine mind and body that allowed it to function. It controlled them in much the same way the conscious part of a human brain controls a human body, via a thick run of optic cable not dissimilar to a spinal cord.

The comparison could be further strung out by comparing the machine mind that underplayed his personality overlay to a human subconscious, though his link to his machine subconscious was far clearer, and his control over it much more absolute.

Also different from our subconscious, his machine mind could perform a myriad of tasks at astonishing speed. It could move his arms and legs with perfect coordination through the most complex of maneuvers while simultaneously using the host of tools and weaponry that was built into the Agents' bodies.

It could react faster and bring more brute strength to bear than any human could possibly imagine. It was, in fact, much faster and more capable than the personality overlay that controlled it. But it did not have opinions, or creativity, or allegiances, and so the machine had been made the willing slave of the personality that was programmed into it.

The machine mind also maintained constant contact with the hub satellites overhead, receiving information from them no matter where the Agent was, and transmitting regularly in return whenever it was within range of the relay, or in case of emergency, by one of several blunter means available to it.

But that was the machine part of each Agent: the control center that managed the shell they each now called home. On this day, though, four days out from Portsmouth, inside a perceived cocoon somewhere in the Agent's head, the personality that called itself John Hunt did something it had never done before. Reaching out to a part of its slaved machine mind, it activated a memory. The memory was of the previous night when, like all his fellow sailors did on their off shift, John Hunt had lain down to sleep for six hours. Though sleep was a vestigial concept for a machine-housed personality, it was necessary to maintain the illusion of humanity, so each night each of the Agents, if they were around humans, stopped moving and lay still for six hours, awaking with their colleagues, or before them, as appropriate.

Recalling that memory of the previous night's 'sleep,' John's mind carefully overlaid the memory of that sleep over the current moment, at the same time disabling the system's recording of his movements by his own slave machine mind.

The sub-computer never questioned the action, programmed, as was mandated, without the capacity to question or override its governing personality; instead it dutifully started reporting to the ever-interested AI that John Hunt was 'sleeping.'

Free now to move without monitoring, John Hunt stood, unlocked the door to the cabin and left, his machine mind still reporting that he was sleeping quietly in his cabin.

- - -

"Hi, Mark, how you doing? As you were." John Hunt said to the petty officer at the door of the engine room.

John's proactive role in the engineering department saw him coming and going from the hot room many times a day, so the petty officer hadn't even really made to stand up as his superior approached.

"Hey, Lieutenant." said the semi-awake Liverpudlian who, like his colleagues, loved that John was one of those officers who didn't stand on ceremony.

John walked through the bulkhead into the twenty-foot deep engine room and slid down the ladder from the gantry to the main floor below. Landing with a clang on the metal engine room floor, he walked toward the two vast, green painted diesel engines, nodding to the two or three men dotted around them.

Walking down between the engines, and out of sight of the others, he extracted a small black disc the size of a quarter from his pocket. At the far end of the engine room, the roaring engines focused into two great driveshafts that drove through and out the back of the lowest point of the hull, driving the two thirty-foot propellers churning under the back of the ship.

John glanced briefly over his shoulder and seeing no one looking, placed the disc on the rim of the giant bearing that sealed the hull around the spinning driveshaft. A red glow appeared on the surface of the disk, resolving into a set of numbers. Running his finger gently around the outside of the disk, John set the numbers to the precise time he desired and then turned and walked away.

As he walked away, the disc's surface went blank once more, its surface began to morph into the color of its surroundings, changing to match the deep, glossy, frequently repainted green of the ship's two engines.

- - -

The next morning, John lay in his bunk until the moment that his machine mind had reached the end of the recording he had placed into it. As it started relaying real-time once more, he stood up and left his room, his two 'friends' snoring in other bunks, heading to the engine room for his scheduled shift.

As he approached the door to the engine room, Able Seaman Julian (Mark had long since gone to bed himself) stood and saluted him.

"Morning, Julian. As you were." John said smiling. Some of the sailors were more willing to relax than others. Nothing that John could say or do would make young Julian stop standing to attention when John walked into the room.

"Morning, sir." said the petty officer, saluting.

Inside the engine room, the small disk, sensing the arrival of the precise moment it was set for, erupted, burning itself into oblivion in the blink of an eye, and creating a spark that would have blinded anyone that had been looking at it. It burned with the intense heat of phosphor, enough to flash-melt a small patch of the military grade steel it had been stuck to.

More importantly, it also burned so hot that, even though the flash only lasted a moment, it ignited the grease on the port engine's driveshaft, starting a grease fire, one of the most dangerous things a ship can face.

The flames surged, immediately searingly hot. At the door, Julian started shouting into the engine room for the men inside to get out. But the explosion had been so fierce that it had knocked out the sensors on the ceiling, so the sprinkler system had not activated as it was supposed to.

Julian's orders were clear: seal the room. The lack of oxygen would extinguish the fire, but it would also seal the fate of anyone left inside. However, clear orders and endless drills were one thing, to actually press the large red button by the door with three friends still inside was easier said than done.

Seeing Julian's hesitation, John stepped forward, slamming his fist into the clear plastic that covered the alarm button. To the astonishment of Petty Officer Julian Billman, the lieutenant then pushed the frantic sailor away from the sealing bulkhead, and stepped through it into the burning engine room as the bulkhead sealed behind him.

As the steel door's pressure seals hissed, the bewildered junior enlisted man was left standing on the outside, wondering why the lieutenant had just committed suicide.

Inside the room John had already leapfrogged over the gantry railing, landing on the floor twenty feet below.

The three men that had been inside the engine room were using small and ineffectual fire extinguishers to try to fight back. There was a manual sprinkler control that would quickly extinguish the fire, and maybe even save their lives, but it was down the side of the very engine shaft that was ablaze.

The fire was quickly consuming the oxygen in the now sealed room, and would, in theory, burn itself out in a minute or two. But by then the men inside would, by definition, have suffocated as well.

As they started to flag, oxygen deprivation slowing their brains, they watched as the lieutenant lined himself up with the side of the engine down which the manual controls were located, and then, at a surprisingly fast sprint, ran and jumped directly into the flames.

- - -

"REPORT!" shouted Captain Bhade running toward the now distraught engine room guard.

Julian stood to attention, "Yes, sir, err, there was an explosion … sir, in the engine room. Lieutenant Hunt, sir, he, err…"

"What, sailor? What did he do?" exclaimed the captain.

"No, sir, no. He didn't do anything, sir, he wasn't even in the engine room when it happened, sir."

"Then what about him, sailor?"

"He, errr, he jumped in to the room after it happened, sir." said Julian, still unable to believe the man had done it. "He activated the door seals then jumped in as the door closed, sir. That was a couple of minutes ago, sir. I'm afraid the door seals haven't deactivated yet, and the intercom is silent."

The captain stared at him, trying to understand why someone would jump into an engine room on fire as the doors sealed. It was insane. Were any of them still alive? Was his hull intact?

He needed to get into that room.

He needed to get in there now.

Where was the fucking chief engineer?

- - -

"Is he awake, Doctor?" asked the engineering officer at the door to the ship's infirmary.

After Bill Shadley had arrived on-scene, he had checked from the outside that the sprinkler system had activated, then manually released the door seals, ready to seal them again if the fire was somehow still burning.

The dry suck of air as the room had equalized had been only momentary. Inside they had found three unconscious sailors clasping fire extinguishers, both they and the entire room covered with retardant foam from the sprinkler system above.

The lieutenant was not among them, and it was only when they looked down the blackened side of the port engine that they had found his also unconscious body lying next to the open sprinkler control panel.

The unconscious sailors had awoken quickly with smelling salts, each of them immediately asking after the young officer. The captain and engineer had listened in astonishment as they had heard about the explosion, the ensuing grease fire and the sprinkler's failure to activate, and the lieutenant's response. And then they had both stared in mute respect at the still slack Lieutenant Hunt as he was carried from the room, the sailors recounting again the way he had leapt into the fire to activate the fire retardant system manually.

- - -

Now, two hours later, the chief engineer was back visiting the boy in the ship's infirmary. The captain and he had stopped by earlier but John had remained unconscious. It was a calculated choice, compounding the sympathy and respect he had planned to glean from the entire façade.

"Yes, sir, astonishingly he seems to be fine." said the doctor. "I don't know how many young officers actually wear that god-awful retardant engine room uniform, but it appears to have worked far better than I would have thought possible. Hardly a scratch on him. He's a lucky boy."

"Luck be damned," said the engineer sternly, stepping past the doctor, "the other survivors are *lucky*, this boy's a bloody hero."

Stepping up to the lieutenant's infirmary cot, he said to the bleary-eyed young officer, "Well, then, I hear you'll be back and bothering me in engineering in no time."

John Hunt smiled at the older petty officer, "Looks that way, sir, sorry about that. How is the port driveshaft, it hasn't warped, has it?"

Bill Shadley shook his head. The young officer's hair was clearly singed, his eyebrows all but gone, and here the little bastard was thinking about the job even now. But the lad's instincts were bang on, the engineering officer had just returned from a meeting with the captain and XO. The driveshaft itself was not warped, hardened as it was to withstand attack by torpedoes and worse, but it would need to be rerun, and the sheathing rings would require a complete overhaul.

"Well, you'll be happy to know you are going to be doubly popular with the ship. Not only did you save three sailors' lives, but because of the need for a dry dock to repair the damage, we're going to be spending two weeks in sunny Virginia."

The apparently recuperating lieutenant nodded somberly. The explosion had happened as they made their way through the Anguilla Straight en route to the Panama Canal, and the nearest allied dry dock capable of taking them, as the Agent well knew, was the US Navy Yards in Norfolk, Virginia.

Chapter 23: The Setting Sun

It had been a difficult two weeks for Neal since India. He had been fighting a rising tide of guilt over the loss of his two friends. He knew his mourning had been cut short by the sheer scale of the challenge he and Madeline now faced. He felt certain that if Laurie and James were here they would tell him to move on and focus on the greater issue at hand; but such speculation was, it turned out, not very much consolation at all.

No doubt at some point in the future he would let the whole event wash over him, allow himself to wallow, to grieve, to crawl into a corner somewhere and sob like a part of him keened to. But he had to fear that instinct, had to set it aside, and categorize it as the base, cowardly urge to flee he was afraid it truly was. No, before he could process the death of his two friends, he had to force himself to face the crisis at hand. He had to find out how deep the situation ran. There were so many questions to be answered; he knew he would have to leave grieving, or running away, for another time.

With that rationalization giving him a form of license to harden himself against the events in Kodikkarai, he had started to form a plan. Working with Madeline both before and after James' funeral in Florida, they were now finally gearing up for his next step.

So, after James' funeral, he had returned to Washington. The job offer was, of course, a godsend, and Madeline had joined the chorus of voices telling him he should go after it. They were going to need access to the halls of power, they were going to need all the information they could get their hands on, and then they were going to need the influence to do something about that information. Having the much increased classified clearance that would come with securing the posting to DC would be invaluable as they tried to subtly move against their unknown foe.

Amongst all of this, the mystery of who had sent him the two letters was, without doubt, the most confounding piece of the puzzle they faced. Whoever they were, they clearly had somehow stumbled on some aspect of this as well, and Neal wondered if it had cost them as dearly. Either way, Madeline and he were beside themselves with curiosity over who it was, where they were from, and what else they knew.

For now, though, they had little to go on there. The only consolation was that their mysterious ally had said they would announce themselves at some point in the future, so he and Madeline would just have to add this mystery to the list of things tugging at their already heavily depleted supplies of patience.

What they had been given, though, was both invaluable and deeply troubling advice. Clearly there was something in space, clearly they were being watched, and clearly their communications were being monitored. To say that this limited his and Madeline's options was a gross understatement. To say it had saved them from making the same missteps that had cost Laurie and James their lives was best left for when, if ever, they had luxury for such speculation.

So, with little else he could really do at this time, Neal had come to Washington focused on the mission of trying his hardest to get the job. In truth, it was not hard to foster enthusiasm for it, such was the scale of the opportunity his last few months' work had inadvertently positioned him for. In a flurry of activity, Neal had revived work on his long dormant thesis, with an ardency he had not applied to his studies in a long, long time. Madeline was a resourceful aide in this, bringing to bear her considerable intellect, and, wherever possible, her resources at the Institute.

Also with Madeline's guidance, Neal had spruced up his appearance. A briskly tailored suit from a low-price vendor in Florida made up for cut-rate materials and far from high-end workmanship with tight lines copied from more talented designers, and a crispness that can only come from being, literally, hot off the press.

It was this newer, shinier version of Neal that had spent the last hour at Laurie's memorial service. He stood alone, Madeline being unable to face another mass so soon after James', but at the wake afterward, Admiral Hamilton had taken the opportunity to introduce Neal to the president, his chief of staff, and several other notable persons. The import of being shown around by the powerful admiral was not lost on Neal, and he had shone with unusual charm and professionalism. Unusual for him, anyway, his efforts not lost on the admiral.

As the crowd started to disperse, General Pickler and Colonel Milton approached him.

"Neal, good to see you again, though I wish it weren't under such circumstances." said the general.

"Indeed, General, how are you?" Neal said, shaking first the general's hand, then the colonel's. Colonel Milton's grasp was firm, and their eyes locked a moment. Neal found the man reassuring, knowing that they shared a mutual respect, though unclear if he deserved it from this auspicious man.

He did not share an equal measure of respect for the general, finding him somewhat bluff. But something about the colonel told Neal he was a man to be trusted, a friend, even, though not one to be gained easily. Yes, Barrett was high on the list of candidates he and Madeline had put together for bringing into their confidence.

"Listen, Danielson," said the general, "this isn't the place to talk shop, but I wanted to make sure you were getting prepped for the upcoming White House staff interviews. I saw the admiral showing you around, which is good, but you should know I have my name on your list of references. I don't want you to make me look bad."

"I will try my best not to show you up, General." said Neal, surprising himself at how well he hid the facetiousness in his voice. The colonel's eyes, though, betrayed the slightest smile. Apparently Neal still needed some work on his diplomacy.

"That said, the colonel here is quite the scientist as well, aren't you?" continued the general, obliviously, "Unfortunately, we can't nominate military men to the advisory positions. So the next best thing will be having him help you prep. I expect you'll have availability while you're here, right, Colonel?"

It was the colonel's turn to mask his reaction, but his politicking was far more practiced than Neal's. With perfect composure, he nodded firmly and said, "Of course, sir, plenty of time."

"Good, good," smiled the general, pleased with himself. "You can make an evening of it. Well, I'll leave you two to discuss … all that, shall I?"

With that, General Pickler was shaking Neal's hand again. Then he responded to the colonel's precise salute with a tap of his hand against his forehead, and walked off.

The two men stood looking after him. Neal smiled, shaking his head as he said, "I imagine you can't say this, so I'll say it for the both of us. What a prick."

The colonel looked down, biting his lower lip to stop smiling. "No, I probably wouldn't have put it quite that way, no."

"Listen, Colonel, if you had plans this evening, don't feel the need to hang out with me, I've got plenty of prep work I can get on with."

The colonel looked at him, trying to assess if the man was just being nice. Then he smiled to himself. No, one thing you could rely on from Neal, he would never say anything just to be nice.

But orders were not negotiable, and he also thought that in the end he could probably come up with a few useful pointers for the rough-hewn physicist. The colonel smiled, without humor. Seeing this, Neal nodded, smiled, and then looked away, acknowledging the futility of trying to get the colonel to ignore the general's 'request.'

Dinner it was.

- - -

At that moment, across the city, Madeline sat in a hotel room across town that she had gone halves on with Neal. Madeline was sitting on one of the two queen beds going through her notes.

They had both decided they would not use PCs for anything to do with their investigation. After all, word files could be easily hacked if the PC was ever linked to the net, even if the files were never actually e-mailed to anyone.

So she had revived to her note-taking techniques from university, making copious, denoted, bulleted, color-coded pages of scribble. She was now trying to categorize them into a file binder she had pilfered from the Institute.

A knock at the door told her that Neal had probably forgotten his room key again, so she stood, straightening her T-shirt, then stopped as it opened from the outside.

It was not Neal. She looked at the stranger, confused, and then her sharp, blue eyes started to widen in fear and panic as she focused on the deep, black eyes staring back at her.

- - -

It had been a fun evening. Surprisingly so. Neal and the colonel had decided to go and grab some dinner together, and the officer had taken Neal to one of his favorite seafood restaurants from one of his three stints at the Pentagon.

They had spent most of the night talking about the job opportunity, but the conversation had frequently veered to stories from the past, with some especially entertaining gossip about the various people working at the array, as seen from both sides of the proverbial fence.

They had both enjoyed the evening more than they would have expected, and Neal had been surprised when, after the third beer came, Colonel Milton had asked Neal to call him Barrett. He had then laughed when the request was followed immediately by another that he only use his first name in private. Which left Neal with the correct impression that, while the colonel was warming to him, he was still very far from trusting Neal to make such judgment calls on his own.

A superfluity of beer and laughter aside, they had nonetheless wrapped things up fairly early, the colonel needing to get to bed for an early meeting, and Neal wanting to get back to Madeline, who had not answered an earlier call inviting her to join them.

The colonel dropped Neal at his hotel in his rental car around 10:30. Leaving Neal rifling through his pockets for a room key, which was, predictably, on the bedside table in his room.

Arriving at the door he knocked twice and waited. There was a moment's pause then a muffled scrambling on the other side. Neal's left eyebrow went up in curiosity about the fuss, then the room door opened suddenly and he was greeted by a very frantic, bleary-eyed Madeline, grabbing him and dragging him bodily into the room.

"Whoa," he said, laughing somewhat nervously, "what the hell is going on?"

She pushed him down onto the bed and then stepped back, glancing quickly at the bathroom before saying, "Neal, something has happened."

He was suddenly concerned, he went to stand up but her look and outstretched hands indicated he should stay seated, almost saying, ''wait, give me a second, this will all make sense in a second.'

"We've had a visitor." she said, and he stared at her. "Neal, I know who wrote the letters." His stare turned into a glare and he was about to speak but before he could say anything the bathroom door opened …

… and out stepped Agent John Hunt of the British Royal Navy.

Chapter 24: Origami's Antithesis

Standing in front of Neal, John offered his hand. Instinctively Neal recoiled from the man, his deep black eyes ringing alarm bells in his mind.

John paused, his hand still outstretched, and looked Neal in the eye. "Neal, I know this is going to be hard for you to understand. It certainly took some time for Madeline to come to terms with what I have come here to say.

"I had hoped to explain this to you both at the same time, but unfortunately I have to leave soon. I can only hope that you can trust me when I say that I am your friend. In fact, I am more than that. I am, without doubt, your only hope."

Neal stared at him, then at Madeline, who was holding out two sheets of paper. One of them Neal instantly recognized as the first of the mysterious letters he had found waiting for him when he had returned home to Arizona. The second was on the hotel's stationary, but as he looked at it, he saw the same handwriting, in fact the same exact words, as the other one: a perfect replica.

She said to Neal, her eyes imploring him to believe her, "Neal, I didn't show him these, after he came into the room he started to write this, as a way of showing me that I could trust him." Neal took the sheet, the writing was identical, disturbingly so.

"I must say again, I don't have much time." continued John as Neal examined the sheets, "I hope by now that you have figured out that you are being watched. Well so am I. I am one of them, Neal, I arrived in one of the capsules you discovered. Mine landed near the Outer Hebrides, and since then I made my way to the south of England and joined the Royal Navy using a false identity created since my arrival by the machines that accompanied me. In the last three months I have graduated officer training school and been assigned as a junior lieutenant on the new Type 47 Destroyer, the HMS *Dauntless*.

"As we were sailing toward the Panama Canal to join the Pacific fleet for exercises I engineered an accident on board, knowing that the captain would be forced to put in at the nearest allied naval shipyard. After we had done just that, I used further misdirection to make my way here to see you.

"The AI above me tracks my every move and communicates it to the others, just as their movements are communicated to me. So I had to fool my monitoring system into believing that I was still on board, pretending to sleep between my shifts. The monitoring satellites believe that the person that left the ship and drove here was one of my roommates, a belief I have compounded by mildly drugging him and leaving him in my bunk, and by using his credit card and ID to get here."

Neal stared flabbergasted, fighting multiple instincts battling in his head, not the least of which incredulity. On the surface he barely managed a nod, deciding that whether he believed this man or not, he still had to listen and keep track of what he was saying in order to decide what to do next.

John took Neal's nod as an indication that Neal was following him, even if he didn't trust him yet, and went on, "So I have until my roommate is scheduled to go back on shift before I have to be back to wake him up. Otherwise the duty officer will go looking for him, find him in his room, instead of ashore, log this, and instantaneously the AI will know something is wrong. That gives me four hours, fifty-two minutes until I have to be back on board, and it takes around three hours, twenty minutes to get back. So all that to say we don't have much time, so I will now ask whether you believe me or need more drastic proof of my credentials."

Neal had never been averse to more proof on the best of days, and he had never had to deal with anything so extreme as this before. So, his fear momentarily forgotten, and his mind engaged, he stood, rising to face the black-eyed stranger. John was several inches taller than Neal, his square jaw and boyish good looks serving as an incongruous frame for his piercing eyes.

"Will it take long to prove this further?" asked Neal.

"That depends," said John, and Neal quirked his eyebrow in a question, to which John replied, "on how open-minded you truly are."

"We managed to figure out that some kind of alien vessel had landed here before you ever showed up, so I think I can handle it." said Neal defiantly.

John nodded, "Very well." He looked directly at the scientist, holding his stare without the slightest hint of a blink. Neal waited for John to say something, then noticed something change in the expression of the stranger.

As Neal watched, the tall officer's left eye seemed to rotate slightly in its socket, then, to Neal's shock and not insignificant dismay, its pupil rolled down, the white of the eye following it like a falling screen. From behind it a black lens slowly emerged, as black as the fake pupil that had covered it until a moment before. Perhaps even more alarming than the emerging lens was the network of microscopic pins and discs that were unfolding around it. As the lens slid out about half an inch from its socket, a series of smaller supporting structures took their place alongside, the whole thing looking like a microscope surrounded by a hundred needles pointing out from the man's eye.

Neal faltered, wanting to run from the vicious looking aberration, but unable to take his eyes from this fascinating device. His broken, meek voice stuttered into the silence, "I, wha … I … err. Are those … are those … communications or …"

"Weapons." finished the Agent, "The central lens is just as it seems, the method by which I see, both in the standard visual range, and in what you would call infrared, ultraviolet, and several other bands that I will explain more some other time. Normally it is recessed behind the cover that duplicates the look of your human eyes, pressed against its 'pupil.'

"The needles around it are what we call a Tactical Contact Weapons Complement. Though small and relatively impotent compared to our more conventional weapons systems, I think you would be surprised at its punch."

With that, John stepped to the right, focused on the bedclothes, and a hazy beam materialized between his eye and the ruffled sheets. Neal and Madeline both stepped back as a spot instantly blackened and sparked into flame where it touched. John, on the other hand, was already moving toward it. The buzzing in the air stopped as John discontinued the beam's attack, grabbed the blanket and smothered the small but bright flame that had sparked to life in the bed's center.

The cleaning lady would later find a hole neatly punched through the sheet and the top of the mattress. She would report that the occupants had been smoking and partying in the room, a story which would fit with the other damage she would find …

"I can also affect electronic equipment, jam radar and radio signals, and create what we call a sonic punch." With that, he appeared to brace himself and turned toward the brown nondescript armchair in the corner.

A dull thud resounded in the room, feeling like someone had driven a truck into the base of the building, and a conical pyramid of air in front of the Agent's eye seemed to waver. The armchair leapt backwards, crashing into the wall, then falling to the floor. A series of dents were left in the plaster where its corners had imbedded themselves.

"That was on about 25% of available power. I can also vary the focus of the wave from constant to an expansion ratio of about 100 to 1, meaning I can knock over a small crowd of people from about eight feet, or put a hole in someone's torso from across the room. The laser I can increase to nearly treble the power of what I just used, but at this range that would have spontaneously ignited the entire mattress.

"There are other features of the weapons system, but those are the most dramatic, and, I hope, adequately demonstrative." And with that, the Tactical Contact Weapons Array folded back into his eye socket, and the façade of an eyeball rose to cover it again.

"Neal, Madeline," he said, looking from one to the other, "I need to know you believe me now, we haven't much more time and we have much to discuss. Hopefully from my demonstration you have extrapolated at least a couple of things …"

Neal raised a hand and John paused. Neal was, understandably, stunned by what he had seen, but as fast as things were moving, he mind was racing, starting to stretch to meet them, and he knew it was his turn to show what he could do.

"Allow me," Neal said, looking earnestly at John, his hand still raised, "Firstly, it is clear that if you meant us harm we would not be alive now. We have no way of defending ourselves against what I have just seen."

John nodded, happy Neal was taking the opportunity to prove he could handle the responsibility John was here to put on his shoulders.

"Second, I am quite certain we cannot produce anything capable of what you can clearly do, so that makes me as close to certain as I can bring myself to be that you are … not … from … here."

John nodded at Neal, who let that sink in, glancing at Madeline, who'd had much longer with this, but was still now only just getting to the place Neal was arriving at now.

It was clear why the scientist had been one of the few to surmise the importance of the meteors, and why he and his friends had been the only ones to figure out how to go after them. It filled John with something approximating hope that he had found these two, or rather that they had been the ones who found him.

Neal seemed about to go on, but John decided to give him a break, "*Not from here*, that is certainly one way of putting it, and maybe that aspect of my story is as good a place to start as any."

John picked up three pads from the desk and handed one each to each of the members of his small but eager audience, keeping one for himself as he said, "You'll need these."

Madeline grabbed a couple of pens from the desk and took a seat next to Neal as John began.

Chapter 25: History of Travel

In the annals of the past, at about the time that the first caveman was accidentally striking a flame to life with what was to be the first flint firestarter, the still evolving people of another planet were also expanding across the continents of their globe.

They were, in many ways, very similar to us. They had evolved on four legs, their front feet eventually adapting to allow them to pick up, and finally manipulate the objects that surrounded them. They were also, like us, hunter-gatherers, the same natural selection bringing their two eyes to the front of what we would call their heads so that they could have the depth perception necessary for pursuing prey.

Their opposable digits evolved slightly differently than ours, with two of their 'fingers' bending backward, and two forward. Their 'hands', therefore, evolved as having two fingers and two thumbs each, making them extremely dexterous, but without anything analogous to our palms. Their wrists simply ending in four flexible joints from which their thick interlocking fingers and thumbs protruded.

Their hind legs were bent backward, lending them to something closer to a rhythmic hop than our own run. Thus their hunting tactic had been more of an ambush than a pursuit, but their powerful legs could carry them over great distances with ease, making migration a natural step in the development of their species.

As time passed, the developing intelligence of this species began to discover the benefits of agriculture, as humanity also would many light-years away. This began with planting crops apparently at random along their path, but returning prior to harvest to reap the rewards.

Their primitive culture continued much like this for millennia, longer even than the Stone Age of the first cavemen. Because of their nomadic way of life, the concept of property came much later, and with far greater brutality than even our own prehistorically violent past. At inherently strategic places at the touching points of their great continents, certain tribes began to settle and fortify. As their still nomadic cousins passed by with the changes of the seasons, these first settlers became traders and primitive hoteliers. As the populations of these first cities and towns grew, the cost of maintaining their ever larger populations grew accordingly, and eventually the concept of tax and levy came to them. With taxation came feudalism, with feudalism came further fortification, and soon the towns became city states, bordered by great walls, imposing their costs upon the still migratory peoples of the great continents they bordered.

Partly as a consequence of these levies, the migratory paths of the remaining nomads started to be pushed into new sea-lanes, a revolution in naval technology and navigation driven by the necessity to survive.

Over time, the fortified city states became nations, expanding their borders into the wide open continents to either side of them, and claiming more and more of the lands of their nomadic cousins. As these burgeoning empires, and their great dynastic families, made the agriculture of the nomads a permanent feature of the land, the nomads were forced into ever more isolated patches along the coast, migrating between distant free lands on their ever improving ships.

Over the next few thousand years, the roles of the two slowly shifted. Whereas the nomads had previously made up the vast majority of the population, the empires now held a greater number. The nomads, relegated to the remaining freelands, slowly became traders, moving first the food, and then the goods of the great empires across the planet's oceans. As they did so, the small ports that had grown up in the freelands began to grow into a loosely allied network of great port cities that housed their meager but growing wealth and influence.

The great empires eventually covered all the land and began washing up against each other. Great wars raged along their highly contested borders, alliances and feuds bending them like the tides of history as great leaders came and went.

Meanwhile, the trading families of the world stood firm in an alliance of mutually assured destruction, uniting as necessary against any over-ambitious empire that tried to dominate one of their brethren. Their ships made up the life blood of the planet, pumping its goods between its nations, and the strict sanctions imposed on any nation that attacked one of their port cities constricted that flow until either control of the port was relinquished, or the interloping empire shriveled, leaving it ripe for destruction at its neighbor's hands.

And so centuries passed.

The warring empires kept a strict control over their populaces, limiting freedom but concentrating their resources into the development of ever-greater weaponry and defenses.

Meanwhile the freer, but much smaller, trading families enjoyed greater inventiveness and creativity, their ships' size and armament growing apace with the perennial potential for attack by jealous emperors.

This might have continued indefinitely if not for the two inventions that would change the planet's fortunes as drastically as they would shape our own when we, in time, also stumbled upon them.

The invention of the steam and combustion engine spurned a new age of productivity and warfare. While the great tanks of the empires raged across the lives of their unfortunate serfs, the trading families' ships underwent an order of magnitude change in size and speed, giving these merchant navies even greater mobility, and with it, independence.

A hundred years later the invention of the nuclear bomb froze every empire in its tracks. After the destruction of a quarter of one empire's population by another, even the victors were forced to concede that their victory was moot at best, the land they had craved having been rendered useless for a generation. But while nuclear power temporarily ended the wars on land in a tense stalemate, the creativity of the trading families saw another use for the great heat of the atom.

The first atomic vessel sailed from the port city of Seilajeh at the beginning of the decade that would change everything. In its holds were the reactors it was shipping to its allied city states. Working together, they had managed to harness the power of the atom to useful ends, and a new age was about to begin. Ten years later, they used the wealth flowing from the electricity they were selling to the great empires to build the first craft to escape the confines of their atmosphere. That first craft was manned by a host of volunteers who had begged to make the voyage, their nomadic instincts driving them all to lust after this first voyage of discovery in an age.

The next century saw the establishment of great lanes of travel and trade across the stratosphere. The trading families purchased from the stagnating empires a series of islands and peninsulas on which to build the planet's first spaceports, and slowly but surely the embryonic technologies of space travel took form.

Fearing the potential for a shift of power, the empires eventually began to rein in on the expansion of the traders and restart their own growth. They leveraged their tight control over the majority of the world's natural resources to buy themselves into space alongside the traders.

But the empires' goals in space were different from their still inherently nomadic partners. The nuclear bomb had put an end to their ability to grow, and their populations were filling their borders. They needed property. They needed space.

First to be colonized were the three small moons orbiting the planet. Then the great space stations started to form, haphazardly at first, until Junta was started, a great hub large enough to be seen from the planet's surface by the naked eye, even in daylight. When it was finished, it would cast a great shadow below, eclipsing the sun as it passed by overhead.

It housed nearly a billion people on its huge, spinning wheel, but it was clear even before Junta was complete that even great space stations would never be enough to house the ever growing population, nor to satiate the hungry palates of the great dynastic families still ruling below.

They needed another planet.

This, of course, was not a new idea, the first thing that the empires had paid the traders to do was send out probes past nearby systems seeking such a prize. But none were found within the range of practical flight.

As technologies for faster travel were explored, the option of subspace or hyperspace travel was exhaustively pursued. While the vast wealth that was ploughed into this avenue would produce no method of travelling faster than light, it would produce fruit of another kind, and so the subspace tweeter, with all its considerable benefits, was born. And it was after creating one of the minuscule wormholes necessary to make the subspace tweeter work that one team of Nomad scientists was able to stretch some of the properties of that subspace strata outward like a bubble in the hopes of creating a doorway into this realm of instantaneous travel.

But the experiment had some strange results. As the subspace sphere enveloped the very engine that was expanding it, its contents temporarily ceased to be governed by the rules that hold sway in our universe.

Scientists were baffled, at first, by the results of the experiment, as the apparatus had appeared to simply vanish. But, after the building they were experimenting in started shaking and then collapsed, the survivors had discovered the remnants of the apparently partially successful experiment merged into its very foundations.

As the sphere had formed, it had, indeed, removed the constraints of the universe on its contents, as had been hoped. It had not disappeared, but had become invisible and intangible, light and matter now passing through it like it was not there. Unfortunately, it was still subject to forces in subspace, and the gravitational well of a planet is so great it affects even the non-space below the skein of reality. And so, without the solidity of matter to stop it, the sphere and its contents had started to fall into the very gravity well it was being designed to escape, rematerializing a moment later, merging with the building's foundations, displacing and undermining them; quite literally bringing the house down.

The next time the premise was tested, the scientists were ready, and the world looked on in amazement as the sphere, dropped from a great height, passed clean through the planet to materialize in open space on the other side, not only unharmed by the passage, but sling-shotted outward by it.

It did not take long to realize the vast implications of this discovery. Seeking to harness the power of the stars, scientists tried to tap into the phenomenal gravitational pull of their sun. The next evolution of the new invention was accelerating toward the sun when they initiated the sphere, blinking back into existence a month later on the other side like a ball shot from a stellar cannon.

It was a steady evolution from there on. Changing the angle of entry into the sun changed the direction of exit, and speed could be progressively increased more and more by stringing together progressive 'jumps' through other stars, planets, and moons en route.

The only limit to the speed attainable was the power necessary to maintain the sphere's integrity during solar entry and exit, and the vast engines that were necessary to decelerate it afterward.

With this technology, new probes were built and fired off through the sun. They each followed carefully planned routes through a series of planets and suns, eventually reaching previously inconceivable hyper-light speeds through the cosmos.

These new hyper-probes would never decelerate. As they began to pass out of the range of the huge onboard subspace tweeters that made up the bulk of their mass, another would be launched along the same path, stringing their communications out across trillions of miles, across light years, the chains of probes extending outward like ethereal tentacles, probing the cosmos and returning what they discovered via subspace. With data relayed back along these ever extending antennae, if a promising planet was discovered, or gas giant with a massive moon that required closer inspection, then the next probe in the chain could tweak its course, still following its cousin, but taking a closer look at whatever might have peaked their interest. Each pass providing greater and greater information on the systems and even the planets they passed through.

After that it was only a question of time until they found what they were looking for. Twenty years later they discovered us, and for the first time in the history of the planet the great empires united, the hope of this prize focusing their resources on the construction of the great fleet they would need to first subdue us, and then colonize our world.

A plan was formulated to build a navy capable of conquering a planet. Ships to carry an army and a colonization force of almost a million would be built to travel within the largest accelospheres that had ever been conceived. They would follow a route through two planets, then into their own sun already travelling at 5% of the speed of light. By the time they emerged they would be travelling at nearly 25% of light speed, and they would vanish from their solar system in a matter of hours en route to the next star as they built up their speed ever further, using the existential properties of the accelosphere to move past the very limitations of relativity. Eventually they would ignite their great braking engines and spend the majority of their actual journey in heavy deceleration, their passengers' bodies immobilized against the colossal pressures.

As the fleet was being designed, tacticians and strategists struggled for the first time with the problem of invading a planet. They analyzed the unique advantages that they had, both from a technological perspective, and also those inherent advantages that came from being the aggressor. It was clear that defending a planet against attack would be a difficult proposition at best, impossible as it is to effectively defend something so large, where all its inhabitants live on its outside, only a feeble atmosphere between them and the void.

That said, the inhabitants of Earth had one notable advantage over their attackers. It was not much, but it was inherent to the fact that the earth, though vulnerable, was the very thing that the invaders craved. For the Mobiliei, as they were called, required not only to wipe the humans out, but to do so without destroying the very world they lived on.

The analogy was drawn to an empire trying to take possession of a fortress from a weaker force. Even if the invading army possessed the artillery necessary to kill everyone in the fortress with ease, it was of no use if they destroyed the fortress itself in the process.

This would not, necessarily, have been an issue had there not been clear signs of nuclear technology under development by the current inhabitants of Earth, its telltale signs clear to the passing probes that even now still studied the planet. The technology appeared embryonic, low yield, but that would change in the years it would take for the Armada to reach them. Not enough to close the technological gap between the two races, not even close, but enough, it was deduced, to threaten the planet should they unleash it in their defense when the Armada arrived.

Though far superior to their quarry in terms of technology, the Mobiliei had found no method yet for subduing or containing the unencumbered power of a nuclear explosion, and the likelihood that humanity would resort to a nuclear conflagration as they struggled to avoid their own annihilation was far too high to be ignored. No, the foe they faced would no doubt unleash any and all of their primitive weaponry in their defense when faced with the military might that approached them.

And even if the ships of the fleet could be shielded against the onslaught, when the humans eventually, desperately launched their nuclear arsenal at their attackers, they would, in the process, irradiate much of the precious planet they were defending.

There was much debate on this. But even the most forgiving models could not eliminate the possibility. After all, Earth would have plenty of warning that the Armada was coming, the great fires of the Mobiliei's engines as they decelerated toward their goal would announce their arrival years before they could bring their guns to bear, shining, as they would, like new stars in the sky.

So the Mobiliei's strategists concluded that brute force alone would not succeed. The option of using biochemical weapons was explored and a virus was developed that could be seeded into Earth's atmosphere before the majority of the Armada arrived.

It was clear that this would be the easiest method of attaining victory. But even such a brutally effective tool of extinction would have the downside of leaving every oil tanker, nuclear power station, jet airplane, and chemical plant on the earth's surface suddenly un-manned. Could this theoretically be timed just so with the arrival of the fleet to avoid an environmental disaster of epic proportions? Perhaps. Again, repeated scenario modeling came close, but would not say, with any certainty, that it could be avoided, and there would be no second chances here, they needed to be as close to 100% as possible.

And so the threat of that pollution and radioactivity soiling their prize brought them back to the original problem. Like a child's innocence, a planet's natural beauty was not something that could be reclaimed easily if destroyed. So again the strategists returned to the drawing board. There would be little or no room for adjustment once plans were set in motion, and so the plan itself must factor all eventualities.

A plan with more finesse was required.

Finally the generals and admirals of the Great Fleet decided that they must send a smaller, more discrete advanced force ahead of them, with the goal of infiltrating any and all military forces with a tenable nuclear capability. With the help of stealthed AI satellites that would accompany this small force, they would strive to clip humanity's nuclear claws, preparing them for quick defeat.

As the plan began to take shape, the emperors and empresses of Mobilius began to lick their lips over our precious world. But amongst all this fervor, not all the world's houses were as enthusiastic as they might seem. In closed meetings, amongst old allies and close friends, the leaders of some of the ancient nomadic trading families grew ever more disquieted by what their race had embarked upon. The images sent back by the probe made them long to visit our planet: not to own it, but to explore it. To meet us and, once dialogue had been established, to open up the greatest trading route of all time. And so, quietly, discreetly, a few of the smaller but very wealthy city states united in a covert effort to subvert the planned attack.

Leveraging their expertise and significant resources, they worked diligently to remain a key part of the Armada's construction, all the while seeding the staff and crews with a network of spies and allies. Their greatest coup was, without doubt, when they managed to focus all of their influence and political capital into placing one of their own minds amongst the prestigious eight selected to have their personalities implanted into the machine Agents of the advanced team.

This double agent would warn humanity about the coming attack, and try to thwart the plans of the other Agents sent ahead to stop Earth from fighting back. It might only delay the inevitable, but the Nomadi's history of persecution and oppression at the hands of Mobiliei fed the trader's desire to help the weaker, unsuspecting humans. They knew they could not be certain of the outcome, they knew that the odds were very much against them. But they also knew they could not sit idly by and bear the shame. They had to resist. They had to find some way to help us in the coming fight for our survival.

Chapter 26: Leaps and Bounds

As he finished describing the story of his race and the method of their coming attack, John Hunt suggested that they focus the little remaining time they had that night as efficiently as possible.

Madeline was clearly overwhelmed. Neal, though, was lapping it all up, clearly fascinated, his desire to let the questions flow from him only stemmed by John's ceaseless speech, never taking a breath, never needing one. The luxury of idle conversation was not available in the little time they had.

"And so, as far as my colleagues and I can see, there are three things that must be done in order for you to have a chance of survival." he said at one point.

"As we have already discussed, we must fundamentally improve the scale of Earth's defenses. Secondly, in order to give those defenses the ability to be effective against what is coming we must introduce several new technologies. I would say that was going to be hard enough, but before we can work on either of those things we must stop the other Agents from accomplishing their mission. Which will mean destroying them, and the satellites we have in orbit even now."

Neal nodded, and Madeline began to ask what new innovations they should be looking into, but John stopped her. "Before we get started on that, I must insist we focus on the task of dealing with the advanced team. I must tell you that my team is very capable of defending itself against attack. The task of defeating the other seven, and the AI satellites that we brought with us, is going to be harder than you know.

"And to make matters more complicated, I have to tell you that we came up with a backup plan in case, for some reason, we were discovered. If all else fails and we are defeated, the hub-satellites have the super-virus I told you about before on board to be used as a final resort."

The two stunned faces opposite him stared aghast at this turn. John went on, "If they perceive that there is a credible threat to the mission, they will release the virus into the atmosphere in a series of cluster bombs. They will not allow you to prepare for the coming fleet. They cannot risk it."

Madeline broke the ensuing silence, "Can we take out the satellites before they can release the virus?"

"Destroying them will require a massive amount of weaponry to get past their defenses, but even if we mount a successful attack without their knowing about it in advance, no amount of firepower could destroy all four satellites before one or all of them dropped their pathogen clusters into the atmosphere. You should know that one successful release would be enough to wipe out up to half of Earth's population."

They both stared, aghast, again. It was becoming a habit.

John labored on, once more, "No, before we can actually attack them, you must develop the antibody and a method of distributing it, and you must do so covertly. To that end, I am going to give you a detailed breakdown of the virus, but more importantly, I am to give you the design for a universal nano-antigen that can be used to combat the virus."

And with that, John handed the pad he had been holding to them. All the while he had been talking he had been doodling on the pad in front of him, or at least that was how it had seemed. In fact, he had assigned a subroutine within him control of his arm and given it a set of data to replicate onto the pad. It had then set to writing a phenomenally detailed dossier for Madeline and Neal while John talked to them, leaving it to its task.

Neal began to leaf through it all. It included a detailed description of the virus and the associated antigen, with schematics and chemical breakdowns. Subsequent pages listed, in exhaustive detail, the other seven Agents, their ranks, locations past and present, mission parameters and interim goals, and a phenomenal set of facial sketches for each, both front and in profile. Neal continued to flick through the pad, coming to design drawings for machines he did not even begin to understand and John reached out to rest his hand on the top of the dossier.

Neal stopped looking through the information and looked up at John, his face meek like a child after the TV has been shut off.

"You can spend time looking at that later," said John, "for now, we have more to discuss."

- - -

That had all been ten minutes ago.

There had been so much to decide, so much to talk about, that John had suggested that they stick to areas where immediate decisions needed to be made, decisions like who they should recruit into the team, and what they were going to need to do to move forward.

When, in the course of the remaining conversation, questions came up which John felt he could answer without debate, he had told them he would add it to his notes, and he took back the pad, his hand once more starting to write and draw at astonishing speed on page after page. Now that they knew what it was doing, it became ever harder to ignore the strange sight, or to escape how cool it was, Neal thought, stifling a boyish grin.

At last their time had come to an end and John had stood, handed them the sheaf of papers he had written, and bid them farewell, leaving to drive back to Norfolk and pretend to the AI that he had just woken from his faux sleep.

They spent the first half an hour after he left just reading through his notes. For now John focused on designs that would help in the fight against the other seven Agents. He had given them designs for jamming devices and body armor, as well as for hand-to-hand combat weapons whose lethality would make any general almost sexually excited.

He had also included the design for the nano-medical device. Madeline tried to wrap her head around it. If they could manufacture this, it would, quite literally, cure almost every communicable disease ever faced. The implications were staggering.

But eventually they had reluctantly set aside these pages, focusing instead on the part of John's lengthy notes, and those that Neal and Madeline had taken, that contained practical advice, the rules of engagement, as it were.

It was clear that for the foreseeable future, Neal and Madeline, and the small but burgeoning resistance they were going to be the seed of, would be at a considerable disadvantage. If any aspect of their enterprise were discovered before they were ready, the results would be quick and bloody. So they must move forward with care.

They were going to need allies. Trusted, skilled, resourceful allies. They were going to need money and facilities. And they were going to need to get all that in absolute digital silence.

Neal had had a glimpse of the way forward when he had first received the anonymous letters from John. Snail-mail, it seemed clear, was going to be the only safe way to communicate, and even then they would have to encrypt just in case.

It was time to start recruiting, and they both agreed who would make the best first ally.

Chapter 27: Hiring Decisions

"Now this is going to be difficult to handle," said Neal, in a different hotel room, in a different part of the city, the next morning. "I have to warn you that what we are about to tell you will force you to break every oath you have made to your superiors, and to become part of a conspiracy that will, in time, need to involve sharing information with other nations without our government's approval."

"Stop there," Colonel Barrett Milton said, "don't go any further. I don't want to know any more. I like you, Neal, and I am already going to have to report what you have said so far. Don't incriminate yourself any further."

Neal nodded, waited for the colonel to settle down a bit. Madeline stood behind him, biting her lower lip. Now that they were here talking to the colonel, she was far from sure they had made the right decision.

For that matter, neither was Neal, but he tried again. "Colonel," he said to the military man's raised hands and bowed, shaking head, "what if I were to tell you what actually happened in India?"

Barrett froze, his eyes rising to meet Neal's once more, then flashing to Madeline's. Her desperate blue eyes were imploring him to listen.

"Barrett, we found something out there." Neal went on, "and it reacted. It killed James and Laurie and the crew of the *King's Transom*, and now it is watching Madeline and me to see if it needs to do the same to us."

The colonel stared at him, incredulous. What had they found, a fucking sea monster? But the faces of his two visitors were deadly serious, and he could not help but feel the weight behind Neal's words.

"Colonel, the meteors, they were not meteors at all, nor were their landing sites accidental. Colonel, we are being prepared. An invasion is coming, and I can prove it to you, right here, right now."

- - -

An hour later, after showing Barrett the photographs which James had managed to stow away before the *King's Transom* was attacked, and several of John's notes, Neal and Madeline stood behind the austere man as he stared out the window of his hotel room, trying to grasp what he had heard.

He was not a stupid man, and he prided himself on being open-minded … compared to his military peers, at least. But this was incredible, literally. It was too much to handle. The more he started to believe the two scientists, the more he had to fight the overwhelming urge to run and report this. To sound the alarm bells and launch everything they had.

But if what he had just heard was true, then that, he knew, would be equal parts futile and fatal.

Just days beforehand, the general and he had discussed at length the incident in the Indian Ocean, and the comment that the victims looked as if they had been attacked by laser had come up twice. Both times the idea had been dismissed as preposterous, but in light of this new information … he was … oh god, what was he thinking.

God Damn It.

He whirled on the two of them and they stepped back involuntarily from the fire in his stare.

"Why? Why have you brought this to me? What am I supposed to do with this? These photos, these notes, god, notes! Do you know what half these things are?!" he shouted at them, "If what you say is true, we don't stand a chance. We cannot defeat this …" he waved the notes at them, then paused, and looked at them again.

"Wait," he said, in a quieter voice, "you never said where you got these from. How did we come across such information?"

Neal smiled, and then he sighed. "Oh, Colonel, that is why I love you so much." The colonel frowned at him, but he continued, "You are absolutely right to say we cannot defeat technology like this. And you are right to ask how Madeline and I got this information."

He walked up to the rugged man and looked him in the eye, his expression becoming serious again, "Barrett, we have some small hope. They are not all as they seem. It may not be much, but we have a friend amongst them. Colonel, one of them is a spy."

- - -

The last remnants of the colonel's resistance gone, they had, eventually, begun to reap the profits of recruiting this new member to their team.

Twenty years in Air Force Intelligence and Surveillance gave Barrett a detailed understanding of the armed forces and intelligence services of both the US, its allies, and many of its enemies.

As he started to wrap his head around the massive disadvantages they faced, his training started to formulate a plan. He explained that it would be like when they first looked to build up an intelligence capability in a foreign nation. It was a slow and laborious process, and it always began with a single, reliable asset. But there was a method here, and they would follow it as best they could.

They would need to carefully recruit allies with specific capabilities. They would need a process for that. They would need safeguards. They would need code words and covert methods of communication. Neal suggested mail, and the colonel concurred, but said there were other methods as well, methods that harkened back to the days of the Cold War, and even the heady days of Enigma and the resistance fighters in Europe. Classified ads in newspapers, and online, would be one way, heavily coded, of course. Trigger calls and e-mails to dummy accounts, disguised as cold calls and junk mail.

For direct action, they could clearly use the highly encrypted 'SurFeR' radios for short distances, but no doubt if they all started carrying those around the Agents would soon become suspicious.

"We are going to need a headquarters." he said at one point, "In fact, we are eventually going to need several around the world, but for now we will need a safe house in Washington. These written notes are all very well, but the kind of research we are going to need to do will need computers. We can isolate them from the net, in fact, that is something we have experts for all over the place."

He stopped, and into the silence Madeline asked, "Should we think about recruiting one of them to the team?"

"Yes," Barrett nodded, still deep in thought, "that is what I was thinking too. But who? I don't know any personally." He thought a moment more, "No, what we need is a counter-intelligence expert, and if, after we get her on board, she still thinks we need a super-geek, she should know who to ask."

Neal looked at him, smiling mischievously in spite of the mood, "She, Colonel? Do you have someone in mind?"

"Yes, actually," said the slightly blushing officer, "an old friend."

"You dog, you!" said Neal.

Madeline laughed, and the colonel looked exasperatedly at the scientist, the tension showing on his face. Surprisingly, Neal became suddenly serious again as well.

"Colonel, you were right earlier. You said that we were foolish coming to you today without a plan. That if you'd reacted differently we could all be dead now. I guess I just want to make sure you have a plan too. In case 'she' doesn't react as well to hearing about all this as you did."

The colonel nodded; Neal was right. Barrett had extolled them on the need to be absolutely ruthless when recruiting. They must be willing to kill anyone that did not agree to secrecy, if not to protect themselves, then to protect their mission, to protect their very species.

The colonel would have to think whether he was willing to risk his friend's life by inviting her into the circle. He would have to think very deeply, it was not a life he would gamble lightly.

Chapter 28: Enemy Within

"Good evening, Chris." said Mrs. Hamilton, smiling graciously as her son came through the door, pecking her lightly on her cheek.

"Good evening, Mother." he said in return, "May I introduce Lieutenant Lana Wilson, currently at Annapolis with me."

"A pleasure, Mrs. Hamilton, thank you so much for having me." said Lana, holding out her hand and smiling.

"Oh, the pleasure is all mine," said Laura Hamilton, shaking the hand, her eyes subtly but thoroughly taking in the cut of her son's new girlfriend. Good hand shake, confident, but not unpleasantly so, nice smile. Hmm.

"Let me take your jackets." said Laura, prompting her forgetful son.

"Err, no, Mom, I can do that. Lana, here, allow me." He somewhat awkwardly helped his lady friend with her jacket, revealing her long but striking black dress underneath. It was quite conservative, in its way, coming up all the way to her neck as it did, and flowing all the way to her ankles without ne'er an inch of skin showing between. But somehow it managed to also say, 'I have nothing on under here,' a factor that was not lost on Chris's mother as she started to realize why her son was so besotted with the girl.

Oh dear, she thought, he is clearly hopelessly outclassed here. I'll just have to make my own judgment of whether she is suitable and ... help him see things my way if I don't think she is worthwhile.

"Come, my dear, come," she said, beckoning to Lana, wafting her into the sitting room, "I'll introduce you to the admiral."

Lana smiled beatifically and followed Mrs. Hamilton into the house proper, Chris rushing with the jackets so that he could be there when his poor unsuspecting girlfriend met the formidable Admiral Hamilton.

Bless him his efforts to protect her, of all people.

"Tim, come and meet Chris's guest, Lana ..." said Laura, then turning back to Lana, she confirmed, "Lieutenant, isn't it?" Lana nodded, and Laura continued to her husband, "Lieutenant Lana Wilson."

Lana resisted the urge to salute; being an informal guest of Chris's in his parents' home, it was considered proper not to treat the admiral as a senior officer for the length of the dinner. But her studies of how to best ingratiate herself made her wait for the admiral to proffer his hand before making a move of her own.

He did, and she meekly leaned forward to grasp it, but then, locking eyes with him, she said, "Admiral, sir, I must confess it goes against my grain not to salute. But I hope you'll not mind me saying thank you to you and Mrs. Hamilton for inviting me. And I hope you'll not be offended if I say it is an honor to meet you."

The admiral smiled, his eyes briefly flashing to his wife, who was smiling ironically, her eyebrows raised. Oh dear, he also thought, Chris is indeed hopelessly outclassed here.

"Dad," said Chris, hurrying into the room, "oh, I see you already met Lana." He saw the end of their handshake, stepping up to her side, and continued, "Isn't she great?"

"A pleasure, Lieutenant," said the senior admiral, keeping his eyes on their guest, "you are right not to salute, you are our guest for the evening. But thank you for asking, nonetheless. Chris, why don't you get us some drinks?"

"Yes, quite, Macallan 18 for you, eh, Dad, Raspberry Stoli on the rocks for you, Mom," his mother frowned at him for making the albeit correct choice in front of their guest, but he blundered on, "and what about you, darling?"

Everyone but him caught the word immediately, the parents raising their eyebrows once more at each other. Lana assessed the comment quickly, and decided on her response in a microsecond. Sending instructions to her cheeks to flush red, she bowed her head coyly and avoided the eyes of her hosts as she said, "Err, a glass of wine, if that's possible, please."

Her hosts could not help but feel for the blushing girl, and the admiral suddenly went into action, stepping past his son towards the cellar door.

"Of course, Lana," he said, offhandedly, "I have a nice Sauvignon Blanc chilling, will that do?" He did not harass her with his eyes as he asked this, but diplomatically avoided looking at her blushing face.

"Perfect, Admiral, thank you."

Good, thought Mrs. Hamilton, at least one of my men can act civilly, some of the time anyway. Now, let's get this girl comfortable and take her mind off my son's brutishness.

- - -

The dinner was a success, Lana was charming and intelligent, and she seemed to like young Chris. His blundering compliments for her remarkable performance at the officer school served two purposes. They could not help but impress the admiral, who remembered his own time there, and they forced both the host and hostess to be especially engaging to make up for the embarrassingly blatant adoration of their son.

By the end of the night, Tim Hamilton, who was the chief of naval operations at the Pentagon, had been impressed by both Lana's apparent capabilities and her ability to handle herself under pressure. She had also proven extremely knowledgeable on naval and world issues, but always stopped just short of expressing an opinion, focusing on the facts. Opinions are for politicians, not the military, he had always said ... and for senior officers, of course, who had to be both.

He would watch the young lieutenant, and his son around her. Neither he nor his wife were fooled for a moment by why she had been interested in the son of one of the most senior admiral's in the US Navy. But then again, he had seen no evidence of manipulation on her part, or condescension toward his son.

She had expressed an interest in submarine tactics and strategic deployment. It was an unusual avenue, and tough to get into, especially for a woman, as the close confines of submarines made them the only remaining unisex branch of the military. That said, she clearly had the mind for tactical and strategic planning, and he was not without the power to help her get where she wanted to be. If she was, indeed, as good as Chris said she was.

Yes, he would watch this one carefully, she had promise.

- - -

Despite the ravages of recent history's judgment, the French military is, in fact, one of the more effective and elite fighting forces on earth. In branches such as the French Foreign Legion, for example, most members of the rest of the world's armed forces would quail at the levels of endurance and toughness required of the young officers and privates.

That said, Agent Jean-Paul Merard had not joined the Foreign Legion, not that he wouldn't have been able to comfortably exceed even their strict standards. But Jean-Paul, like his seven other cohorts, wanted the fastest way to his target nation's missile command. Combat experience was the key to getting there, and the elite Rafale fighter pilot division of the French army was one of the best ways for him to get it.

During his training he had made sure he showed especially high proficiency in both hand-eye coordination and tactical target selection, placing him on top of the list of his class's candidates, and now he was profiting from that proficiency.

Arriving at the Dassault Rafale Training Base in southeastern France, he parked the small Citroën he had bought and went to survey his new environs. Complementing his vantage point was the AI satellite's aerial view being sent to him via the relay in his car, and he followed various paths till he came out against the tall wire fence that hemmed in the actual fighter planes. Most of his initial classes would be in a simulator, but he wanted to see the storage place for the actual machines.

The Dassault Rafale was France's answer to the Eurofighter, as the impatient country had dropped out of the development of that plane early to work on its own machine. It had managed to complete the plane nearly ten years earlier than the European consortium and the result had been small, sleek, and lethal. They were, in the opinion of Jean-Paul's overlaid personality, a strange combination of primitive brutality and pure, functional beauty. The now space-born warcraft of his own race had long since become so distanced from the actual battle by the range of their weaponry that the concept of seeing your enemy through glass seemed at once terrible and wonderful.

Despite his machine soul, he could not help but think this was going to be … fun.

"Can I help you, sir?" said a French sergeant on regular patrol around the central landing and hangar facility. Though these training craft carried no functional weaponry, they were still $45 million each, and access to them was closely guarded even inside the base.

"Just looking at my new job," said the pilot trainee, smiling at the sergeant and extending his hand. "Lieutenant Jean-Paul Merard, plaisir."

The sergeant was surprised by the officer's casual attitude, but he instinctively took the smiling man's hand, the ice inevitably melting between them.

"New trainee, sir?" the sergeant asked.

"New *pilot* trainee," corrected the lieutenant, laughing a little. "Beautiful, aren't they?"

The sergeant could not help but smile a little. He had wanted to be a pilot himself, but his eyesight had not met the strict standards required. By the time Lasik had come around he already been too old for the training program anyway. In the past he had usually begrudged the new trainees their job, but this one was so openly happy that the sergeant was momentarily caught up in it.

"Yes, sir, beautiful indeed, but quite hard to handle, I hear."

"Ah, we'll see if I can't make her sing for me," said the lieutenant, laughing. The sergeant laughed as well, and began to walk away, continuing his patrol.

Nice human, thought Jean-Paul, his eyes following the chuckling soldier. It was a pity they were all going to die, he thought offhandedly. But the thought passed and his gaze returned to the lethal fighter. He smiled.

Chapter 29: Willing and Able

Every time the doorbell rang at Neal's new house in Georgetown, his heart skipped a beat. He had been sitting in the plush living room, working on the finishing touches to his rushed dissertation so that he could hand it off to Barrett Milton to push through the approval process at Neal's own university, a place where the colonel clearly had far more influence than he. He would return to defend it to the review panel, the final step in any dissertation, once it had been tacitly accepted by the dean.

Putting his laptop aside, he climbed from the easy chair and went to the door. As he did so, he heard the colonel coming down the stairs from the room he was temporarily using in the house. It had seemed easier for him to stay with Neal while in DC, and it had meant he could contribute to the extremely high cost of renting the house while he was here, too.

Neal opened the door and was greeted by a lady in an Electric Company uniform and cap, probably in her mid-fifties, introducing herself as Madge. Her dark, Persian looks made her seem more like an Isabella or Maria, but Neal nodded and waited for her to explain herself.

"I'm with the electric company, Mr. Danielson. Need to check the meter, may I come in?"

"Oh, right, of course," said Neal, stepping aside to let her pass. He heard the colonel coming down the stairs behind him but kept his eyes on the electrician, who was looking up at the colonel and smiling.

"Well, Barrett, you are in more trouble than your message betrayed." she said, taking off her hat, and shaking her long, black hair free. The action made her look younger and more virile than she had appeared to be. But Neal was too disturbed by her change of attitude to notice.

She turned back to face him, smiling, "Don't worry, I'm a friend," then looking back up at Barrett, she went on snidely, "for now, at least."

She nudged Neal aside, and closed the front door firmly behind herself. She locked it, and said in an aside, "You'll need a dead bolt and a much stronger chain. Maybe a steel crossbrace. Anyway, let's get away from the door so you can tell me what's going on, shall we?"

"Who are you?" said Neal, almost angry at the way she was taking control. He looked at Barrett as she walked into the living room he had occupied a moment ago, "Do you know this woman?"

"Yes, Neal, you'll have to take my word for this, she can be trusted explicitly. She is the old friend I mentioned to you a week ago."

"And how does she come to suddenly be here, at my house?" asked Neal in an almost whisper.

At this, the woman in question returned from the living room and answered the question herself. "Neal, Barrett and I go back a very long way. A week ago he sent me a note asking me to come to DC, and saying he wanted to get back together."

Neal digested this for a moment, and then said to the tall officer shaking his head beside him, "You invited an ex-girlfriend over to my house?"

"No," she answered for Barrett again, before he could open his mouth, "he said he wanted to get back together. The last time I saw Barrett was five years ago, and I had joked then, however sadly, that I would never hear from him again. He had said he would contact me again when he was ready to get back together. Both of us knew that was impossible, so I had said that if he ever asked me back that I would know he was in trouble. He asked, so I knew he was in trouble."

Barrett and the woman looked into each other's eyes for a moment, the practiced understanding of many years of intimacy needing no words as they greeted each other and let each other know the gravity of the situation with their expressions.

She nodded, "Well then, Neal, I have been watching you for two days. You are clearly in hiding, though from what I do not know. And Barrett here is clearly concerned for your well-being, and maybe his own, but that never made him ask for my help before." She looked around for something.

"Does this place have a basement? I'm not comfortable talking with all these windows around." she said, waiting for Neal to respond.

"Err, yes," he said, jolted into action, "it's a bit of a dump, but it's certainly not got any windows."

"We shouldn't have to worry about being listened to up here or down there." put in Colonel Barrett, "I brought over one of my bug detectors from the Pentagon when Neal moved in, the place is clean."

"Good," said the delivery woman, following Neal and the colonel into the basement, "good."

- - -

It had not taken long for their guest to see how worried Barrett was. But ten minutes into their dialogue about the surveillance they feared, it was painfully obvious to her that they were not telling her the whole story.

"OK, guys," she interrupted Neal during a sentence about encrypting e-mails, "OK, I guess I need to know some things before we go any further." They looked at one another, and it was clear to her that Neal was relying on Barrett to make a decision about how much to tell her. That, in and of itself, was very interesting.

"Firstly, you have carefully not told me who is trying to monitor you, or why. Now I have worked in many situations where that was the case … in my previous life. But always under orders from someone else who I had to leave the big decisions to. Needless to say, I am retired now, and so I make those decisions for myself." She waited while they absorbed that, and then went on.

"So, here is what I can surmise from your … limited explanation so far. You do not just suspect, but are clearly quite certain you are being watched. You know that the organization watching you can hack your e-mails pretty reliably, if not with ease, so that makes it one of … ten or eleven countries in the world. You are also surprisingly certain that you are being monitored by satellite surveillance cameras, which brings it down to three countries in the world, including your own."

Neal noted the use of 'your' own. She was not an American, apparently, though her accent was perfect. She knew that she was being evaluated by them both and noted that she had given Neal that piece of information. She decided it did not matter, as Barrett already knew it, and they were clearly very much in each other's confidence.

"Now, gentlemen, if you are being watched closely by either the US, China, or Russia, you must be someone very important, the question is: important to whom, and why? The fact that you are also clearly afraid for your lives makes you either A) important enough that China or Russia would risk an assassination on US soil for the first time in nearly ten years; or B) dangerous enough to the US that you think they would kill a colonel in their own air force, not unheard of, but hardly standard operating procedure either.

"Unfortunately for you, the courses of action open to you are inherently different for each option, so in order to help you, I am afraid I need to know which it is. I am sorry, that is my price."

She sat there, impassive, and watched the cogs turn over in their heads. Neal looked from her to Barrett, and back to her. Barrett, however, kept his eyes firmly on the floor, clearly very deep in thought. After about a minute of absolute silence, he looked up, and she saw immediately the conflict in his face. He wanted to protect her from whatever it was they had to say to her. She had never seen such a thing from him. She was touched, but she was also deeply disturbed by this level of emotion from a man such as he.

He broke the eye contact, clearly coming to a decision and moving forward with it immediately, before he could change his mind. "Neal, she is ready. Tell her the truth, all of it, and do not spare any details. She is easily as intelligent as we are, even you, so give it to her straight. We'll worry about her loyalties afterward."

Neal nodded somberly, looking at his friend and taking his cue from him, then turning, almost sadly, to the guest. "Maybe you could tell me your name first, your real name?"

She smiled. Then she decided that she was clearly about to be let into something that Colonel Barrett Milton, with all of his years in the Pentagon, considered a big secret. If Neal was willing to trust his life to her on Barrett's word, she was willing to meet him partway.

"My name," she said, "is Ayala Zubaideh. I am retired now, and I live in Denver, Colorado, which I have called home for five years. But I was born in Israel, grew up in Saudi Arabia, and worked for HaMossad leModi in uleTafkidim Meyuḥadim, the Mossad to you, until my retirement five years ago. I met Barrett when he was stationed in the Gulf in 1991. He did not know who I worked for until I retired, when he decided he could not, in his position, stay with a member of a foreign intelligence agency, even a retired one, however close an ally Israel may be at this particular time. We got divorced and I have not seen him since."

Neal struggled with the idea of the colonel married, and to such an exotic woman, and then with the fact that he had ended it so utterly. Finally, Neal struggled with the fact that he had just been told he was sitting in a room with a member of the feared Israeli Institute for Intelligence and Special Operations. The Mossad to its friends, and its enemies.

Not for nothing, but Holy Shit, thought Neal.

"OK, well, yes, I can see, upon reflection, that what you just said was not something you would have said at the door." Neal went on, noting the colonel pacing behind his ex-wife.

"That said," continued Neal in a pensive tone, "as much as I am grateful that you have …. opened up to me about who you are, I must ask that you brace yourself." She looked at him, puzzled, her instincts pricking in mild alarm. "Because what I am about to tell you is, I am comfortable saying, far more important than anything even you have ever been told before."

And with that, he set about thoroughly blowing her very experienced mind.

- - -

Thirty minutes later Neal stopped his monologue.

She sat, still holding the probe's photos of the capsule he had handed to her, and she asked her ex-husband to stop pacing behind her. She was quiet and introspective, but she was also calm. The colonel paused behind her, and Neal could see the officer's fear and sadness, the tension of the last thirty minutes had clearly taken a toll on him. The colonel had been absolutely explicit on what they must do if they recruited someone who did not immediately completely understand and agree to the enterprise's strict secrecy.

Neal could see the colonel's service pistol from here, its black matte metal lethal in his hands, the safety off. He had taken it out after Neal had started talking in earnest, staying behind Ayala and keeping the gun out of sight.

"Barrett," Ayala said, not taking her eyes off Neal, "you can put your gun away, now." Neal and Barrett both flinched, "You were right to be cautious, but you need fear nothing from me." They both held their breath.

"If what you say is true, and from what Neal has shown me it most certainly looks like it is, you had no choice but to send for me, Barrett."

She stood, turned, and walked slowly over to the shaking colonel. Her left hand came to rest lightly on the gun, as she cupped her right hand softly against his cheek. Something in him seemed to give ever so slightly, and a single tear ran down his face. She took the gun, clicking the safety on with her thumb without taking her eyes off the man she clearly still loved, and he turned, temporarily broken, and climbed the basement stairs without a word.

Neal rose to follow his friend, but she stopped him. "Don't," she said quietly but firmly, "leave him a moment. He has spent the last half an hour waiting to see if he was going to have to kill his wife. Let him be for a while."

She shook her head, then she walked over to Neal, tucking the gun into the back of her pants as she came, and said, "We have much to do, and I should leave here soon, before whoever they are start to think it suspicious that an electrician has stayed so long. In fact, the first thing we are going to need to do is arrange a way in and out of here that will allow us to come and go without them knowing. I can take care of that, and while I am at it, there are some other things we are going to need, all of which will require money. So, let's talk about ways to channel funds."

Seeing his expression at the mention of funds, she chuckled and said, "OK, first let's talk about some ways we can discreetly generate them."

- - -

Across the world, in a cold cave in the northern mountains of Pakistan, Agent Shahim Al Khazar sits and prays. In many ways his prayers are more genuine, and certainly more immediately effective than those of his fanatical colleagues. As he bows forward, dipping his forehead to the soil, his machine mind relays, in real-time, his thoughts and actions to his four godlike cohorts soaring far above.

At the entrance to his cave, a nervous cleric awaits. The fighter has gained a fierce reputation in the four months he has been with the Liberation Army, proving as deadly to any of the other freedom fighters who stood in his way as he has to the infidels.

Twice he had begged forgiveness from the army's leaders for fighting and killing a rival Islamic brother, though in both cases it had been clear to all that the fights had been started by the other man. That said, few would fight him again, as both of his victims had received crushing injuries, one man's neck being snapped clean to one side by a kick from the deadly fighter's foot.

But now the junior cleric had been dispatched to summon the fighter to an audience with the clan's chief cleric and general, and the poor messenger was not sure who he feared more.

Respecting the prayer time of the kneeling fighter as much out of fear as religious doctrine, the junior cleric stood and waited until Shahim eventually opened his eyes.

"Honored soldier of the cause, you are summoned to an audience with Cleric Mashadi Amar immediately." said the junior cleric, with as much authority as he could muster.

"Why did you not tell me sooner?" said the brusque man, "You have been standing there for nearly five minutes."

The cleric could not bring himself to respond, his shrug turning into an involuntary shake as the large, powerful man propelled himself straight from kneeling to a brisk run, pushing bodily past the cleric and out of the small, carved cave that was his home.

Arriving in the underground hall that was the home of the chief cleric, he bowed.

"You must forgive me, Cleric. I was not informed you wished to see me until a moment ago by the fool that was dispatched to summon me." said Shahim, his clothing wrapped thickly around him, but still barely disguising his bulk. He stood in the cave's only entrance, all but blocking out the stark sunlight leaking through it.

"Shahim, all my clerics speak directly for me, you will respect them, all of them, as though they are my own blessed kin." the chief cleric was quick to put the fighter in his place. He was used to dealing with men who could kill him if they wanted to. Indeed, they would be of no use to him if they could not. The trick was to dominate them, they were tools, strong of heart but weak of mind, and they needed leadership.

"Forgive me." the warrior bent his head lower.

"You are forgiven, my child." said the cleric curtly, "But now I have a mission for you. And maybe an opportunity to prove you truly believe in our cause, Shahim." Though the warrior did not look up, the elderly cleric hoped his words were driving home. In truth, they had rarely had such a bold, fierce, or effective warrior amongst them, but Shahim was still relatively new.

It was a facet of the dangerous tactics forced on them by the infidel oppressors that many of the cleric's recruits died in their first missions. Those that did not, either by guile, intellect, or even cowardice, though that would never be said, formed all of the higher ranks. They were often much older, and always untrusting of newcomers. Power was a limited commodity in these regimes, and they did not give it over to newcomers easily.

Shahim Al Khazar had proved to be as relentless, brave, and merciless as he was brutally effective, and the elderly cleric knew that there would soon be those among his force, and outside it, that would consider whether the young warrior might prove a better general than he. Indeed, they may already be thinking it. Well, the cleric had not survived the brutal life of the jihad for forty years without dispatching a rival or two. No matter how good a warrior, it was clear he had to get rid of this man, and he thought he could see a way to make it look like the warrior's fault.

"For many years now we have been subjects of a weak, corrupt, puppet government of the West," the cleric began, starting to pace, slowly, around the room, "They have been brought to power by nonbelievers and heretics. We have bargained with them and taken their stinking money, but the time has come that we remind them of our divine purpose."

Shahim studied his leader closely. The man was talking of an attack on the Pakistani leadership. This was not part of his plan. A direct attack on the government would, eventually, be necessary for the Agent to take control of the nation's nuclear weapons, but only after Shahim had achieved control over some portion of the freedom fighters army, and trained them to the level necessary to make the attack successful.

Shahim could already see that this was going to be a halfhearted attempt, which the cleric didn't really believe would work. Whatever their target, sending a new warrior such as himself meant that he was meant to fail, sacrificing himself to show the Pakistani government that they were serious, or probably just to dispose of said warrior, and the internal threat he represented.

"I have seen you fight, and I have seen the results of your operations. But these were small fry, not a test of a real martyr. So…" the cleric looked the warrior in the eye, holding his gaze as he said these next words, "…I am sending you to make an attempt on the prime minister's life, or die trying. Is that clear?"

Shahim stared at him, then at the floor. It would do no good to argue with the cleric; he either had to kill the elected leader of the country, kill the cleric in front of him, or kill himself. There was no other option now that the order had been given. Neither avenue was desirable, but that was precisely the dilemma the cleric had intended to force on the man. He would need to consult with the Council to decide what to do next.

Chapter 30: A Very, Very, Very Fine House

Upon returning to DC from a quick trip back to Florida, Madeline had been shocked to see so many changes to the house, and to meet its new resident.

"Of course, officially," said Neal, as he introduced her to Ayala and took her bag, "she lives next door."

Madeline looked at him confused, and he laughed, walking off upstairs with her two heavy bags. "What the hell do you have in here?" he groaned as he climbed the stairs, his out of shape frame wilting under the weight of the clothes she had bought from home.

Ayala rolled her eyes at Neal then turned to Madeline, saying, "I'll explain everything to you in a moment, my dear, but first, do you want a shower, or a cup of coffee maybe? You've just gotten off the plane."

"No, thanks though. It isn't a long flight and I do it all the time."

"OK then, maybe it's best if I give you the tour, then?" said Ayala, looking at Madeline, who nodded, curious and a little wary. Ayala took her arm and led her to the entrance to the basement, Neal running back down the stairs to join them once more. A moment later, Madeline stood at the bottom of the basement steps, even more baffled now as she looked at the messy, dusty space.

"Well, what do you think?" said Neal, stepping past her toward the washing machine in the corner.

"Err, I guess I kind of expected you to have, you know, cleaned this place up a bit," Madeline said, "weren't we going to put our computers down here?"

As she watched them, confused, Ayala smiled, somewhat proudly, and Neal opened the washing machine lid, reached inside, pulled something and then grabbed the corner of the big machine. Clearly on rollers, it slid gently out of the way, revealing a rough hole in the wall about three feet high.

"After you." Neal said to Ayala.

"Such a gentleman!" she said, walking over and getting down on her knees to crawl through the space.

Neal indicated for Madeline to follow, and she did, ever more perplexed.

She now stood in a parallel basement, clearly belonging to the house next door. It was dominated by two things, a line of computers, each clearly hubbed together, though Madeline assumed not connected to any external network or internet link, and several racks of clothes.

"Welcome to our new headquarters, Madeline." said Neal, as he crawled through after them, pulling on a metal lever next to their ingress that clearly pulled the washing machine back into place behind them.

"But..." Madeline started, before Ayala cut her off, sensing her confusion.

"We couldn't risk all of us coming and going from the main entrance of Neal's house, it would be too easy to track our movements, and even easier to link us all together. We are going to need to have some freedom of movement, so I rented the basement apartment off the house next door. They hadn't been planning to rent it out, but after a few days looking into all your neighbors, both to each side and the house behind, I found a little leverage over these ones which I could use to encourage them to accept my offer."

Madeline looked at her. Who the hell *is* this woman, she thought, but after seeing Neal grinning like a boy with a schoolyard crush, she decided to leave that question for later; maybe Barrett would be able to shed some light on the whole situation.

Choosing to ignore Neal's childlike wonder, and Madeline's current confusion, Ayala went on, "So we have a separate entrance, which the AI has no way of knowing is linked to Neal's house. And in order to make sure it does not recognize someone entering one house and leaving from the other, we have a series of disguises here. It is very important to note that these red racks are for when you leave through this entrance, this empty rack here is for the clothes you arrived in. DO NOT MIX THEM UP." She was very stern on that point, and Madeline felt like a school child, even as a part of her noted the sense behind the point being emphasized.

But Ayala wanted to make sure this was not lost on Madeline, and it wouldn't hurt to reiterate it to Neal once more as well, given what was at stake.

"If, just one time, an orbiting satellite sees a person it recognizes as having entered through *that* house," she pointed back at the main house they had come from, "leave through *this* entrance," she pointed at the basement's separate entrance, "then we must assume it will take it precisely half a second to figure out that the two houses have been linked for some reason. It is such a very small leap from that conclusion to realizing that we are trying to fool it, and then the only reasonable reaction we can expect from it is a quick death. For all of us. Is that clear?"

Madeline nodded, wide-eyed. Clearly Ayala had thought this through.

"So," Ayala continued, slightly calmer, but no less emphatic, "red rack for leaving here, this rack for your normal clothes. Also, you *must* wear either a hat or a wig when leaving here, and you must not look up when outside. I would say you should get out of the habit of looking up altogether, as strange as that seems, but at the very least, never, ever present your face to the satellite when in disguise."

Madeline nodded. This woman was good. Neal's crush seemed more and more understandable. Madeline may have one of her own, she thought, smiling.

"Over here," Ayala said, walking over to a chest of drawers, "you will find what we shall call your 'basement' identities." Each drawer was marked with one of their names, starting at the top with Madeline's, then Ayala's, Neal's, and finally Barrett's.

"Inside, you'll find everything you'll need to get around on the outside without using your own name. Judging by what your visitor John Hunt said, we have good reason to believe you are both being tracked. So if the AI thinks you are at home and then all of a sudden you use your credit card in some other city, it will figure out something is wrong and we are back to the whole 'death from above' scenario."

How had this woman done all this, thought Madeline, looking at the four ziploc bags in her drawer. It was, wow, she didn't know what it was, but she realized she had developed a childlike grin of her own. She looked more closely at each of her 'basement' identities. Each bag contained a driver's license, social, credit card and, in two cases, a passport. One of the passports was not American. She picked up that bag.

Inside she found her photo on all its contents, but a strange name, and someone else's details, even on the Australian passport.

"How?" Madeline was astonished, and she brandished the passport in the air as she stared incredulous at the woman. A week, for god's sake. A week. In that time Madeline had managed to quit her job, pack a few bags, give notice she was breaking her lease, and get back on a plane, and it had felt like a very full seven days. This woman had fabricated sixteen personalities, broken more laws than Madeline could name, and bought clothes to dress the five thousand.

Ayala ignored the question of how, it was not important, or even recommended, that they know the ins and outs. Instead, she took the passport from Madeline and smiled at the name it had so neatly printed on its pages. "Yes, for you, I've revived some of my old names. I had plenty. I haven't used these identities in a while, but they are still good," she said, handing the document back to Madeline. "The back stories are infallible, they've been out there for twenty years and I fabricated them myself. The credit cards are new, you'll need to maintain those. As one of a host of tasks associated with maintaining all this, we will have to follow a process to remotely pay all these. Can't have them all associated with this address so we will have to log in remotely, using ghost IPs. But that is for another day, the important thing is that we don't miss a payment, not one, no matter how small. It seems petty but we want to avoid any unnecessary attention on these identities. They must all be model citizens, clear? So that also means no speeding, running red lights, stop signs, not even jay walking."

Madeline nodded again, returning the passport to its bag and placing it back in her drawer, somber again at the severity of it all.

But Neal broke the mood, piping up like a boy who wants his mom's approval, "Ayala had to fake the colonel's and mine from scratch, I have an American and British one." He put on an appalling British accent for a moment, something between cockney and heat stroke, "Yoo kan caull muy Jones, Maark Jones." he said, and laughed.

Ayala and Madeline half-smiled, half-frowned at each other, then shook their heads and decided to ignore the man. "Now, that's the logistics out of the way, let's talk shop." She took Madeline's arm and said, "How much do you think you understand about this nano-medical device that Mr. Hunt gave us the design for?"

This woman didn't mess around, Madeline thought. OK, she could keep up. She was a professional engineer. She had three different masters in Chemical Engineering, Marine Biology and Physics. Let's see if this woman could beat that, "Well, Ayala, I think I have a pretty good grasp of how it's supposed to work. It is essentially a biomimetech device that takes the concept of an antibody to its logical, if exponentially more advanced, conclusion, employing various, frankly very straightforward, if very, very small tools that each facilitate and enable selected functionalities of autonomous diagnosis and treatment. It is self-replicating, and operates using a hive mentality, each unit being but a part, albeit a very versatile part, of a greater system, which alters and develops itself as it senses new threats. Once deployed, it is, by design, almost completely self-sufficient."

Madeline took a breath, then went on, "Once we develop the manufacturing tools that John also provided specs for, I think we can make it. In fact, I think we must. This machine...well...there's really no way to overstate its importance. This machine, if it works as John says it does, will be, by far, the biggest medical advancement in history."

Madeline stopped, looking at Ayala to see if she was impressed. But Ayala was not one to compete with people. In her field she was as good as any, but nano-mechanics was most certainly not her field.

"Good," she said, "because I didn't have a fucking clue about any of it, so I think you are going to have to come to Japan with me."

Japan? Madeline glanced a question at Neal, as she was led to the computer bank by the formidable woman, but he just shrugged. He had grown somewhat used to the way the ex-spy worked, and he found it was best to just stop worrying about it and try to keep up.

- - -

A few days later, Madeline and Ayala were, indeed, on a plane to Japan. Ayala had explained that if they needed production and research facilities, the best way to get them was to 'seed' the idea.

It was an old concept, used most effectively by the Nazis before World War II. In order to speed up the development of tools and technologies that Hitler had envisioned needing for his planned expansion, he and his Third Reich had seeded German companies with subsidized scientists to fuel their research in specific areas.

While Ayala and Madeline had no subsidies to offer, they had something much better. They would offer the actual, finished designs, piece by piece, of course, to certain organizations, in return for certain concessions.

First, Ayala and Madeline, under assumed names, would offer details of the basic manufacturing technologies that they were going to need, under the guise of corporate espionage.

The technology would be offered, at significant cost, as part of a package to hire Madeline's fake persona as a consultant. Madeline, who would pose as a US government scientist, would say she was willing to help the Japanese manufacturing magnate in secret because she felt that the technology she was working on was just too important not to be used for the benefit of all.

She would be telling the truth to a degree, but that portion of the truth would be all they would need. They would stipulate that they must work directly with the CEO and his senior research staff, and even then only if he agreed that Madeline's involvement remain strictly confidential.

The vast profits the company could hope to gain would no doubt be sufficient incentive for the CEO to keep from divulging the source of his inspiration. But if not, and the CEO was careless, then the added layer of anonymity given by their use of pseudonyms would hopefully keep them from being discovered for long enough for them to get their job done or get out.

They had settled on their particular target company for several reasons. Firstly, the company had a reputation for real technical creativity that would lend credibility to the sudden manufacturing improvements that would soon start coming from them. Secondly, their non-US headquarters would help mask the link between Ayala's friends and the work. And thirdly, because the significant manufacturing and research facilities they did maintain in the US for their American contracts would make it easier for Madeline to stay involved in their 'research.'

If they were able to get the president of Matsuoka Industries to take the bait, they would return home and Madeline would relocate to whatever facility the CEO assigned the project to. If not, Ayala had three more potential companies lined up, each hungrier than the last, but Ayala doubted that they would find much difficulty in persuading the man they were going to see. She had made a career out of persuasion, and she knew the power of the hand she had to play.

Before even getting on the plane, in a seeming aside, Ayala had already also begun the process of selling her house in Denver, which itself had been purchased under a dummy name, more out of habit than anything else.

Whichever company they got to take the bait, she would put the entire value of the house into shares in that company. Only she could do this, none of the others could be seen linking themselves so clearly to what was about to be such a game changing organization.

But between the considerable wealth they would get from the share price sky rocketing in the near future, and the 'consulting fees' they would ask for in return for Madeline's time and expertise, they would gain a significant additional source of funding for the other work they needed to be starting on.

Chapter 31: Officer's Club

Going for a meeting in the office of General Pickler was usually an exercise in self-control for Colonel Milton. But today was different for several reasons, thought the colonel as he stepped through the Pentagon's security screen and replaced his cap.

Waiting for the elevator, the colonel considered what he had to accomplish today. For the first time in his twenty-year career, he had called a meeting with a superior for personal reasons. He needed to relocate to DC, at least for the meantime, so he could work closely with Neal, Madeline, and Ayala in building their plan.

He also needed to regain access to military hardware and personnel. Though they were a long way from being ready to do it yet, in the not too distant future they were going to need to launch an attack on the four unseen satellites John Hunt had told them were watching them from space.

The satellites' capability outline that the mysterious double agent had provided was, frankly, horrifically long, and as long as those satellites were in space, they were not going to be able to start preparing for the larger threat that they represented.

So, to that end, Colonel Milton needed to start building the contacts he would need across the globe to eventually coordinate that attack. For now, that started here, in the US.

He sighed as he considered the scale of the job, comparisons to Everest seemed woefully inadequate, but that wasn't all he had to do, not even close. Also begging for his attention was the disquieting problem of getting some kind of handle on the other Agents that were at work across his blissfully unaware planet. John had given them the Agents' names and countries, and the basics of their progress to date.

The colonel would have to be careful, but he would start by very subtly locating the operative in the US.

His senior rank in a NATO force should also allow him to keep a quiet eye on the French Agent, and maybe even the Israeli one. After that, well, getting people in place near the Agents in Pakistan and India was going to be much harder, not to mention infiltrating the Chinese and Russian armies.

But that was for another day. Putting that seemingly insurmountable task aside for now, the colonel arrived at the door of the general and knocked.

"Colonel, come in," the general gestured at a seat and waved off the salute of the more junior officer, setting aside some memos on his desk.

"Well, Colonel, what is all this about? Looking for a raise?" the general laughed at his own joke, as he so often did, and Barrett waited for it to subside.

When it finally had, Barrett began, "Sir, thank you for agreeing to see me. As you know, I have been in DC for a short while, since Dr. West's funeral, in fact." The general flinched at the reference, but nodded at the colonel to proceed, "Well, sir, I have asked for this meeting to ask for a … favor."

The general was instantly suspicious. He did not like favors, he did not like owing or being owed. The colonel had never bothered him with personal requests and whining before, and that was why he had kept the man around.

He did not like where this was going.

"General, sir, I hope we have worked together long enough that you know I do not take lightly the mixing of personal wants and the needs of the service. But, this once, I have found that I must ask if it is possible to consider … a move."

"A move? What move, Colonel? What, from the Array? Impossible. What? Why? Why is this happening?" sputtered the general.

Damn it. I should have been more circumspect, thought Barrett. But no, small talk with General Pickler would only have served to annoy him further. No, you know that it was best this way, thought Barrett. Now, let's give him the bait as planned and hope he takes it.

"General Pickler, sir, I can't stress enough that I have never before allowed my personal life to interfere with the air force. The service has always come first. But … well sir, my ex-wife and I are trying to make a fresh start of it." At the mention of the colonel's ex-wife, the general balked. He had not even known the colonel was divorced. He would need to kick some intelligence officer firmly in the ass for leaving that out of the colonel's file.

The colonel went on, "She is living in DC now, we met again while I was visiting, and, well, needless to say, I am not a young man, and we have decided to try to make it work between us."

The lie pained the colonel more than he had thought it would have. He had protected enough classified information to be well practiced in the art of dissemination, but this was different. Most of all, because seeing Ayala again had indeed reawakened feelings he did not know how to control. Maybe it pained the colonel most because, in many ways, it was not a lie at all.

The general was aghast. Such a display from so senior an officer, and such a stalwart one at that, was disconcerting to him. "Colonel, are you asking for retirement or reassignment?"

"No, sir, no, not retirement. No sir, my dedication to the service remains absolute, but reassignment would, indeed, be very … welcome, and hopefully a little closer to Washington, if that might be possible."

The general's mind raced. This was an unfortunate display, and the idea of having Colonel Milton in the Pentagon, even if he was an excellent officer, was suddenly unappealing.

Meanwhile, the colonel watched the senior man's face tell the tales of his emotions. He was flushed red, his blood pressure clearly even higher than normal.

The colonel knew that there was a chance that he would not be reassigned, and that if he was it might not be to DC itself. He was OK with that. Anything in the NE would, by the very nature of the bases up here, probably be more tactical than his role at the Array.

The general eventually broke the silence, "Well, this is very irregular, and not something I would normally entertain. But, as you say, this is not something you are given to, and so I am inclined to consider it. It would mean transferring you out of my command, of course." As he said that, he hesitated a little. The colonel was a very effective and reliable officer. While having some nauseating lovebird at the Pentagon sounded like a bad idea, he had another option, and one that didn't make it seem like he was bending over backward to meet the needs of some colonel.

"Or maybe not. Colonel, your expertise might, actually, lend itself to another assignment within my division," the colonel's eyes narrowed, he had considered that this might happen, "and I believe you have worked with the folks up at ESC before."

The ESC, or Electronic Systems Center, based at Hanscom Air Force Base in Massachusetts, was in charge of developing and testing the air force's command and control, communications, computer, and intelligence systems. Its location was not ideal for Barrett's needs, but it would give him more than enough access to the information he would require.

Even more than that, it was the only base in the air force that had more officers than enlisted men, and it housed some of the finest minds in the US. Ripe recruiting grounds for the colonel and his friends.

As the colonel contemplated the assignment, the general waffled on. He made sure that the colonel knew he would be receiving a very large favor, and that the general was a very generous man for giving it to him.

The colonel nodded until his neck hurt, and thanked the general enough to tan his nose, but he didn't push hard for it. He let the general make the final call, and once he did, the interview finally came to an end.

OK, thought the colonel, time to move house.

Chapter 32: Excess

The Agent that was Shahim Al Khazar laughed to himself at the paltry force that had been assigned to the mission. To say that these men were inadequate to the task of effectively making an attempt on the prime minister's life would have been a gross understatement. The twenty-six men were nearly all new recruits, the remainder being once-great warriors, now too blind, too slow, or too fanatically insane to be of use to the cleric who had dispatched them.

In the days since his orders had been handed down to him Agent Shahim had requested that the AIs convene his peers for a Council. When they had met in the virtual void they had discussed at length what he should do. While there was no doubt he could accomplish the mission, even with the poor tools he had been given, the thought of destabilizing his nation's government at this early stage in their time here had been far from ideal.

But neither could he return to the mountains unsuccessful, for he would be an outcast. The remaining option, killing the cleric that had ordered the attack, was also fraught with risks and uncertain outcomes, the only certainty being that it would gain him a reputation for disloyalty, not ideal, by any means. No, taking the mission had been the lesser of three evils. And so he had accepted, feigning stoic bravery in the face of what the cleric assumed was certain death, or worse, capture and ignominy.

Once in the capital city, Shahim had fought the urge to simply forge onward and get it done. Instead he had maintained the guise of needing this sham of a team, and after two days of improvised strategizing and planning with them, Shahim had laid out an empty husk of an attack plan for his men to follow, knowing full well the futility of everyone's part in it but his own.

With orders set, they had left their staging base, a disused warehouse in the old part of Islamabad, an hour ago. Shahim had ordered several of the most useless of the older warriors to stay behind, seeing that they would actually limit the already minimal efficacy of the team he had.

He had then split his remaining force into three groups. The majority of his forces had been concentrated into two groups that would attack the main gates of the prime minister's compound. Their mission had been clear, distract the bulk of the guards, and take down the transformers powering the deadly electrified razorwire that capped the wall around the remainder of the complex.
Now he sat, waiting in silence, in an old battered Morris Minor they had stolen earlier that day. He had taken three men with him to form the third, much smaller force. He would not need them, but it would have seemed strange for him to go alone.

Down the street from them he could see where the neighborhood's residential buildings ended, and beyond them the road that ran along this side of the compound. The area on the other side of the road had been cleared of trees to remove any cover for attackers on the thirty feet or so between the road and the perimeter wall, its top proverbially sizzling with the electric razorwire that the two main teams were supposed to disable.

The sound of sputtering, angry gunfire sprang to life in the distance. The AI overhead informed him that both attacks on the main gates were now in full swing, and Shahim started the car's engine, his face set as he pressed down hard on the throttle.

The old car accelerated slowly but steadily over the two hundred yards to the wall. Overhead, the satellite was monitoring traffic and told him it was all clear, but the three men he was with did not know that, and they started to shift in their seats nervously as they approached the junction, unable to see either way on the road ahead because of the buildings lining their street.

Bursting out from the side road, their relief was only momentary as they crossed the main avenue unharmed. Now doing thirty miles an hour, they quickly covered the short, open patch of grass between the road and the wall. We are not slowing, they all thought, why are we not slowing? One man managed to release a scream as they flew headlong into the reinforced barrier wall.

This should deal with these incompetents, thought Shahim, as he locked his phenomenally strong arms and legs and braced for impact. The man in the front passenger seat of the car had not worn a seat belt, as there wasn't one for him to wear in the old junker, and he flew straight through the front windscreen, shattering the glass and his skull as he went. His journey was short, ending a moment later as he connected with the thick concrete wall that had so effectively stopped the car.

Even as his head and upper body splattered into the wall, the heads of the two men in the back were forcibly wrenched forward under the stress of the seat belts they had been slightly more fortunate to have. The one who had been behind the front passenger's seat suffered severe but not fatal chest and neck injuries as the force whiplashed through him, but the one behind Shahim shot forward into the seemingly brick wall of the driver's inhumanly strong shoulders and neck. Shahim's head did not even move as the other man's cracked open on the back of it, his skull shattering and crumpling against the Agent's like a melon colliding with a cannonball.

The car's rear wheels were still spinning in air, not half a second after the impact, as the man's crushed face began falling away from the back of Shahim's head. The very instant Shahim felt the momentum shift, energies in the car settling, he released his left hand's grip on the wheel, itself bent back under the pressure, and slammed his elbow into the driver's door. Wrenched it from its hinges, the door was sent flying away from the car. Shahim's hands flashed up to grasp the car's roof with vice like strength, he then pistoned his thighs, launching himself up and out of the side of the car, and onto the roof in one fluid motion.

Shahim's feet were already landing on the car's roof as its wheels finally came to rest. He was about to set off when, moaning, the car's rear passenger stumbled from the open door on the other side of the car. Ah well, the Agent thought, the 'freedom fighter' would be of one more use to him. Stepping over the car's roof, he picked the bewildered man up by the back of his neck.

"Congratulations, martyr, you can be the final show that this team struggled for the cause."

And with that, he braced his legs, and with one thrust of his arm propelled the man bodily up into the air to land on the charged fence that ran along the wall's top.

The man shouted as he flew through the air, insensible at the way he had been manhandled so easily by the superhuman below. But his shout turned to a short, blood-curdling scream as he landed on the curled razorwire, its knife-sharp blades cutting into his outstretched hands and delivering the might of the fence's charge straight into his burning veins.

The last of his doomed team now limply twitched and shook on the wall above Shahim, but he wasted no more time on them. Bending his legs slightly, he leapt easily over the wall and the dead man on top of it, landing with a tuck and role on the other side. He could already hear approaching guards, and from his ever-vigilant satellite's view he could see each team of soldiers as they converged on the site of the car's impact, their speed increased now that the alarm from the fence had been triggered.

No worry. Moving with quick, silent steps, dotted with sudden ducks behind bushes and leaps into tree branches, he avoided each group of men in turn, getting steadily closer to the main complex.

Meanwhile, the AI above was monitoring the radio traffic of the frantic guards, and informed him that the prime minister and his family had been moved to the bunker under the north wing of the building. It was on the other side of the compound from Shahim's position, but that shouldn't pose too big a problem.

Maneuvering to the nearest side of the large main building, he braced his legs once more and took a giant leap up and onto the flat roof of the main building. He would not go through or around. It was much easier to go over.

The roof was dotted with riflemen and one of them was stunned to see Shahim's determined face rise suddenly up out of the panicked night. Shahim had seen the guard waiting on the roof from the satellite image that was being relayed to him by the AI, and, in mid-flight he was already reaching down and drawing one of the twelve-inch hunting knives he had strapped to his calves. He landed in another roll to minimize the noise of the impact, just past the shocked guard, and immediately turned into the sights of the guard's rifle. As the stunned man began to squeeze his trigger, the long, sharp blade of the heavy knife drove straight through his forehead, the force of it repelling the instantly dead guard backward toward the side of the building.

Shahim, still grasping its hilt, wrenched backward viciously, the motion pulling the blade free, and dragging the body of the guard away from its impending, noisy fall to the ground, to crumple, instead, quietly on to the roof where it had stood moments before.

It would, no doubt, have been easier and quicker to use one of his built-in weapons systems to burn a neat hole through one of the man's eye sockets, but such a strange injury might have aroused unnecessary suspicion, and using the sonic punch when in midair would have thrown him back just as hard as it would have hit the soldier. No, primitive instruments would be preferable for now, until the intensity of events forced him to use more deadly tools.

- - -

The prime minister of Pakistan was incredulous. An attack? Were they mad? He had nearly four hundred men stationed in the compound as part of his personal guard, and more at a nearby barracks. Certainly, it had been attempted before, but all it had ever accomplished was the needless death of the few insurgents stupid enough to try it, and the loss of several of his brave guards.

He frowned at the captain of his guard for having dragged him and his family down to the bunker for what was, no doubt, another futile attack, and then turned to his wife and children, smiling reassuringly as he explained that there was nothing to worry about.

The sound of two of the rooftop guards hitting the top of the bunker after a forty-foot fall was little more than a series of dull thuds, but it nonetheless knocked the reassuring smile from his face.

The guard complement that had joined the prime minister and his family in the room spun around and trained their machine guns on the door. Forming two rows, the front one kneeling, they aimed ten powerful assault rifles at the fifteen-inch-thick steel portal while their captain called to his counterpart outside the door for an update.

"The guards at the gates report all insurgents dead, sir, but some must have made it into the compound. Two guards have just been thrown from the roof. We are sending a team to … wait, you there, one of the fallen guards appears to have survived … go help that man, fetch a medic … wait, he is getting up … dear Allah, what is happe …" gunshots could be heard through the radio, then the guard on the other end shouted: "Die, You Bastard, Why Won't You Die?!" then the radio went dead, a few more shots still just audible through the thick walls.

The firing stopped.

"Captain!" shouted the prime minister. "What is happening out there? What is happening?" the children were crying now, huddling by their mother, but their father was focused on the door.

"Prime Minister, the door is over a foot thick and can only be opened from the inside." The captain was clearly deeply shaken, but he had a procedure. "We will wait until the garrison arrives from the barracks. They have a code word to confirm they have control of the compound, only when I hear it will I open the door. They cannot get through this door, sir." The captain's voice waivered, but he was firm, his training centering him and holding him steady.

Shahim could, probably, have wrenched the door free, but the massive structure's formidable tensile strength might have strained even his phenomenal muscles. Even if he could, though, it would have left even more evidence that this was not the work of insurgents.

No, brute force was not the primary method of the advanced team, despite the massacre he had just wrought on the really quite brave guards. Nonetheless, in preparation for what was to come next, he rolled out the Tactical Contact Weapons Complement from behind his left eye, its menacing needles emerging from the eye socket as stepped up to the door.

Back inside, behind what they thought was an impregnable door, the radio came to life again.

The voice was familiar, an exact duplicate of the captain's now dead colleague on the outside, it said, "Captain, the insurgents have been suppressed, we have control over the compound and all sectors report secure. Also, the East Gate reports that the rest of the garrison has arrived and is manning the walls. You may open the door, code word 'alshahad75.'"

The captain hesitated, but he had known that voice for the over thirteen years, and the code word was, of course, correct. He turned and smiled weakly at the prime minister, "All is well, sir, the threat is over," and he turned back, ignoring a nagging sense of dread inside him, and pulled the lever to release the monumental door's locking mechanism.

His only reprieve was that he would never know what he had done. Brandishing both his twelve-inch blades, Shahim flashed through the opening gap moments later into the long room. Before he even realized what was happening, the captain's head had been severed completely from his body.

As he decapitated the poor soldier, Shahim's right foot came up and braced against the reinforced wall just inside the still opening vault door. Firing his right leg's phenomenal string of muscles, he launched himself headlong at the ten men formed in front of him.

Even as they reacted, even as their training kicked in and their fingers began to close on their assault rifles' triggers, the flying warrior collided with the still formed line of guards, and they washed from his onslaught like paper before a hurricane.

Shahim landed straight in their midst. His left foot flashing forward to ram into the head of one kneeling soldier, snapping his neck back, as his right foot brought all the rest of his momentum to bear on another's stomach, flattening him backward and driving his right boot through the man's torso to the ground beneath.

His arms were already flashing up as his feet connected, the two blades in his hands lashing out in wide diagonal arcs, slicing like scythes through the soft abdominal flesh of the four remaining men in the center of the formation.

It was a blur of death. As six of the soldiers' hearts completed their last beats, their blood spilling from their opened bodies, Shahim brought his terrible eye to bear on the two men still standing to his left. Their rifles were still turning to follow the path of the intruder, only a second having passed since hell had breached their haven.

The needle-thin antennae of his deadly stare focused an arc of super-low frequency sound into an oval, one meter across and a foot high, and laid it across the torsos of the two men.

To the petrified prime minister, it looked as if the two men had been struck at their waists by a spinning helicopter blade. They flew backwards, folding completely in two as they did so, then smashed into the bunker's walls with brute pain and crushing force.

He saw, with the last of his hope, the final two guards finally start to fire at the beast, but the bullets thudded into its back without effect. Whatever power it had used to break the two other men seemed now to push the beast back into the only two men left, the blades in its hands rising behind it as it went. It did not even look at the last of its prey before slaughtering them. The ineffectual gunfire stopped. It was over.

With the final two guards dripping down the bunker walls behind him, Shahim turned. He was drenched in gore. His team member's skull fragments still dripped down the back of his head. His right foot was soaked to the knee in the blood and guts of the soldier it had crushed. Both his arms ran wet with coarse, red blood, from his shoulders to the tips of his blades.

The prime minister was about to say something, he knew he had to, but what? What do you say to such a thing?

Shahim saw the man's mouth open and, without ceremony, hurled one of his slick blades right at the man, felling the target of the wild attack through the chest.

Shahim paused. Then walked slowly up to the man and retrieved his knife.

It was done.

With obvious effort, he turned to the cowering family on the cots arranged against the wall.

Despite it all, despite the way he had dispatched so many tonight, the Agent who called himself Shahim Al Khazar had never thought of himself as an evil man.

Until now.

The man whose personality had been chosen to overlay this particular machine's mind had been a lord of the Hamprect Empire. He had thought he was a noble, not only in name, but in deed. For though he had been a decorated warrior on his home world, war had never been his passion, let alone this massacre of the defenseless. These were, he was forced to admit, sentient, if primitive, people.

But as he looked down at the shaking, weeping family, he knew his duty. He had been too fast, his attack too wild, the killing too easy. He could not leave any witnesses.

- - -

He made his way carefully through the waking city cloaked in a stolen shawl. The attack had awakened the population like a hornet's nest and over the next few weeks the entire place would be combed, house by house, by a furious and hateful national army.

After two hours skulking from back alley to doorway, he arrived back at the warehouse where his few useless old warriors still remained, too stupid or too afraid to run. As he recounted the story of their victory, they whispered hoarse cheers, some of them crying with an orgiastic, fanatical joy. He removed the clean smock he had thrown around himself to cover his gory clothes and they cheered again at the sight of his victims' blood drenching him.

As he walked toward a waiting van to leave, one of them asked after the fate of the prime minister's family. As Shahim told them, they leered and cheered once more, whispering vulgar epithets about the dead woman and children.

Shahim's huge frame froze for a moment, then he carefully placed his clean smock in the van, closed the door, and turned to the once proud warriors.

The sight of his left eye sliding back into his head, and the aberration that replaced it, shocked the levity out of them.

If they loved death so much, Shahim thought, he would give it to them, and his weapons flashed out once more before he finally left the warehouse, alone, his shame masked only by a murderous fury.

Part 3

Chapter 33: Counterpoint

Neal sat looking at the large corkboard on the basement wall. It seemed like every time he did it was more formidable. Over the last six months they had managed to confirm the identity and location of nearly all seven of John Hunt's fellow Agents. They had slowly and discreetly acquired varying amounts of information on each of them, and Neal had arranged this information on a large corkboard in his basement headquarters.

In that time, their small team had also grown and split into three somewhat liquid groups. Madeline was now living almost full-time in North Dakota. Their cover company Matsuoka Industries had a large facility there and she had become a regular in their research department, helping them develop the new micro-manufacturing technology that was set to make them all very rich, for what that was worth. While the rest of the team there was unaware of it, they were actually also now a vital part of something far more profound. Even now they were close to completing the first step in the long process required to develop and deploy an antigen to the virus that hung, quite literally, over their heads, waiting to fall like a guillotine once they initiated their attacks on the satellites.

Once this stage of their work was complete, Matsuoka Industries would be able to manufacture microchips that were smaller, more reliable, and most of all cheaper than anyone else, and all in a fraction of the time per chip it took more conventional facilities. That was how they had sold the idea to the company's overjoyed CEO. But as the technology mogul licked his lips over his new toy, he had no idea that the manufacturing device they were going to make at his facilities was capable of far more than even he imagined. So much, in fact, that in time the microchip would be made defunct by the incredible abilities that the new resonance technology would give humanity. But for now that was all moot. They needed the new tool in order to build the tiny and impossibly complex bio-devices that the group needed to bolster humanity's defenses against the almost inevitable biological attack they were going to invite.

While Madeline had been playing corporate spy, Colonel Milton had moved to his new posting at Hanscom Base in New England. Unbeknownst to General Pickler, he had also started to recruit a small but highly capable team from among the many officers stationed there, giving him access to some of the skills and resources he would need to coordinate an international attack on the network of satellites above.

Ayala, meanwhile, had taken on the role of intermediary, for which her training made her uniquely qualified. She travelled almost constantly between North Dakota, Massachusetts, and DC, updating each arm of the team on progress, and sharing crucial information, while helping each maintain their all-important cover stories.

Neal remained, for now, the lone member of the team's third branch. His role was more esoteric. Firstly, he had looked for ways to find and track the satellites above them, relying solely on passive sensor data gleaned without ever referencing what he was really doing. It was an intricate ballet, to be sure, forever dancing around his real goal, taking almost comically convoluted routes to track down four devices that were already, by design, pretty damn hard to find.

He had made a brief return to his old job at the Array in Arizona timed to overlap with a similar trip by Colonel Milton. They had tested some of his theories using its phenomenal network of antennae, but while they had been able to detect one of the satellites on a couple of sweeps, it had soon become clear that to track them accurately they would have focus far too much of the array's attention on them, and risk alerting the constantly vigilant devices to the Array's newfound affection for them.

So Neal had started to pursue another avenue. Using his new role as part of the White House Science Advisory Team, he had parlayed access to several super-telescopes in Hawaii, the Philippines, Chile, and Australia. Using the combined imagery from all of them he began to set up a triangulated image of anything that was nothing. Armed with the knowledge that the satellites were cloaked beyond any capability we had to actively track them, he had instead used that fact against them and tracked pieces of near space that were blank, seeking moving patches where stars momentarily vanished, or, disconcertingly, seemed to shimmer, even if only for a fraction of a second. Taken in isolation these instances would provide little or no solid information, but taken as a whole they began to show paths in the sky. They were certainly very slippery, but once consecutive hits on each satellite started to come, he was able to plot an initial track using this passive method.

Eventually he had mapped the exact orbits of each of the four craft, and all without using any active radar. But the complexity of the process had only improved his respect for the advanced team's abilities. They had not made it easy.

As Earth's rotation gives the equator a relative speed of about one thousand miles per hour west to east, it is far easier for us when launching a satellite to use that latent speed as a catapult, so that we only have to gain roughly five to ten thousand miles per hour more to reach the relative speeds needed to enter low to mid-earth orbit. To go the other way would be like paddling upstream: you would have to work that much harder just to lose the momentum you already had from launching from Earth's moving surface.

But an object arriving from somewhere other than Earth did not have to worry about accelerating into orbit, only decelerating. Unaffected by the earth's natural spin, they had used this freedom and designed their satellites' approach vectors to make the orbits retrograde: going against the earth's spin.

It meant that no spot was ever far from their view, Earth revolving beneath them as they circled it in the other direction. Orbiting just above the Hubble telescope and Iridium satellites in low-earth orbit, the AI satellites moved at just over fifteen thousand miles per hour, using the additional rotational speed of Earth below them to allow a rapid, virtually constant vigil over the bulk of humanity. Each satellite passed the same point on the planet below every three hours, and that same point was also passed over three other times by the three other satellites during that time.

And so the increased relative speed of the satellites made it both harder to track them and harder to escape them. No matter where you were on Earth, every forty minutes a satellite soared overhead, unseen, its eyes upon you, its weapons ready. Only at the poles were you relatively safe, but still the satellites' orbital distance allowed them a constant, if oblique view of all but the most remote parts of each pole, and they could, Hunt had warned, adjust their orbits to some degree, should they need to follow some unfortunate soul into colder reaches.

After reconciling this and compiling some semblance of a tracking algorithm, Neal had set up one of the online computers in his office to continuously gather a sea of seemingly inconsequential data from each of the facilities he now had access to. The online computer did nothing with the data, remaining impartial should it be scanned by the probing virtual eyes of the satellites many viral systems. But it did store the data on a drive that was also accessible, via a hard-wired, passive link, to one of his bank of offline computers. This secure PC then culled the information it actually needed from the sea of decoy data and parsed it through the algorithm Neal had designed. It was a long and convoluted process, and one that would no doubt need many tweaks and adjustments before it was capable of providing tracking data of targeting quality, but already it had given them a real insight into the movements of their quarry.

Colonel Milton and his small but elite team at Hanscom had then been able to use this information to extrapolate various options for destroying the orbiting threat. Given the information provided so far by John Hunt, a brute force attack using ICBM nuclear missiles would no doubt work, but it would be very difficult to gain access to nuclear weapons, and there was always the huge risk that launching them may facilitate World War Three, thus replacing one extinction scenario with another. Clearly nuclear weapons were, at best, a last resort. But they had some other options; quite a few, in fact. The large selection of long-range ballistic missiles in NATO's arsenal included many that were non-nuclear, but which were designed to traverse the globe like their radioactive cousins, their chemical engines carrying them to some predetermined point in low orbit then cutting out and relying on gravity to bring the warheads crashing back down to earth. It was this ability to travel long distances outside the atmosphere that made them a strong potential option for attacking a target in space.

The information that Neal had supplied to the team at Hanscom had also given them a totally new set of options outside of extra-orbital ballistics. While the satellites' retrograde orbits made them very hard to track, and harder still to run away from, this same fact could be used to the group's advantage when trying to destroy them. If they could get something big enough, and explosive enough, into their paths, the satellites might do the work for them, rushing headlong into whatever trap the group was able to set.

It was a possibility, and one which depended on several assumptions they had made using the excellent but still limited information John Hunt had given them to date. Not least of these assumptions centered around the defensive capabilities of the satellites, and their ability to maneuver around the munitions being thrown up into their path.

Those assumptions, among other things, would be confirmed, or denied, tonight.

A week ago Neal had received another letter from his enigmatic contact within the alien conspiracy. The letter had said that, for the first time since the brief visit to Madeline and Neal's hotel room a few months beforehand, John Hunt was going to be able to return to the

States. In the letter, the double agent had expressed the need for Neal and Madeline to discreetly get to a specific small airfield in Virginia. They would meet in a hangar at that airfield, at a set time and date laid out in the letter.

Using two different classified ads, one in the *New York Times* and one in the *Enquirer*, both of which Neal arranged from separate pay phones, Neal used the code words Ayala had given the team to instruct them all to meet. He used the codeword for an all-hands meeting request, and another that referred to a predefined covered car park in DC. He then added a phone number, which, translated per Ayala's instructions, would tell them the date and time for the meeting. Finally he added ONO, which Ayala had asked that they use just to say if all was well. She would come loaded for bear either way, as she did to any meeting, but it was wise to let folks know that this was not some dire situation. It was best to minimize any additional stress on their, some might say, slightly fraught psyches.

It was time, thought Neal, as he glanced at the system clock on his screen.

Standing, he went to the empty clothes rack near the door and removed the clothes he was wearing down to his T-shirt, underwear, and socks. He then donned jeans, a sweater, and sneakers from the full red rack to his right.

Stepping to the basement identity chest, he pulled his own credit card and ID from his wallet and left them in the drawer, just in case, and replaced them with his English alias's driver's license and Visa card.

A wad of cash from the drawer in his pocket, a pair of thick, plastic-framed glasses he had bought recently, Orioles cap, moustache, a chuckle at his appearance in the mirror, and moments later Mark Jones was stepping out of the basement entrance, his jacket collar up, his cap pulled down, and setting off down the street at a brisk walk.

He would take a taxi to the local U-Haul and rent a moving van under his pseudonym. Then he would meet his friends at the specified car park, and drive them all to the meeting with John.

- - -

Sitting in the rental van in the parking lot of a nearby mall, Neal considered his new life, and how quickly he had become inured to the constant threat he now found himself under. While in disguise, he had to constantly be on guard. If he glanced upward when outside, or took off his cap, or his face was caught square on by a security camera or the like, it was very possible he would die … unpleasantly.

The concept was profoundly disconcerting. Neal felt he had some small idea of how people felt in war zones, or in London during the blitz, or Sarajevo under siege. Somehow, he was not sure how, you just got used to it. Death might well come at any second. So why waste a moment worrying about it? Sure, whiskey and cigarettes had helped. After all, the need for healthy living seemed somewhat less important when you knew all the things that Neal now knew. In truth, he had really wanted to buy some weed as well, but the risk of getting arrested either in disguise, or as a White House advisor, was simply too great.

So here he sat in a rented U-Haul van, the window ajar, the engine off, smoking a cigarette for want of something stronger. He had parked deliberately in front of the small parking lot security camera, using the van's bulk to block the camera's view of his colleagues as they arrived.

Ayala was the first to turn up. She surprised him by quietly coming down the driver's side of the van, approaching from the back.

As she stepped up to the window stealthily, her hand lashed out and whipped the cigarette out of his hand.

Neal, focused on the door to the mall across the parking lot, spun around in shock. "Shit! Ayala, you scared the living crap out of me." He breathed a sigh of relief and laughed.

"These are very bad for you," she said self-righteously in her sultry Mediterranean accent, then she took a long drag of the cigarette and flicked it away. He smiled, opened his door, and stepped out. As he did so, she glanced up at the camera on the pillar next to the van, noting how Neal had planted the big rental right in front of it. She smiled.

"Nice work," she said, returning his hug. The hug was strong and genuine. Sharing deadly secrets and living with the threat of annihilation made for strong friendships, and over the last few months the four of them had started to think of each other as family.

"Am I the first to arrive?" she asked, and he nodded. "Well, let's get back in the van and you can tell me why you've summoned us all." They both climbed back in, Ayala sliding over into the passenger seat.

"You'll have to excuse the lack of chairs," he shrugged, indicating the open flatbed behind them.

"Not at all," she said thoughtfully, and then smiled, "there are two very comfortable chairs I can see, so you and I will be just fine."

He chuckled. Then, just as Neal was starting to explain why he had called the meeting, another car approached, this one clearly a government van, black with darkened windows.

Ayala went quiet, tensing almost imperceptibly, catlike.

When the car pulled up alongside, they saw Barrett's unflinching visage through the driver's window, but two men they did not recognize were in the car with him. After the three had shuffled into the back of the van leaving the locked government SUV to wait for their return, Barrett made brief introductions. They all greeted each other somewhat reservedly, and then an awkward silence fell while they waited for the final member of the team. Fifteen minutes later, Madeline walked out of the mall elevator dressed like a college undergrad. They did not even recognize her till she approached the van and took off her huge sunglasses. It was disturbing how effectively she had disguised herself, not least of which to Neal, because of how much he had been admiring her figure as she walked up.

- - -

It was a three-hour drive to the airfield. The group was hesitant to talk at first because of the two new men the colonel had brought along. But soon their trust for Barrett's judgment, and the obvious fact that the men already knew a lot of key information, allowed the group to relax their guards a little.

By the time they approached the small private airfield, they had all gotten to know each other fairly well, but the anticipation of meeting the mysterious John Hunt silenced the group once again as Neal pulled up to the main gate.

"Hi," he said to the attendant there, producing one of his fake driver's licenses from his pocket, "my name is Mark Jones, I'm meeting a friend here."

"Yes, Mr. Jones, I have you on the list." the guard nodded, after checking a handwritten sheet on his clipboard. He walked to the single gate and raised its red and white bar, allowing them through. Neal shouted a thanks to the guard, his friends remaining out of sight in the back of the van.

Neal drove across the small and antiquated airfield, dotted with small two- and four-seater propeller planes in various states of upkeep. It was a strange sarcasm of circumstance that while owning a plane would appear to be the pastime of the rich and the famous, the truth was that the wealthy owned private jets, and those far more often flew out of larger airports. So despite the alluring moniker, 'private' airports were usually fairly relaxed affairs. These airfields weren't for people who wanted to own planes as status symbols; they were for the people that wanted to pilot them. Many of the small planes here were owned by two or three people in a kind of timeshare, and they were all owner maintained, owner piloted, and all loved like the proverbial Harley or well-used sailboat. Amongst these labors of love, Neal drove the team over to the two slightly dilapidated hangars that lined the far end of the airstrip.

As they approached, Neal saw that the first hangar contained two men working on an old four-seat Cessna, so he drove on to the next. The fact that the two small planes inside it were covered by tarpaulins told them that the roof probably leaked, which pretty much defeated the point of a hangar, but at least it reduced the ravages of the sun on the paint on the planes' wide wings. Most important for the team was that it was bereft of people, and as it was already 8pm it was unlikely any would arrive anytime soon.

They sat in silence for a few minutes. They were a little early. Then Neal thought of something.

"I brought some snacks, a flip chart, and a few reference binders for the meeting." The group brightened at the thought of a distraction. "Shall we get set up?"

They all nodded and Neal got out and opened the big doors in the back of the van allowing his five groaning fellow conspirators to tumble from its confines and stretch their aching limbs. They were wary, unsure of what to expect from the coming meeting. Only he and Madeline had actually met John Hunt before and they had so many questions, so many preconceptions. Neal smiled, knowing that they could not be prepared for what they were about to see. This was going to be interesting.

Chapter 34: Rough Hewn

It was starting to get dark. The day was at that strange point where the ground is darker than the sky, as if in anticipation of the coming night. The airfield was quiet, as was the group, who were all staring off toward a point in the evening sky. Off in the distance the twilight was punctured by two small lights, wobbling slightly as the small plane they were attached to adjusted its approach.

Ayala had reminded the expectant group that they should all remain under the roof's proxy shelter, keeping their presence safely hidden under the cover of the hangar's old corrugated iron sheeting. So they all stood behind this invisible but nonetheless tangible line, facing the approaching plane. They could see it clearly now, its wings were mounted above the cockpit, typical of smaller models, and it was clearly a civilian plane.

The small plane swooped down the runway in a textbook landing, its precision giving some clue to the abilities of its pilot. In truth, until that day, John had never flown a plane, but personal experience was hardly the measure of him or his peers. At the end of the runway, the plane turned sharply and began to taxi back to where the group stood in anticipation. Any doubt they had of whether this was their contact was assuaged when it came to a halt in front of them, its right wing stopping just under the roof of the hangar, over their heads.

Everyone but Neal and Madeline literally held their breath as the small door of the four-seater opened. With the engine still cooling and hissing after the long flight, John Hunt leapt expertly through the small door and landed, standing under the plane's wing for a moment. Then he walked, staying under the wing, into the hangar, without ever stepping into the view of the satellite eye he knew was even now scanning the earth from above.

Once under the shelter of the hangar roof, he went up to Neal first, reaching out his hand. "Neal, how are you?" he said, shaking the now White House science advisor's hand firmly. To everyone's surprise, he then turned to Madeline and gave her a big hug.

With the rest of the group exchanging confused glances, he turned to Barrett, "You must be Colonel Milton." he said, "It is a pleasure to finally meet you."

The colonel's confusion was clear as he shook the Agent's hand, unclear of the protocol when talking to a machine, a fact he had to keep reminding himself now he was face to face with the handsome, charming, and seemingly very human John Hunt. Ayala was just as baffled by the young-looking man, but also quite fascinated.

For his part, John smiled at the confusion of his hosts. They had clearly been expecting some fake human, some inherently flawed imitation of themselves. Maybe even some burly weightlifter with a heavy Austrian accent and fake tan. To think that the young, attractive, engaging man in front of them was a machine must indeed be very disconcerting.

No, the stares of the group were not lost on John, but he chose to relish it, taking no small amount of encouragement from Neal's obvious amusement at it all. Yes, thought John, you should learn to deal with it. Because if you think this is strange, my friends, you should try waking up one day in an alien body, feeling every bit like the person you had always been, but now having these strange hands, flexing your legs and having the knees bend unnaturally forward. If you knew how disconcerting that was you wouldn't complain at having to just meet a humanoid robot for the first time, John thought. He'd had to deal with *being* a robot.

But the strangest thing had been meeting himself, the real him, the Mobiliei who had volunteered to have his personality inserted into this machine to govern it. They had exchanged a few code words. The real John Hunt had needed to check that this copy of his personality retained the secret purpose it had been put there to serve. It had been the strangest of days for both of them.

Of course there were perks. There are few people, either Mobiliei or human, who would not enjoy the power the machine body gave the Agents. Never hungry, never tired, never struggling to recall a memory. The weapons, the speed, the sheer unadulterated power. It was a heady feeling right up to the moment you remembered the genocidal purpose behind all those abilities, and the danger of your mission, not only to your quarry, but, in John's case, to everyone he knew and loved, were he to be discovered.

Setting the thought aside John turned to the three remaining members of the group, "While the colonel had been mentioned by Neal and Madeline when last we met, I am afraid I do not know the three of you at all, which, no doubt, is a very good thing." John said, inducing frowns on the group's faces.

But Neal nodded and smiled at John, explaining it to the group as he ushered them all farther into the hangar, "If John here doesn't know who you are it means you have not been flagged as being associated with Madeline and me. Trust me when I say that is definitely a *very good thing*." They all nodded appreciatively and Neal continued, "John, let me introduce our three new friends.

"Ayala here has been with us since soon after you first approached Madeline and me. I hope she will not mind me saying she is uniquely qualified in the art of both discovering and keeping secrets. I think it is safe to say she is a very big part of why Madeline and I are still alive."

Ayala was not bashful and nor did she feign modesty. She smiled and shook John's hand, her eyes clearly assessing the man even as she gripped his hand with somewhat excessive firmness. He smiled in return, unfazed by her scrutiny or her applying her considerable strength to his hand.

"To her left is Dr. Martin Sobleski, a projectile engineer who has spent the last two months working with Colonel Milton on long-range missile options to take out your friends above us."

Several of the group inadvertently glanced skyward at the rusted roof while Martin and John nodded at each other and the scientist gingerly shook the Agent's proffered hand.

"And, last but not least, we have Captain Jack Toranssen, of the US Air Force. The captain served under Colonel Milton for several years at the beginning of his career, but now he is a B-2 Mission Commander. He is normally based out of the Whiteman Air Force Base in Missouri, but he is on loan to the Hanscom right now, at the request of Colonel Milton, of course." John Hunt nodded, and the captain stepped up to face the Agent, displaying the same lack of reticence as Ayala had moments before.

He stared straight into the eyes of the young-looking Agent and said firmly, "Good evening, Mr. Hunt." the lack of rank was notable, if only to John and the Colonel, "I think I'll go ahead and say something I assume the others are all thinking. The colonel has shown me a lot of frankly circumstantial evidence of this conspiracy. Persuasive evidence, certainly, especially considering the man it was coming from, but now that I'm here … I think it's reasonable to say I want to see something more … concrete."

The captain spoke without spite, but with enough force and bluntness to make the words a form of threat, and Neal and Madeline flinched a little. Knowing some small measure of the Agent's abilities, they knew that facing off against the machine was nothing short of suicide. Of course, neither of them thought for a moment that John would actually hurt the captain, it was just disconcerting to see a proverbial Jack Russell barking at a Rottweiler, no matter how well restrained that Rottweiler might be.

The British officer stood firm, meeting Jack's inquisitive gaze head on, and Neal half expected the Agent's vicious left eye to metamorphose again. Because of that, Neal found he couldn't help but stare at that orb, his morbid fascination taking over.

But instead, John smiled, then shrugged, apparently deciding that the captain would respond to something rather different than the display he had given Neal and Madeline.

"If you'll excuse me a moment. Maybe this will help." said the Agent.

He walked over to one of the old planes in the hangar, crouched under it, positioning his feet under the fuselage as best he could. He then grasped one of the reinforced arms that went from the bottom of the plane to about halfway along the wing, and placed his other hand under the plane's fuselage. Without strain or much in the way of obvious effort, he then lifted the plane from underneath, raising it entirely over his head in one smooth movement.

They all stared. He smiled, and a moment passed while he looked at each of them in turn to see if there were any other takers.

"In fairness, that was a very reasonable question, Captain Toranssen," said the Agent, gently placing the plane back on the floor of the hangar, "and I am glad you asked it. It gets any doubts you might have out of the way."

He walked back to the group, seemed to reconsider something, and then with a sidelong glance at Neal, he said to Martin Sobleski, "I know Neal wants to see this again, and maybe this will interest you too, Doctor." and without further ceremony, his left eye slid down, exposing his weapons system. The doctor's head jerked away instinctively, then the scientist in him reacted and he peered closer.

Neal came to stand next to Martin and they both stared at John's transformed eye socket for a moment, "Awesome, isn't it?" said Neal and Martin nodded, equally agog. John smiled at the two, then Neal gathered himself, remembered that there were other people present and said, "Yes. Thank you, John. Someday we'll have to have another demo of what it can do. But for now, if everyone is … comfortable with John's credentials, we have a lot to cover and not much time."

Neal looked around the room getting nods from everyone, most of them still astonished by the nonchalant hefting of a plane into the air like so many sacks of potatoes. Neal merely smiled as he looked at each of them in turn, until his eyes returned to rest on John, who also nodded.

"Yes," said the Agent, "If I may, I would like to get an update from each of you on how things are moving along, and maybe I can go over any plans, schematics, or theories you are ready to discuss as well. Then I have some important updates I need to give you while we have time." He looked around the group, "Well, who would like to start?"

The colonel spoke up. "I have been watching you, you know." They all turned to Barrett. "Not overtly, I've never run a search on your name, or anything obvious like that, but I had my office start to monitor your ship, under the very reasonable auspices of it being one of the new Type 47 Destroyers which we are also looking to develop here in the US as well. I must say your name does seem to come up a lot in the ship's bulletins, Lieutenant First Class Hunt."

Barrett emphasized the new title John had acquired in his short but storied time on the ship, and carried on, "But that is not the point of my speaking up. If my information is correct, the HMS *Dauntless* is currently docked in Hawaii, so I have to ask: how the hell did you get here?"

John nodded, "The Cessna is a surprisingly capable little plane, but no, it would not get me from Hawaii me to the mainland, let alone all the way here. No, Colonel, I was selected by my captain to attend a seminar in San Diego at your Naval Academy there. I then convinced my fellow Agents during one of our Councils that I needed to have a … liaison with a female to stop some rumors that have been spreading that I am either celibate or gay. And rumors of the like have indeed begun to spread aboard the *Dauntless*."

Some of the group flinched a little at the mental image of this, well, machine, sleeping with some unsuspecting lady. Ayala was not among the more squeamish in the group. It would be hard for a covert agent to describe the offhanded way with which one approaches such things as sex after a long time in the field. Because of this, Ayala was notably not one of the people in the group who had a problem with the fact the alien Agents were apparently fully functional in that department. In fact, it spoke of an alarming level of preparedness on their part.

Moving past any such conjecture on the part of his audience, John continued, "At this moment, there is a female officer who was also attending the conference in San Diego unconscious in the hotel room the navy provided me. When I return, I will report the same thing to my fellow Agents that I will tell my fellow officers aboard the HMS *Dauntless*: that I spent the weekend locked in my room with her, in flagrante, as it were."

Madeline was clearly dismayed at the thought of the unconscious woman waiting in the Agent's hotel room and glanced at Ayala, who feigned equal disdain of the Agent's tactics. But inside she was still noting the efficiency with which this man … this machine … had used his surroundings to his advantage. She noted this all with a mix of professional respect and equally professional detachment, her mind reflexively gathering information on the abilities of this ally, and what this told her about what she should expect from the other seven Agents that they were going to have to face.

But Madeline only saw that this man had done something her morals said was, at best, distasteful. To drug the poor girl was admittedly very effective though, and if she pressed the issue in her mind she knew she would have to acquiesce that this unknown woman's reputation was an unfortunate but more than acceptable price for getting John Hunt here to help them.

John quickly finished his explanation, mentioning the borrowing of an unaware fellow officer's Cessna from an airfield in southern California, an officer John knew was still in Hawaii, the brief fuel stop in Kansas, and then the flight here.

Formalities aside, they got down to business, ignoring the tensions that clearly pervaded the group. They did indeed have a lot to cover.

- - -

An hour later they were in the thick of their conversation. Enthusiasm, fascination, and the vital importance of their work kept them all focused. They had started at the beginning, discussing how to handle their single biggest threat: the satellites. First on the agenda was a review of the satellites' defenses in detail so they could decide how best to circumvent them. It would be difficult, expensive, and very unsubtle, but hypothetically the orbiting platforms could be brought down.

They had analyzed the various options in the US arsenal for hitting an extra-atmospheric object. They had discussed the country's large stockpile of Inter-Continental Ballistic Missiles (ICBMs) and Submarine Launched Ballistic Missiles (SLBMs). Armed with nuclear warheads of various lethality, ranging from devastating to earth-shattering, these devices all wrought appalling destructive power.

If they could penetrate the satellites' laser defenses to within the blast radii of one of these leviathan missiles, then John told them that there would be nothing that the satellites could do to stop them. A nuclear blast would destroy them; there was no question of that, the Mobiliei could no more build a machine capable of resisting a close proximity thermo-nuclear explosion than humanity could. Unfortunately, as they had already surmised, detonating multiple warheads in low-earth orbit would have devastating effects on the planet below too.

So Neal and Martin Sobleski had concluded that launching a volley of Ballistic Missiles at them was 'less than ideal.' This was where Martin's more advanced missile work came into play. Taking the floor, he started to work through their other options, such as they were.

He presented on the various satellite killer missiles, both experimental and in place, in the US, its allies, and even its enemies.

There were not many. It was not an easy task to shoot a fast moving target hundreds of miles away in space. So he turned to the GBMD system, or Ground Based Mid-course Defense system, the US's primary defense against a nuclear attack. It was a system designed to track incoming missiles' paths and intercept them using a battery of kinetic collision and high-power explosive devices.

Normally this system, which covers the whole contiguous US, wouldn't have the range needed to chase down a satellite, but the information Neal had managed to get on the satellites' orbits provided one small advantage: the AIs were moving so fast in their retrograde orbits that a missile did not need to chase them down. Hypothetically, the missiles just needed to get into their path and the satellites would come at them at the equivalent of about Mach 15.

Hypothetically.

Martin's theory had one huge flaw, though. Well, actually, it had many flaws, but the main one was that is was based on an assumption. An assumption only John could confirm or deny. Could the satellites maneuver quickly enough to avoid the missiles?

John Hunt did not let them wonder long. He smiled and said: "No, now they are in position they do not have the capacity to alter their orbits that quickly. It was a one-way trip for us all, they are all but stuck where they are."

Martin, Captain Toranssen, and Neal all sighed and shared smiles bordering on the triumphant. They might have something.

But the Colonel was far from ready to celebrate. There was much left to confirm and the discussion veered to how much of the defensive net's capability would need to be co-opted.

The answer was daunting. Even firing the majority of the system's munitions they would still only be able to take out two of the satellites, at best. With shielding they could boost their chances of success, but not the number of the AIs they could destroy using that tool alone.

So they moved on to ... other options. Discussion veered to Russia's Gorgon interceptors and Gazelle missiles. But there was no way of shielding them in advance, and anyway, there was the small issue of gaining access to a launch system built specifically to defend Moscow from the US.

As moods darkened once again John decided to offer them one more measure of hope, "Gentlemen, I have a partial solution: the *Dauntless*. Missile defense is, after all, what the Type 47 was designed for, both at long and short ranges. I'm sure the British government will object pretty strongly, but ..." he smiled sarcastically and the room smiled with him, briefly.

"The *Dauntless* carries over a hundred and fifty defensive missiles," John went on, "but specifically it has forty-six with exo-atmospheric range."

"The *Dauntless* has *that* many exo-atmospheric missiles?" said the colonel, whistling at the scale of the armament. Jesus, the British took the navy seriously. That ship was a veritable missile barge. But if what John had said about the amount of missiles they would need in order to take out the satellites was true, then even the massive arsenal aboard the *Dauntless* would not be enough. He went to speak but John was one step ahead of him.

"It is classified, but yes, the *Dauntless* has that many exo-atmospheric Ship Launched Anti-ballistic Missiles, or SLAMs" he smiled at the acronym, "Now, that is still not enough to get through the satellites' laser defenses unless all forty-six are shielded, a process that will be even harder aboard a ship than it will be at the GBMD sites, and one which I will need help with from outside."

He went on. The room listened and each person spoke up as other points came up. There were recaps of a sort but no one needed to point out the vast holes that still remained.

They bandied other options around: launching a battery of Nuclear Ballistic Missiles from Turkey or the Black Sea and hope that Russia does not retaliate; find a way to assume control of either the Royal Navy's second Type 47 Destroyer or one of the US's new Arliegh Burke class satellite killers, neither of which was even afloat yet.

They were stalling, everyone could see that. They clearly needed to do more research here and rather than let the meeting flounder on the seemingly impossible task of co-opting the Russian missile system the colonel moved the agenda on to other areas.

They each had a role on the team, a niche they filled, and leadership was the colonel's. He was a decision-maker, and for the next twenty minutes or so helped focus their attention on planning the next nine months of everyone's life. As he did so, it was clear to them all that those nine months were going to be the most challenging they had ever known, and yet still even a glimmer of true hope seemed almost too elusive to grasp.

- - -

As the meeting entered its final hour John's internal clock let him know how little time he had left for his long journey back to San Diego. He had one very important topic he had to discuss with the team, and it was time he got to it.

"If I could change gears for a moment, there is something I need to update you on while before I need to leave." They turned to John Hunt, "I hope you have been able to use the information I gave you on my seven colleagues around the world to track some of them down, and hopefully without incident."

The colonel confirmed his assumption, "To a degree, we have. I was able to find Lana Wilson here in the US via discreet means, and Jean-Paul Merard in France. Ayala has also managed to track down Raz Shellet in Israel via her remaining Mossad contacts. Unfortunately, the others have been harder to get accurate information on without arousing suspicion, but we know their names and rough assignments, all except one."

John nodded, "Except one." He said gravely, "Yes, one of us is not following the same path as the others, and is, perhaps not surprisingly, having a less … predictable time during his stay on Earth."

The colonel, Ayala, and Neal all knew who he meant, and they were a little worried where this was going.

"Shahim Al Khazar" continued John, "has been causing quite a stir in Pakistan. He has been a little too successful, perhaps. And because of this he has been forced to call more attention to himself than the Council would have preferred at this stage. I should tell you that it was him, and him alone, who assassinated the prime minister of Pakistan earlier in the year."

The room was stunned. The incident had rocked the world, and security had been vastly increased in the region because of it. But the freedom fighters had also been emboldened by the unexpected victory, leading them to ever more violent, if often futile, acts.

John did not pause while the news sunk in, "The attack was an attempt by a power-hungry cleric to get rid of the Agent, who he perceived as a potential rival. When Agent Shahim succeeded in the impossible scheme and managed to survive to return to the insurgents' base in the mountains, the cleric was forced to admit he had ordered the insane attack. He died ignominiously in the Waziristan Mountains the next day, but Shahim's star rose sharply with his success. The leaders of the Taliban and Al Qaeda have decided that such a capable fighter should be sent somewhere where his skills would be of greatest advantage."

John paused a moment and Ayala spoke up, "He is heading to Iraq?" she asked.

John shook his head and said, "That would be problematic, yes, but more for us than for you. No, actually it is much worse. The exact location of Shahim is difficult to say as he has had to leave his relay behind in Pakistan, but he is updating the satellites regularly using the laser built into his eye, and according to his most recent reports, he landed in New York a week ago."

Chapter 35: Nobility Overall

After he surprised everyone with his success in Pakistan, it had been decided that Shahim Al Khazar should be sent abroad. Partially because the powers that be wanted him causing damage in America, and partially because Pakistan was so up in arms over his actions that neither he nor anyone else could achieve very much for the foreseeable future.

As they rushed to prepare him for his new assignment, Shahim had shocked all of the teachers appointed to him with the speed with which he picked up the skills he would need. Of course, the truth was that Agent Shahim Al Khazar could easily speak any language on earth, and master any technique they chose to teach him in seconds, but he had to maintain a pretense of being human, and so slowed his uptake to a more believable pace. Being sent to America was an unfortunate detour, but delaying it with a feigned inability to learn English would only have postponed the inevitable, while also frustrating the very people Shahim was trying to impress.

He had arrived in New York as a stowaway on an Oil Tanker from Saudi Arabia after being smuggled across the border from Pakistan with a group of refugees.

Security was tight after the attack in Pakistan, and he had told his superiors that he would need to lay low and plan his next mission more carefully. At this particular moment, however, he was literally lying flat on the roof of a tenement building in Queens, staring at the sky. His weapons array was folded out of its niche in his left eye socket and he was using a low-power, focused beam from its laser to send a signal to the satellite ranging above. Though it was not high bandwidth, and had a slight delay to it, he would be able to participate fairly effectively in the Council meeting that was about to start.

<Welcome.>

The eight avatars stood in their circle. John Hunt had just made it back to the HMS *Dauntless* waiting in Hawaii after his supposed conference in San Diego. Despite Shahim's not being fully connected, his avatar appeared just like the others, but the limits of his connection would not allow a full range of expression to be expressed on the virtual Agent's face.

<The Agenda has been created, and supplemented by two items from Agents: first for discussion is the reassignment of Agent Shahim Al Khazar to America. We need to discuss strategies for getting him redeployed to Pakistan.>

Mikhail Kovalenko spoke first, "It seems pretty clear to me that he must either fail in America or be discovered in order to have him sent home. It also seems clear that failure may bring some unwelcome consequences, so instead we should look to engineer Shahim's discovery and subsequent escape to force his leaders to bring him home."

"I agree," said John Hunt, "surely Lana can easily arrange for his identity to be discovered. Have him arrange a low-level attack, and be caught on video. The image would make him a liability to their cause in America and force them to bring him home."

Lana spoke next in her usual haughty tone. "I have been considering this reassignment, and before we rush him back to Pakistan, it seems to me that we could take advantage of his being here while also helping his credibility and standing with his leaders back in the mountains of Pakistan. I propose to the Council that we have him take out some of the more capable officers in the US's leadership ranks. If he kills a few senior folks, then it ramps up the US's anti-terrorism work, which takes the focus off Pakistan for a while, softening it for attack when Shahim returns there in due course. Of course, it also helps with my own progress up the ranks here, especially if I end up being the one who identifies him."

Pei Leong-Lam asked, "What targets would you want Shahim to consider taking out?"

Before Lana could answer, the voice of Shahim interjected. Because of the machine speed the conference was being conducted at, compared to the slow speed of his laser communications, Shahim was only just now responding to the AI's original question.

"Fellow Agents, it is clear that I have the most … irregular assignment among us all. The process of promotion within a guerilla army is far from predictable, and this detour to America is a direct result of that lack of predictability. Maybe it is time to rethink our strategy here? If the Council approves, I could easily make some minor adjustments to my appearance and join the Pakistani army as a junior officer as you have all done in your respective countries. With my knowledge of the insurgency, I could quickly get promoted simply by helping the regular army defeat the remaining Al Qaeda forces."

The AI responded as soon as Shahim finished talking. <As we know from our initial analysis, the threat of the insurgency has lead the Pakistani government to institute a policy that no member of the military is allowed access to their nuclear deterrent for a minimum of fifteen years after joining the service. There are many other stipulations, but that time limit alone prohibits our achieving our goals in Pakistan before the Armada arrives.>

Most of the team decided to wait and allow Shahim the time he needed for his inevitably delayed response to come back. Most of them.

"Listen," Lana said, "this conversation is moot. Of course we are not going to reassign Agent Shahim now. Instead of simply looking at the downside, I wish to discuss what this might buy us. We have an opportunity here and I think we should use it. Shahim can do what I cannot: start to disrupt the defenses of one of our three greatest threats right now. With the US's responsiveness damaged, we can then focus more of our efforts on China and Russia. I, for one, am very afraid of the sheer scale of China's war machine. Can one Agent really disable such a leviathan alone?"

Pei's avatar looked at her. The Agent that was Lana Wilson was overlaid with the personality of none other than an emperor's daughter. The princess had lobbied hard for the position, and several of her competitors from within her nation's own populace had mysteriously disappeared during her campaign to secure the prestigious role. She sought glory and fame, and eventually she sought her father's throne, and having her personality selected as one of the eight was as glorious a first step as she could envision.

In short, she was a pretty serious bitch.

But the strict parameters of the Treaty of Conquest, which all the world leaders of Mobilius had signed, dictated that while she was on this mission, she was one of the eight. Equal among her fellow Agents. At home, Pei Leong-Lam represented three much smaller empires, whose combined influence amounted to far less than the power of Lana's mighty Balachai Dynasty, and Pei would have been no match for her, but here, the treaty Lana's own father had signed made them all equals. He smiled at his condescending but temporarily impotent fellow Agent. He need stomach no shit from her here.

"Thank you for your concern," said Pei, his avatar more than adequately delivering all of the thick sarcasm he had layered the words with, "but my assignment to the Hong Kong Intelligence Division puts me well on-track for promotion to Missile Command within our schedule. In a few years I will have access to significant proportions of the Chinese nuclear arsenal. It is, I believe, only in America and Russia that control of the nuclear arsenal is spread over all three branches of the military. Maybe I should be giving you some tips on how to handle your little country, Lana?"

John let them bicker. All the better. He assumed that Lana had some reservations about him as the only Agent nominated by the Nomadi clans. It was just her snobbery as a royal princess. Luckily though, she was just as patronizing to her other cohorts as she was to him and that suited John just fine.

It had been less than half a second of real-time since Shahim had last spoken, but the equivalent of nearly five minutes in the meeting of the machine-based minds when Shahim's signal returned to guide the response of his avatar once more.

"I know the safeguards that the Pakistanis have put in place to guard against infiltration, but if I were to help them to defeat the insurgents once and for all then I would be a national hero. Surely an exception might be made for me at that point and I may be promoted early?"

The group thought about this. John hoped they would agree with Shahim, if only because John himself thought the idea was inherently flawed. But unfortunately they were not idiots, and one by one their avatars started shaking their heads.

Raz Shellet spoke from Israel, "No, Shahim, that plan relies too much on chance. Your reputation amongst the rebels grows ever stronger. At this rate, you may even be able to take over the insurgency completely at some future date, at which point you would be able to command the suppression of Pakistan's nuclear capability yourself. Remember, Shahim, we do not need to get control over their weapons, only to stop them from being used in the coming war."

She stopped talking and the room waited once more, giving their low bandwidth colleague time to respond. Even Lana was silent this time, waiting for the room to turn, happy that it looked like she was going to get her way.

But impatience eventually got the better of her, "Have we decided then? Shahim will stay in the States." She looked around the room, bullying them into responding. But they ignored her as best they could and waited for Shahim's response. It was his assignment they were discussing and they would let him have the last say before they voted.

When Shahim's reply eventually came, they were lucky that they could not see the true emotion behind it. Shahim had lost his taste for helping the insurgents fight their war. He would comply with the decision of the Council as was his duty but he was wearing down. This was not what he had signed up for, and not what he had been trained for. He was a general, a hero, and a fierce patriot, and this job deserved none of those titles.

Reluctantly he replied, "Very well, I will continue to fight the insurgents' fight for them, but I have been told to select my targets from a list given to me by the grand clerics. I would appreciate the Council's input on which of these I should destroy first?"

Though they could not see his expression, Lana thought he sounded broken, malleable. Good, she disliked being spoken back to by the host of commoners and low-ranking nobles that made up the Council. Back on Mobilius none of them would have dared to speak back to her. So hearing Shahim's lack of fight was fine by her, it was just one less among them to resist her will.

John Hunt also felt that Shahim Al Khazar sounded defeated. Something had changed in him since the beginning of the mission. Long ago all of the eight had been privy to the Councils of War that preceded the launch of the Armada against Earth. During those sessions John Hunt had taken the opportunity to carefully study the people who would be his fellow Agents. The man that inhabited the body of Agent Shahim Al Khazar was a noble of the Empire of Hamprect, and a captain of their armadas. During their planning, he had proven to be thoughtful and incisive, and had appeared every inch the proud warrior: honorable, in his way, and fiercely loyal. Maybe the ugliness of his assignment had shaken the man that had been a lord. Interesting, thought John Hunt. He could only hope it would make the other Agent easier to kill once the time came.

Chapter 36: Suppression

Shinobu Matsuoka had been born of a powerful family and his father's company was already an important international conglomerate when Shinobu started working for the firm out of college. The pretense had been maintained that he was starting at the bottom of the firm and would have to work his way up, but no one had ever been under any misconceptions about his rightful place in the company, least of all Shinobu himself.

After a fast rise through the ranks, Shinobu had eventually become chief operating officer of Matsuoka Industries two years before his father's planned retirement as CEO and chairman. He had been the heir apparent in more ways than one, winning allies in the company's senior leadership through the weight of his presumptive claim to its throne coupled with an ambition and intelligence to rival his entrepreneurial father.

The ensuing fifteen years had witnessed the sad passing of the father, but they had also heralded in a surprisingly successful new king. Matsuoka Industries had become one of the top companies in several fields, from computing and chip manufacture to shipping and submarines. But while their diversity of portfolio had helped them weather the vagaries of the world marketplace, it had also stopped them from becoming a true leader in any given field. A commitment to quality and the fierce ambition of their president driving them to be persistently one of the best in all areas, but never *the* best. Until now.

He stood looking at the machine. It was actually here. He had been promised so much. The investment had been risky but relatively minimal: only $6 million. And the speed of development had been unparalleled. He had seen so many research projects come and go. All hope and glory at the beginning but the fuse usually fizzled before anything came of it. It was par for the course. But early on during this unusual effort, his project manager had reported that this was no façade: the theory had a depth and solidity that shocked the diligent man whose task it had been to oversee.

But then this particular project had been unusual right from the very start. The two mysterious ladies that had approached him not long ago had come not with an idea, but with a fully fledged plan. More than just fledgling, in fact, the designs they had shown him had been thoroughly fleshed out and, apparently already realized, the product of research they said was being conducted in secret by the US government. Well, they had never actually said it was the US government, but even though the dark one might have been European, the blue-eyed one was most certainly an American, and she was the one who actually knew how the system was supposed to work.

Fearful of the recriminations of an angry US military, he had willingly and faithfully observed the strict censures of the two ladies. No e-mail, no telephone. Handwritten letters only, or personal visits. And here he was. A letter from the project manager Shinobu had assigned to oversee the development of the device had stated simply: "We are ready for you. Please come as soon as possible."

He had rerouted the company's private jet and had it whisk him from his estate outside Kobe to the research plant in North Dakota, deep in America's Midwest. And now here he was. Staring almost lustily at the machine that promised to take his company to the next echelon.

The research lab was large. It was stereotypically oppressively white: white walls, white floor, white ceiling, with only some metal tables and several computers to add some limited color. Well, those and the big, ugly device that dominated the center of the big laboratory. Several things leapt out at the initial observer. Firstly, that the machine had a clearly spherical core, about one meter across. Next that the core was heavily ordained with various clamps and protrusions, none of which seemed to follow a particular pattern, but which were all hitched by various cables to a series of computers and transformers, all humming away with inconspicuous energy. But by far the most notable feature of the big, strange-looking machine was that the sphere at its center seemed to be made of solid, gleaming gold. Shinobu stood staring at it. His project manager, Ito Hanso, stood just behind him, wringing his hands and glancing at the lab's hermetically sealed double doors.

For a while Shinobu just stood there, transfixed by the golden center of this extraordinary machine. The design schematics that he had been shown not three months ago had detailed what that central sphere must be made of, and why. But that had left him no more prepared for the sight of that smooth, shimmering gold shining back at him. After a moment's contemplation of what the golden sphere was going to give him, he gathered himself, composed his voice back into the commanding tone he had been born to utter, and spoke to the project manager.

"Well, Hanso-san? Start the machine, please. Show me what it is that has made you request my visit," said Shinobu. His composure was impressively resolute, like a man of his stature should be, but the project manager seemed agitated.

Bowing several more times than was strictly necessary, Ito Hanso stammered, "Yes sir. I will have the team show you immediately, sir. I assure you, you will not be disappointed, sir. It is ... well, there is just one ... minor ... consideration."

Consideration? The team? They were the only people in the room and Shinobu was becoming impatient. He had been there for several minutes and he was used to his people being prepared for his arrival. He interrupted the junior man's explanation, as was his right, and made his displeasure known. "Mr. Hanso, I have come a long way. Where is the team? Why are you not ready?"

Ito Hanso shook visibly with concern. He had been under strict instructions to tell the president if there was progress on the project. He had also been under equally strict orders not to discuss the details of the project over the phone or via e-mail in any way, but merely to send a letter to the president telling him if there was anything that required his attention.

That all seemed reasonable. He had previously been working on a sonar jamming device for the submarine division of Matsuoka Industries so he was used to secrecy, even if this was a little more stringent than most. What he was not used to was working with someone who did not seem to be as beholden to the company's president as Ito Hanso was. The truth was that he had been utterly unprepared for the Western woman's refusal to update Mr. Matsuoka herself, and very uncomfortable at having to go behind her back to get the president to come and see their progress.

And now here he stood, stuck between his professional obligation to his superior, something his culture took very seriously, and the upstart American woman who had so boldly driven the project to its current state, its current *very successful* state. He was obligated to tell his superior that the prototype was complete, but that did not mean that he also had to confess his duplicity to the fearsome American woman. So he had decided it was best not to anger her, even if only to save his own hide from her considerable wrath.

It had seemed like the best solution when he had come up with it. But now he stood facing Mr. Matsuoka, unable to operate the machine without Madeline's assistance, and to make things worse he knew that Madeline would be arriving any moment, like she always did. A quivering in his gut told him that this was not going to be pretty.

"Mr. Matsuoka, if I may," said Ito meekly, "while the team has been working very hard to build the machine to the specifications given to us by Madeline-san, she has also been careful not to reveal all the details of its operation to us."

Shinobu whirled to face the man, staring at him, "You mean I have invested $6 million dollars in a machine that not one of my employees knows how to use? This is unacceptable, Mr. Hanso. Completely unaccep ..."

Matsuoka stopped as Ito Hanso turned suddenly to the laboratory's door. He had been alerted by a faint beeping. Someone was using the keypad outside to type in the entry code.

Oh dear.

The door swung open and in wafted Madeline, all focus and purpose, her excitement at the experiments to come leading her to thoroughly ignore the two men as she headed for one of the tables to deposit her jacket, hat, and gloves. October in North Dakota was very different from the balmy weather she had enjoyed as a child in Florida, and she had been forced to bulk up her insulation accordingly. Glancing up, she took in the project manager standing looking concerned but did not really register the president of the firm standing over by the machine.

"Ah, Ito, good. You're here. Let's get started, shall we?"

She was already powering up her computer when Ito finally drummed up enough confidence to talk. He was being made all the more nervous by the clear indignation the president was showing. The important man was not used to being ignored.

"Umm, Madeline-san, we have an honored visitor." said Hanso quietly, stuttering slightly as he did so.

Madeline turned her head and saw the president, pausing a moment to let his presence sink in. Seeming unperturbed, she then turned her whole body to face him and composed herself. An ingratiating smile spread across her lips. "Ah, Mr. Matsuoka. How wonderful to see you. To what do we owe the pleasure?" she walked over to him and extended her hand. He begrudgingly shook hers in return.

Speaking with the force of his position as chairman and CEO, Shinobu Matsuoka said, "Hanso-san informed me that the prototype was complete. I have come to inspect your work."

"Oh, he did, did he?" she gave Ito a sideways glance, her smile faltering for a moment but still staying valiantly upon her cherubim face. She would deal with that little pen-pusher later. For now she had to deal with this one in front of her. "Well, we are honored to have you here. Please, Mr. Matsuoka, come. Take a seat, and we can discuss the project's progress." She was about to continue when Shinobu interrupted her.

"Ms. Cavanagh, Hanso-san has told me that the prototype is fully functional. Before we discuss anything I would like to see a demonstration, please." The president stood firm.

"Of course, Matsuoka-san. If you will just take a seat I will initiate the system. It is just a prototype, you understand, but I think we can show you some very strong progress." As Ito Hanso brought a chair for his superior, Madeline went to one of the computers on the other side of the room and logged in.

Calling over from the far side of the lab, she said, "I'll just be a minute, gentlemen, I am just … initiating the system. We should be ready to go in about an hour. Ito, maybe you can offer our guest some refreshments?" Hearing Ito quickly respond and take some cursory requests from the uppity Mr. Matsuoka, Madeline quickly pulled up the web browser on one of the lab's few PCs that was hooked up to the internet and logged into an anonymous gmail account she had set up after arriving in North Dakota. Ayala and Madeline's plan had accounted for eventually having to deal with the president of the company and Ayala had told Madeline to let the other woman know if the president was asking questions. They hadn't exactly accounted for him turning up unannounced like this, but nonetheless Ayala had asked to be informed and Madeline would take any assistance Ayala might be able to provide. Suppressing a surge of anger at Ito Hanso, she selected Ayala's equally anonymous e-mail address, selected 'new message' and then typed simply: 'have an old friend over today. looking forward to seeing you soon.'

With that innocuous sounding proverbial distress flare sent up she closed the browser and turned to one of the labs offline PCs to start the procedure of switching on the mysterious device in the center of the room. She would take her time as she did not want to get through with this any faster than she had to, but clearly Ito had told the man that the big unwieldy looking machine had worked. And almost on the first test. Of course, he couldn't know that she had been just as surprised as he was when it had.

- - -

'looking forward to seeing him. landing at 4pm.'

That was all Ayala's reply read and it was all Madeline needed. Ayala had seen the message and gotten on the next flight from wherever she was to Minneapolis, which was a two-hour drive from the facility. Somewhat luckily for Madeline, Ayala didn't really mean she was landing at 4pm, she meant she would be arriving here at the Matsuoka plant at 4pm.

Unfortunately, she could not delay the demo till Ayala arrived, especially as her team already knew the machine worked. If it had been just her and the president she could fake a system failure, but while she had been able to keep the team in the dark about the full workings of the machine, she was not really that knowledgeable herself either. Rather than risk doing anything that might damage the machine or tip her hand to the rest of the team, she would have to give the CEO a demo. Well, part of one.

Like the machine's original inventors back on Mobilius, her team had also not realized the full potential for the machine when it had first been invented. But John had told her what it would truly be able to do and now that she had seen it in action she could not help but believe him.

So despite her reluctance, it was with genuine excitement that she prepared the machine. An excitement that was clearly visible on her face when she announced that they were ready a little over two hours later. She came to stand in front of the president and smiled. The rest of the five-person team was there by now, busying themselves with the various measuring and tracking devices that they had set up around the big machine in the room's center like orbiting satellites around a robotic sun.

She stood there smiling for a moment, she might as well enjoy it, and then turned to an extremely clean-looking man standing in a stereotypical white jacket to her right and asked him to open the sphere. The technician bowed, turned on his heels, and walked over to join three other similarly dressed men standing around the large machine behind her.

Standing between the CEO and the machine, Madeline faced her lone audience member and cleared her throat a little before saying, "Allow me to welcome you formally, Mr. Matsuoka, and thank you for your patience. You have been most gracious.

"Now that we are ready to begin I will talk you through the process you are about to see. Please feel free to stop me if you have any questions and I will answer them to the best of my ability. But for now I will explain what the technicians are doing and then we will begin.

"First the technicians will introduce several raw materials to the machine. These are the basic building blocks of a typical microchip. Notably among them we have this solid piece of material." With that she produced what appeared to be a small blackish-green coin from her pocket, holding it up between her finger and thumb. It was a tiny piece of silicon half the size of a penny.

"Matsuoka-san, please note that I am holding this silicon in my bare hands without wearing gloves. I am sure I do not need to tell you that doing this just before using a piece of silicon to make a chip using current chip manufacturing methods would most certainly introduce all kinds of foreign impurities to the microchip being built. Leading inevitably to disastrous results for the chip's efficacy. Because of this fact, Matsuoka Industries and all of her competitors observe strict precautions both before and during the manufacturing process. *Expensive* precautions."

The CEO looked stern as Madeline emphasized that last statement. Behind her, the technicians activated a control on the ugly machine and a seam around the equator of the golden sphere twisted and unlocked. Two of the techs then heaved the top half of the big dome open on the large steel hinge it was mounted on. As the meter-wide sphere cleft neatly in half along its equator, a perfectly polished hollow interior was revealed. Smooth gold shining brightly: the most expensive globe in the world.

Turning, Madeline walked over to the open orb and simply tossed the tiny piece of silicon into it with practiced nonchalance, raising Matsuoka's eyebrows at her indifference to the rigorous cleanliness and precision that was typically the hallmark of all microchip manufacture. For even a single speck of dust in the inner workings of a microchip would render it useless.

"My colleague here has the other key ingredients of a basic integrated circuit or microchip: planarized copper and our substrate." She pointed to two more pieces of material, one coppery, the other a tarnished green, that were clasped between tweezers in the hands of one of the white-coated technicians. She nodded to the man, smiling a little, and he placed them in the big sphere. When they had first tried this it had seemed so strange. Like adding a few grains of salt to a meter-wide paella dish, one grain at a time, or pouring a jug of water into an empty swimming pool. She looked down into the lower hemisphere of the open machine where the three pieces lay in its golden apex. How little we knew. She smiled and then glanced at Mr. Matsuoka.

Oh, my stern-looking Japanese friend, you look so doubtful. You have no idea what you are about to witness. In about five minutes your mind is going to be thoroughly blown.

She came back to stand in front of the president and smiled as she heard the three techs carefully closing the sphere again, the big machine sealing with a dull thud. Matsuoka was starting to look anxious, glancing every now and then at Ito Hanso standing at his shoulder. He wasn't sure whether he should really believe what he was witnessing. It had seemed plausible in theory, and the ladies had been more than adamant. But now, as he sat facing this monstrous machine with its gaping, hollow core, he found himself worrying if he had fallen pray to biggest prank in history.

Returning to their computers, the technicians activated the machine. After a moment's anticipatory silence, a bass hum could be felt around the room as the big machine came to life. More than one of the technicians looked from side-to-side, a little concerned, as this was still only the fifth time they had powered up the miraculous machine. Matsuoka did his best to remain impassive and Madeline smiled. She had done this several more times than the rest of the team, wanting to test the more elaborate applications of the machine when the others were at home or asleep. It took longer to set the machine up without assistance, but it could be done. She had done wonderful things with the beast. It was going to change the world, in more ways than one.

"Now," said Madeline suddenly, making several of them jump, "we cannot see anything inside the sphere as there is absolutely no light inside that block. But the devices attached to its outside, by the very virtue of the way they control what occurs inside, can show us what is happening to the objects inside as well. This information is shown to the machine's operators in a graphic representation which allows us to operate the machine, and for your edification we are going to show you the same view which they enjoy."

On a large LCD screen to one side of the big machine an image came to life. It was in full color, but something about the scene it displayed looked awry: though the image appeared to have texture, the coloring appeared to be two dimensional, like an old photo that has been retouched, or an image from an atomic microscope. The latter comparison was, perhaps, the most apropos, as the images were a magnified view of the three objects that had been had introduced to the sphere. But not seen using light. Instead they were being viewed using vibrations varying from the audio down to the gamma. These were sonar images.

Looking at the screen it appeared as though the objects were hovering in midair inside the sphere and this was, actually, exactly what was happening. They were being held there by the focused resonance being pumped into the sphere by the devices that radiated from its exterior, and as the tech adjusted the fields, they were able to flip the three objects over and move them around relative to each other.

As Matsuoka stared in silence at this parlor trick, Ito Hanso saw the childlike fascination creeping into the man's expression and a reflected smile spread to his own lips. He had been right to send for the president of the firm.

Madeline rolled her eyes at this sycophantism and carried on with her explanation. "OK," she said suddenly, making them jump once more, "for this next part of the demonstration, I would like to ask if you have a Matsuoka Industries cell phone, Mr. Matsuoka?" Shinobu Matsuoka looked at her confusedly and then nodded.

She then held out her hand and he stared at it a moment before realizing that she meant for him to give it to her. Disconcerted but keen to see where this all was going, he dipped his hand into his jacket pocket and withdrew a high-end but nonetheless fairly standard smartphone. Standard excepting that it was a platinum-plated version made especially for him. Madeline glanced at the extravagance a moment, then smiled and turned it over, glancing at the model number on the back.

"Domo Arigato." She bowed to the man. "With your permission I will return this at the end of the demonstration." She smiled. She was not used to being a showman, but it was easy to run a circus when you had an act like this.

"The image you see on the screen is, as I said, a representation of what is happening to the objects inside the sphere. Using super-low frequency waves, resonated and focused within the sphere, we have perfected a way to hold these objects in place at the very center of the sphere. The method does not work outside of a confined area like the ceramic and gold sphere you see here, and the area must be tightly sealed for the sonics to be accurate and effective. But once you have that sphere sealed ... well, let's just say you can do wonderful things." She smiled again, almost laughing with joy at it all.

"First, can you see the discolorations highlighted on the magnified objects? Those are impurities on their surfaces, left by my fingers and by the manufacturing process. The machine knows this because, while the low-frequency waves are holding the materials in place, another set of far more precise waves are probing them, from microwave all the way down through the gamma range. You see, all materials have a specific sonic signature, a way they vibrate under pressure that tells the machine what the contents of the sphere are made up of. Tells it right down to the molecular level.

"As I mentioned earlier, the impurities on the outside of these objects normally present a significant problem for Matsuoka Industries and other chip manufacturers, forcing you to maintain a stringently clean environment for chip production.

"Because the sphere can detect the sonic signature of any material, it can identify which materials are part of the specifications of a given chip design, and which are not. This, in itself, would be of no value, of course. Unless you can also do something about them. But detection is not the only application of this resonance technology."

Madeline turned to face the screen and said, in the most professional voice she could muster, "OK, gentlemen, remove the impurities, please."

On the screen, Matsuoka saw each object in turn begin to shed its coating of what Madeline had described as impurities. The discolorations simply flew away from the materials.

Shinobu Matsuoka was stunned. That was incredible.

You are impressed with that, thought Madeline. Ha! He thinks it is a cleaning device. Oh, if only I could get away with just that. But Matsuoka had been promised more, and Ito would tell the powerful man if she held anything back. Well, he would tell the president about the things he knew, anyway; she still had some very important secrets they could not possibly have guessed at yet.

"Now, if I may return your focus to the phone you so kindly lent to me," said Madeline, holding up the ostentatious but innocent flip-phone, "I see that this is one of your MVC-416Ns, slightly modified, of course. The flagship phone of the company, for its flagship chief officer." She smiled at the president who merely nodded curtly. Turning and stepping over to one of the computers, she said, "If you will excuse me a moment, this is one of the steps in the process that I am afraid my colleagues do not yet fully understand." She sat down at the machine, focusing on the computer screen. As her hands moved quickly over the mouse and keyboard, she carried on explaining what she was doing, speaking offhandedly the way parents do to nagging children, and teenagers do to nagging parents.

"What I am doing now, Matsuoka-san, what I am doing now is calling up the schematic for the main processor in the MVC-416N.

"We have loaded into the computer controlling the machine the designs of all of Matsuoka Industries' standard processor chips so that we can use them as test subjects." She typed and clicked furiously, taking the schematic and inputting it into the machine's control screen, assigning material types and build parameters.

After about five minutes studious dragging and clicking, she announced that she had the schematic locked in. The room became excited once more. Standing, she checked the screen one final time and then straightened, bringing her focus back to the man for whom her little circus was performing. "If you are ready, Matsuoka-san, we will initiate the design into the system and begin."

He remained still a moment, a slight quiver of his lip betraying his well-masked anticipation. But after a moment he managed a nod, trying to appear as nonchalant as possible. With that the technicians inputted the routine Madeline had created, instructing the machine to begin imposing the chip's design on the materials in the sphere. Suddenly the noise from the machine became markedly louder, shaking the room on a fundamental level. But as the noise grew, and the rest of the room began to sensibly shake, all of its occupants were transfixed by what was happening in the big screen. The three objects in the sphere seemed to freeze in midair, and then appeared to go soft, almost to liquefy. Their sides became viscous, vibrating infinitesimally like a cup of coffee resting on the bonnet of an idling car.

Matsuoka stared at the screen, trying to make out if he was seeing it correctly. After another moment the machine was satisfied that the substances in its grasp were at the correct malleability and it began. Without ceremony, the now gelatinous objects started to morph, tiny strands starting to lift from their surfaces like a wool sweater coming unraveled. Imagine a bucket of viscous liquid into which a complex wire structure has been submerged. Now imagine that wire being slowly exuded from the liquid and you have an image of what appeared to be happening on the screen.

It looked some complex construct was being pulled slowly out of each of the three objects, coated in viscidity like melted chocolate. But it wasn't something being pulled from the materials at all. The machine was shaking the very bonds that held the substances together, freeing them like an earthquake settling a desert, making their constituent molecules shake freely from each other. Violating and undermining their solidity.

Once the material bonds were deconstructed, the machine then used the same gamma tendrils to bend and twist the now malleable objects to its own end. The big machine was imposing its will on them via the focused force of the resonance being drummed into the dome. It was beyond imagining. In fact, the very concept was at the fringes of humanity's scientific understanding, and if it seemed incredible to the people in the room, that was a reasonable reaction. For unbeknownst to anyone but Madeline and her fellow conspirators, the magic they were witnessing on the screen was not of human origin. It was a gift from above. A gift of knowledge given so that we might build the tools of our salvation.

As the impossibly minute structures started to take shape, the machine began to move them into each other. Like pieces of a puzzle, the computers controlling the machine began to intertwine them, winding them into each other like a thousand minuscule metal snakes merging. The bounds of gravity negated by the resounding waves in the sphere, its impossibly precise pulsing fingers were able to manipulate the material in any way its programmers chose.

Within a few seconds the chip was taking shape. After five seconds it was done.

As the machine finished, it calmed the now melded block on the screen, allowing it to regain its solidity. Then the complete object dropped slowly off-screen and it was over. The screen went blank, the machine came to a stop, and the vibration slowly dissipated. The room was left unnaturally silent like a garden after the lawn mower has been silenced. The recipient of the whole demonstration sat mutely, his body still reverberating from the machine's bass thrum as his mind vibrated from the shock of what he had seen. It had been beautiful and fantastic to behold, and he sat mute.

After allowing him to mull for a moment, Madeline nodded to the technicians who proceeded to open the sphere once more and retrieve the chip from it, taking more care this time with the finished product. They brought it to her and she spoke as she held it aloft. "The chip we have just made is perfect in every way. Pure and accurate down to the molecular level." One of the technicians stood to her side opening the president's cell phone expertly with a small metal shim designed for just that job. In front of the still visibly stunned Shinobu, the tech used a set of tweezers to remove the phone's primary chip from its small motherboard and set it to one side, taking the new chip from the smiling Madeline.

"Identical and perfect, in every way." reiterated Madeline, "Only this new technique allows us to duplicate the circuit's specifications at a significantly smaller scale."

The technician finished slotting it in, reattached the phone's cover, and handed it to the president who pressed the power button and waited for it to switch on. When he saw that it had found a signal, he dialed a number on it. A moment later a ring could be heard and he smiled as the project manager scrambled to get his own phone from his pocket. As the phone rang the team started to applaud.

Shinobu Matsuoka laughed, bowed deeply, indicated for his technicians to do the same, and then stood and faced Madeline. "Thank you, Ms. Cavanagh. You have delivered all you promised and more. Matsuoka Industries is forever in your debt. Now, I have much to do, so if you will excuse me I will allow you to have your lab back. "

She nodded and returned his small bow, the technicians around her basking in the reflective glow of the president's obvious satisfaction. But before he could leave, Madeline stopped him.

"Um, Mr. Matsuoka, I am glad that we have been able to meet your expectations." said Madeline, searching for the right words. For her part, Madeline did not want to let the president out of her sight now that the man knew what the resonance manipulator could do.

"If I might," she went on, "I would like to discuss something with you, regarding the next delicate steps in the development process." She smiled innocently. He looked at her awry for a moment. But the sheer awesomeness of the display he had just witnessed gave her the benefit of any doubt he might have, and so he smiled accommodatingly. They walked out side-by-side, Madeline working hard to craft the beginnings of a long and involved explanation of why the president should wait just a day or two longer before making his plans to go public with the new technology.

Ayala would be there in four hours. Madeline hoped she would know how to handle the situation from there.

- - -

For the rest of the day, Shinobu Matsuoka mulled over the implications of the new technology. The obvious happiness of the president had given the project manager new found confidence. This, combined with his guilt at having gone behind Madeline's back, gave him a bolder voice than he would usually have been capable of, and for now that voice had joined Madeline in stressing to the president that the new manufacturing technique was far from ready for production. Shinobu had acquiesced but demanded a timeline for the machine to be ready. The debate had gone on like this for hours, Madeline eyeing her watch occasionally as she waited for her friend Ayala to arrive.

After a while, Matsuoka had tabled the timeline discussion, confident that he had his own plans for how to take the machine to the next level. They had spent the rest of the afternoon discussing the implications of the new device. The immediate difference the new technology would make was a dramatic reduction in the cost of manufacturing complex microchips. This would be achieved through reduced inaccuracies and thus reduced waste, and from no longer needing the expensively sterilized work environments that had been the trademark of chip manufacture for so long.

After the initial cost savings had been realized, it was hoped that chip designers would start to take advantage of the freedom the new technology gave them as well. The machine would allow the construction of truly three-dimensional chips, layers upon layers of semiconductor in relational, organic designs that would push the boundaries of integrated circuit design.

Once the device was released, Matsuoka's competitors would no doubt be quick to realize that this was an industry changing event, and frantically start to look for ways to duplicate the process. In due course, they would find information on the new process surprisingly easy to come by, as Ayala and Madeline had no desire to hand Matsuoka a monopoly. But it would take them all years before any of them realized the full potential of the new manufacturing technique, just as it had taken its Mobiliei inventors a decade to make the leap. The capabilities and potential applications of resonance manipulation were actually far more widespread than microchip manufacture, and it was along one of these branches of possibility that Ayala and Madeline now needed to take their new toy.

It had taken millions of dollars to develop the first working prototype of the resonance manipulator from the schematics John Hunt had given them, millions of dollars that Madeline and Ayala had not had. For this reason, it had been essential to engage a proxy that would provide them with the resources they needed. This, of course, had come at a price, and the team had been under no illusions that using an outside company to develop this crucial device had been a large potential gap in their security. But they had neither the money nor the materials to build such a machine. They had considered attempting to tap into the military's seemingly bottomless research funds, but while it was going to be difficult to manage a private company's curiosity, that was nothing compared to what it would have been like trying to restrain a general or admiral once he had seen what the resonance manipulator could do.

Nonetheless, the chance that the development of the machine by Matsuoka Industries would be discovered by the Agents or their guardian angels overhead had been a constant threat. Because of this, Ayala had enforced strict controls on Madeline while she was working at the Matsuoka plant in North Dakota in order to protect her identity while there. She had carefully mapped each of the security cameras within the facility itself, as well as at the nearby extended-stay hotel where Madeline had taken up residence.

Ayala had then shown Madeline ways to come and go from each building without her face being seen by any of the cameras. She had done the same for two restaurants nearby which Madeline was then cleared to eat at. It was a limited lifestyle and Madeline had never felt so constricted in her life, but she knew all too well the consequences should she stray from the path. The only place where she could move at ease was in the highly secure research lab at the facility. There were no cameras there, by design, the programs that were conducted in its confines being highly confidential.

Hours had passed since the demonstration, but eventually Ayala had arrived. It was 4:15pm before Madeline finally met with Ayala in a back room of the Matsuoka facility in North Dakota. Madeline excused herself briefly to talk with Ayala when the woman arrived at the building. It only took a few moments for Ayala to get up to speed and then the Israeli woman told Madeline what they were about to do. There had been no discussion, once Ayala had told Madeline what she must do she had opened the door and sent for the Matsuoka CEO to join them. As they waited for him, Madeline found she was even more worried now, having some small idea of what Ayala was willing to do to keep the emboldened CEO in line.

With haste and no small amount of bravado, the CEO brushed into the room, bowing to the two ladies. He was alone, and he was smiling, seemingly unfazed by the sudden appearance of the second of his two mysterious friends. It had been a good day for Shinobu Matsuoka and he was a very happy man, all the happier to see the two women who had made it all possible.

"Good afternoon, Ayala, it is most pleasing to see you again." said Shinobu, seating his smug little self down in the small room.

He was not used to being in such discreet confines, but for these two angels he felt he would do almost anything right now, almost. The two women across from him looked at each other, like conspiring sisters, and Madeline nodded almost imperceptibly at the older Israeli, who took the lead.

"Matsuoka-san, thank you for responding so quickly to our request for a meeting, we know how precious your time is." said Ayala, well practiced in the unwritten rules of polite dealings, no matter how covert they might be.

"A man would have to be a fool not to want to meet with two such ladies as yourselves, especially ones who have brought such good fortune." said Matsuoka, his English excellent, if accented. But, now that he saw the expression on the face of the darker lady, he realized he did not feel as convivial as he had thought.

Madeline had always seemed to be exactly what she said she was, a scientist from some entity, probably the US government, but that was not certain, who had decided that the technology she was working on was too important to be kept under lock and key. And now that he had seen it in action he had to agree. But her friend was not so easy to read. She was nice, and very polite, following all the Japanese rules of social engagement with surprising alacrity for a Westerner.

But under that he sensed, well, he sensed that there was something he couldn't quite sense. She was not easy to read like her partner and that unsettled Shinobu. And now, after he had surprised Madeline this morning with his visit, she had returned the favor with her own sudden appearance not six hours later.

His instincts told him that their deal was about to change. He didn't like change. He liked innovation, oh, he liked that very much. He liked it when his company stumbled on the most important new technology since the microwave, that kind of change was most welcome. But he didn't like it when the person who had given it to him wanted to change the nature of their agreement. No, that kind of change was very unsettling indeed. And he sensed already that this was the direction of this conversation. Bracing himself for a heated discussion, he readied himself to hear what they had to say, and to defend his contract if need be. They had as much to lose as him at this point.

"Maybe you can tell me what this is about?" Matsuoka asked, somewhat cagily.

"Of course, Matsuoka-san. We have asked you here today because we would like to negotiate a new contract with you." said Ayala like she was ordering a latte.

He withheld an ironic smile, his eyebrows rising only slightly as he placed his elbows on the table, his fingers interlocking slowly. He had been a man of considerable influence for many years, and he felt even more like a sovereign now that his company had in its possession a technology that would catapult it to the top of the computer industry, and probably many other industries as well. But as he thought of his position, he decided he was not too proud, nor too foolish, to know how much of his good fortune stemmed from these two ladies. Maybe they had something more for him, he tried to tell himself, though that seemed hard to imagine.

He decided he was willing to listen to their proposal, not that he would let that show, of course. He was not an amateur negotiator; he knew never to show the other party what power, if any, they had over you.

"Ladies, while I thank you for your help to date, we both know that this relationship was as beneficial to you as it was to me. And of course, you have been adamant that this is as much about your releasing the technology your current employers held hostage as it was about my firm making profits. We are still in the same position as we have always been. I see no need to renegotiate our agreement, nor will I entertain such a topic."

"You misunderstand me, Shinobu," the use of the senior man's first name was like a slap in the face in Japanese culture, made all the more powerful by Ayala's previously careful adherence to the cultural rules of his country. As he reeled from the snub, she continued, "we do not seek some retroactive change in compensation, your money is not important to us, though do not think for a second that you would not be forced to give us more compensation if we demanded it."

She smiled ingratiatingly, "But Matsuoka-san, we do not want to make this confrontational. We simply want to take our professional relationship to the next level."

He waited in silence. This was not how he had expected such a negotiation to go. She carried on, her voice lathered with irony and political grease, "You are a powerful man, Mr. Matsuoka, but soon Matsuoka Industries is going to grow exponentially more powerful, and you are going to become very rich, very fast. This is good, but it is not why we have given you this technology. Now that you have seen what resonance manipulation can do, we are sure you are going to start planning the next step in its deployment. No doubt you are already thinking of the plethora of ways it can be applied to your business to make you more profitable. And you will get the chance to pursue all those avenues, trust me. This machine will make you every bit as rich as you hope it will. In fact, once you know the full extent of its abilities, I think you will agree that even your substantial ambition will be more than satiated by what is to come."

She paused and he allowed himself a hesitant smile. She was giving him good news, wasn't she? Then why was he afraid? But the moment he opened his mouth to reply, she spoke again, leaning forward to look at him more intensely.

"But not yet, Shinobu. We need some more time. Not to develop the tool. We had hoped to string that out longer, but the efficiency of your project manager has put pay to that. You see, Matsuoka-san, you cannot have the machine yet." Ayala saw Shinobu move to speak again and pressed on, making sure she dominated the conversation. It was a delicate art, and though she had done this many times before, coercion was different with every person. She carried on, playing the man as she worked to slowly break him down. Choosing her moments. When to relent, when to hit home.

"Shinobu, we thank you for your support to date. But unfortunately we cannot have you running off half-cocked. In fact, soon you will see why a premature release of this technology can absolutely *not* be tolerated. Matsuoka-san, we think it is time you knew exactly what it is you have helped us develop."

Mr. Matsuoka sat motionless, stunned. He felt a wave of heat emanating from his core. A bead of sweat ran down his forehead, and he had an overwhelming desire to open windows that the small room did not have. He was starting to feel like he had signed away his soul to the devil. And apparently she was cashing in on the contract.

"You see, Shinobu, manufacturing chips is a very complex and detailed science, but it is child's play compared to what resonance manipulation is capable of. While your project manager ponders the implications of cheap, high-powered circuitry, we are going to be building something altogether more important, in secret. And you are going to leave us alone while we do it."

"I am?" managed the executive, tapping his considerable indignation as a source of bravery, "You forget yourself, young lady. You cannot make me, or my company, do anything."

But his heart was not behind his posturing, and Ayala knew it. He rose sharply, wanting to get out of the room and regroup. He needed to find out what this machine was really capable of. Was it some weapon? Had he unwittingly helped some terrorist organization build some kind of doomsday device? He shivered and turned to leave the room.

"Sit down, Shinobu." said Ayala quietly, but with an authority that welled up from her very core. He froze. He was angry, and maybe even a little afraid, and his emotions were starting to become overwhelming. For reasons that he could not quite explain, he turned back to her and saw that she had stood as well and they both faced each other, in silence, for a moment. It was a moment that passed like an age.

To the man's surprise, it was Madeline who eventually spoke up. As the Japanese businessman stood face to face with Ayala, Madeline had seen the moment Ayala had told her to look for, and so she began.

"I suggest you take a seat, Matsuoka-san. While I may be the harmless scientist you have been told I am, I am afraid my friend here is definitely no mathematician. Perhaps more importantly she is far from harmless either, by any stretch of the imagination."

The man looked at the Israeli woman as if for the first time. While she had seemed so pleasant in all their previous dealings, he suddenly saw the violence she kept caged inside her. Her supremely confident eyes locked with his, and she smiled a cold, merciless smile, her face hard as ice, her brows set, her body tensed and ready.

He maintained his poise for a moment longer, not out of bravado, but paralyzed by this woman's stare. In it he saw an unyielding desire and capability to hurt him, hurt him in ways he struggled not to envision, and for a moment he was frozen by a wave of fear he had not felt since he was a child. He waited for her stare to relent, for some sign of civility in her eyes, but there would be none. He sat down.

Madeline went on, softly, even as Ayala came and stood over the seated man, "You see, Shinobu, you don't mind if I call you Shinobu, do you? Well, Shinobu, I do not work for the US government, nor did I steal this technology from some research institute, in fact I don't work for anyone except myself right now. My colleague and I have decided it is time you found out exactly where your new technology came from, and why you are going to do exactly what we are going to tell you, or suffer a quick and ignominious death."

His eyes widened, darting from the ex-Mossad agent standing over him to the calm, seated lady who had just threatened his life. But Madeline was just getting started and over the next half an hour his reality slowly caved in around him. He listened intensely as Madeline began to explain the depth of the conspiracy they had drawn him into.

Carefully, slowly, and deliberately, she laid it all out for him. All of it. The eight capsules, the conspiracy, the discovery in the Indian Ocean and the subsequent death of the crew of the *King's Transom*. He shook his head occasionally, he dismissed the photographs of the capsule they produced from Ayala's case, and though he was fascinated by some of the design schematics John had given them, he still seemed to maintain some small grasp on his previous world. But the design of the nano-machine, if it could be called a machine at all, that they wanted to start manufacturing with the resonance manipulator was beyond anything he could have imagined.

It was impossibly complex, and its minuscule dimensions were even harder to grasp. It was not a machine at all. It was a cellular construct. They weren't using metal, or silicate, they were using proteins and polysaccharides and fatty acids. They wanted to use his wonderful machine to make what could only be described as a creature. A tiny, vicious-looking cellular weapon that shook him to the very core.

It was the explanation of this terrible device and its purpose that finally broke his resistance, allowing the full extent of their story to wash over him. It was like he had been staring at the truth through glass, unreal and distorted. But this final piece, this cracked that shield like a shattering aquarium, the liquid realization his mind had held at bay suddenly flooding over him. He sat there, bewildered, fear and lack of hope soaking his psyche as he gave in to the truth.

After a moment's more explanation from Madeline, Ayala saw that it was done and raised her hand slightly. Madeline fell silent. Her role was done; she had played her part excellently. Ayala waited a moment more and then said softly, "You see, Shinobu, we do not need your money. We never did. We needed something that we could not buy. We needed access to complex research facilities and expensive materials. And now we need to use the product of our work to move on the next stage: fabricating, testing, and then manufacturing the smallest, most advanced machine man has ever created."

She let that information sink in a moment like she was spooning medicine into him, and then she gave him his final dose:

"So, Shinobu, I am afraid we have used you. I am sorry to say that but it is true. And now I am telling you that you are going to help us to build what we need. You can do it because we are trying to save the world. Or because your competitors would be more than happy to help us in return for the detailed designs of the resonance manipulator.

"Or you can do it because if you don't … you will die. Either at the hands of the alien force already here, or the far more powerful Armada that is hot on their heels." Then Ayala leaned in close, saying her next words right into his face in a barely audible whisper, "Though if I am honest, if you do not do as we say, your death will far more likely be at my hands, and trust me, you have as much chance of escaping me as you do the satellites that watch us even now." Ayala straightened slowly once more, with lean menace.

Madeline felt for the poor man. But she played along, acting out her part as Ayala had planned it, "So, Shinobu, are you with us?" Madeline said, like she was his advocate, his protector from the assassin standing between him and the door.

It … they … shinjirarenai … the old executive's mind spun. He thought of the threat to his life and shuddered, but in truth his mind was racing with the thought of the greater threat above. The end of everything he knew. All his work building up his father's company, all for nothing. He thought of his arrogance, and how pleasantly ignorant he had been before he came into this room today.

He mourned his broken innocence, and as he contemplated it all he found he hated these women for bringing him to their circle. They were damned: damned by their knowledge, damned by their complicity in the earth's defense, and now he was too. But underneath that layer of resentment he knew they were all damned, everyone of them, unless he did what these women asked.

A part of him could not help but lament the wonderful device he would be giving away as well: the greatest invention of all time, a panacea for every communicable disease known to man. He sagged into his chair at the thought and Ayala saw that he was theirs. She saw that he was no longer thinking of how to resist, or whether to believe, he was thinking of the consequences of what he knew he must do and that meant they had succeeded. And as the final touch, she would cauterize the wounds they had given him just a little by giving him one small spark of hope to light the way through his despair.

"Of course, these machines that you will so kindly be giving away, these cells that will cure AIDS, and Malaria, and Polio, you should know that they have a shelf life. And if one man were to help us give humanity this first mass release of them to protect us from the coming viral attack, then I see no reason why that man wouldn't be able to sell the next release … for profit … if you like."

A patent on the greatest medicine in history, and on the only way to manufacture it. He swelled with the very concept of it and with that Ayala saw that she had pulled him through to the other side. Like threading the eye of a needle, she had pushed and prodded him through that impossibly small hole. But now she had a hold of him on the other side and he was hooked. Now they could truly use him and his vast resources to help defend humanity.

She had known that he would never have been a willing ally. They had needed to break him of that which he valued most, his personal power, and then they had needed to show him a route back to it, a route back to that by which he had always defined himself.

The fear of losing what he had now would make him theirs today. The promise of wealth and prestige beyond measure would keep him true tomorrow. Months from now, when their purpose was served, he would eventually discover that the machines they were going to release were self-replicating. But by then it would be too late for him to take them back. His purpose would be served, and they would cut him loose.

Madeline glanced at Ayala. She had doubted the older woman's strategy when they had discussed it earlier, but there was no doubt in her mind now that this lady had broken men far stronger and far more capable than this poor specimen.

She thought about the fact that this woman had been Barrett's wife and found that she had to admire the man that had captured the heart of such a force. For now, though, Madeline was simply grateful that Ayala was on her side. She was a good friend to have. And they needed the very best.

Chapter 37: Hans On

The colonel pulled up the collar of his pea coat as he strolled across a large quad. He was well inside the confines of Hanscom Base. The October wind was not strong but it carried the first chill of winter. It was the kind of chill that folks still warm from the Indian summer might call invigorating. In a few weeks those same people would no doubt be complaining about how long the winter already was, but the colonel was not one to talk about the weather, good or bad. As he approached the entrance to the hangar where Dr. Martin had set up their equipment he saw Captain Toranssen standing outside, looking pensive.

"Good evening, Captain." he said as he walked up, slowing as he approached, but not stopping until he was fully covered by the large metal awning that sheltered the hangar's double doors. He came to a halt next to the captain who was also well covered from prying eyes above by the metal sheeting that made up the wide awning.

"Good evening, sir." said Jack Toranssen, his hand coming to his forehead in a quick and informal salute as the older man approached. The small group of people that was now privy to the alien presence on Earth was very diverse, spanning different backgrounds and areas of expertise, but they had several key things in common. Firstly there was the knowledge of the threat, a knowledge that bound them together. That burden also drove a shared dedication in all of them to fight their common enemy to the end. And while they came from diverse parts of the country, even the world, and each contributed very different things to the team, they had also all taken on several notably similar habits in their various locations.

The families and friends of all six had seen a sudden and marked increase in the numbers of letters and postcards they received, an increase that was matched by a proportionate decrease in phone calls and e-mails as well. All six of them had also given in to some luxuries that they would previously have denied themselves. A new Omega watch for Colonel Milton, a vintage Corvette for Jack, and two pairs of Prada shoes for Madeline. For Neal it had not been a single purchase. Instead he had taken to drinking through his local wine store's collection of vintage ports. At around $400 a bottle, these weren't the most expensive splurge of the group, but they were by far the tastiest.

Another key trait they now all shared was that they no longer lingered under open skies a moment longer than they had too. Though there was little that would protect them in case of an attack by one of the satellites, their instinct to stay under cover still had grounding in common sense: as long as they were under any kind of shelter, the chances of their conversation being viewable from space was significantly reduced. So this spot under the big metal awning was among the closest places that either of the two men came to getting some fresh air each day.

"Taking a break, Jack?" asked the colonel, standing next to Jack and looking out at the twilight sky.

Jack smiled. Like his cohorts, he hadn't been able to truly let go for months now. When Ayala visited she always insisted on having a glass of wine or three with them, trying to help them let off steam. No doubt it was harder on Neal, as most of the time he was unable to talk openly with anyone in his location. Nodding reticently, Jack replied to the colonel, "A break, yeah. I guess, Colonel. They're not doing much I can contribute to right now in there so I thought I'd get some fresh air." The colonel raised an eyebrow and the captain continued, "Permission to offer an opinion, sir?"

"Captain, I think we're a little past that, don't you? Besides, you didn't seem to have any trouble expressing yourself with John Hunt last month." As he quipped about the captain's minor confrontation with the Agent, Barrett found he was actually frowning slightly at the memory, reviving as it did his sense of hopelessness about their situation. He would never show that though. Deal with each problem as it arose, strive for the success of the mission. What else was there to do?

But the captain's melancholy was grown from the same seed, and in a rare moment of candidness he decided to confide in his superior officer, "Sir, I don't wish to be … pessimistic, but I am afraid to say that I think there may be some … holes in our plan."

Barrett kept his expression even but inside he was deeply unhappy to hear the captain voice his concerns. Sadly he was also not surprised that the young captain had seen some flaws in their plan, hopefully there were no more than the colonel had already noted himself.

Jack kept his eyes focused on the distant sky, and taking the colonel's silence as permission to carry on, said, "Sir, if I set aside, for a moment, the problems of getting control of the missile defense system, not an insignificant task I'm sure you'll agree, there is still the glaring gap in our attack plan around how we are going to handle the fourth satellite. We simply do not have enough munitions in our GBMD system to mount a third attack and maintain security on our borders." Barrett nodded and went to speak but the captain carried on, "Of course, this does not factor in that we will have to wait to attack the final satellite till it is in range of our missiles, by which time it will be alerted by the destruction of its cohorts.

"Something tells me that if it knows how we took out the other satellites it will be markedly more proactive in its defense than the first two will have been. Colonel, I shudder at the thought of the kind of damage that final satellite will do to our defense network before we can even get our missiles to it." And with that, Jack did actually shudder. It would have been funny if there were anything even vaguely funny about the thought of a high-powered laser cutting up military targets in Western Europe and the eastern US like a hot knife through so much butter.

The colonel stood firm, baring so little as he always did. He was not insensitive, but he had long ago learned that he must remain resolute in the face of unavoidable casualties, disconnecting his mind from human ramifications in order to focus on whatever role he had to play. But he had considered this at great length, and he had done his share of soul searching, and he would not stop his search for an alternative.

Until one came to them, though, he had reconciled himself to the cost they would pay. But he had developed an even bleaker worse-case scenario than the captain, "Jack, I'll be frank, it is clear to me that if we leave one of those machines up there, then the remaining components of our missile defense system should be considered compromised. We should assume that if we allow it to, there is a good chance it will obliterate any remaining GBMD arsenal before we can even bring it to bear.

"The only upside is that if we come under attack from space then it will negate the need for secrecy, at which point we can call upon our friends in Russia to launch their A-135s and the Chinese and Indian missile defense systems can also be deployed. If what we know about the satellites is accurate, then that would surely be the end of the fight. Between them, China, India, and Russia have more than treble our defense network, so the upside of our network being decimated would be the eventual destruction of the fourth and final satellite."

"Assuming John Hunt is able to deploy the HMS *Dauntless*'s munitions, and they are successful."

"Assuming John Hunt is successful, yes." Neither of them doubted John's ability, but to put so much faith in one man and his one ship was not the kind of redundancy upon redundancy that military men were trained to strive for. The fact that the man was John Hunt did make it easier, but even one of Britain's cutting edge new Type 47 Destroyers had only so much exo-atmospheric firepower.

The captain recapped the conversation so far, "So, *if* we can destroy the four satellites, and that is a big if, we are still left with a best case scenario where the continental United States will, most likely, be left with virtually no long-range missile defense system."

The colonel shook his head, staring at the ground. He had come to the same conclusion. It was an appalling strategic position for any military man to consider.

Jack looked a little desperately at the colonel and then regained his composure. His back straightening again, he said, "Not desirable, I think you can agree, sir. Even if it is successful, which is far from certain. But Colonel, even that scenario is not the greatest of my concerns." Jack paused, waiting for his mentor to react to that, but the colonel merely stared off into the distance. So he has seen it too, thought Jack, then continued slightly resignedly, "Clearly Madeline's work with that machine she is working on is moving even faster than we could have hoped, and that is great, I don't question that for a moment. No doubt Ayala and Madeline have now begun co-opting the new manufacturing abilities to produce the first prototypes of the antigen.

"But, well, I have thought long and hard about it, sir, and it just doesn't add up. I just cannot see how we can spread the nano devices quickly enough, and diversely enough, to initiate the immunization of nearly seven billion people in time. It just isn't possible."

The colonel stood silently for a moment, looking out at the twilight sky over the base. It was mutely beautiful, its high-cloud grays brought into deep relief by the sharply angled light, the moment's peace made it all picturesque and peaceful. His planet, so huge, it had seemed so impregnable to him, so vast and so strong. Now it felt so fragile. Everything hung in the balance and the solidity of the ground had gone from under his feet. As he had the last few months, he found solace in his tactical process, thinking through his response to the all too incisive comments of his prodigy. After a moment's silence, a distant test engine fired, its contained fury a muted roar echoing across the base, and the colonel's thoughts fired in unison, focus returning to him with a hidden shiver.

Barrett had assumed that many of his fellow conspirators would have done the same calculations he had, but the unspoken rule had always been that they should just do the best they could. "Captain, since you have been candid with me, I shall do the same for you. As you know, my team, of which you are now part, has tried to balance the need for resources, and to mobilize an effective resistance to the threat we have discovered with the constant chance of discovery and destruction. We've done this, as I am sure you know, not just because we don't want to die, but because we have to assume that if we are discovered, our deaths will mean the end of one of Earth's few hopes of salvation in the coming conflict. Even worse, there is a chance that if a conspiracy as deep as ours is discovered, the virus may be released before we have any of our plans in place." He left that statement unfinished, the finality of that concept able to speak for itself. Doomsday. Extinction. A mess for the Mobiliei Armada to clean up, no doubt, but that would be no consolation to an eradicated humanity.

"Now, as long as we remain undetected, we have months, maybe even years to do this properly. As we only have one shot at this, we cannot afford to take risks by bringing too many people into our circle. Because of that we have been more ... cautious than we may have liked. This will limit the speed with which we can spread the antigen, but weighed against the risks ... well, I'm sure you understand."

"I do, Colonel, I hope you know that I understand that, but ..." he caught his breath, clearly struggling with a demon. Reining it in after a moment, his surface calmed again, and he went on, "Colonel, I have reviewed our plans for dispersion of the devices, I know we have to get about a hundred into a person for them to be effective, and I know that once a group of the cells reaches critical mass in a host the antigen will be able to start using our own immune system to start manufacturing duplicates of itself."

"And no doubt you remember the timeline we are looking at?" asked the colonel. The captain nodded, so the colonel left the topic alone, he knew the captain was not really looking for resolution, only to air his fears. Barrett let him go on.

All of the team had been told that the tiny biomorphic devices worked by identifying the DNA of their host. Once that was identified, they essentially moved through the blood system rooting out foreign bodies and destroying them with a simple but effective cellular lance laced with toxins and a minuscule but relatively potent electric charge that caused the target body to disintegrate at the nuclide level, to be absorbed and reconstituted by the body. Assuming that nearly all communicable diseases were transmitted around the body via the blood, or at least could not effectively attack the host systems without access to the cardio-vascular network, a team of these minuscule bio-constructs patrolling your blood vessels would permanently immure you to everything from the common cold to rabies in about a day or two.

In order to maintain and grow their numbers, the incredible devices also entered and manipulated their host's bone marrow with a virus of their own, turning immunized bodies into factories for further nano-device production. Within a week of infection, a host started turning out their own defenses, and infecting others with the super-cells. Along with the standard white blood that was produced in the bone marrow under normal circumstances, each human host could also produce enough of the 'devices' each week to infect at least one or two more people, who would also then start producing the panacea.

That meant that each week, each immunized group would roughly double in size: two, four, eight, sixteen ... from the first infected person. Given enough time, the process would slowly but surely wipe away nearly every infectious disease known to man, while also inoculating us against the lethal virus the satellites had on hand. Given enough time.

But even with exponential growth, the infected group grows very slowly at first. It would take a single starting case eight months to spread to 5% of the population, even though it would then spread to the remaining 95% in just the following five weeks.

More starting hosts sped up the initial stages, but by incrementally smaller amounts. If they started by injecting around five hundred people, for example, they could accelerate through the first four months. But after that, even if you doubled the starting number to one thousand, you only gained one more week. The next week would need two thousand people. That was two thousand opportunities for discovery. So after five hundred, the marginal return of manually infecting people would be far outweighed by the speed of the infection's natural spread.

So once the drug was ready, they were going to need nine months. No matter what they did, it would take at least nine months to spread to the entire population. And so the danger, as both the colonel and now the captain had seen, was that the vast majority of people would not be immune till the very last stages of the spread. If their plan was discovered just a month before they were ready, more than three quarters of the planet would still be defenseless. That was five billion lives in the balance.

That was equivalent to the population of America, times fifteen. It was four times the entire continent of Europe. These were the odds the team was faced with. Only a week before they were ready and half the planet would die. Six weeks early and it was effectively still genocide.

Even this disturbingly slow uptake did not factor in that the spread would be far from regular. A person could only 'catch'" the cure if they were near an immunized person who was producing it. It would not leap easily from country to country, and certainly not from continent to continent. So they needed to seed the process evenly across the globe.

If this disturbingly fragile part of the project succeeded before they were discovered, they could then, to some degree, come out of the shadows and be more proactive in their attempts to destroy the satellites, the threat of being wiped out abated.

But if they didn't …

They both stood stoically, considering all this. Eventually the captain shook his head, the colonel was waiting for him to get it all out. And so the captain decided to finish his thought, now he had started, "There is something else, despite it all, despite the power of the satellites, and that damn superflu they want to drop on us.

"Even if I forget how incredibly easy they seem to find killing all of us, we seem to be ignoring the fact that there are eight of their Agents amongst us even now. And they can pick up fucking planes, Colonel, planes, and that didn't seem very strenuous for him either."

The captain shook his head again, and laughed somewhat shakily before continuing in a quiet tone, "I saw the report you had on this Lana Wilson. She is dating Admiral Hamilton's son. He has personally seen her posted in the Atlantic Fleet Submarine Command in Georgia. That puts her two promotions away from US Missile Command.

Plus we have a trainee Rafale fighter pilot taking the French army by storm, the most dangerous terrorist the world has ever seen living in New York, and god knows what their Chinese and Russian cousins are up to right now."

The colonel placed his hand on the captain's shoulder. It was a gesture of friendship and reassurance he had never felt the need to show before now. "Jack, I know. I know what it looks like. Trust me, I have wrestled with this for even longer than you have."

Barrett took a deep breath, and decided to give it to the young man as straight as possible: "The chances are that we won't be able to save everyone. And I'll be frank, even if we actually manage to launch a trillion dollars of our country's military hardware into space and our attack is successful, then our own government will probably be more willing to go after us than they are John Hunt's seven deadly friends.

"But for what it is worth, don't forget that one of those plane-lifting bad-asses is on our side," he smiled and the captain laughed momentarily, meeting the colonel's eyes and nodding, "and Jack, our friend Lieutenant Hunt has something they don't; he knows who they are, but they don't have any idea who he really is. As long as that is true, and as long as our efforts stay secret, we have a chance. I believe that. Really I do."

Speech made, his tone changed back from patrician to officer. He lowered his arm and he said to the young man, "In the end, we have a mission, Captain Toranssen, and though difficult, our objective is clear. Are you with us?"

The captain saw the question in the colonel's eyes and filled with determination. The call to arms seared through his veins. This was not just a mission; it was the most important thing any of them would ever be part of. As the captain filled with determination, the colonel saw in the young man's taught frame and set face that he would, indeed, give his last drop of blood to stop the coming storm.

With all the gravity Jack could deliver, he met his mentor's stare and said with the very meat of his soul, "Please do not mistake my reticence about our odds as reticence about the necessity of our mission, sir. I am absolutely with you, to the end. Believe it, sir. Do not doubt that for a second. The odds may be against us but so be it. Me whining about it won't improve things one iota. I am here, and I will fight these bastards to the end."

They looked at each other a moment then both turned to look back out at the evening sky. Jack smiled a bit and then decided to add a little addendum to his last sentence, "... preferably theirs."

Barrett laughed a little and then shook his head. Good man, he thought, and nodded. Yes, the kind of man you wanted in a situation like this. Barrett took a deep breath. It was surprising how therapeutic it was to talk about it all, even if all they did was come to the same grim conclusion.

He wasn't sure which cliché applied more: 'a problem shared' or 'misery loves company,' but either way he did feel less despondent than he usually did these days. He thought about his team. They didn't have much, but what they had was good. In the end they were probably all royally screwed, but with a bit of luck they would at least make the bastards hurt before it all ended.

Emotional moment over, he coughed a little and they both decided it was time to move on, "Now then, Captain, why don't we see what Martin and his new team are up to?"

Jack nodded, opening the door, "Very good, sir."

- - -

"What we have here, Colonel," said Martin Sobleski inside the lab hangar, "is a deuterium fluoride laser, which I have to say is pretty damn cool. It goes some way to duplicating the type of missile defense system that we think the Chinese are developing."

Neither the colonel nor the captain nor Dr. Sobleski made eye contact with each other as the doctor cursorily mentioned their cover story for the project. In truth, the colonel did not really need a cover story at this stage. Being one of the primary military research facilities in the world, Hanscom Air Field had several lasers on site that they could use to run their tests and more than enough expertise in that field to fill a conference room.

But if Dr. Sobleski was going to consult with all the field experts he wanted to, he needed a classified project code to work with in order to secure the scientists' silence. It was either have a code or tell yet more people the real reason for their research, which they had decided to avoid unless absolutely necessary.

In truth, the project code the colonel was using referred to an upgraded GPS-based missile guidance system he was supposed to be testing. But the various civilian scientists Dr. Sobleski was consulting with didn't know that. They just knew that any disclosures they made about their work here would be covered by the same threat of a lifetime behind bars that came with all highly classified work. Assuming none of them were spies, this should stop them from chatting about what went on in the lab to anyone, even other base personnel.

At some point, no doubt, the team was going to have to actually work on the GPS project whose budget the colonel was burning, but the senior officer would string it out for as long as possible.

"So," continued Martin excitedly, "my colleagues here have set us up with a pretty potent device." The laser the man was poring over looked like a medium-sized spotlight, about fifty centimeters across and a meter deep.

It was mounted on a motorized rotating frame designed to point the big device at airborne targets. This was because the lethal device was in fact a beta test of a now obsolete missile defense system. At the request of Martin and the colonel, it had been revived for this test, though, and it was now pointing across the room at a series of sheets of metal mounted on a twenty-inch-thick concrete block.

"OK, gentlemen, it's time we started our control test. Colonel, those sheets represent a rough approximation of the military grade steel that a missile defense laser would have to penetrate or buckle to render one of our munitions inoperable. Now, we know that as of now, our missiles carry enough shielding to protect them from low-level laser attack. But apparently the Chinese are looking into ways of increasing the power/heat output of their systems and our job is to make sure our missiles stay one step ahead of them."

"Sounds good, Doctor. So what are your initial thoughts about how to increase the shielding's resistance?" asked the colonel, playing along with Martin's charade. He knew that they really only needed the laser so that they could design and then test the mounting of the new armor plating they would need. They already knew the primary method they would use for buffering the missiles against the satellites' scything laser. All they really needed to do was design the shape of the plates they would need and then supply that to Madeline. The real benefit would come when she then used the resonance manipulator to morph a wide array of raw materials into the plates with the same properties as the superconducting alloys the alien satellites were coated in. The task would then fall back on the team to take these plates and get them installed on enough of the GBMD missiles to make them able to penetrate the satellites' defenses.

Either way, though, they needed a control so they could track the way the missile components that were behind the shielding plates would react to the onslaught. Today they would conduct that control test.

Martin continued his explanation, "Well, Colonel, for now, we have the standard missile shielding attached to that block. We are going to introduce various reflective and heat resistant materials to it and test their effectiveness, but first we need a point of comparison." The doctor smiled like a kid. "In other words, Colonel, we need to measure, very accurately, how long it takes this deuterium fluoride laser to utterly destroy these armor plates here."

With that, he walked around the back of a big a protective glass shield, highly polarized and armored to protect them from the coming test. As they all put on darkened goggles, the scientists began to initiate the laser. It warmed up slowly, taking about thirty seconds to come to life and warm the long, thin gas tube that would stimulate the light emission, the very thing that made a laser a laser.

At a beep, the machine innocently notified the team that it was ready, like an oven saying it had reached the selected temperature. Flicking a switch, the machine thrummed to life, then suddenly a tight green beam bisected the room. The beam lanced into the metal on the concrete block. For about two seconds it stayed still, seemingly pinned by the light, then it buckled sharply with an audible twang. After that nothing happened for about ten more seconds, and then there was another, louder snap like an axe hitting the side of a ship. They felt it through their feet, and a moment later the concrete block behind the plating started to smoke.

The laser was deactivated, its cooling fans whirring, and with a confirming wave from Martin, various scientists began to emerge from behind the shield to check the powerful device. The colonel followed Martin over to the test block and they examined the damage. The smoke had been the concrete burning once the layered shielding had been completely penetrated.

"Dr. Sobleski," said the colonel in a whisper, "how does this laser compare to the specifications that John gave us for the satellites' defenses?"

Martin looked at the general and frowned a moment. Then he replied, also in a whisper, but one that belied the gravity of his response, "The best way I can think of to describe it would be to tell you that this deuterium fluoride laser compares to the power we face above us in roughly the same way a CD player's laser compares to our deuterium friend here."

The colonel stared at him.

"If you want an equally scary comparison," said Martin, as excited as he was disturbed by his own words, "according to John Hunt, each of our Agent friends have a laser almost as powerful as this deuterium beast built into their left eyes. More than amazing even than the size factor, the implications that statement has for the kind of power sources they must have inside them are phenomenal."

The scientist's eyes widened at his own statement as he thought about the Agent's technological prowess, and then he got back to examining the burn marks on the plating and the scale of the buckling. With the detachment of a scientist, he was able to find the whole concept of the invasion fascinating. That was his objective point of view. But when he lay in bed at night and thought about his one-year-old nephew, or his widowed mother, about them being slaughtered by the alien army that even now hurtled toward Earth, Martin Sobleski shivered with the same fear and anger that haunted the rest of the team.

Chapter 38: Little Princess

As always, New York was busy and vibrant. The city was one of the busiest places in America, on Earth even, and Times Square was one of the busiest places in the city. In the weeks since his arrival, Agent Shahim Al Khazar had taken to walking through the bustling crowds in this mecca of commercialism. Having spent his first months on Earth mired in one of its most unforgiving and brutal regions, this was a stark comparison. His original mission had been clear: infiltrate the ranks of the insurgent army that occupied the mountains that covered northern Pakistan and Afghanistan. Now that mission had taken a sharp detour, but the end goal remained clear. Shahim needed to move this mission forward, balancing carefully a need to expedite his return to the Kush mountains without being too successful and accelerating destabilization before the rest of the team, and the Armada, were ready to sweep in.

So his missions now refocused on the United States, and the range of potential targets his brief had laid out for him.

One of his proposed missions was to build and deploy a dirty bomb in New York. Both he and the Council had been appalled at the thought of deliberately releasing a radioactive device in any place, not for ethical reasons, but environmental ones. But Shahim's superiors in Al Qaeda had insisted that it remain on the list of options.

A Pakistani businessman visited him each week. He was a genuine businessman, with genuine interests in New York and very real financial interests and holdings. But everything about the man was, in fact, a cover. Despite the man's own high ideals about his role in Al Qaeda, and his limited understanding of the true ramifications of the agenda his associates were pursuing, he was really no more than a donkey, ferrying information and money to Shahim for the length of his stay in the US.

His choice of targets was simple and unimaginative, and in truth, he suspected that his superiors were really shopping for another miracle. They were still unclear on how he had managed to successfully complete his mission in Islamabad, and they were trying to see if the man was just lucky.

With various attacks on New York's financial and commercial centers on the terrorists' Christmas list, he had found that he had cause to spend lots of time walking around the city, which his tortured machine-bound personality found surprisingly relaxing.

The curse of a machine memory was the ability to recall, at any time, in perfect color, even the most painful of events. And he had found himself reliving the death of the prime minister's sobbing family many times over the months since it had happened.

He was not sleeping. True, he did not need to, his machine brain did not need to rest or recuperate. But the effect on his psyche of being awake for weeks at a time was disorienting. He noted the passage of time not in days but in the weeks between visits from the businessman that was his only 'friend.'

A week ago a stranger had called him a 'rag-head' when he was getting off the subway at his stop in Queens.

In a microsecond his arm had flashed out with all his might, flaring toward the man's face. At the last moment he had relented, withdrawing the bulk of his might from the blow and stopping it from crushing the man's face into the back of his skull. The softened punch still connected though, snapping the man's nose and sending him reeling backward into a wall.

He had stepped up to him and pinned him to the wall with a single vice-like hand and whispered, "If you ever say that to one of my brethren again, I will find you, and I will rip your very soul from your stinking guts. Then I will find everyone you know, everyone you love, and they will all die slowly at my hands. Do you understand me, you disgusting piece of shit?"

The man had nodded frantically, tears streaming down his face. As soon as his neck had been released, he had fled. It had been a phenomenally foolish thing to do, and Shahim had erased the twenty seconds from his reports to the hub satellites, stopping it from being transmitted to his colleagues.

He wished he could erase his memory from Islamabad so easily. But he needed it. If he was to remain honest to his mission and his country he must not go cutting valuable information from his memory banks. The eight Agents' purpose here was far too important to the future of his species for him to give in to the whims of his conscience.

Returning from his daily trip to the city, he mounted the subway steps once more and wandered out into the autumn evening. The street was alive. People were standing on corners and congregating around the doorsteps of their apartment buildings. Latin music, both old and new, blared from various small stereos and a couple of cars, their doors open to let the sound out, even as its high volume corrupted and warped the car's cheap speakers.

Shahim navigated the groups of people that always populated the streets of his neighborhood in Queens, finally stepping through a group of three laughing Puerto Rican men at the door of his building. They ignored him, as they always did; he was harmless, the poor rag-head.

Entering his walk-up, he climbed the steps three at a time to the third floor and stopped at the door to his studio apartment. As he always did, he scanned the door handle, the frame, and the tattered mat in front of it before entering, the risk of discovery ever present.

On the handle were three fingerprints that had not been there that morning, his resolved sight picking them up as he scrutinized the metal with his eyes' wide spectrum. Seeing this, he looked up, and through the wooden door. Activating the advanced radar and infrared beacons in his right eye, he reviewed the room behind the door. The radar passed back limited information through the cheap wood, but his infrared heat sensors returned confirmation that there was no one in the room.

It was entirely possible that one of his more dubious neighbors had merely tried the door on the off chance that it might be unlocked.

But there were other possibilities, and the Agents, like any covert operative, tended toward assuming the worst. He activated his weapons array in his left eye, but kept it in its sheath.

He could deploy it in a moment if he was, indeed, in trouble. Then he stepped forward and inserted the tendrils in his forefinger into the keyhole and opened the door.

No clicks, no electronic signatures indicating an explosive device had been activated.

He entered. His sensors had confirmed that there was no on in the single-room apartment so he was momentarily confused by the sight of the woman sitting on his only chair.

Only momentarily, as he very quickly recognized her from his records and numerous Council meetings. There was no heat signature in the room because there was no human in the room. An Agent was, by design, much harder to detect than the humans they mimicked, unless it chose to mimic a human's warmth, or project an X-ray skeleton onto a panel in a mockery of the way one would have shown there if they weren't thoroughly impervious to them.

"Good evening, Lana. How are you?"

She smiled thinly, "Let us not use these plebian names, I grow so tired of them. You will address me by my appropriate title, my noble Hamprect cousin."

"I thought we were under strict instructions to use only our Agents' names, even in our Council meetings. Something about the fallibility of our frail personality overl …"

"Enough, Lord Mantil!" she did not shout, but force and venom soaked her words as she spat them at him. "Save the petty irrelevancies for the Council and an AI that cares for such things. You will address me by my title!"

Even though she had no power over him here, even though she was just a copy of the monumental bitch that was the Princess Regent of Balachai, a lifetime of accordance with the strictures of his standing made him comply.

"My apologies, your majesty." inadvertently he even bowed a little.

She bristled, the man's obsequiousness like a drug to her spoiled veins.

"Good. Now, let us speak openly, Lord Mantil. The Hamprect Empire has long been in the good graces of the Emperor Balachai, even before the peace that this noble enterprise imposed on Mobilius. I hope you feel the same fraternity of purpose that we enjoy toward you?"

"Of course, your majesty." it was surprising to him how quickly the old ways came back, how natural they were. His home of Hamprect had indeed long been a semi-servile ally of Balachai, the wealthiest and most powerful of the great empires. But it had not been a marriage of equals, and he, like his countrymen, had long resented the superiority of the Balachans.

This Princess Lamati had been the worst of them. She clearly believed in her own divinity, and her personality's election to the eight Agents had been mourned by many, including Lord Mantil; though in silence, of course. But she was here now, or at least, the substrate of her personality was. And he had attended at her father's court enough times to feel the weight of her inherited power upon his back.

"Now, Lord Mantil, I find that you have ended up in my ... area of control. Naturally, it is not through any fault of your own, but your mission was in Pakistan, and mine in the United States. I am sure you will return to your own lands soon, but I am sure you will also agree that while you are here I have a certain right to ... express my opinions on your actions." She let that hang out there for a bit.

Shahim was quite sure that she did *not* have that right, or anything like it. "Your majesty, while my undying allegiance to my king, and his treaties with your father, make me ever your willing servant, I feel it my duty to point out that, by the purview of every emperor and trading family that signed the Treaty of Conquest, we are all equals while on this mission." He stood firm and did not bow again, in the hopes that this would reinforce his message.

"Lord Mantil," she smiled demurely, itself quite a disturbing sight for anyone that knew her, "I do not mean to rewrite the sacred decrees of my father and his fellow rulers. I merely mean to offer ... an opinion on your enterprise here. I would never dream of imposing my will or that of my family upon you. We are, as you say, equals, for the length of this mission, and when this copy of my personality is reunited with my royal self on Mobilius years from now, I would not dream of holding any of your actions here against you, or your family."

To call the threat veiled would be a profound insult to veils. Lord Mantil of Hamprect nodded to the woman in front of him. He was painfully aware that he was, as of now, not speaking with a fellow Agent, but with the beloved and conniving daughter of the most powerful man on his world.

"So, Lord Mantil, as I was saying, I came here to discuss the mission at hand, and your actions as they affect my mission here in my target country. You see, my lord, I have decided that we have an opportunity, an opportunity to accomplish something. Your arrival here allows us some freedoms that the AI and our fellow Council members were too scared to pursue when it was most pressing." She paused, but not long enough to invite a response. This was a diatribe, not a conversation.

"But," she sighed and smiled beatifically, "better late than never. Lord Mantil, as expected we have encountered precious little resistance since our arrival here. And no one's actions have shown how weak the humans are to greater effect than your attack on one of their leaders. One day I will no doubt do the same to the leadership of this country, but till then I have to work within their pathetic society's laws."

She locked eyes with him and delivered her next words with regal weight, "But you are not hobbled by such things, Lord Mantil, young freedom fighter that you are. So you have the ability to close those loose ends that my respectable colleagues and I cannot."

"Your majesty, what, exactly, is it that you believe I should be doing while I am here in your country?" he put a little emphasis on the word 'your' but she did not allow his subtle insolence to phase her.

"Oh, nothing very important, Lord Mantil." She smiled pleasantly. "On the list of targets your leaders gave you were two ambitious options thrown in, no doubt in the hope that your improbable success in Islamabad might be something close to divine intervention, a thought that is more accurate than they realize.

"I merely point out that one of the people who we suspected of discovering our arrival here spends a lot of time at the White House and the Pentagon. So why don't you use your time here to plan an attack on, say, the Pentagon, and while doing so, kill one of the men that may have some level of suspicion that we are here? It is merely a case of two birds with one stone."

It seemed almost reasonable. But she had always been able to couch her schemes and ambitions in logic. It was a skill she had applied with a broad brush to get her personality elected to this mission in the first place. But Lord Mantil knew that this was, in truth, just the whining of a spoilt child, still frustrated that her attempts to have this man killed in India had been voted down.

Lord Mantil knew that her spite was limitless. He had seen too many good people, in her own government and his, fall to her whims and petty acts of vengeance. But that said, this knowledge that her proposal was actually motivated by her seemingly bottomless well of spite wouldn't necessarily stop him from playing along.

After all, this man she wanted killed was going to die at the Armada's hands even if Lord Mantil spared him. Why incite the fury of the Princess of Balachai? And so, Lord Mantil bowed, his 'noble' roots remembered, and said, "Your majesty, I can see no reason why a lord of Hamprect cannot do this thing for such an honored ally."

She beamed, stood, and walked over to him, placing her hand flat against his chest, a gesture of blessing from a member of the royal family such as she.

"Thank you, Lord Mantil. I will not forget this accommodation in the future." She nodded slightly to him, then lowered her hand. "Now, I must return to Washington, I have a flight tomorrow to Georgia to start as a junior lieutenant at King's Bay Submarine Base. Getting closer, Shahim, soon I will try for a posting at US STRATCOM in Omaha, or failing that, Fleet Command in Virginia."

She smiled and he bowed slightly. She spoke once more, in an offhanded tone, "I see no need to report this conversation to the Council. I will duly support you when you announce *your* plan at our next meeting.

"The Pentagon would seem an easier target than the White House, anyway, and you can simply kill Danielson as he enters the building. But of course, I will leave the details in your capable hands."

She smiled once more then left the room.

Shahim Al Khazar was left standing in the small, dirty slum, alone once more. Now, to prepare for his move to DC. His contact would be here in a few days. Shahim would give him a list of requirements and some specialists he would need to request to make the show complete. Can't have it seem too easy to his superiors. Nor did he want the cowardly terrorists to be without loss in the coming attack. If he had to kill unsuspecting civilians then he would sacrifice a few of their so-called 'warriors' to the altar as well.

Chapter 39: Newborn

Shinobu Matsuoka had been more than accommodating since their last conversation a few weeks ago, dedicating the whole branch of the facility in North Dakota to their needs.

The facility manager had been told in the strictest possible manner that he was to follow Madeline's orders to the letter and that he was to subdivide the entire enterprise under the same research cost brackets he had worked under to date. Above all, he had been told that under no circumstances was he to ask any questions about the purpose of the team's work.

Under the guise of keeping the company president happy, Ayala had also asked that he come by at least once a month to check on their progress. In truth, this was more so that Ayala could keep checks on him and assess his mood, making sure that the man stayed in line.

After they had co-opted an angry and then scared Shinobu Matsuoka into their conspiracy, Ayala had left on another of her tours to DC and Massachusetts, leaving Madeline for a few weeks to the arduous process of creating a computer schematic of their cellular warriors. In that time, Madeline had also decided to carve out a new appearance for her prolonged stay in North Dakota. It was this new Madeline that greeted the returning Ayala inside the building's lobby, smiling at the Israeli woman's double take.

"Hello, my old friend," said Madeline, reaching out her hand and smirking. She was wearing a frilly white blouse that buttoned up to her neck, and a long blue pleated wool skirt. But the real coup de grâce was her hair. She had shed her wigs and done something more fundamental, dying her hair a dark blond color, and perming it into a broad, eighties semi-fro. Ayala looked at her, flinched, then stifled an involuntary laugh. Madeline kept her face completely deadpan to increase the other woman's struggle.

"Something wrong, Ms. Zubaideh?" Madeline asked.

"No … wow … I … umm …" Ayala looked to either side and was further disconcerted to see that the receptionist sitting across the room was in a disturbingly similar outfit. Ayala doubted that the other woman had also been going for irony when she got dressed this morning so she merely nodded and looked back at her friend. A laugh tried to escape her lips again and her brow furrowed, her lips pursing as she held it inside.

Madeline relented on the poor woman and allowed herself a small smile. Leading Ayala through the security doors with her badge, they made their way in relative silence to the small office that had been the site of their meeting with Matsuoka.

Closing the door behind them, Madeline turned to her fellow conspirator.

"Well, what do you think?"

Ayala allowed herself to laugh openly now, a tear of mirth even running down her face, "My lord, you look … delightful." Madeline looked at her, laughing as well, while also feigning indignation and defending her new look.

"What? This is a very nice blouse, I'll have you know. Some women in a local church group make them." This new twist made Ayala redouble in laughter.

"Oh, it's lovely," said Ayala between giggles. "And how is your husband the vicar?"

"Well," said Madeline, laughing, "he's fine. You know, the vicar thinks I look beautiful." Madeline reached up and cupped her hands under her new hairdo, puffing it lightly.

"Oh I'll bet he does, the horny devil."

"Yes, well, he's always had a thing for women in industrial strength wool skirts," laughed Madeline.

Ayala started to get her laughing under control, and looked again at the woman. Shaking her head as she wiped the tears from her eyes, she sighed. "Thank you, Madeline. Oh, wow, I needed that." Still laughing, she went over and hugged the younger woman.

Madeline returned the genuine sisterly affection, and they squeezed each other tightly for a moment before Ayala stepped back and looked Madeline in her deep blue eyes.

"How is it going here?" the Israeli asked. "Are you really going crazy or is this just the vicar's wife talking?"

"No, I'm good, very good actually. It took some late nights, but we are on schedule. We have been producing test batches for a few days now, and I've introduced them to a couple of our little buddies to test their effectiveness."

Ayala nodded. John Hunt had told them that the cellular construct would work equally well with most primates, as well as pigs and several other higher mammals, so they had requisitioned some monkeys for trials. It had raised some eyebrows with the facility's staff, but they were not paid for their inquisitiveness, as they well knew, and it had not been questioned.

"Why don't you come and check out the results? I've given my staff the day off so you can come and see the process without having to meet them," Madeline asked.

"Great, let's get down there."

Madeline opened the door and Ayala grabbed her small bag once more. She travelled light, maintaining a small stash of clothes at each location so she could move easily between the various pockets of people she supported.

As the older Israeli woman walked past Madeline out the door, she paused, shaking her head and laughing once more, noticing the reading glasses on a thin gold chain around Madeline's dainty neck.

Madeline laughed too, "Oh, those." She smiled and put them on, completing the Mary Tyler Moore look Madeline had gone for.

"Yes those." They both laughed as they walked down the corridor, locking arms with each other as they went. "Oh my lord, what have I done to you. You were such a pretty girl."

"Price of admission, Ayala, price of admission."

- - -

If Ayala had been struck by Madeline's striking change upon arriving, she was equally taken by the way the young woman's demeanor changed when she entered the test lab. She was at home here. This was her domain, and with its distinct lack of cameras and windows it was truly one of the few places she could really relax.

The resonance manipulator's home was still the same large white lab where Madeline had demonstrated the prototype system to Shinobu Matsuoka not long ago. It was still dominated by the large sphere that had been the focus of the room's efforts for so long now. Same white walls, floor, ceiling; same metal tables dotted with several computers.

But since that day, the austere concrete and metal decorations had received a splash of color in the form of four brown chimpanzees in large cages against the back wall. They all started clamoring and yapping when the two women entered the room, and the two women went over to greet them.

"In another couple of days they should become infectious, according to John's information," said Madeline, taking one of the young chimps out of his cage. He wrapped his legs around her, draped one powerful arm around her neck, and reached out with the other to touch the new woman.

Ayala smiled at the cute little guy, and stepped close so the he could touch her face and inspect her. As she gently extricated her long black hair from his playful grip, she said, "So, how have they responded so far? Have you seen a decrease in pathogens in their blood?"

Madeline smiled, expertly throwing the monkey up and over onto her back so she could pick up the clipboard hanging from his cage. He squealed, almost like laughter, and the other three rattled their cage doors, wanting to join in.

"Calm down, you three," said Madeline in a motherly tone, then, flipping a few pages over she found the graph she was looking for and showed it to Ayala.

Ayala studied it, looked back at Madeline, then back at the chart. "Is this correct? Nothing, they have none?"

Madeline nodded, handing the chart to Ayala to study while she manhandled the excited little chimp off her back and back into his cage. Closing the door, her soft voice placating the monkey, she turned and started walking toward one of the computers, Ayala following incredulously.

"Yes, Ayala," Madeline said, signing in to the PC, "nothing. We have run a battery of tests on the little guy and as far as we can tell his blood is completely clear of any pathogens. Turns out that when you have detailed schematics to work from it really isn't that hard to build it right first time. Well, maybe not first time, the cell walls of the first fifteen constructions collapsed as soon as the resonance chamber was deactivated, their internal pressure too great for the casing I had designed to coat them. Of course, I didn't know that until I got the test tubes under a microscope.

"Turns out I had misread a section of John's notes in my haste to input what I thought was the easiest part of the cell's design, basing it on my knowledge of human cell structure rather than the much higher pressures required to contain this little bad-ass's internal bio-machinery."

Madeline pointed at two diagrams she had called up on the screen and Ayala tried to follow along, the entire conversation seeming like Russian to her. Actually, her Russian was pretty good, this was more like Finnish, she didn't speak a lick of Finnish.

Madeline continued, "So once the superstructure was stabilized, the cells seem to have worked pretty much as advertized. I don't know if they are self-replicating yet, well, I know there are more in their blood than I put there, but they haven't become infectious yet. The two control subjects are unaffected by the antigen so far."

"So?" asked Ayala.

"So ... we're moving forward well?" said Madeline, confused.

"So ... let's get to the next phase." Ayala looked at her, waiting, but Madeline did not see where she was going. "Madeline, umm, what do you think we should do with this?"

"We should see if it communicates to the other monkeys then we should infect some unfortunate guinea pig, probably you or I, and see what happens."

"Madeline, my dear, once we get this out into the population, there is only so much we can do to speed up its spread. No matter how far and wide I travel, there are only so many people I can infect, and only so much affect that will have on our timeline. But every week we wait to start the process is a week added to the end date, plain and simple. And in those final weeks that could translate to billions of people."

Ayala stared at the younger woman. Madeline knew what Ayala was suggesting, and she understood the logic, but her scientific training was making her balk at what seemed like a simple decision to Ayala.

"Madeline, give me the drug," Ayala said, already starting to look around the room.

"No, wait, it is only just starting to spread in the monkeys, this thing may still kill them all. We need to see if it is safe, you can't risk it, not yet!" Madeline pleaded but the other lady ignored her, looking round the room and spotting the two large stainless steel refrigerators in the corner.

Madeline followed her over to them, trying to talk to Ayala as she pulled open the first refrigerator's door. It contained blood samples so Ayala closed it and opened the second. It was lined with vials filled with clear liquid, and several large bags marked as plasma were hanging on a rack at the bottom.

Ayala turned to Madeline, "Which is it, Madeline? Which one is the agent you gave to the monkeys?"

Madeline stared at the woman, defiant, and in response Ayala's face transformed, setting into a resolve that, over the years, had been many a person's last sight before they felt the full force of Ayala's lethal training. For a moment Madeline was taken aback, then her instinctive fear turned to offense at the thought that her friend might actually hurt her. Ayala saw her young friend's shock, and she softened.

"Madeline, I'm sorry. Please, of course I would never hurt you, don't be silly. I may have bristled, but no, not you, I would not have resorted to that with you. You are like family to me. We are in this together, you have to believe that." Ayala placed her hands on Madeline's shoulders and felt the tension flow out as Madeline relaxed, the unexpected fear going from her.

"But please also know that I do not intend to wait for one moment more for this test to run its course. Do not let the scientist in you forget what we are facing here. We were given these designs by an alien agent. Possibly the only person risking more than we are, and for much less reward. He would not have given us some halfhearted design. I am going to take that drug today. I am going to take it right now, and then we are going to make a batch for me to take with me. This thing starts now. Whether you want it to or not."

Madeline's fear subsided to be replaced with resignation. She was not foolish enough to think she could stop this woman from getting what she wanted. How did Ayala do that? She seemed so …. nice … but then she had this beast inside her. What must she have seen to make her capable of such inherent violence?

Ayala waited, but it was clear she would not wait for long. Madeline relented and lifted a rack of vials from one shelf and walked over to a large, empty metal table. A rack of powered syringes was mounted on one side tethered to a gas tank under the table.

Madeline opened the valve on the tank and the lines running to the syringe guns pressurized. She then unwrapped a clean needle tip from a box to one side and picked up one of the guns, clipping the needle prick to its mounting on the front of the gun. As she loaded one of the vials into the top of the vicious-looking device, Ayala rolled up her sleeve and came to stand by her friend.

They looked at each other. Madeline looked into the resolute older woman's eyes and warned, "Umm, not your arm."

Ayala's eyebrow rose.

"I need muscle." said Madeline, "Your shoulder would do, but your backside would be best."

Ayala smiled wryly and turned, unbuttoning her pants. She was not modest so she simply dropped her trousers and underwear to the floor and hiked up her sweater, bending over the table to expose her rump.

Madeline was a little shocked at the sudden exposure of flesh; most people pulled down one side of the pants just enough to allow access, but she soldiered on. "This will hurt a little." she said.

"I'm sure." said Ayala, knowing that after she had bullied Madeline into giving her the dose the other woman probably wasn't going to be gentle.

Placing her left hand on the small of Ayala's back, Madeline pressed the needle gun's tip hard against one of Ayala's cheeks and fired. There was a pop and a hiss as Madeline depressed the trigger, and the thick grey liquid was forced into Ayala's flesh in a moment. Madeline would not admit it, even to herself, but she was a little disappointed that the other woman hadn't even flinched. Pulling her pants back up, Ayala turned and faced the other woman and gave her a smile.

"I've never been shot with a vet's gun before." said Ayala.

"Oh, right. Yes, sorry about that. Can't rely on young chimpanzees staying still so it's a little more … intense than the machine I'll give you for use on everyone else." said Madeline, stifling a smile.

Ayala nodded and said, "Hmm, well, I hope you'll be able to recover," Madeline looked at her confused and Ayala went on, "you know, from being so torn up about it."

Madeline smiled innocently and went over to a couple of office chairs and sat down, Ayala careful to favor her good cheek as she lowered herself into the chair opposite.

They were silent for a moment while the seriousness of what they had just done settled in. Then Ayala said, "You know I'll need a lot more of that to take with me, Madeline. We can start with a batch for me to go to DC and Hanscom with, and I'll make a quick trip to Europe and Israel while I am at it. That should be as much as I can take in one go. After that I'll come back and get some more so I can go to Asia and India. Then I'll take one final long trip out to Australia, by way of Eastern Europe, Russia, and Africa."

Madeline nodded, doing the mental calculations of the numbers of batches involved. They had said that they would try to get the panacea seeded to about five hundred people in the first month or so. That would knock about four months off the diffusion of the drug, the first part being the slowest. After that time, the margin of return of infecting people by hand would be so low that it would not be worth the risk anymore as the infection would be spreading so fast on its own.

It was time to look forward to the next stage. By the time Ayala returned from her three convoluted trips, the team at Hanscom would hopefully have completed their designs for the missile shielding using the initial pieces of superconducting material Madeline had already fabricated and sent to them. Even if they weren't ready for Madeline to start mass-producing the shield components with the manipulator, she would at least be able to start on the designs John Hunt had already sent to her for the missiles on board the HMS *Dauntless*.

- - -

Neal was never ready for the door to his basement lair to open. Without fail, it scared the living shit out of him. Ayala tried not to laugh when she found him on one knee, pointing the Glock she had procured for him at her, more than a little shakily.

"Now, now, Neal, that seems a little excessive, doesn't it?" She smiled as he replaced the gun in his drawer with his bags of IDs, including one that had a gun license among its various erroneous, but otherwise perfectly legal, documents.

She rummaged around in her bag as he did this then came over to him and said, "Don't move, Neal, there is something on your neck." Neal froze, his eyes instinctively trying to look down to where her outstretched finger was touching him just under the chin. In a swift movement her hand flashed downward and grabbed his arm firmly while her other hand whipped out from behind her back. Before he had even registered the small and vicious-looking needle gun in her other hand, she had it pressed against his shoulder. He flinched as the needle punctured the skin and then, a moment later she was walking away like nothing had happened.

"What the hell, Ayala?" he said, pulling up his sleeve to touch the tiny wound and looking at the trickle of blood on his fingers afterward. She was already replacing the gun in her bag, making sure it was loaded with another of the many doses she had with her before closing the little pouch it travelled in.

"Stop whining, you big baby." Ayala had known he would balk at the injection, so she had decided not to negotiate it with him. She would have to find numerous excuses and underhand ways to discreetly inject countless people with the drug over the next two months. She wasn't about to waste time on a member of her own team.

"Well," she said, ignoring his hurt face, "I am glad you were here. I couldn't exactly call in advance, so it was fifty/fifty whether you would be at home. As it is, though, I can go right back to the airport and catch the next shuttle to Boston."

"Wait, you still haven't told me what the hell that was." Neal asked.

"What do you think?" she said, her hand on her hip while she waited for him to figure it out.

Light dawned and his face lit up, "Shit, that's it! We have it!" he exclaimed, rubbing his arm again, this time with reverence, "That's awesome!"

Contemplating a troop of those tiny warriors coursing through his veins was strange for him, and he took a moment to think about it. But Ayala was already picking up her bag again. He stared at her. He had been a little thrown by being unexpectedly jabbed, but he had a lot he wanted to discuss with this woman, and information he needed her to share with his colleagues working at Hanscom as well.

"Ayala, wait. I have some materials for Martin in Hanscom. Let me get them together for you. Actually, they are on one of the isolated PCs, so let me put them on a drive." he walked over to one of the PCs and sat down, quickly inserting one of the many blank flash drives he kept handy for just this purpose.

He carried on talking as he moved files to the drive, "Look, I know you are in a rush, but while I have you here there is something that I wanted to discuss with you." he paused a moment, focusing on the screen while he dragged the last of the documents he wanted to copy, until all he was left with were a series of time-remaining screens as the bulky files filled the solid state device.

Turning to face her once more, he gathered his thoughts and then said, "I have been thinking about something, and I imagine the colonel will have been struggling with the same thing too, but I think it's time we got someone more … senior on the team if we are going to get the GBMD system online and prepared for D-day."

Ayala nodded, she had considered the same thing but had assumed that the colonel had it under control. "I know what you mean, Neal, but I am assuming Barrett's got that part of the plan under control. I'll mention it to him, but I think that he probably is the most knowledgeable among us on US military protocols."

"Of course, of course." Neal glanced over his shoulder to check the progress of the file copy then looked back at Ayala. "I just, well, I think he may be hesitant to take the cause further up the ranks because, well, not to put too fine a point on it, but I think we all know his immediate superior is a bit of an ass."

She smiled, even laughed a little. She had heard about General Pickler from Barrett long before Neal had even met the man, but Neal was right, the general was not the right man. Neal saw the last of the copy windows close and clicked on one of the files now on the drive to make sure it had copied fully. Happy with the result, he grabbed it and stood up, coming over to face Ayala.

"Look," he said, "I absolutely agree that this is 100% Barrett's call, of course, but maybe we, and by 'we' I mean you, could suggest that he think of another senior officer other than General Pickler who might be able to help us."

She looked at him a moment and he took the hint and got more specific, "I know it will go against the grain for an air force guy to go to another branch, but, well, I think that Admiral Hamilton could be our man."

She thought about this for a second, then nodded and said, "And who is going to approach the admiral? It isn't easy to for an air force colonel to get a meeting with a senior admiral without his superiors knowing about it, you know."

Neal smiled, "True, but a White House science advisor can arrange a meeting easily enough. If the colonel just happens to be at it, then so be it." he shrugged, then his expression became much more serious and he added, "And if he happens to be carrying a gun …"

He left the thought hanging out there. She did not need reminding about their recruitment policy, she had been ready to kill Shinobu in a moment if their meeting had gone differently. Killing an admiral, however, would be a different matter.

"OK, I'll talk to him about it. For what it is worth, I think you may be right. But military recruitment is Barrett's field, and I will go with his decision here."

He nodded, turning the now full USB drive over in his hand and then handing it to her. She unbuttoned the bottom of her blouse and slipped it inside a nook in her pants, tucking it down before rebuttoning. Neal always tried his hardest not to enjoy seeing her do this, but the truth was Ayala had encountered countless strip searches and worse, including her run in with a veterinary vaccination gun on her all too recent trip to North Dakota, and she was not shy. She didn't care whether he looked or not. She did enjoy catching him pretending to look away though.

Straightening her jacket, she thought about what Neal had said. She would share his thoughts with Barrett when she got to Hanscom, along with her own recommendation. After that …

She looked at him, "Anything else?"

He shook his head.

"Good." then more gently, "And you, Neal, are you OK?"

He smiled and nodded. Though her comment may seem cursory, he knew that her concern was genuine. She did not banter or politic, not within the team. Outside the team he was sure very few people saw much of the real Ayala, but once she had told someone who she really was, she had a way of conveying that underneath it all she was a very clear-cut person: an open book. Once she let you see the real her, that was it. After that, what you saw was what you got.

She gave him a quick hug, then slung her bag over her shoulder and left.

Chapter 40: Guilt Plating

"The rivet gun, the large one." shouted Martin Sobleski from under the mammoth shell.

Captain Toranssen hefted the bulky and lethal-looking device under one arm, using the other to pay out its thick wire, and made his way round to where Martin's feet were sticking out from the bottom of the missile casing.

The GBMD system that the US had spent countless trillions constructing around its borders was made up of several overlapping and complementary layers. These included various radar and sonic sensing devices, satellite monitoring, and other less advanced but equally important methods of sensing and tracking incoming threats. But while sensing and following incoming missiles was maybe the most technologically complex part, it was relatively pointless without the more tactile side of the system.

The business end of the GBMD was made up of two different but equally deadly missile batteries. The first was kinetic. It relied upon building up a lot of momentum and focusing it into a small point, delivering a crushing impact to an incoming missile. While each one of its warheads had a relatively small area of impact, it used what was called a cluster effect, deploying hundreds of the needle thin projectiles in a destructive maelstrom. This gave it a large chance of interception. Despite this, it was relatively cheap per unit, meaning lots could be launched at a target; the aim was to blanket, to carpet bomb the skies.

The second type of weapon in the shield was a battery of much larger, much more expensive, and much more lethal anti-ballistic missiles. While they were still smaller than the long-range ballistic missiles, they were designed to intercept, and their payload significantly less potent, they were still much larger and more expensive than their kinetic GBMD counterparts.

With the size of the missile barrages in question, it had been clear to the team that they could not hope to manufacture, distribute, and install the one thousand or so missile shields they would need to protect all of the missile battery they would be sending against the satellites. So they had decided to focus on shielding the larger and much more destructive anti-ballistic missiles, with their small tactical warheads.

If all went to plan, the satellites would spend a lot of time trying to take out the smaller and more numerous kinetic missiles before it got around to the larger tactical ABMs. By then, hopefully it would be too late for even the powerful lasers aboard the satellites to penetrate the shielding on each of the remaining missiles, and at least a few would get through their defenses.

Hopefully.

It was from under the disembodied nose cone of one of these tactical behemoths that Martin now lay, requesting that Jack pass him the rivet gun. He was attaching a mock-up of the layered shielding they were designing so they could verify its specifications.

The captain grunted slightly as he lowered the powerful industrial rivet gun into the waiting hands of Martin lying on his sliding palette, ready to roll back under and start riveting the shield in place.

"Holy shit," said Martin, as he took the weight of the machine off of Jack. He wheezed as he slid back under the big nose cone, the gun's weight squeezing the air out of him.

"OK, plug her in." he shouted, grunting as he maneuvered the big gun into place over the holes in the shielding.

The missile casing was mounted on a pallet that held the hefty chunk of steel from the inside, allowing the team to work on its outside. The focal point of the missile's armor plating would need to be in the warhead case, the very front of the missile. After all, the lasers that would try to destroy each of their missiles would come from their targets, the satellites, and therefore would impact the front of the missile as it approached.

"OK," shouted Captain Toranssen as he connected the power for the rivet gun. He heard one last grunt from Martin as he pushed the riveting machine into place against the casing and then a rending metal sound that was highly disturbing, followed by a resounding snap as the rivet's central mandrel broke off. They were unpleasant, but thankfully those were the sounds the gun made when it worked properly.

"I'll never get use to that." shouted the captain, shaking his head and walking over to a second layer of shielding that was on a separate pallet to one side. It looked like another version of the structure Martin was under, the same shape. But it was critically different. Martin had just finished riveting a thin ceramic layer to the inner nose cone structure. Now they would overlay that with the composite layer of superconductor that Madeline had fabricated for them.

Due to the size constraints of the resonance chamber Madeline was working with, she had been forced to construct the superconducting sheath in overlapping sections with four shaped plates joined by a central nose cone. These had then been fixed into place on the inside of the standard outer casing of the missile.

Now they were going to bolt that whole structure, case, superconductor and all, over the ceramic insulating layer. The design, which John Hunt had helped them with, was supposed to sacrifice the missile's standard outer casing first. It would evaporate almost immediately under the laser's attack, despite its quarter inch of military grade titanium, before the laser came to bear on the superconducting sheath beneath. This revolutionary alloy was held together with chemical bonds that were unlike any material Martin had ever seen before.

Through mechanisms none of the team entirely understood, the material did not absorb energy in the normal way, and within reason did not react to it. This made it tremendously resistant to heat. The plan was that this layer would take the brunt of the laser attack, shielding the warhead beneath for as long as possible. Apparently the material would be able to survive for about forty-five seconds under the satellites' concentrated glare. Comparatively, the ceramic below would only survive for a fraction of a second longer once the black shielding was finally ruptured. But the ceramic layer was not part of the defense, it was just there to deflect the heat that even the mysterious alien alloy would emit under the magnificent power of the satellites' attack. Before it eventually ruptured the superconducting material would become phenomenally hot and the ceramic heat tile would protect the warhead within from that terrific heat.

"OK, Jack, might as well slide the outer shell into place and I'll get this lower bolt in while I'm down here." said Martin, breathing heavily as he wielded the big rivet gun.

"OK," said Jack, heaving under the effort as he pushed the big structure of the outer shield casing over the inner shield. He moved slowly, taking guidance from Martin.

"Good, that's it, OK, now straighten up, you are coming in a bit from the left." said Martin as the two touched.

They started to squeeze together, the fit necessarily extremely tight. Slowly but surely the inside of the superconducting shell slid over the smooth white of the ceramic heat shielding. It was a strange sound. The superconductor siphoning off the energy as it slid and muffling any scraping sound. They had learned early that this stuff did not behave like anything they were familiar with.

Martin shook his head as he considered the material. "Weird stuff, this," he said, careful not to touch it as it slid in. It would not hurt him, but it would deliver all of the friction energy it was generating in a static shock to Martin, such was the perfection of its ability to siphon energy.

"OK, nearly there, slowly does it." said Martin, watching the two big cones come together from underneath. Jack heaved, pushing against the titanium outer shell. The shell alone cost over $200,000, he thought as he heaved. Not something you wanted to dent.

"That's it," shouted Martin, and Jack heard him grunt once more as he shifted the rivet gun into place over the next join hole.

- - -

"I have to say it, Colonel, it looks good." Martin said, not looking up from his computer. The colonel had come to join them. They were behind schedule, the need to ship the advanced material components from North Dakota, and to do so discreetly, was hampering their efforts. But today was hopefully going to be a good day.

"Give me the details, Martin, if you don't mind." asked the colonel, looking over Martin's shoulder at the screen.

"Well, Colonel, we have locked in the shell casing and I have been scanning it with the ultrasound for the last four hours. We have two small air gaps which I need to fix, but with minor adjustments I am confident we have our design."

"And we can use the existing outer casing?"

Jack spoke up, "Just as you see it, Colonel, we have managed to use the outer casing and the standard heat shielding from the original missile armor. All we needed to do was change the mounting slightly to account for the sandwich of superconductor between them."

Barrett nodded. They were close, but he had to balance the need for expediency with the need for accuracy. He needed to know if it worked. Screw it, he thought.

"Captain, Doctor, time to check if this thing works. I know we've checked the superconductor against the laser before, but I need to know this structure will work under pressure." he looked at them both; Jack seemed skeptical, but Martin was grinning. Barrett prompted them, "Well, gentlemen?"

They sprang into action. OK, the man wants to destroy $200,000 of titanium, who were they to argue.

Both the modified missile casing and their deuterium fluoride laser were ungainly devices, but they soon had them facing off against each other, locked in place, the big chemical laser powering up.

"Are we ready, gentlemen?" said Martin, as they all donned their dark glasses and arranged themselves behind the mobile, polarized Plexiglas shielding, itself thoroughly out of sight of the actual laser.

"Ready." said Captain Toranssen.

"OK," said Martin, "activating laser." the humming from the already warm laser grew suddenly louder, and then its terrific green beam lanced at the big nose cone across the room. The twang and snap of the titanium casing came just fifteen seconds later, and the laser started to hammer at the thinner, impossibly black superconducting layer beneath.

"Just to reiterate, gentlemen," said Martin over the loud thrum of the laser and the hiss and creak of the missile shielding heating up, "let's remember that our target time is forty-five seconds under the much more powerful attack of the satellites' defensive laser. That means it needs to be able to withstand this lesser attack for about six minutes."

They went silent, their eyes moving in unison from the missile casing to the clock and back again like a parody of a tennis match.

Two minutes passed. They had a camera mounted behind the shielding. Not directly behind, because they had a large concrete block directly behind to absorb the laser attack once it broke through, but from its spot just to one side the small camera was still able to relay an image of the ceramic of the inner casing.

It was starting to glow, temperature sensors inside the casing showing the heat rising. The outer casing that was still intact was also starting to absorb the incredible heat of the superconducting layer, warping slightly and even starting to glow itself.

At three minutes, the metal of the outer casing was visibly orange and the large room they were in was starting to get noticeably hotter. Sweat was forming on the brows of the three men for two reasons as, at four minutes, the remaining outer metal casing started to slag, pieces liquefying and dropping to the floor to melt the concrete.

At five minutes, the airmen had shed their uniform jackets and all three of them were dripping with sweat. They had disabled any smoke detectors in the room weeks beforehand, and it was lucky that they had. The remains of the $200,000 titanium casing were now in a smoldering slagheap on the floor.

After what felt like days of endless heat, it happened in a snap. The superfine tethers of superconducting shielding started to fray ever so slightly as they reached and surpassed their maximum effective temperature. The slightest gap was all the laser needed, and in an instant the sliver of killing light broke through and hit the already superheated ceramic beneath and the whole structure shattered. As the laser at last reached the block behind the cone and started to burn it as well, Martin reached out and hit the kill switch and the beam died.

Five minutes forty-eight seconds. It was not what they had hoped for. It was within their range, but not as far into it as they had, in truth, hoped. But pipe dreams aside, it was functional and within parameters. It was time to clean up the mess. And it was time to go to full production.

- - -

Four hours later, a tired but satisfied Barrett Milton entered the apartment the navy had provided for him and slung his jacket on the floor. He noticed her smell first, recognizing it instantly, and his heart leapt.

"Pushpin?" he said, "How long have you been waiting?" he used his old nickname for her, for the way she had always been able to bring so much pressure to bear on such a small spot. He had always thought she should have been more annoyed by it than she had. That was before he had known what she truly did for a living.

Ayala came up from behind him, smiling softly, "Not long, cushion, not long." He laughed softly, her retort reminding him that she had been the only person who had ever thought of him as soft. He turned to her. Their resistance to their mutual attraction had not lasted long after they had been reunited, but as he looked at her now he felt that his feelings were changing once more. He found that as he looked at her now he felt not only the passion that he had forgotten, and the love he had denied himself, he felt that thing he had lost when she had revealed her past to him.

He knew that now, embarked as they were on this seemingly suicidal venture, he trusted her once more, and as he took her in his arms and kissed her she knew it as well. She pulled back for a moment and looked into his eyes, savoring the sight. She had lied to him, endangered him and his career, she had even cheated on him when her duty called her to do so. She had done it all with a clear conscience, knowing the importance of her work, but she had never doubted the risk to their relationship, or the importance of her love for him. He had been the only luxury she had ever allowed herself.

Now, in this new crisis, she knew that all her previous missions may have been for nothing, and with this new perspective she saw that they had been on the same side all along. He, in turn, now knew that when faced with something important enough, he had found himself willing to betray all he had held dear in the name of something greater, just as she had.

He had lied, cheated, stolen, all for the greater good, and in doing so he had become that thing he had spurned in her. She saw that he had not so much forgiven her, as realized that he had nothing to forgive. Reading him as she always had, she realized that the pain she had caused him had come to an end and that they were one again, and she was overwhelmed with how much it meant to her.

He lifted her in his arms and she allowed herself to be a woman, his woman, forgetting all the training, the violence, the killing of her past. He carried her to bed. He was sweaty and smelly and alive. She laughed at how young she felt, how it reminded her of when they had met twenty years before. No more lies. For these precious moments she had no layers, only Ayala Zubaideh as she truly was. And she could think of no possible reason why she would ever lie to this man again.

Chapter 41: A Higher Echelon

They did not meet outside the Pentagon. Colonel Milton had been careful to enter by a different entrance and had also arrived several hours before Neal. Sitting in a bank of cubes reserved for visiting officers, he thought about how to play the crucial meeting he was about to attend. He was relying on Neal to bring the documentation they were going to rely on as proof, while for his part Barrett had also brought a sheaf of superconducting material to show their potential recruit.

Neal, arriving as he always did through the civilian checkpoint, went to his office and then pulled up the daily check-in sheet on his computer, locating the cube the colonel had been assigned for the day.

Seeing Neal approach, and noting that no one was in sight, the colonel did something he hadn't done in years. Standing as he saw Neal approach, he took the man's proffered hand and then put his other arm around his shoulder in a brief hug.

Neal was surprised, touched even, but he kept a serious face.

"Colonel," he said, the moment seemingly passing, "it's good to see you."

"You too, Neal, you too, and I thought we said it was Barrett when no one was around."

Neal laughed quietly, "Of course, Barrett." It felt strange to say it, but somehow good as well, like calling a parent by their first name. Neal asked, "How are things at Hanscom?"

"Good, we have the shield design finalized and we have sent Martin to North Dakota to help Madeline with production. We are about a week behind schedule but I am hoping we can make a good deal of that up in deployment, we had some necessary contingency in that part of the schedule." He smiled as he said this next part, "I understand Ayala attacked you with the antigen."

They both laughed a little. Ayala had taken a bit more time and care before injecting Barrett than she had with the unsuspecting Neal, but only so she could enjoy winding him up about how much it was going to hurt. It had ended in a brief tussle when Barrett had tried to get the hypodermic gun off her. Not a good idea, it turned out. Moments later, he was face down on the floor with her astride his shoulders, her legs pinning him down as she rather ignominiously wrenched his pants down. The actual injection had been rather anticlimactic, in the end, but the, err, tussle that followed it wasn't.

When they had gotten back to the task in hand, she had given him a hundred doses for him to administer as he saw fit. He would take a few flights to visit various friends and family across the country, and then he would make a long, looping trip through Mexico and South America as well, under the guise of visiting War Colleges in various allied countries, culminating with a brief but fortuitous speaking engagement at the Argentine Naval

Academy. Diplomatic status would help him bring the small dose cases with him, liberal anaesthetizing beverages with colleagues in each location would help him administer them.

Moving past the spread of the antigen, Neal brought them back to the topic at hand, "So, how do you think we should go about this? Do you want to lead the conversation or should I?" asked Neal.

"I think it's probably best that I kick it off, introduce what we are doing, and give some background. Then you can take the lead on the technical part, he will trust that more coming from you, and you are better at explaining it. After that ..." the colonel looked blank for a moment. He didn't really know how they were going to handle it if things did not go as planned. He knew what he would have to do, he knew that all too well, and that is why he had not wanted to have the meeting in the Pentagon. But he also knew that to ambush the man anywhere else would probably be just as risky and far harder to arrange in secrecy.

"OK, Barrett, we'll go with that." agreed Neal, "How about you let me start with a brief explanation of why I have brought you in as well, seeing as he isn't expecting you to be there."

Colonel Milton nodded, and they stood silent for a moment. Neal inhaled deeply then raised his eyebrows expectantly, "Well, Colonel, shall we?"

"Absolutely, Neal. I forget where the admiral's office is, so why don't you lead on?"

"Oh, please, Barrett, you think that I know my way around this rabbit warren?" they laughed.

"OK, I'll get us to the navy STRATCOM section and we'll go from there, how about that?"

Neal nodded and they set off.

As they arrived at the Naval STRATCOM section, Neal noticed that it was not the same section of the building as the one he had met Admiral Hamilton in after returning from India. His suspicions were further confirmed when an assistant directed him and the colonel to the admiral's office and they arrived at a wholly different location than he had remembered from before.

"Colonel," Neal said, taking Barrett's arm to get him to stop before they went in, "should I be concerned that the last time I met with the admiral he was in a completely different section of the building?"

"He hasn't changed jobs since then?"

"I don't think you can go much higher than head of Fleet Operations."

Barrett realized what had happened and shook his head, "I've heard of the general doing this too. Leave it to me, I'll find out whether it is anything to be worried about." and with that they turned and went into the admiral's receiving area.

They didn't have to wait long, and soon they were being ushered by one of the admiral's aides into his large office.

"Wow, this is nice, Admiral," said Neal, shaking the older man's hand, "much bigger than the office we met in before."

Admiral Hamilton smiled, not thrown by the comment, but clearly intrigued at the presence of an air force colonel in his office without a pre-call from the man's supervising general.

"I was having this one redecorated when you last came by, you'll have to excuse the loner they gave me." said Tim Hamilton, now staring openly at the colonel, who went ahead and spoke.

"My apologies for being here unannounced, Admiral Hamilton. I'd like to request that you withhold judgment on that point until the meeting is over. After that, if you feel I have overstepped my bounds by coming to you, I assume you will contact General Pickler as you see fit." The admiral's eyebrows rose in surprise, but his face also betrayed a hint of impatience. He was not one for office intrigue.

Barrett noted this and went on, "I hope you'll see soon why we did not supply an agenda for this briefing in advance."

The admiral knew protocol demanded that he call the general before speaking further with the colonel, but he was not fool enough to ignore the tone of the decorated airman's voice. Nor was he naïve enough to believe for a moment that General Pickler would immediately call him if a naval commander were to approach *him* in secret.

The admiral nodded, giving his tacit consent to the colonel's request, for now, and the colonel went on, "Before we begin, sir, I have to ask something. If you were in a different office when you met with Mr. Danielson before, I am assuming that it was the other office that was the interview room, not this one."

The admiral looked blankly at the colonel for a moment, not allowing his fury at having senior military protocol discussed in front of a civilian. But clearly the colonel was unfazed. Very well.

"Colonel, Mr. Danielson, I will hear what you have to say, since you are clearly very keen to say it to me. And I will set your mind at ease by saying that my real office, which we are indeed now in, is swept daily by Naval Intelligence: you will not be heard in here." The admiral leant back in his chair, looking pointedly at each man in turn before he delivered his final proviso.

"That said, gentlemen, I do not take kindly to being ambushed with interagency gossip. You have my attention, for now. I hope, for your sake, that what you have come to me with is important enough to warrant this highly unorthodox behavior."

Barrett looked at Neal, who was nodding appreciatively and biting the inside of his cheek. Yes, quite, interagency gossip. Barrett was proverbially biting his tongue as well. The admiral wants to be impressed with the gravity of their purpose, they thought in unison, I think we can oblige him, and without further digression Barrett begun.

"Admiral," said the colonel in an official tone, "the events we are here to discuss with you start just over seven months ago, when the *King's Transom* was shot at and sunk by an attack from space, killing all aboard."

The admiral stared wide-eyed at the man, then at Neal, who gently nodded, pensive at the memory but clearly resolute.

"Admiral," the colonel continued, before the other officer could find the words to reply, "since that day a small but dedicated team has worked hard to identify and classify the source of that attack, and have discovered some extremely disturbing facts that we are here today to share with you.

"We have chosen you very carefully, aware of the fact that the slightest misstep by us, or anyone we share this information with, will have disastrous and far reaching consequences. But we cannot go much further with our work without informing either yourself or some other member of Strategic Command."

He let that sink in for a moment, but when he saw the admiral about to speak he again preempted him, using a trick Ayala had taught him to control of the flow of the man's thoughts, "Admiral, we have come to you today with proof that we have been infiltrated by agents from an extraterrestrial force. That, along with the vastly more extensive documentation we have compiled offsite, will show you, conclusively, that they have already penetrated deeply into our world's key military institutions."

With that, the colonel began to take a photo of Lana Wilson from a file in his lap, but Neal stopped him, "Colonel, before we get to that, why don't we discuss in more detail the attack in India, and what has happened since. We'll get to the agents themselves in good time."

The admiral stared at them both. Were they mad? They clearly meant what they were saying. If this was a joke he would have them both thrown from the building, and the colonel would be dismissed from the service when the admiral had finished with him. But even as the indignant admiral thought that, he knew that they weren't joking at all. Neal may have been capable of such a thing, but not this man Colonel Milton. He had met a thousand men like him. He did not play with admirals and generals. He knew his duty too well.

The admiral's mind raced; had he just heard the colonel correctly? Admiral Hamilton knew that he had sensed something profound in Neal all those months ago after the attack, and had assumed the man would come to him when he was ready. But Jesus Christ. Aliens. Really? This was the purpose of this meeting?

He looked at them curiously, "Colonel Milton? Mr. Danielson? I am waiting."

The colonel nodded at Neal, seeing the wisdom of not throwing the photo of the admiral's son's girlfriend in front of the man just yet. He sat back and watched as Neal took over. To a certain degree, they knew, it was now out of their hands. There was no way they could control the reaction of a senior naval admiral. Nor, realistically, could they contain him if he did not see things the way they did.

It was down to them to convince him. A part of Neal wished Ayala was there, and he assumed Barrett felt the same way, but that would have been close to impossible. It was fairly difficult, and fairly treasonous, to bring a foreign spy into the Pentagon. They would just have to give it their best shot, and then put their faith in the man they had chosen.

- - -

The three men did not travel across town together. It had come down to proof, as it always did. Neal left by his usual route and returned home. Meanwhile, the colonel and a bemused admiral drove out of the Pentagon's secure basement garage in Barrett's rental car. They drove in silence, stopping first at a separate apartment the team had retained across town, where they changed clothes and went the rest of the way by bus. They eventually arrived on foot at the basement entrance to the house next door to Neal's.

Neal was already in the basement when they came in from the street. He had booted up two of the offline PCs to show some of the information they had compiled since India, as well as the probe's findings that had cost Laurie and James their lives.

It took several hours, and the admiral had to be talked down from fury and disorientation several times. But the hardest part had come when he had turned to the wall where Neal had posted all the information they had on John's seven counterparts around the world.

"Jesus, is that … Lana. Good God, it can't be." he had said as he looked at the woman who was dating his son, who he had entertained in his home … whom he had personally seen deployed to the Atlantic Fleet navy yards in Georgia.

"It's true, Admiral," said Neal, trying to be gentle with the man, "these are not suspects, the double Agent John Hunt has specifically identified each of these people. How do you think we got any detailed information at all on the activities of members of the Chinese and Russian military?"

"How do you know he is not just trying to undermine key people in our armed forces?" said the admiral, a sickness overcoming him. His son. It was too much to come to terms with.

"Admiral," said the colonel, "if you were trying to spread dissent about key military personnel, would you name a fresh-faced naval lieutenant? Look at the dates, sir, look at when they each started Officer Candidate School."

Hamilton looked at them. They were all within a couple of weeks of each other.

Neal stepped up to the admiral and stood just to his side, wary of the man's emotions, "Admiral, just to reiterate, the meteor shower that started us all on this path was October 4th. Five days before the first of these individuals checked into OCS. All but one of them were in schools around the world within a month. And then three weeks after they arrived we saw the attack on Bachamir Air Base in Afghanistan that we now know initiated the last Agent into the ranks of Al Qaeda."

The admiral looked around the board. The Agents. The probe's findings. The superconducting material. The virus. Jesus Christ. And to think he had threatened these two men with wasting his time.

For their part, Neal and Barrett waited. They sensed that the admiral's mood had reached critical mass. Soon he would crack. The question was: what would be left afterward? Would he be one of them, would he be broken, or, worst of all, would he be a liability?

Admiral Tim Hamilton thought. The evidence they had compiled was widespread and exhaustive. The sources were as close to infallible as you could hope to see in such situations. A senior White House advisor, an air force colonel previously in charge of the

Deep Space Array, sourcing every major skyward facing asset they or any of their allies had. The meteors' trajectories and landing sights. The markings on the remains of the *King's Transom*'s crew. The schematics of the virus and its antigen. The plating, its utter lack of reaction to heat, cold, or, more demonstrably, to Barrett belting it with a large hammer and no small amount of malice.

As pie in the sky as it all might seem, the Pentagon had, of course, white-boarded scenarios just like this. He had been part of the briefings, at first jovial, then serious, and then jovial again. Their laughter seemed so naïve now.

Finally, face set, he looked at the photo of Lana Wilson one more time. She had come into his home. She had used his son to get ahead. He thought long and hard.

The silence was like a cloud in the room, a mist that veiled everything but the lack of response from the admiral. Eventually he spoke quietly, his eyes still locked on Lana's picture, "How do we kill them?"

The colonel looked at Neal, who nodded, clearly still holding his breath. The colonel spoke, "Well, Admiral, first we have to break their key defenses. We have to destroy the satellites which they have orbiting above us. Once they are destroyed, we can start arming ourselves with the tools we will need to attack the Agents."

The admiral nodded, "I hope, gentlemen, that you have not brought me here and thoroughly ruined my day without also having a plan for how to accomplish that."

He turned to Neal, and he was an admiral once more. An air of confidence and leadership rising up, his spine regaining its steel like rigidity that all military leaders learn from long experience.

Almost consoled, this now left Neal and Barrett with the decision about how much of their plan to reveal to the admiral at this first meeting. Should they reveal the full insanity of their plan, with all its diplomatically and physically explosive parts? Neal thought a moment, holding the admiral's stare, like a child thinking whether to ask for a kitten or a pony.

"Actually, Admiral, it is precisely because we have a plan that we approached you in the first place. Tell me, sir, how much do you know about the workings of the GBMD system?"

Yup, might as well go for the pony.

- - -

Shahim did not take notice of either the arrival or departure of the heavily disguised colonel and admiral through the basement entrance of the building next to Neal's. The neighbors, and countless others that came and went on the street, were ancillary to his interests. He sat perfectly still in an apartment across the street, his face just visible in the second-floor window. He watched Neal's house.

Knowing how much harder it would be to monitor the entrance to the Pentagon up close and personal, he had decided to watch Neal's house instead, to get an idea of the man's patterns of movement. Once he knew when his target typically went to work, he could follow him to work and then focus on studying the exact entrance the man used. After that he could plan his attack around that.

But as the days passed, Shahim watched his prey and he saw that something was not quite right. Neal Danielson would come home from the Pentagon or the White House, typically around 7pm. Then he would disappear for at least a couple of hours, sometimes longer. The day before he had not even gone to work, and yet Shahim had not seen Neal through any of the windows all day.

He knew the layout of the man's house and he suspected that Neal was taking the stairs in the center of the house that led to the basement. But why? His floor plans told him that the basement had no windows, and Neal had a large office upstairs.

Shahim could not help but be curious what the man was doing down there.

Chapter 42: Sowing the Seed

The street in Tel Aviv was filled. The large crowd of people in the local market milled and moved like water gently washing between rocks on a calm shore, ebbing and flowing, filling every space, dotted with pockets of movement and rest like the eddies and currents of a stream. Ayala was in her old neighborhood. She had spent so many years here as a child that she could taste the place, like a long forgotten recipe, or the smell of a loved one. She had been born a Yemenite, daughter of a long line of pioneers who had settled this part of Tel Aviv long before it was Tel Aviv. Kerem HaTeimanim had always been a relatively observant neighborhood compared to the more secular districts that now surrounded it. This orthodoxy had been the cause of her mother and her being forced to leave the area when they were younger, and later the source of a teenage Ayala's rebelliousness.

Her father had died in a car accident when Ayala was six, leaving her mother to depend on Ayala's grandparents for support. Ayala's mother shared her fiercely independent nature, and she had railed against this dependence, eventually spurning tradition and taking work in the Kirya, an area of government buildings just across the then burgeoning city of Tel Aviv.

Three years after Ayala's father had died, in the summer of 1964, her mother met and fell in love with an Arab working for the Israeli government, in and of itself a great controversy, both then and now. They had kept it a secret for many months, but secrets are hard to keep in a tight-knit community like the Yemenites of Kerem HaT. When Ayala's mother had been discovered, rage had spread throughout the neighborhood in a matter of days, shaming her family and friends.

She had been faced with a choice: stay with a family who was ashamed of her, and face curfew and moral outrage from everyone she knew, or take her now nine-year-old daughter Ayala with her and leave, going to the man she loved, surely the only way she would ever be able to see him again.

For a couple of years it had been good. Ayala was more at home in the secular world of their new neighborhood across town, and she basked in the happiness of her mother and the good man she had found. Ayala's memories of this time had been the soil into which she would eventually plant the seed of her relationship with Barrett, the only fertile part of a life otherwise bereft of affection.

But it had not lasted. Her stepfather was an alien here, he had taken work with a construction company as a younger man, but growing tensions between Israel and its Arab neighbors made it ever harder to find work. In 1967, the six-day war marked the start of renewed open aggression in the Middle East, and the outward expansion of Israeli borders as far as the Suez Canal. Though the war was officially started by Egypt and Jordan, the Israelis were prepared, and it was during this brief but lopsided conflict that they took control of the West Bank and Gaza Strip. Hostilities would continue to flair until the last major Arab-Israeli conflict in 1973, when the armies of Egypt and Syria, backed by a host of other nations, would invade Israel once more. That war would, ironically, lead to Egypt becoming the first Arab nation to recognize Israel as a state, but by then Ayala's life, and that of her small family, had been changed forever. Without work, or hope for support from Ayala's family, they had left Israel and gone to her stepfather's home nation: Saudi Arabia.

As an Israeli, Ayala's mother was a leper in the community, and stayed indoors for most of the day. Meanwhile, Ayala was forced to survive by becoming her surroundings. The first fights and struggles of her days at school made her extraordinarily tough. She discovered inside her an innate ability to fit in, and two years and two different schools later, she walked and talked like all of her new Arab friends. Her mother went slowly insane, grief at her fate and her daughter's denial of her roots wrenching at her in her long days behind closed doors and drawn curtains.

By the time Ayala was eighteen, there was nothing left of the mother she had once loved; fear, grief, and paranoia driving her to fits of rage.

But Ayala's mother was wrong about the young Ayala. She had not forgotten her roots in Tel Aviv, either in HaKirya or even in Kerem HaTeimanim. She had not forgotten who she was. She had done what was necessary to survive. To this day she still thought of it as her first mission, and her most complete success. Her ability to fool even her own mother into believing she was something she was not giving her the confidence she would later need to walk into a den of hornets, look them in the eye, and say, "I am one of you."

To her mother's surprise, she had announced on her eighteenth birthday that she was returning to Israel to fulfill her commitment to the armed forces there. The day they had parted, she had looked into her mother's eyes and given her some measure of peace. Speaking in their mother tongue, she had told her she was a Yemenite and she was returning to the homeland to take up arms in its defense. She had left and never looked back. To this day she had no idea what had happened to her mother or stepfather, they were a sadness necessarily left in the past.

While her Israeli colleagues in the army may have been standoffish about the apparently Arab woman in their midst, her superiors had seen her value immediately. She had been earmarked for recruitment into the Mossad from the start, and her performance in her first few months of service had only heightened the ardency of her unseen suitors. They approached her after close combat training one day and asked her why she fought with such vigor.

The nineteen-year-old dark-set Ayala had not hesitated, "Because no one will come to my aide but me." If she had been looking to impress them, she could not have said anything more apropos. But she had no idea what they had in store for her.

She was a Jew who could speak fluent Arabic, both the Standard, Nadji, and Hijazi dialects, and she had no close relatives in Israel. The only hesitation they had was the fear that she was simply too perfect. Their test: she had been forced to return to her old district of Kerem HaTeimanim and find one person who recognized her. The difficulty of finding one had almost broken her, but a cousin had eventually seen in her now-hardened eyes the nine-year-old who had left the district with her shamed mother and they had even spent one strange afternoon reminiscing of old times.

But it had been a brief reunion. After setting their considerable resources to vetting the cousin in question the Mossad had been satisfied. And Ayala's course would not be of her own choosing for the next thirty years. As the years passed, she developed a way of envisioning herself that helped her to remember who she was. This helped her center when she needed to, and more importantly, to forget when she needed to as well. She saw herself like a Matryoshka doll, her consecutive lives and personas piled atop each other like rings in a tree, dating back to her earliest memories.

It had been twenty years since she had last walked the streets Kerem HaTeimanim, and now she sat looking at the passing people of her childhood. The place had been gentrified and developed since she had been here. But it was still the old neighborhood. Unlike many Western cultures, the Jews tended to change less than their surroundings, not more, and many of these people looked shockingly similar to their parents and grandparents so many years ago, even as the buildings around them had evolved.

But there were many more unorthodox people here now than there had been in her childhood, and she was one of them. She sat in a café, outside. The dry, pleasant heat of the Israeli afternoon on her, and she allowed herself a rare luxury. She opened the many layers of her Matryoshka doll, and shed light on the very smallest core of her. A nine-year-old girl looked out on the surroundings she had once called home and smiled.

If her father had not passed away, she would no doubt still be here now. Married, probably with children. No doubt happy, but also completely innocent of the way the world really worked. She would think of herself as a woman, no doubt, but she would still be a child compared to the woman she had been forced to become. She would never have killed. She would never have known the horrors, or the power, or the fear, or the truth. She would never have shot a man in the face even as he leapt on her, knife ready, to have his head explode over her. She would never have allowed a target and his guards to rape her so they would eventually sleep, allowing her to wrap her legs around his neck and rip the life from him, killing his cohorts next as they slumbered, slitting their throats one by one with unparalleled satisfaction.

She shook her head. In so many ways she would still be that nine-year-old child. Ignorant even of how much she did not know, perhaps even longing for some adventure. She smiled coldly and sipped her coffee.

Out of the corner of her eye she saw him. He was not looking at her, nor would he. He would have seen her sitting at the café table from a distance and now he would walk by her, on the other side of the street. Maintaining this same lack of open acknowledgement, she stood, finished her Turkish coffee in one swig, left some money for it, and started to walk in the same direction as him, the bitter taste of the thick coffee grinds still in her mouth. He walked for a while. She stayed on the other side of the street, but soon he crossed in front of her and walked down a side street to her left. She followed, pretending to dial a number on her cell phone and start a conversation. He turned into an alley about three doors down, and for the first time glanced back to check that she was there, only momentarily, but confirming she had followed him, he walked into the alley and disappeared from view.

She stopped by its entrance, still talking into her phone, and looked up and down the street like she was receiving directions from her fictional caller, then, comfortable that she had not been followed and that she recognized no face from the café where she had picked up his trail, she turned and followed the man. He was waiting in a deep-set doorway ten meters down the alley, its stone arch ample cover in the slim, dark space.

"Ayala Zubaideh, I didn't really believe it was you until this moment." said the man.

"Saul, how have you been?" She hugged the older man who had been her handler for the majority of her career. He was in his sixties now, but handlers tended to live much longer than agents, and retirement was rarely an option for them. There was simply no way to fully transition an asset from one to another without great risk to both parties.

But unlike him, Ayala had indeed retired, hoping that she would return to America to her husband and he would forgive her the lies she had told him. But she had not been completely surprised when he hadn't. So she had gone into a kind of mental hibernation. Her days had consisted of running and writing, she had found she was very good at crosswords in any of the five languages she spoke fluently, and had even started to write them for a local newspaper in Denver. But now she had been reborn with a new purpose. She was her own handler now, but this man was still an important man in the Mossad, and a man who could be useful to her.

She had called the man she knew as Saul from a payphone after landing in Tel Aviv that morning, and he had not missed a beat at hearing her voice. It was difficult to surprise a man who had sent as many people to their deaths as he had. He had simply set the time and place of their meeting as he always had, using the old code words she knew so well. She had suggested a different spot, using the code word for the café in her old neighborhood and he had agreed, then they had hung up.

"You disappeared, 'yala, I assumed you would be living in wedded bliss by now." he smiled, his broad bearded face and wise eyes full of genuine affection, despite the lie he had just told.

"You know as well as I that I never got what I went to find in America, old friend." she looked at him with pensive eyes, but they were not as sad as he would have expected given that his reports on her told him that her relationship with Barrett had failed. He had been faced with the potential for having to order her termination after her retirement from the service. He knew her well and he had been relatively sure that she would confess her true job in Israel to Barrett once she had retired. But despite that fact, Saul also knew that the Ayala he knew would never tell the man any details, or betray any of her colleagues. This fact, combined with the fact that he also knew from the agency's extensive file on her unsuspecting husband that he was not a threat to them had led him to let her go in peace.

He had let her live as a reward for thirty years of unfailing service to Israel. It had been a rare concession on his part.

But now here she was, standing in front of him. And she had a secret in her eyes, one he knew she was not going to tell him. Well, 'yala, he thought, let's see what you have come for. What do you know that you want me to know, and, more importantly, what do you know that you do *not* want me to know.

Ayala looked at the man and knew he was going to try and get from her everything she had, whether she was willing to give it or not. She was, to some degree, prepared for that, but she was not here to recruit the man. He could not be relied upon to act as he said he would, and the chances that he would attempt to verify what she said if she told him the truth were just too great to be risked. But knowing she should keep the details of their plot from him was not the same as actually succeeding in doing so. This was no pompous executive or political buffoon, he was her intellectual match in every way and she would have to be careful.

She would have to give him just enough information for him to be useful to her, and hint at the severity of what he did not know so that he would not feel comfortable researching too vigorously the facts of her story. Most important of all, she had to use his own perceptiveness against him. She would not for a second expect him to believe her lie, but she would try to make him worried enough at what the truth was behind that lie that he would not go alerting the ever vigilant satellites above them to the fact that their presence was known to her and her colleagues.

"Saul, I have asked you here today to tell you I have become aware of something while in America that affects Israel. The people I am working with intend Israel harm, and I have discovered an aspect of their plot that worries me deeply."

He looked at her. This was, perhaps, not a topic for an alleyway, but he had used this block on occasion, and unbeknownst to her he knew that the doorway they were standing in was the back door to an old safehouse of his, and was in fact bricked up. Their hushed voices would not be overheard here with the sound of the busy streets of Tel Aviv in the background.

She continued, "There is a plot afoot to spread a biological weapon in Israel. It may not come to fruition, and there are those of us who are trying to stop it, but my being here endangers us both. They have the ability to listen with ease to both our e-mails and our telephone calls."

While his face remained impassive and pleasantly curious, his mind raced with this information, just as Ayala's mind had when Barrett had first told her of the plot in Neal's basement. He, too, quickly surmised that there were only a few countries that could monitor them that way, and among them, only Russia had ever shown any enmity toward Israel. Even Russia could not truly keep tabs on them in the way that Ayala was describing. But who could. He knew who could, of course, and he knew where Ayala now lived, and this was very disturbing to Saul.

She carried on, "I cannot tell you much, not yet, but there are some things I need you to do. Firstly, there is a woman in the Israeli armed forces who works for this group. I need you to work on holding her back from advancement, and I need you to do it without being discovered."

He nodded, "And the name of this agent?"

"Raz Shellet, she is a new officer training to be a pilot in the Israeli armed forces. When the time comes, she will be in charge of distributing the virus. As long as she is ground based, she cannot do any harm. The people I am working against cannot get a military plane into our airspace without being destroyed by our extremely extensive defenses. Slow her, and you slow them. But do not try and kill her, they will simply replace her, and I may not know who that replacement is. Better the enemy we know."

He nodded again, what she said seemed reasonable, for a lie. "So, 'yala, are you going to tell me what this is really about, or are you going to lie to me all day?"

She smiled, then opened her bag. He flinched as he saw the syringe she was taking out, and fear momentarily took him. He reached for the small revolver in his jacket pocket involuntarily and she smiled.

"Saul, really?" she laughed a little, holding the syringe up and flicking its end, "If I wanted to hurt you do you really think you could protect yourself from me?" she looked at him with the implied threat and he lowered his hand. God, this woman, she was serious. What was she doing here? For that matter, what was *he* doing here?

"This is an antidote to the drug they intend to spread. I am going to inject you with it now." she said this as the fact it was, and he clearly took it as such, nodding somewhat reluctantly and rolling up his sleeve. "It will not hurt, and within a week you will begin spreading this cure to others, I do not have time to explain how or why."

He saw she was serious, and they locked eyes as she expertly jabbed him and depressed the needle. "Now, once again I will stress that if I wanted to hurt you I would have to come to you in the night and done what I wished to do. You now live, as you always have, at 55 Kersiliya Street." Why had he thought for even a moment that she did not know as much about him as he did about her? He thought about it and concluded that it was, indeed, highly unlikely that this was just some method of hurting him. Good, he thought, as he watched the plunger go down, forcing the thick grey liquid into his muscle.

"Now," she said, still holding his gaze, "there are ten more doses of this drug in my bag. You are going to distribute these doses widely around the country. If you don't, then everyone in Israel will, most likely, die quickly and ignominiously in a few months. I also have forty more doses that you are going to administer as soon as possible to agents of ours deployed in Syria, Jordan, Egypt, and Iran. Do you understand?"

"I imagine you are saying that this will spread the immunity in their countries as well. I cannot help but think …"

"Do not think that, Saul. Do not for one moment entertain the thought of keeping this antidote within our borders. If that happens, I will know, and I will find you, Saul. Know that your fate and that of all you hold dear rests on whether you get this drug spread to all the countries in this region. I will be working on getting it out to surrounding areas as well, but do not doubt that I will be able to tell whether you have done as I have asked today. This is not a time for Zionism, old friend, this is a time for practicality. If Israel survives the coming attack and all around her die, they will say we did it, even though we were in fact the intended target. How do you think the world would react to such a genocidal act?"

He nodded. He knew her well enough to know she was not telling him the whole story, but those same instincts worked both ways. He felt certain the threat she described was absolutely real. What was most worrying about it was that if they were indeed able to crack all of their e-mails and telephone calls, well, that only really meant one country was behind this. He had known for many years that America had established a strong CIA presence among them. They had allowed it because fighting it would have meant alienating their greatest ally. Now, he knew, that presence was too intrinsic to be countered. He would monitor this Raz Shellet, but he would do it extremely subtly, as he knew that even the slightest report of his interest in her would alert the foe that Ayala was trying to protect him from.

She watched his mind work and she knew she had him. He had taken the path she had wanted and she had seen the moment that he had made the incorrect but perfectly logical leap to America.

Good. If he suspected the CIA, he would take the necessary care to avoid detection. That was all she needed. She had sown the seed.

- - -

François-Xavier Marchelier walked down the street to his office. He liked to do this on occasion, especially in the first onset of winter. The cold made him feel alive. He knew that Lieutenant Jeanette Archalle was not far behind him, and neither were the two men who followed him around sullenly all day. The brutes were such a burden. But such were the dangers of his position in the French government. At least as he entered the Ministry the two thugs would leave him behind. The big doors swung easily at his push, and he walked up to the security detail at the metal detectors, noting and trying to place the familiar face of the striking woman standing just inside. She seemed to recognize him too. She was about his age and she was coming over. She was smiling and he knew that face and that smile. Those lips, God, was she a lover of his? No, wait, she was …

She approached him, "Monsieur Le Minister, comment ça va? Madame Winstel, Bettina Winstel." she introduced herself and tilted her head slightly to one side as he automatically went to kiss her cheeks in greeting.

"Of course," he said, recognizing her now as the woman who had so notably dazzled him years ago when he had just been appointed to his post. She had not gotten any less beautiful since then, her dark hair and stunning eyes were still offset by her clearly Middle Eastern looks in just the right way, making her mysterious on so many levels. They had only spent an evening together, she had romanced him at the inauguration ball for their new president, which, in a way, had been the minister's own inauguration ball as well. But what was she doing here?

Ayala had never been assigned to France formally by the Mossad, her French was not as perfect as they demanded, but when a new government came into power in any major global power, it was customary to send a few of the Mossad's more 'charming' agents to get some leverage on its key members. They had not slept together that night at the ball, but the recording she had of his detailed and imaginative proposition to her had been a valuable addition to their file on him, should it ever be needed.

"I was in town unexpectedly, and thought of you." she said in lilting French, her accent intoxicating, "Might you be able to have dinner tonight?"

He was supposed to attend a gala tonight, but not a very interesting one, or a very important one, for that matter. Maybe he could excuse himself early, "Madame, I am honored that you thought of me." he smiled charmingly, "I have an appointment that will detain me until about nine, would it be at all possible to meet me at that time? I know of a wonderful restaurant that we could rendezvous at."

She seemed to think a moment, smiling coquettishly, then nodded, her eyes conspiratorial. "I like to eat earlier than that, I am afraid, my minister," his spirits sank a moment, but then rose as she touched his arm gently, "maybe you could meet me for a digestif instead? They carry a Martell XO at my hotel. Say at ten? I am in room 1909 at the Renaissance Trocadero."

He was stunned, she had resisted even his most ardent advances at their first meeting. Oh my. The part of him that was naturally cautious said it was too easy, but that part of him that was more amorous said in rebuttal that if she meant to blackmail him she would have done so long ago. The amorous side won without much of a fight.

- - -

She had spent the day travelling by train to Brussels and back, jabbing various unsuspecting people in crowded train stations, often to shouts and rebukes. But none saw what had actually jabbed them as she expertly blamed their momentary pain on a sharp handbag she had purchased precisely for its impractical points and buckles. On her long flights to Israel and then to Paris she had also drugged several people on the plane with minor soporifics and administered them the antidote as they slept.

As the ardent minister entered her hotel room, she already had a similar draft made up for him. But first she had some business to discuss. He was shocked at her story, but believed it. As France's defense minister, he had responsibility over all military spending, and she managed to bake into conversation how she had heard rumor in her home country of Turkey of a plot that was afoot to steal one of the expensive Rafale jet fighters from the French army. He was suspicious, but she had a document with details of the career of one Jean-Paul Merard with her, and a disturbingly large amount of information about both this pilot and the minister himself.

He was sad for a while that she had not really wanted him here because she found him charming, he was even angry for a moment at being used this way. But she was very charming, and very sincere. And very beautiful. When, after outlining her strategy for stopping the Turkish agent, and including a couple of veiled threats of what she would say to the French press if he did not do exactly as she said, she offered him a drink and apologized sweetly for being such a bully.

He smiled meekly and accepted her peace offering.

When he awoke a few hours later she was gone, and there was a folder by his side. It contained several clearly recently printed photos of him in this very hotel room, quite asleep but also quite naked, in various creative poses that would quickly end his career if released.

The folder also contained an almost mockingly sincere written apology, barely veiling a reiterated threat to his career should he not pursue the subtle, if effective, course she had described the night before. More importantly, she stressed the consequences would be no less severe should he tell anyone of their encounter. He cursed her and his own gullibility, but he had no intention of straying even one iota from her instructions. He would follow them to the letter.

Unbeknownst to him, she had not undressed him just for blackmail, or even for the considerable fun she had had posing and photographing his slumbering body. She had also saved his life: through a tiny needle mark on his ample posterior, she had introduced the drug that would actually make him the unwitting bearer of the greatest panacea in history to everyone he loved and held dear.

Chapter 43: On the Street Where You Live

<Welcome>

Eight Agents were arrayed in their circle once more, the nothingness of their backdrop emphasizing the esotericism of their virtual meeting.

<Agent Shahim Al Khazar has requested a reassessment of a previous Council decision.>

John withheld his look of concern, not transmitting his personality analog's emotions to his avatar in the virtual meeting. He did not know what decision the arbiter was referring to, but he knew that Shahim Al Khazar was in America and that made him nervous.

Given that he had called the meeting, Agent Shahim took the lead, "Eight months ago we struggled with the decision of how to handle the remaining members of the group that discovered Agent Preeti Parikh's capsule in India. Along with the majority of you I voted for allowing them to live, but with the stipulation that if we found more reason to suspect them we would complete the job the hub satellites started." he paused a virtual moment, then continued, "I have called this meeting because I believe I may have found just such a reason."

<Agent has uploaded some video and analysis for Council review, sending to meeting participants now>

"There is not any concrete evidence per se, but I saw something over the last three days that has made me suspicious. I have been watching Neal Danielson in his home in Washington, DC …" he went to continue but John cut in, his virtual voice perhaps betraying the sudden concern his face was programmed not to show.

"What do you mean you have been watching him? Why? What are you doing in Washington, DC?"

There was a pause and then Shahim went on, "I went there to assess the potential of attacking the Pentagon and White House as part of the package of target options given me by my superiors."

John restrained himself, hoping someone else would say the obvious response to that statement. Preeti Parikh spoke up a moment later, "But the Council agreed that both those targets were too noticeable and would initiate a weapons build up by America and others, something we certainly do not want to encourage. Why were you looking at them?"

Before he could respond, Lana spoke up, clearly displeased at the direction the conversation was going, "What does it matter why he was there? He has not initiated any attacks on those locations. And by the sounds of it he has discovered something that will require further examination. Agent Shahim, please talk us through this information you have uncovered."

John knew Lana had no compunction about killing, either here or on their homeworld, indeed they had all been selected at least in part because they were capable of maintaining a detached perspective toward their prey. But the princess was also famous for being just that, a princess. She was used to getting her way and John Hunt had always suspected that she had harbored some level of animosity toward Neal and Madeline simply because she had been outvoted by the Council on her suggestion that they be killed back in the fishing town of Kodikkarai. Indeed, it had only been because John Hunt and a few others had supported the AI's push for prudence that the two of them had survived this long.

At Lana's insistence, Shahim continued his thoughts on Neal, "As I mentioned, I was in Washington, DC, and I took it on myself to follow Neal Danielson simply because he had been of such interest to us before. I have not approached him, but I did gain access to the house across the street from his for several days and observed his movements."

<Agent Shahim Al Khazar, since the incident in southern India, I have continued to monitor the movements of both Neal Danielson and Madeline Cavanagh and have found no reason for further action. Nothing in their movements or in their telephone or e-mail traffic indicates any awareness of our existence.>

"Oh, I do not question that the AIs have been more than proficient in monitoring the two humans remotely. And Neal's movements outside his house certainly seem perfectly reasonable." said Shahim, "But what about the amount of time that Neal spends at his house? What is he doing there?"

Becoming increasingly more perturbed by the conversation, John interjected, trying to defuse the situation, "Do you have any actual information on the actions of Neal Danielson, Agent Shahim? If not, I see no reason to take this topic further."

"Agent Hunt, forgive me for being so circumspect, but my experience both here on Earth and back on Mobilius has told me that there is rarely smoke without fire, and the smoke I see here is this," said Shahim, "Neal Danielson spends anywhere up to ten hours a day in his basement. We have the schematics for the house, and they have no record of any computer connections or hookups down there. Plus there is no activity on his e-mail accounts during this time. This would not normally be enough to rouse suspicion, but combined with his pivotal role in the development and deployment of the probe that located Agent Preeti's landing capsule, it is enough, I believe, to warrant further investigation."

John was about to respond, trying to select his words carefully when Lana took the conversation in a new and equally disconcerting direction, "And this Madeline Cavanagh, is she also acting suspiciously, Shahim?"

This was not good.

"As for the woman that was with Mr. Danielson in India, I have not seen her come or go from his DC residence during the time I have been observing him. Maybe the hub could update us on her whereabouts." said Shahim.

<My records show that Madeline Cavanagh boarded a plane to Florida to stay with her mother at the Sunny Valley assisted living facility six months ago. She has remained at that location since that time.>

"She hasn't visited her friend Neal once?" asked Lana.

Before John could interrupt, the AI said, <No. She has remained inside the facility for the entire time.>

Fuck. He had been concerned that Madeline's dropping off the radar might spark suspicion, but it had been an even greater risk for her to be seen flying back and forth to North Dakota regularly, so they had gone with this lesser of two evils with the assumption that John could warn her if the Council's suspicions became aroused. As his avatar remained outwardly calm, the real Agent Hunt was already sending a coded message to her via the agreed upon channels. If Madeline reacted immediately, she might be able to stave off further investigation.

But when Lana had the scent of something she pursued it with singular purpose, saying, "Are you telling this Council that this woman has stayed indoors for the last six months?" said Lana indignantly, "That is ridiculous. You must be mistaken. I have spent enough time with these people to know that they could no more remain in one building for that long than I could. She must have left without you knowing, you must have missed her. She could be anywhere right now."

<Agent Lana Wilson, we do not rely solely on visual surveillance to track subjects. That would be, as you suggest, inherently open to error. To supplement the position that she has remained in the building for that time, we can also tell you that we have no record of any use of any of her credit cards, ATM cards, driver's license, or passport at any other location during that period. Unfortunately, the home does not have an extensive security system so I cannot review internal footage to confirm her whereabouts, but it would be difficult for a person to go that long without appearing on my grid if they were moving about the country.>

Lana was incensed, like a dog on the trail, "Unless she knew we were watching her!"

John went to respond but the AI's reply was almost instantaneous, <To suggest from the information available that either Neal Danielson or Madeline Cavanagh have discovered both our presence and the extent of our capabilities to the degree necessary to circumvent our surveillance systems is highly unsubstantiated. That said, we concur that her behavior does not fall within accepted norms and may warrant further investigation.>

Despite the AI's restrained tones, Agent Lana Wilson took the statement as more than enough rope to run with and said in an authoritative tone, "It is clear that we must confirm the location of this Madeline Cavanagh immediately, and it is also blatantly clear that we must find out what is going on in Neal Danielson's basement. Agent Shahim, I order you to apprehend Neal Danielson and investigate his house."

Luckily for John, the AI reacted immediately, saying in markedly more diplomatic tones what he and several others thought about Princess Lamati's 'orders.'

<Agent Lana Wilson, we respectfully remind you that you are not empowered under treaty to give orders to any member of the Advanced Party. All decisions brought before the Council must be approved by majority vote of all members.>

It was lucky that the AI had no avatar of its own, or it would have felt the full brunt of Princess Lamati's regal stare at this impudence. Instead, she turned her wrath on the pathetic Nomadi's representative, Agent John Hunt, using him as the proxy for the source of her impotence.

"What is the meaning of this? We had a clear vote back when these two humans came to our attention that if there was *any* further evidence of malfeasance on their part, they would be eliminated. I initiated the vote myself and it was unanimous."

Shahim, through a combination of wanting to disassociate himself from Lana's attempted steam rolling and an equally powerful desire not to be seen as her proverbial bitch, spoke up, "In fairness, Agent Lana, we do not have anything that could be considered 'evidence of malfeasance.' Merely some conjecture supplemented by mildly suspicious behavior."

Both Lana and Shahim were silent for a moment, their avatars gazing at each other with equal but opposing intensity, and Agent Mikhail Kovalenko made the mistake of putting his opinion forward into the proverbial fire, "Maybe we should investigate the two of them more discreetly for now, and if there is cause I am sure we will all support further punitive action ..."

"Obviously there is cause, you fool," said Lana with venom, "six months! She has not been seen for six months! What more do you need?"

John tried to play the reconciler, hoping to curry some favor with the group while also trying stave off a closer investigation of Neal's house, something that could only have truly disastrous consequences, "Clearly we need to investigate this further, we can all see that Agent Lana has more than ample reason for suspicion. But at the same time I think it is clear to the Council that we do not have enough information to warrant an attack on the more prominent of the two parties at this time. So may I suggest that we start by confirming the location of this Madeline Cavanagh? Lana, Shahim, would it be possible for either of you go to her location in Florida and confirm her whereabouts?"

Lana looked at him. Was she being dispatched on some errand now? She was about to nominate Shahim for the job, as John had hoped she would, when Mikhail spoke up. He was still justifiably annoyed at being called a fool and he decided to exact a little revenge, "I propose we vote on sending Agent Lana Wilson to investigate this Madeline Cavanagh's last confirmed location in Florida."

Shit, thought John, that leaves Shahim in Washington. John had hoped to get him out of there at least until he could get a message to Neal to cleanse the site.

"Seconded." said Shahim. Lana was shocked. This was the first time she had been ordered to do something in her life. But the orders of the Treaty that her father had signed were abundantly clear. If she refused a direct order of the Council, it would appreciably affect the Empire's holdings on the soon-to-be conquered Earth. The consequences of such an action on her part were too grave to think of. Even a princess would find herself in dire circumstances if she cost her empire such an exaction.

The ensuing vote went as she feared, with only two dissenters, and the moment the last vote was cast, she felt the AI download the address of the nursing home into her memory along with the personal details of one Madeline Cavanagh.

But Agent Lana Wilson was not done yet and John listened resignedly as she directed her indignation at the one thing he had hoped against hope to avoid. Despite several further objections on his part, she quickly cajoled the group into a vote for Shahim take further steps to find out what Neal was up to. It was a somewhat diminished version of the action she had originally suggested, but while the Agent would not actually abduct the suspect, he was still ordered to enter Neal's house as soon as possible and investigate what activities were consuming so much of the human's time. As the conversation continued, John's mind raced. He must react, and he must do so immediately. In the end, it was decided that Shahim would enter the house the next morning after Neal had left for work.

John could risk a direct message to Madeline's secondary e-mail in North Dakota to warn her of the coming investigation, but with Neal under a renewed microscope, the chance of any message being sent to that house, or its neighbor, being traced back to anywhere near the HMS *Dauntless* was too high.

John had fourteen hours to warn Neal. He was already moving when the AI closed the meeting, setting off at a run down the corridor outside his quarters.

Chapter 44: London Calling

Like everyone else, Admiral Hamilton had taken the news of their predicament badly at first. His incredulity had soon turned to outrage as the mountain of proof they had amassed swayed him to the same inevitable conclusion they had all come to.

But unlike the rest of the team, the admiral was in a position of incredible power and influence. Here was a man who had personal experience ordering large scale attacks with potentially massive consequences. Here was a man who had commanded a carrier fleet during the first Gulf War and the first two years of the US invasion of Iraq. A fleet with three times the combined firepower of the entire Allied force that had landed at Normandy on D-day. Perhaps most importantly, here was a man who had both the authority and the necessary strategic experience to command the vast swath of the US military under his command. He was their greatest ally to date, but because of his political and military might he was also, by default, now their leader. His power and influence was simply so much larger than anyone else's on the team.

To have approached him before they had a complete plan in place would have been to give control of the entire enterprise to him. Now that they had a clear set of tasks that that required his assistance, they had at least been able to have some influence over the direction that he took. But from here on it was a ride they could not stop. Now they had him involved they were not driving the car anymore, Admiral Hamilton had the wheel, and they had to hope he liked the route they had laid out for him.

After their initial meeting with the man, the admiral had convened a council of some key military leaders for the afternoon, including General Pickler, telling Neal and the colonel that he planned to present a carefully edited version of their plan to them. It would include details of a missile threat, and a plan to counter it. But the proposed threat would be from China, not space, and the counter would include no details of the alien-materials they would use to defend themselves against it.

Martin Sobleski would be there, as would Colonel Milton, who the admiral would suggest as an excellent candidate to be put in charge of the counterplot they were proposing. They were hoping that this would have the double benefit of getting their man in place to pursue their goals while also appeasing General Pickler by giving the colonel, and thus the air force, proxy control of the project. That was the plan.

Neal would also be in attendance at the meeting and would support the various aspects of the plan as a seemingly disinterested third party, with the additional role of offering up some seemingly innocuous suggestions that would help them achieve some of their other goals.

Standing in the foyer of his Georgetown home, Neal grabbed his portfolio of documents, which was carefully filtered to include only that information that might support their case, and stepped out of his front door to catch the bus across town.

He locked the door behind, activated the alarm system, and went through his checklist in his mind: keys, standard cell phone, the correct ID and cards. No additional IDs or cards, and no gun, he was, after all, going to the Pentagon. After a moment's reflection, he decided he was ready and set off down the street.

Shahim was crouched amongst the branches of a small bush in the front garden of the building across the street. He had been there, perfectly still, for the past eight hours. In Shahim's mind, he used the satellites bird's eye to watch Neal walk down the street, waiting in perfect silence until the human had boarded his bus and it had moved off from the stop. Shahim's legs then smoothly extended, his joints not showing the slightest fatigue at being bent for so long, and he emerged from the bush and walked slowly and deliberately up to Neal's front door.

His unnaturally capable eyes told him there was an electrical circuit inside the door wired to the lock, possibly some kind of alarm system. He could not just break the lock, he needed to circumvent the alarm as well. With his back to the street, his left eye rolled down and he deployed his laser system, setting it to a low power. Then he placed his fingers around the outside of the small pane of glass in the window to one side of the door and held them there. Directing his gaze at the caulking that held it in place, he focused his laser array on it. As he applied extraordinarily precise pressure with his hands to all four corners of the glass pane, his laser started to slowly heat the caulk. After a moment of this combined pressure, the pane of glass started to slide inward, the suddenly more malleable caulk bonds no longer keeping it fixed in place. With even the slightest variance in pressure, the glass would have shattered, but Shahim's control was perfect to within a fraction of an ounce of torque, and the glass evenly strained against the softening sealant until it slowly, inextricably pushed free.

As it came loose, it started to fall inward, and in the blink of an eye Shahim had whipped his hand through the gap where the pane had stood to catch it before it had fallen even an inch. He then twisted it and pulled it back though the hole and reached his left hand back in through the gap. A fine tendril on his finger extended and projected a beam of ultraviolet at the keypad on the inside of the door frame, highlighting the still warm fingerprints Neal had left there when he activated it not ten minutes beforehand. Sensing the necessary keys and seeing from the angle of the fingerprints the order they had been pressed in, he tapped the keys without ever even looking at the pad with his actual eyes. A moment later he sensed the alarm deactivating and he withdrew his hand so that he could use another of the tendrils that ran inside his fingers to open the lock and enter.

Within a minute he was inside the house, replacing the windowpane against the still soft caulk to reseal it in place. After all looked well once more, he retracted his weapons system back into its socket and his left eye slid up and back into place. He was inside and there was no sign of a forced entry. Neal had been on the bus for only a few minutes.

Shahim quickly found the entrance to the basement but was surprised to see very little of interest down there. After briefly scanning its empty boxes and other sundry junk, he decided to check the rest of the house, parts of which were not visible from across the street. For the next twenty minutes, he carefully searched the house, focusing on specific parts of rooms that he could not see from outside. He found Neal's laptop and downloaded its hard drive just in case, his machine mind analyzing it as it was parsed into his mind and telling him that there was nothing of interest there.

After twenty-three minutes, he had completed a thorough sweep of the entire house, every drawer had been opened, every closet explored in every room on both floors, and he had found nothing of interest. If Shahim had not had specific reason to be suspicious, he would have been forced to assume that Neal was not a threat. But the fact remained that he had not found any viable explanation for why Neal had been out of sight for such long periods of time.

He reviewed the feed from the AIs overhead. He could not contact them directly while he was in the house, but he could receive information from them anywhere, and among the steady flow of data coming through subspace, the AIs were providing him a running update on Neal's whereabouts. Seeing that his quarry's bus was still en route to the Pentagon, he thought about his options. He had plenty of time, and he still needed an explanation to take back to the ever-pleasant Princess Lamati. So he decided to return to the basement to examine it once more before calling the search off.

Coming back down the thin wooden stairs, he started to review each box that was stacked in the big room in detail. They had all appeared innocuous on his first review, and he found nothing on a second pass to change that evaluation. He scanned the walls as he had in every room already and found, as he had before, that they were riddled with the same holes and pipes that wove under most houses.

But there was one particularly large hole behind the washing machine, too big to be explained by the piping that attached to the back of the washer and dryer. He went over to the washing machine in the corner and scanned it. It contained nothing of interest, not even clothing, which was not surprising as it appeared to be broken: it had a shaft going through the base of the tumbler inside that would clearly render it useless. He adjusted the power and wavelength of the X-ray coming from his eyes to change how far it penetrated into the machine, following the shaft into the base and seeing through its casing to where the metal bar came to an abrupt stop. His infrared showed signs of recent stress, some kind of fracture, heat still emanating from the pressure of whatever had broken the shaft. He scanned behind the washing machine again. The large hole in the brick seemed to be blocked by a sheet of some metallic material.

Shahim stepped up to the machine and pulled. It appeared to be bolted to the floor, but under pressure something in its base gave, and suddenly it hinged outward. He saw now that the shaft he had seen earlier had been blocking its movement. He became even more curious when he surveyed the sheet covering the hole behind it. He could see the heat emanating from the screws around its edge. It had been put there within the last few hours, there was no doubt about that.

Reaching down, Shahim pressed his fingers into the gap between the plate and the wall and pulled. The screws' hold on the mortar put up some small measure of a battle but soon they were wrenching free one by one, the metal, an aluminium sheet about a quarter of an inch thick, bending and rippling under the stress until he had wrenched it free.

He saw the hole behind it. He knelt and looked into the basement on the other side, then he began to climb through.

- - -

The previous afternoon, Madeline was busy with a complex schematic rendering in the resonance chamber management system when her phone beeped.

She looked down at the small device, which rarely made any noise save for her frequent alarms and very infrequent calls. Apparently she had received a response to her profile on a dating site. Knowing what this meant, she checked the site immediately. They all had false profiles there, allowing any other member of the team to ping them whenever they wanted, while remaining relatively anonymous in the process. It was one of many covert methods they used, somewhat at random, to blur their lines of communication to the eyes of those that were watching. The site's servers added a layer of complexity to the task of tracking their sources, and combining this with the innocuous code words and phrases Ayala had provided them with, and they had a relatively safe method of sending the occasional message to each other when something could not wait for the next of Ayala's regular visits.

"Loved your ad. You look cute. I am from the South as well. I am hoping to go back very soon. Maybe we can meet up. -Mr. Little"

Madeline recognized the meaning of the message as soon as she read it: that her cover in Florida was in jeopardy and that she had to return there immediately. Madeline stared at the monitor for a moment, then checked her other dummy e-mail accounts and even looked at the various classifieds where they also posted information. Nothing. No more information.

She had to act, she knew that. She had to move. Now. But she was frozen with, she did not know what.

She stared, a sense of numbness settling over her. A small part of the back of her mind began thinking about flights. She realized this and watched it, almost remotely, as this part of her stepped up and went through the schedule of flights back to her hometown, one of the many things Ayala had made her memorize for just such an occasion. She knew what she had to do. As if by default, she eventually stood, went to a drawer, gathered one of her fake persona packages with its complement of credit cards and matching driver's license, and slipped her real ID and credit cards into a purpose made slit in the lining of her purse. Thus prepared, she turned for the door. There was nothing else for it. She walked out as if impelled. She had just over three hours before the last flight to Tampa. She had to go.

- - -

John could not risk sending such a message to Neal with the increased attention that was now being paid to him. If a phone pinged while he was being watched so closely it might alert the AI to the fact that he was getting messages from a source other than the ones it was monitoring. It would then only be a matter of some targeted tracing, something the AI was disturbingly good at when it had cause, for it to find John holding the cup at the end of the string.

So John's second note went to Ayala instead. It had been quick, and it had been the first time any of the team had used the code in question.

Ayala reacted instantly, she was out the door in less than a minute, and was on a plane not two hours later. She had to get to their headquarters, save what she could, and then burn the rest. Then they had to move. Where, she did not know. How, she did not know. They had created the code as a worst-case scenario, an all-else-has-failed option. In truth, they had never thought they would survive very much longer if it was ever used.

Her only solace was that John had not said they were definitely discovered, but that it was imminent and probable. She hoped they were relying on more than just blind luck to avoid it, but didn't hope very hard.

- - -

Shahim's bent frame knelt at the hole that linked the basement he was in with what must be the neighbor's. He looked through. He could see clothes on two racks, the underside of a row of tables with a host of computers on them. He could make out the back of a corkboard. It had been turned to face the opposite wall.

He scanned the room for signs of life. None. He scanned for alarms, electronic or otherwise. No sensors, heat or movement. The computers were all off, though heat signatures showed they had been on recently, and had been working quite hard. He saw the corner of a readout from an Array scan in the trashcan, and signs it was not alone in there.

This was a hidden entrance to a secret room. It was, almost certainly, where Neal had been spending so much of his time, the place he had gone to when he went to the basement. It was not conclusive, but Shahim could think of no reason why the man would have this room other than to hide a secret, a secret he felt could not reasonably be hidden even in his own home.

Neal must know something. Shahim felt more and more certain of it.

With resignation to the fact that he would probably soon be killing again, Shahim leant forward to climb through into the other basement, noting with some curiosity the large, metallic seeming pillar that his sensors told him was just to the right of the entrance, but seeing a moment too late that it was wearing clothes.

- - -

Just inside the door, John Hunt stood above him. He was not using active scanning so as not to alert the other Agent to his presence, but Shahim was pumping out so much IR, X-ray, and microwave pulses, he was like a beacon.

He saw the other Agent's head start to come through the gap. He had hoped that it would not come to this. He had hoped that Shahim would not look behind the curtain.

- - -

Shahim saw the front of a shoe, he did not see any heat from it so he assumed it could not be on someone's foot. He saw, overlaid with heat imaging, that it was dead and metallic inside. No, not metallic. What was it made of? He turned his head, looking up. His scans told him with certainty that this was not a person, so what was it, a mannequin?

Fractions of a second passed as his eyes moved up the side of the object just inside the room, while his tactical analysis tried to reconcile the information being returned with known human material science to provide some kind of reasonable conclusion.

As John saw the threat was not going to pass, he knew it was time.

The scene changed with blinding rapidity.

John flexed his hand down in an impossibly fast movement, his fingers aiming for the other Agent's left eye.

Shahim's machine brain registered the threat coming at him a moment later, tactical analyses springing to life in the nanosecond before his consciousness could even work out what was happening. The analysis showed the only conclusion it could: he was being attacked by another Agent.

Several automated responses kicked in, and within a tenth of a second Shahim's weapons array was already starting to deploy, John's hand flying through the air in front of him, even as Shahim's fake left pupil started rolling down.

Shahim started to pull away, back through the hole he was coming through, and John reacted. Shahim could not be allowed to escape. Redirecting his hands' movements, he went instead to grab the other Agent's head, turning and dropping to the floor as he did so, to try and get the purchase he would need to drag Shahim into the room by force.

As John began dropping into view, Shahim's head was still coming up, his left eye still receding, his weapons array still emerging. This was only the first tenths of a second, but these moments were vital, as the two combatants made their first moves in the deadly game, getting in position, pawns moving forward to try and establish control.

As Shahim saw John come twisting into view, his face angling toward him, the Agent recognized its features even as it registered the needlepoints already fully deployed from John's left eye. With fear and astonishment racing through his mind, Shahim's machine sub-consciousness noted the deployed and powered up weapons array that was targeting his own and automatically began to wrench at every muscle in his neck to try turn his head away from the weapons now zoning in on it.

He knew he must protect his array until it was fully deployed. He needed two-tenths of a second to complete it. But John's initial gambit was too quick, and the first pieces to fall in this game would go to the Englishman.

As John's hands grasped either side of Shahim's head, he had barely a millisecond to lock on and target Shahim's eye. He knew he only had one shot. Then his advantage of surprise would be mooted by Shahim's fast responding systems. Finding the target and locking in, he fired everything he had, focusing his entire destructive wrath into the inch-wide aperture of his opponent's left eye.

Shahim's entire body registered the blow, alarms flaring as his still vulnerable weapons array superheated almost instantaneously. The sonic wave followed a millisecond later, smashing into his suddenly scorched eye socket. With the complex structures suddenly heated to extremes, the focused sonic punch brutally warped their intricate superstructure and they jammed in mid-deployment, their systems frying under the focused barrage.

It was an initial score for John, but they were already both thinking about their next moves, tactical options filing through their minds with probability analyses and damage potentials. John's feet were already coming up on either side of the wall as his hands clenched on either side of his enemy's head, getting ready for his next play.

Shahim sensed that he was about to be pulled bodily into the room by his neck. It was too late to stop it, so instead Shahim went on the offensive, thrusting two of his most powerful pieces on the board forward.

John felt the shift. Shahim's head was suddenly no longer pulling away, but surging forward, toward John, and Shahim's fists were now firing ahead like pistons.

John felt the dual blows register throughout his body like an earthquake, a seismic event that shook every structure in him. His vision actually shifted, his eyes momentarily realigning under the duress. He could redirect his hands downward, sweeping Shahim's flying fists from his midriff, but that might allow Shahim to get away.

So he also changed tacks, opening his ranks, drawing his opponent in. Redirecting his torsion musculature to pull from the very points where Shahim was impacting him, he directed all his strength into closing the gap between his hands and his stomach, every fiber of his being suddenly and entirely pulling inward with herculean power, even as every ounce of Shahim's strength was focused in the opposite direction, driving his attack forward.

The change in tension was titanic, and because of the way they were both thrusting, that tension was applied, as John had intended, directly to Shahim's neck. Alarms wailed inside Shahim as the forces shifted, his frame registering the pressure even as his own arms amplified it. John's move had turned his own strength against him. He was effectively now trying to rip his own head off.

He knew he needed to free himself. He withdrew his attack, his fists stopping their firing progress through John's torso as suddenly as they had started, and flashing inward, between John's own forearms, looking to break John's hold on the center of the board.

John's body quite literally thanked him for forcing Shahim to relent some measure of the force behind the cannonball fists that had been driven into it. Shahim had delivered the equivalent of an artillery shell fired right into the center of John's frame. It would have ripped a human clean in two.

The game continued to change millisecond to millisecond. Shahim was a writhing mass of muscle and wrath and John had only marginally damaged him. He was breaking John's grip. While both Agents shared equal strength, Shahim's arms' momentum as they came up gave him the fractional torque advantage he required.

His head free, Shahim moved to bring his rooks into play. Starting to flip himself, pulling his head back and bringing his feet forward. Both Agents were now in midair. The momentum from Shahim's first attack still driving them upward and back into the wide-open room.

John saw the new attack. Shahim's fists were bad enough, but an Agent's legs contained exponentially more power. John's tactical analyses scrolled.

He looked for a way to counter. There. Maybe.

While Shahim wanted nothing more than to beat John into submission, he knew that victory in a straight fight was far from certain, especially with his weapons system gone, his proverbial queen. But he did not need to win. He needed only to get out alive, and bring the AIs into the fight, and this match would be all but over.

His systems told him that when his legs connected with John, who was flying backward through the air just ahead of him, they would catapult his enemy at the far wall. Any moment now. Almost there.

John saw Shahim's knees come up. He did not stop them. John opened himself to them, inviting them in.

As Shahim's castles surged forward, John enclosed them, and at that same moment, began firing his sonic pulse, repeatedly, at the wall Shahim had just come through, using it to propel his body back and down. And suddenly, Shahim was not attacking, he was being pulled in once more. His whole self, king and all.

Shahim felt his body wrench upward, successive pulses from John into the wall and then the ceiling sending the British Agent down and under Shahim, while John's grip on Shahim's ankles was now redirecting Shahim's own strength and ever increasing momentum up and over John. It didn't seem all that bad at first, but Shahim's onboard computers were already telling him how it would end.

John held on as long as his machine fingers would allow him, flipping his enemy with all his might. John was attempting to wield Shahim like a transcendent sledgehammer. They both saw the forces at play.

The concrete floor literally rippled under the blow.

John had not been able to hold on any longer, and he was sent scurrying across the floor as his opponent impacted, trying his best just to keep his eyes on the scene.

It was spectacular. Shahim hit hands first. He had set them, as pawns, to attempt to alleviate and redirect some small measure of the impact. But in the end he knew he was going to have to take the brunt of the blow directly and hope his armor could withstand it.

For the most part, it did. The superconducting shielding spread the pressure across every inch of him, and every system buckled and sang under the blow. His machine brain shuddered within its protective cradle and his systems flickered. It was momentary, but highly disturbing. He could not feel pain, but his systems never slept, never, so when they went offline even for a second it was a profoundly unpleasant sensation, like somebody switching off the sun for a moment in the middle of the day.

But it was not quite over yet. Shahim, his position shattered, his pieces decimated, scrambled for purchase. If he could only get a signal to the hub satellite. He looked for a gap in his opponent's position. The wall he had come through was all but obliterated, but there was still the basement's main entrance.

As they both regained their footing, John saw Shahim trying to claw his way out, broken, but still full of fight. And as Shahim began to turn toward the door, John focused a sonic wave at the Agent's feet and fired.

Shahim felt his feet fly from under him, the impact spinning him in midair. Reacting smoothly, he threw his arms back to connect with the floor once more. Even if John could stop his legs from running, Shahim would happily use any of his remaining strength to get out of this fight.

John knew his shot at Shahim's feet could only delay his opponent for a moment. He needed to end this. He needed to get to mate. He looked for position.

He was now in the far corner of the room from the only exit still intact, so as Shahim flipped in midair, John pressed his hands back at the corner wall, bringing his feet up so that he could push off with all four limbs at the same time.

His feet connected with the wall a moment after his hands did, and with unified precision, all four bionic limbs powered at once, the drywall caving and cracking under the compound pressure as John propelled himself backward in a high arch, angling up toward the ceiling in a massive backflip.

Shahim saw it and flexed his damaged muscles once more, using his arms to try and throw his upside down body upward into the path of his opponent.

It was a desperate move, and John brushed it aside with a deft sonic punch. Not too powerful, not too much, a well-protected knight swatting back an errant king.

And in a moment it was done. John was past Shahim. He landed and turned in one fluid movement. It was almost beautiful. And as Shahim clawed and kicked to get at him, John turned his queen upon his opponent's lone king and thrust him back again.

The full-powered sonic punch sent Shahim reeling. John slowly rose from his crouching position and stared intently at the prone Shahim Al Khazar, cornered and alone at last.

Three and a half seconds had passed since Shahim had entered the room.

The battle was over. Shahim had no pieces left. The two meters that lay between them was all John needed to stop Shahim from bringing his remaining brute force to bear. But still Shahim would not surrender. He would try against hope to escape. He bent his legs to launch himself away but John fired another pulse at his feet flinging him onto his front. Without pause, even as his feet rolled beneath him, Shahim was already trying to use his arms instead. But John fired another pulse under the man, flipping him once more and sending him sprawling across the floor.

Again Shahim tried to power himself upward but John was stepping slowly toward him now, beating each limb down, forcing Shahim into the corner, into mate at last.

Shahim registered components of his machine frame starting to break down. Too much pressure, too many hits, his systems were failing. But John did not relent. He did not let Shahim move a muscle without immediately smacking him down. For his part, Shahim did not stop either. He was ready for death but he would not give in to it. Why did the other Agent not start attacking with his laser as well? Why did he not finish it?

Eventually Shahim stopped fighting, refusing to move again, or to acquiesce, and glared at his opponent with his one good eye.

"Why?" said Agent Shahim Al Khazar.

John paused a second, tactical systems still running. But this was not a problem for them. This was for the man alone, and he considered his reply.

"You ask me why, Lord Mantil of Hamprect?" John said, eventually. "You ask me why I am doing what I am doing? You have the audacity to ask me why I am trying to *stop* you killing seven billion innocent souls so that the Princess Lamatis of our world can have more lands to fight over? Well, I do not need to explain myself to you, you genocidal bastard. Tell me, Lord Mantil of Hamprect, what reason do *you* have for attempting to bring about the death of an entire race of intelligent beings we have never even spoken with? How do you excuse *your* behavior?"

Shahim stared at John Hunt. His machine mind was listing the extensive damage he had suffered, still striving to come up with tactical options. Among those options, and now disturbingly close to the top of it, was his self-destruct sequence. It listed his chance of successfully detonating before Agent John Hunt could disable him at 12%. Shahim switched off the display, and disabled his defensive systems, facing his destruction with what dignity he still had left.

As he thought of how he was going to die, he thought about John's question. Why was he here? He thought of the family of the prime minister of Pakistan. The humans were very different from what he had previously thought of as intelligent beings: they walked strangely, their strange hands were disturbingly long and slender, they ate meat, sometimes even raw, something no Mobiliei had done in an age, and all these things repulsed him. But he could not deny that they were intelligent, and nor could he honestly say that he had been untouched by the innocence of the prime minister's young daughters. But he had killed them. He had slaughtered them unflinchingly after killing their father in front of their horrified eyes, and as he thought about it, he knew that it was one thing to kill a soldier with a gun or missile. But this, this was something different.

"I have no answer for you, Agent John Hunt." said Shahim with the few scraps of pride he could muster, "End this, I have disabled my self-destruct mechanism, end this and leave. You have your victory. The rest of the Agents will think that somehow the humans killed me and they may well retaliate against them, but you may still be able to survive this if you leave now."

John Hunt looked at him. Of all the warriors that had been chosen for the advanced team, Lord Mantil had struck the Nomadi conclave as the most reasonable and pragmatic of the group. But no one had ever doubted his resolve. He was a brutal and effective champion of Hamprect, a hero who had led countless battles in the various insurgent wars that sprung up from time-to-time in the crowded empires of Mobilius. But he had never executed those tasks with relish, never displayed the psychotic zeal that was so evident in the eyes of Princess Lamati and her like. For what it was worth, Lord Mantil had always seemed a noble and honorable man.

John looked at him, "Tell me, Lord Mantil, what is your justification for eradicating all of these humans? What threat do they pose to you and your nation?"

Lord Mantil flinched at the remark, but he could not answer it. Over the last six months, he had been forced to admit that there was no true honor in this war they were planning. The last shreds of his enthusiasm for the enterprise had died with the Pakistani prime minister, his brave guardians, and his innocent family.

As John spoke, a message from his machine mind was trying to come through the temporary moratorium he had set on his system. Shahim could feel it too. The ever-watchful AI above them was requesting an update from Shahim. It had not heard from the Agent for too long. In its ever-implacable way, it was worried.

As Shahim considered the message from the AI, John shook his head and spoke, "You will not be replying to that message, Agent Shahim Al Khazar. Once I have killed you, I will fake an explosion here. Nothing will be left of you or the plot you found. We will rebuild it somewhere else and our work will continue."

Shahim said nothing, but just lay on the ground stewing in the broth of his defeat. As he lay there, his machine mind continued to try and prompt him to action with tactical suggestions. The Agents' bodies were designed for a long deployment in a hostile environment, and over time nano-machines built into their superstructure could repair even the most drastic damage. Shahim felt his machine mind updating him on its status. It was diverting all its resources to the laser component of his weapons array, which Shahim was informed would be online again in one minute. It was not much, but it would allow him fight back a little, and to send an accurate signal to the satellite if he could get outside for even a moment.

John bent down to look into the other Agent's one good eye. With his own augmented sight, he could see the machine inside Shahim's left eye reconstituting itself and his own machine mind was estimating the amount of time it would take for the eye to regain some measure of its operational capability. He knew he did not have much longer.

"You have an honorable reputation, Lord Mantil, surely you can see that you have been dispatched on an errand that is evil to its very core. I know that asking you to betray your orders goes against everything you believe in, but I also know that you are not a blind or stupid man, that you have always been known as fair and just. Your observance of the rights of your foe, even when they do not observe your rights, is well documented. So I will give you this opportunity. Swear on the name of Mantil, on your Lord Protector, and on the soul of your father that you will help me stop this genocidal butchery and I will … well, I will believe you. Such is my faith in your inherent honor."

Shahim was stunned. Surely this man could not put such faith in the strength of his character. Shahim certainly no longer had such faith in himself after what he had done in Islamabad.

"You know what I have done, Nomadi. So tell me, why? Why would you believe me? What is there to stop me from saying the things you ask and then betraying you the moment I leave this building?"

"In truth, Lord Mantil, nothing would prevent you. So if you think me foolish for asking for your help, Lord Mantil, then prove me wrong about you. Swear on your father's soul that you will help me and then break your oath and betray me. After all, you have already betrayed all that you hold dear. You have already killed women and children, coldly and without mercy. Why not break an oath in your father's name while you are at it. What do you care for that man's memory?"

Shahim's fury at this insult ignited a deep-seated rage, rage that was truly directed at himself, but which he allowed to burn in John Hunt's name. He reactivated his systems and launched his fist upward, but John was ready for him, he stepped back and away from the wild swing, shouting fiercely as he went, "Do you deny it, Lord Mantil? Do you say to me that you believe in this enterprise?"

Shahim went to rise, but John fired another crushing wave into him, pounded him to the floor again, still shouting, "Well, Lord Mantil? What do you say?" John hit him with his lethal left eye again, "What do you have to say in your defense, Lord Mantil?" again the needle eye pounded Shahim to the floor, "What? Lord Mantil? What would your father say about this massacre?" Again the pulse drove into Shahim as John screamed at him, "WHAT WOULD HE SAY?"

Shahim broke, not stopping any of his emotion from showing on his face, or in the broken wail he let out, "He would have killed himself rather than do this. He would have killed anyone that brought such massacre to such innocents as these." John stared at Shahim, resting his sonic fury a moment and allowing Shahim to carry on, spite and venom and shame filling the broken man's voice, "For God's sake, even the soldiers here are innocents. They do not even know they are at war. They cannot fight us because we cower in the shadows like thieves and petty bullies. We are nothing." Lord Mantil's final words ebbed from him quietly as he broke, "We are no better than assassins and grave robbers."

Shahim went silent and John looked down at him, "You are wrong, at least about one of us, my lord. I am no coward. I am no bully. I fight for the innocents." He looked at Shahim and his mind raced. Really, could he really trust this man? The risk was massive, but then, in truth, he could not explain the destruction of an Agent by a human anyway. They were already in more trouble than he could imagine. In the end it was all about the individuals who made up the resistance. The few people who risked everything to stand up for what they believed in. Shahim was no different. The only way this strayed from his own recruitment back on Mobilius was that John alone must decide whether to accept this man, where a committee of conspirators had decided John's fate, with equal risk to themselves if they were wrong. Here he had his instincts, and only his, to rely on.

Cautiously, John Hunt said to the beaten and battered Shahim, "Together, you and I might help these humans defend themselves. Together we might stop our race from committing the greatest crime in history. Trust me when I say this, Lord Mantil, I do not do this just for the humans. I do this for us. I do this so that our generation does not have to answer to our descendents for committing this genocide on the first sentient species we ever meet. How will you explain it to your children, Lord Mantil? When this is all said and done, which side will you have stood with?"

The words penetrated through to Shahim, and he looked up at John like the savior that in many ways he was. Like the only man who could help him redeem himself for what he had done.

John saw this and put the fate of them all on this last statement, "Help me save our race from ourselves, Lord Mantil. Help me stop this madness."

Shahim was still for a long, dry moment. And then he nodded.

John extended his hand and Shahim reached up and grasped it. As the beaten Agent arose to his feet, his list of tactical options sprang to life once more, unbidden. The list surged with new proposals. Shahim had a grip on his opponent and his machine mind thrummed with ways he could spin and throw the man, using his weight against him, negating John's intact weapons array with physical blows to his head and face. But as Shahim looked into his would-be ally's trusting eyes, he knew that the man had been right about him, and he was glad of it.

Deep within the substrate that housed his operating systems, he reached out and opened the virtual heart of his machine sub-consciousness. With precise mental movements, he began to reprogram it. He had an enemy, but it was not this man in front of him. It was time to put his crimes to right. It was time to salvage what honor he had left.

- - -

Fourteen hours beforehand, as he had closed the connection with the Council, John Hunt had debated his options. It had become riskier than he had ever wanted it to be, and he had considered rolling the dice and letting the team be discovered, allowing them to die if that was what happened. He could, hypothetically, start a new resistance, maybe even here in England, with all the additional access that would give him to them, but if he was discovered trying to save the American team, then John would be destroyed along with them, and, realistically, any chance for Earth's survival would die with him.

He had debated it long and hard, for over a minute of real time, an age to his synthetic consciousness. He had wrestled for relative hours. But in the end, it came down to the same emotions that had swayed him to the resistance's cause back on Mobilius: these people no more deserved to die than the billions of humans who remained completely unaware of the threat that hung over them.

In fact, given their bravery in the face of annihilation, they deserved his loyalty all the more. And so, after John had sent his notes to Madeline and Ayala, he had requested and been granted shore leave from a surprised Captain Bhade. The captain was not one to give out passes willy nilly, especially not to junior officers asking that they immediately be allowed twenty-four hours away from the ship. But they were, for now, briefly, in Portsmouth for systems maintenance, and the junior officer in question was the man who had not too long ago saved three of his sailors' lives and possibly his entire ship. Given that John had rarely, if ever, requested shore leave before, the captain had allowed the junior to cash in whatever credit he might have, and made an exception. In fact, if the captain remembered correctly, the boy had not taken leave since his famous visit to San Diego, when he had apparently bedded an American female naval officer, and for two days straight, or so the rumors had gone. Smiling at the memory, Captain Bhade had waved the man out the door to whatever conquest he had in mind.

So while Madeline had been rushing to catch the last flight out of Minneapolis, John had been using a fake passport and credit card Ayala had given him to discreetly head to Heathrow Airport, boarding the last of the daily flights across the Atlantic en route to Philadelphia. Landing at one in the morning, he had then taken the train to DC.

He had approached Neal's house emanating a healthy, humanoid warmth to assuage any suspicion from the Agent he knew was, even then, watching from across the street. Entering through the basement, John had met Ayala there, already hard at work cauterizing the room. They had formulated a plan, John bringing her up to speed on the full scope of the threat.

They had left Neal be, in order to avoid any sign of fear or concern on his face when he left for work the next day. They knew that if he came to the basement in the morning they would have to tell him what was going on, but fortuitously Neal had a late start the next morning, and he left unhindered and unencumbered, just as they had hoped.

When Neal had boarded the bus from Georgetown, Ayala was already rushing to catch up with him. If things did not go as they hoped, they might still have to disappear. They had a plan for that. He would need to be warned, and she had his documents with her along with five loaded hard drives containing his combined research to date culled from the now magnetically scrubbed PCs in the basement. Along with the disguise he would need to get out of DC alive, she had everything they would need should they have to flee.

Waiting to hear from John was as tense a fifteen minutes as Ayala had ever experienced, and she had known more than her fair share. After fifteen minutes, she had assumed the worst, as planned, and pulled Neal from the bus.

They would eventually hear from the English Agent, and return from their aborted escape run, frazzled and more aware than ever of the fragility of their entire enterprise.

- - -

Meanwhile, as John gambled their scheme on the honor of one Agent, a thousand miles to the south another Agent was arriving at the assisted living facility, which Madeline's mother called home. As she approached, Lana was receiving the AI's reports of a lack of contact with Agent Shahim Al Khazar. The AI had not received any distress call or anything that might indicate there was an issue, but it had been nearly twenty-five minutes since Shahim had entered the building. The AI was not speculating, merely conveying facts. It was aware of nothing in the human's arsenal that could harm the Agent, short of prolonged heavy weapons fire from a large team of highly trained soldiers, and it saw no reason to believe such a group was hiding in Neal's basement.

Given that it was unlikely that Shahim could have found anything that could pose any threat to him without destroying the building itself, the delay was merely being noted as unusual, and the AIs were monitoring. Despite the AI's pragmatism, Princess Lamati felt a surge of self-righteousness. They should have killed the other humans back in India. Now she was here, she would go in and find out where this Madeline Cavanagh was. Maybe Shahim was even now interrogating one of Madeline's cohorts, and Lana could imagine nothing more satisfying than doing the same here. Without a hint of her malice showing on her beatific face, Lana parked her rental car and got out, strolling toward the front entrance of the Sunny Valley Assisted Living Apartments.

Across the parking lot, Madeline was watching as Lana got out of her car; she had only just arrived herself. She had seen so many photos. She had even had nightmares about these Agents, but it took a moment for her to reconcile those images with the beautiful young woman she was watching walk up to the entrance of the nursing home.

She fought a wave of panic welling up inside her. They were here for her, she thought. She should run. She should hide. She fought an instinctive desire to glance at the sky and the threat that loomed there. Instead Madeline sat there, staring at the Agent Madeline knew as Lana Wilson as she opened the door and went into the nursing home.

Steeling herself, she thought about the situation as clearly as her rising panic would allow. If there was a threat on her life, then the code phrase that would have been sent to her would have been different. She would not have been warned to return here, but instead to never come back here, or ever use the name Madeline Cavanagh again. That was a contingency they had planned for and it had a different trigger word altogether.

But the message had not said to stay away. Instead it had said that she should return here immediately. They were checking her cover story. Lana was here to confirm that Madeline was inside the big assisted living apartment complex.

And while the alien assassin walked up to the front desk Madeline was sitting outside.

Shit, Madeline thought, and started to move.

- - -

"We have a *Sarah* Cavanagh on record here," said the receptionist after Lana's polite inquiry, "and I see Madeline marked as her next of kin and a caregiver, though I haven't seen her in a while. Wait … let me call Ms. Cavanagh's apartment for you."

Even if Lana had not already found Ms. Cavanagh's apartment number in the AI's extensive database, she could comfortably read the receptionist's screen by its tiny distorted reflection in the older woman's thick spectacles.

"No, don't worry about it." said Lana, "I have her cell number. I don't want to risk waking Sarah with the house phone." said Lana smiling idyllically, "You know how loud those things can be, and I kind of wanted to surprise them."

The receptionist nodded and smiled in return, she had always liked seeing women in uniform. She was so proud that they were taking advantage of something that had never really been an option when she was young. Good for her, thought the receptionist and she leaned in conspiratorially, "Listen, do you know their apartment?"

Lana nodded, "Sure, I see them all the time, apartment 258 in the Serenity Wing, right?"

The receptionist smiled at this sign that this clearly clean-cut officer was obviously a friend of the Cavanaghs, "Why don't you just go on back, sweetie?" she winked.

Lana tilted her head to one side and smiled innocently, "Oh, are you sure that would be OK? Well, that is just so nice." she flashed the woman a big, perfect, and thoroughly fake smile and winked as well, inwardly thinking what a fool the old lady was, and then she headed back toward the Serenity Wing.

Serenity Wing. What a ridiculous name. But then this was a ridiculous place. The concept of welfare, of caring after those who no longer contributed to society, and had no intention of doing so in the future, repulsed the princess. She reassured herself, as she always did, that places like these, along with their residents, would soon be eradicated.

Running down a side corridor on the far side of the building, Madeline rushed to change her appearance. If only she hadn't gotten this preposterous haircut. She brushed it back fiercely with her hand, trying to smooth it down, and used the same keycard that had gotten her in through one of the complex's side entrances to enter her mother's room. Luckily her mom was out, probably in the TV room or playing bridge by the pool. Thank fuck for that, Madeline thought. Hopefully it would stay that way. Madeline didn't know how long she had before Lana arrived from the front desk, so she didn't even try to change clothes. Instead, she just started ripping off her things and stuffing them under the bed.

The doorbell rang all too soon and Madeline grabbed a towel from the room's bathroom and threw it around herself, grabbing one of her mother's shower caps and covering her hair with it. She took a deep breath, opened the door and found herself standing face to face with the machine that called itself Lana Wilson. It was the single scariest moment of her life.

Madeline stood there, sweating and panting, half from exertion, half from fear, "Yes?" said Madeline to the woman who she knew had come to Earth to kill her and everyone she had ever known.

"Hi," said Lana Wilson, pleasantly, "oh, sorry, is this Jane Matthews' room?"

Madeline looked at the Agent, but the other woman's face was unflappable. Madeline realized that between her mad rush to get to the room and her innate fear of facing this woman she was dripping with sweat. It was lucky that she was pretending that she had just come from the shower. Madeline's blue eyes looked into Lana's deep black eyes and Madeline thanked god she did not have to feign being confused by the other woman's sudden appearance, "I'm sorry. Who did you say you were looking for?"

"Is this apartment 258?" asked Lana, pretending to check the door number again while she scanned the room with radar and reflective X-ray. It was not a large space, there was a mid-sized living room and kitchenette with a small bedroom off to one side. It seemed unlikely to Lana that two women lived in it. But, that said, here was Madeline Cavanagh, Lana had scanned her facial structure against the AI's records and confirmed the woman's identity the moment she had opened the door. It appeared the computer had been right, and the woman had been in here all this time.

But that was ridiculous. There was something wrong here, and Lana longed for the simple authority to just kill the woman and set her mind at ease, a power she had always enjoyed as the daughter of an emperor.

The clearly naked human stood in front of her, wrapped in one of her mother's well-worn pink towels. How had Madeline stayed off the grid for so long, thought Lana? She needed more information, so she decided to press her pretense of being in the wrong room further.

"I know for a fact that my aunt, Jane Matthews, is in apartment 258. What the hell are you doing in here?" Lana started to push past Madeline into the room.

Madeline was stunned with fear. She knew this woman could kill her in an instant, and from what John Hunt had told them, this Agent in particular would probably enjoy it. But she could not let this woman into this room if for no other reason than the simple fact that her mother could be back any moment.

"Look, I don't know who the hell Jane Matthews is," said Lana, allowing the panic she had been suppressing to show, "but she does not live here. This is my mother's apartment, Sarah Cavanagh, and she has lived here for several years now."

"And you? What are *you* doing here?" quizzed Lana, standing face-to-face with Madeline and challenging her.

Madeline's towel was slipping and she thought about letting it fall, but knew that such an act would not faze this woman, if you could even call this thing a woman. No, Madeline had to say something believable, she knew that she needed a reason that she had been staying here for almost six months, and her mind did not have to work hard to find one.

As she opened her heart to the only reason that she might have been in hiding for so long, the tears that came to her eyes were genuine. It was compounded by a deepening fear and stress and that helped her emotions run free, but when she allowed herself to think about James, about what had happened to him, she found she was still filled with unprocessed grief. And now here she stood facing one of the people who had ordered that death, and she could do nothing to avenge the man she'd loved. She could not hurt this murderer. She had no weapon at her disposal that would bring this bitch down. Though she wanted nothing more than to lash out at the almighty cunt standing in front of her, Madeline knew she could not hope to win that fight. Not today, not yet.

But nor did she have to completely suppress her anger and hatred for this murdering, unholy bitch. The woman had barged into her mother's room and because of that Madeline had every right to be angry, even if she bought the cover story Lana had used. So Madeline took a deep breath, allowed her rage to build up inside her, and then let it rip:

"Look, bitch, I don't know who the fuck you are, or what the fuck you are doing in my mother's room, and frankly I don't give a shit. This isn't your room, this isn't your friend's room or your aunt's room, this is my mother's room, and I have been staying in it since my boyfriend was killed in an accident in India a few months ago."

Lana instinctively stepped back from the suddenly enraged woman. Lana was born a princess and she was not used to being spoken to this way. As she began to consider how good it would feel to punish the human for her tone, she suddenly registered a message coming in from the AI. Apparently Shahim had reestablished contact. He was OK, he had been forced to hide when an internal alarm sensor had registered his presence, but he had managed to disable it. Lana was being ordered to stand down and return to her post in Georgia per the stipulations of the Council. Shahim had completed a thorough search of Neal's affairs and confirmed that it was a false alarm and there was no need for further investigation.

Lana stared back at the furious human in front of her and cursed her impotence. You'll get yours, she thought, keeping her face passive, soon you will all be dealt with. It's coming, you peasants, and when it does I'll be there to ensure the thunderbolt hits you the hardest.

Outwardly though, Lana remained calm, and Madeline wondered whether she had gone too far. But she was enjoying herself too damn much so she decided to go for broke. Stepping right up to the Agent, she grabbed the woman's shirt and said into her face, "Now I suggest you go back to reception and check that room number. But that is really up to you. You can go fucking swim for all I care. All I know is that you need to get the fuck out of my room, and you need to do it right fucking now."

Madeline didn't know if she was about to die, and at this point she didn't really care. That had just felt so deliciously good.

But Lana had her orders, and the rules of the Treaty that governed the advanced party were extremely clear. Very well, the princess would stand down, for now. It appeared that these two humans were, indeed, innocent. But she would not forget the words of this lumpen commoner. No one manhandled Princess Lamati and lived.

Madeline sensed Lana's hands coming up with more than a little trepidation, and she felt them wrap around her own. She felt them squeeze with smooth force and was reminded that the woman she was manhandling could easily crush every bone in her body. Now that her pent-up rage was released, the initial fear came flooding back.

But it was not necessary. Lana was leashed, for now, and Madeline would be allowed to savor her small victory. Limiting her phenomenal strength, Lana simply pulled Madeline's hands off her shirt, stared at the human for a moment, and then turned and left.

Madeline stood there in the Agent's wake, the door ajar, her heart racing, sweat beading her forehead, and butt naked except for a shower cap and a threadbare pink towel. She smiled and thought about what she had just said to the alien assassin. Her adrenaline soaked fear slowly turning to relief. She tried to contain a sudden urge to laugh. That was fucking awesome, she thought. Then she closed the apartment door.

As she went to get dressed, she stopped, changing her mind. Taking the towel into the bathroom, she removed the shower cap and climbed into the shower to rinse away the stress that she could feel permeating every part of her. The heat was a sweet release; it washed over her. There was so much to do, so many hurdles, and she knew that would not be the last time she faced death so closely, not by far. The worst was no doubt yet to come.

But the littlest victories resounded all the more in a war as hopeless as theirs. Taking a deep breath, she allowed herself to relish this one.

Part 4

Chapter 45: Raising Glasses

The sun was setting on Pearl Harbor Naval Base in Hawaii. On the side of a large storage hangar on a wide pier, a small door opened, casting a long shadow along its aluminium walls and the concrete surface of the pier. The newly promoted Major Jack Toranssen stepped out of it, bidding a final good night to the forty or so officers and enlisted men that made up his new team. He was leaving them to finish cataloging the shipment of modified tactical missile casings that they had been busy putting together in Hanscom. As he closed the door, he turned to stroll pensively toward the pier's edge, squinting into the sunset as he went. The sun's reflective sparkle danced on the diamond surface of the water as his gaze wandered out over the harbor's breakwater and out to sea, blinking into the blood orange glow of the setting sun. Slipping on his sunglasses, he surveyed the storied harbor.

It had been three months since the fateful day when the enemy Agents Shahim Al Khazar and Lana Wilson had come so close to discovering the plans of the team. Much had happened in that time. Though Jack had not even known about the day's events until days afterward, it was clear that John had truly saved them all. His quick thinking had been extraordinary, as had Madeline's equally daring response. Both of them had faced imminent death without thought and it had been a reality check for the whole team. Though the world would never know it, they had been a hair's breadth from triggering a response that might have wrought the eradication of the entire human race. It had been inordinately close, and since then, they had pursued their security measures with renewed vigor.

But from the jaws of utter failure they had managed to grasp an unexpected new ally. For many on the team, including Jack Toranssen, the thought of bringing the infamous terrorist into their midst had been difficult to stomach. The man had killed so many innocents, women and children falling in the face of his callous attacks. During Shahim's brief stay on Earth, he had become an international symbol of everything that Jack despised. But the strategic and tactical options opened up by John's induction of Agent Shahim Al Khazar to their ranks were undeniable.

No, there could be no doubt that it had been a coup for the resistance and it had paid off tremendously. But to achieve it John Hunt had risked everyone's fate on the integrity of an Agent responsible for the brutal execution of countless innocents, and, in truth, Jack still felt that it had been too great a risk for the man to take independently.

In the days following the fateful fight, Shahim had apparently also met with Neal, Ayala and Admiral Hamilton. Given that he already knew Neal's complicity, and John's, it seemed moot to keep the rest of the team from him. If he planned to betray them, then they were, to all intents and purposes, already sunk.

Shahim had approached Neal even as the dust still settled, even as John Hunt had rushed to get back to the HMS *Dauntless* before his absence became suspicious, and he had been introduced to Ayala not long afterward. Later, now with Ayala's approval, they were able to involve the admiral as well, and though the meetings between them all had been strained, it had apparently led to some significant improvements in their overall plan of attack. Ayala had said she was very excited at the new options that Shahim had been in a position to propose. But after an all too brief time with Neal and Tim Hamilton, the enigmatic double agent had been forced to vanish back into the underground. By design, they would not hear anything from him again for some time.

There had been stories in the news about Shahim. Stories about the FBI locating him and his terrorist cell in DC. According to the news they had not apprehended Shahim himself, which was lucky for the FBI agents involved, of course, but since those initial frenzied reports, there had been nothing. If all was going according to plan the notorious killer should be back in Pakistan by now and they would have to hope the man was true to his word. True to his word, and indeed able to do all he had promised. Because now that they had him on their side so much depended on him being every bit as fearsome as his terrible reputation suggested.

An unsettling feeling rumbled in Jack's stomach, part hunger, and part discomfort at having to rely on unknowns. Jack did not like variables, he liked known entities and detailed intelligence. He liked his plans to be layers of redundancy upon redundancy, and his brow furrowed at the thought of leaving so much to the efforts of one man, let alone this particular man. But John had been insistent that the Agent that they knew as Shahim Al Khazar was both extremely reliable and amply resourceful. No, his abilities were not in question, thought Jack, they had seen plenty of evidence of what he could do. And despite concerns on the parts of Jack and Barrett, Neal and Ayala had mirrored John's opinion that Shahim could be relied upon, and had even expressed cautious optimism about the new plan.

Jack had wrestled with it all for months but had failed to come up with a better solution, or a way to mitigate the risks he saw in their current course, so, like he had numerous times before, Jack set his doubts aside and returned his focus to the sky, contemplating the satellites which his friends and he were quietly plotting against. A mental image of the earth rotated in his mind with a caricaturishly large version of himself standing on the Hawaiian isles as the planet revolved.

As he visualized the planet revolving, he tried to switch his mental perspective, just as Galileo had first done hundreds of years beforehand. Locking the sun in place, he instead envisioned Earth as it span relative to it, the inhabitants on its surface racing at a thousand miles per hour toward the sun in the morning, and away from it each night. When he had first learned of the satellites from Colonel Milton all those months ago, it had been difficult to imagine how the four satellites fitted into that picture, but after many months of thinking about them, Jack's mental image was now clear. The satellites were orbiting against Earth's rotation, in retrograde orbit. As everyone on Earth revolved into the east to meet the dawn's sun, the satellites came round in the other direction, flying overhead at phenomenal relative speed and effectively overtaking the sun and the moon as they went. He knew, for example, that at this very moment one of the deadly platforms was soaring far above him, tracing its long arc over the earth. Soon it would head toward the horizon to catch the rapidly receding sun, only to be replaced by another satellite perennially chasing it from the east, and so it went on.

But hopefully not for too much longer. His team's arrival in Hawaii meant that in just a few more months they would be ready to launch their attack: a massive barrage of missiles flying up into the satellites' paths, carrying the hopes of humanity with them. Hopefully it would be enough.

For his part, Jack Toranssen was leading the Western arm of the effort to modify the huge battery of GBMD missiles. It was this mammoth job that had brought him to the Hawaiian archipelago where the southern branch of the tactical explosive arsenal was based. There were similar arrays of missiles in Alaska and California, and this was matched on the Eastern seaboard by batteries in Florida, the Carolinas, and Maine. Finally, a string of batteries in the northern US and Canada served to protect the country and its neighbor to the north from long-range missiles that may come over the North Pole from Russia, or, of course, should China get uppity all of a sudden.

For the task at hand the team would only be able to utilize the two large batteries in Hawaii and Florida because of their proximity to the orbits of the satellites. So Jack's team had travelled with the shipment of the new missile nose cones in a C-17 Globetrotter military airlifter from Hanscom Base, leaving behind an equally large team under Colonel Milton that was continuing to work on more shielding for the Eastern batteries.

But the massive airlift plane had carried more than just GBMD shields, and as Major Jack Toranssen looked out over the harbor, his eyes came to rest on a particular ship moored across the bay. As part of the long standing alliance between the US and Great Britain dating back to the Second World War, the two navies shared an uncommonly liberal access to each other's dockyards. So it was as normal to see a US naval sub in one of the berths at the British naval base in Gibraltar as it was to see a British ship in port here.

As Jack looked at the HMS *Dauntless*, he noted that it was a strange-looking ship. The ordinariness of its pragmatic bluff bows and grey paint served only to emphasize the two significant differences between it and most any other warship afloat. Firstly there was the huge tower amidships, capped with its unwieldy looking radar dome. The tower housed one of the most advanced tracking systems on earth, capable of sensing and tracking the tiniest of objects over the greatest of distances, and it was the nerve center of the ship. The second thing that made the ship stand out amongst other warships was its apparent lack of onboard armament. There were no great artillery guns on board like on the various ships that crowded the busy harbor, only large grey boxes like cubist sheds. But the strange-looking grey structures that covered the deck were in fact the housing for the vast and deadly array of missile systems that made the new destroyer such a powerful beast.

It could track and intercept incoming missiles and planes at vast distances, guiding and controlling multiple warheads simultaneously in complex vectored intercept patterns to shatter the path of anything unfortunate enough to incur its wrath. It did not even try to be a conventional warship, thus freeing every member of its highly skilled crew to be dedicated to the identification and destruction of anything the HMS *Dauntless* did not want flying in its airspace. That said, this singularity of purpose left it quite vulnerable to torpedo attack by another ship or by a submarine, which was why it always travelled in complement with at least a small but lethal orca-class attack submarine.

The submarine in question remained carefully hidden in one of the covered sub-docks of the harbor, entering and exiting its berth without ever showing its head above water, just like its larger nuclear cousins it shared the dock with.

Gathering his thoughts back to the moment, Jack nodded to himself, tapping his head as if to reset it on the task at hand. OK, time to go. Tonight he was going to be getting his hands very dirty indeed. And in order to accomplish the seemingly insurmountable task at hand, three men were going to be joining him, among whom was the alien Agent John Hunt.

The base was vast, and it was a long walk back along the pier and across the large parade ground to the barracks where he and his team were being put up. He had refused the offer of officer quarters from the dockmaster, preferring to stay in a small private room in the large barracks where the master had placed his men. It would give him more freedom to get the job at hand completed. Entering the barracks, he headed to his room, closing the flimsy door to the small, sparsely furnished bedroom as he stepped in. He poured himself a small glass of whiskey and settled down to calm his nerves. He was about to embark on the closest thing to espionage he had ever undertaken and he found that up close it really wasn't as glamorous as he had thought.

He looked at the two other glasses he had procured from the mess and thought of what he was about to do. The plan seemed simple. John and an operative that Admiral Hamilton had assigned to the operation were going to head over to the shed where the new warhead casings were being stored and commandeer the two trucks that Jack had ordered his men to load with twenty-six of the large crates they had arrived with earlier. They would then drive to the Royal Navy pier to unload their contents on to the HMS *Dauntless*.

But the plan was far more convoluted once you got into the details. Firstly, British naval warships did not let other nationals, even members of allied military organizations, on board without the express written permission of the captain. Secondly, the loading of large pallets onto the ship was always orchestrated by either the boatswain or the ship's engineer, Bill Shadley, without exception. And of course, like a perverse cherry on this mountain of obstacles, there was also a satellite cruising above them watching their every move, and if it spotted John Hunt doing something it did not consider appropriate, even the Agent would not be able to survive the destruction it would rain down upon him.

Their plan to counter these obstacles was fraught with risk and it was going to require some less than officer-like behavior on the part of one Major Jack Toranssen of the United States Air Force. Jack knocked back the last of his whiskey then reached for a refill. His glass full, he placed the half-empty bottle back on the table and picked up the small metal vial Ayala had given him before he left Hanscom. Inside were several small pills. He took two of them and dropped them into the neck of the bottle of whiskey and watched the pills dissolve in the potent brown liquid.

He was still swirling the bottle to dissolve the last of the soporific draft when there was a knock at the door. He put the bottle down, grabbed his own glass, and went over to open the metal door to his austere quarters. Two men in British Navy uniform stood in the hallway outside.

"Major Jack Toranssen, right?" said Lieutenant John Hunt, "We met at the naval strategy conference in San Diego a few months ago."

Jack nodded, "Yes, that's right. Wait, don't tell me … John, right?"

John smiled, "Yes, that's it. How've you been? Hey, sorry to drop in on you like this, but I saw your name on the duty roster when we came into dock and thought I would drop in and see if you wanted to join me and my friend here for a drink?"

Jack nodded and looked at John's 'friend.' He was a big burly man in his forties with a rugged face that had been hardened by countless years of salt air. He was clearly also English, and they discreetly sized each other up while John introduced them.

"Major Jack Toranssen, United States Air Force, this is Warrant Officer William Shadley, chief engineer of the HMS *Dauntless*," said John. Jack put out his hand as Bill Shadley instinctively saluted the senior officer. Jack smiled, politely returned the salute, then put his hand out again.

"No need for that, William," said Jack, trying to establish a relaxed tone, "we may be on the same side, but we have very different bosses."

They both chuckled conspiratorially and Bill, relaxing a little, took Jack's hand and said, "Very kind of you, sir. In that case I'd prefer it if you called me Bill. Only me 'mam calls me William."

They all smiled at each other and Jack waved them into the room, feeling a pang of guilt at abusing this clearly good man's trust. But he did not let it get in the way of his objectives, and his smile remained warm as he said, 'Bill' and 'John' ... that sounds good to me. After all, I can't drink with people who call me sir."

"Listen," he said as they seated themselves, "before we go out, I've just poured myself a whiskey. Why don't you two join me for a quick one and then we'll head out." He indicated the bottle and two glasses and said to Bill, "Help yourself, and don't be shy, I get it free from the officer's mess."

Bill wasn't known for being shy with whiskey, in fact, they were very close friends, and he half-filled the two glasses. Jack went a bit wide-eyed, worried for a moment about the strength of the draft, but they all raised their glasses, took a sip, and then sat down, Jack sitting on the single cot, and Bill and John taking the two metal chairs that came with the small room.

John decided to hasten proceedings and looked at Bill, "Looks like we're playing catch up to the major, Bill. Shall we?" He raised his glass and downed it with aplomb, following his mammoth gulp with a satisfied gasp and a mischievous smile.

"You're a bugger," said Bill, staring a little disconcertedly at the two or three shots of whiskey in his glass. He had suffered more than once from trying to keep up with the young lieutenant, but that didn't mean he was going to roll over and admit he was less of a sailor than the boy in front of him.

"Your health, Major," said the chief engineer, then, raising his glass, he grumbled, "why do I listen to you, John? Jack, I hope you know what you're in for with this one."

"Oh, I am painfully aware, Chief." said Jack, thinking that it was Bill Shadley who was sadly innocent of what he was signing up for. He watched as the big man knocked back his drink and smiled sympathetically as the stocky British sailor cringed at the burning in his throat. The chief engineer of the HMS *Dauntless* whistled and looked into the bottom of the empty glass appreciatively as the alcohol singed his throat, unaware of the powerful soporifics already working their way into his body.

- - -

Ten minutes later, John and Jack were walking out of the barracks, leaving an unconscious Chief Bill Shadley snoring on Jack's bunk. John had examined him and estimated that they had about ten hours. Ten hours to get twenty-six half-ton crates on board the HMS *Dauntless* without her captain knowing. Then they had to get back in time to return the British naval uniform Jack Toranssen was now wearing to its owner, who was sleeping happily in his underwear.

For reasons known only to the administrators and planners of the world's great military forces, the US is virtually unique in that its soldiers, sailors, airmen, and marines have nametags on their uniforms. Jack had praised the lack of nomenclature on British uniforms as he had quickly slipped on the Royal Navy breeches and jacket, knowing that the guard detail on the HMS *Dauntless* would have no way of recognizing the uniform of their chief engineer later that night. The insignia on his sleeves and collar would only tell them that he was a relatively senior warrant officer. They would hopefully then take the word of the well-respected and well-liked Lieutenant John Hunt to bolster the realism of the fake Royal Navy ID Ayala had procured for him.

But getting past them was probably still the easiest challenge they faced tonight.

- - -

Entering the low, almost surly looking shed where the missile casings were being stored, they were greeted by a bright flashlight in their eyes. It hesitated only a moment on the major before concentrating on John Hunt. But the light did not faze the Agent, both because his eyes saw easily passed the torch's beam and because he had been expecting the greeting.

"He's with me." said Major Toranssen with a sternness that hinted at the urgency of the situation.

The man holding the torch lowered it and stepped forward, coming up to face the stranger with the full might of his muscular presence. John met the other man's stare in the night without flinching, but spared the man the humiliation of simply brushing him aside. Master Chief Mike Lombardi of the Navy Seals believed he had faced death in his life. Twenty years beforehand two frightened officers in the Iraqi National Guard had pulled three of Mike's fingernails out and crushed one of his molars with a pair of pliers. After two months in a clandestine prison, the 'war' had ended and Mike had been released, but the ordeal had proven to him that he was immune to anything short of actual death. Pain is weakness leaving the body, the Seals said. But standing face-to-face with the young and soft-looking John Hunt, the Seal could have no idea he was facing death incarnate. All his training and conditioning, the burnished shield earned through years of pain, none of it would protect him for a second if John Hunt were to accept the implied threat that Mike Lombardi was making.

The master chief had been told in absolute terms by the single most senior officer in the United States Navy that he should trust no one but Major Jack Toranssen, and he was ready to kill this stranger in front of him if the major gave even the slightest hint of an order. John Hunt waited patiently while the major figured out that he had to intervene, the hot breath of the master chief in his face as the Seal attempted to dominate him. Eventually Jack figured out what was happening and said, "It's OK, Master Chief, he's on our side. Mike, this is John. John, Mike."

John held his ground until Mike stepped back a touch and then they both shook hands, Mike somewhat hesitantly. But with the same speed at which Mike's ire had risen, it dissipated. For now, he was attached to Jack like a proverbial guard dog, and with Jack's approval John became persona grata. They turned and set to, their task clear, all working quietly and efficiently to get ready.

- - -

Two lumbering M927 trucks grumbled across the yard. The dark green, canvas-topped, 6x6 army trucks growled as their monstrous diesel engines drove them up onto the long, wide wharf that the HMS *Dauntless* was moored against. It had taken considerable coordination to align the arrival of Major Toranssen, his team, and his assistant Mike Lombardi in Pearl Harbor with the brief stopover of the HMS *Dauntless*. In the end, Jack, Colonel Milton, and Martin Sobleski had had to work through the night getting the final shielding components ready for shipment once the *Dauntless*'s schedule was confirmed. But when you had the explicit support of the US Navy's senior admiral, and thus the Pentagon Security Council, you could open a lot of doors. Jack's orders had been written and rewritten in order to factor in the plans of the HMS *Dauntless*, though neither the crew of the *Dauntless* nor the satellites watching them all had ever been aware of it.

But orders from the US Navy could only get them so far, and while they had debated getting some of the Royal Navy's senior command involved in the plot, they had decided that this would open up the group too much to the risk of discovery. Once they had destroyed the satellites, they could start to disseminate the news of the coming attack more widely, but if the deaths of their friends in India, and the more recent confrontations in DC and Florida, had done nothing else, they had taught them that the need for secrecy was paramount.

The two trucks pulled up next to the *Dauntless*, and John jumped down, running up the main gangway to the two armed ratings zealously guarding the top of the gangway. The two men presented arms as John approached.

"No, no, lads, no need for all that, it's just me. Listen, I've got a favor to ask. Bill and I were supposed to get these pallets on board today for stowing before the captain rejoins the ship tomorrow morning, but they weren't ready on time. Now they are, and if the captain finds out they are ready and we haven't loaded them, it will be my arse. I'm going to sign them in and get them loaded, OK?"

The two ratings did not need reminding that they were stuck on board while most of their friends were off drinking, and they eyed the officer suspiciously. Lead Rating Peter Killarney summoned up his resolve and said to the well-liked officer, "Loading up, sir? Well, if you have to load then you have to load, but you'll understand of course that we can't leave our post to help you." The man glanced at his colleague for support and they both stood firm. It was one thing to be stuck on board on guard duty when in port, especially in Hawaii, but it was a whole other level of punishment to have to work as well.

John, meanwhile, had counted on just this response, "Now, now, guys, I'm not asking you to step away from a lowered gangway, you think I want to explain that to the big man?" They all laughed a bit and the two other men were visibly relieved at the lieutenant's reaction. John went on, "They aren't heavy and it shouldn't take more than an hour or so. One of the yard's crane operators is still on duty and he will work the gantry. We'll load them in the forward bay and then I'll take care of it in the morning." He looked at them and shrugged.

It all seemed harmless enough. The forward access bay was sealed from the upper deck down, so it was just a holding bay for now anyway. Without a reason to question the well-liked and famously competent officer in front of them, they both nodded and waved the lieutenant on his way. They were already distracted by their previous conversation when the lieutenant returned from for'ard and the now open loading bay and then jogged back down the gangplank to the wharf. As he saw John coming back down off the warship, Mike Lombardi stepped down from the driver's seat of the second truck and met him on the pier.

They came close and talked quietly, "All right, Mike, you've got the keys to the crane?" Mike nodded. He had procured the keys along with a cursory lesson in the crane's operation through a sternly worded letter from Admiral Hamilton to the base commander demanding the strictest of secrecy on his part. It was the kind of letter that, when backed up by an otherwise innocent sounding phone call from the admiral using a certain denoted codeword, could open pretty much any door on the base.

"So, we've got twenty-six crates to load in two hours." said John.

Mike nodded once, hesitated, and then shook his head as he took in the scale of what was being demanded, "Wait, I thought we had *ten* hours?" he said quietly.

John shrugged, "Yes, but I want to get the casings all fitted tonight, plus the longer we spend loading them the greater the chance we could be discovered."

Before Mike could comment further, John went on, "Look, that crane is rated up to twenty tons, that means that if we are smart about it we can do this in four goes."

Mike shook his head, "But they aren't set in four pallets, they are all crated separately." he said with outward calm but inward confusion.

But John smiled, "Leave that to me, Mike. I'll get them hooked up, you just lift them and drop them like we discussed."

Mike shook his head. But John felt confident they could do it, and so with a final nod of assurance, he stepped passed the master chief and went around the back of the truck to peel back the awning that covered the flatbed. Mike steeled himself and walked over to the foot of the rail-mounted crane, launching himself into the long climb to the control cabin.

In the back of the first truck, John bent and grasped the first of the twenty-six crates. The satellite watching above inquired what was going on and he replied via his relay onboard the *Dauntless* with a story about loading last minute supplies. He had recalibrated his built-in weight sensors so that the information being sent back to the satellite would show the crates as weighing only fifty pounds each, more fitting to the report he had filed with the AI.

He bent and picked up the first of the hefty crates and placed it on top of the one behind it. Then he turned to the next one and put that on top of the first two. He continued doing this till he had a block three crates high, two crates wide and one crate deep. Six crates, good. Now he picked up one more and hefted it over his head. Flexing his vastly powerful arms and legs, he thrusted the half-ton box into the air and deposited it on top of the stack to make up the seven crates he would need to get this done in four goes.

The tall, shore-mounted crane above started as easily as it had that afternoon, thought Mike, its electro-diesel engines powering up under the master chief's unskilled but quick-to-learn guidance. If a dockworker came along, he would have to decide how best to handle it. But his orders were clear. His utmost concern was the secrecy of the mission. Mike was authorized to use lethal force to protect that secrecy if necessary, and he was both willing and able to do it.

It would not be as tidy as he preferred, and the thought of silencing a dockworker, or worse a navy man, did not sit well with him. But the mission had been given to him with the utmost gravity, and if it came to it he would not hesitate. Ours is not to reason why, he thought, ours is just to do and die. With a wry smile, Mike set aside his concerns and watched John manipulating the crates far below. Those had seemed a shitload heavier earlier that night, he thought.

As the large cradle and hook swung over the truck, John reached up and grabbed hold of it, guiding it down and unhooking the two loading cables from its huge steel grapple. He jumped down and quickly ran them through the lowest pallets on the stack and then jumped back up, reattaching both ends to the grapple above and giving the thumbs-up to Mike in the cab. As the tension came on, John used his phenomenal strength to stabilize the load, riding up with it high into the air and slowly out over the ship's wide deck.

The ship loomed wide below him as John swung out, standing atop the crates like Ahab on the bow. Controlling the big load's progress with the plethora of levers in the control cab, Mike stopped the crate's outward movement with a clunk as he saw it range over the yawning forward bay on the *Dauntless*. As the package stuttered to a sharp halt over the entrance to the *Dauntless*'s hold, John felt the huge load start to swing like a pendulum. Mike was a fast study but he was no crane operator, and he had stopped the stack far too abruptly. The sudden stop had set its vast weight swinging back and forth, and at this rate it would collide with the sides of the hatch as it was lowered in, with potentially disastrous results.

John moved fast from his spot on top of the crates, grasping one of the supporting cables and clambering down the side of the stack. On the deck, one of the armed guards that was patrolling the seaward side of the ship stared in disbelief as the officer dropped down to hang from the side of big stack of crates and dangled from it as it swung from side to side.

From Mike's position in the crane's cab, it was not possible to see how much the package was swinging until it was almost level with the deck, but as it got closer to the entrance to the hold, Mike suddenly registered the movement and froze. A professional operator would have instinctively stopped the engine that was lowering the crates but Mike had to spend precious moments trying to think of which lever to pull. Shit, what the hell was he doing here, he thought, scrambling to stop the stack's slow drop into the hold. He could now see the apparently insane John Hunt hanging from the side of the unwieldy stack and trying to get between it and the fast approaching hatchway. A part of his brain registered respect for the brave way the Englishman put himself in harm's way, but Mike would only appreciate it later, long after he had gotten down from this damn crane.

Dangling from the bottom of stack, John sensed the course of the package, calculating with precision its momentum and the slowly increasing radius of its swing. Sensing which side of the yawning hold entrance the stack would swing into first, John agilely flung himself into place with his back to bottom of the stack, grasping the bottom crate with both hands so he could swing out both his legs to brace himself.

There were now two of the ship's armed deck guards watching the crates as they swung perilously close to the deck. Having caught a glimpse of the lieutenant throwing the boxes around down on the jetty earlier, they were woefully misinformed as to their real weight and so they did what they thought was best and reached out to help control the package as it came down. But before they could get their hand on it, the two men were astonished to see the lieutenant brace himself between the boxes and the steel lip of the hold. Surely he wasn't going to … fuck me, he was, they thought, as he extended his feet out to take the pressure of the coming collision.

John had braced his legs, and spread out his arms to spread the weight out over the side of the crates as much as possible but this impact was at the limits of even his machine strength. He felt his powerful body register the forces on each of its limbs. In his mind the deliberately miscalibrated pressure sensors rated the pressure at five hundred pounds, but he knew it was closer to five tons as it forced his feet into his chest. If his emotions had naturally registered on his face, he would have been straining and grunting at the effort, but an unnatural smile remained throughout, looking quite out of place as the hatchway and crate stack groaned with the pressure.

But his legs did absorb the blow, driving the huge force of the stack's momentum into the reinforced deck of the ship like shock absorbers. The two guards could have sworn they felt the 50,000-ton ship move slightly when John's feet hit it, but that was ridiculous. Thirty feet below them at the waterline, the ship swayed slightly, sending a tiny ripple out across the still harbor waters.

- - -

In the end it had only taken them about an hour and a half to load the four stacks of pallets into the ship. Afterward, John Hunt had thanked the various guards and waved to the master chief as he walked off into the night. In the bowels of the ship, John now stood amongst crates and scanned them. Sensing the one that was notably lighter than the rest, he stepped up to it and pried it open. Inside, a disheveled and slightly disconcerted Major Jack Toranssen sat, holding onto some tools and a weak smile as light shone in on him for the first time in nearly two hours. He was wearing Bill Shadley's uniform, which should help facilitate his departure from the ship once they were done, but getting an unknown man *onto* a naval vessel without the captain's express permission would have been next to impossible.

Climbing out of the crate, Jack smiled at John and surveyed his surroundings. The hold was large and smelled of grease and diesel, an almost inescapable smell aboard a navy ship. It was a wide rectangular space, ten feet deep, with walls of steel. The now closed bay doors took up the bulk of the ceiling, but under his feet Jack knew the floor could also be opened up, either in sections, or all at once, to give loading access to the lower decks of the ship. In port these more sensitive areas of the vessel were essentially sealed, with only the captain or chief engineer having access rights.

But John was no ordinary junior officer and he had been preparing for this day for several months. Stepping over to a stout-looking metal box on one wall, John placed his forefinger on the fat keyhole and allowed the microfibers that lay hidden inside it to snake out into the complex lock. With practiced ease, they found the necessary purchase and the lock opened with a dull clunk, to reveal a small keyboard and screen beneath.

John had long since hacked into the ship's central control systems and planted a virus that gave him access even the captain did not enjoy, and he had also supplemented this with a second program that allowed him to erase the evidence of his activities should he need them to remain secret. His fingers worked the keypad at whisper speed, his hands communing with the machine as he accessed his dormant programs and activated them, essentially opening up the sealed vaults of the ship to his control, at least until the captain returned or the chief engineer woke up.

Jack watched curiously as John worked on the pad and was startled when a large hatch suddenly thudded underneath him. John turned and smiled, stepped over to the previously locked platform, and hooked one of his fingers through a latch that usually accepted a special hook designed to allow the sailors to lever open the heavy trapdoors. But John did not need such tools. His mechanical muscles registered the weight without concern as he wrenched the massive door up and heaved it away to rest against the far wall, revealing a far deeper hold beneath them. As Jack came up to stare down into the twenty-foot-deep cavern below, John smiled at him.

"Wow." said Jack, steadying himself against an instinctive vertigo.

"Welcome to the bowels of the HMS *Dauntless*." said John.

Jack stared into the dark hole beneath them, aware that it extended back under his own feet. Trying to remain calm, he stepped discreetly back from precipitous drop, saying, "What happens if someone comes down here while we're working?"

"Once we are down there no one will be able to come looking for us." replied John as he started to carry the boxes, one by one, to the edge of the hatch, "the more sensitive areas of the ship are sealed by a network of armor-plated doors, each with a code lock. Access is strictly controlled and monitored. Even if the captain opens this door or any of the other ones that we will be going through in a while, an alarm sounds automatically on the bridge and in the captain's cabin."

Jack looked slightly horrified at the comment and had to stop himself for looking for an escape route, but John's easy smile and relaxed attitude calmed the US officer.

John went on, "The doors we are going to go through are also made of two-inch-thick blast-resistant steel and have permanent surveillance cameras mounted on either side of them, recording twenty-four hours a day."

Jack looked no more comforted at the addition of this good news, but John carried on talking as he moved the crates, "Of course, we have access rights rather better than those the captain enjoys." He paused to look at the major, his smile broadening, "No alarms will be going off tonight, trust me, and the cameras have just entered a ten-hour-long loop." Of course John's own internal monitoring devices had also entered a loop as soon as the hatch above had closed, telling the AI satellites above them that John had gone to bed and was even now lying, in the dark, asleep in his cabin.

Back in the hold, John finished his explanation of their strategy to Jack, "Once we have closed this access hatch, we will be essentially sealed off from the rest of the ship. With the captain ashore and Chief Engineer Bill Shadley … 'detained' in your quarters, no one can open these ports without one of the sealed emergency codes which are reserved for active combat. In fact, even if there is an emergency tonight, the first lieutenant and acting captain will find that even the emergency codes will have mysteriously ceased to work."

Jack shook his head a little and thanked the gods, not for the first time, that this man was on his side. Then he shrugged and smiled resignedly. John returned the major's smile with one of his own and nodded toward the crates, saying, "Now, I've lined up the first eight of these along the edge of the open hatchway. Now I am going to jump down to the bottom of the main hold and you are going to stay here and push them, one by one, over the edge. I'll catch them below and stack them up, then come back up here and line up the next eight. Sound good?"

Jack's eyes widened once more, "Wait a …" he managed to get out, but before the rest of his objection registered, John had grabbed one of the crates, hefted it over his head and stepped off the edge. Jack stepped quickly to the side of the hole and looked downward in time to see the top of the crate stop with a thud at the bottom of the dimly lit space below him, then shift to one side revealing an unharmed John Hunt as he placed the heavy box in a corner.

John looked up expectantly and Jack stared at him. He couldn't believe he was about to do this. But after a moment of looking down at the sweet-looking face of the Agent, he shrugged and set to. Stepping back he jammed his shoulder up against the first crate and heaved. It slid slowly forward, and then, with a sudden flood of speed it was gone, falling down into the darkness. Again Jack watched in amazement and again the crate seemed to hit solid ground, but this time without any perceptible noise. It just stopped, hung there for a moment, and then was hefted aside easily by the comically innocent-looking lieutenant.

Jack shook his head, reconciled himself that he was a long, long way from Kansas, and started heaving the big boxes over, one by one, into the waiting arms of his superhuman friend below.

- - -

They did not pause once they had the materials at the bottom of the hold. After John had resealed the hold from prying eyes, they cracked open the crates and began stacking the big super-conducting armor plates ready to carry them to the six main missile silos. From the bottom of the hold, a long, spinal corridor could be accessed through thick, steel doors that ran almost the length of the ship. It was through this strictly controlled access way that the ship's vast arsenal passed outward from the loading bays, moved on pulleys that hung from railings running along the roof of the dark hallway.

"Can I suggest," said John, being careful not appear patronizing, "that you let me carry all the plates to the various silos while you start removing the bolts on the nose cones of the forward SLAMs. I'll hack each of the access hatches and disable the cameras and then we should be able to move about pretty much un-noticed down here."

Ship Launched Anti-ballistic Missiles, or SLAMs, had to be one of the greatest military acronyms ever coined. But Jack was not thinking of such things as he looked at the Agent. Jack had been a college football player before he had become a pilot, and he had never experienced the sense of being utterly outclassed by someone, physically. It was not a pleasant sensation, but nor was it a particularly useful one either, he thought as he set such considerations aside. Jack knew that his strength was like a child's when compared to the Agent in front of him and he was not too proud to admit that his time was better spent wielding a power driver than trying to maneuver the huge boxes around the ship.

Jack nodded his agreement to the plan, unable to come up with much more enthusiasm than that, and with that John picked up one of the six huge stacks he had piled up and turned the corridor that led aft. They walked off, stepping through several bulkheads where the corridor could be sealed in case of a breach. Three times John had to put the stack down to type in a complex code into another armored door, red lights spinning ominously above his head as he hacked the system and temporarily disabled the ship's advanced security. Once they were completely done, he would check one last time that their movements had been completely removed from the records and then he would send his programs to hibernation once more, leaving no evidence that either Jack or John had ever been in the weapons hold.

Following behind the Agent, Jack Toranssen studied the ship that formed such a key part in their plans. He knew that the ship was recently launched, and he knew it was the very latest in naval technology. But he was only academically impressed. Deep down he knew why he had joined the air force: he felt constricted and claustrophobic in this confined space and longed for the wide open feeling of flight. They came to an abrupt halt after another stretch of steel corridor, and John placed the large, heavy stack on the floor once more. Typing for the last time, he opened the final bulkhead and urged Jack through into the missile room that marked the end of the corridor. They had passed others to each side along the way back through the ship but they would start back here and work forward.

Stepping into the massive space, Jack was stunned once more. The two men now stood at the bottom of another space like the one they had lowered the crates into, but this one was a military man's dream. Lining the walls on complex railings and movable brackets were a host of missiles of various lengths. Jack recognized a couple of Tomahawks and other cruise missiles, but those were just gravy; the meat of the room was an array of deadly ship-to-air missiles and finally the massive SLAMs.

These leviathans had chemical boosters and were capable of sustained supersonic flight and atmospheric egress. They were tipped with various warheads with technical names that went some small way to describing the havoc they were designed for: Tactical Electro-Magnetic Interruption Device and Explosive Deployed Cluster Kinetic Collision Warhead. But these were just names. In practice they were badasses. And each automated silo was designed to allow the rapid deployment of up to six of them a minute. At any time any one of them could be selected by the firing control computers and automatically lifted and braced into the bulky launch tubes at the top of the chamber, ready to be fired within a tenth of a second of the tube being sealed.

To be in this space during a missile deployment would be suicide, as the motors necessary to move this arsenal's massive weight would mutilate anything as flexible as an arm or leg without compunction. But when the room was not action ready, a central shaft about a meter in diameter was kept free of missiles. Down this shaft the main clamp tube ran, a thick, well-greased steel tube like a giant fireman's pole which the missiles were latched to for lifting to the tube launchers above. Jack stared at the vast array of firepower and considered how much more this one silo held than even his huge B-2 bomber's large bays. Suddenly he had an appreciation for the role this powerful destroyer would be able to play in the coming attack, and a more profound appreciation for the navy as a whole.

While Jack stared agog John headed over to a small compartment set just inside the bulkhead and grabbed one of several large wireless bolt drivers from the charging brackets inside. "There," said the Agent to the major, handing it to Jack, "now, let's go on up to where the SLAM missiles are stored up top and I'll show you how to start unbolting the nose cones."

John and Jack climbed onto a small removable lift platform at the bottom of the shaft and John pressed a foot pedal that sent them up through the core of the missiles. Jack felt small next to these billion-dollar death bringers, like an ant climbing amongst bullets in a Titan's handgun. At the second of three levels of missiles, John stopped the lift and Jack noted that he could easily step to either side and plummet thirty feet to a painful death below, but he stayed calm as he watched John Hunt step expertly onto a set of rungs mounted on the side of the brackets holding one of the SLAMs. Jack noticed that all of the brackets were designed so that a lone man or woman could stand on their sides and it would place them exactly level with the nose cone of that missile. Smart.

John took the bolt driver and placed the bit against one of the bolts.

"Now," said John Hunt, holding the bolt driver steady, "you must start with this bolt here with the small yellow arrow next to it. You will notice there are also red and blue arrows next to some of the other bolts. It is a small security measure, but unscrew the wrong bolt first and you will set off a small explosive device inside that will disable the missile and almost certainly kill you at the same time. Just our little way of stopping people tampering with the equipment.

"There are other failsafes inside the warhead, but we aren't going to even touch the actual warheads themselves so don't worry about those. Yellow, remember, the yellow arrow." Jack nodded to the Agent and John nodded back, then he expertly removed the first bolt and handed it to Jack.

"I'm assuming the driver is magnetic." said Jack, putting the bolt into his pocket.

John glanced down at the floor far below and nodded, "Yes, it is, you wouldn't want to drop anything in here."

With that John handed the driver back to Jack and stepped back onto the lift platform. Jack in turn took his place on the missile frame and went to the next bolt. After he lined it up, a little nervous about the explosive, he turned to John, who nodded.

"You are good to go. Don't bother trying taking off the cones once they are unbolted, they weigh fifty pounds each and they are fitted very tight. Just remove all the bolts on the missiles on this level and then come down. Once you're done I'll take the shield components up, take off the cones, and fit the superconducting shields between them and the warhead's ceramic heat shielding underneath."

Jack nodded, focusing on his task, and John went on, "In the meantime, I'll finish getting the boxes stacked in each missile silo. This is one of six. When you're done here you can get started on the next. Sound good?" They nodded at each other once more.

"You'll need this to get down," said the Agent finally, indicating the lift mechanism he was standing on, "so I'll leave it here for you. Just shout if you need me, or walk back down the main corridor and you'll find me soon enough." He nodded once more, Jack smiled back at him, and with that John stepped off the side of the lift platform and slipped between the platform's side and the missiles. He plummeted the thirty feet to the floor and Jack stared after him, his heart skipping a couple of beats until he saw the man land with a loud clang on the floor below. Jesus Christ that was weird to see. John glanced back up momentarily, waved and then walked off to grab another half-ton crate, leaving Jack to his work.

- - -

Jack managed to keep up with the Agent for an hour or two. It took a while for John to carry all the shielding to each of the six missile silos, but there were eight SLAMs in each of the tall loading rooms, and it was already 11pm when they started. He continued to work even as John started to catch up to him, finishing whole silos in just the time it took Jack to remove the bolts. By one in the morning, Jack was exhausted, a profound, bone-deep fatigue that he could no longer ignore. He had worked his way through three of the missile rooms, clambering over twenty-four of the huge missiles to remove the tight-fitting bolts, eight bolts a piece.

For each missile, Jack only had to take off the bolts, while John had to carry up the thin, black shielding components, remove the fifty-pound nose cone, place the sheets in precisely the right positions, weld them there using his onboard lasers, and then replace the cone. The pressure required to squeeze the cone back into place alone was roughly three thousand pounds, roughly the weight of a small SUV, which had to be evenly and consistently applied. Jack had kept ahead of him for a while, but now John was able to do all this in less time than it was taking Jack to unscrew the bolts from each missile.

As the night wore on, Jack got steadily slower. But John Hunt never tired, never lost concentration, never stopped for breath or to go to the bathroom. Soon the Agent had caught up with the determined but flagging major and so he went back and picked up the large pile of bolts Jack had left in the first missile silo, took another of the bolt drivers and started reaffixing the bolts.

By 5am they were nearly done, but Jack was a shell of a man. He could barely lift his right arm anymore, and his body was screaming at him to rest. He went looking for his indomitable colleague with the resignation of the outclassed. He could hear the whine of the bolt driver in the fifth missile silo as he stepped through the bulkhead and into the big room.

"John," he shouted up into the shaft of the fifth missile chamber, "you got a sec?"

As he shouted, Jack noticed the lift platform still on the floor, but was certain he had heard the sound of the bolt driver coming from the room. Jack heard the whoosh a moment before John landed on the steel floor, his legs flexing abnormally low to take the blow while his face remained passive.

Jack looked at the Agent. The relatively fit and healthy Major Toranssen felt as tired and beaten up as he ever had. He was bruised and battered all over, and he ached from his hair down. His hands were bleeding and sore, blisters rising on the inside of his right hand while welts from the battle-grade steel bolts lined the fingers of his left. But this young-looking man in front of him looked as bright and cheerful as a six-year-old on Christmas morning. Not a drop of sweat, not a single puff of exertion to show how hard he had been working. A slightly hysterical snort escaped Jack's lips as he stared at John, bewildered.

"Tell me something," Jack said to the Agent, "I know you are a machine, but you have also said that you have a copy of a person's, I mean a Mobiliei's personality in you." John nodded and Jack went on, "Do you … I mean … is it … well …"

"Strange?" prompted John.

"No, no, not strange. No. I just wondered, well, is it fun? You know, being able to do all the things you can do?"

John looked at the major for a moment, assessing the exhaustion of his human friend. Then, after a moment's consideration, he answered, "There are times when, yes, it feels good. There are times when being able to run and jump and lift anything I see is … well, it's enjoyable. We have this kind of technology back home, of course, but it's illegal to use android bodies in public unless you are a member of the military, and even then usage is extremely restricted, for obvious reasons. The power it gives you is truly awesome.

"But … well … I guess I would compare it to being a king's favorite general: I have huge amounts of power, I can go anywhere and do anything to anything, and it feels good. Only I am still subject to a higher power, and in this case that power is, frankly, a ruthless, soulless son of a bitch. So any time this body's abilities seem enticing, I find myself reminded that this is a co-opted power, taken at a price I still have trouble wrapping my head around."

Jack looked at the Agent, sobered suddenly by his words, and Agent John Hunt went on, "I am sure you feel in no small measure the weight of the secret you bear, and the danger you and everyone you know is in. And because I see that danger too, and I am not a monster, I am going to try and stop my world from doing this terrible thing. But think on this a moment, Jack. Think about what kind of selfish, power-hungry, almighty asshole would order the death of an entire race. Once you have that image in your mind, you will have some idea of the kind of people I am disobeying to help you. Imagine an alliance of Hitler, Khan, Mussolini, Yung Il, and bin Laden all united by one thing, they *all* want to kill every human alive. Well, something akin to that alliance commands the forces arrayed against you, Jack.

"So, I guess when you ask me whether I am having fun, I …" he laughed introspectively and shook his head a little, "well, I worry that you and the others really think of me as a disinterested outsider just trying to help out." Jack went to shake his head and deny it, but the truth was that he did think of John like that. Like some kind of movie star going to Africa to help the poor, only to return on his private jet the next day to attend an award ceremony. But John's expression was stern and Jack waited for the Agent's next comment. "Jack, have you ever wondered what that group of bloodthirsty motherfuckers that rule my world are going to do when they find out that I have betrayed them?"

Jack stared at him, stunned and mortified by the man's words, but John wasn't finished, "Jack, what do you think they are going to do to my family? To my three children. Those children are grown up by now, back on Mobilius. Maybe they have children of their own. Grandchildren of mine who I will never meet. Grandchildren of mine who, if my complicity is discovered, will pay a terrible price for the actions of a man they have never even known."

Seeing the human's discomfort at his words, John lifted his hands as if to downplay what he was saying and went on, "Jack, I'm sorry, I'm not trying to make you feel bad, goodness knows you are putting yourself on the line as well, but when you asked whether I am enjoying myself … I guess … well, I guess I just wanted to set the record straight."

The two men looked at each other and Jack nodded. They were silent for a moment and then Jack took a deep breath and said, "You're right, of course. I can't speak for the others, but I guess I always felt a bit patronized by you and your … well, your charity. Maybe I even resented that we were so dependent on you." They both smiled ruefully at each other and Jack finished, "For what it's worth, though, thank you. For all of us, for my family and my friends, and for me: thank you for what you are doing."

He held out his blistered hand and John's synthetic hand met it in a firm grasp. One day, Jack hoped, he would get to shake the real hand of the person inside Agent John Hunt, whatever that creature actually looked like. Maybe if they survived the coming war it might happen. Who knows?

Till then, though, Jack vowed never to take this man's sacrifice lightly again.

Chapter 46: Spread Your Arm(ament)s

It had taken Shahim a long time to recover fully from the fight with John. But John Hunt had not been able to hang around and help the battered Agent repair. After a brief but brutally honest discussion of what they needed to accomplish, John had left, trusting his instincts about the lord of Hamprect and hoping he had not doomed them all.

At first Shahim had found the fact that he was now a traitor a difficult pill to swallow. But the river of doubt and remorse for what he had done in Pakistan ran deep within him, and once its banks were breached there was no way it would be contained again. He had known the Nomadi was right from the moment the Agent had started to berate him for his role in the whole enterprise.

Since that day Shahim had rediscovered a lost sense of pride and meaning as he began to pursue his new mission. Now, as he stood on the soils of Pakistan once more, he knew he was steering the right course. That fateful day in Washington DC was three months and seven thousand miles away now, and any semblance of doubt Shahim might have had in his decision was long since laid to rest.

Getting back to Pakistan had been a long and arduous task. It had started simply enough: an anonymous phone call from near his hideout in DC had brought the authorities with surprising efficiency. The FBI took the three men who had been sent to assist Shahim in an angry but one-sided struggle while Shahim himself slipped out a window into the night.

The AI had heard of the raid well in advance, even though it was unaware of the source of the FBI's information. Shahim had pretended ignorance as the AI had informed him of the approach of the authorities and had stepped onto the fire escape as the bureau's cars came down the street, leapt up on to the roof, and then from there he had jumped the thirty feet across the night to the top of the next building. For his own edification, he had waited there a moment and watched the men fight as they were apprehended. He had heard the struggle and watched the heat signatures of the men as they were wrestled to the ground and dragged away.

It had felt good. He had already helped humanity a little. Not enough to make up for what he had done that dreadful night in Islamabad, but it was a start, and soon he would have ample opportunity to atone for the rest of his sins.

While his Al Qaeda 'brethren' in the US and back in Pakistan assumed he had been captured with his cell, he had evaded the authorities and made his way slowly back to Pakistan. With no identification or money it was a long journey, even for a man of his talents. But after countless cargo ships, freight trains, and hitchhiked rides in the backs of trucks, the warrior had eventually made it back to his adopted home country. Predictably, his sudden reappearance in Peshawar three months after his assumed capture in America had brought immediate suspicion and accusation. How had he escaped? How had he evaded capture for so long? What had he told the infidels to buy his freedom?

Standing in the warehouse where he had been brought after he had approached one of his old contacts in the city, he sullenly but humbly answered their questions. But with his newfound purpose came a certain leeway he had not enjoyed before. The truth was that the Agent that called himself Shahim Al Khazar didn't like these people. He did not agree with their cause or their methods, and while neither side in the global struggle the insurgents were involved in was above reproach, these so-called freedom fighters were, in Shahim's opinion, a horde of hypocrites and tyrants. So when the impromptu tribunal that had been arranged to judge him began to criticize the integrity of the man that called himself Shahim Al Khazar, the Agent decided that it was the justification he needed to wreak some havoc upon the mockery of justice that stood before him.

"No one," he said quietly, "no one should dare suggest I am not a faithful warrior. I have failed in my mission, and for that I am ashamed, but if anyone dares to say I am not still Allah's faithful servant, I swear to his holy name that I will kill that man where he stands." His eyes slowly swept the room, their fierce burn spitting dread at the gathering.

But there were those in the tribunal who saw this as a potential opportunity to establish their dominance over the formidable Shahim Al Khazar. Among them, two clerics considered speaking up and one of them finally drummed up the courage to confront the bound warrior. It was not that great an act of bravery given the circumstances, or so the cleric thought. Shahim stood in the center of the large concrete floor, bared to the chest, his face dirty, his arms tightly clasped behind his back by thick rope and the grip of two burly guards.

Cleric Bin Amar stepped up to the bound Shahim. It had been Cleric Amar's brother that had ordered the attack on the prime minister's complex all those months ago. Shahim's unexpected success had brought the swift execution of the cleric who had ordered such a foolhardy attempt. For the brother of the man who had attempted the power-grab, Cleric Bin Amar, had also seen his political clout falter noticeably since the day Shahim had managed the impossible. This and the death of his brother had left him hungry for revenge, and this opportunity was simply too good to pass up.

"You say to me that anyone that accuses you of weakness will die where they stand." said Cleric Bin Amar, posturing for the crowd, "Well I say to you that I do not fear death in God's name. Unlike you I would not sell my faith to you or the Americans for my freedom."

Shahim stared at the man and allowed fury to glow darkly on his strong features. As the room followed the cleric's 'brave' speech, Shahim's hands began to apply a discreet pressure to his bonds. As his powerful muscles started to apply their smooth, massive tension, Shahim felt the rope start to split, clearly unable to contain the machine might of the warrior. But the unwise cleric was not alone in his misguided showboating. Another ambitious sect leader, Barakahto Wa-Alahd, was not about to be upstaged. It had been he who had called this tribunal, and it would be he who garnered the fame for bringing down the notorious Butcher of Islamabad.

So Barakahto Wa-Alahd stepped forward and tried to claim his portion of the limelight, "Cleric Bin Amar, while no one doubts your faith, please remember that it was I who called this trial of the traitor Al Khazar." Then, turning to the prisoner, he said, "Yes Shahim, hear me when I call you traitor. For you could not have escaped the Americans any more than you can escape the bonds that now hold you," he paused for a meaningful look around the room and then finished his point, "without selling your loyalty in return for your freedom."

Inside his head, Shahim smiled. Oh dear, my friend, be careful what you say, he thought, and he slowly and steadily pulled his arms apart, the taut ropes parting at his will like they were made of candy floss.

The two guards behind him suddenly realized that the movement of the famous warrior's arms was not the pointless struggle of a bound man, but in fact the suddenly unimpeded movement of their prisoner's arms. Their grip tightened on the man as Shahim stepped forward, but he barely even registered their efforts.

His first accuser, Cleric Bin Amar, had struck a brave pose facing away from Shahim, talking to the crowd. That left Barakahto Wa-Alahd to stare wide-eyed at Shahim as he stepped up behind Bin Amar and grabbed him by the back of his neck.

Frozen on the spot by the apparently unconfined prisoner's sudden freedom, Wa-Alahd did not even have the presence of mind to turn and run as he watched the warrior's left hand manhandle the other cleric, and in a moment it was too late to run anymore, as the prisoner's other hand flew out at his own throat to seize him as well.

The two guards pulled and punched at the bared might of Shahim, trying to wrestle his arms back while the two pinned Clerics struggled vainly at the fingers ensnaring their necks. Eventually the guards gave up trying to grapple with the prisoner, his arms just did not give, and they both stepped back and pulled their rifles from their shoulders, pressing the butts of the guns into Shahim's sides.

The room was alive with shouting and panic, but Shahim's bass voice boomed out over the hubbub and silenced the crowd. With the two clerics' necks clasped in each hand, he bellowed, "These men have said that I am a traitor, even though I warned them of the consequences of decrying my loyalty. They have said they do not fear death in God's name. I tell you now that God has filled me with the strength to test that claim."

The room was silent but for the shouts of the two struggling clerics. The two guards were transfixed by the sight of the two powerful leaders writhing in this man's hands. Surely he would not kill the two men. That would be suicide … surely?

Cleric Bin Amar tried in vain to turn and see the man holding him, all the while screaming as he grappled futilely with the warrior's vice-like grip. "Shoot him!" he wailed, "Shoot the prisoner! In Allah's name, I order you to shoot him!"

The second accuser was facing Shahim, though, his neck grasped from the front, and he was silent. The grip around his neck was tight, his very breath barely wheezing through his constricted throat. Shahim planned to deal with them in the order they had accused him and he did not want Cleric Barakahto Wa-Alahd interrupting the first cleric's brief trial.

Shahim's voice boomed out once more from behind the first man's head, "Cleric Bin Amar, you say that you would die for God, and you accuse me of being a traitor even though I told you I would kill you for doing so. Therefore I will grant your wish to meet our glorious maker. Allah, accept this man's sacrifice to your cause, allow his faith to guide him to you."

The cleric scrabbled frantically at the fingers of his captor, his eyes wide at Shahim's words. Dear Allah, the bastard was going to kill him, but, no, wait, no, this cannot be! His fear was palpable and he screamed, "No! No! Stop him you fools! Stop h—"

With machine ease, Shahim snapped the cleric's head to one side like a giant light switch, shutting the man's life off instantly. Shahim liked the image. He had switched the evil man off, permanently. Shahim released the cleric's now limp neck and the body slumped to the floor. Shahim allowed his raw pleasure at what he was doing to show on his face, and the other man imprisoned by his grasp began to weep at the site of the grin now etched into Shahim's dark features. Why had he accused this beast so lackadaisically?

The sudden death of the first cleric awoke the guards from their vacillation and they started shouting at the prisoner with renewed vigor. No one was prepared for this. No one was willing to fire the first shot. Not here. Not during the tribunal. This was simply unprecedented. But the men continued thrusting their guns into Shahim's ribs in the hope the man would desist.

Shahim ignored them, his eyes glued now on his other victim, who was weeping with fear, urine dripping down his quivering legs and pooling at his feet. Shahim shouted at the remaining man, "Do you still doubt my ability to escape the Americans, Cleric Wa-Alahd?"

The man shook his head as best he could in the man's grip and whimpered his response, but he couldn't be heard over the shouting of the two guards. Shahim needed silence. Killing the first cleric had left Shahim's left hand free, and without warning he whipped it around behind him and grabbed the muzzle of one of the rifles poking into his back. The guard felt the gun be powerfully wrenched from his grip and then watched in amazement as Shahim tossed it smoothly into the air, catching it again a second later by its grip. A part of the guard's mind registered the precision with which Shahim's finger slipped into the trigger mount of the rifle but his awe turned to shock in a flash as the gun swung back to point directly between his eyes.

Shahim shot him at point-blank range without qualm and then swung the gun under the outstretched arm still holding the struggling cleric and fired another single bullet through the other guard's chest. All the while never taking his eyes of the doomed cleric in his grasp.

The gun's loud reports echoed around the enclosed space, the crowd now utterly silent as they looked in disbelief at the center of the room. Shahim stood grasping the rifle in his left hand, the whimpering cleric still gripped in his right. Three bodies lay sprawled around him and his once tight bonds lay behind him in a pile where only moments beforehand the warrior had seemed so … contained.

The room's stunned silence allowed Shahim to say his next words calmly and quietly, "Wa-Alahd, do you wish to recant your statement? Do you wish to beg for mercy?" Shahim lightened his grip ever so slightly, allowing the man to speak.

The openly crying cleric gasped to the silenced room, "Yes! Please, I beg of you! Let me live! Hear this man! Please, hear him! He is innocent! I tell you this man is a true servant of God!"

His eyes were pleading and pathetic, and a stench spread around the room as the cleric soiled himself. Shahim spoke once more, lacing his words with cold, bitter disdain, "You are pathetic, begging like this. Would you choose ignominy over death, Cleric? If I grant you forgiveness for your statements against me, will you renounce your position and leave this place forever?"

The cleric was spastic with fear, sobs wrenching his body as he writhed in Shahim's iron grip. He screamed, "Yes, please, forgive me. I will leave here, I promise. I will never return. Do not kill me, I beg of you."

Shahim nodded, "Very well, I forgive you for your accusations." The man struggled a moment longer but then paused, trying to see if his attacker was really going to let him live. A look of childlike hope filled his face, a hope he had never given the hundreds of people he had murdered, raped, and abused in the course of his patently hypocritical life.

The rest of the people in the room were reeling at the cowardly display. Shahim was not just killing the cleric, he was destroying him. As a sense of disgust washed through the audience at the display of the pleading cleric, each one of the onlookers couldn't help but wonder how they would behave in the face of such righteous fury. Having seen this, no man present would ever stand against this warrior in the future, he had purchased their fealty with the threat of utter humiliation. His resolve was clearly absolute, his wrath terrifying.

Shahim stopped talking to the broken man in front of him and addressed the whole room, "Here me, tribunal, I forgive this man for his statements against me. But I tell you now that if any of you ever question my faith again I will not be so lenient. Is that clear?" The room's silence was his answer, and Shahim looked back at the man in his grip and smiled.

"That said, the punishment for renouncing Allah's holy jihad in order to protect your own irrelevant life is and should be immediate death. Wouldn't you agree, Cleric Wa-Alahd?" The cleric's fear surged up inside him once more and erupted in a final scream as he looked into the vicious smile of the warrior, but his curdling wail was cut off as Shahim's hand tightened around his throat once more.

The crowd stared in shock as the man's head turned purple, and they recoiled in horror as each of the gurgling man's eyes popped from his head, the pressure forcing the tissue from his neck up into his skull to crush his brain.

After a final squeeze to drive any hint of remaining life from the little shit's body, Shahim tossed the man's limp frame aside, and wiped his hands on the shawl that still lay around his waist. Then he pulled the shawl back up over his shoulders, restoring some measure of dignity, and slung the dead guard's rifle over his shoulder.

"Now, I believe this tribunal was summoned to vote on whether I should be considered a faithful servant of the jihad. Are there any among you who wish to say I am not?" He looked at each of the remaining men in turn and they each shook their heads vehemently.

"Good, then I humbly submit to the will of Almighty Allah and ask that I be sent back into the service of our Holy War. In fact, if the tribunal would care to hear them, perhaps I may even suggest some ways in which I might continue to serve our great cause?" With four bodies lying still warm at his feet, Shahim smiled pleasantly and bowed to the panel arrayed in front of him. The anathema of that smile scared them in ways even the brutal slaughter they had just witnessed could not.

- - -

Three weeks later the warrior Shahim Al Khazar clambered once more into his old cave deep in the Hindu Kush Mountains. His long buried relay now back in his possession for the first time since his departure for America, he placed the device in one corner and knelt to pray. Two men had apparently taken residence in the cave since he had left, but when news of Al Khazar's return began to spread, they had quickly evacuated the chamber, fleeing his now legendary wrath.

As Shahim knelt on his prayer blanket, he felt the Council convene once more, and settled in for his first full-bandwidth Council meeting in months.

<Welcome.>

The eight Agents floated in their virtual circle and waited for the AI to detail its agenda. <I have prepared an agenda. We have six items to discuss.>

The Artificial Intelligence that chaired their meetings went through its list, various assignment changes, and new business. First on the list was the revised location and status of Shahim Al Khazar after the Agent's return to Pakistan. His next moves would be discussed by the Council, but both Shahim and his new ally John Hunt were clear on what they thought had to happen next. The team had a defined, if risky, course to steer during the buildup to the impending attack on the satellites, and Shahim's role would be pivotal. Now it was up to John and Shahim to subvert the Council's will in order to align it with their own.

As Shahim and John thought about this in silence, the AI continued its agenda review, and they were both shocked from their reverie when the AI reached item number six on its list, <Finally, recent reports from four separate Centers for Disease Control in Europe and America have reported several cases of unexpected recovery from incurable communicable diseases, most notably there have been cases of unexplained and complete recovery from the Human Immunodeficiency Virus. It is our opinion that this should be investigated.>

Neither John nor Shahim allowed their shock to show on their faces, but nor could they believe that the antigen's effects were registering so quickly. Had Ayala really been that effective in getting it out to the population? They sat in silence, allowing the meeting to run its course so they could learn more without showing their hand.

<Agent Shahim Al Khazar, please report on your progress reintegrating into the forces in Pakistan.>

They had all seen his updates on the trial in Peshawar, and things had moved quickly from there. He began his report, "Things have progressed well since my trial. Many are afraid of me, and though I believe some of the old guard still plot against me, the bulk of the fighting force here has taken my name as anthem, and I am heralded as invincible. A nickname has started to spread that I am 'Osman Returned,' a reincarnation of the legendary Islamic warrior Osman Gazi, who was so victorious against the Byzantine Empire in the 1300s.

"It is clear that in order to promote my success here I am going to need to capitalize on that developing hero persona, possibly by discreetly encouraging an internal war between some of the factions in order to eliminate some of my rivals. Once I have declared for one side, I can swing power to the leader of that group in a series of lopsided victories. That will remove my naysayers and also leave me as heir apparent and right-hand man to the remaining leader. The distraction will also serve to help the Pakistani government to relax a little, softening them for the coming blow.

"Currently they are still very much on their guard from my attack in Islamabad, and the fast spreading rumors of my return have only bolstered their paranoia."

Lana spoke, "It's hardly paranoia, Agent Shahim, you did kill about 150 of them in one night." His avatar merely nodded, but inside Shahim cringed at the memory while Lana continued snidely, "Of course, we can only hope you will continue to be as successful now you have returned to Pakistan, and not repeat the errors of your time in America."

She looked at him and he was reminded of the conversation they had had in his apartment in New York when she had wielded the echoes of her royal influence over him. Oh, Princess Lamati, you think you are disappointed in me now, just you wait, thought Shahim.

But outwardly he looked grave and bowed slightly to the princess who called herself Agent Lana Wilson, averting his eyes in respect.

<Very well. We believe the Council should consider the motion proposed for Agent Khazar to initiate a faction war within the Taliban and Al Qaeda forces. Do we have a second?>

John Hunt nodded and the AI registered his accession, automatically initiating a vote. As Shahim had hoped, it was not a controversial topic, and the motion passed easily. So far, so good.

The meeting moved on, through discussion of the various topics left for them, winding its way excruciatingly slowly toward the all important final item on the agenda. Finally they got to the elusive topic and John allowed himself a brief glance at his sometime partner Shahim across the room as the AI introduced it.

<Reports from several Disease Control Centers across the world have noted significant increases in recoveries from serious diseases, including some previously incurable diseases. Most importantly there has been a small but statistically relevant increase in survival rates from Malaria in southern Africa and Egypt, and a significant number of cases where previously HIV-positive cases in Europe and America have shown a sudden recovery from the disease.>

<The HIV recoveries are of particular concern to our operation here as it is upon a combination of this virus and the disease humans call Influenza that we based our own viral bio-weapon.>

John and Shahim watched the room as this information was relayed, and to their surprise and relief the Council did not seem particularly worried by the AI's comments. Hoping to avert further investigation John decided to play upon their lack of interest, "I am unclear why this is relevant to our mission here." he said, "The virus is only a backup plan at best, a last resort. We have no intention of using it unless we are discovered, and so far, in over a year on the planet, we have successfully remained hidden. If you remember, we easily dispatched the only people who ever came close to discovering our presence when they stumbled on Agent Parikh's capsule in India. The *King's Transom* was sunk over nine months ago and there has been no further sign that the humans even suspect our presence since then."

He let that sit out there, then decided to try and get an ally from the group's most outspoken member, "Agent Lana Wilson and Shahim Al Khazar proved this even further with their investigation of the two survivors of the incident not three months ago."

Ever happy to hear her name used, Lana spoke up, "I agree. So what if a few humans have recovered from a disease. It will hardly protect them from what is coming."

The AI persisted, <Mission Parameter: If human's show signs of technical improvements in critical areas, Council is instructed to act in order to suppress such technology. If this spread of immunity to noted communicable diseases is linked to a deliberate act by the humans, it clearly falls within one of the critical areas noted in our mission parameters, and as Arbiter of the Council we table a proposition that we look into these incidents.>

Not wanting to go too far out on a limb, John glanced at Shahim in the hope that he would offer up some point to support John's and Lana's statements. The other double agent took the hint.

"Arbiter," said Shahim, "what numbers are we talking about here? Is this a large sampling or merely anecdotal?"

The AI responded immediately and without emotion. It was no more capable of being frustrated at the persistent refusal of the Council to acknowledge the problem than it was of caring when it was being asked to provide information that would refute its own argument. <The number of incidents that have been reported by the CDC in America are fifty-seven. Other disease control centers do not have as accurate information and are limited to isolated cases.>

Shahim threw his virtual arms in the air and several others joined him in expressions of skepticism, but both John and Shahim knew that it was a cheap trick. To have fifty-seven reported cases was actually a very significant number. Only fifteen years beforehand, Great Britain had slaughtered and burned four hundred thousand cows because of only fourteen fatalities from Creutzfeldt–Jakob disease. And reported recoveries, like reported cases, are always only the tip of the iceberg. Fifty-seven represented a relatively significant threat. These things always started small, but for now the Council did not know that the immunity was actively spreading through the population, and they could only hope they remained ignorant long enough. With less than two-tenths of a percent of the American public living with AIDS, that meant that nearly one tenth of a percent of that population was already seeing the effects of the antigen. And that was just the cases that had been reported. People may go months without blood tests if they were not showing symptoms. The antigen appeared to be moving quite quickly.

But any good debater knows that statistics are far from infallible, they are a tool of the politician, and John took Shahim's lead and ran with it.

"My friends on the Council, with seven billion humans on Earth, such a small number of cases are hardly relevant. This is a waste of our time. I propose that we move on. Is there a second?"

Shahim did not have to offer up his hand as several of their colleagues were equally unimpressed with the AI's point.

But they both knew it was only a matter of time now. They were getting close. The cases of miraculous disease recovery were only going to increase and that was going to translate into media coverage and eventually someone was going to discover what was causing it.

While that meant they were getting close to being ready to openly attack the satellites, they were still hobbled by the fact that the last few weeks of the antigen's spread were going to be by far the most important.

Once the spread reached critical mass, it would go like wildfire through the population. But between now and then they were at their most vulnerable. So few were already immune, and once the AI saw the antigen up close, events were going to snowball fast.

Chapter 47: Little Dutch Boy

Ayala looked pensive as she stood against the wall of the large hangar at Hanscom. She and Colonel Milton had stepped off to one side to discuss the team's progress in hushed tones.

"And how is Jack doing?" she asked.

"Good." said Barrett, "According to his schedule, he should be back in a couple of days. We haven't spoken openly, of course, but he called yesterday and said that he was 'tired from a long but very fun evening out with an old friend,' so that means they completed the installation on the HMS *Dauntless* as planned and he and his team are moving on to the GBMD sites."

Ayala smiled at the news, but the colonel's thoughtful look remained and Ayala looked at him, sensing a disquiet underlying his casual tone. He smiled, but with worried eyes, and answered her unasked question, "The work that they must have put in to refit all the SLAMs on the *Dauntless* must have been phenomenal. Even *with* John's abilities. Things *seem* to be going well. I didn't think it would be possible but we're on track with the missile upgrades. I leave for Florida next week with the next shipment of casings. We're … well … we're progressing. But …."

She raised her eyebrow, and he looked about the huge space, clearly making an effort to mask his emotions. "Ayala, don't you think that we have been … well, extraordinarily lucky just to make it this far?"

She nodded slightly, a matching pensiveness spreading across her own face, but rather than answer she let him carry on, hoping it would help the man if he got it all off his chest. After a moment he continued, "We barely escaped with our lives the last time the Council became suspicious enough to begin nosing around. Now we have this letter from John saying that the CDC reports on HIV recoveries are raising new questions amongst the Agents. We're so close, but … shit, pushpin, if they find out about the antigen now … well, it will literally mean disaster, absolute disaster."

They both looked sideways at each other, their faces remaining as passive as they could, then she stepped in front of him, putting herself between him and the rest of the large room so she could speak frankly. With their eyes connected, her expression reached out to him, fondness and support radiating from her and he felt her love for him like a warmth.

"Barrett, darling, you need to remember that this is not a burden you bear alone. We are a team. Let's not talk about problems or concerns, but about solutions. You say they might find us too soon; well that is certainly a possibility. But if it is, then let's decide what we will do if that happens."

He looked at her and tilted his head ever so slightly in a question. He didn't have to verbalize it; they both understood what the implied risk was: what, my dear, do you propose we do if 90% of the world's population is wiped out by a plague that would shame the old testament? She pursed her lips and nodded. Through a pragmatism born more of necessity rather than choice, she focused on what she could affect, rather than what she could not.

After a moment's thought, she said, "The antigen spreads quickly now, but not in some areas. We feared this might happen and Martin and Neal have no doubt been trying to think of other ways to counter the viral attack, should it come before all areas are immunized. Those two always did like a challenge. Instead of fretting about this, why don't we get Neal up here, sit down as a group and talk this through, with all the facts at our disposal?"

- - -

To an outsider, the movements of one Mark Jones from England might have seemed irregular. He would appear one day at a car rental agency or airport in or around DC and buy a ticket somewhere or rent a car for a few days. He would then be prominent on the grid for a couple of days, travelling wherever he needed, paying for hotel rooms, food, and fuel before returning to DC and vanishing again for some indeterminate amount of time.

If someone had been watching him, or if he had been flagged for some reason, then they may have thought this strange. But his behavior was far from being actively suspicious. No, Mark Jones had never done anything important enough to call particular attention to himself.

Well, nothing except dying two years beforehand in a car crash on the M5 near Hammersmith.

Shortly before his untimely demise, though, Mark Jones had applied for and been granted a green card to come and live in the US. The widely diverse national record systems around the world being as, well, widely diverse as they were, news of Mark Jones's demise never found its way to the US, and thus his visa remained valid. The passport that bore Mark Jones's name was also good, as long as its owner never tried to use it in Europe where records, by reason of proximity, were more up to date.

Combine the fact of Mark's untimely demise with the fact that there are more than sixty thousand Mark Jones of varying sizes and shapes wondering the globe, and you had yourself an identity that would happily get you around any American airport, car rental agency, or credit card application without incident. At this particular moment, the man pretending to be the deceased Mark Jones was Neal Danielson, and he had used Mr. Jones's credit card to buy a ticket on a train from DC to Boston.

After arriving in Boston, he had taken a brief walk to a nearby mall, using some of the city's numerous overpasses and underground walkways to get there without spending too much time under an open sky. Once he had reached the car park of the mall, he had spotted the black sedan idling in a prearranged spot. As he approached the car, flashed its hazards once, and Neal slipped into the backseat.

"Martin!" Neal said, in surprise at seeing the diminutive rocket scientist in the driver's seat.

"Good evening, Neal, I'll be your chauffeur today. Where to, mi'lord?" said Martin in a dubious English accent and they both laughed, Neal clambering up and into the front passenger seat as they pulled out of the car park so they could catch up.

- - -

Half an hour later, in another covered parking lot at a Marriott Courtyard near Hanscom Base, the two scientists parked their car and took the elevator to the hotel's third floor. Martin led Neal down the corridor to a hotel room. The door was opened by a smiling Ayala Zubaideh, who ushered them in quickly. Colonel Barrett Milton welcomed them once inside with a fatherly smile, and after Neal had greeted the two proverbial parents of the group he turned finally to the recently promoted Major Jack Toranssen leaning against the wall by the drawn curtains. Neal had saved a handshake for Jack, congratulating him on his promotion, and following it with an even more emphatic word of thanks for his work in Hawaii aboard the *Dauntless*. Jack blushed slightly and swept the compliment aside. He had no time for congratulations, especially when it had been John Hunt who had born the lion's share of the task.

The curtains were closed and there were various pieces of equipment in the small hotel room. A projector threw a dim image from a laptop onto the wall, a flip chart dominated one corner, and various binders and folders covered the bed and filled two large boxes on the floor.

They set to immediately, Neal taking the floor so he could show some of the modeling he had been working on. He had used his position to discreetly glean several reports from the CDC and from various health organizations in allied nations around the world.

"OK," said Neal plugging a flash drive into the laptop Martin had provided for the meeting, "I have been extrapolating the numbers of reported infections against population demographics and typical spread patterns and I have to tell you that, for the most part, I have good news."

He smiled at the group, but it was a weak smile, because he knew the disconcerting end that was going to follow this pleasant seeming start. "OK, so, on the upside, I can tell you that based on the models I have put together, the antigen is spreading with surprising efficiency. In Western Europe, for example, I predict we are only a few weeks away from an effective 100% immunization. The same is true in North America, Japan and most of urbanized Indochina. I also register strong progress in Southern and Eastern Africa, South America and Australasia."

The group nodded, but Ayala was not encouraged by Neal's comments. He paused, done with the good news, and she spoke almost immediately, "And what of Northern Africa, the Middle East, the Urals, the Tibetan plateau?" He looked at her and she read his reply from his eyes.

She saw that things were not going as planned in all areas, as she had feared. Her shoulders sank and she spoke quietly, with an almost defeated tone, "But I spent weeks trekking through those godforsaken places. A Jew. And a female one at that." She shivered slightly at the memory. It had been an unpleasant and dangerous time, even for someone with her background and abilities.

Gathering herself, she looked back up at Neal and said, "Tell us, Neal. What are we facing?" She was desolate. She had risked her life, and done so willingly, but to find out it had been for nothing was ... demoralizing.

"Listen," Neal spoke in placating tones, "it is not that bad, for the most part. In Northern and Western Africa the spread is strong in urban areas, but in Sahara and the central plains it has been slow, most likely because of the limited travel and communication in those regions. It is worst in the sparsely populated regions of the Middle East, as it seems to be more pronounced there, despite the much larger populations involved. I think that the same causes are true there as in Northern Africa but I suspect they are being compounded by the ongoing conflicts in Afghanistan, Pakistan, and Kashmir. I suspect that the limits these are placing on the natural movements of the local peoples are further limiting our antigen's spread."

"How much longer do we need?" said Ayala, "How much longer till we have some effective level of coverage?"

Neal shrugged, "It's difficult to say accurately, but I fear that in Kashmir, Pakistan, Afghanistan, and Iran, the spread is disturbingly slow. It will take several months, maybe more, before the majority of people in that region are reached by the antigen."

He met Ayala's gaze frankly, not sugarcoating his news, but she knew that it was not just a matter of patience.

"So we can just wait?" said Jack, shrugging, but Neal shook his head slowly and Ayala lowered hers, disappointment mixing with frustration.

"Unfortunately, no." said Neal, slowly, "The cases of recovery from serious infections are increasing, and as John's last letter pointed out, the satellites are taking notice. Shahim and John may have been able to avert the AI's attention for now, but it is only a question of time before the entire process becomes too widespread to ignore. Within the next few weeks new incidences of the flu and common cold will pretty much stop in Europe and North America ... completely. Every hepatitis, tuberculosis, measles, and mumps patient will see a complete and total end to their symptoms.

"In places like Kenya, South Africa, Malaysia, all across the tropics, malaria and HIV will simply cease to be. Current estimates have HIV rates as high as 33% in some African nations. Millions of people will be better over night, their white blood cell counts returning to normal, which with the antigen backing them up will make their immune system better than it was even before they contracted the virus in the first place. With events that unprecedented, the world is going to notice, and so are the satellites. It is only a question of time before they go looking for the source of the change.

"We have to face the fact that at some point in the next few weeks this whole situation is going to go critical. The remaining Agents are going to find out what we are doing and ... well ... we have to assume that they are going to launch their virus ... at the very least. They may not be able to kill us all, but once they know that we are becoming immune, we have to assume that the AIs will react by either attacking immediately, hoping the immunity is not too widespread, or attempting to circumvent our antigen and build a new virus. John has said that if they get hold of a sample of the antigen they could, hypothetically, develop a pathogen that can withstand the antigen's defenses. And if we delay our attack on the satellites long enough for that to happen ... we will be done. End of game."

They sat silent. Ayala and Jack Toranssen instinctively looked at the colonel, but he was as stunned as they were.

After a moment it was Martin, somewhat hesitantly, who offered up a thought, "So what you are saying is: we have up until the moment that the AIs figure out what is happening.

Once that happens we have to launch our attack, whether the antigen is fully dispersed or not, we have to launch. If they can potentially counter the antigen we cannot give them the opportunity to do so. We will have to save whoever is already immunized."

At Neal's nod, Martin then asked, "I am assuming we cannot further speed the spread of the cure?"

"That is statistically impossible." said Ayala, shaking her head, "I personally injected over three hundred people with the vaccine. That was an average of ten 'covert' injections a day. I also enlisted several friends and ex-colleagues to distribute a further 250 of the doses, including the colonel."

"But it has been months since that effort. It is out there. Each week it is spreading to millions of people. If we have less than a month left to the reach 100% dispersion in Europe, that means that ten percent of the population is already immunized. That's one hundred million people in Europe alone. To noticeably speed the process up now we would need to manually immunize millions ... and there is simply no way to do that, not without alerting the Agents to their actions. It is simply impossible."

There had always been a diminishing marginal return from further injections, which they had matched against a serious and steadily increasing risk of discovery every time one of the team or its proxies stabbed another stranger with the drug.

A sad resignation settled over the room. People who had worked round the clock for months under the constant threat of discovery were now somewhat inured to it all, and faced with facts like these they knew they had to simply accept the potential for mass casualties, just as they had accepted the potential for their own. And so no one expected the next question.

"Umm, there is another thought," said Martin Sobleski, "but first I have to ask: when we launch against the satellites, can I assume the gloves are off?" The group stared at him. His glance moved between Neal and the colonel and they both shrugged and nodded.

"What do you have in mind?" said Jack, voicing the room's curiosity.

"Well, I was just thinking that maybe instead of looking at ways to speed the spread of the cure, maybe instead we could look at ways to slow the spread of the disease."

Slow the spread? How do you slow down a doomsday virus released from space in a thousand capsules, each one of which is programmed to detonate in the stratosphere? But Martin didn't seem to notice the group's lack of enthusiasm and carried on, "Tell me, how many of you are familiar with thermobaric grenades?"

Jesus, thought Jack. Firebombs? A smile spread across his lips. This was going to be interesting.

- - -

It was their most ambitious plan yet. Martin would leave the remainder of the nose cone shielding deployment to Jack, Barrett, and the team that Admiral Hamilton had assigned to the project. This would allow him to redirect his considerable expertise to a new avenue of research. Ayala would go with him to North Dakota and once they were there they would use the resonance chamber to build a new type of warhead.

The AGM-158A was an already existing air-launched cruise missile that could be deployed from a B-2 bomber, the bomber type that Jack Toranssen had been a pilot of up until Barrett had recruited him to the team.

The plan was to build an entirely new set of warheads for these stealthy missiles. Ayala would help with the procurement of materials, Martin would work with Madeline to meld these materials in the resonance chamber in North Dakota, and once these new and highly explosive warheads were ready, Martin and Ayala would deliver them down to Whiteman Air Force Base, where the main US B-2 bomber wing was stationed. After that it would be up to Jack, the colonel, and their ally Admiral Hamilton to pull the necessary strings to discreetly get the upgraded warheads onto the base.

Even after that set of fairly considerable hurdles, the final step would be by far the most dangerous. John had shared with the team the plan for how the satellites would drop the virus. They could see that, of all the areas that still remained vulnerable, the largest unprotected populace was also directly within the arc of the satellites' pod drops.

And so, once the warheads were fitted onto a series of the cruise missiles, and the missiles were loaded into one of the B-2 bombers, Major Jack Toranssen would get behind the wheel again. They were going to attempt to shoot down the virus pods as they entered the atmosphere. Not all of them, that would be impossible. But those pods that were dropped over the area still left untouched by the antigen's spread. They would strive to save some of the millions of innocent people that lived in those areas: the rural peoples of the Hindu Kush, the Afghan mountains, and the plains of western Iran.

They would focus there because they fell directly within the drop paths of the viral pods. They would use the stealth of the B-2 to carry him deep into enemy airspace. Once there, they would start the biggest fireworks display in the history of humanity, and once they started firing, they had no doubt that those same people they were trying to save would no doubt do all they could to stop them.

Chapter 48: Catalyst

"Thanks for that update, Mike, looks like more rain, huh?" the anchorwoman beamed a paper-white smile, shrugging as she laughed with practiced cheerfulness. "Now for our next story we're going to head over to Jacksonville General where Robin Jacobson has a report about a medical miracle."

The view switched to her co-anchor whose face became comically quizzical, "A miracle, Bethany?"

The view switched again to show both anchors for a moment and they looked at each other as Bethany replied, "Well, Simon, reports are coming in from around the country about what *some* are calling the *miraculous* recovery of some previously seriously ill patients." They both smiled and tilted their heads with the sheer joy of it all and Simon took his cue, "Wow, sounds like a miracle to me. Why don't we go over to Robin at Jacksonville General and find out what it's all about? Robin?" They both smiled, their sparkling eyes wide with faux curiosity as the scene shifted.

A smiling woman stands in a hospital room holding a large WPPI News microphone up to her beautiful face.

"Thanks, Simon and Bethany. Yes, that's right, folks, I'm here at Jacksonville General with Armondo Zorilla, a patient who, until recently, was in near critical condition with effects of advanced Acquired Immune Deficiency Syndrome." The reporter frowned a moment, because that is what reporters have to do when they mention AIDS, and then turned to the patient, who was standing in his regular clothes to her right.

"Mr. Zorilla," she said to him, still very serious, "I understand you were diagnosed HIV positive some years ago?"

She thrust the microphone under his chin and he stammered a moment, unsure whether to look at the camera, or her, or the floor. Choosing the floor, he said, "Yes, that's right, Robin, I was diagnosed back in 2006 with HIV, but apparently I had already had it for a while and it progressed to full-blown AIDS last year."

Robin did not like her interviewee's sullen tone, or his use of the acronym AIDS, which research showed was not good for ratings. For that matter, the fact that the man had used the term 'full-blown' was also far from what they had discussed before the interview. She decided to redirect the conversation.

Reclaiming the microphone when Armondo paused to breathe, she turned to the camera again, and said, "But things have taken a turn recently, isn't that right, Mr. Zorilla? Can you tell us a bit about that?"

She turned back to the patient and he stammered again, "Err, yes," he managed to aim a small smile at the camera, then looked down again as he went on. "There's been some, well, some good news over the last three weeks." He smiled again and then stared at the camera in silence, apparently having to choose between speaking and smiling.

Robin's smile remained plastered on her face but inside she growled quietly in frustration and gave up on the patient, turning back to the camera. Her cameraman took her cue and focused in on her again, "Well, isn't that just great?" she said, "And for more information on that, I have Armondo's doctor here, Dr. Lawrence." She turned to her other side and the camera zoomed out again, this time to include a young, tired-looking doctor.

"Doctor," said the reporter, "this all sounds very interesting, maybe you can tell us a bit about the case?"

The doctor nodded, looking at the camera. He looked a little disconcerted, but it was really the case, not the camera, that was baffling him. He shrugged for a moment and then said, "Well Robin, it's a heck of a thing. The patient was in an advanced stage of Acquired Immune Deficiency Syndrome associated with infection with the Human Immunodeficiency Virus. As I'm sure you know, HIV is, in and of itself, not fatal, but its effects on the immune system make the sufferer much more susceptible to other infections that our bodies' white blood cells would normally be able to handle."

The reporter nodded and then, feeling the need to say something, she put in, "And in this case, Doctor, what has happened that is so unusual?"

"Well," continued the young doctor, "actually, we really don't know." He shrugged again, "Since the patient's last check up a month ago, there has been a dramatic reduction in viral and other foreign bodies found in his blood, and this has been matched by a notable increase in his white blood cell count, though not by nearly enough to account for the drop in foreign bodies."

Robin knew the network would expect her to stick in her line now for the masses and prompted, "A miracle, Doctor?" glancing suggestively at the screen and smiling.

"Well, if you want to think of it as a miracle, then I suppose you can do that," said Dr. Lawrence, slightly impatiently, "though I can tell you that we have also seen a similarly anomalous set of symptoms in two other patients in the last month."

Robin froze. Wait, what did he just say? More cases? More cases meant a bigger story and her long-subjugated journalistic instincts kicked in. She responded in a serious tone, "So there have been other cases of this, Doctor? Could this be an epidemic? Should folks at home be worried?"

Dr. Lawrence stared at her a moment, mildly perturbed by the chopped logic that Robin had applied to his statement, then replied, "No, Robin, the public should not be worried that people with potentially fatal diseases are showing signs of remission. That is, I think, a good thing. And nor should we start using words like epidemic. A few folks have had some extremely good luck, and that is great. We'll continue to monitor them and hopefully they can have some measure of reprieve from their difficult prognoses."

Robin picked up his mood and matched his air of respect and sobriety, thanking the doctor seriously, but then turned back to the camera with a big smile and said, "Well, folks, there you have it. Some good news for some of the suffering people here at Jacksonville General.

A Miracle on Richard Street? I'll leave it up to you to decide. This is Robin Jacobson reporting live for WPPI News, back to you in the studio."

Agent Lana Wilson turned off the television and stood up. It was one thing to have random reports filling up CDC filing cabinets, but now this thing was in her backyard. The last thing she wanted was humans living longer. There were far too many of them as it was.

Jacksonville was twenty-five minutes from the naval base she was stationed at. It had been a few weeks since the AI had introduced the topic at the meeting, and she was hearing more of these reports every day. As usual, the local news station was the last to get the story, having been relegated to more of a tepid regurgitation of local weather and sports than an investigative news source, but now it was so widespread that even this nescient outlet had been forced to take notice. This was no longer a phenomenon, it was indeed an epidemic, and it was time that Lana found out what it was that was spreading longevity amongst the very people whose lives she was working so hard to shorten.

- - -

<Welcome>

<This emergency meeting of the Council has been called due to information that has just been brought to our attention by Agent Lana Wilson. I am uploading a report to you now. Agent Wilson, please proceed.>

It had been nearly a month since John and Shahim had managed to stave off a detailed investigation into the rapidly spreading antigen's effects. They had done their best, and in truth the time they had bought had translated into the effective completion of the antigen's spread in most urbanized nations. The same was true in the rural areas that were linked to those urban centers by the trains and roads that gave the cities their life. But just as the team had predicted at their meeting in Boston, this same success was inevitably going to be their downfall. And sure enough, events in Europe and America were now beyond the team's ability to dissemble. With local news stations reporting 'miracles' and anomalies in previously critical AIDS, Diphtheria, Lyme Disease, and Hepatitis patients, and the number of new cases of other infectious diseases dropping off dramatically, Shahim and John had known that the time was coming when they would no longer be able to delay the inevitable. As Lana's report uploaded into the Council's minds, John and Shahim both braced themselves.

Lana Wilson's avatar spoke, "After the observations of the AI a few weeks ago I have continued to hear of these anomalous cases. This culminated in a report I saw on television yesterday from a hospital near my location. After hearing the report I travelled to the hospital and managed to procure a blood sample from one of these 'miraculous' cases. Though I was unable to conduct a chemical analysis without proper equipment, I was able to scrutinize the blood visually at high resolution. I have since uploaded my imagery of it to the AI for confirmation of my analysis. The images are in the reports that have been provided to the Council."

Here it comes, thought John. Shit. His avatar remained outwardly calm but the Agent himself subtly cued up a response routine he had laid in for this moment. He had several protocols that he had planned out with Neal and the rest of the team. He knew that the team wasn't completely ready yet. The antigen had spread far faster in heavily populated nations than others, and in certain pockets tens of millions were still defenseless. Every day they waited more people would be safe from the attack and maybe he and Shahim could delay things just a few days longer.

But as Lana's report went on, John's heart started to sink, "The results were disturbing. The man's blood contained significant numbers of some kind of cellular defense mechanism. This cellular construct appears to have capabilities similar to those of the Bio-Immuno-Defensive-Constructs that we have long relied on back on Mobilius.

"Now it was our understanding that this kind of technology was far out of the grasp of the humans, in fact, our own viral attack weapon that we hold in reserve here relies on just that fact. We have assumed to date that they were unable to even build this kind of defensive cell, let alone disseminate it on this scale. If the humans now have such a technology, then we urgently need to review our own progress to see what options we have. In fact, I believe we may need to take drastic action, and very soon."

The room was silent for a moment, then Agent Mikhail Kovalenko from Russia spoke up, "Wait. I am confused. How did this construct come to be in the human's blood? Surely if the humans had developed such a breakthrough there would have been a huge public announcement. Unless …"

His thought was finished by Jean-Paul Merard, "Unless they have been doing it in secret, Mikhail?"

The room was silent a moment, then several people turned to Agent Wilson. She responded as if accused, "I have no idea how the constructs came to be. I only discovered their existence."

<We have no evidence at this time that would suggest that the humans have the necessary technology to build such a complex device. This suggests two things. Firstly it could imply that the humans have a degree of technological prowess that they have managed to keep hidden from us. Secondly it suggests that they are acting in response to a perceived threat by keeping the development and release of the cellular defenses secret. It is the opinion of the AIs that this could imply that the humans are aware of our presence and our plans against them.>

The Council was in an uproar. Several of the Agents spoke at once but John and Shahim stayed silent. This meeting of the Council was proving to be everything they had feared it might be. John looked around the room and realized that any further delays would probably be impossible. His avatar remained outwardly calm as he tried to think of ways to keep the group away from any further extrapolations and eventually he said in a loud but placating tone, "Fellow Agents, let's not get ahead of ourselves. There are many reasons that the human's may have developed these constructs, and even more reasons that they may have kept the work secret. We all know the properties of the construct, but let us not forget that our own history shows that such things are often born of military research. Scientific research into biological weapons is as taboo on Earth as it is on Mobilius, if this was originally planned as some antidote to a proposed weapon then it would have been kept under the strictest confidence, even from the population of the nation that was working on it."

John took a proverbial breath and looked around the room. He needed an ally, and Shahim saw it too and stepped up.

"Agent Hunt is right." said Shahim, "Clearly this is a very disturbing turn of events, and we should all thank Agent Wilson for discovering it. But before we jump to wild conclusions based on this purely circumstantial evidence, we need to know more about what the humans are up to. Agent Wilson has the right idea, we need to gather more information on the matter and gain a deeper understanding of how widespread this condition is. I suggest that each Agent acquire a sampling of various humans' blood, let us say one hundred samples, over the next week, and then we can reconvene and assess how widespread this phenomenon really is."

Some in the room were nodding, but many were clearly not going to be mollified by this plan. Preeti Parikh offered up a point, "I feel I should point out that reports of Malaria and digestive illnesses have dropped off significantly in India, it is all over the news here. The government is calling for an inquiry. It seems unlikely that the two incidents are unlinked, and if they are born of the same cellular defense, then that would indicate that this would appear to be very widespread indeed."

John kept up the pressure, trying to keep the room with them, "Indeed, this is clearly an epidemic of some sort. We must get more information and we must do it now. I second Shahim's motion to have each Agent gather a hundred blood samples and provide them for analysis. We do not have much time. We should do this in no more than a week and reconvene then to decide if we need to take forceful action."

The AI responded to the seconded motion by automatically initiating a vote, but Lana sat firm, silent and unresponsive. The AI ignored her silence, the votes of the other Agents enough to pass the motion.

<Motion passed. All Agents are ordered to obtain a hundred blood samples from their surrounding areas and submit detailed imagery within the next seven days. We suggest that a random sampling method be used when selecting donors, and that no samples be taken from humans that Agents have daily interaction with to avoid unnecessary risk to the mission.>

Well, that should keep them busy for a while, thought John. But Agent Lana Wilson was still silent and John's avatar glanced nervously at Shahim for a second. He was about to speak again when Agent Lana spoke, "While that is a … pleasantly conservative plan, I would like to suggest an alternative."

She looked around the room and then said, "Arbiter, what options do we have to counter this cellular defense if it is as widespread as it would appear?"

<In order to counter the defensive cellular construct you have discovered, Agent Lana Wilson, we would need to perform a detailed chemical analysis on the cell's structure and makeup. If the sample were on board one of our satellites we could accomplish this very easily, but as we have no practical method of getting a sample to us, we would need to take operational control of one of you on the surface and conduct the analysis remotely.>

Both John and Shahim immediately saw an opportunity to interrupt the operation and went to volunteer to be that proxy for the AI, but the arbiter was not looking for volunteers. It had an Agent in mind.

<As Agent Lana Wilson already has a sample of the cells in her possession, I can execute the tests as soon as she can get to an appropriate facility.>

Lana's avatar looked disgruntled by the fact that she was to be a puppet of the AI, but she could hardly refuse. It had been her line of thought, after all. The AI's disembodied voice continued with the counter proposal Lana had initiated.

<We have located a facility one hundred sixty-seven miles north of Agent Lana Wilson's current location. It is a private medical research facility and relatively primitive, but according to its description in the company's annual report it has all the tools we would need. We will need approximately three hours to conduct our tests once the sample is delivered to the facility. If this plan were to be approved by the Council, when would Agent Lana Wilson be ready to leave her current location?>

Princess Lamati thought a moment and then said, "I am officially on duty at the base until tonight at 6pm, I can leave any time after that."

<In that event, we propose the motion that Agent Lana Wilson bring the blood sample to the facility we have identified. We will facilitate entry past the minimal security and then we will be able to use the body of Agent Lana Wilson as a proxy to conduct the necessary tests.>

That's it, then, thought John, his personality reeling at how suddenly it had all come to a head. This was it. John knew perfectly well that the design he had supplied to Madeline and Ayala for the antigen was not inherently different from the one that coursed through the veins of every Mobiliei, just modified for the humans' different bio-chemical makeup. Once it was properly analyzed by the AI it would not take long for the powerful machine mind to devise a way to circumvent it. After all, before it had even been released on back on Mobilius, every nation had already had their war departments working on ways to outwit it.

The room voted on the AI's motion. John and Shahim waited till the last moment, but the other six all voted for Lana to help the AI analyze the antigen, as the two double agents would have in their place. It would be pointless for them to risk their cover by being the only two Agents on the other side of a losing vote; and so, begrudgingly, but with well-feigned enthusiasm, they acquiesced.

"Arbiter," said John after voting, still keeping his concern hidden behind his virtual face, "I am worried about how long it will take to develop a counter to this antigen once you have analyzed it. What would the turnaround time be for production of a response to the humans' immuno device?"

<We estimate that once a chemical analysis has been completed it will take at least a further twenty-four hours to design and synthesize a counter-measure for deployment, though it may be longer based on how complex the device is. We will then need a further seventy-two hours after that in order to produce the necessary quantities and prepare our deployment pods to use the new construct. Therefore we estimate approximately four days from the end of our analysis before we are ready to deploy a virus capable of having the same 100% kill rate that our previous viral attack mechanism had been designed for.>

Four days. John looked at Shahim. As there was really no way for the two conspirators to communicate with each in secret during these meetings, they had agreed on a simple method of signaling using their virtual body's movements. It was a limited form of communication, little more capable than the hand motions of a batting coach in baseball, but they had only planned to use it to make some basic signals to each other while in Council meetings.

While looking at Shahim, John tilted his avatar's head slightly to the left, then nodded, blinking his eyes once. Shahim kept John's stare. This was it, then. Among all the codes they had developed, this was by far the most important one. Shahim acknowledged with the same movement, and they both blinked once more.

They had no more time. Within four days the satellites would have a new bio weapon capable of wiping out humanity. Worse, now that they were alerted to the humans' ability to defend themselves, the AIs would not wait to use the new virus. The team would not have another chance to build and spread a new supercell in response.

For better or worse, this was it.

Chapter 49: A Dark Night

Silence. The only noise is the gentle mountain breeze wafting through the desert night.

Nothing disturbs the darkness deep in the mountains of northern Afghanistan.

A cold mountain wind sluices up and through a high valley deep in the Hindu Kush range that bridges northern Afghanistan and Pakistan. The valley is one of thousands that dissect the range, different from the rest of them only because of the men who lie sleeping in its myriad of hidden caves. Amongst these sleeping warriors are two members of the senior leadership of Al Qaeda. In order to avoid detection, the leaders of the insurgent forces move location every two nights, and rarely stay together. But tonight had been one of those rare occasions when two of them had met.

Around the outside of the camp, guards lie concealed in strategic spots, on the lookout for approaching planes or any other light at all in the settled night. This night was particularly dark. The moon had not risen yet, and nor would it for another three hours.

Among the many half-awake men dotted around the outside of the camp was Ushant Prabalah. He was twenty-two and he had lost his father, mother, and brother in a firefight between freedom fighters and the invading infidels in his village four years beforehand. He was smarter than most, he had learned to read and write and had been well on his way to a university education, but that had been before the fateful night his world had died. He did not know that boy anymore, that boy was as dead as his parents. As dead as the countless people Ushant had killed and seen killed since that tragic juncture.

Now he lay still. Unlike many of his fellow guards, Ushant's eyes were vigilant. Many considered the nighttime lookout duty to be ignominious, but tonight two great generals were staying at their camp. A breeze washed over Ushant and he shivered. He could not see a thing. It was utterly dark. Only the stars provided any light. The land was black, the horizon barely discernable against the sky.

Silence.

Shahim could barely hear his own approach as he stepped lightly up to where Ushant lay. The boy was awake and watchful. He was staring out across the desert, but he was looking for sources of light: men clambering over the rocky terrain with torches, or planes or helicopters. But Shahim carried no light, and he had run the final two miles to the camp in perfect silence. Despite the darkness that shrouded him, Shahim's sensitive eyes could see everything. Shahim approached the boy from the side and stood over him. He could hear the young guard's breath. His heart beat. This boy was awake and keen. It was cold yet the boy was hardly moving. He was a believer, without the sullen complacency of the older men. This warrior was good at what he did and Shahim was going to need plenty of fighters like him for the coming task.

Unbeknownst to Ushant Prabalah, death was standing over him, looking down on him and judging him. But instead of ending the boy, the harbinger simply turned and walked silently away. Walking straight toward the hidden caves in the valley below even as Ushant so valiantly guarded them.

Shahim's feet fell on the rocky surface with a precision not even the most highly trained human soldier could replicate. He had removed the sandals that the mountain warriors often wore, allowing his bare feet to adhere softly to the rocky surface, never slipping, never displacing the slightest pebble. Like a cat he, moved down into the sleeping valley.

His heat sensitive eyes told him that there were several groups of men in various tunnels and caves around the valley. But two groups stood out. In these two caves, he could see individuals sleeping apart from the rest of their groups, in both cases at the back of the cave, behind a wall of other warriors.

Ah, the two great generals. Such brave warriors … cowering behind their minions.

Shahim stepped slowly toward the first cave. The fully repaired and operational weapons system behind his left eye was already unsheathed and ready as he gently stepped into the cave, two long knives also brandished in his hands. Two guards sat just inside the door, barely awake as they peered into the darkness and tried to make out the black shape wafting in through the small entrance. But it made no sound, and carried no light, so they dismissed it as a trick of the night. Shahim neatly and silently decapitated the two men in unison, catching their severed heads before they touched the floor and resting them on each man's lap.

Less than a minute later, Shahim was emerging from the cave once more. The first general was dead. After killing the guards, he had turned to the rest of the men sleeping peacefully on the ground. He had stepped over them carefully, walking to the back of the cave to lean in close to the man who slept alone behind them. The general had been wrapped in more blankets than all the other men combined, but his warm breath had been visible from the gap in his thick insulation. Shahim had focused his deadly stare on the man's closed eyes and then fired a tight beamed sonic punch straight through the soft ocular tissue, crushing the eye easily and driving inward through the pulp to pulverize the grey tissue behind. The general's head barely moved against his pillow as his brain was pulped, wiping his mind out in a silent second.

On his way out of the cave, Shahim had carefully extricated the rifles from each of the two dead guards along with several grenades from each of their belts and then he had stepped back out into the night.

His black shape now moved stealthily up and around the other general's cave to a spot on the shelf of rock just above its entrance. Once there, he quietly unpinned one of the grenades he had pilfered from the dead guards, angled his arm back behind him and pitched it with a powerful throw in a high arc to land well outside the camp's perimeter. A moment later the explosion shook the night, awakening a hornet's nest.

Just hoving into view in the sky above, one of the satellites noticed the disturbance. The AI still believed Shahim to be sleeping peacefully in his cave many miles away over the border in Pakistan. The sudden explosion at the encampment brought the AI's full attention and Shahim registered as it informed him of the situation, unaware of its complicity in it. It began scanning the area closely, broadcasting a live signal of the unfolding events into his head. It also told him it did not know the source of the commotion. Good, thought Shahim, let us hope it stays that way.

On the ground, the camp sprang to life, warriors running from their caves, and lookouts searching the night sky for the attackers they assumed were upon them. Shahim silently unpinned another grenade as the men started to run about, hoarse whispers racing throughout the night. A moment later the night was rocked once more by a fresh explosion twenty degrees around the perimeter from the first. The night-sensitive eyes of the fighters that happened to be looking in that direction were stunned, leaving them blinded and disoriented as an even more profound darkness settled around them now. Several started firing, confusion and fear fueling their madness. Finally, Shahim sent a third grenade into the top half of the valley, near the entrance to the first general's cave, careful so as to avoid having it land too close to the men running out from it.

Amidst the shouts, explosions, and random gunfire, he now sensed that there were only three people still remaining inside the cave under his feet. He had no doubt that the second general was among them, probably cowering with some of his personal guard. He took his fourth and final grenade and uncorked it, bending and tossing it into the chamber.

He was already stepping away when the explosion, contained and amplified by the cave's rock walls, obliterated the three men inside. The blind fear and anger of the fighters reached critical mass. Different groups of the same army were shooting at each other in the confusion and Shahim compounded this by shouting into the madness, "The generals are dead. Run! Run for your lives! The Pakistanis have killed our beloved generals!"

After a few more well-placed shouts spelling out the propaganda he wished to spread, Shahim began to walk about among the flood of men now fleeing the hail of bullets coursing through the base. Several men came clambering past him through the blackness, stumbling on rocks as they fled. They were completely unaware of Shahim's presence in the night as they streamed away in fear. He looked at them running out of the night, analyzing their faces until he saw one that he recognized from his time in Pakistan. He grabbed the man and threw him to the floor, pinning the man down and covering his mouth to silence him.

Shahim whispered into the frantic man's ear, "Silence, soldier, I am one of you. They are near." The man under Shahim froze. "I heard some of them shouting to each other and I think they are Pakistani soldiers. Here, I killed one of them and managed to take his jacket. We must take it. We must take it back to the fighters in the Hindu Kush and tell them what has happened here." Shahim grabbed the man and lifted him bodily to his feet, still holding him tight to stop him from running off or making a noise. But the man was paralyzed with fear and was not going to argue with this single voice of reason in the enraged night.

Shahim led him away, "Come, I will lead you to one of our jeeps. You will escape this attack and live to fight another day."

Walking through the crags in the valley, Shahim led the man, navigating the darkness with ease. He guided the soldier to where two jeeps lay well covered with camouflage in the next valley, helping the man push one of the off-road vehicles onto the dirt track that led to the encampment. He signaled for the man to get in as the car started rolling down the track and leapt into the driver's seat himself. He let the car roll at first, not starting the engine but relying on the steep slope of the road to get them started. The last thing he wanted was to draw fire from the melee tearing through the encampment and get his patsy killed.

"What are you doing?" whispered the other man, staring into the darkness ahead of them, "How can you see the road?"

But Shahim ignored him and went on. Shahim could see that the road leveled out ahead so he put the car into second gear and popped the clutch, allowing the car's own momentum to jumpstart the engine. As soon as the pistons were firing, Shahim gunned the throttle and the car surged forward. He drove off at inhuman speed through the mountains, his charge holding on for dear life.

Several hours later the now bright moon was starting to give way to the first blues of dawn. They had made good headway and had already crossed the unmarked border back into Pakistan. Reports from the AI told Shahim that throughout the mountain range insurgent forces were awakening to radio reports from the destroyed encampment and stragglers from the mad firefight were stumbling out across the bleak mountain range. Shahim assumed that many of the surviving fighters there now knew that most of their casualties had been caused by 'friendly' fire, but he was happy to hear that this was not what was being disseminated.

There was news of an attack, and there was news of the deaths of the two generals who had been encamped with the decimated force, but few would be willing to admit that there had been no sign of an actual attacking force. Few would be willing to admit they had been part of some misconceived gunfight that had killed two prominent generals. Instead, stories of the nonexistent Pakistani force became distorted and overwhelming, as Shahim had hoped they would.

The reports the AI was relaying to Shahim even included details of the flight of two men in a jeep, the AI unaware that Shahim was one of them. From these images, Shahim confirmed that he was, as he had thought, approaching the camp that he called home, the camp the AI believed he was still in. Without warning, Shahim pulled the car to a halt.

The other man was delirious after the brutal punishment of the drive, but he came to as the car stopped and turned to Shahim. Shahim spoke as he climbed from the car, "You must go on from here on your own, my friend. My home is near here, but you must take news of this attack back to the main camps deeper in the Kush. For my part, I am going to rejoin the Great Shahim Al Khazar who camps near here. He will know what to do about this attack. When you get back, listen for word of his response and make sure your own brethren join the cause."

The other man stared at Shahim and nodded. This man by his side knew the Great Shahim Al Khazar! No wonder he had known what to do when the attack came.

Bolstered by the mention of the now legendary Shahim, the weary soldier smiled and climbed over into the driver's seat, saying, "Praise God, my brother. I will listen for news from Shahim Al Khazar. Thank you for saving me, you are indeed a messenger from almighty God. I will make sure everyone knows who perpetrated this great injustice this night." said the grateful soldier, still clutching the Pakistani army jacket Shahim had given him early in the night.

Shahim looked seriously at the man, bowed slightly, and then turned and ran off into the last remnants of the night. He did not look back at the man, the image from the AI told him that the soldier was getting ready to drive off as Shahim climbed up and over the high ridge that lay between him and his own encampment. He considered the seed he had planted.

Naturally he would get his own group to mobilize in response to the attack, but this additional source of verification that it was the Pakistanis that had perpetrated the attack would help fuel the fire he hoped to start.

He did not go to his own cave. He needed to bamboozle the satellite still watching his movements. He ran into a larger cave and into the waking group there as they heard about the attack over their radio. He called on them to gather in the valley below, even as he exchanged his shawl with one of them. None of them argued for a moment with the fearsome warrior, and he joined them as they then all flooded out of the cave to go and gather the rest of the camp's forces.

The satellite noted them all leave the cave from above, still unaware that Shahim was among them, and now loosing the trail of the man that had come to the camp as they all went this way and that. With the satellite now watching one of the wrong men, the real Shahim ducked into his own cave and changed once more before making his own way down into the valley to incite the gathering horde.

- - -

By the evening, Shahim had agitated and enraged a string of encampments, summoning them to his banner. The deaths of the generals had decapitated a huge part of the region's militia, and Shahim had stepped into the vacuum. And so, not eighteen hours after he had flicked the first proverbial domino, he came to be sitting in the back of one of fifteen trucks bearing an angry company of warriors down from the mountains.

The reports from the AI were now starting to show signs of concern. It could see the growing convoy descending on the Peshawar Army Base, and its requests that Shahim intercept the insurgents had gone unanswered.

Too late to turn back now, thought Shahim. The dominoes would fall as they may. They had so little time and the plans of John Hunt and the team of humans depended on him initiating the chain reaction here in Pakistan.

But he also needed to continue to dissemble until the last, for the AI and the rest of the Council must not know what he was doing until it was too late for them to stop him. He smiled at his fellow warriors in the back of the truck as it rumbled toward the unsuspecting Pakistani army base, and then stood and clambered toward the clattering old vehicle's back.

Lifting the tarpaulin flap that hung over the back of the truck, he leaned out and looked skyward. Then, using his left hand to shield his eye from drivers of the trucks behind, Shahim unsheathed his laser and locked on to the satellite ranging unseen, far, far above them. The tight beam connected with the orbiting platform and he opened a direct channel to the AI. Providing a carefully edited version of his activities over the last twenty-four hours, he informed the AI and thus the Council that he was travelling with the warriors to make sure that they did not go too far. He posited, quite truthfully, that it would be very damaging to his credibility within the insurgent force for him to suggest that they not retaliate against the Pakistani army, and by instead assuming a leadership role in said attack he would be in a position to stop the soldiers before they became too emboldened, while also reinforcing his own reputation.

This was, after all, a natural consequence of what the Council had planned for him, he assured the AI. He would allow the rebels to break into the army base, even helping them to penetrate the base's defenses, but he would stop them from getting hold of any of the serious weaponry. It would be just enough to give the insurgents the confidence that they would need to do it for real when it better suited the *Council's* purposes.

Message sent, he pulled the awning back down and walked back up to the front of the truck's flatbed.

The AI's continued tracking of the convoy told him that there were two checkpoints between them and their destination. Time to run interference for his small force, thought Shahim. He had gathered over 450 men, but there were over five thousand stationed at the base fifteen miles down the road. He could even the odds for them, but he could not afford to have his force waste its momentum on small firefights at pointless checkpoints.

"Tell the driver to pull over!" he bellowed over the noise of the grumbling diesel. The message was passed and the truck duly pulled to the side, its fourteen fellow convoy-mates forming up in a long idling line behind it amidst the dust and diesel fumes.

Shahim jumped down from his truck, noting who followed him from amongst the fighters in his lead vehicle. Good, these brave souls would be his vanguard. Turning, he saw two junior leaders running up from trucks back down the trail. In the confusion after the devastating attack in Afghanistan only thirty-six hours ago, he had made sure his was the strongest voice. He was their proxy leader now. And he was shepherding them toward the fight of their lives.

The first of his new generals approached, asking, "What is it, Al Khazar? Why have we stopped?"

Shahim looked at him and then placed his hand on the man's shoulder, a sign of great friendship, "There is a roadblock ahead, designed to give advanced warning to the base of any approaching force. I intend to take three men and destroy that roadblock. Hassim Bin Maktala, I name you general in my absence."

The man froze a moment, Shahim had never taken another man into his confidence in the storied year since he had first joined the army. Now he, Hassim Bin Maktala, would have his own destiny tied to this star's ascension. He bowed his head, but Shahim was not finished.

"Hassim, you will bring the rest of the force to the main gate and meet me there. They have their forces spread wide around the base's perimeter to ward off small attacks. Leaving their pathetic roadblocks to give them enough warning to gather their troops at any given point to resist a more concerted attack." Shahim smiled, "I will see to it that they do not get that warning."

Another leader, Dakar Wakin, came running up, but Shahim and Hassim stayed focused on each other as Shahim carried on, "Though we have only four hundred and fifty to their five thousand, we will crush the unsuspecting forty-five men that make up the standing guard at their main gate. By the time the rest of the base is alerted, we will have spread out into three groups.

"The first, led by me, will take a hundred men to the right and work our way around the perimeter, taking out the on-duty guard teams as they converge on the main gate. The second force, led by Dakar here," Shahim looked at the second man standing expectantly at their sides, "will break left with another hundred men and sweep along the perimeter in that direction, destroying the reinforcements coming from the north.

"With gunfire spreading around the outside of the base, the remaining bulk of the base's off duty forces will not be able to focus their response and so they will resort to their standard response pattern once the perimeter is breached, which is to retreat to the missile silos in the northern part of the base to defend the nuclear weapons that are stored there. This will allow you, Hassim," Shahim looked at his first general once more, "to take our remaining warriors into the southern part of the base, where the non-nuclear munitions are stored."

The men half smiled, half gaped at the large warrior in front of them, who went on, "Hassim, you will take your force there and secure the area. Even with the bulk of the remaining forces concentrated in the northern part of the base, you will still have a fight on your hands. I estimate that at least five hundred men will be tasked to defend the armory, which is why I will then bring my force up from the perimeter to flank them, helping us secure that area.

"Once we have the armory, we will … procure some of their hell-sent anti-personnel mortars that are stored there and set up a reinforced battery aimed at the main bulk of their troops surrounding the silos and bunkers in the north. That should awaken their complacent souls, eh?"

The two recently promoted young men nodded, smiling while the other men gathered around began nodding and started to get riled up. Shahim decided it was time to set them going. He was pretty sure that once they started launching mortars into the three thousand or so men dug-in in the northern part of the base, then they would soon find that the force up there had some pretty unpleasant surprises of their own. But at that point he would have accomplished everything he needed to with these unwitting assistants. After that it would be up to him and him alone.

Pitching his voice above their heads, he used his phenomenal volume to deliver a rousing speech to the amassed soldiers. He told them that they would all be famed for this day. That from this moment on they would all be remembered as the greatest of all Allah's faithful. He wound them up, giving them impetus to drive them into the heart of the base's defenses ahead of them. He had no doubt they would make a real dent in those forces. But he also knew that his message to the AI about the futility of the attack was, in essence, true. In the end, such a small, disorganized force would be crushed by the army that awaited them. But that did not factor in what a fully armed, fully weaponized, and singularly resolute Agent could do in the chaos that would ensue.

- - -

Across the mile-wide base, huge explosions blossomed like flowers, shedding fire and death like pollen. Night had fallen once more, but the evening was lit with detonations that rocked the soil beneath the fighters' feet. Hassim could feel his knees shaking. He could not believe the sheer force of their attack. The column of trucks had indeed driven through the checkpoint on the approach to the base without hindrance. There had been no sign of Shahim, but nor had there been any sign of resistance from the checkpoint's guards. Some kind of explosion seemed to have rocked the area.

The guards were spread far and wide from the small huts they had manned, which were, in turn, flattened. But though the guards' bodies were crushed almost beyond recognition, they were not burned. It was as if they had been blown outward by some mighty force. But Hassim was not about to ask questions; he had simply thanked God for the might of his leader and spurned the convoy onward. As Shahim had promised, the trucks had approached the front gate of the large army base unhindered.

As the evening fell, the sleepy guards had seen the column of trucks approaching. No one had mentioned this. Why hadn't they heard about this from the checkpoint? But as they went to report the approaching trucks, they had been even more surprised to see the lone man that suddenly stepped out from the sparse brush not twenty yards from the front gate. He carried no gun and made no noise. He seemed utterly harmless. As he walked up to them, they had shouted at him to stop, arranging themselves in a line in front of the main gate and leveling their rifles at him. Some had even had time to notice that something seemed to be wrong with the lone man's left eye, it was missing, replaced by some dark spiny object that they could not begin to describe.

Back in the cab of the first truck, Hassim had seen the blinding flash. But there had been no noise, no explosion. Just a momentary bright light, illuminating the front gate like the biggest camera flash he had ever seen. For a moment afterward he still had the image on his retina, and he was sure he could make out a single man silhouetted against it, standing in the road just in front of the gate.

For the twenty-five base guards that were actually facing the flash, it was impossibly bright, the white heat of the broad span laser flare emitted from Shahim's eye blinding them instantly and permanently. Shahim was not happy at having to do it. These men did not deserve such brutality, and they would be only the first of many casualties tonight. But even if they all died in the coming battle, it would be for a greater purpose. He was trying to save a planet. Even five thousand deaths would be acceptable compared to the billions that would die if he failed in his mission.

The blind men had screamed and stumbled, but by the time Hassim had arrived with the rest of the men, Shahim had already killed most of them. The force had then split into three parts as planned and the attack had begun in earnest.

Once the battle had been joined, Hassim had found himself unprepared for the stupendous noise of it all. He had been involved in countless firefights and attacks, but somehow this was so much more … pervasive. The air shook with frequent explosions that seemed to be spreading with ferocious speed from his right, where Shahim and his team of one hundred men had started their branch of the perimeter attack. Hassim had wondered at what was causing those great explosions, but had pressed on toward his objective, eventually coming up on the garrison protecting the armory. After a brief firefight in which his poorly armed and poorly trained troops were clearly loosing ground, the defenders had been flanked by Shahim and his one hundred fighters.

For his part, Shahim Al-Khazar had not waited long for the one hundred men that had come with him on his run around the perimeter. Sprinting ahead of them, he had taken out the Pakistani soldiers in his path with machine efficiency, cutting through their skulls with his laser as he ran in his long loop around the inside of the lower part of the perimeter fences. He was firing the rifles he carried in each hand as well, shooting into the fuel tanks of jeeps and trucks to detonate the petrol and diesel they contained. It was mostly for effect, but that effect was a wave of quick death surging through the base.

Shahim's aerial view told him where each of his teams were. It also told him where the Pakistanis were. He could see the Pakistani troops gathering around the armory and the much larger force taking up positions around the silos in the predefined defensive stances he had described to his cohorts earlier that night. He could also see that Hassim was pinned down by one of the groups defending the armory. Dakar, for his part, was continuing his fight north, around the perimeter closer to the silos, but he was still well outside the ranks of the three thousand soldiers now guarding those precious nuclear missiles.

Amidst the destruction, he spotted seven of the army's new Al-Khalid battle tanks sitting in a yard a few hundred yards up ahead. He knew that three others were already on the move around the base, and even now converging on the silos to support their defense.

They were three-man tanks: a driver, a gunner, and a comms man who doubled as a second gunner. He ran toward the nearest of the big tanks. He did not need to wait for the rest of his group to catch up so he could steal one; he could perform all three tasks with ease himself, but he would, however, need a moment to break into the well-secured tank and load its mechanical loaders with explosive shells. Sure enough, by the time he was ready, some of his now spread-out force had caught up with him. He shouted for one of them to man the 12.7mm machine gun on the top of the tank and for the rest to form up behind him, and without further ado he set off.

He wielded the tank more like a car than the multi-ton beast it was, not aiming the tank's cannon independently but instead veering the entire tank to point at the various pockets of resistance they encountered as they made their way toward the back of the armory.

He needed to spread a little confusion, to make the Pakistanis feel like they were under attack by a much larger force. So in between taking out outposts of Pakistani soldiers along their route, he also lobbed shells out over the base to land apparently indiscriminately. He had fifty explosive shells in the tank's loaders and he disposed of forty-two of them in less than ten minutes, sending fire and fear to fall like rain throughout the base.

Hassim crouched against the side of a building hiding from intense gunfire. His team was pinned by large-caliber fire being laid down from two entrenched machine-gun posts near the armory. He had dispatched two groups to try and flank the gunners but they were well dug in. More than fifty of his men had already fallen and they had only been inside the base for about twenty minutes. He could not keep this up much longer. He was well inside the camp and enemy forces were starting to come at him from every direction.

Hassim heard the tank approaching from behind the posts and shuddered. Dear Allah, the tank must be coming from where Shahim's force had been. So that had been the source of the explosions. It had been the sound of Shahim and his men dying. Very well, if their leader had faced one of the tanks, he and his followers would follow him. Screaming a battle cry at the top of his lungs, he sprung from his position just as a shell from the tank hammered into the first machine-gun post that had blocked his way. The explosion rocked him back, followed a moment later by another as the tank swung bodily on the other machine-gun team in their path.

He could see the tank in the square next to the armory. He could see the freedom fighters around it cheering. And as he started to run toward it, he could see Shahim Al Khazar climbing out of it and heading toward the armory's entrance.

Fires burned in a wide circle around the armory, the night was ablaze.

"It is Osman Returned! The great warrior leads us! Come, my men, come!" screamed Hassim, running across the broad open space to the armory building. His remaining soldiers joined him, flooding the square around the large squat building, as hope filled their souls.

- - -

Shahim targeted the mortar teams himself, giving brief instructions on how to fire the simple but effective weapons and how to change the target slightly each time. In short order, ten mortar teams were in place on the roof of the armory and raining down explosive shells on the missile silos half a mile north of them. More teams were moving out across the base to spread the fire, and machine gunners were setting up on the roof to defend the main position. The shells would not damage the incredibly well-armored silos, not even slightly, but the soldiers around them were suffering terribly, and the generals commanding them stirred.

The AI informed Shahim that the three other tanks that were active in the base were starting to move toward them from the embattled silos to the north, along with a large force of soldiers. He turned to Hassim and shouted over the explosions.

"My general, you have fought well tonight. Now we enter the final stages of our battle to avenge the deaths of our leaders in the mountains. You must hold this position for another twenty minutes and then leave. Send fifty men to fetch the trucks and bring them here. When the twenty minutes is up, load the trucks with what is left of your forces and leave. Do you understand these orders I have given you, Hassim?"

Hassim nodded but then stopped, confused, "And you, Great One, where will you be?"

Shahim looked angry for a moment. 'Great one.' There was nothing great about this barbarous massacre. Maybe, if he succeeded at this next stage, he might be something better than a murderer, but until then …

Shahim took the man's shoulder, "Hassim, hear me. We like to think we are fighters, but we are, in truth, little more than cowards. We hide in caves and then attack without warning or control. We massacre innocents under the banner of God and insult His name every time we do so. This fight," Shahim waved his hand around the burning night, "this fight is more important than you could possibly know, but not for any of the reasons you think. If you survive tonight, then I beseech you to return to your home, and give yourself over to peace. We are not worthy to take on His work, and we insult Him when we take up arms in His name. If these men here deserved to die for some Holy War, would He not smite them? Who are we to act on His behalf?"

Hassim stared at the man, dazed. What was he saying?!

"For my part, well, I am beyond redemption." Shahim continued, "I am going to face whatever judgment awaits me. I promise, Hassim, with absolute certainty, that you will never hear from Shahim Al Khazar again after this night. No matter what else happens, that man dies now."

And with that Shahim turned away from the dumbfounded Hassim. The burly warrior took a few steps back from the edge of the roof, and then, to everyone's astonishment, ran and leapt off the roof of the two-story building, landing with a roll on the concrete parade ground below. They watched as he tucked and then came to his feet in one smooth motion and set off at a run across the quad. He was heading north, right into the hailstorm, and they stared after him as he disappeared into the violent night.

Chapter 50: Hidden Pathways

On the far side of the planet, it was still early evening in Washington, and the president was sitting and cupping a hot mug of coffee, and looking in confusion at the collection of people in his office. An hour beforehand, the president's chief of staff had informed him that Admiral Hamilton was requesting a private meeting with the president immediately. He was told that the admiral had not said why, but had stressed that it concerned national security and that it was imperative that the meeting happen without delay. The president had found himself in his Oval Office just before he was supposed to be getting ready for dinner with his family, sipping his coffee and bracing for whatever news the admiral might be bringing.

The meeting had started strangely and only gotten stranger. The president was no newcomer to sudden emergency meetings being called by any one of a number of his inner circle of advisors, aides, and close political allies. But to have such a meeting called by the senior admiral of the navy was very unusual.

What was even more unusual was the list of people that had come with the admiral: some colonel in the air force stood in one corner, and the intelligent but slightly off-color White House Science Advisor Neal Danielson stood in another. His chief of staff Jim Hacker sat on one of the Oval Office's beige couches across from the unusually enigmatic admiral.

The president focused on the navy man and said, "Well, Admiral, would you care to tell me why I am late for dinner with my wife? I mean, couldn't this have waited till morning?"

The admiral glanced over his shoulder at Neal standing in the corner. They had rehearsed this moment for some time, but the admiral was finding that no amount of practice made it any easier to actually say what he was about to say. Neal gave the senior military man a nod of reassurance and the admiral turned back to the president. He took a long, deep breath and then said, "Mr. President, Mr. Hacker, I am sorry that I have dragged you in here tonight, but I am afraid the information I have to share with you will not wait."

He ignored the questioning looks the men gave each other and carried on, "Sir, for about nine months now, a small team of scientists and officers have been tracking a hidden threat to our security, and preparing for the day when we would be able to respond to that threat. During that time, this team has worked to put in place a response that would be both effective at neutralizing the threat while also coming up with frankly unique and unprecedented methods for minimizing the collateral damage we fear will come once we initiate our plan.

"The team's goal .... or rather, *our* goal," the admiral spared a brief smile for his two associates and then went on, "has been to prepare for the day when we would be ready to strike with lethal force, for we will only have one shot, and it must be 100% effective."

The admiral paused for a moment, and then said with as much authority as he could muster, "Mr. President, we've come to you this evening because today is that day."

- - -

An hour later, the president was still in the grips of the admiral's presentation. Neal had provided Admiral Hamilton with a plethora of information prior to the meeting, and he and the colonel stepped in to support the admiral or answer any particularly technical questions whenever it seemed prudent. The president was taking it reasonably well, as was the chief of staff, but while they were not totally incredulous, they were far from convinced. The team had wanted to get the president on his own at first, but that had proved impossible. Jim Hacker was very good at his job as the president's gatekeeper: to get to the president, you had to go through him.

"I'm sure you understand that this is all very … hard to accept, Admiral." said Jim Hacker, and the admiral nodded. He understood better than the chief of staff did, and they had notably left out the details of the whereabouts of all eight Agents, focusing instead on the satellites that were their first priority.

Jim Hacker continued, "You've shown us a lot of compelling material, but I hope you'll understand when I say that, in my opinion, it is all fairly circumstantial." Again the admiral nodded, and Jim went on, "I guess I am saying, Admiral, that, again, in my opinion, while such a theory from such a man as you cannot be taken lightly, I think it is my duty to say that I cannot recommend any action on the part of the United States government without further evidence and information."

"Wait," said the president, "action? I am not ready to even begin talking about action."

The president went on, "We have talked a lot of theory, and you've shown me lots of photos of nothing in space and nothing on the bed of the Indian Ocean and insisted that all this nothing means something very important. I know you are clearly absolutely convinced of this information's efficacy, and that, in and of itself, is very powerful, I don't disagree. But so far I have to agree with my chief of staff's analysis. I respect each of you enough to accept that you clearly believe you have something concrete here. But none of you have talked about action. What action do you want me to take exactly? What is this 'response' you mentioned earlier that you want to make to something so … incredible?"

The admiral nodded again thoughtfully, reflecting that he was probably doing that too much, and then checked his watch.

Good, they should be getting the report any moment. After a moment's pause, the admiral spoke again, slowly, as if filling time, "Mr. President, the response I have spoken about is just that: a response. I concur that your chief of staff makes a good point. While my colleagues and I have seen enough by now to come to the strong conviction that this threat is very much a reality, we did not expect to convince either of you without significantly more … *concrete* evidence."

The admiral glanced at his watch again, aware that it might now be starting to look like an affectation, then went on, "Plus, we knew that if we had approached you earlier you would have been forced to pursue this, possibly in ways that we know would have been detected by them, causing them to react in ways that I do not wish to contemplate."

The admiral paused, and the two other men looked expectant for a moment, waiting for the military man to go on, but he didn't. Jim Hacker lost his patience first, "So? That doesn't quite explain why you are coming to us now, Admiral."

The admiral shook his head. When he reflected on it, he was about to admit to being part of an international conspiracy that ended with the firing of billions of dollars worth of military hardware into space. He smiled. Well, here goes nothing.

"You see, Mr. President, Jim, we had actually come up with a plan that did not necessitate involving you at all. We had devised a way of, well, using the resources at our disposal to attack the satellites without going through your office." He found he was no longer having trouble looking at them as he spoke, a weight starting to lift from his shoulders as he said, "But that plan was not a good one. For one it did not include a method for destroying all the satellites, only three of them. We have a different plan now. Part of which is even now starting to unfold."

They looked at him, concern spreading across their faces even as a peace spread across his. He had not liked lying to his commander in chief. Now, at least, he could say that the lying was over.

The beeping of the admiral's phone caught them all by surprise, as did the fact that he didn't ignore it but calmly picked it up and glanced at it.

The chief of staff looked awry at the admiral, "Admiral, what could possibly be important enough that you would …" but he was interrupted by his own phone. He paused. There was a very short list of reasons that both of their phones would go off at the same time, and as he went to look at his own phone's screen there was a knock on the door, which then opened just a crack. The president's personal secretary poked in her head, "Mr. President, gentlemen, I am very sorry to disturb you but your presence is requested in the SitRoom, sir, as is the admiral's."

The chief of staff looked up from the similar message on his phone and looked at the president, then they both looked at the admiral, who was sitting serenely on the couch waiting for them.

"Mr. President, you are about to be told that there has been an incident in Pakistan. When you hear about it you are going to be stunned, and with good reason. It is, by many measures, one of the worst things any president can imagine happening on his watch. But we are here to tell you that it is not as it seems, and that we have a very specific response that we need to make to the events about to unfold across the world.

"Like I said, we have been preparing for the day when we would be able to respond to the threat that is coming our way. Whether we like it or not, today *is* that day, and we are as ready as we will ever be. Both you and the joint chiefs are about to see irrefutable proof that what we have said is true. What you do with that evidence will, of course, be up to you. But we are here to tell you that we have a plan. And that everything is in place to execute that plan tonight."

- - -

Agent Mikhail Kovalenko drove at speed to his office in the center of Moscow. It was four o'clock in the morning, and he had already phoned the majority of his department, waking them up and telling them that their senior officer needed them at work immediately.

While he dedicated one subroutine of his machine mind to calling his colleagues, another part of his highly capable mind was focused on driving the car through the still sleeping city. Though the city appeared calm, he knew that all across it hundreds of men and women were responding to the rapidly unfolding events in Pakistan. While senior government officials were busily awaking the premier and his staff, others were activating and arming the country's powerful defenses.

But even with all their spies and agents, Mikhail still knew more about what was happening than the vast Russian military. Even as Russian, American, European, and Chinese satellites were redirected to fly over Peshawar, Mikhail already knew what they were going to see when they got there.

He knew that they are going to see the site of a brief but bloody battle. That they will see fires raging across the badly damaged base. They will no doubt make out the three burning hulks that had been the Al-Khalid Battle Tanks sent to take out the freedom fighters and they may even see the last of the freedom fighters fleeing back into the mountains. For in the end, those same insurgents who had so boldly attacked the base had been just as shaken by how it had all ended. Even the most bloodthirsty of them had been as surprised when they had seen the six huge HATF-VI missiles thunder up out of their buried bunkers, and upon seeing that terrible sight they had fled. Even their boiling insurgent rage had been blanched clean at the thought of what those missiles would do to whatever target they had been sent to destroy. As a whole, the remaining fighters' wills had faltered and they had run, leaving the base to shake with the aftereffects of the launch.

Back in Russia, Mikhail knew that soon the satellites of the world's great military superpowers would confirm the broken reports each country was getting. They would find six of the long-range missile silos open. And soon Russia's advanced ABM radar would detect six inbound signatures heading in its direction.

For his part, Agent Mikhail Kovalenko was not yet part of the upper echelons of the Strategic Command Force. The relatively unimportant analysis group he was assigned to had not been called to handle this crisis but Mikhail needed to be involved. He needed to stop the Russians from going too far in their response. He needed to make sure the wishes and needs of the Council were adhered to, and that a full nuclear conflagration was not sparked by this unprecedented action.

So while one subroutine in his machine mind called his colleagues, and another handled the task of driving his car for him, the personality that governed the entire machine mind used the relay in the back of his car to connect to yet another emergency Council meeting, the second in two days.

<Welcome.>

<We have called this emergency Council meeting to discuss the important events unfolding in Pakistan. It should be noted by all members of the Council that this is not a complete session of the Council. We have not had contact from Agent Shahim Al Khazar since the beginning of the attack on the Peshawar Army Base, despite ongoing attempts to locate him.>

They all looked about the virtual meeting room. Never before had they met as an incomplete group. It was disconcerting. John remained silent. He knew more than the rest of the group what Shahim was up to, but he could not know how successful the other Agent had been. So he literally and proverbially sat back a waited.

<At this time we must assume he is either destroyed, severely damaged, or unable to move from his current location. All the above options seem unlikely, but Agent Shahim was last seen entering an area with significant firepower and weapons-grade nuclear materials so all possibilities must be considered. We believe it should be a high priority of the Council to discover what has happened to Agent Shahim Al Khazar, but before we can attend to that we have an even greater issue to discuss.>

<The latest update on the situation in Pakistan is that Agent Shahim has clearly lost control of the insurgent forces there. While most are dead, some clearly made it into the bunkers. We are unclear how they managed to bypass the security or obtain the launch codes, but they clearly have, and they have managed to launch six HATF-VI Long-Range Nuclear Missiles. We are tracking response protocols in China, America, England, France, Turkey, Iran, India, Russia, Saudi Arabia, and Israel. There have been no additional launches as of yet, but Indian forces are on high alert and their missiles have been put on launch ready status, as have the Russian, Israeli, and Chinese offensive and defensive missile systems. The Pakistani government has reached out to key global leaders saying the launch is accidental and that it is not possible that the weapons have active warheads as the terrorists do not have the activation codes.>

<As of now, most countries' internal communications indicate that they believe the launch is not government sanctioned, but also that they do not believe the warheads are definitively inactive. The fact that the launch occurred at all clearly diminishing their faith in Pakistan's pleas.>

<Our analysis of the missiles' trajectories shows a likely projected target of Moscow. Although Moscow is outside the missiles' tested range, some tests have shown that it is inside their theoretical limit.>

<Based on our analysis, we have two response options to disable the missiles, and three options for gaining further information on the status of Agent Shahim Al Khazar:>

<The missiles' flight path will intersect with the orbit of one of our orbital satellites in four hours' time, as we are adjusting our orbits to allow for optimal viewpoints in the coming hours and days. When we cross paths with the missiles, we would be able to use our onboard defense systems to destroy them. However, with the ground-based and satellite surveillance of the world's superpowers focused on the missiles, there is a disconcertingly high chance that our intervention would be spotted by the humans.>

<Russia has already initiated response protocols and placed its A-135 missile defense system on high alert. With the Pakistani HATF-VI missiles apparently aimed in Russia's direction, Agent Mikhail Kovalenko could be provided with additional analysis information with which he can encourage a prompt Russian response using their midrange Gorgon Interceptors. These have been retro-fitted with relatively advanced laser guided non-nuclear warheads and would have an 89% probability of destroying the inbound missiles while they are still exo-atmospheric.>

<At this time, we recommend relying on the Russian A-135 response, which can be encouraged and directed by Agent Mikhail Kovalenko. If, for some reason, we are unable to goad the Russians into responding with enough of its Gorgon missile armament, or if the

missiles prove ineffective, only then do we recommend using our laser weaponry to destroy the errant missiles, and rely on disinformation from each of you to stop any unwelcome inquiries into the fate of the missiles within your respective countries' governments.>

<Does the Council agree with the analysis as we have presented it?>

The seven people around the room nodded their assent. It was the most danger they had been in since the *King's Transom* had discovered one of their capsules off India, and no one in the room felt the need to have their voice heard in connection with such an unprecedented risk to the mission. Several among them had already begun thinking of how they would make sure any blame for problems arising from the incident were placed firmly at Agent Shahim's feet, but bar that they were happy for the AI to take the lead here.

The AI recorded their assent and moved on to the job of finding the missing Agent, listing its three options for doing so.

<In order to locate Agent Shahim Al Khazar, we have three potential options. As you all know, your bodies were specifically designed without any active locator beacons in order to avoid the chance that their signals would be picked up by the humans. Because of this, we have relied on the small subspace tweeters built into your human analogs, and the larger relays you were equipped with to maintain contact with you. Shahim is not currently near his relay and therefore we cannot pick up signals from him and discover his current status.>

<Shahim was last seen in a firefight with three Pakistani tanks in the middle of the base. After disabling them, he entered a building nearby and we have not been able to positively identify him since. The Pakistani army has already dispatched two large forces to converge on the base and retake it, though there are, in fact, very few insurgents still alive there.>

<As you all know, three of you are currently in the same region as Agent Shahim. Agent Raz Shellet in Tel Aviv, Agent Preeti Parikh in New Delhi, and Agent Jean-Paul Merard currently stationed in Afghanistan with the Eighty-Second Fighter Wing of the French Air Force.>

<We believe that with the region on high alert, it would be very difficult for any Israeli to leave that country on short notice and make it across Iran and Afghanistan to Peshawar. Though Agent Merard in Afghanistan is closest to Shahim, his body analog is what the human's term Caucasian, and we believe that would make it equally challenging for him to covertly gain access to Peshawar Base at this time.>

That left one, and the room turned to Agent Preeti Parikh. Her avatar looked a little surprised; this wasn't the kind of attention you wanted in a time of crisis. But she was ready to attend to her duty, and she started formulating her response to the suggestion that they could all see was coming.

Among the six virtual faces looking at her, John Hunt's looked as concerned as the rest, and in truth, he *was* concerned, though for very different reasons than his colleagues. As the AI continued with its analysis and Agent Parikh discussed how she could realistically get to Peshawar in the shortest possible time, Agent John Hunt pondered the news the AI had provided. So, there were six long-range nuclear missiles heading for Moscow.

The question was: would they make it?

Chapter 51: Launch Protocols

Major Toranssen sat gathering his thoughts in the officers' break room at Whiteman Air Force Base. Across from him sat Dr. Martin Sobleski, his chest heaving with exertion, sweat gathered and beaded on his forehead.

"How you doing there, Doc?" asked Jack, smiling at his partner in crime, and quite a few crimes at that.

"Hmm, Jack, let's review," said Martin, panting a little. He glanced around and lowered his voice to a measured tone, "We've just finished loading sixteen of the most explosive and unpleasant devices I have ever worked on into the belly of the single most expensive plane the air force has ever built. And now we're sitting and waiting for confirmation that we should go ahead and steal that plane and break pretty much every international treaty the world has ever known."

He sat back, clearly still reeling from the mental and physical exertion of loading and affixing the huge air bombs into the clamps that lined the huge hold of one of the menacing stealth bombers that sat in hangars across the base. They had done it. Using every available lie and con they had, using the major's seniority and B-2 experience, along with faked orders from General Pickler, all supplemented by phone calls from Colonel Milton to the base commander.

But they had gotten the sixteen warheads Martin and Madeline had manufactured in North Dakota onto the base and over the last two nights they had loaded them into a series of ASM-158As, an aircraft launchable stealth cruise missile with a payload weight of about one thousand pounds. Martin's design had filled the missile's warhead bays as he had planned, and they were going to set off a heck of a bang when they went off. But the bang wasn't what Martin was actually going for. It was the aftereffect. Using a cluster of thermobaric explosives, he had designed a deployment weapon that would create a huge torus of superheated oxygen, burning hot enough to create an implosive vacuum. If all went well, this would create a vortex of superheated air that would destroy the pathogens right at their point of deployment. It would only work a few times, as no amount of stealth would be enough to hide the great detonations once their attacks began, but if they could get themselves into position over the right areas at the right moment, then maybe they could stem the flow of pathogens to the least protected areas.

According to Neal's estimates, they might save as many as five or six million people if all went well. But no pressure, or anything.

Jack suddenly froze, looking at Martin, who instinctively held his breath. Jack felt in his pocket and extracted his cell phone. It was vibrating. Jack answered it, keeping his eyes on Martin as he spoke.

"Colonel?"

There was a pause while he listened to the man on the other end, then.

"Yes, Colonel."

Another pause.

"Yes, Colonel, I understand. We're ready at this end. The bird is prepped and awaiting your orders. Sir … Barrett, can I ask, does everyone know now?"

Martin waited a moment longer. The major nodded somberly as he listened to the man on the other end of the phone.

"Yes, Colonel. I understand. We'll be ready."

"Good luck to you too, Colonel … it's been a pleasure."

He hung up and looked at his colleague, took a long, deep breath, and then said, "Well, my friend. We'd better get into position." He thought for a second and then went on, "Listen, Colonel Milton told me that as of an hour ago, the president and the Security Council know everything. He told me that they know about the missiles and that they are willing to initiate the GBMD protocol once they see the first satellite destroyed. But as we feared, they didn't approve our part of the mission."

Martin stared at him, deflated, and Jack bit his lower lip for a moment while the other man came to terms with it. "They simply weren't ready to accept sending a heavily armed bomber into hostile airspace when the world is already on tender-hooks after the incident in Pakistan.

"We always knew that this was a possibility, just as we knew that the army chiefs could also have refused to fire the GBMD system. We had a plan for how to handle that, and we have a plan to handle this, but we both know what this means. The colonel said to me that in the end we have to make the go/no-go decision for ourselves. And you have a right to make this decision for yourself, just as I am going t—"

"Stop, Jack." Martin interrupted him and Jack went silent, "Like you said, we always knew that this was a possibility, but we're talking about millions of lives here. We both know that neither of us could walk away from this." Martin took a deep breath and looked resignedly at the major, "You know what my answer is, just as I know yours."

They nodded at each other, paused a moment as if something else might need to be said, but then thought better of it. The B-2 bomber was among the stealthiest machines ever made, but they were about to fly it over some of the most war-torn countries on earth, and once they were there, they were going to launch firebombs into the atmosphere. To top it off, they were going to have to steal said bomber in order to do it. Admittedly, the way they were going to steal it would mean that the US government would not know about it until long after they had done what they had to do, but eventually they would realize what had happened. And after that they were on their own.

They were under no illusions as to how this night might end. But they also knew why they were doing it, and neither of them could think of any way that they could not try, at least try, to slow the coming plague. In the end, the only thing less appealing than the task at hand was the thought of living with themselves if they didn't accept it.

They stood and left the room, silent and resolute.

- - -

Captains Billy Kellar and Jennifer Falster jogged across the hangar floor, staying between the yellow lines that ran in front of the vast bombers which the massive hangar sheltered. The B-2 faced outward, as large as a football field. It was designed to be flown by two people, a pilot and a mission commander, who sat in a cockpit mounted at the apex of the vast Delta wing that gave the B-2 its unique profile. There was no door on the B-2. Under the nose was one of the three large hatches on the bottom of the plane that housed the landing gear. Two much larger bay doors allowed the plane to deploy its huge payloads. At rest, the nose gear hung down from the very tip of the plane's nose, exposing the space where the big wheels tucked away during flight. With the gear deployed, a small secondary hatch on the inside of the wheel housing was the main access hatch to the cockpit, and it was through here that the pilots climbed in and out of the plane.

Billy and Jennifer came to a halt in front of their plane, B-2 21070, codename Ice Maiden, and started to go through their preflight checklist. Billy and Jennifer had received the scramble order along with ten other flight crews and were two minutes into the ten-minute countdown to takeoff. They would be briefed en route, but their order package had said that they were being set to DEFCON 2, and dispatched on standard defensive vectors in the Atlantic and Pacific arenas.

Jennifer Falster, the pilot for this mission, began her customary inspection of the outside of the plane while Mission Commander Billy Kellar climbed into the cockpit and began his preflight weapons check. As Jennifer walked around the huge plane, she chatted with various ground crew members doing final preflight on the plane. They had six minutes to takeoff, but even in critical times like these the flight crew was trained to take these last few minutes slowly, making sure everything was set. In the end, when all was said and done, they were responsible for the safety of the plane and they needed to be confident that everything was as it should be.

Finishing her wing inspection, Jennifer bowed her head and walked under the plane to the payload doors. At this point in the preflight protocol, they were already closed and sealed, the technicians actually painting over the door seals with a waxy, absorbent grey paint that would help further minimize their radar signature. She nodded to the tech who said, "Two minutes, ma'am." from behind his facemask, prompting the captain to get on board.

The captain nodded. That paint smelled awful anyway, she thought, and went to join Billy in the cockpit. As she mounted the ladder under the hatch, she heard the thrumming of the four leviathan engines starting up, echoed by the engines of her colleagues' planes powering up to either side.

Go time, she thought and ducked through the hatch. Once at the top of the ladder, she turned to climb the two steps to the cockpit and was greeted by the sight of a gun in the hands of ... wait, "Major Toranssen, what the hell are you doing?" she exclaimed, stunned at the incongruous sight.

"I'm sorry, Jennifer, now, don't make a sound. Just turn around and open the door to the head." said Jack Toranssen, indicating the small on-board toilet directly behind where Jennifer Falster was standing. Jennifer's mind raced as she tried to think of what to do.

One thing she knew, there was absolutely no way she was giving this plane away. Not on her watch. No fucking way.

She spotted the tech from the missile door walking under the hatchway. The man turned and saw her standing in the small space aft of the cockpit. Jennifer raised her hands like she was being stuck-up in an old cowboy movie, hoping the tech would raise the alarm. The man paused. Good, maybe this guy would figure it out. Wait, no, shit, the tech was walking toward her. Fuck. No! Don't come up here, you idiot. Go and get help, chock the wheels, sound the alarm you fool, but sure enough the man came over and started climbing the small ladder that folded down from the cockpit hatchway.

OK, maybe when the tech showed his head in the hatchway Jennifer could grab the gun away from the apparently deranged Major Toranssen. Maybe she would get shot doing it, but so be it. The gunshot would bring people running and then at least the plane would not be co-opted by this apparently insane ex-Captain Toranssen. But then Major Toranssen did something that Jennifer did not expect. As the tech's head and upper body appeared through the hatchway, the major fired.

There was no bang, more of a whoosh, and Jennifer felt a stabbing pain in her neck. Fuck, I've been shot, the bastard shot me, her mind raced. What the hell did he do that for? What about the risk of damaging the plane? Jennifer's hand instinctively came up to her neck to feel the wound but something was wrong. Wait, what the hell was that? She felt her vision blur as she pulled the dart out, but the dart seemed to melt away as the world began to swim and flow around her.

"Damn it, Jack!" said the tech climbing into the cabin as the female pilot slumped forward on top of him. Martin, disguised in the overalls of a technician, heaved under the weight of the unconscious woman while the major reached over the top of them and opened the toilet door at the back of the small space. In it was the already unconscious body of Captain Kellar, and the major helped the straining Dr. Martin to heft the limp body of Captain Falster into the small space with her sleeping colleague. They would attend to the two pilots in good time, but for now, they had to get seated and get this bird airborne.

Martin hastily climbed the rest of the way into the cabin and stripped off his overalls, revealing a flight-suit underneath. Stuffing the overalls in with the two sleeping airmen, he climbed into the unoccupied seat next to the major, where even now the man was performing the final flight prep.

As Jack worked diligently and expertly to prep the plane, he filled Martin in on what was about to happen, "OK, Doc, get your helmet on. In a moment, a ground commander is going to poke his head through that hatch and confirm we are flight ready. Do not turn around, just sit there and move your arms a little, like you are getting the plane ready. From where he'll be looking from, he won't be able to see much of you anyway, just the back of your shoulder. When he says, 'are we a go?' you just stick your thumb out like this. Once he gets the OK from us, he's going to order the hatch sealed and we'll begin our taxi.

"If we can get to the runway, we are pretty much home free. There is pretty much nothing they can do to us once we are airborne as they won't be able to see us. After all, that is basically the idea of this beauty."

Martin was about to make a remark about how taking off was the least of their worries when they heard clanks on the hatchway ladder as the ground commander climbed up. Jack and he exchanged a few words over the growing roar of the engines and Martin heard the shouted question, "Are we a go?"

He gave his best Top Gun thumbs-up, reviving some remembered pilot stereotype, and then the man was gone and the hatch was being sealed. Though he would not admit it, a part of him had hoped they would be caught. Deep down he knew that he was probably going to die tonight, or, if he was lucky, spend the rest of his life in a military jail. And he couldn't help but think that maybe just cutting straight to the military jail bit might have been preferable.

But that option was gone now. Three minutes later they were taxiing into the still warm jet wash of the B-2 in front of them, watching the white burn of his four turbojet engines as they propelled him down the runway. This was no civilian airport; as the plane in front was just lifting off they were already in place and gunning their engines to catch it. Martin was thrown back in his seat as Jack fired the plane's great engines and the powerful beasts catapulted them forward toward whatever fate the night had in store for them.

Chapter 52: Flash Exposure

The earth below passed by like a wooden globe spun by a child. Hub Satellite Number 3 orbited high above southern China, flying westward as it overtook the sun.

The four AIs that circled the earth operated as one mind. Their systems were thoroughly integrated, the instantaneous communication made possible by the subspace tweeters each satellite was built around making fluid operation a possibility. Therefore the unified artificial intelligence that was the four satellites watched the planet they were orbiting as one mind, its four acute eyes scanning the globe and creating a composite image from all the data that flowed up to them. As one satellite's orbit took it away from Middle East, to soar out over the Mediterranean toward the Atlantic, another was already coming around behind it, bringing its eye to bear on the object of their attention. The focus of the AIs' combined mind shifted seamlessly to the next satellite's eye as it took in the six missiles soaring up out of the atmosphere ahead of it.

As the AI watched the six errant missiles streak across the Middle Eastern dawn, it broadcast the image to its eight Agents on the surface below. The AIs' eyes also watched eagerly as various nations responded across the planet's surface. They watched as the US, China, and Russia deployed their long-range bomber fleets. They saw the F-35 strike bombers being fueled and prepped with long-range cruise missiles on French, English, and US aircraft carriers in the Mediterranean.

With computerized calm, the AI hivemind tracked and monitored tens of thousands of ships, submarines, planes, tanks, and battalions of soldiers as they all began to move in an impossibly complex dance. The world was readying itself for potential nuclear holocaust. The earth had stockpiled an estimated twenty to thirty thousand high-yield nuclear missiles: enough to destroy mankind forty-two times over. Each of the fifty or so nuclear submarines that England, France, the US, China, and Russia had in the world's various oceans had enough firepower to wipe out half of humanity on their own. If any proportion of that arsenal were fired en masse, the satellites could not hope to stop it. Nothing could. It was just this realization that had brought the team of eight Agents to this world in advance of their Armada. The last thing the Mobiliei wanted was a broken and charred planet; they just wanted an empty one. They needed us gone, but they needed to eradicate us methodically, in an orderly fashion.

Their plans were predicated now, as they had always been, on the premise that as long as their presence remained unknown they might still infiltrate the world's nuclear powers deeply enough to mitigate their might from the inside. But not if there was a war tonight. Not if the insanity of a few insurgents started the conflagration that would render the earth both uninhabited *and* uninhabitable.

Even with the world's great powers unsheathing their claws and baring their fangs, the AIs operated under the assumption that this could still all end peacefully. Study of Earth's history as well as their own showed that this was not the first time either planet had been pushed to the brink of nuclear war. Like the Mobiliei, the humans had discovered that the atom was as powerful a deterrent as it was a weapon. Both races had only ever dared to use it once, the sight of the weapon's power showing each world that if two nuclear capable nations ever went to war it would be the last thing the race ever knew. But even with such a massive deterrent staying the hands of the world's super powers, events like the Cuban missile crisis had still been one of many events that had taken the world to the very brink of annihilation.

So on this night, as the world once more teetered on the edge of the precipice, the four satellites roaming above were ready to take on the role of unlikely guardian. They would watch over the humans and try to ensure that this was just another false alarm. Under no circumstances would they allow the six Pakistani missiles to reach Russia, but nor would they risk exposure unless it was absolutely necessary.

As Hub Satellite Number 3 continued up over Tibet toward Azerbaijan, it tracked the Pakistani missiles as they left the atmosphere and began their brief, ballistically doomed orbits. Their rocket engines still burned with fury, though now in the silence of vacuum, the sound lost as though drowned out by the expanse of space they were so briefly escaping into. As the satellite eye flew toward the six HATF-VI missiles from the east, it also registered as Russia launched its counterstroke from the north. Out of the heart of Northern Asia came thirty-two flaring rocket signatures. The big missiles, known as Gorgons, were the long-range component of Russia's massive missile shield. They were capable of exo-atmospheric travel, and they were armed with the latest kinetic cluster warheads. They were blunt tools, they were huge, and they were lethal.

The stealthed AI satellite came surging over the horizon, and watched the two great arcs forming just ahead of it. At this rate, the hub would be right over the surging missiles in a matter of minutes. As it watched, the two arcs continued to form like sides of a massive bridge coming to meet in the middle, a bridge of fire large enough to connect Moscow to Pakistan, over two thousand miles to the south.

The HATF-VI rockets had reached their theoretical peak altitude, with a documented range of two thousand miles they were about eight minutes from disengaging their rocket boosters and beginning their plummet back to Earth. But instead of leveling out and preparing for their freefall, they continued to rise.

Mikhail Kovalenko had spent the last two hours convincing first his superior, then several of that man's superiors that the missiles could make it to Russia, even though it was outside the effective range of the weapons. So sure enough, the Russian missile control was ready when the Pakistani missiles continued to rise.

Their own missiles adjusted accordingly and they continued their meteoric rise out of the atmosphere to lay their spectacularly destructive munitions in the path of the onrushing missiles. The AI watched the two trajectories continue to angle farther and farther upward, until its own subroutines started to alert it to a new possibility. The paths: they were going to intersect. The Russians had indeed fired high and wide enough, and the giant Gorgon missiles' onboard tracking systems were now able to plot an intercept course that would lay them in the path of the six aggressors.

But the AI satellite would also be in that path. The machine laid route plan after route plan but the closer it came to the missiles, the plainer it became. The Pakistani missiles were not leveling out. They were continuing their rise. The missiles' powerful boosters were sending them up into the path of the orbiting satellite, and the thirty-two Gorgon interceptors were coming to meet them.

The AI computed its options, it called the Council, it had simply not accounted for an option where it could be destroyed accidentally. In the event of an attack it was allowed to defend itself. It had a protocol for that. But no scenario had been envisioned where it would be faced with the fact that defending one of its four satellites against attack might result in detection. In all its scenarios it would only have to defend the satellites *after* they had already been detected. This was outside its parameters, and without a preset and preapproved response pattern it called the Council and waited.

If it had been capable of being frantic it would have been scrambling to get the seven Agents whose whereabouts it knew together, but with the infinite machine patience it calmly sent the summons to the Agents. With one Agent unaccounted for, it needed all the remaining seven to attend in order to reach a consensus, such were the limits of its mandate.

John Hunt busied himself on the deck of the HMS *Dauntless* feeling the urgent summons to Council from the AI ring in his head. He smiled. He knew that for a satellite to use its active weaponry while under close surveillance it would need a unanimous consensus. With Shahim out of pocket all John had to do was take his time. In a few hours the other Agents would no doubt all know the truth anyway. Might as well stick it to them while he still could.

Eventually, though, he knew he had to respond to the AI's calls, otherwise the Council could vote him unavailable and count his vote in proxy. So, sighing a little, he politely excused himself from the group of sailors he was standing with and stepped to the ship's railings. They were at sea, about two days outside Sembawang Naval Base on the island of Singapore. Looking out over the afternoon waters, he was struck by the magnificence of the planet. No wonder his race craved it. It was, without doubt, an exquisitely beautiful world. He knew this abstract of himself that lived in the Agent's body would never see Mobilius again, but he could not deny it was a fine consolation. Worth his life, should it come to that.

For no matter how beautiful the prize, it was not worth genocide, nothing was. Somewhere behind his machine eyes he braced himself one last time, and then his eyes stared out over the water and glazed over, his mind connecting with the other Agents in Council.

<Welcome>

<Emergency meeting of the Council to review options to avoid imminent destruction of Hub Satellite Number 3 over Azerbaijan. The missiles that were launched by the insurgents in Pakistan are converging on the satellite's orbit, as are the interceptors launched by Russia. At their current rate they will cross the satellite's path at the same time that the Russian interceptors are timed to detonate and destroy the incoming HATF-VI missiles. We have only two options: destroy the missiles using the satellite's onboard defensive lasers, while under the strict scrutiny of a significant number of human military satellites, radars, and observatories; OR accept the likely destruction of one of our four satellites.>

The room was hesitant, the risks of either scenario being equally profound. But Agent Lana spoke up, "This is too much, first the incident in India, then the discovery of the antigen in the human's blood. Now we have lost contact with one of our own and are faced with this thinly veiled attack.

"Enough of this. It is clear to me that they must know we are here. I do not know how, but there are simply too many signs that they do. In light of that fact I move that we release the virus immediately. Even with the antigen in some of the humans it should still take a significant toll on them, and we can release the updated pathogen when it is ready in a few days and finish the job."

The room was even more shocked by this blatant overreaction than it had been by the news the AI had delivered. The conversation was, as always, being conducted at machine speed, so even if they discussed their options for what seemed like several minutes, it would still only use a few seconds of the time left before the satellite entered the kill zone.

But as much as Lana may have finally seen through the counter conspiracy, her colleagues were not so keen to admit that they had been discovered by the humans. The debate went on. Without support for her more drastic response, Lana decided to at least second the AI's motion that it be allowed to defend itself. Even if the room was not with her in her suspicions of the humans' awareness, surely they were not ready to sacrifice one of their satellites to the increasingly unlikely position that their arrival on Earth remained a secret.

She was, in the end, very persuasive, and the room voted eventually to allow the satellite to defend itself. Except one. As the room came to what it thought was a consensus, Agent John Hunt's avatar waited placidly, biding his time.

<Agent John Hunt, we have no vote from you. For an attack while under surveillance, our mission parameters dictate that we require full consensus. Please indicate your vote.>

The room looked at John's avatar. He waited a moment longer, debating whether he should even maintain the pretence any longer, but he needed his cover for a few hours more, however thin it was about to come.

"Umm, no. My vote is definitely no. We have four satellites and only one chance at success at our mission here on Earth. I believe the satellite should not defend itself."

The room was stunned and Lana responded immediately, "Agent John Hunt, this is not acceptable. The rest of the Council has voted that the satellite destroy the missiles before they detonate. That is six to one. Who do you think you are to vote against the will of rest of the Council?"

John considered this point a moment, a smug smile spreading across his avatar's lips as he replied, "Well, I guess that's the problem with consensus votes, isn't it Princess Lamati? You need to get *all* of the votes to move forward. You ask who am I to vote against the rest of the Council, well I'm the one person you don't have any influence over, Princess. The one person who doesn't care what you think. And in votes where unanimity is required that means I am the man who decides that this isn't worth the risk. Let the satellite die, I do not intend to bring about the failure of this mission so that you can have one more pretty little satellite in orbit."

The group stared at him, Lana with fierce anger, and several of their colleagues glanced at her to see what she would do. For John's part, he held her stare with equanimity. Though they were miles apart both of them knew that she had figured it out, that she knew who was behind their building troubles. She looked at her nemesis and she fumed.

"Traitor!" she screamed, but he only smiled in return. She had nothing. She couldn't prove a thing. Not yet. And by the time she did have the proof she would need to override him, it would hopefully be too late for all four of the satellites. Though Shahim wasn't here, he had clearly succeeded, and if all else went to plan, the world might soon have a temporary reprieve from the machinations of the Mobiliei.

"You did this." Lana said with infinite venom, "You … you … Nomadi *scum*. You did this. You were never one of us, just as your pathetic tribe had never been one with the great Empires of Mobilius." She stared at him but he replied only with quiet complacence. Realizing there was no way he was going to be baited into a response, she turned to her colleagues. "Can you not see? Is it not obvious? This trader scum never had any intentions of supporting our claim to Earth. He has conspired against us from the start. He probably had Shahim killed in Pakistan somehow and then he initiated the attack on the satellite." She stared wildly from person to person and some of the faces even began to show signs of acquiescence.

Sensing that she might sway the room before he had time to complete the last of his plan, John spoke up, feigning anger and incredulity at Lana's comments, "Enough, Lamati! Your hateful prejudices against my people are well known, as is your vaunted pride and the disdain you have openly showed for the other nations represented in this room." He noted with satisfaction as his comments hit home, several of the other Agents' anger turning back on Lana as she festered and boiled with rage.

"Silence, scum!" she shouted in return, "I will not stand for that tone from the likes of you."

"And so we see it." sneered John in reply, "So the truth comes out. You have always thought you were better than us, haven't you, Princess? You've never thought of us as true equals. Well, shout all you want, your precious title means nothing here and it's time you started respecting us for what we are … your equals.

The princess's face flamed red and started to twitch as her personality raged at the limits of their virtual conference. She wanted to tear into her opponent. To rip out his eyes. To pound her foot into his balls until they were crushed to a pulp. Images reeled through her mind, her machine brain feeding her scenarios like a pusher in response to her rabid lust for vengeance. She was silent a moment as she reveled in the perfectly rendered image of smashing his accursed skull under foot and jumping up and down on its mangled remains until they were but a red smear across the world.

But such violent acts were not within the parameters of the virtual construct they were meeting in, so as her avatar tried to interpret and relay the ultra-violence she craved, her body seemed to convulse and spasm in its place. The rest of the room recoiled from the spectacle.

While this confrontation boiled impotently, the AI remained aloof. It was not part of any emotional contest. With infinite patience and calm it awaited any further resolution from the Council while maintaining its vigil on the progress of the munitions heading toward one of its own. Though the argument raged on, the vote was over and the AI was not interested in or capable of mourning the impending loss of a quarter of its very self. Instead it focused on what preparations it could make for the now inevitable amputation. It attempted to back up some measure of the swathes of data stored in the doomed hub; the behemoth hammers of its huge subspace tweeters thundering across the subspace void with exabytes and zettabytes of data, like the drums of the satellite's death knell.

In front of the orbiting satellite's path, the six missiles hove up into range from the south as the thirty-two flaming fires of the Russian Gorgon missiles came in from the north, coming together like the hands of a giant, to collide in the most thunderous clap the world had ever felt.

As the final seconds ticked down, the Agents fell silent and watched the images coming from the satellite in disbelief. Lana's avatar was suddenly mute and unmoving. Its emotions essentially disconnected from the conference, leaving the remaining Agents to watch in silence.

John smiled inside himself. Well done, Shahim, he thought, you have proven yourself beyond any possible doubt. You have given these people a chance, and may have saved more innocent souls than we can imagine.

Many miles below, deep in a bunker in the smoldering army base in Peshawar, the Agent once known as Shahim Al Khazar lay, dressed in the uniform of a dead Pakistani soldier, waiting, unmoving, as the Pakistani army arrived and began to clean up the destruction he had wrought. So many dead, he thought.

Though Shahim was not talking to the satellites himself, he was still receiving the images they were broadcasting to the other Agents. He had seen John vote against allowing the satellite to defend itself, and even now he watched as the orbiting platform soared inextricably into the trap they had set. In a moment, he hoped, the world would reap some small reward for the death he had brought to this unsuspecting place.

Lana and John's avatars locked eyes one last time. She looked like she was still contemplating attacking him and John wished it was that easy, he would love nothing more than to fight her. To rip her limb from limb. But they were, in reality, thousands of miles apart. She would have to wait, she thought.

But she knew that if another attack on the satellites came she would not have to rely on his sullied vote. No one would believe that this could happen twice by accident, and once the satellites were allowed to defend themselves, the humans' pathetic arsenal would be crushed. Either way, she would win in the end. And when the Armada arrived she would upload this copy of her personality via the chain of relays they were laying in their path to the real Princess Lamati back on Mobilius. Then she would find and fucking eradicate the traitorous bastard John Hunt: his real self, his family, his name, and anything he had ever held dear.

She smiled at the other Agent's avatar and John shuddered at the site. Oh, go ahead and plot away, you bitch, make your plans. You'll get yours soon enough, he thought.

When the two converging groups of missiles were half a mile and a quarter of a second apart, the Russian interceptors decided with computer precision that the time was at hand, and thirty-two kinetic warheads simultaneously detonated, firing an unholy storm of tiny titanium needles forward into the path of the Pakistani missiles. Like grenades lobbed by a god, the massive munitions exploded and created a hurricane of destruction designed to consume and eradicate the oncoming missiles … and anything else unfortunate enough to get in their way.

The satellite's systems registered the blast, documented every impact in the thousandth of a second before its shielding started to fragment, noted as it was flayed, nano-second by nano-second, its huge internal systems disintegrating and vanishing as the kinetic cyclone eviscerated it, until its very core was penetrated and the giant subspace hammer, magnificent even as it was delicate, sublimed in the combustive tempest.

- - -

From Earth's surface, the explosion could clearly be seen as a wall of white fire in the sky that spread quickly south into the path of the six missiles. Under orders from US STRATCOM, the nuclear submarine USS *Achilles* had broken protocol and surfaced while on station in the Black Sea, pointing its phenomenally acute SLBM guidance systems skyward to watch the explosion.

While the captain of the ship believed he was there to make sure that all six HATF missiles were destroyed, he was actually there to capture proof of something vastly more clandestine. As the admiral and his coconspirators had predicted, the images of the kinetic storm showed an object amidst the destruction. Something very big and very black that was clearly caught in the cross fire. An object that had not shown on any radar before that moment.

As the object was consumed by the furious cloud, along with the six HATF-VI missiles, the USS *Achilles* sent the series of images, per their orders, directly to the Pentagon, without comment.

Four of the Agents that had been attending the virtual Council meeting had been connected to rest of the group via the now destroyed satellite. Back in the virtual meeting room of the Council, those four Agents' images suddenly vanished. The Council was left with three disquieted members. Pei Leong-Lam, Lana Wilson, and John Hunt stared at each other in silence. The AI spoke without emotion.

<Destruction of Hub Satellite Number 3 confirmed. The agenda of this emergency meeting of the Council is now finished. As quorum is no longer possible with current coverage, this Council meeting is hereby terminated.>

Chapter 53: Consequential

For the key players in the events unfolding across the globe, the next five hours were very strange. For the time being, they stood in something like a calm between storms, the sunny pupil of the hurricane's angry eye. The conspirators had to wait for all their systems to be brought online, their approvals confirmed by the now all-too-aware president. Then the three remaining satellites had to be allowed to complete another circumnavigation until they were in place.

The first part of the plan had relied on surprise and subterfuge. The unshielded Russian missiles would not have been able to penetrate the defensive lasers of the satellite if it had been allowed to defend itself. But no amount of subterfuge and misdirection would make the remaining satellites sit idly by when they were launched upon. As the next phase of the plan could not rely on surprise, it would rely instead on overwhelming force. And in order for it to work, it needed to be executed at precisely the right moment. That moment was five long hours after the first satellite had been brought down.

For the US joint chiefs, it was a time of impatience. The White House Situation Room was, by the admiral's recommendation and then the president's order, on lockdown. No one could be allowed to leave who knew the full scope of what was about to happen. The admiral had now fully briefed them on the situation. A briefing that had been starkly reinforced by the shadow of the huge satellite in the images from the USS *Achilles*.

For some present it had been nothing more than a strange phenomenon at best, but the team's earlier meeting with the president and his chief of staff had planted the seed they had required. The admiral had watched both men as the images had come back from the Black Sea. The satellite was there, exactly as the admiral and his colleagues had said it would be. Its existence could no longer be argued, and according to the supporting evidence of the admiral and his team, it was not alone.

The joint chiefs and the rest of the room had taken the president's lead and listened to Admiral Hamilton and the White House science advisor as they explained the next stage of their plan. As the opinion of the room had swung in their favor, they had eventually agreed that the launching of the shielded GBMDs was, if not desirable, then at the very least a valid next step to take when the scale of the threat was laid before them.

The admiral had not been surprised when, once the president was convinced, the hardest thing had not been mobilizing the rest of the joint chiefs, but holding them back. With one satellite even then flying over the western US, they had wanted to launch immediately and then wait for the next two to come around in order to fire on them as well. It had even seemed like they might get their way until the colonel had stepped in, producing a piece of the superconducting material they had used for the missile shields. He had conducted a brief demonstration of the shield's phenomenal properties with the drill he had brought for just this purpose, and the room had been silent as the unscathed plate was handed around the table.

His demonstration was followed with an explanation of how thick the satellites' version of this plating was, compared with how few of their missiles were clad in the alien armor. It had served its purpose, and the joint chiefs had agreed to the more concerted effort the team had planned for.

Preparations for the next phase were not limited to the US, though. As the other members of their pan-global conspiracy waited through the seemingly endless hours of respite before the main battle, one of their ranks was getting his way by far more nefarious means.

- - -

John Hunt knocked on the captain's cabin door with one hand, his other holding a tray with a cup of hot chocolate steaming happily. For the marine guard stationed permanently at the captain's door, this was the hardest time of the day. It wasn't that he had a sweet tooth, per se, but the smell of that chocolate getting delivered each evening was simply torture. Why didn't they give that stuff out to the ratings? I mean, they got hot chocolate, but it was out of a sachet. The captain got the real thing.

John looked at the guard and smiled wryly. Poor guy, you wouldn't want what's in this mug, trust me. But still he smiled at the marine and gave the man his best 'woe is me' eye roll. The barked order to enter came through the metal cabin door and Lieutenant Hunt followed it. Captain Prashant always liked to keep people waiting for a second to establish his control over the situation, even when those people were bringing him his daily dose of the only vice he really allowed himself.

"Your mug of chocolate, sir." said Hunt, setting the mug in its holder on the captain's chart table.

"Where is Ensign Grimes, Lieutenant?" said the captain, asking after his usual aide-de-camp.

"Minor problem with a spill on his uniform, sir, I offered to step in." John replied, smiling angelically.

"Very well, leave it there." said the captain, waving John away.

"Will there be anything else, sir?" said Hunt.

"No."

No, thought John, after you drink that hot chocolate there most certainly will not be anything else. John stepped quickly away down the thin corridor that ran from the captain's cabin to the bridge. Dropping the tray behind some piping, he took the stairs down to the master's cabin and checked on him. Snoring away, and his whiskey was finished, good, that was him out for the night as well.

For the next thirty minutes, he made his way around the ship. He had been careful to drug each of the senior officers and warrant officers that ate separately from the rest of the crew in their own mess, and now he had to check and see if they were all sufficiently disabled. For the crew he had not needed to be so subtle. There were two seatings for dinner for the bulk of the ship's complement, served each side of the change of watch. The watch that currently manned the ship had eaten earlier, before their watch started, while the other had eaten just after they had gone off duty.

As the crew 'on deck' started to falter and pass out, the off-duty crew still had a groggy twenty minutes before their liberal doses of flunitrazepam kicked in. Basically John had given the entire ship a rufie. Standing on the bridge now, John watched as each crewmember started to flag. He walked around catching them and laying them on the ground. Deactivating their stations and the ship's controls as he went. As the comms guy passed out, John reached over and flicked the kill switch on the ship's radio and its intercom, disabling them both, and then entered in a kill code that he had programmed in weeks beforehand. The ship's comms were now utterly disabled, its regular pings to the Admiralty back home now going off automatically via the same viral subroutine that made any other form of communication to and from the ship temporarily impossible. They were cut off.

Like every other important military asset actively deployed around the world, the *Dauntless* had been a hive of activity that day, responding to the events in Pakistan and Russia. Now John raced around the ship, checking key stations and making sure open systems were shut down as the officers and ratings that usually tended them collapsed slowly to the floor. He also shut off ovens and cooking ranges in the galley, deactivated and set the engines to idle, as he ranged all over the ship watching its officers and crew collapse.

As he finally ran toward the ship's weapon control center, he came across two frightened sailors. They had been off duty but they had gone back to their station to collect some magazines they had left behind. They had found the crew unconscious and been unable to wake them. Since then they had found several other people asleep. But even as they spoke John could see they were starting to flag as well, their eyelids drooping and their speech starting to slur. But he didn't have time to argue with them. He cut them off, and told them he needed their help.

"You," he said, pointing at one of them, "get to the bridge immediately, wait there for me and make sure it is secure. Don't lock the doors, but make sure no one comes or goes without the orders of a senior officer." He waited for the man to react, but he was clearly already struggling to stay awake, as was his colleague. He watched them a moment, mildly sympathetic, and then changed his tactics.

"You know what, I order you both to sit down … right here." They both looked at him and the relief on their faces was palpable. Mumbling their acquiescence, they lowered themselves gingerly to the floor. They were asleep by the time their arses touched the cold steel.

At the lightest possible dose John had doled out, he estimated he had about three hours. Any of them who had eaten a larger portion at dinner might be out for closer to six or seven. Longer than that and they would be in danger of cardiac arrest and possibly even paralysis. That was not desirable, but it was also unavoidable.

He came to a halt in the weapons con and stepped inside. John approached the main control board and noted the flashing red light on the console. The weapons officer had been proactive and diligent. Clearly he had sensed that he was unable to stay awake and had reacted accordingly. Unable to maintain his station, he had activated the ship's alarm and locked his console. If the ship's communications had still been active, a warning would even now have been sounding at every Admiralty outpost in the world. Only the captain and first lieutenant knew the code to unlock the weapons console. Not even the weapons officer knew it. That way, if he thought he was going to be coerced into activating the ship's weapons systems, he could remove himself from the equation by activating the alarm.

Unfortunately for him, but fortunately for humanity as a whole, John had long since hacked the captain's personal files. He had learned the code and now he pulled the weapons officer out of the way and reinitiated the console. It had to be reactivated on the ship's bridge as well, but first John pulled the launch key from officer's neck and inserted it into its sacred slot.

Next he placed a small device he had co-opted from his own supply of tools and gadgets. It could loosely be described as a servo, not wholly dissimilar from one found in a remote control car, only it was a little more capable than that. While it was, in fact, one of the stupidest robots you would ever have the pleasure of meeting, it was still phenomenally flexible, versatile, and only an inch tall. And it was strong for its size. It had three limbs, each with three knuckles, and a pincer at each end with rubberized sides. It could grip, open, climb, twist, and do pretty much anything you could imagine an inch-high robot doing, as well as quite a few things you probably couldn't. But most importantly, it could do all these things remotely, acting as an Agent's eyes and fingers when they couldn't be there in person.

Setting the small drone next to the key, he opened a mental link to it and instructed it to grip the key with one of its pincers and brace its two free legs so that it could turn the key on his command. Then he ran from the room, wrenching the door shut and bending its handle sharply so that it would stay that way. That should stop any person who was somehow still awake on board from interfering. Stepping over the two sleeping sailors sitting in the corridor, he ran to the nearest staircase and started to ascend to the bridge once more. His internal clock told him he had one hour. Good, he was ahead of schedule. He only hoped the GBMD system was ready too.

On the bridge he sat and waited. Once the Weapons Console Key was turned in unison with the Command Key he now held, John could operate all the systems he needed directly from here using programmed viruses he had implanted long ago. But like everyone else, he now had to wait. If they did not take out all the remaining hubs in their next attack, then whichever was left would have a mandate to return fire. Its presence obviously revealed, it would not only release the viral pathogen they knew was coming, but also bring its laser systems to bear on any and all military targets it could before it was also destroyed. Thousands would die, hundreds of thousands, under its blistering attack. So John knew he had to wait for the Americans to launch, or allow the satellites to pass overhead unhindered until they were in place once more.

The irony was that the only way he would know if the Americans had launched would be because the AI satellites would tell him. So he sat and he listened. He listened to reports and information that the AI and his fellow Agents were supplying while they were within range of the now broken chain of satellites around the planet. He listened to Lana's accusations of treason as she documented them formally. She was now accusing Shahim as well, which was interesting, but she was also accusing Mikhail of being an accomplice. Oh dear, that was nearly half the group, and Mikhail was from an Empire that was, historically, one of Princess Lamati's greatest allies. But then, John thought, so was Lord Mantil, the personality that possessed the body of Agent Shahim Al Khazar.

John sympathized with Lana with a smile. I guess you just can't find good help these days, how will the universe's genocidal maniacs survive, he thought.

While waiting for confirmation of a launch from the US, John also listened to the latest reports from Agent Preeti Parikh as she made her way through Pakistan toward the last place Agent Shahim had been spotted. John frowned a little at the thought. That should be interesting. He had little against Agent Preeti, but she was one of them and he did not spare her too much pity as he thought about what she was walking into. That said, he had faced a surprised Agent once before, and while that element of surprise had been enough to clench victory for him, it had still been a far closer fight than he would have liked.

- - -

Fires still burned in the remnants of Peshawar Army Base as Preeti Parikh drove up. She had 'borrowed' a Pakistani officer's uniform and now she walked through the base with a flashlight, searching for her missing colleague. She answered questions and shouts from the other soldiers patrolling the base in perfect Iranian, which was, interestingly, the most common language in western Pakistan. She was carefully making her way closer and closer to the bunkers and silos in the northern part of the base. They were the last place that Shahim had been seen, but they were also under incredibly heavy guard, and she was having to navigate through the maze of tank groups, machine-gun emplacements, and artillery teams that now surrounded them. After several laps walking in ever decreasing circles around the silos, she had finally made her way to the inner cordon. This was the innermost perimeter around the silos, and there was no way she could just walk passed it. Searching her databases, she came up with a name.

"Good morning, Sergeant, I am part of General Abashell's team. He is expecting me." They all knew the reputation of the general, and immediately set to locating him. The man was a legend, but more than that he was a veritable asshole and known for his furious temper. They didn't even know he was here, but in the confusion after the attack, every unit in the vicinity had responded. It had been a mess, but they had secured the area. It was a little late, perhaps, as the cat was out of the bag, so to speak, in fact, six of them were, but there were ten more HATF-VI on the base, and they did not intend to lose track of any more of them.

As various junior officers inside the complex scrambled to locate a general that wasn't even on-site, Preeti feigned impatience, eventually stepping up to the guard and saying, "Well, have you found him yet?"

The guard shook his head and was about to speak when she carried on, "Incompetent man, find him and tell him that his daughter Sowmya is here."

The man balked. The only person more feared than General Abashell was his daughter. She implicitly carried with her all the power of her formidable father, and was not without considerable military experience and standing herself. Waiting a moment, she assessed the affect she'd had on the poor man and then said, "Fool, I will find him myself." and she pushed passed him into the inner base.

On any other day the guard would have known which senior officers were and were not on-site and no amount of posturing would have convinced him otherwise. But this was no ordinary day, and the guard post, in fact the entire inner perimeter, had only been reestablished a few hours ago. So Preeti's practiced impudence overrode the guards' hastily given orders and they looked after her with a mix of fear, shock, and confusion as she walked into the silo complex.

Unknown to her, the man Preeti truly sought was actually watching her. She was regularly updating the AIs with her position when she could so Shahim had known she was coming from miles away. And now here she was. He was also dressed in a Pakistani army uniform, and also speaking either perfect Iranian or Urdu as circumstances required, so he had managed to blend in with the soldiers as they arrived to defend the base. Now he stood with his back to the small lantern that his guard troop was using while manning the inner perimeter not far from the checkpoint. Silhouetted against the lamp, he watched Agent Preeti head to the bunkers and smiled. While the satellites still roamed overhead, he could do nothing. But thanks to him there was now a yawning gap in those satellites and it was fast approaching.

He felt the AI's call to the Council just as she did. He knew that the gap in the satellites' coverage was now over the Indian subcontinent and coming his way. The AIs could not hope to get Pei Leong Lam online from China so it must have good reason to be calling a Council meeting when it could not get quorum. Shahim hoped he knew the reason, he knew it should be happening any time now.

He watched as Agent Parikh stepped off the path from the checkpoint and discreetly looked up. She angled her face slightly westward toward where she knew the nearest satellite was even now heading for the horizon. Shahim would not look up to join her in Council. He had no answer to the questions they wanted to ask him, and no intention of making some up. But he listened in on the meeting as he had earlier when the first satellite had been destroyed. Soon the others would join as well.

He saw immediately that it had indeed begun. The AI conveyed images to the Council without emotion as the eyes of its three remaining satellites tracked the launch of two hundred missiles from each of the GBMD sites in Florida and Hawaii. While the remaining Council members argued over the source of this new attack, the AI prepared to begin destroying the projectiles using the multipurpose laser systems on each of its three satellites. But as this went on, Shahim noticed Agent John Hunt go silent and his avatar become perfectly still. Hello, this is going to be interesting, thought Shahim as a new set of alarms went off in the meeting. There was a third launch cluster being detected, this time in the western Pacific. The satellites were tracking forty-six objects in the new launch, but they all seemed to be coming from the HMS *Dauntless*.

"Wait," said Agent Lana, "the HMS *Dauntless*? Isn't that your ship, Hunt?" she stared at him, the extent of his betrayal sinking in. Well, no point maintaining pretenses anymore, thought John and Shahim in unison.

As the three banks of missiles drove up through the atmosphere to intercept the orbits of the remaining satellites, John's avatar smiled. He then raised his virtual middle fingers in a very human gesture at Lana and allowed himself a long, hearty laugh before vanishing from the meeting, disconnecting from the Council for the last time.

Shahim, meanwhile, started to walk toward the Agent standing off the road, walking around behind her and deploying his weapons array. She sensed a person approaching but assumed it was simply another guard and so she disconnected her laser link with the satellite, which was rapidly disappearing over the horizon anyway, and closed her array. She was still in shock over the fact that they were under attack again. Without much thought she turned toward the approaching steps, thinking more about the satellites than the man she could hear coming.

Sorry Preeti, thought Shahim as his hands powered toward her head. Time slowed as he focused on the attack, his systems readied and braced. He had been here before, he thought, but before he had been the one caught off guard. His systems blithely factored in every mistake he had made into his tactical options, and also John's errors. John had waited a fraction of a second too long, allowing his hope that he might avoid the fight to delay his attack for the millisecond it had taken Shahim to register that there was, in fact, something wrong.

Shahim displayed no such hesitance.

He let Preeti turn into the blow, but no more. It began the instant his systems said it was time. His left hand came up hard and fast at her face, his first and index fingers pointed, his right hand coming up on the other side to grasp the back of her head and hold it in place. By the time she registered an attack, his fingers were microseconds from impact. Her view flashed an alarmist red as tactical came online, but already his thumb was driving into her eye, stabbing with vital force and precision.

Her hands came up to grab at his forearm as his thumb penetrated her eye socket. Shahim pushed inward with all his strength, focusing all his might on crushing the weapons array and grinding it backward, fighting to crack the lobe behind it and get at the substrate and neural cortices that lay in her skull.

As her hands focused on pushing outward against his left arm, Preeti's right foot came up and over at lightning speed, gathering centrifugal momentum as it went, her high kick connecting with his head like a cannonball. He flinched away, tucking his head down as he saw the blow coming, then felt it resonate through his skull like a struck bell.

He could feel her eye orb breaking, as could she. She bent, shifting her weight and bringing both legs up, hoping to get one between them for leverage. He saw it coming and mirrored the action. For a nanosecond they seemed to hang in midair as their legs all lifted as one, then they were falling, exquisitely slowly, their tactical systems darting and twisting in response to each other as minute, seemingly inconsequential twitches rippled across their bodies. All the while Shahim continued to drive his fingers into her brain, and she fought to gain some purchase against him.

When they hit the ground, they became a writhing mass that seemed to leap this way and that as one limb or another fired outward in their battle, hers ever more frantic, his focused beyond measure. An attempt to lock her foot in between his arms, a parried blow from his sonic punch to deflect her; each sent them skittering in the dust or thumped them both upward to spin and twist in midair.

When he could, Shahim was sending focused sonic needles at her right ear, pounding at the drums there, racking her audio systems and the connected accelerometers that fed her onboard attitude indicators. It would not fool her tactical systems completely, but it gave him microsecond windows when he was working off more accurate information than his opponent.

She knew it too, she knew he was gaining a greater and greater advantage every moment, and she knew her skull would not withstand the punishment much longer. Every time they impacted the ground, she knew her lobe might shatter under the megaton per inch pressure Shahim was still exerting against it.

As alarms continued to blare in her head, she stopped trying to pry his hands free and let her fists go, landing terrific blows even as her options faded. He felt his body register the damage as she pounded his torso and even tried to punch his head with her powerful fists, but he could feel her skull cracking now. It would be over any moment.

He stopped trying to block her feet and fists and instead brought his legs up now to wrap them around her head and neck as well, adding their weight to the pressure his fingers were exerting.

Armed guards were finally converging on them, as if in slow motion, shouting at him and raising their guns. What was he doing? Why was he attacking the general's daughter? Shahim was tired of all the violence but knew he had to stop them. Even as Preeti still wrenched her powerful body this way and that, he set his deployed laser to wide burn flash.

Keeping the setting low so the effect wouldn't be permanent, he fired four flashes in quick succession, turning his head as he did so. In the ensuing confusion, the blinded soldiers clawed at their singed eyes. Preeti registered the flashes, she had not hoped for much help from the soldiers, but it had been a small probability option flashing in her tactical list. It went out. There were not many options left, she thought.

And then were none, as the rupture she had feared finally happened and Shahim's thumb finally penetrated to the infinitely softer substrate within her head. He drove it inward, grinding his thumb around in her skull to crush her synthetic brain.

As her systems started to shut down one by one, she gave in. Her machine consciousness was fazing in and out, shuddering as parts of her mind were torn from her. Deeper within her brain, her personality overlay sent a simple message through her small onboard subspace tweeter to leap the small distance between her and Shahim.

"Why, Lord Mantil, why?"

The Agent did not reply. He might want to try and convert her, as he had been converted, but in the thick of the base's defenses, he'd had neither the luxury of a prolonged debate nor the prolonged battle it would have taken to subdue her without destroying her.

She went stiff. Her mind no longer registered. It was done. As he pulled his thumb from her eye socket, and pried her rigid dead fingers from his arm, he silently considered her question. I asked the same thing, he thought, as he rolled the now stiff, defunct body of Agent Parikh off him and stood up.

He did not ponder it too long. There was much still to do. Hefting her up and over his shoulder, he set off into the night at a fast run. He had to bury the machine that had been his colleague out of sight of the many prying eyes now converging on the site of their bitter little battle, then he had to go and fight another.

Chapter 54: Well Done

The AIs worked with speed and precision, a thousand stimuli driving smooth calculated reaction. They tracked the approach vectors of each of the missile barrages rising into their paths, determining risk potentials and reaction parameters. With this open declaration of war, their gloves came off and instantaneous programming kicked in. Without emotion or regret, they moved forward with standard response protocols, no longer hindered by the whims and bickering of the politically charged Council.

Their goals were no longer of espionage and subversion. Now their mission was one of oppression and disarmament. Inside the three satellites' hulls, vast generators churned, yielding massive swarms of power that thrummed into the satellites' laser systems. Extending the laser mechanisms from their casings, the satellites turned on their own axes, aiming themselves bodily at the incoming missiles.

They selected their targets dispassionately, taking them out in order of approach. While they started picking them off they continuously calculated the chances of destruction and weighed them against other responses. Inside their plated shells they initiated preparation for the launch of the viral pathogens: warming, filling, and prepping the cluster modules and then loading them into their atmospheric entry pods. They had not completed their analysis of the human antigen, and they now surmised correctly that the missile attacks had probably been prompted by the fact that they had discovered the antigen and were planning to counter it.

- - -

On the planet's surface, Agent Lana Wilson had no intention of continuing business as usual either. If these humans wanted war, she would give it to them. She had been stationed at the Atlantic Fleet Submarine Base in King's Bay, Georgia for months now and many people had come to know and like her. She had befriended them and worked her way into their trust. They thought they knew her.

But a wholly different beast walked onto the base today, and she gave but cursory salutations to the people who greeted her as she headed to the main Z Berth building. The Z Berths were a long set of large sheds that abutted the heavily guarded harbor waters of the naval base. The long flat buildings were in fact armor plated and frequently patrolled. They were staunchly guarded because they housed the US Atlantic Submarine Fleet, the greatest concentration of nuclear weaponry on earth. In order to keep their movements secret, the big sheds had no approach above water; no surface ship could enter them or see into them. Great doors both above and below the water's surface guarded the sheds' entrances, and they only ever opened at night, allowing blackened hulls to slip unseen to and from the great berths.

As Lana walked up to the buildings, she saw a group of people staring mutely at the southern sky. Hundreds of miles to the south lay one of the GBMD launch sites that the conspiracy had chosen to fire from. The whole country, indeed the whole world, was abuzz with the news that a massive barrage of missiles was heading into space. But even more amazing to the billions of people watching was that the missiles were even now starting to detonate in mid-flight. The massive cloud of fire rising into the sky was being steadily whittled down. She smiled. Pesky humans and their pathetic weapons. Even now, even when it was clear that they had discovered the satellites in orbit, they still did not have the courage to launch their nuclear missiles at them. GBMD indeed. Nothing but a bunch of kinetic warheads and tactical oxidizing weapons. That may have been enough to destroy the first satellite, but only because the satellite in question had not been allowed to defend itself.

Well, humans, now you get to see what our satellites are really capable of. Now you will see what happens when we bare *our* claws, you impudent fools. And now that you have shown us your true colors, there is no way I am going to carry on lurking in the shadows. New game, new rules. When this attack fails and you eventually get around to launching your nuclear weapons at my satellites, I intend to see to it that you have several less of them left.

As she approached the Z Berth sheds, she felt a surge of disdain for the personnel who were staring at the missile barrage soaring into the sky. She smiled. Enjoy the show, you plebeians, things are about to heat up.

Inside the huge shed, she walked along one of the long concrete jetties that ran between the behemoth Ohio class submarines. As she did so, she continued to review the data being sent to her by the satellites. It was mostly good news, but not all of it. The missiles fired by the GBMD were being destroyed easily, and every calculation showed that they would all be disabled long before any got within effective weapons distance of the satellites they were targeted at. Good, she thought. But something was different about the missiles coming up from the *Dauntless*. They were proving more resistant than they should be, and the AI was unsure of whether they would all be taken out before they impacted their target.

Lana frowned. It was yet another sign of how deep the counter-conspiracy went, but it was also all the more reason for her to upgrade her activities on the ground.

She reached the first submarine's gangplank and stepped up onto the ship's smooth black deck. Of the fourteen Ohio Class nuclear-armed submarines in the fleet, seven of them were maintained and deployed out of King's Bay, with five at sea at any one time. That left two in harbor for maintenance and the mandatory rest period that the crew got between eighteen-month deployments. The Minnesota and Arkansas were in dock at this time, but their normally relaxed refit and resupply schedule had been stepped up because of the unprecedented events of the last two days. With the crews rapidly preparing for sea, Lana was able to slip aboard with little more than a cursory glance at her very real access badge.

She didn't stay for long. She was only going to leave a small device in each. It looked so innocent, she thought. But where she planned to leave it would hopefully prove devastating. The devices in question were the same white phosphorus disks that Agent John Hunt had used to disable the HMS *Dauntless* a year ago. Back then, the disk had proved relatively harmless against the steel of the driveshaft, but inside the chemical boosters of one of the twenty-four behemoth ballistic missiles that each submarine carried, it would be the fuse for a titanic explosion. Igniting the missile's chemical fuel inside the confines of the ship would be like throwing a grenade into a fuel tank, and Lana relished the image of the damage it would do.

Thirty minutes later, as she finished planting the second disk deep within the second submarine in dock, she climbed back out of the long thin vessel. In just half an hour, she had effectively disabled two of America's fourteen nuclear submarines. When she was ready, she would have the satellites send the kill command to the disks using their large subspace tweeters. The signal would find them wherever they were and the submarines would be destroyed. She should have started doing this a long time ago, she thought as she stepped back down to the jetty. By now she could have set charges on over half of the Atlantic fleet. Admittedly, that was only one part of the United States' vast nuclear capability, but it was still something. She was bored with this covert tiptoeing. With the satellites under attack, it was time to start fighting in earnest.

Suddenly she stopped in her tracks. Something was awry. It had been thirty minutes since she had entered the base and her charges were now set. It was extremely unlikely that they would ever be found by anyone, they were simply too small and appeared too innocuous. But now something else was happening. The satellites were worried, something was very, very wrong. Her eyes glazed over as she communed with them, seeing with their eyes, their machine thoughts melding with her own.

Just as the missiles fired by the *Dauntless* had proved more resistant than the AI had anticipated, something now seemed to be wrong with the second phalanx of missiles launched at the other two as well. After they had finished destroying all of the initial kinetic missiles, they had begun to focus on the fewer but larger tactical explosive missiles behind them. But the second wave was proving just as resistant as the javelins the *Dauntless* had thrown. With cold-hearted precision, the calculations changed. Predictions were reevaluated.

The whole world of Agent Lana Wilson had revolved around the capabilities and information the satellites had given her. Because of them she saw the world with omniscient eyes. She had been able to see around corners. She had been able to see the movements of her colleagues and her prey. She had been able to read any e-mail, access any file. The thought of losing these abilities disturbed her on a fundamental level.

It was painfully clear now that there was a pervasive counter-conspiracy in place and she knew that she needed to find these conspirators and make them pay. She would start with Neal Danielson and Madeline Cavanagh, she thought. To think that she had talked to that petulant little bitch Madeline and then let her go. She had listened to the whining of the Council and allowed herself to be duped by the machinations of the traitors that must have infiltrated it.

Most notably, John Hunt, that Nomadi shit. Yes, I know who you are, you lying bastard. You fucking snake. I'm going to kill everyone you ever spoke to on this god-forsaken planet. And then, when our glorious Armada arrives here to wipe this planet clean, I'm going to send a message back to Mobilius and see to it that every member of your family is raped and butchered. You bastard in your shroud, John Hunt, now I only hope I find you before the Armada gets here so I can kill you myself. So I can rip you apart with my bare hands. And once I have torn your limbs from your machine body, I will stake what's left of you to the ground and make you watch as I wipe this pathetic race from the face of this planet. I'll make you watch as I make it my planet, traitor. My own, personal, fucking world.

As these thoughts coursed through her, she considered the charges she had just placed. The thought of losing the satellites was like contemplating an amputated limb, but she had to be practical. If they were gone, they would not be able to detonate the disks remotely. Changing her plan slightly, she activated a link to the two disks, setting a two-week timer on each of them. Good. The submarines should be at sea by then, fully submerged and en route to whichever station they were assigned to. The charges would go off while the ship was deep undersea and with any luck they would kill everyone aboard.

Now, what to do next. She walked away from the gangplank along the concrete jetty and headed for the exit. But something else was amiss. Where was everybody? The jetty had been a hive of activity only fifteen minutes beforehand when she had boarded. Where was everybody now? No doubt they were all looking at the death throes of her satellite guardians. Yes, she thought, they must be outside.

But something in her told her that could not be right. Surely all of them wouldn't have left their posts. Without breaking stride, she pulled a pair of sunglasses from her top pocket and put them on, deploying her weapons system from behind her left eye as she did so.

As she exited the big shed to the quad outside, she paused. What the hell was this? The quad was deserted. But arranged in a wide semi-circle around the door were twenty-six men in full combat armor. Her tactical computer scanned the area and assessed the threat. Four of the soldiers were lying prone on the ground behind M249 tripod-mounted machine guns. The rest were carrying CAR-15 commando assault rifles. All of them were focused on her.

A voice rang out from one of the commandos, "We have you surrounded. We have orders to shoot you if you do not comply with our demands. Lana Wilson, you are to lie down and spread your arms out. We will secure your limbs and you will be transported to a secure facility for questioning. You have been under surveillance for some time now. You cannot escape. We know who you are."

She looked at them. Machine guns? They wanted to take her down with machine guns? So her cover was blown. Of course it was. John Hunt must have supplied it to them. So, you think you know who I am, do you? OK, let's see.

Her machine mind was already calculating her tactical options. As she contemplated her response, it was arranging its recommendations into escape and evacuation, or E&E options, and Stand and Fight options. Like she was going to flee these children. Dismissing the E&E list, she looked at her Stand and Fight options, noting the computer's analysis of the weapons ranged against her. The CAR-15 rifles fired at a rate of seven hundred rounds per minute and carried thirty rounds in a cartridge. No doubt they would fire in two teams, one half of the twenty-two soldiers waiting till the first had exhausted their cartridges before firing, allowing the first group to reload while maintaining a constant rate of fire. That was what she would do.

Assuming these were trained Navy Seal troops, as they clearly appeared to be, she should expect a high hit rate from each of them. That meant that she should anticipate being hit by an estimated 128 rounds in the first second. OK. She could take that. She should assume they would be using armor piercing rounds, but they didn't know the kind of armor they were dealing with here. Her tactical analysis continued on to the four prone men with their belt-fed machine guns. The M249 fired one thousand rounds per minute, and unlike the assault rifles, they could fire continuously. At a glance, the belts they had strung were two to three hundred rounds long … each. They also had a higher caliber and higher muzzle velocity than the CAR-15. They would come at her at around 915 meters per second.

Those would hurt. Combined with the assault rifles, that would mean she would be facing around 180 bullets per second.

Half a second had passed since the ultimatum. It was more than she had needed. She selected her response, locked in the attack protocol and initiated, telling her machine mind to select its targets automatically.

The automaton that controlled her body took over. Wide beam flash laser first: blind assailants. Bang, bang, bang. The machine mind turned her head, spreading her white hot laser flashes in a wide coverage arc. Not hesitating a moment, it then focused the laser's beam and ramped up the power, simultaneously initiating her sonic punch. Starting with the machine gunner lying where her head was already facing, she braced her stance and fired, blanketing the prone man with blistering heat and a powerful shockwave. The unfortunate man and the two men holding assault rifles either side of him were thrown back, their faces ablaze with laser heat, all of them dead before their bodies came to a halt, but as she annihilated the first machine gunner, the others opened fire. They had not been totally unprepared, it turned out. They were wearing heavily polarized goggles to protect them from the flash beam.

Twenty assault rifles and three machine guns roared at her, and a wall of lead rammed her against the shed behind her. Lana was stunned as the bullets hacked at her torso and upper legs. As she hit the wall of the shed, the fire continued, thudding into her like hail into a sandbag. Though the bullets were not doing her significant damage, the rate of fire was massive and unrelenting, and she flailed under the blows, trying to bring her weapons systems to bear on the remaining attackers. After two seconds, she had been hit by over three hundred rounds, each travelling at over a thousand miles per hour. Her human clothes were shredded. Her human analog hair blasted from her head as she raged against the punishing blows.

Her reactions were absolutely perfect though, information cruised through optic fibers in her body at the speed of light as she used all her phenomenal muscle power to focus her weapons on another of the big machine guns. As the first wave of the assault rifle team exhausted their magazines, the rate slowed almost imperceptibly before the second wave took up the slack. But in the millisecond gap, she was able to get her head round, and as her vision blurred across one of the remaining M249s, she fired immediately, blasting the placement and killing the gunner and three other seals standing near him.

Two of the big guns left, she thought. Now the fire was noticeably lower than before, but the pounding abuse was starting to fray and tear at her compound skin. They were getting to her. Five hundred rounds of armor-piercing lead, each round igniting as it hit her skin. The few bullets that either just missed her or careened off her toughened shell slammed into the shed wall behind her. From the other side of the wall, her crouching silhouette could clearly be seen against the armored plate where she was pinned. With the massive rate of fire, they were starting to hit the same exact spots on her body two, three times in a second, and even her resilient armor was not able to recover in time. She screamed inside at the flood of machine pain.

Bucking under the blows, her mind was registering each and every hit, and updating her on her status. Fucking gnats! Fucking mosquitoes! I'll kill you all, you fucking bugs! Beneath her woven skin, a layer of black superconducting shielding was starting to show.

In her mind, a portion of her anger was saved for herself. When the blinding flash beam had failed, she should have immediately changed tactics, she thought. But she turned her fury at her own complacency on her attackers and screamed, then selected another tactical option. Instantly her legs braced and launched her on a high-arching trajectory. The fire immediately subsided as the gunners' target suddenly went airborne. The highly trained seals instinctively kept their guns on her as she jumped, but the machine guns were tripod mounted, and it would take precious moments to point them skyward. Even the few rounds still hitting her were enough to throw her body back as she flew, but she had accounted for this in her calculations, and her sharp angle still had her coming up in an arc to land amongst the line of seals still firing at her.

Then a wholly different round hit her.

Her machine mind informed her instantly, flagging the round that had just slammed into her chest, even as the impact stopped her in midair. At four thousand miles per hour, that last shot had been vastly higher in power than the others. Then another hit her from a slightly different angle and she slammed back to the ground not five feet from where she had jumped from.

SHIT FUCK ASSHOLE MOTHERFUCKERS. They had her pinned by snipers as well. At least two .50 caliber, rail-mounted guns were targeting her position, her machine mind informed her. It was already calculating their positions from the angles of impact and it would have them in a moment. As if to help her calculation, two more rounds careened into her, and, along with the resumed fire from the two machine gunners prone on the ground, the blows sent her body rolling and sliding along the concrete quad floor back up to the wall she had been pinned against only three seconds ago.

FUCKING BASTARDS! she screamed in her head. She was losing. Soon they would have stripped through her outer skin to the superconductor shielding beneath. They couldn't keep this fire up forever, but with the snipers now bringing much higher power, higher caliber rounds to bear, she was in serious trouble. She called out to the satellite above her. It was furiously attempting to take out the missiles that were closing in on it, and its outlook was looking ever bleaker than hers. The missiles were not coming down as they should, it reported to Lana and the others, the secondary barrage was shielded somehow, and they were getting close. Too close.

She ordered the satellite to stop protecting itself and redirect its laser to take out the gun placements around her. If it was doomed, at least it could save her. But it was not taking orders from Council members any more. Its protocols were set. Now that the humans clearly knew that the satellites were there, it had a new mission protocol and Lana saw the view from above as it initiated the viral deployment. As the upper atmosphere over Florida, Hawaii, and Singapore burned with the explosive fury of the approaching missile barrages, the satellites were already firing tiny missile pods out to their left and right, sowing the seeds of viral death onto the humans below.

Fucking machine, Princess Lamati thought, not noticing the irony, and she looked at her tactical options once more. As another set of high-power rounds hit her back, she crouched into the fetal position and protected her face. Her metal ribs were cracking, her skull was dented in two places, her left shoulder had been hit by three bullets at once and it was dislocated. She was dying.

But her hatred for the filthy race she had been sent to exterminate gave her options no sane person would have considered. OK, you little fuckers, she thought. You think you have me? You think I am down? Well, ask yourselves this: what, exactly, do you think I was doing at the base in the first place? And with that she reached out with her internal subspace tweeter and found the two tiny disks she had planted inside the Ohio Class submarines behind her.

Why don't we see ... how you like ... this, she thought, and she sent the kill code.

To the Navy Seals arranged around her, the dull thuds of the initial explosions could not be heard above the barrage of fire they were laying into the seemingly indestructible woman on the ground. But those seismic rumbles were but a precursor. Each disk had each been placed inside of one of the submarines' many massive ballistic missiles. When their white heat encountered the chemical fuel stored in the missiles' engines, it triggered an exponential chain reaction. The fire ripped through the reinforced steel plating of the huge ships like paper, engulfing their hulls in less than a second and igniting the remaining twenty-three missiles' chemical boosters on each submarine as it went. From overhead, the huge shed suddenly ballooned at two points, the roof expanding outward even as it was absorbed by the two expanding balls of fire coming from the submarines' missile tubes.

Sixty years of perfecting missile design meant that not one of the nuclear warheads on board actually went thermonuclear, but the sheer volume of explosive material on each submarine created a blast radius over three hundred meters wide. This solid wall of flame washed outward from the submarines like a wave of death, covering the area around the sheds in a matter of seconds. The team that had been firing on Agent Lana Wilson was instantly baked at a thousand degrees as the fire engulfed them.

Within two more seconds, two thousand men and women in the surrounding buildings were dead.

And in the middle of the hellish cyclone, the Agent lay, curled in a ball, her skin flayed from her body, the midnight black of her core exposed to the nightmare. She remained crouched for a moment as the shockwave passed, protecting her relatively fragile eyes from the blast.

All her touch sensors had been built into the fake skin that had coated her and so she watched the scene using the satellite's doomed eyes. She saw the explosion clearly from space as the shockwave washed outward. No doubt they would report that one of the submarines had suffered an accident. Either way, the combined nuclear material from two nuclear submarines would soon irradiate all of Georgia and northern Florida before it started its path northward.

In its last few moments, the AI informed Agent Lana Wilson that by deliberately setting off nuclear weapons she had violated the mission parameters. It was a pointless accusation, but the AI did not understand such things. Even as it counted down to its own destruction, and that of its two remaining cohorts, it still diligently logged and categorized the information in a database that would be obliterated within moments.

The final missiles closed in, and at the last moment the surviving rockets detonated. As if in response to the huge fireball that Lana had set off, the upper atmosphere answered with three silent but massive explosive clusters around the globe, each consuming the last of the Mobiliei's satellites.

Lana lay alone. The silent aftermath of the submarine eruptions matched by the eerie silence of the now extinguished satellites' data feeds. Her view from space was gone. She felt the loss of their vast databanks and aerial weaponry like the loss of a parent and mourned.

Carefully she uncovered one eye. Her calculations told her that the initial blast should be washing upward now, creating a small mushroom cloud above her. With her eye's sensors reporting that the fire had dissipated, she stood and surveyed the scene. The black of her body matched the charred remnants of the base. A huge steam cloud rose from where the shed and its two wards had been, but bar that the base was flattened for about a quarter of a mile. An eerie silence lay over everything, matched by the deafness of her collapsed eardrums.

A lone black figure in a circle of obliteration, she stood. Hairless, skin burned off, deaf and lame she alone had survived the blast. She stepped forward gingerly, balancing her good leg against her broken limb, and she felt vulnerable for the first time in her life.

She needed to get away from here. They would be coming with everything they had and she could not survive that again. Soon they would be evacuating Jacksonville and the surrounding area and she needed to get out before they set up radiation checkpoints.

Limping away, she came to the edge of the blast radius and found the first of the explosion's survivors. The man was moaning and crawling away, as if to escape his own charred, mangled legs. She ignored his cries for help and limped onward until she spotted a Humvee. The base was slowly responding, variously running toward the disaster or away from the aftermath, depending on how much they understood about the radioactive cloud that was even now bathing them all with certain death. Jumping into the Hummer, she ignored the lack of keys and tried to use the sheathed wires in her finger to start the vehicle, but like so many of her systems, it was unresponsive. She accessed her memory banks and quickly retrieved information on how to boost a car.

A minute later she was driving away from the base at speed, running down anyone who got in her way. Her machine mind estimated that she was going to need approximately three weeks to reconstruct the systems that the attack had destroyed. Princess Lamati had never had to run from anything in her life. But now she needed to hide. She needed to repair and regroup. And then she needed to decide how best to punish the humans for what they had done.

Chapter 55: Violent Reactions

The large Situation Room under the White House echoed with cheers. Gone were the doubts of the past hours. Gone was the skepticism of the last few nonbelievers. Neal and Barrett shook hands. Neal was laughing. They had done it. Barrett looked him in the eye.

"Enjoy it, Neal. It's our first victory. We can relax for a bit. We are safe … for now."

Neal's smile faded a little but remained strong, his eyes becoming pensive at his friend's proviso. He nodded slightly, repeating his coconspirator's words, "For now." Then after glancing around the room, Neal asked in a quiet voice, "Any news of Jack and Martin?"

The colonel shook his head almost imperceptibly and took a sip from his glass of water, his eyes telling Neal to leave the subject alone. Barrett noticed something across the room and Neal picked up on his sudden consternation and followed his stare. Admiral Hamilton was talking on one of the room's many secure phones and he looked deeply concerned. Neal and Barrett glanced at each other and then turned as one to make their way over and see what was happening.

Halfway across the room, they were intercepted by an excited Jim Hacker, all smiles and pats on the back.

"Gentlemen," he said, stopping them in their tracks, "wow, I must admit, I had my doubts. But when those missiles started to get picked off. Holy shit!" he laughed, "Half a million bucks a pop and those bastards were swatting them like flies. But then they came to your bad boys in the rear and no more easy takedowns for them, huh? Slam! No more, huh? Bam! Wow, what a thing. I tell you, I would love to have seen their faces when they realized we had that advanced shielding, right?"

Barrett looked at the man and smiled, as did Neal, his infectious enthusiasm warming them. The colonel replied pleasantly, "Yes, Jim, hell of a thing."

Then Jim became suddenly serious again, his expression changing with an ease only politicians and actors are capable of, and in a businesslike tone he went on, "Listen, Colonel, Neal, I know you've told us this is just the beginning, and I think I can speak for the president when I say that this effort is going to enjoy the administration's full support from now on. We're going to need to start a task force to handle this, and I know the president will want you and your team involved."

Vindicated by explosive proof, Neal listened to the man's words and knew he was no longer the outsider trying to be politically sensitive in order to be accepted. He had been proven right beyond all reasonable measure. And now the president, this man, and this entire room all knew it. Something in him gave a little and his smile changed minutely from an ingratiating one to one bordering on patronizing. He no longer needed to bend to these people; they needed to bend to him. Placing his hand on the chief of staff's forearm, he looked the politico in the eye and interrupted the man's calculated overture.

"Jim, you don't mind if I call you Jim, right? Listen, I think that we should get something very clear. My team and I have been working on this for nearly a year now. We have had direct contact with the Agents, we know who they are, where they are, and what they are capable of. Now, don't get me wrong, I appreciate your sentiment, goodness knows having the support of the government, and hopefully of other world leaders as well, in time, will be essential as we start hunting down the remaining Agents and preparing for whatever is coming next."

Jim nodded and was about to reply but Neal pressed on, getting to the crux of his point, "But as we enter the next stage, Jim, I think it is very important you remember that you're involved in this solely because we needed something from you. Now that this first step is complete, you are absolutely right to say that we are going to need a task force. But I think you are a bit off the mark about our level of involvement."

Jim looked at Neal and raised his hands placatingly, "Neal, my friend, whoa. I'm not trying to say you aren't the sole reason we were successful here today. Goodness knows I am sure I speak for the president when I say you have our deepest gratitude. There's no reason to be defensive, Neal. Make no mistake, we're going to need you for the next phase. You have …"

"Jim … Jim," said Neal, his smile becoming even more patrician, "please, stop, listen to me, Jim, listen. I'm not saying for one second that we won't be involved in the next stage. You couldn't stop us if you tried." Neal glanced at the colonel who was staring at him agog and fought the urge to smile as he said, "What I am trying to say, Jim, is that you were mistaken in saying we would be merely 'involved' with your 'task force.' Jim, right now you are talking to the people who are going to be *in charge* of that task force."

Light dawned on the chief of staff's face as Neal finished his point, and Neal's voice became deadly serious, "Over the past year, my friends and I have successfully planned and executed a massive military operation right under the noses of both the American government and the very satellites we have just destroyed. If you think we are now going to become some ancillary part of this 'task force' of yours, you are sorely mistaken."

Neal held the man's stare a moment and then his smile returned like sun from behind a cloud. He patted Jim on the back once more and said, "Now, Jim, I am sure you will have lots of questions, and we can get started on those soon enough, but for now I want you to listen very carefully to the colonel here. As head of the air force branch of the new task force, he has a detailed list of the key people we are going to need on the team, and a plan for our initial projects. For my part, I am going to leave you in his inordinately capable hands as I have some other matters to attend to." And with that, he nodded, grinned broadly at the colonel, and walked off to check in with the obviously distressed admiral still talking on the phone.

In the wake of Neal's newfound confidence, Jim looked at the colonel as if searching for some sanity in a world gone mad. Jim Hacker was a political puppeteer of the highest order. He got people to do what the president needed them to do by any means necessary. And he realized now that being told his business by a political nobody was actually harder for him to swallow than the events of the last few hours had been.

For the colonel's part, he was only slightly less shocked. It was a side of his scientist friend that Barrett hadn't seen since they had first met back at the Array so long ago. Now he was seeing it with the weight of a hard-won reputation behind it and he had to admit that it was good to see the old Neal Danielson again. He was surprised only because Neal had been absolutely right when he said that Barrett had a plan. Ever the organizer, Barrett did indeed have a list of the people the task force would need, a preliminary one at least, and some initial action items that they should be working on.

He allowed himself a brief smile and then returned his thoughts to the stunned Jim Hacker, placing a conciliatory hand on the chief of staff's shoulder, "Jim," Barrett smiled in spite of himself, "don't look so distraught. Look at it this way. The man who just saved humanity has offered you the opportunity to approach the president with a comprehensive list of action items for his new task force, and a strong recommendation for its leader. Something tells me you can find a way to make that work for you?"

Jim looked at him. He had just been chastised by a White House science advisor and now he was being offered political advice by an air force colonel. But he wasn't foolish enough to miss the fact that said advice was sound. He had no intention of being the man that stood in the way of the people who had just orchestrated the destruction of the single greatest threat humanity had ever faced. Nor had he gotten where he was by allowing pride to get in the way of taking credit for someone else's good ideas. And so the White House chief of staff looked at Colonel Barrett Milton with surprisingly genuine deference and asked politely how he could be of assistance.

Across the room, Neal came to rest at the admiral's shoulder and looked at him. The senior man looked discomforted, like he had just heard that he had a terminal disease and the incongruity of the expression on a man such as the admiral made Neal uneasy. Neal's first thought was that something had gone wrong with the attack on the satellites, and that somehow one of them had survived. But no. This was not a face of despair, it was a face of regret. The admiral had done something wrong and it was clear that whatever the consequences were they were shaking the man very deeply indeed.

Only a truly significant loss of life could perturb a man with the admiral's extensive combat experience. But what could the admiral have done that would have cost people their lives?

It came to Neal in a moment and he shook his head. Both he and Ayala had worried that they would not be able to control Tim Hamilton once he was on the team, and they had been right. Looking at the senior officer, Neal knew that the man had gone after Lana Wilson, his rage at her having come into his home, and her use of his son as a pawn in her scheme, it had all been too much for him to overlook. And by the looks of things, whatever he had done had gone horribly wrong.

"Admiral, what did she do?" Neal said quietly.

The senior man looked at the scientist and tried to assess how much the man knew. Then he looked around the room. The colonel and Neal had established clear ground rules when they had brought him into their conspiracy, but he was the most senior officer of the United States Navy and he did not take orders from a colonel, let alone an air force colonel. But now he knew that he had betrayed their trust. More than that he had done so at huge risk, and the results had been worse than he could have imagined.

He drummed up his strength and readied himself for the other man's righteous anger, "Neal, I … I was very discreet, and I listened to everything you said. I prepared the team using all the knowledge we had about them. I told them all her …"

Neal didn't judge, but he was not gentle either, "Admiral, you went after Lana, didn't you? You sent a team after Agent Wilson." the other man did not nod, but he did not deny it either, his eyes were firm. Neal carried on, "What happened to them, Admiral? What did she do to them? No, wait, don't answer that. I know what she did to them." He shook his head, "How many did she kill, Admiral? What are we dealing with here?"

"More than you can imagine, Neal, more than you can imagine."

Neal stared at him a moment finding himself unable to be angry in the face of the violent distress the admiral was clearly suffering. After a second's pause, Tim Hamilton took a very deep breath, composed himself, nodded to Neal, and then stepped past the scientist into the center of the room. Neal looked after him wondering what he was doing. His answer came when the admiral, speaking with the full force of his authority, took the floor.

"Excuse me. Everyone. Everyone, can I have your attention, please?"

The room fell silent at the admiral's booming voice. Neal, standing behind him, noticed that several worried-looking aides were handing out sheaves of papers to key people in the room. Whatever news the admiral had, it was clearly starting to come through official channels as well. That did not bode well.

The admiral spoke to the attentive faces staring up at him in a clear contralto, "The brief given earlier highlighted that the satellites we have just overcome were only one part of the team that was sent to subdue us. Well, while they were by far the most lethal part from a destructive point of view, they were, in fact, only the minders of the real team. We had one of that 'team' among us here in the United States." The room reacted predictably, glancing instinctively at their neighbors, but the admiral held up his hands in a calming gesture, "No, no, not in this room, though if she had have been left unattended she would almost certainly have ended up here in good time. The Agent assigned to America was named Lana Wilson, and up until an hour ago, she was a lieutenant in the United States Navy."

He seemed to catch his breath a moment and then went on, "I myself actually had the displeasure of meeting her, and I can tell you that she would have had no trouble fooling each and every one of us if the good Colonel Milton, Neal Danielson, and their team had not warned us." Some folks glanced at Barrett and Neal, but for their part Neal and Barrett's eyes remained fixed on the admiral.

"With the destruction of the satellites, I took it upon myself to attempt to apprehend this Agent, assuming that she would go into hiding once the satellites were destroyed and we may never get as good a chance to take her.

"At this point, I would like to stress that neither Neal nor Colonel Milton had any knowledge of the operation. Only myself and the head of the navy Seal team I dispatched to apprehend her were aware of it."

The room was silent. The president looked concerned, and in any other room the chief of staff or one of the joint chiefs might have silenced the admiral so he could be debriefed in a controlled environment. But this was the Situation Room. The only person who could silence the admiral was his only superior—the commander in chief himself—and the president had no intention of cutting the report short.

"No doubt we will be receiving more detailed reports shortly, but at this time I can tell you that the team attempted to apprehend the Agent as she departed a Z Berth shed in King's Bay submarine base just under an hour ago." There were several gasps and a couple of whispered expletives as the location sunk in. "Details are sketchy but it is clear that only one of the thirty-person team survived. The rear comms man contacted me from a car on a highway, heading north. He had been in charge of comms relay and thus had not been part of the actual team that engaged Ms. Wilson. From his report, the team was actually partially successful in suppressing the woman, but ..." he paused, obviously emotional, then pulled himself together and continued, "but as they closed in to engage her at close range she apparently somehow managed to set off some kind of explosion aboard one of the Ohio Class submarines docked at the base."

Several people spoke at once, but the president's voice soon trumped them and he asked the question everyone was trying to vocalize: "What kind of explosion, Admiral? Those ships carry ... Jesus, Tim, they carry enough firepower to destroy half of Florida."

The admiral looked at the president. As they both well knew, each and every Ohio Class submarine carried twenty-four ballistic missiles, each of which was armed with a 475-kiloton warhead. By comparison, the missile that destroyed Hiroshima was only 22 kilotons. But the admiral did not feel like correcting the president by saying that each Ohio Class submarine in fact carried enough firepower to destroy the Western Hemisphere, and instead set the room somewhat at ease by saying, "While my man reported that there was no thermo-nuclear detonation, an observation his survival definitely supports, it is clear at this point that the radioactive material aboard at least two Ohio Class submarines, including that in their onboard reactors, was compromised."

The president found a nearby seat and lowered himself slowly into it, stunned into silence, trying to catch his breath as he stared at the floor, "Jesus h. fucking christ." he whispered.

While the room considered the ramifications of the admiral's comments, Neal glanced at the colonel, and then spoke to the room as whole, "OK, ladies, gentlemen, may I suggest we reconvene this meeting immediately? Let's take our seats and get some more information in front of us. We have a lot to discuss."

The room responded instantly, protocols kicking in as well-rehearsed roles came in to play. Reports had already started to come through and for a couple of minutes no one spoke as aides shuffled and copied briefs, and superiors got updates and prepared to answer questions. The president stayed in the chair he had collapsed into and the room arranged itself around him, setting the scene for the second part of the most extraordinary meeting of the United States joint chiefs in history.

As the room reacted to the crisis, directing the country's mammoth military and governmental machine as it went, Neal kept a part of his thoughts on his two friends flying silently, unseen, on the other side of the planet. America may be focused on the fires burning in southern Georgia, but any moment now Martin and Jack would be starting fires of their own. And the people they were trying to save would probably not be grateful.

Chapter 56: Thermobaric Defense

"Jack. Jack!" Martin shouted from his seat at the controls.

"Yes, Martin, I'm coming. Is everything OK?" said Jack, wiping sleep from his eyes.

The flight deck of the B-2 was split into two small sections. With the long patrol missions the B-2 was designed to fly often taking upwards of twenty to thirty hours, the crew needed some basic amenities onboard. There wasn't much, a small cot, a bathroom, and several small lockers packed with dried foods, an extensive medicine cabinet, and plenty of powdered Gatorade. These pleasantries were located in a small compartment aft of the cockpit, with the access hatch through which the pilots entered the plane coming up between the two.

For this particular flight, the space was made even more cramped by the addition of the two unconscious pilots on the floor of the rear section of the flight deck. The dart gun that they had used to sedate the plane's real pilots was only designed to last ten minutes or so, so Martin had administered an intravenous sedative soon after takeoff and every five hours since then to keep them under, a timer on his wristwatch warning when the two bound pilots needed to be re-dosed.

Martin had done his best to arrange the two sedated people as comfortably as possible while Jack had taken the plane up to its cruising altitude of 40,000 feet. As the attack on the satellites raged above southern Florida, they had flown southeast over the US to the Atlantic, where the plane was supposed to fly a patrol pattern over the Mid-Atlantic and Caribbean.

The US had spent billions of dollars in order to make the B-2 Spirit Bomber virtually invisible to radar and they had been so successful that they had actually had to install a beacon that made it visible to air traffic control while it was in US airspace. Theoretically, they were supposed to use it in Allied airspace as well, but typical mission parameters required that the beacon be turned off when leaving US airspace unless otherwise directed, a policy that suited Jack and Martin's purposes just fine.

After a rendezvous with a KC-135 tanker plane about three hundred miles off the coast of Florida, they had begun their long flight east. Flying high over northern Morocco, they had been careful to stay out of sight of the extensive NATO military presence at Gibraltar, and then they had angled north up to the Mediterranean so they could trace a long path east over the sea, bypassing the airspaces of Southern Europe and Northern Africa all the way to Cyprus. Preferring to risk a flight over Turkey than either Israel or Egypt, they had then flown up over western Turkey, and from there they had entered the final part of their convoluted journey to the skies over Tibet and far northern India.

After eight hours in the air, Jack had finally acquiesced to the pleas of both his copilot and nature's call and taken a break, leaving a nervous but resolute Martin to mind the plane's systems and autopilot. Jack had insisted that he not be allowed to sleep more than an hour, and then he had clambered over the sleeping pilots into the bathroom.

The bathroom was a small cubby, three feet by two feet, with small seat built into the wall. Like a commercial airplane bathroom, only distinctly less luxurious. There was no sink, no running water of any kind, in fact, only some disinfectant wipes in a dispenser attached to the wall. Because of their two unwitting passengers, there was no way of closing the door to the toilet anymore, making the process even more demeaning, but military people were not known for their coyness, so Jack had matter-of-factly dropped his pants and done what he had to do before stepping back over the comatose captives and into the cot that ran the length of the small rear section of the flight deck.

Nearly three hours later, Martin felt he had gone as long as he could without Jack's input. Reports had been coming over the radio of the conflagrations above Florida, Hawaii, and Singapore, and if their information was correct, then they should be approaching the first pod deployment area soon. When, after thirteen hours in the air, the plane's powerful radar system started to pick up the first of the virus pods entering the atmosphere over the former soviet state of Turkmenistan, Martin knew he had given his friend as long as he could. He needed him on deck.

Though the satellites were now destroyed, they had left a terrible legacy. In their final minutes, they had begun deploying the viral pathogen that Madeline and Ayala had worked so hard to counteract. As the team had predicted, their antigen to the super-virus had not spread as quickly as it needed to in some of the more sparsely populated areas of the world. John had described to the team the way the aliens' virus would be deployed using viral cluster pods launched in a wide spread pattern to either side of the orbital path of the satellites. The pods would then fall to Earth in two bands three thousand miles apart, sweeping east to west. Once the pods were in the lower atmosphere, they would break apart, releasing their deadly cargo, which would then filter slowly to the ground to seed the world with a plague of biblical proportions.

There was a specific point in each pod's descent when the pathogen was most vulnerable, and it was in that window that Martin and Jack now intended to try to stop some of them.

Working in the team's favor was the fact that the pods were only being actively distributed in that three-thousand-mile-wide band, though 'only' was used loosely here. Once the pathogen was on the ground, it was designed to spread the old-fashioned way, through the sputtering coughs and sneezes of the sick and dying. So outside that pod's band, it would be subject to the same limitations as the antigen, which had the advantage of being deployed months ago. But any countries that were inside that three thousand mile wide band and were not already sufficiently protected by the antigen would be devastated by the disease. Their populations would be literally wiped out in a matter of weeks.

With less than 40% of the populations of several countries in the Middle East immunized with the antigen that would mean a 60% kill rate. Tens of millions of people dead.

So into this weakest spot in the world's defenses flew a single B-2 Spirit Bomber armed with more explosives than a flotilla of World War Two flying fortresses. They knew it wouldn't be enough to completely stop the killing, but it might limit it, and that was the best they could hope for.

"Jack!" shouted Martin, somewhat impatiently.

"What, Martin? I said I'm on my way." said Jack, swigging some Gatorade as he climbed back up to the cockpit. Settling into his seat the empty pilot's seat, he checked the instruments with experience bordering on reflex.

"Three hours, Martin!" he exclaimed when he saw the mission clock, "Shit, what the hell were you thinking? I said not to let me sleep more than an hour. God damn it, we're nearly over Tibet." he did not look at Martin as he said this, he was using the plane's nine-screen control system to page through the extensive information available to him. Any moment now they were going to hit their target deployment area and this whole mission was going to come to a head.

Setting his mind at ease that they had indeed not had any radar hits from ground-based units yet, Jack turned to the upper atmospheric radar with which they were hoping to track the pods as they entered the kill zone.

All across the planet reports were coming in about the debris from the massive conflagration that had transpired above humanity's heads. From the initial face-off in the skies above Azerbaijan between the HATF-VI Missiles and Russia's Gorgon Interceptors, to the three massive missile storms that had been launched from Florida, Hawaii, and the disabled HMS *Dauntless*, no part of the sky had been left unblemished by the fires of Earth's arsenal. Rumors abounded about the cause of the great conflict being raged in the skies, but within the world's great militaries, the return fire of the alien satellites had not gone unnoticed.

Over the next few days, the international team that had been born of the curiosity of a hitherto unknown scientist named Neal Danielson would reach out to those governments and let them see the critical information that they had gathered. They would all hear of the double agent John Hunt and what he had done for them. But for now the world was at the highest level of alert since the end of World War Two, missiles were prepped, fighters were fueled and on the tarmac, armies were gathering, and the weapons of doomsday were poised and ready. No one was under any illusions as to how difficult it was going to be to get the world to finally lower its guns and to turn their focus to the real threat that was on its way.

But Jack and Martin had no time to wait for political stability. True to their word as only machines and monks were, a widely spread volley of viral pods were even now making their long, slow falls towards Earth, showing as evenly spaced blips ahead of the B-2. The pods they were seeing had actually been dropped way over the horizon, but the speed of the satellite's retrograde orbits had slung them around the globe as they fell toward the surface. All across the globe these pods were slowly falling, except over Europe and Africa, which would have been the drop zone of the satellite Shahim had long since dispatched.

Jack stopped talking as he surveyed the tactical radar readouts in front of him, then looked at Martin, "We have about five minutes left before we launch the first rocket. You ready for this?" He looked very seriously at his friend, "You know what happens when we launch, don't you?" Martin nodded, but Jack elaborated so he could be sure his friend knew the consequences, "All our stealth goes out the window. We will be launching munitions over foreign soil without their permission, heck, without even their knowledge, or that of our own government. We will be shot at by everything that they can mobilize against us, and eventually they *will* hit us."

Martin did not make light of it. He got it, and he held his friend's stare. They both got it. The looked at each other for a moment longer, then Jack nodded, his respect for his colleague's bravery showing in his eyes. Jack reached across and held out his hand. Martin looked at it a moment, then extended his own. The two doomed men shook hands across the central console of the plane and then put their concerns behind them.

"OK, Martin, switching to deployment mode. Strap in and put on your face mask."

They both secured their straps and pulled on their helmets. Jack had his in place in seconds, but Martin fiddled with his face mask for a moment before he got it settled. The oxygen now flowing, they were prepped for maneuvering, and Jack reached down to switch the plane's screens to deployment mode.

The view on the screens in front of Martin changed instantly. As a missile specialist, he was more familiar than most with the missile deployment systems on US warplanes, but he had never had as good a view as this before, and he whistled. Paging through the screens in front of him, he selected the target acquisition screen and started to plot in the first pod's trajectory, setting the computer to track its course and plot a path to intercept. Next, he switched to the armament screen and began activating the first of his one-thousand-pound AGM-158A cruise missiles. The system automatically initiated fuel stirring and warming devices and a thirty-second deployment pre-system check started. Sensors and systems went to work making sure the engine would ignite when it was dropped from the cargo hold of the plane.

"OK," said Martin, "I've plotted the target path on screen."

"I see it, time to launch window … six minutes." said Jack, "How are we doing on missile prep?"

"Green light in thirty seconds. Transferring coordinates to the missile now." Martin moved slowly but methodically through the process, double-checking himself as he went. Speaking to no one in particular, he said, "Select target coordinate package … target coordinate package selected; assign package to missile bay … package assigned to missile bay; select missile … missile selected; lock-in target coordinates … target coordinates locked; awaiting pilot approval …" he looked up at Jack, who was smiling.

"Pilot approval awaited?" said Jack in a lighthearted mockery of Martin's grave tone.

Martin eased up a little, chuckled, then raised his eyebrows, "Well?"

"I'm on it, Martin, cool your jets." said Jack, still laughing.

Jack looked at the screen and checked the numbers. Martin did not mistake Jack's levity for brevity, and saw the experienced pilot deliberately review all his entries, as he was trained to do. "Looks good, package approved, launch approval set. Ready to lock in?"

"Ready." said Martin, looking at him and taking a breath. They both readied their hands on the switches to either side of them, deliberately designed to be as far from each other as the cockpit's width would allow. Jack glanced at Martin and said, "Locking in … now." He turned the key on the left of his console as Martin turned the key on his right and the control screen beeped, a countdown timer appearing a moment later.

It was out of their hands now. They could stop the launch any time up to the moment the missile left the bay, but unless they changed their minds, the plane was now going to do everything else itself, the possibility of human error removed from the equation.

It was a long few minutes. Martin occupied himself by scanning for the next pod, higher in the atmosphere but coming at them fast as it headed west. Once the first missile was launched at the first pod 250 miles away, they would bank hard and send another missile after that second pod, then a third, and onwards until they had used up their payload or been shot out of the sky.

Jack went through his prelaunch routine. Running through his maneuver and responses in his mind, preparing his reflexes. The B-2 had a significant armory to defend itself, including everything from decoy flares, to explosive jacket air-to-air missiles; they could fool incoming missiles and even disable enemy planes. They were mostly delaying tactics, rather than actual game changers, but they might be the difference between life and death, between being blown up and having enough time to eject.

At one minute out the cabin started beeping loudly, the plane was preparing to open the missile bay. It would significantly reduce their stealth capability, but then, so would the huge rocket flare of the missile they were about to launch, not to mention the explosion that would light up the sky fifteen minutes later.

The screen counted down and Jack positioned his hand over the autopilot switch. He already knew the course he wanted after the launch: a one-hundred-sixty-five-degree hard turn to starboard. Heavy banking turns always made the plane more visible to radar, but they were already going to be announcing their position to the world and he intended to get his turn completed at the same time, rather than giving those that would soon be trying to kill them a second radar blip to aim at.

The whole feeling of the plane changed as the huge doors in its undercarriage opened. The smooth lines of the delta wing were suddenly interrupted and the two men could instantly feel a ripple in their world.

10, 9, 8, 7, 6, 5, 4, 3, 2, 1.

A camera in the bomb bay showed Martin the missile as its clamps released and it dropped away. Two seconds later its ramjet engine ignited and it rocketed ahead. Jack was watching the same image from his console and the moment the missile's engine ignited, he flipped off the autopilot and wrenched the plane off its heading. The G-force pressed Martin into his seat and he grunted, "Jesus, Jack, is this thing supposed to turn this hard?"

He strained at his belts as his view changed dramatically. He had a brief glimpse of the missile powering off into the distance out of the cockpit window before the horizon angled to more than forty-five degrees and their hard bank obscured his view of their first launch. Oh well, Martin thought, remembering the long nights he and Madeline had spent building the warhead, I hope the damn thing actually works.

With the big hold doors straining shut behind them, Jack leveled the huge plane out again and Martin took a breath.

"We should call that first one Sylvester." Martin said to Jack after a moment's silence.

Jack looked at him, confused, and Martin smiled, feeling a strange peace now that they had sealed their fate and it was out of their hands. He chuckled as he looked back at his screen, saying in an aside, "Because the cat's out of the fucking bag now."

Chapter 57: Red Sky at Night

Alone now, unleashed, the missile surged forward with singular purpose. Fully one-third of its mass was given over to the ramjet engine that drove it forward. Its body was white and completely encased in fiberglass. Halfway along its length, two stubby wings swept back from its midriff, matched by an equally short tail fin. An air intake emerged from the top of the missile just behind the wings like a mouth gasping for air. That mouth fed the missile's ramjet with supersonic oxygen, which was then superheated and fired out of the rear of the missile at blistering speed. A long, blue-white jet trail streamed from the nozzle at the rear of the missile like God's Bunsen burner, propelling it forward at over a thousand miles per hour.

Two hundred miles ahead the first viral pod continued its descent through the atmosphere, itself burning with the heat of atmospheric deceleration. At the missile's breakneck speed it covered the distance between them in only ten minutes, descending on the pod with fury. As the missile got ever closer, the pod hit an exact point in its descent and, just as Agent John Hunt had said it would, the pod began to break apart. With most of its initial velocity now spent, the heat screens were no longer needed, and now it could release its cargo to disperse on the winds onto the unsuspecting populace below.

The pod and the missile flew toward each other.

The final mile between the AGM-158A and its target would be covered in only three and a half seconds. As this threshold was passed the missile reacted, triggering the explosion that would rip it apart. In perfect coordination, the engine cut out and two small bar explosives halfway along the missile's length detonated, slicing the missile neatly in two. The heavier rear started to fall away immediately, taking the spent engine with it. A moment later a much larger explosive in the core of the front half of the missile fired. The remaining fiberglass casing of the fuselage disintegrated as fifty smaller cylinders were blown outward by the shaped central charge. The small cylinders flew outward and forward, forming a wide circle, the explosion propelling them away from each other, even as the missile's massive momentum continued to carry them forward and down over the descending viral pod in a wide circle, like a massive rope lassoing the alien capsule in midair.

As the small cylinders fell level with the larger alien pod they all ignited. With machine precision they detonated at once, their thermobaric payloads exploding in a ring of fire around the pod. The fire swelled inward, sucking in oxygen in a massive gulp. At the center of the blast a vortex of flame was created, rushing upward. The disintegrating alien pod was swept up by the 100m wide inferno, the beautiful and terrible fire roasting its target's deadly cargo to a harmless crisp.

A moment too soon and the pod would not have begun to disintegrate yet, leaving its shielding in place to absorb the heat of the blow. A moment too late and the virus would have already been too dispersed, flowing on the wind in ways the computer tracking systems on board the missile could not have predicted.

But John had been very precise about the altitude they had to hit the pods, and Martin had listened. With this prescient knowledge of his enemy's behavior, Martin had designed the missile to meet the virus pod at the exact point it needed to, creating a massive storm of fire in the sky over Kashmir, and saving almost two hundred thousand people in the rural farms below from certain death.

- - -

On the ground, the first of the people of Kashmir to wake in the predawn darkness looked to the sky and shook once more with fear. Seeing the fiery ring above them, the farmers and shepherds out with their flocks amongst the cold dew assumed that one side or the other was up to no good once more. They had long since stopped caring which side it was that was firing, as long as they survived. The only thing they cared about now was how the other side might retaliate.

For those in the military, this new fire in the sky was something unknown, as it was for the insurgents still running into the mountains to escape the wrath of an incensed Pakistani government. Knowing all the horrors they had each wrought on the region, the sight of this new, unknown weapon was disturbing.

As reports of the explosions started to run around the region, all of these groups wondered and worried about what new way their enemies might have found to attack them. But two the Agents that still hid among them knew precisely what was happening.

"They know about the viral pods." thought Jean-Paul Merard, standing in a briefing room on the Allied Force Military Base near Kabul, Afghanistan. Over the last few hours, his world had changed completely, as it had for all the Agents. There could no longer be any doubt that John Hunt had betrayed them, and Jean-Paul fumed at the thought.

But his desire to find the traitor was, for the meantime, secondary to what Agent Jean-Paul Merard should do right now. It would be foolish to think that Agent Hunt had not also revealed the identities of his colleagues. Therefore he should assume that his cover was blown and that he needed to get off the base, and soon. His immediate instinct was to reach out to the Council and get their opinion on his next steps, but that was no longer possible, and he realized that for the first time since his personality had been implanted into this machine he was now free to make decisions of his own. Now that the satellites were dead, the Council was all but moot.

He needed to act, and he needed to decide what to do without input from the others. Looking into the night sky he knew that he could serve multiple goals with one plan. Get off the base, hurt the military force he had been sent to infiltrate, and find out what was taking out those viral pods as they attempted to deliver the final stanza in the satellites' requiem.

Turning, he started to make his way across huge base. He wasn't going to wait for the world to come for him, he was going to take the fight to them, he thought, as he rounded the corner and the fenced-off Rafale Fighter hangar opened up in front of him. Six of the powerful beasts sat there, prepped and ready to go. There was lots of activity on the base, which had been on high alert since the attack on Peshawar had begun. The small, nimble fighters were on standby, fueled and loaded. Their standard armament was mostly air-to-ground, but they also carried four sidewinder air-to-air missiles. Flashing his pilot's ID, he walked past the doubled guard, and into the quad.

The six fighters were deadly, capable of wiping a field clean of a hundred men in a matter of seconds. Like the American F-22 and European Typhoon, they mounted Gatling guns in their forward wings that could tear through steel with devastating ease. Unlike the F-22, they were not stealth capable, but were still much harder to pinpoint than any previous generation of fighter in the sky.

Jean-Paul reviewed the mission log for the next patrol. He was a copilot for now, supposedly learning the ropes from a more capable pilot. He chuckled bitterly, like they could teach *him* anything. He was not assigned to the next patrol, but he turned and headed to the pilot's locker room anyway, to talk to the next pilot and copilot team as they prepped for their patrol mission.

"Michel, Etienne, ca va?" he shouted, as he glanced briefly around the room to make sure no other pilots were showering or getting changed. With pilots on long shifts, he knew it was unlikely any of them would be in the locker room unless they had to be, and he soon confirmed they were alone. Stepping back to the locker room door, he flicked the latch and returned to the aisle where Michel and Etienne were putting on their flight suits.

The two men looked up as Jean-Paul approached, smiling before continuing to pull on the bulky, one-piece suits. Stepping between them, he reached out with his left hand and grasped the neck of Michel, while simultaneously bringing up his right leg and whipping his booted foot out into the jugular of Etienne. He registered the feeling of the man's neck snapping through the sole of his boot, and turned his gaze to Michel, who was scrabbling pointlessly at the hand around his neck.

As his instantly dead copilot slumped to the ground, Michel stared wide-eyed at the man he had known as Jean-Paul Merard, struggling at the hand pinning him against his locker.

"I want the takeoff clearance code, Michel." said Jean-Paul.

Michel glanced from Jean-Paul's steady eyes to the body of his friend and copilot on the floor. "What the fuck are you doing, Jean-Paul? I will have you court-martialed for this." He wrenched at Jean-Paul's hand once more and called out to his colleague with mounting anger and concern, "Etienne? Etienne, are you all right?"

The other man did not move, and Michel became enraged. Ignoring the extraordinary strength of the hand pinning him against his locker, the pilot's left hand grabbed Jean-Paul's shirt and his right fist barreled into Jean-Paul's face, colliding with it with all the force the burly pilot could muster. But the Agent's head did not give an inch, and Michel's fist splintered and cracked against the immovable skull of his assailant, the bones shattering as if he had slammed them into a brick wall. The pilot screamed as the incredible pain tore up his arm, forcing his whole body to spasm.

Michel's face wrinkled in agony, tears streaked down his face, and Jean-Paul smiled, "Michel, please, let's not make this more painful than it already is." He reached out with his free hand and wrapped it gently around Michel's broken fist. Applying the slightest pressure to the shattered ball of flesh and bone, he saw Michel tense and convulse with the pain, his eyes rolling back into his head as the fractured joints ground together.

Jean-Paul saw that if he applied any more pressure the man would pass out, but that wouldn't be acceptable. When a pilot was given his flight assignment, he was given a unique, mission specific, six-digit code to call in to air traffic control before take off. Together with the flight plan given to the tower by fighter command, they must have this code to take off, or the tower was under strict orders to shoot them down. There were no exceptions in a hostile war zone like Afghanistan. The base had numerous SAM sites and anti-air cannons ranged around the base and they would shred anything that didn't have a preapproved code.

Jean-Paul reduced the pressure on Michel's fist a little and watched the pilot suck a breath in through strained lips, a small sob escaping his mouth as he despaired.

"Michel, if you don't give me the code, I'll just have to do this to the mission control sergeant instead. Either way I'm getting that code. Do you want to be responsible for another man going through this as well?"

Michel wept. A moment ago he had been chatting about his next home-leave. He was scheduled to return to France in two months. It was not that he was not prepared to die for his country, but not like this. Not at the hands of one of his own men. Rage came over him again, "You motherfucker, Merard, we don't have enough troubles here already? Fuck you, kill me, I'm not helping you …" but his rant was cut off as the Agent began to squeeze once more.

The man bucked under the pain, tensing and wrenching at the hand holding his neck as his broken fist was squeezed, but to no avail. Jean-Paul desisted again and smiled, "Michel, please, death is the least of your worries. Death is going to be the gift I am going to give you when you tell me the code. No, no, Michel, you have to *earn* death. If you want to say something brave it should go something like this." Michel stared at the mad man and was horrified to hear an exact copy of his own voice come out of Jean-Paul's mouth, "Torture me all you want, Jean-Paul, I will never tell you the code."

The Agent mimicked Michel's strained face as he mocked him, then laughed coldly, "Michel, I am not here because I want some irrelevant plane. I am here for reasons you cannot imagine. And I am going to get what I want. Even if I have to kill everyone on this base." At the last words, Jean-Paul's face turned vicious, his next words coming in a venomous whisper as his civil veneer cracked to show the monster beneath, "So why don't you give me the fucking code, you pathetic little cockroach, or I won't just kill you; after I am done here I will go and find your wife and children in Nantes, and I promise you that once I find them I will brutally skull fuck all three of them. Do you understand?"

The pressure returned to Michel's hand and he tried to scream, but the noise was stifled as the Agent's other hand tightened around his throat. Despair flooded into Michel's mind as he started to black out. His remaining good hand grabbed desperately at the zip pocket on the arm of his flight suit. Jean-Paul looked at it and released the man's crushed fist, reaching up and opening the pocket and withdrawing a small printed slip, six digits neatly printed at its center.

"Michel, Michel, tut tut. You are supposed to destroy this as soon as you have memorized it." Without ceremony, he then twisted his left wrist violently and snapped the pilot's neck, killing him instantly. But he did not let go of the man just yet. After slipping the sheet of paper into his own pocket, he opened the pilot's tall locker and jammed the man's limp body into it. It was a squeeze, and he felt a few more of the dead pilot's bones break as he thrust his body in there. But soon he was closing and locking the tall thin door and turning to the other dead man lying on the floor.

"Away we go, Etienne." Jean-Paul said, hefting the still warm body of the copilot up and opening the dead man's locker. Unceremoniously, Etienne was wedged into his proxy coffin as well.

- - -

It had been a strange four months for Dassault Rafale pilot trainee Serge Latral. Not long ago he had been a happy, hopeful inductee in the French Armee de l'Air, on track to join the prestigious Rafale Attack Group. He had worked hard. He and his young wife had sacrificed a lot. But a few months into his training he had met an attractive, well-dressed executive in a bar, exactly his type, and the beautiful man had attempted to seduce Serge. Tempted after three years of monogamy, the drink had broken through to his vigorously suppressed bisexual urges. The next morning had been one of regret and worry. The beautiful man was nowhere to be found, and Serge had snuck from the anonymous hotel room.

All had seemed well, but it was not long before another, older man approached him from the Direction du Renseignement Militaire, the secretive French military intelligence service. He carried photos of the fateful night and threatened to release them to Serge's wife and his military superiors, ending the man's hopes of moving forward in the career he had dreamed of for so long. It was not that the French military was biased against homosexuality; long before such ridiculous policies as 'don't ask, don't tell' the French military had taken up the stance of France's population as a whole: your private life should be just that. But having a given proclivity revealed once you were already a powerful person was very different to having a reputation hanging over you when you were trying to break into those higher ranks, and such a revelation would have damned Serge in the service as much as it would have in his home.

But the French spy had not been there to crush Serge's ambitions. He was there at the bequest of a certain French foreign minister to enlist young Serge for an important job. He was needed to shadow another recruit in the Dassault Rafale training program ... that is, if he wanted to stay in the program at all.

Having agreed to do what they were asking, Serge now found himself stationed in Afghanistan with Jean-Paul. It had seemed innocent enough at first; a relatively innocuous, if distasteful task that he had completed with ease. But now all hell was breaking loose around them and Jean-Paul Merard was nowhere to be found. So Serge had gone searching for the other pilot on the large Allied base.

During his infrequent communications with his agency handler, he had been told again and again that a time may come when the other man, Jean-Paul, might try to leave the base, and that this would happen in tandem with some notable world events. He had not been told more than that in any of his cryptic briefing sessions, but if ever something had qualified as 'notable world events', it was the last two days.

He searched the base frantically, checking guard logs at each of the three main gates. His ward was not in the officer's mess, or in their barracks. At last he headed to the briefing room where they had advanced tactical classes each day with the senior pilots. But as he walked over to the low prefabricated building he passed the fighter hangar.

Wait, was that, holy shit, that was Jean-Paul now, in a flight suit, heading to one of the planes. They weren't scheduled to go up, and they certainly weren't scheduled to go up without a pilot. Sergio broke into a run, heading to the guard post. Flashing his pilot's ID just as Jean-Paul had, he called out to the other trainee.

"Jean-Paul, qu'est-ce qui se passe?" Jean-Paul did not turn around at first, but as the other trainee approached him, he stopped and turned to him.

The quad was wide open and flood lit at all times. It was surrounded by guards, and the airfield's tower was just next to it, between the hangar and the nearby runway. While theoretically Jean-Paul could easily handle the base guards with his onboard weaponry, his short-range lasers and sonic punch would be useless against whatever was taking out the virus pods above. The base's air defenses, meanwhile, were an active matrix, meaning that if the tower didn't actively stop them, they would shoot any foreign object out of the sky. Which all meant that he needed the powerful jet fighter to take down whatever was up there, and he couldn't take off if the tower had any reason not to allow him safe passage. So in the middle of the wide-open quad, he turned to his fellow trainee and smiled like an old friend.

"Shh, Serge, not so loud." Jean-Paul whispered, reaching out and taking the other man's hand as he ran up. Serge looked at him, confused, and was about to speak when Jean-Paul carried on, "Thank God you are here." said Jean-Paul conspiratorially, "Michel and Etienne are drunk, they didn't know they were scheduled for a patrol. They begged me to take their flight so they don't get grounded. Now that you are here you can join me, come on, get suited up. It's just a standard patrol route."

This wasn't right. This was a long way from right. Something in Serge told him that this, right now, was the reason that he had been assigned to watch the other cadet. It was happening. But the same instinct also told him that he needed to tread very carefully. He had three choices. Shout out for the guard to come over, go with his fellow recruit and attempt to discreetly alert the guard that something was wrong, or say that he didn't want to go, and hope that Jean-Paul let him go quietly.

Jean-Paul did not let go of Serge's arm while the other man considered his options. He stood there waiting, a smile on his face like he was trying to get Serge to do something as innocent as go for a beer.

"I don't know, Jean-Paul. Maybe I should talk to Michel, make sure he is OK with me going along too?" Serge said, fighting to keep the quiver out of his voice, but Jean-Paul was taking something out of his pocket. Serge looked down. It was the slip the captains were given by fighter command with the clearance code. There were only two ways Jean-Paul could have gotten it from Michel: either he was telling the truth and Michel really did want Jean-Paul to take the patrol duty, or ... Serge set the thought aside, to think along those lines was just paranoid.

But in truth, either conclusion brought Serge to the same response. He had to stay with Jean-Paul and try to alert someone when he had a chance.

And so, reluctantly, Serge nodded to the other junior officer, and eventually responded with a weak smile. Jean-Paul's smile broadened in reply, "Great, my friend, great. Come on, let's get you suited up quickly and get aboard." Not letting go of Serge's arm, Jean-Paul set off toward the locker room once more, and the twenty-three-year-old felt himself propelled along by the powerful grip of his erstwhile friend.

Once in the locker room, they came across two other pilots suiting up. Jean-Paul cursed his luck with inner shouts of frustration, but externally remained beatific. He would have to actually take Serge with him. One more complication, but not an insurmountable one, by any means. Another pest to be dealt with once he was away from this place.

- - -

The black sky seemed to shudder with the fourth explosion as the B-2 tracked down its targets one by one. It had been thirty minutes since Jack and Martin had fired off the first missile and they had enjoyed a quick run of successful hits since then. Having banked after the first strike, they were now on the same course as their targets, heading east over Kashmir and northern Pakistan. As the fourth fireball ballooned upward, Jack veered slightly to avoid the worst turbulence, but the plane still bucked as the explosion-induced vortex warped the atmosphere.

Jack turned to Martin briefly. The other man was staring mutely at the massive plume of flame with a mix of reticence, professional pride, and childlike awe. Jack smiled with him but was disturbed by a sudden beeping from his console. Paging through the screens, he came to the radar and located the source of the alarm. Multiple bogies inbound from astern.

"Martin, I have multiple contacts at vector four-niner converging on our position at Mach 1." said Jack in a worried tone, "Pull up the radar analysis screen and read off the diagnostics to me."

"Radar Analysis Screen … got it." said Martin, as calmly as he could manage. He selected the view and scrolled through the information on screen, assessing what they were facing.

"I make it six bogies, converging on our position in a v-formation. They're coming up from the southwest so it looks like they were scrambled out of Peshawar."

"That must be the Pakistan air force coming to check us out." said Jack. He glanced at the mapping screen and checked his readouts, his face creasing into a frown as he checked their position.

"Shit." Jack said, "They're only 300 clicks out, at that speed they'll be on us before we reach the border." He shook his head, "how did they scramble a response so quickly?"

"Well, we knew they were going to come looking." said Martin, as calmly as he could manage.

"Yeah," replied Jack, "but I guess I had hoped that Shahim's rampage down there would have delayed them more … or even grounded them permanently."

Martin nodded, but then replied, in as hopeful a tone as he could muster, "We were either going to have to face these guys or our own fighters scrambling from our bases in Afghanistan. Surely these guys don't have anything too serious to throw at us?"

Jack barked a sarcastic laugh at the air, then shook his head.

"They didn't have too much a while back, maybe," he said, "but that was before we sold them thirty-six more F-16s a few years ago. I have no doubt that is what they have sent to check us out."

Martin stared at Jack aghast, but the other man merely nodded. Then they both turned back to their respective screens.

"Just F16s, then." said Martin quietly.

- - -

"Command Central, this is squadron leader Pelishar One. What do you have for us?" The voice of the lead F-16's pilot came in clear over the radio in the command bunker.

It had been hell on the base for the last two nights, and god knows what new horror these latest aberrations foretold. Luckily for General Abashell, he had not been here for the worst of it, but he was here now, and the legendary commander had been directing the battered base's defenses since his arrival a few hours earlier.

After bringing the base back under some modicum of military lockdown, he had faced a slew of preposterous rumors about the seemingly superhuman nature of their attackers. That had culminated in reports that his own daughter had been killed on the base, something he had quashed with a stern call to her real commander back in Islamabad, a quick word directly with her just to be sure, and then a diatribe on what he would do to the next person who brought him a report that include the word 'superhuman.'

After events had seemed to be somewhat under his control, reports of an even greater wave of launches had started to come in. They had heard of the missile launches in the upper atmosphere around the globe, and god knows he knew of the earlier launches from the very base he now commanded. As he had feared, the Russian military machine was reportedly now mobilizing in response, and the Kremlin was calling for full access to Pakistan's nuclear arsenal. Then, of course, there were rumors that all the missile launches were somehow linked.

But General Abashell had even more pressing concerns. Three hours earlier, as news flooded the world's television and radio networks about the explosions in space, they had started to pick up some sort of debris falling into the upper atmosphere over Eastern Pakistan and sweeping west in a long arch. It had been hard to tell how big the objects were, but there was a string of them coming down in a line stretching as far as their radar could see.

Then, without warning, one of them had detonated, forcing them to dismiss the theory that this was merely debris from some rogue satellite's demise. The explosion had been so high and so bright that people from over sixty miles away had reported it. A massive circle of flame in the night sky blossoming inward and upward in a great plume. He had not seen it himself, as Peshawar was hundreds of miles to the south of the line of falling objects. But radar and surface-to-air missile installations along the Chinese and Indian borders had sent back images of the detonation.

Maybe it was some weapon he did not know of, some leftover munitions from the attacks over Singapore, Hawaii, and Florida. Either way it was clearly something that demanded immediate investigation. That had been half an hour ago, but he had responded as quickly as the base's depleted capabilities would allow.

Scanning the command bunker, he quietly cursed the absent air force colonel that was supposed to be his liaison. He had dispatched the exhausted man to personally oversee the launch of six of the base's remaining F-16s. Many had apparently been damaged by the insurgents' attack, yet another example of the supposedly superhuman efforts of the vermin attackers, or the equally phenomenal failure of his own people.

His chest surged in anger, but he wrestled his frustration under control as his aide de camp looked askew at him. There was no point in shouting any more than he already had, so instead he mastered his mood and said quietly to the efficient major by his side, "Go and find that bloody air force colonel, Major Duranda, and get him back here. I am tired of doing his job for him."

The major nodded his head and left without ceremony, making for the guarded doors of the command bunker as the general turned back to the panel of computer screens in front of him. At least his birds were in the air and en route. Soon he would have more information. Hearing a bad report was better than not having a report at all. Information was everything, and he needed to know what the hell was going on up there.

An operator at one of the consoles spoke up, "We're receiving reports of a fourth explosion, sir, same as the first three."

"Same altitude?" asked the general.

"Yes, sir, forty-nine and a half thousand feet." said the operator with brisk efficiency.

Good, thought the general as he regarded the operator in question, at least somebody knows their job. So, same altitude as before, then there is a pattern. General Abashell liked patterns. He liked predictability. In his opinion, everything was predictable if you had all the relevant information to hand. So, he thought, let's look for the next logical step in that pattern.

"Get me a line on the next object and an anticipated point where it will hit the same altitude."

The operator did not respond for a moment, and the general felt his ire rising once more in the second before the man reeled off his response.

"I already have estimated coordinates for the next explosion, sir, and a bearing for the squadron to intercept."

Hmm, thought the general, his next order anticipated. Not bad. He glanced at the nameplate on the top of the operator's console and made a mental note.

"Sergeant Gupta, inform the squadron commander to come to that heading and altitude, and give him an estimated time to detonation. Let's get some eyes on one of these explosions." said the general, and the operator acknowledged quickly, already reaching for the comms key in anticipation of the command.

- - -

"Acknowledged, Command Central." said the squadron leader a moment later, then, flicking a switch to go to tight beamed plane-to-plane comms, he passed on his orders to his pilots.

"Pelishar Wing, this is Pelishar One, come to nine-zero-niner, on my mark. Line up on the parallel, vertical recon formation, 2K splits from 40,000ft. I have the point."

The other pilots acknowledged briefly and efficiently, and the squadron leader initiated the maneuver. With cool precision the planes broke formation and started to spread out. They were entering a vertical search pattern with the lowest plane at 40,000 feet and the next two thousand feet above him and so on, up to fifty-two thousand.

As the planes climbed and spread out onto their new search grid, the command bunker operator updated them on the latest information. The squadron had actually seen the last explosion as a yellow-orange spark on the horizon, and now they were starting to get intermittent blips from the next pod as they closed on it. If it followed the same pattern as the others, they should be in visual range when the next explosion occurred. It was still night, but the sky was starting to be permeated with the first deep blue hues of dawn. Soon the line of the horizon would resolve itself against the brightening sky and the stars would bleach and fade behind the coming day.

Maybe the new day would bring some clarity to the strange tori of fire punctuating the sky over their violence stricken country.

Fifteen more minutes passed as they closed on their objective, then suddenly the top four planes in the formation reported seeing a blue band streaking through the sky. At that precise moment, a second radar blip registered briefly on their radar screens, too small to be visible to Central Command. There was something else out there, but a moment later it was gone again, leaving only the faint blue band ahead of them.

The squadron leader had heard about this. They had received reports from Afghanistan of the radar ghosts formed by America's advanced stealth fighters and bombers, and the squadron commander's curiosity grew as he considered what they might be about to find.

- - -

General Abashell nodded as the operator gave him the reports of a fresh radar signature being patched from the fighter's radar arrays, and reached up to stroke his chin. Only the Americans had planes equipped with proven stealth technology, though the Europeans and Chinese each claimed some level of it themselves.

"Get me the liaison to the Allied forces, I want to speak with him immediately." said the general to the air, expecting an automatic response from his aide de camp. But none came and he remembered that he had dispatched the man to look for the errant air force colonel.

"Radio," he barked in anger, "contact flight control, and find out what the hell is going on over there. Where are Major Duranda and that colonel?"

The operator at the radio console spoke briefly into his headset and then turned to the general.

"Sir," he said nervously, "I have Major Duranda online, sir, and he is requesting to be put through to you."

"Very well, put him on speaker."

The operator patched the radio connection through the main speakers and the voice of the general's aide de camp filled the room.

"General," said the unnaturally amplified major, "I have a disturbing report from the air field, sir."

The general paused a moment, waiting for the report, then realized his assistant was being diplomatic, hoping to give his report to the general in private, as was customary. But the general had no time for such niceties, "Well, Major, go on." he said loudly, "We are in the midst of an active engagement; where is that god damned colonel?"

The major's voice was clearly strained as he reluctantly gave his report, "Sir, the colonel is unconscious, sir. They found him a few minutes ago. He has received a serious blow to the head and is not responsive at this time."

"What!" said the general, incredulous.

"Yes, sir, they found him near to the runway, sir. We are moving him to one of the field medical facilities being set up on base, sir, but there is no information at this time as to what happened to him, as he was not injured in the original insurgent attack." The voice hesitated a moment, then went on, "But that's not all, sir, they found another unconscious officer with the colonel."

The general's mind raced, he had personally toured the base perimeter twice since they had gotten it back under Pakistani army control. There were over seven thousand troops in and around the base at this moment, actively deployed; to think that an insurgent had managed to escape detection was beyond imagining. But the aide was not done.

"Sir, the other officer—" came the aide's voice once more. There was a pause, the room silent in anticipation as the aide prepared to deliver the last of his report, "The other man they found, sir, is one of the F-16 pilots; one we thought was even now in command of Pelishar Four, sir. I have checked and rechecked the pilot's lists extensively, sir. I am afraid we have no idea who is flying that plane."

The general paused a moment and then spoke quickly, his mind resolving to action, "Major Duranda, get things under control there and make sure that news of this does not go any further than is absolutely necessary. Radio, get me a closed link to the squadron commander on Pelishar One. Mission command, I want another squadron in the air, stat and en route to their position. Under no circumstances is that plane to leave Pakistani airspace in one piece."

The radio operator acknowledged and the general's face creased in focused anger. Time to find out who the hell was flying that plane.

Chapter 58: Showdown

Shahim's acute hearing registered the flick as the fixed link to the squadron leader was broken, and started to wonder why that had happened. They were fast approaching zero hour for the next detonation and his advanced eyes could see the blue streak of Jack and Martin's latest missile in the distance, even as his radar picked up the supersonic missile as another green blip on his increasingly crowded screen.

At this point there was no reason for the squadron leader to drop off comms, not at such a critical juncture, unless he was talking on a closed loop with Command Central. He twitched as his radar started to show a slight shift in the formation. The squadron leader was starting to drop back from his position at the bottom of their 12,000-foot-high stack, and he was climbing as he did so.

Shit.

Shahim needed to see what was going on. The plane's radar was more effective than his eyes over long distances, but at close range he trusted his robotic eyes more, despite the darkness. Without shifting his plane's position in the formation, he gently teased the stick to the right and his plane rolled smoothly, the horizon spinning in front of him, and with his head bent backward, his eyes panned the air behind and below him to pick out the blue flare of the squadron leader's jet as it fell out of formation. In the momentary blur as his plane spun, his powerful vision zoomed in on the other pilot, thousands of feet below, and saw the man looking up at him. Shahim could see the other man's lips moving as he stared up at Shahim's plane.

They know, he thought.

- - -

"I see him, Command Central, wait, he just rolled his plane. Wow, that was tight." Squadron Leader Anish Nagaraja whistled silently as he watched the maneuver. To spin that tightly without breaking formation was difficult, and required extraordinary precision. "This is no amateur, Central, he knows what he's doing."

"Squadron Leader, this is General Abashell," came the response through the squadron leader's dedicated radio connection, "I want you to position yourself astern of him, and then we'll open a link and order him to return to base. Then you can escort him back here. Whatever happens, I am ordering you not to let that plane out of your sight. It must not leave Pakistan. Is that clear, Captain? You are under strict orders to bring Pelishar Four down if the pilot attempts to leave Pakistani airspace."

The squadron leader acknowledged. He was furious. The rightful pilot of Pelishar Four had been seriously injured, and some imposter had infiltrated his command. All his pilots were a tight-knit group, and the now comatose Captain Mysore Kumara was also a friend. Captain Nagaraja would have no qualms about firing on this interloping bastard if the need arose.

- - -

Ahead of them, still unseen, the B-2 surged on. Jack scanned the horizon as Martin updated him on the squadron's movements. The fighters were closing fast, and darkness would not hide the big bomber much longer. They were still 150 miles from the Afghan border. They had to stay hidden for just twelve more minutes.

But their ability to be subtle was becoming an ever more distant memory, he thought, as their fifth missile reached its target: 3, 2, 1 …

The sky lit up with another violent detonation ahead of them as the circle of thermobaric grenades cooked another of the alien virus pods at two thousand degrees Fahrenheit. Five minutes to the next missile launch. The B-2 would still be in Pakistani air when it fired again, and the fighters would be in visual range of them when that launch lit up the big bomber's position.

Jack and Martin knew that no amount of stealth could hide a 172-foot-wide plane in a morning sky if you were close enough to actually see it.

- - -

"Pilot of Pelishar Four, this is Central Command. You are ordered to return to base immediately. Is that clear? You will be escorted back to Peshawar Base and taken into custody. If you do not comply with these orders, you will be shot down. Is that clear, Pelishar Four?"

Oh, it's eminently clear, thought Shahim, while noting the fifth explosion far off in the distance. He had regretted the need to knock out the F16's pilot, but the need to be in a position to help Jack and Martin was far more important. As he considered his position, he wondered if he should reply. But then his tactical systems alerted him to another option: he could turn the fact that he had been discovered to his advantage.

If he made a break east, away from the B-2's course, then the squadron might follow him, giving Jack and Martin the precious time they needed to get over the border. After that, his colleagues would be in Allied airspace, and less likely to be blasted out of the sky. They would still be actively pursued, but even a stolen B-2 was still worth $22 billion, and Allied forces would be far more hesitant to destroy it than the Pakistanis would.

Choosing this over the array of tactical options his mind was giving him, Shahim decided not to respond to the repeated calls from his squadron leader, well, not in words, at least, and instead he jerked his plane hard right, accelerating as he did so. Let's see what this thing can do, he smiled, as the jet powered away, the thick blue flame focusing to a needle point as his afterburners kicked in.

- - -

"Central, this is Pelishar One, he is breaking formation, banking hard right. I am pursuing. Shit, he has engaged his afterburners while still in the turn. This guy is crazy, Command." Then, flicking his comms to include the rest of his squadron, he went on, "Pelishar Squadron this is Squadron Leader, break hard right, now, get on my tail. Pelishar Four is rogue, I repeat, Pelishar Four is rogue. Pursue Pelishar Four. Go weapons hot." The sounds of the squadron leader straining in the hard turn came over the radio in the command bunker, and General Abashell cursed.

"Pelishar Squadron, this is Command Central, belay that order." the general shouted into the radio. "Pelishar Three and Five: pursue Pelishar Four on Pelishar One's point. Pelishar Two and Six, stay on track for intercept with the target. We are registering the fifth detonation. Relaying estimated coordinates for sixth now." He nodded at the operator and Sergeant Gupta began diligently calculating the next point of detonation.

- - -

"Wait, what the hell?" said Martin in surprise as he stared at the radar screen, "Four of the fighters are breaking off!" he continued, incredulously, and Jack's head jerked back to his console. He had been diligently watching the horizon for the first visual signs of the squadron and trying to figure out their chances of getting across the border alive. Staring at the radar screen, he saw the squadron separating. What are they doing, he thought?

Two of the F-16s were still tracking with the big bomber, climbing and turning slightly to converge with the next pod as the B-2 continued on its course toward the same spot, still unseen in the night. During training, Jack and his fellow B-2 pilots had been told again and again not to put all their faith in the stealth technology. In theory it made them virtually invisible to radar, but there were certain angles where the plane showed up like a beacon, and then there was always good old-fashioned eyesight. The sky was getting ever so slightly brighter behind them, and soon the fighters would be coming up alongside the big bomber. If they got within a thousand feet of Martin and Jack then the plane would be painfully visible as a big black silhouette against the first light of dawn, and then things could only get ugly fast.

- - -

"Come on." said Shahim, to no one in particular, as he continued his supersonic turn. He was monitoring the radar to see how many of his cohorts came in pursuit. But as he watched, it was clear that two of the fighters were staying on track to intercept the B-2.

He considered his options. He couldn't risk the bomber being discovered. And neither could he waste all his fuel in some Mach 2 pursuit. He needed to get this chase over with so he could return and fend off the two planes descending on his colleagues.

He sighed in an unusually human gesture. As he had feared must happen, he reluctantly engaged attack options in his mind once more. Forgive me, he thought as he scrolled through the tactical options in his head. Selecting the most fuel-efficient attack plan, he felt his body tense up in preparation for battle. An instant later, his machine mind engaged.

- - -

They saw the plane break upward before they registered the speed with which it was doing so. The squadron leader instinctively matched the maneuver, as did Pelishar Five on his tail. Pelishar Three was too slow responding, though, and instead started a long loop to intercept their target once he came back down.

The squadron leader could feel his weight increase as the G-force drove him into his seat. The planes rose together, the two pursuers in a tight phalanx about half a mile behind their quarry as their rogue cohort screamed upward. But the climb was too hard and too fast, and the leader felt himself starting to black out as his cockpit alarms flared. He was about to pull out when the front plane started to airbrake.

As the brakes engaged, Shahim throttled back and almost immediately his fighter started to stall, amidst a squall of alarms, as his engine struggled against the steep climb and sudden loss of thrust. Without the power it needed to counteract its steep angle, Shahim's plane quickly lost momentum and started to fall, and he allowed the plane to turn downward as its weight took control. His two pursuers stared in disbelief as they raced up toward the stalling fighter above them, and the leader broke off immediately, angling right in an inverted curve to bring him back to the perpendicular. But Pelishar Five powered onward a moment longer, veering slightly as he sliced toward the other jet, the nose of Shahim's plane falling lazily downward toward him.

In a flash, Pelishar Five thundered across Shahim's view, the other plane's jet spasming fire as it surged past. Shahim was ready for it. His plane's 20mm Gatling gun lashed out like a claw, forty bullets slicing a line down the other plane's belly in half a second, striking home at extreme close range. The big air intake under Pelishar Five's cockpit erupted as the plane was ripped apart, the pilot screaming as a bullet tore up through his thigh, shattering his hip bone as it speared up his side. Within a fraction of a second, the large lead bolt had powered up through his torso, popping the poor man's ribs in quick succession as it made its way up and out of his shoulder, flying out through the reinforced glass dome above him even as it splattered his blood across it.

As the last of the bullets broke into the ballistic plane's combustion chamber, it released the superheated fuel from its confines and the plane consumed itself in fire. Within a second of opening fire, Shahim was already hundreds of meters below his first victim, angling downward and falling fast now as his engines sucked in new air and his plane regained its legs. His mind deftly assessed his remaining targets.

Shouts and screams were coming through the radio at him. Pelishar One and Three were cursing him, even as the booming voice of the general at Command Central tried to find out what was happening and reestablish some control over the situation. The squadron leader was still recovering from his own brush with Shahim, coming around in a long arc as he watched to see what the rogue jet would do next. But Pelishar Three had not followed Shahim on his crazy climb and had had plenty of time to bank left in a smooth circle. Now he was closing fast from the north and Shahim heard the telltale ping from his radar as Pelishar Three got missile lock on him. The other pilot didn't hesitate, firing off two AMRAAM missiles in close succession at one mile out. Shahim didn't bother checking his radar, he had seen the launch, and he gunned his afterburner, his plane accelerating straight downward in a powerful nosedive as the missiles closed on him.

The squadron leader stared in disbelief as the other jet powered downward, plummeting toward the appropriately named Kush Mountains thousands of feet below them. The man was suicidal.

Shahim reached Mach 2 in record time, but the supersonic missiles continued to close, unperturbed by his mad downward rush. As an internal clock inside Shahim's head counted off the fleeting seconds, his speed increased, the ground rushing up to meet him. At the last possible moment, he pulled up hard, releasing decoys to blend with the peaks as the two missiles raced down to find him. The jet's engine screamed like a tortured demon as he pulled up into a twelve-G curve, the jet-wash and shockwave lifting dust from the hitherto peaceful valley as he rocketed through.

Confused by Shahim's sparkling decoy flares and the approaching peaks and valleys, the two missiles darted into the ground at over three thousand miles per hour like cosmic hammers, rocking the deserted plain which only moments before had born witness to Shahim's thundering passage.

Pelishar One and Three surveyed the explosion site from their lofty height to see if their enemy had somehow survived the desperate nosedive. It was impossible to confirm it in the predawn mist, but the plane's trajectory and speed had been insane, and the ensuing explosions huge. The squadron leader had just begun hesitantly reporting the rogue plane's destruction when a fleeting blip registered on his radar screen.

"Let's go down and take a look, Pelishar Three." The other pilot acknowledged and the two powerful fighters both rolled and entered a steep-angled dive of their own, though without applying the afterburner of their maniac adversary.

Without warning, Pelishar Three's radar suddenly blared with a radar lock.

"Someone is locking on to me!" he shouted in surprise as two missiles came streaking up out of the pluming cloud of smoke on the ground, quickly followed by the demonic plane itself.

"Dear Allah, he—" the pilot stopped talking as he frantically tried to maneuver, but there was no time. The missiles streaked upward at over two thousand miles per hour, even as he rushed toward them at several hundred.

As his colleague tried to break off, the squadron leader flinched, sensing the hopelessness of the maneuver. The missiles detonated on either side of Pelishar Three, ripping along its wings like a can opener and clipping the great bird. The pilot was somehow spared, surviving for the moment, only to realize his agile jet had just become his coffin. The man frantically started to pray as the plane continued to accelerate toward the ground: his systems fried, his eject sequence blown.

Trying to blank out the pure terror in his friend's voice as it sputtered though the radio, the squadron leader focused his rage on the plane still rocketing up toward him, and Shahim in turn altered his course to lock on to the last F-16. They raced toward each other, both firing their Gatling guns in a Mach 2 game of chicken, seventy bullets per second ripping across the rapidly closing gap between them. But fury blinded the brave captain's eyes in his last second before a hail of lead ripped his cockpit apart, mincing his body in an instant as it raced aft to do the same to his plane. As Pelishar One disintegrated, Shahim was already breaking upward in a spiraling turn to go after his American colleagues once more.

His face was resolute and he used his absolute control over his machine body and mind to blank out the last screams of the wingless Pelishar Three as it finally plummeted to the ground.

- - -

The general struggled to get his voice under control. Three F-16s gone in under a minute. Dear Allah, how could that be? Radar reported that the rogue Pelishar Four was now chasing after the remaining two planes of the squadron and he shook his head in despair. Why was this man doing this? How had some insurgent imposter managed to take out three highly trained pilots with such brutal dispatch? He shook his head, not even turning as his aide de camp finally came back into the room after his ill-fated trip to flight control.

"General Abashell, sir," said the aide, trying to catch his breath, "the reports from the tower indicate that the pilot on Pelishar Four used the correct call signs and even emulated the voice of the pilot he apparently knocked unconscious."

The general stayed staring forward, unsure how this new information helped the situation. So he was dealing with a very talented, well-informed imposter, who could fly better than any of his actual pilots. He frowned and summoned up his strength.

"Radio, call off the remaining members of Pelishar Squadron. Instruct them to join up with the support squadron coming up from the south and come under that squadron leader's command." He sounded resigned, almost defeated, and the room was quiet as they tried to ignore the bitter sound of their general's waning tone.

He gathered himself, then said, "Bring up Missile Control, quadrant 7."

The operator nodded, typing into his console to raise Missile Control on the main screen. The border with Afghanistan was dotted with small, mobile anti-air missile outposts designed to intercept any incursion from their neighbor. There weren't nearly as many as there were along Pakistan's contested border with India or their closely watched border with Iran, but as the big main screen changed to an aerial view of the northwestern border with Afghanistan, a series of red dots showing their current anti-air deployments appeared. On top of this view, the operator overlaid the path of the rogue F-16 and the remaining objects falling down into the atmosphere, and the general quietly praised the sergeant's efficiency once more.

So, he thought, we have a rogue F-16 with three kills tracking to intercept a series of objects that seem to be blowing up all by themselves. And based on the reports of the squadron, before all hell broke loose, we may have some kind of stealthed plane out there too. What the hell did it all mean? The rugged old Pakistani stared in consternation at the screen and tried to analyze it all. If there was a stealth plane out there, that meant the Americans, but what the hell would they be doing here? And the pilots had also reported seeing the blue streak of a jet-propelled rocket approaching the last explosion.

He shook his head. He was a veteran of countless military clashes with Indian forces in Kashmir, the long and arduous Russian occupation of his neighbor Afghanistan, and of course the more recent and equally bitter conflict that had almost laid waste to every country from here to Jerusalem. But this was something new. It was something outside his extensive experience, and he was at a loss. And at this point, with three more men dead to add to the sea of dead and dying from the insurgent attack on the base, he was at a point where he almost didn't care.

With the resignation of a man without options, he raised his voice and gave his next order, "I want all anti-air crews along that border line put on missile-ready status. They are to lock on to any object in range and shoot to kill. Bring our remaining forces onto a patrol run along the outside range of the anti-air platforms missiles and then issue the command."

He turned to his aide and saw the normally placid man's harried expression.

"Time to wipe the skies clean, Major Duranda." he said in a quiet voice, resignedly, "Time to wipe them clean. Now I need you to get hold of the Allied Forces Command in Afghanistan and tell them about the explosions. They seem to be heading across the border so it is their problem now. Oh, and Major, I do not see any need to tell them about our encounter with Pelishar Four at this time. That should be resolved soon enough."

He turned back to the big screen and braced his hands behind his back. Major Duranda nodded briefly and then spun on his heels and headed out of the room. The general would leave the Americans and Europeans to handle this latest phenomenon. His people had too many wounds to tend to.

- - -

As the remaining fighters disengaged and turned away, Shahim breathed a proverbial sigh of relief. He had no desire to fight any more of these men, any more than they had a desire to die at his hands, no doubt.

The burly warrior settled his fighter's course to bring him on an intercept path with where he assumed Martin and Jack were flying. On cue with his internal time clock, he saw the B-2's sixth cruise missile appear on his radar screen with a rapidly vanishing blip. Martin and Jack were clearly not leaving their bomb bays open for long in order to minimize their exposure to detection. But it was long enough to confirm his assessment of their location and he refined his course accordingly.

They saw him coming in and started to fret. It had been a confusing fifteen minutes as the squadron ducked and died on their radar screens, four of its planes seeming to fight with themselves in a spasm of movement that left only one of the four standing. When the two that had stood safely apart from the battle had broken off pursuit, that had been equally confusing. But that still left that sole survivor, and he was now closing in on Jack and Martin. Not on the next pod, and not on the missile they had just launched to destroy it, but on their supposedly invisible plane.

Their radio, silent for so many hours, suddenly spat out a voice, making them both jump.

"Jack, Martin, can you hear me?" said the disembodied voice and they stared at each other, shock turning to curiosity at the voice suddenly coming over their comm.

"That is a tight band," said Jack to Martin, before opening the comms channel to respond, "that means it is close range. No more than a few miles." He looked at his radar and realization dawned on him with a smile of overwhelming relief, as he clicked on his own mike and spoke in return, "Good morning, my friend. Agent Shahim, I assume?"

The reply was quick and sounded relieved, "Good morning to you. And please, call me Lord Mantil. I've had enough of that other name: it is time it was laid to rest."

Jack and Martin looked at each other and shrugged, and Jack replied, "Happy to make your acquaintance, Lord Mantil. Well, it looks like we owe you a debt of gratitude. Thank you. What is your status, my friend? Did you sustain damage?"

"No, my plane is undamaged, though that is little consolation. I am sad to say I have just downed three Pakistani pilots to add to my list of crimes. I had hoped to head off more death, but I'm afraid it seems to follow me wherever I go. Anyway, that is in the past now, and they appear to be withdrawing the rest of their fighters."

Jack confirmed that his radar showed the same thing, and then Lord Mantil, formerly Agent Shahim Al Khazar, suggested their next move. "Looks to me like you'll have a clear path across the border, gentlemen. But after that we should assume that the Allied forces will come to check you out. No doubt Peshawar is informing them of the situation even now, at least the part about the explosions, and they will want to come see."

"That had been our assumption. Once they're in range, I imagine they'll figure out what we are pretty quickly and then the shit will hit the fan back home. But that said, they should be very hesitant to shoot down an American bomber, even a rogue one, without express permission from the White House, so that will buy us some time. My bigger worry is what happens when we get close to the border with Iran. There is a large Iranian base near Mashhad in northern Iran and they have heavy strike capabilities. We won't get far past them."

"Agreed." said Lord Mantil in return, "but by then you will have taken out nearly a thousand miles worth of the viral pods. You can't have expected to do much more than that."

"True, but there are hundreds of thousands of unprotected people there as well, Lord Mantil," said Jack, somewhat dejectedly. "We have to try and get as far as we can."

"Very well, Major Toranssen, I won't try to dissuade you. Goodness knows you are saving more lives than we can yet count," came the other pilot's answer across the dawning sky. "But that said, I think it is best that I bid you farewell. I am afraid a rogue Pakistani plane will get an even worse reception in Afghanistan than a rogue US one, and I wouldn't want to compromise you by accompanying you across the border. I will stay with you a little while longer to make sure the Pakistani air force doesn't try anything else, and then I will probably head north and take this plane down in the mountains. If I eject late enough they shouldn't even see that I made it out and I'll be able to disappear before the army gets to the scene."

Jack looked distressed. This man, or whatever he was, had just saved their lives, and they were going to leave him to crash land, alone, probably to be hunted like some fugitive. But as he considered trying to talk the Allied forces into letting the other man fly into Afghanistan, he knew that he and Martin were going to have a hard enough time negotiating for their own lives without the specter of a lone rogue fighter pilot on their wing.

Recognizing the wisdom and the selflessness of Shahim's ... Lord Mantil's actions, Jack was about to wish the other pilot luck when he heard the fighter's alarms sound through the radio. Shit! That sounded like missile lock.

"What is tha ..." Jack began into the radio, but was cutoff by Shahim.

"I have been locked on by ground-based air defenses, Major, they must have been given the green light to launch on me. I am a sitting duck up here. That explains why the other fighters pulled back. Listen, I haven't much time. I have to pull away from you or they may pick up your jet stream and take you out as well." There was a brief hesitation as the alarm changed, registering launches now. Jack and Martin saw it too, four blips appearing below them as the missiles began their climb to intercept Shahim's fighter. But the warrior had one more comment before he left.

"Before I go," Lord Mantil said, "I just wanted to say I'm sorry."

Jack and Martin both spoke at once, "Sorry for what!" they both exclaimed.

"Sorry for bringing this all down on you. Sorry for coming here and starting this war … Sorry for all the death I have brought with me." Martin and Jack tried to speak but the Agent did not pause long enough for them to break in, going on to say, "Thank you for trying to save as many as you can, Major, Dr. Sobleski, I am afraid the virus is still going to exact a terrible toll, but at least you tried, and before the week is out, countless men, women, and children will owe their lives to you. This is Commander Mantil, Lord of the Hamprect Empire, Guardian of the Mantilatchi Heartland and Second Arberator of the Orbital, bidding you farewell and good luck."

And with that, he rolled his plane earthward once more, soaring downward toward the coming missiles, breaking the tight-beamed connection with his fellow conspirators as he flew out of range, and leaving Jack and Martin in silence. The ground-to-air missiles were bigger and more powerful than anything a fighter could carry, relying more on brute force than the agile finesse of a fighter plane's AMRAAM air-to-airs. But he came at them nonetheless, with the confidence of the phenomenally skilled, and the abandon of the just.

As he approached them, he spun his plane into a wide spiral as the wall of missiles came up at him, confusing their systems as their paths crossed and re-crossed. The first missile flew by within twenty feet, its detonation a moment too late as it exploded harmlessly behind him.

A quarter of a second later, the next was too far away to connect with him as it flew past and it didn't trigger, instead starting a tight, powered turn so it could pursue his engine trail once more. But the third and fourth came in together, detonating as one on either side of him. A wild maneuver saved him from a direct hit, but the detonations rocked his plane like a die thrown across a backgammon board. Before alarms had even had a chance to go off, his canopy had shattered, air racing in like a thousand hurricanes and ripping his puny helmet off his head to snap the vestigial oxygen tube from behind his back.

His remaining instruments told him that his right wing had been perforated in three places by the explosion, and that he had lost missile control on that side. His engine was down to two-thirds power and he had lost a large part of several of his flaps, as well as a majority of control of the trailing surfaces of his wings. Continuing down the growing list of other problems, he could not help but be amused by the fact that he had also lost control of his landing gear … like he was going to get to use it anyway.

Back on the bomber's flight deck, they did not have long to mourn the loss of their friend as the beeping of their radar began afresh. Jack glanced down at his screens once more, but Martin already had a fix on the new source.

"I have another set of bogies inbound from the east," he said, "coming in hot, Mach 1.3. Jesus, those things are supersonic." He whistled in spite of himself, but Jack was less nonchalant.

"They can't be missiles that far out." Jack said, studying the screen himself. It tore at him not to spend a moment on what he had just seen happen to Lord Mantil below them, but his training told Jack to focus on what he could affect, and he did so.

"I have them at three hundred miles out, but closing fast." said Martin, "At that rate they'll be on us in no time." he went on, turning to face the major, "But they can't see us, right? They can't get missile lock. They're just coming to investigate … right?"

Jack paused a moment then said, "Well, it's true that they can't get a bead on us too far out, but once they close enough, they're going to be able to go to guns, and that is bad. To be coming in that fast, they must be either F-22s or one of the European Typhoons, Rafales, or Gripens."

"So, they're on our side then?" said Martin, hopefully.

"Well, not quite: the moment we stole a B-2 Bomber, there ceased to be anyone that was on 'our side' … except Mr. Mantil," he said, soberly, "but either way, I can tell you that there are also no F-22s currently deployed in Afghanistan. Which means it must be either the French or the British."

Jack looked pensive, then changed tacks, "Martin, do you have the sniffing salts to hand?" Martin looked over at his friend and then back at the two pilots unconscious behind them. Then he nodded and rifled around in his flight bag to find the small canister.

"You want me to wake them up?" said Martin, retrieving the salts.

Jack nodded, "We have only a few minutes before those planes are in visual range, and once they see us I don't know what is going to happen. Under the circumstances, I think those two deserve to be awake for this. In case it goes badly."

Martin nodded, unbuckled his restraints, and started to climb out of his chair, Jack suggesting that Martin recheck the ties binding the pilots' hands before he woke them. Martin agreed and then set about waking the two unwitting combatants. They were about to find out that they were deep in enemy airspace, on the other side of the world from their patrol route, and about to be assaulted by several of the most deadly war machines on earth. Not quite your morning cup of joe, but what can you do?

Chapter 59: To the Heart of the Matter

"Enjoying yourself, Serge?" said Agent Jean-Paul Merard into his mask. Their 'regular patrol' had turned into something much more when their Dassault Rafale had been redirected shortly after takeoff to join a small squadron made up of two British Typhoons, and one other French Rafale. They were all breaking the sound barrier in a race to get a bead on the objects apparently exploding above Pakistan, but only one amongst them knew what the pods were, and that the explosions were not a planned part of their deployment. Pilot Jean-Paul Merard, flying the second of the two French Rafales, intended to find out who was blowing his satellite's viral pods out of the sky. Then he intended to return the favor, even if it meant destroying the squadron around him to do it.

The British fighters were led by Captain Sarah Hutcheson on Lightning One, with Lightning Two flying close on her starboard wing. The Eurofighter was faster than the Dassault, and slightly more heavily armed, but not significantly, and the two more maneuverable Dassaults were keeping up, flying behind and to the left of the Typhoons in a V-formation. Jean-Paul and his unwilling copilot Serge Latral were in the left wingman position, and they could see all three other planes arranged out to their right in an extraordinary display of destructive power.

Jean-Paul surveyed the other planes with a predator's eye and weighed his options. Soon they would come into range of one of the pods and then it would not take long to see whatever it was that was shooting them down. Jean-Paul wasn't certain, but the fact that no other plane was showing up on his radar was sign enough that it was some kind of stealth plane, possibly an F-35 or a B-2. What either of those was doing out here he had no idea, but either way he would happily blow them out of the sky. The only question was whether he would need to kill his 'allies' before or after he went after the culprit. He thought a moment. He didn't know yet what was out there, or if it was alone. If it was a B-2, then that shouldn't pose too great a problem, but it could be a wing of F-35s, in which case that could strain even his extensive abilities. If these two Typhoons were to come in on his side because of a miscommunication he could engineer, well, that could even the balance. So whether these three other fighters were a hindrance or a tool to be used depended on what he was about to find out there.

But his decision process was suddenly thrown into disarray when a new factor entered the scene.

"Balbuzard One and Two, this is Lightning One," came the voice of the British pilot leading their formation. "Ground radar reports another signature crossing the border at extreme low altitude. Also they are reporting several missile signatures across the border in Pakistan. We are being asked to drop our ceiling to 10,000 feet on a course of one-five-eight and intercept."

As he was the wingman, Jean-Paul left it to Balbuzard One to reply, and his colleague did just that, confirming the new bearing. The small squadron broke right in a rolling turn, dropping to the new altitude with a roar of their tumultuous engines.

The mild-angled dive, combined with their already supersonic speed, combined to close the distance to the border even faster, and soon they had a radar bead of their own on the object darting between the mountain peaks far below. But Jean-Paul's attention was elsewhere, his powerful eyesight was scouring the sky for whatever was firing on his virus pods, and suddenly he saw it. Far, far above them, its profile was distinctive, its silhouette like no other plane in the world, old or new.

The flying wing configuration of the B-2 Spirit Bomber could mean only one thing: the Americans were attempting to take out the viral pods, and as his squadron had been dispatched to investigate them, the bomber must be working without Allied approval. Most likely the pilots were members of the same organization that had launched the attack on Jean-Paul's four support satellites, destroying his entire defense and communications network in one harrowing night.

He would not need his squadron mates, after all, but he could expend whatever bullets and missiles he had left killing them later, if they still posed a threat. First things first: time to slice up that bomber.

Before the squadron even realized what was happening, Jean-Paul had pulled back hard and engaged his afterburners, soaring back up into the sky like a bullet, homing in on the distant bomber. His copilot Serge Latral strained in his seat behind him and tried to grasp a breath as the massive G-force crushed him into his harness, driving the air from his lungs. His hands were heavy, he could barely speak, let alone engage his external comms, as he strained to ask his colleague why they had suddenly broken formation and gone rogue. The other pilots barked questions into their radio, but Jean-Paul stayed eerily silent, driving the plane upward and away from the other three fighters as he started to engage his weapons systems.

Jesus, thought Serge, staring at the weapons screens as they went active. Why is he doing this? We don't have permission to go weapons hot. Holy shit, it's happening. This is what Serge had been warned about. And now he was onboard while the crazy man in front of him engaged the multi-million dollar arsenal of the Dassault and flew like a demon into upper atmosphere.

Serge struggled to master his hands, switching on his comms he spoke in rasps, "Jean-Paul, what are you doing? Where are we going?" the strained voice went out over the airwaves, and the other pilots in the squadron called in alarm bells to mission control back in Kabul, asking for orders. The other French pilot also registered confusion at the name Jean-Paul. Weren't Michel and Etienne flying Balbuzard Two?

Hearing Serge's strained voice over the comm, Jean-Paul remembered that the copilot was back there and threw the plane into a violent turn. The overwhelming power of the twenty-thousand-horsepower engine forced Serge's eyes back into his head. The poor man tried to control his body's reaction, to master its instinctive responses to the pressure wrenching at him. But it was too much. As the blood was forced to the back of his head, his heart struggled to keep the oxygen pumping, but it was an impossible task for any human, and in a few moments the man blacked out.

His final act had been singularly important, though. For the pilot of the other French fighter was not the only one surprised by the mention of Jean-Paul's name over the radio.

- - -

With little left of his cockpit, Shahim wrestled to keep the hurtling hulk of his F-16 off the ground as he tried to stay low and keep the other pilots guessing as long as possible. The remains of his communications systems were dying or dead, and his comms were barely audible over the titanic scream of the wind about his ears. But his ears picked up bits and pieces through the storm, and the name of the French Agent rang out like an alarm.

Jean-Paul. The name was not unusual in France, but the fact that it was here, and it was the name of a pilot breaking formation to fly up toward Jack and Martin's B-2 could only mean one thing. Like it had been catapulted from the grave, Shahim's plane came launching up out of the valley in a blur of smoke. The two Typhoons reacted instinctively, their advanced weapons systems got a lock on him almost instantaneously, and the two pilots stopped shouting at their errant comrade long enough to bark a warning at the foreign plane to disengage.

But Lord Mantil was also locking on as he tried to get as many of his remaining weapons online as possible. The two Typhoons and Jean-Paul's fellow Rafale also changed course, pulling back on their controls to send their planes arching upward to intersect Shahim's, all combatants now banking upward to converge on Jean-Paul's jet stream. Shahim could no longer get his relatively antiquated and thoroughly perforated F-16 to break any speed records, and he could sense the other planes coming at him even as Jean-Paul started to stretch away. He knew he didn't have much longer. Punching at his semi-responsive control board, he fired all his available missiles in unison, the four explosive lances belching from under his wings and racing ahead with a speed he could not hope to match.

Jean-Paul registered the launch immediately and was surprised. Surely they would not fire on him so soon, he had assumed. But turning his attention back to his pursuers, he did not spare much time to assess which plane had fired on him, or why. Instead, Jean-Paul pulled a hard G-turn and tracked the missiles' pursuit with the same machine skill Shahim had used to avoid his own destruction at the hands of the Pakistanis.

Though Jean-Paul's Rafale jet was slightly outclassed by the British Eurofighters, it was still an evolutionary leap above the F-16, and Lord Mantil looked on with a mix of jealousy and sadness as the fighter completed an impossibly tight turn. With the Agent at its helm the plane would fly faster and with more agility than its designers could possibly have dreamed of, and Shahim knew the aging missiles he had sent after it had little hope of taking it down. Lord Mantil's only remaining hope was that Jean-Paul did not know that he was facing another Agent. And so, factoring in how beaten his plane was, he set his machine mind to a tactical analysis of the other's flight path and response patterns, and began defining an intercept course.

Lightning One shouted as he registered the firing of missiles at the Dassault that had broken formation, reporting the incident quickly and cursorily to Allied Force Command. Their response was equally fast. An unidentified foreign plane had fired on an Allied jet. Their orders were clear. Take the unknown pilot down.

Jean-Paul's own mind was offering up tactics at a blinding pace, and he selected them as they arose. The plane dropped decoys earlier than would have been tactically wise, but it was not to fool the missiles, but to throw off further missile lock from whatever had fired on him. As he spun his plane hard back down toward his pursuers, he noted the mangled F-16 coming up behind him and allowed his tactical computers to assess the plane's threat potential, while he came nose to nose with the other three Allied jets.

Lord Mantil sensed rather than heard the alarm from his battered systems denoting missile lock on him, and broke right as hard as he dared, banking away from the returning Jean-Paul. His plane was no longer capable of much, but his sudden movement was fast enough to throw off the lock before the pilot could fire, and he followed his new course as his mind continued to look for tactical opportunities to defeat the powerful Rafale.

Lightning One followed the battered Pelishar Four as it banked outward, leaving Lightning Two and Balbuzard One to continue their burn upward toward Jean-Paul. But the other plane was now coming back down to face them, its agile design and inhuman pilot bringing with him four streaking missiles hot on his tail. Jean-Paul brought his plane on a downward arc to pass between the remaining two planes, and as he did so, Lord Mantil cursed the simple but ingenious maneuver. It was exactly what he would have done with a plane capable of such a sharp turn, and he and the other pilots watched as the seconds unfolded and the maneuver's game changing results became apparent.

Jean-Paul's Rafale rocketed between the two jets and his jet signature vanished in their combined jet stream. The missiles on his tail lost lock and searched for another heat signature, finding the other planes in an instant. The two men had only a moment to pull apart from each other as blind fate chose one of them and the four missiles reassigned their trajectories to meet him.

The Typhoon erupted in a blaze of fury as four simultaneous explosions tore it to shreds. Wings flying apart as the fuselage disintegrated in white-hot flame.

But as Jean-Paul then pulled up, he followed the precise trajectory Lord Mantil's own computer would have chosen for him, and the double agent was waiting for him. Jean-Paul saw the broken jet an instant before the other pilot's course fell across his own and registered the threat in a flash. Machine reactions taking control, he rolled his plane but Lord Mantil was already firing, emptying the last of his Gatling gun's belts into the flicking silhouette of Jean-Paul.

The bullets clawed along the Rafale's left engine and wing, and the plane's advanced computer systems instantly shut down the torn left thruster, cutting off its fuel supply before it killed the entire plane. Lord Mantil was allowed a second of pleasure at the hit before another radar lock found him, and this time Lightning One's pilot was immediate in her response. She fired two of her latest generation, fighter-killing missiles at close range and every tactical option Lord Mantil saw told him he was doomed. Without hesitation, Lord Mantil literally ripped his own seat out of his plane and catapulted himself clear in the fraction of a second before the missiles flew up his jet stream, fucking his plane's engine with two hundred pounds of explosive fury.

He was just clear when the missiles struck, and he felt more than saw the explosion as it drove him outward. His tactical options gone, his part in this contest over, Lord Mantil began his long hard fall to Earth with a tinge of regret. He had enjoyed piloting the jet, and he had enjoyed firing on Agent Jean-Paul Merard. He hoped it would not be the last chance he had to bring his vengeance to bear on the man, or the rest of his remaining colleagues for that matter.

For his part, Jean-Paul was far from done. The desperate maneuver by the mysterious F-16 had significantly reduced his Rafale's power, and the damage to his left wing would affect his maneuverability severely as well, but he was still in the fight. Lightning One was climbing to take the height advantage from him, but worse than that he could not see Balbuzard One on his radar at all anymore.

Shit, he thought. All the advanced fighters in his squadron had some of the ingredients of a fully stealth fighter. Nothing like the F-22, B-2, or the F-35, but if they got on the right vector, they were very hard to find. Clearly his French cousin intended to give him the run around. Very well. In mimicry of the maneuver Lord Mantil had made earlier that morning, Jean-Paul rolled his plane, his acute eyes scanning above and below him as his view rotated. There. A quarter mile behind him, and fifty feet below.

Balbuzard One barely registered the turn as Jean-Paul started his loop, such was his confidence in his own shroud at this angle of approach. He was still programming his missiles with his intended attack vector when Lightning One's voice came over the radio.

"Balbuzard One, Balbuzard One, above you!"

The other French pilot glanced up in a reflexive jerk to see Jean-Paul's plane had vanished from his field of view. An instant later, the rogue jet was barreling down on him from above, guns blazing as he ripped the other plane apart. Jean-Paul had pulled a fifteen-G inverted loop to bring him up and over the jet pursuing him, coming down on the other fighter like the sword of god.

Like Pelishar's commander not two hours earlier, Captain Sarah Hutcheson's emotions swam as the last of her small squadron was rent asunder by the bullets. The plane did not so much explode as get decapitated, and there was no report from its pilot as it began to fall to Earth, its battered nose a mockery of its slick, graceful, former glory.

But Sarah was no amateur. She had seen what this other pilot could do and she had seen the damage the fragmented F-16 had done to it before she had finally killed it. She could take him, but she would not rely on old tactics. They clearly would not work against a pilot this daring and capable.

Breaking off the pursuit, she started to race for home, hoping that the rogue Rafale would continue on whatever mad mission had caused it to turn rabid in the first place, but knowing she could outrun him even if he chose to pursue. Sure enough, the other plane did not come after her, and she noted with satisfaction its smooth turn as it started to climb again to pursue some other goal. Maybe a defection? Who knew? She only knew it had killed two of her command and she was going to exact her retribution.

Lord Mantil, his parachute just opened, was beginning an almost serene drop to Earth when he saw her breaking off the engagement. "You can take him!" he screamed at the howling air as she flew off toward the horizon. "He's damaged, and you have a superior plane. Goddamn it he's trying to kill the very people you are here to protect!"

But his shouts of frustration echoed pointlessly across the sky, and Jean-Paul raced onward, without concern. The dogfight had delayed the French Agent, and while the five planes had ravaged each other, Jack and Martin had flown by unheeded, their stealthy plane soaring far ahead to carry on its mission of mercy.

Well, you conspiring bastards, thought Jean-Paul, your mission of mercy be damned.

There was a stirring behind him as Serge Latral started to come to, and with utter contempt for the other pilot and his entire race, Jean-Paul ripped a small piece of metal from the underside of his chair and slung it over his shoulder with massive force. The jagged metal slammed into Serge's neck just under his chin, semi-decapitating him and pinning his head back against the chair. The man never knew what had hit him. His blood spurted from under his lolling head, spraying the back of the cabin with thick red spurts.

The final beats of the man's heart sent gobs of it up to splatter the glass dome. Jean-Paul flew onward, a smear of gore behind him to symbolize the death in his wake as he closed in on Martin and Jack.

- - -

Major Jack Toranssen crouched in the rear section of the B-2's flight deck and tried to reason with the recently awoken pilots that still lay bound there. He understood their anger more than they could know, but his patience was starting to wear thin. He had explained their situation to them as clearly and concisely as he could, but he was moments away from knocking them out again, anything to stop their insistent shouting and bickering.

"Look," he said, trying to keep his frustration under check, "it boils down to this: you can be angry all you like. You can shout and scream and force me to knock you out again. Or you can accept that something has happened that pisses you off royally, but that a decorated US Air Force major from your own unit is telling you that it is more justified than you can possibly grasp, and is trying to give you a chance to face this awake and conscious, instead of in a dribbling lump on the flight deck floor. Either way, I am afraid I don't give a shit anymore. I have to get back to the mission, so here is your choice … either shut the fuck up or I will knock you the fuck out."

They stared at him with a mix of shock, and now somewhat restrained fury, and he saw them resigning themselves to at least being conscious for whatever was about to happen. But the moment was broken by a call from Martin in the cockpit, "Jack, we have a problem. The fighters seem to have torn each other apart again, and once again it looks like there is only one survivor. Only I get the sense that the survivor this time is far from friendly." They had each seen something they hoped was their friend Lord Mantil rising up into the fray as the Allied fighters approached them, but their hopes had been dashed as the clearly damaged fighter had flung himself headlong into the swarm of hornets and vanished in a haze of missile fire and explosions. Only two planes had left where five had entered, and they had both been moving too fast to be the old and battered F-16.

Jack gave the two groggy and sullen pilots one more stern look, then climbed forward to glance at the radar screen. One of the remaining fighters had vanished into the dawn, but the other was coming in pursuit of the bomber as it continued to fire upon the viral pods dropping down from above. It was not quite supersonic, and maybe it had been damaged in the fight, but it was coming on hard, harder than the F-16 would have been able to fly with its remaining fuel, and it was slowly gaining on them. It would not be more than fifteen minutes till the pilot was in visual range.

Miles astern of them Jean-Paul calculated the coming kill. The minutes ticked by slowly and he decided on the tactics for his attack and started to think about how best to escape after he had killed his prey. He would take the jet north as far as his remaining fuel would take him, he decided, and then eject as close to the border with China as possible. After that he would try to regroup with Agents Lam and Kovalenko so they could assess their remaining strategic options.

The time of attack approached, his machine mind informed him, and he started to scan for the plane he knew must be out there. After a few minutes, his eyes found it even before the ghost blips started to show up on his radar. From directly behind, even the stealthiest of planes become somewhat visible as the four big jet engines driving the bomber spewed their heat and left their indelible signature on their air behind. His missile systems found the heat source a couple of miles ahead and locked on, giving a literal green light to his fire control.

- - -

Slowly, slowly, Captain Sarah Hutcheson crept up on the rogue jet. She had shut down her radio systems, disabled her active radar, and even put her missile systems on standby, relying on passive radar and line of sight to bring herself up to Jean-Paul in his singular blind spot. She was waiting till the kill was guaranteed. Till the bastard that had slaughtered her friend and their French colleague was dead in her sights. She was only a quarter mile behind him now and she allowed herself a smile.

But her moment of satisfaction was cut short as she then also registered the big bomber off in the distance. She had a moment to contemplate what she was seeing before she saw Jean-Paul's jet launch his missiles. Shit. She had waited too long. She had allowed the rogue fighter to launch on another hapless victim. Her rage boiled over in her and she went weapons hot in a flash. Engaging her systems at point-blank range and locking on in less than a second. As she fired her missiles, she went to guns and opened up her powerful Gatling gun, bringing her nose across the other plane's tail and sending everything she had after him.

Jean-Paul heard the lock and missile alarm as one and started his bank before he even registered where it was coming from. But his silent pursuer had been too close and too complete in her attack. The four missiles came in a tight phalanx and followed his hard turn with ease. While the missiles sought the heat of his tail-fire, Sarah's bullets flew into the space he had occupied only a moment before, followed quickly by Sarah's plane itself, but the missiles stayed true.

Jean-Paul's head span round in surprise and shock as the explosives closed in and was granted a moment's regret at his complacency before the fire ripped through his plane and blasted him outward, charring and flaying his flight suit and synthetic skin as he began the long, hard fall to Earth. The plane's carcass dropped past him like a metal meteor, a sad echo of the Agents' arrival on Earth eighteen months beforehand. The fall was going to hurt, probably destroy even his robust body, for unlike Lord Mantil, there was nothing left of the eject mechanism and parachute that he would have had if he'd had the time to eject.

Without tactical options, he set his fate aside and turned in the air to watch as his missiles cruised toward their more distant target. At least he would get to watch these bastards go down, he thought.

Onboard the B-2, Jack, Martin, and the two bound pilots scrambled frantically into the two ejectable pilot seats in their last few moments. Jack was strapped in and clipping Captain Jennifer Falster's jumpsuit to his own with the reflexive automation his training had imbedded in him, while Martin tried ineffectually to do the same for Captain Billy Kellar. The missile lock alarm had sounded moments before the missiles launch had registered on their screens. There was not enough time, thought Jack, glancing across at Martin and Captain Kellar, and he saw the despair in the other captain's face as the female pilot in Jack's lap screamed at them to strap in.

The pilots knew they only had a few seconds. Jack glanced over at his friend and thought he saw the man give the thumbs-up, but later he would curse his uncertainty as he reached for the eject lever, wrapping his spare arm around the female captain in his lap as she rolled her head back onto his shoulder to avoid breaking both their necks when the seat's booster engaged.

The canopy blew off and air rushed out. There had been no time for oxygen masks and the air was sucked from all four people's lungs as the cabin pressure equalized. Captain Billy Kellar screamed. He was not fully strapped in yet and his body flew upward as the air blew explosively from the cabin. Martin was incoherent with fear as he gasped for breath in the suddenly thin air. He pulled the chair's eject lever. The chair flew upward, wrenching Captain Kellar by the lone strap that was properly attached and snapping his spine like a rag doll. The massive tug broke off the captain's scream as it broke his back, the instantly dead man's weight unbalancing the seat's propulsion and pulling Martin's seat around as it launched upward out of the cabin.

Martin was already unconscious when the missiles hit. They flew up the B-2's engines and erupted in the flow of jet-powered air, igniting the plane like a tinderbox. Within a fraction of a second, the detonation reached the bomb bay and the fresh addition of the remaining missiles' fuel and munitions sent the explosion supernova. Martin was consumed along with Captain Kellar's body in a mile-high pyre.

Chapter 60: Fallen

Where the plains of northeastern Iran meet Afghanistan, they are all but unguarded. But despite the lack of obvious border installations, regular patrols and surprisingly advanced radars still diligently sweep the skies for any encroachment by Allied forces into Iranian airspace. They had long since alerted the authorities of the airborne conflagration approaching from the east. But no one noticed as a lone man ran, unbidden, over the border in the aftermath, chasing the fiery shells of the fallen planes with reckless abandon.

In the middle of a wide, sandy plain, the burning wreckage of a Dassault Rafale fighter burns and smolders. A little over a mile away lies the remains of its pilot, equally blackened, equally charred, but not equally destroyed. A cinder of life still burns in its machine mind as it tries desperately to repair some of its systems. The lone runner sees the black outline of the body and veers wildly, coming to a skidding halt not far from the smoking remains. He approaches the body slowly, examining it closely as he does so. He is cautious despite the stupendous impact the body has suffered, aware of what the battered hulk was once capable of.

Stepping gingerly up to the blackened shape, the redeemed Lord Mantil of the Hamprect Empire kicks it over and scans for signs of life. A part of the wreckage that was Agent Jean-Paul Merard's mind stares back at him and recognizes him, trying desperately to compute some tactical option. Their black eyes connect for a moment and Shahim smiles bitterly. After a pause filled with all the tension of retribution, Shahim's left eye rolls back into his head, and a lethal array of needle-thin spines emerge from its socket. Agent Jean-Paul experiences a last moment of despair before the laser cuts into his head to cleanse his machine body of life. Within a few moments, the white-hot syringe finally smites the Agent's infectious presence on Earth, and Lord Mantil turns and walks away.

Epilogue

As the planet reverberates in the aftermath of the attacks, its effects spread across the globe.

In America, a cloud of radioactive dust from the explosions at King's Bay washes up the Georgia coast. Born on the wings of the northern Atlantic trades, the cloud carries death and mutation to the scattering population. Amid the millions fleeing its silent lethality, a scarred and battered Lana Wilson drives west into the heartlands of America to heal and recover. She needs shelter, she needs time. But her machine body's convalescence will also give her time to focus her fury, forcing it to fester and boil inside her. Her rage is tumultuous, her thirst for vengeance palpable. She wishes death to the world, but for now her enmity is focused on three individuals: Neal Danielson, Madeline Cavanagh, and her former ally John Hunt.

The loss of the satellites' sight and protection is like the loss of a sense for all of the surviving Agents. In China and Russia, the suddenly isolated Agents Pei Leong-Lam and Mikhail Kovalenko reach out to each other via phone. They know they have been discovered, that much could not be clearer, and like Lana they suspect that Agent John Hunt is the Mobiliei's Judas. The discovery of the antigen just before the satellites were destroyed indicates that the humans were somewhat prepared for that branch of their attack as well, and they must assume the coming viral attack will only kill that small slice of the world's population that is not already inoculated against it.

Deciding that John must surely have also revealed their own identities, they conclude correctly that their own discovery is probably imminent. So the two Agents agree upon a remote meeting place in the mountains of eastern Russia and close their brief call. Without ceremony or hesitation, they gather their remaining equipment and vanish, fleeing the backlash they know must find them in a matter of days, maybe even hours.

In a naval base in Singapore, the now awake and disgraced crew of the HMS *Dauntless* is still unaware of the vital role they have played in Earth's defense. Furious and humiliated, their captain turns a blind eye to the beating that his crew is giving the prisoner deep in the ship's hold. For his part, John Hunt takes the blows, ignores the mental abuse, and blanks his mind while his former shipmates and friends urinate and defecate on him as he lies in chains in the ship's brig. He hopes that at some point soon, Neal or the colonel will reach out to the British government and secure his release, but until that time he will not fight his captors. He has abused their trust, and though he knows that he did it all for their own good, they cannot be aware of that yet, and he does not begrudge them their revenge.

All around the globe, the final weapon of the now destroyed satellites floats down through the upper atmosphere. The small pods contain the worst virus the world has ever known, and while the antigen has already reached the vast majority of the world's population, several large bands remain unprotected. The desperate efforts of Major Toranssen and his now dead friend Dr. Martin Sobleski have saved millions in the most exposed zone of all, but the mission has cost Martin his life, and many more will also die before the antigen stops the spread of the synthetic plague that now falls, unseen, upon the ignorant and innocent.

The Agent that had been known as Shahim Al Khazar has done much to atone for his sins. Preeti Parikh and Jean-Paul Merard lie dead at his hands, and the earth owes the destruction of one of the four mighty satellites to his savage attack on Peshawar Base. But the deaths of a thousand innocents weighs heavy on him as he walks away from the mutilated body that was Agent Jean-Paul Merard.

He saw only one parachute drop from Jack and Martin's B-2 bomber, and that at great altitude. But if there is even a slight chance that one of the brave men is still alive then he must do what he can for them. Unfortunately for the lone parachutist, its greatest peril lies ahead it as it floats to the ground, for it is a highly visibly remnant of an illegal US Air Force flight deep into Iran's skies. Long festering anti-American hatred, fueled by fear and confusion from the past days' aberrant missile attacks, awaits any who survive the long drop, and Shahim has no illusions as to the welcome they will receive if the Iranians get to them before he does.

In Israel, Ayala Zubaideh's old handler from her days in the Mossad follows the Israeli Mobiliei Agent at a safe distance. He is nominally aware of some of Raz Shellet's extensive abilities, and so he watches her from afar as she calmly walks away from her post, and from the double life she had led up until the satellites were destroyed. Each week he has been reporting her movements in regular coded letters mailed to a post office box in Boston, but those reports are about to change dramatically.

As the world spins and the many players in the great game take their new positions, another vastly more powerful foe is eyeing them from afar. Just starting to become visible in the night sky, a small cluster of new stars are shining. Still ten years away, they bring with them untold firepower and merciless purpose. At this great distance they are too far away to have been inside the range of the subspace tweeters that had beaten aboard the now destroyed AI satellites. They do not know that the advanced team is discovered. But they have always assumed that we will not go quietly. In virtual conferences of massive scale, the admirals and generals of the Mobiliei meet and discuss their plans, and behind the great fires of their decelerating engines, the huge Armada readies itself for war.

Look for Volume Two in The Fear Saga: *Fear the Survivors*, coming in late 2014.

Stephen Moss would love to hear from you. To share your thoughts on *Fear the Sky*, or to sign up to receive updates on The Fear Saga, and Stephen Moss's other work, you can find the author on Facebook.

Read on for an excerpt from the next installment in the series: *Fear the Survivors* . . .

Excerpt from Volume Two in The Fear Saga: *Fear the Survivors:*

"   Though it was waterproof, impervious to bacteria and viruses, and imbued with all the protective technology the Mobiliei possessed, Samuel still felt a volt of vulnerability every time he touched the strange-feeling gelport on the back of his neck. A sense, perhaps, of the fact that this was a proverbial well that reached down directly into his brain; an opening to his being, that bypassed every ingrained and instinctive barrier, to touch at his core.

He shivered a little, then shook his head slightly and smiled at his foolishness. He had done this a thousand times during the construction and testing of the ship. He took a moment to tuck his legs under their straps in the soft, cradle-like Captain's chair he lay in, and checked the straps across his torso. He then brought the cable's tip up to the back of his neck, feeling the gelports reach out as they sensed each other's presence, binding.

He waited while the system synced with the spinal interface buried in his neck.

<Open connection?>

Three, two,

His world curved. The ship sunk backward and exploded outward at once, his view distorting and moving out of focus even as his mind told him he was seeing everything more clearly than before. Everything suddenly went blue with a blink. Firewall.

Captain Harkness felt his identity being validated as his preset limits and time checks came on line: his anchors to the real world. He checked them as they scrolled across his brain and then, authority confirmed, he moved on, not by action but by will, simply stepping through the blue wall that enveloped him, popping it as he did so, and entering the vacuum.

His universe expanded outwards exponentially, all walls gone, and he felt the vacuum of space on his skin as the ship became him, his arms and ears and eyes, his fingers and toes. He felt it, flexing his muscles delicately he felt his systems respond. He sensed the other crew as they embodied their respective systems, and by thinking of them he brought them to him, their minds providing him with system status in magnificent color and glory, the smell of green light pervading him as he absorbed the ship's readiness in his bones . . . *as* his bones.

In the nearby space station, Birgit hung suspended in a cradle of her own, her link also active, her body limp as she connected with the ship across subspace. She linked with Captain Samuel as he joined her and greeted him in the strange communing that was seeing someone's personality in cyberspace. Over the course of several generations on Mobilius, the Agents' ancestors had created complex graphic interfaces to ease their populations' acceptance of the concept of direct interface with a computer, but this was no public system, no game, this was pure, and the primal rush of power it gave you was not for the faint of heart.

After careful consideration, checking and rechecking, the Captain told her it was time. At the Captain's request she turned her attention to the eight great engines that made up the bulk of the ship's mass. She was here to guide the final preparatory step the ship would make before it left Earth forever. She was here to switch on the preposterously powerful engines that would propel New Moon One further and faster than any man-made ship had ever dreamed of going. She prepared herself. Once ignited, the engines would drum with an energy it was not possible to contain. It would need to be spent, and spent it would be. This was the last chance to stop it. They had cycled the engines in testing. Teasing them with the promise of ignition, but they had not let them reach critical mass. Each one of these mighty beasts was capable of generating enough power to supply Mexico City's thirty million inhabitants with electricity indefinitely.

They were specifically designed to run at two different capacities, the first being only a tenth of the power they would use once they were leashed to the asteroid they intended to bring back to Earth. Any more and they would crush the ship's crew to pulp in an instant with the sheer force of acceleration. As it was, the crew was strapped into cradles in their various compartments. Muscle relaxants already pumped through their veins, oxygen rich blood supplementing their own via tubes passing to and from veins in their arms. Their breathing was slowing, their bodies preparing for the coming surge. It would only be for a few minutes at first. Enough to start them on their journey before the accelosphere engaged and they vanished into Earth's gravity well for the first powerful leap toward their goal. But that was all to come. First was ignition.

Steeling herself, Birgit turned her mind to the engines. As she did so the rest of the crew faded, replaced by the cold hearts of the eight massive generators. Her thoughts went coursing through their systems like fingers, feeling them, bracing them. They were cold now. Hollow. Shells of potential. She started by engaging the fuel systems. They worked only on demand. Giving only when their contents were wanted, and even then withholding their full potential. They responded begrudgingly, their safeguards querying her request in a hesitant loop that would help harness the roar of the engines once started.

Next she needed pressure. Massive pressure. Wave generators began to warp the inside of the engines, forcing inward, pushing the vacuum, focusing nothingness into an intense magnetic and gravitic pressure centering on the very heart of the engines' cores. A spine-like needle reached from one side of the engines' cores into their centers. It could retract as needed, coming close to, but never touching that center of force at the heart of the engine. Through it a tiny amount of liquid oxygen, hydrogen and nitrogen coursed, harvested over the past weeks from the upper atmosphere by the climbers as they rose toward Terminus. It was the engine's fuel, and it would be injected into the fusion core. As it ejected from the end of the needle it was caught instantaneously by the wave field and became hyper-weighted, swarming into a ball of ever-greater pressure as it gathered to critical mass.

This was the most delicate phase. Birgit managed it with finesse, with literally her whole being focused on the process. Too much, and the reaction would surge out from the fields and overwhelm them. It would still be contained, at least theoretically. Sensors would control the supply of fuel and the ship would survive. But the engine wouldn't and the whole project would be set back precious weeks as another generator was fabricated and sent up. Too little, and the pressure would overwhelm the core and smite the reaction. Not deadly in and of itself, but beyond a point she would not be able to stop the other engines powering up, and the ship would be torn apart as seven of eight engines fired and sent the ship off in a warping spin that would certainly kill everyone aboard.

She felt them coming close. She felt it like fire on her skin, a growing warmth that she could feel, not as pain, for none of her sensors were so crude as to send such blunt signals, but as pure, hot information telling her every source and magnitude, instantly analyzed, meanings and implications forecasted and presented directly to her cerebral cortex as her own knowledge. As the energy mounted, so did the feeling of power in her veins as ever more potent signals thrummed through her synapses. It was building to a surging crescendo, balanced, perfectly in tune. Supply and demand singing in harmony as the reactors went energy positive and started to fire. The feeling pounded through her, and even as her mind swam in perfect clarity with all the information coursing through her, the sense of it all drove her to something close to orgasm, sweat breaking out on her brow, her face and neck flushing as she lay, cradled in the Terminus station, some two miles from where her mind was sparking eight new suns to life at the center of New Moon One's engines.

Captain Harkness felt some echo of the life in his engines from the ship's systems and sensed as the eight massive reactors cycled and notified him of their readiness. He felt as Birgit disengaged from each in turn and handed them off to their various techs, turning each into separate entities so they could be managed by their respective onboard teams.

As they came online, the Captain flexed them and tensed his machine body, feeling it respond. It was almost time. Checklists filled as feelings of strength in his mind, his health was the ship's tested newness, his breathing its fuel and life support systems, his eyes the far reaching sensors and onboard cameras that covered the hull, inside and out. A presence met him, stepping into his world from outside and greeting him. It was Birgit, linking in one last time from Terminus station, head of the 'ground' crew that had helped build and prepare New Moon One. Her checks had completed as his had: her team's minds scouring the ship like dockhands were satisfied and signing off: and so they were ready.

The countdown began as planned. The computers sought his approval and got it, a second surging feeling came as Birgit gave her approval and she was gone, a single message left in her wake. He would read it later.

Birgit retracted her view as the ship came to life, the countdown running toward zero, and she engaged with Terminus' external cameras and sensor suite to view the launch. Joining numerous others using the station's eyes and ears, she watched as the spherical ship began to glow. It was just outside Terminus' own orbit, sitting above it, and it would need to clear their range before beginning its descent. The eight cigar shaped engines came to life in unison as the counter reached zero. Only mildly at first, Captain Harkness feeling his way before ramping up their power. Eight blue streaks began to resolve behind the ship. Tiny atomic particles accelerated to near light speed, catapulted from the ship to give their momentum to it. Such tiny masses, but fired with such monumental power that they began to drive the mighty ship forward, pulling ahead of Terminus' orbit and starting to accelerate around Earth's equator.

Confidence building, the Captain throttled the power upward smoothly toward his operational maximum, the eight blue lines from his engines forming into sharp blue blades, white hot like super novae. Inside the ship, twenty-three bodies were pressed into their gravity cradles as the ship thrusted forward. Pulling away at a rate of nine gravities the ship was a hundred miles from Terminus in under a minute, travelling at a relative nine hundred miles an hour already.

Varying the output from each of his engines ever so slightly, the Captain began to curve the ship downward. Arcing smoothly toward the huge globe beneath them, even as the ship continued to gather speed, gravity adding to their flight now as they began their mad plummet into Earth's gravity well. The accelosphere engineer began his preparations. It would come up fast now, and they would only have a brief window for the coming translation.

From SpacePort One, Neal and a host of dignitaries and staff watched the ship turn earthward and the tension began to mount. Silence was broken only by the regular report of the mission commander updating on speed and altitude, and the occasional heavy sigh as someone remembered to breath. The ship had now surpassed every speed record known to man, and it was barely four minutes into its journey. It entered the atmosphere not on a ballistic trajectory, as it was not coasting downward, instead it was punching through the air like a cosmic spear, the wild blue flare of its engines overshadowed now by the fireball of our atmosphere wasting itself on the ship's meter thick shielding. But even that thick shield could not stand too much more, for unlike previous spacecraft or meteorites plummeting to Earth's surface, New Moon One was not slowing, it was getting faster still, and the pressure and fire would only build until they rivaled the fire in the stellar cores of its eight engines.

The moment came. They knew it would. They could see the timer ticking slowly to zero. But despite this no one was quite prepared for it. With an intense suddenness the fireball imploded, a shock wave resounding outward across the upper atmosphere as the source of that massive turbulence heat vanished, literally into thin air. A vortex of smoke warped the upper atmosphere like an inhaled cloud.

And then there was silence.

They knew that somewhere the ship's engines were still firing. They knew that the ship was, in fact, still coursing downward, and even now beginning its ultrasonic flight straight through the planet. But for everyone in the control room and in the many powerful offices monitoring the event, New Moon One had simply vanished.

A new counter showed now, and screens were already switching to a new view as the effects of New Moon's abrupt departure wafted ethereally on the wind. Now the view went to a camera mounted on a stratojet on the other side of the planet. The jet was circling high above the central Pacific Ocean, about three hundred miles North of the Marquesas Archipelago, its pilot, Major Jack Toranssen, already in position for the next big step. He was waiting, transmitting his view via humanity's growing subspace tweeter network to audiences in SpacePort One, Terminus, the Research Group in their bunker in Japan, and a select few heads of state around the globe.

- - -

Complete blackness surrounded Captain Harkness and his team. Weightless and isolated, they watched their internal clocks and hoped their calculations were correct. They could have no way of knowing their location. They had no instruments capable of penetrating the void outside, for they were enveloped in a sphere that placed them outside the normal universe. They were passing through the seemingly dense core of the planet like sound through water, unencumbered, unnoticed, their presence muted but still vital, waiting to reenter the universe when they were safely clear of Earth's fiery core. For now they were as ghosts. Ephemeral. Awaiting translation back into reality even as they harvested Earth's massive gravitational well to slingshot them right through it.

They counted down.

- - -

Fourteen minutes after New Moon One had vanished from space, the majority of the most important and powerful people on Earth had returned from whatever task they had busied themselves with and were once again routed to their various screens, mute and transfixed as the counter went to single digits. Jack circled the anticipated spot, his stratojet flying at over sixty thousand feet and his cameras pointed higher still into the purple blackness of the exosphere. Countless models and experiments had led them to this precise time and place on the far side of the planet.

The time came. Whether clear of Earth or not this is when New Moon One would disengage its accelosphere. Acute cameras on Jack's plane showed a lucky few hundred spectators the spot as it happened. Space seemed to warp and then explode outward as 700 tons of fusion-fired madness was reintroduced to the universe. A thunderclap was heard across a quarter of the planet as the shockwave buffeted the Earth, but New Moon One was not waiting to see the aftershock of its rebirth. Catapulted outward at over seventy thousand miles per hour, Captain Harkness and his crew shot out away from Earth. Fired out like a cosmic cannonball, using Earth's entire mass for gunpowder.

New Moon One surged out, and aboard her Captain Harkness felt their course resolve now, not theory but certainty, a future they were hurtling toward at ever increasing speed. Powering in a wide arc they would now begin to dip inside Earth's orbit toward the Sun's vastly more powerful embrace. They would not penetrate that massive orb as they had the Earth. Such extreme catapults as stars were reserved for achieving interstellar speeds. But New Moon One would veer inside Earth's orbital path so they could cut the corner on the orbit that would take us a full year, and in doing so they would catch up with their quarry from behind.

And so, the ship surged outward like a blue missile spat from the planet's very soul. Still accelerating, it soon outpaced the telescopes tracking it until Birgit and her colleagues could only see the angelic blue flare of its engines vanishing into the blackness.

The crew, jubilant at their monumental achievement, settled in for the longest journey any human had ever undertaken, either in terms of time or distance, and Captain Harkness remembered the message left for him by Birgit as they departed. Opening it he heard her voice in his mind. 'God speed, Captain. You fly on the wings of the combined accomplishments of two races. A hundred light years have been crossed to bring you the technology that powers your magnificent ship, and she is, without doubt, the most amazing thing humanity has ever built. Take her and enjoy her, Samuel. Take her out and when you come back, bring Earth a New Moon.'

Made in United States
North Haven, CT
03 May 2023